Jenny Colgan is the author of seven bestselling novels, most recently *West End Girls*, which is also published by Sphere. She is married with two children and lives in London.

For more information about Jenny and her books, visit her website at www.jennycolgan.com

Praise for Jenny Colgan

'She is very, very funny' *Express*

'A delicious comedy' *Red*

'Witty and clever' *Heat*

'Fast-paced, funny, poignant and well observed' *Daily Mail*

'Hugely entertaining and very funny' *Cosmopolitan*

'A funny, clever page-turner' *Closer*

'A quirky tale of love, work and the meaning of life' *Company*

'A smart, witty love story' *Observer*

'A Colgan novel is like listening to your best pal, souped up on vino, spilling the latest gossip – entertaining, dramatic and frequently hilarious' *Daily Record*

'An entertaining read' *Sunday Express*

'The perfect summer sunbather, easy to read, packed with gags and truths' *Irish News*

Also by Jenny Colgan

Amanda's Wedding

Talking to Addison

Looking for Andrew McCarthy

Working Wonders

Do You Remember the First Time?

Where Have All the Boys Gone?

West End Girls

Operation
Sunshine

Jenny Colgan

sphere

SPHERE

First published in Great Britain in 2007 by Sphere
This paperback edition published in 2008 by Sphere

Copyright © Jenny Colgan 2007

The moral right of the author has been asserted.

A CIP catalogue record for this book
is available from the British Library.

ISBN 978-0-7515-3762-8

Typeset in Caslon by M Rules
Printed and bound in Australia by
Griffin Press

Sphere
An imprint of
Little, Brown Book Group
100 Victoria Embankment
London EC4Y 0DY

An Hachette Livre UK Company
www.hachettelivre.co.uk

www.littlebrown.co.uk

For someone due out the same week as this book —
we cannot wait to meet you.
Well, two of us can't wait to meet you. The other one would
probably prefer a new bicycle and some apple juice.

Acknowledgements

Huge thanks and respect to Ali Gunn, my sensational agent, of Gunn Media, and Jo Dickinson, my brilliant editor. Both of you were right about everything, as ever!

And thanks to everyone at Little, Brown, especially Tamsin Kitson, Antonia Hodgson, Helen Gibbs, Alison Lindsay, Louise Davies, Peter Cotton, Hannah Venn, Ursula Mackenzie, and all the sales team who've done so much and worked so hard – thank you.

To all the yachties who have been so friendly and kind to me over my years of hanging about and getting in the way, particularly the crews of *M/Y Golden Cell*, *M/Y Leander*, *M/Y Jo* and *M/Y Deniki*.

Jonny Popper, whose excellent and lucid poker game was too long to make it in here, but will somewhere else; AME-LISA and Roni for being such great friends during our year abroad, and Jojo Moyes for chocolate and sanctuary on so many occasions; Mrs Doctor Karen, Katrina, Wesley, Dan and, of course, everyone on the board, as well as a big shout out to Feb Mums.

Huge thanks to Marina, and the staff of Kozie, de Drukkery and Zeeuwse Bibliotheek.

Thanks to my wonderful family for everything, and special thanks to Mr B & wee B, my two favourite people in the whole wide world.

Chapter One

'Holidays suck,' Lydia was proclaiming loudly, stabbing her straw into her drink to make her point. We were in a new West End bar which had been recommended in *Time Out*. Places like this normally intimidated me, but Lydia loved them; her dark eyes flashed at the cheesily good-looking barman, and her movements got more emphatic. You'd notice her.

'They SUCK!'

'Well, that's your opinion,' I said, a little stiffly under the circumstances. But I was the one who had brought up the subject of holidays, and now I was being told that, therefore, my dreams and desires were effectively a big pile of steaming dog turds that I'd just deposited between us on the bar.

'It's not an opinion,' she said. 'It's a fact. Everybody

knows. You've got to fly in a shitty plane, which is always shit, sit on some stupid bus for nine hours, sleep in some stupid room that's nothing like as nice as your own, listen to other people shouting all night, get sunburnt, get hungover, spend all your money, have a shit time, get knocked over by a car, remember you forgot to buy travel insurance, get your leg amputated and get flown home on a cargo plane to face three years in debtors' prison.'

'And that's what always happens, is it?' I said.

'Pretty much.'

I sighed. This wasn't going exactly as planned.

You always see, don't you, other people's holiday snaps, where they're patently having the most fabulous time some-where incredibly exotic, and you ask them about their holiday (if you have a lot of time on your hands at work, which I do) and their faces go all slack and dreamy and they get a faraway look in their eyes and say something stupid like, 'Well, we'd get up early in the morning and go running along the surf on the empty pink sand, then pick coconuts and fruit for our breakfast in the hammock.' And you think, Eh? How come I got vomited on by a child all the way from Gatwick to Fuerteventura and ate chips every night for a week?

Or they organise massive gangs of chums.

'Oh, yes, thirty of us are going sky hiking in the Peruvian Andes, then we've taken a luxury villa for a month in a cloud forest.'

How do people do that? Do I have the wrong friends? I

can't get any three of mine to commit to going to the cinema on the same day without two cancellations, one cancellation retraction, one falling out between two people who then refuse to sit together, a skirmish over the M&Ms and nobody paying me for the booking fee.

'My last holiday,' said Lydia, tossing back her long black hair, 'I copped off with a bloke who lives two doors down from my mum. Ten years of my life getting away from that place, and then what happens?'

'Well, if you knew that, why'd you cop off with him?'

'Durr! Because ON HOLIDAY they make you drink big goldfish bowls full of spirits until you're nearly unconscious, that's why. Chalk another one up to "why holidays are shit" by Lydia Li.'

'Well, THAT is why you have to listen to me,' I said.

I was doing my best to be assertive, whilst not being blinded by the retro disco lighting. It's important to be assertive with Lydia. Not that she's the most insanely competitive woman that ever lived. OK. She's the most insanely competitive woman that ever lived. If *you've* broken your leg, *she* was once skiing in St Moritz with Prince William and she did the world's highest ski jump and broke her neck and the doctors said it was a miracle and they gave her the Nobel Prize for prettiness.

You never ever wear new clothes if you're going to see Lydia. If she likes them she'll say, 'Oh, I like your outfit – very WAG.' (Even if it's, like, a grey sack made out of plasticine.)

And if she doesn't, she'll say, 'Oh, that was seventy per cent off down the King's Road – is that where you got it?'

We work next door to one another. We're receptionists on Harley Street in London, where all the plastic surgeons reside.

Lydia is 50 per cent convinced that one day a rich man is going to come and pick his wife up from surgery but instead get blasted by a lightning bolt and fall in love with her instead. I've told her this is both unlikely – rich men NEVER bother to pick up their wives, and their wives wouldn't want them to – and immoral, but she won't be moved. Her other 50 per cent is convinced that she's going to pull a young doctor. She doesn't date very much. No wonder she went mad on holiday.

So being assertive, my friend Bailey says, would help me no end. Growing up with three evil brothers in a very small house meant I had to develop a very loud mouth to even get fed, or rescued when the horrid beasts I had to share a home with, also known as John Jr, Patrick and Cassandro (Mum went a bit mental at the end), had alighted on some new form of torture involving holding me down whilst they shut the automatic door of the garage on my head, or setting fire to one of my pigtails, or threatening my pet rabbit with dire dis-memberment whilst tying me to a tree. It wasn't what you'd call idyllic. I'm only stunned (and occasionally disappointed) that they're all now rational adults roaming free and not in some prison somewhere.

We didn't go on foreign holidays when I was young, partly because we didn't have much money for all six of us, but mostly because Mum and Dad knew the boys would behave so unbelievably badly that we'd all end up getting deported.

So we always ended up in a caravan park in Wales, where the boys would instantly turn feral and run free, returning only for frequent top-ups of sausages and ice cream. We always stayed one week in one place and one week in another so that the boys didn't get enough time to form an international criminal conglomerate with all the other children on the site.

I'd sit inside with my parents and we'd eat crisps and play card games as the rain beat against the window whilst I indulged my fantasies of being a cosseted only child. It wasn't bad, but it wasn't the same as returning to school sporting a suntan and ankle bracelet with ribbon braids in my hair, and talking about mysterious dark waiters and romantic young men on motorbikes and staying out all night, like the other girls in my class.

When I was seventeen and just about to start college, I had my first all-girls' holiday, to Malaga. I looked forward to it for months. I stuck the tickets above my desk and fantasised solidly with my friends about the gorgeous boys who were going to fall madly in love with us, and spent every Saturday going in and out of Dolcis and Ravel choosing exactly the right pair of white stilettos. Tanya and Claire promised that we'd get free drinks everywhere and that it would be sun, sea and snogging all the way. I pored excitedly over letters in *Jackie* that said, 'I fell in love on holiday but now I don't know if I'll ever see him again,' and vowed to take the problem page's wise advice, and not put too much hope into a holiday romance when it probably wouldn't work in the rainy days back home (although I was sure mine would).

So it did come as something of a disappointment when it turned out that our one hundred and twenty-nine pound special was a room in a grubby white building next to a small pool filled with pissing children and surrounded by bull-necked families who'd brought their own packets of lard and deep-fat fryers.

This wouldn't have mattered if we weren't chased around by tragic-looking reps effectively begging for a huge share of our holiday money to take a 'party cruise', which we duly did. Tanya pulled one of the reps, who it then turned out Anne-Marie, another, slightly plumper girl, had a thing for, precipitating an enormous row which split the camp and lasted the whole of the rest of the holiday. Which hardly mattered to me, I was so shivery and shaky with sunburn (I had covered my mousy locks in Sun In and sat out through the heat of the first two days) I couldn't think straight, and Los Animalo's only disco, the Slutty Slug, gave me a pounding headache the first five thousand times they played the 'Macarena'.

Between hugely intense levels of secretive bitching, dirty

looks, Anne-Marie showing how over the club rep she was by snogging a different bloke every night, until they started hanging around outside our apartment like stray dogs, it was not what you might call the holiday of a lifetime, particularly after I got home and my finkish brothers developed a new game called 'Peel the Skin Off Evie'.

Since then I'd kind of sworn off holidays. At college, whilst other people went off Interrailing and trying to make it through Italy on five quid a day, I worked in the local pub and tried to look interested when people showed me pictures of the lions they'd seen on safari in Namibia, or of the Tuscan villa they'd hired, or of them falling hilariously off a big yellow banana and I'd think glumly about the night Anne-Marie got sangria sick on Tanya's new coat and they went for each other's hair.

And now, well, I was older, Bailey had got me a job in London working for some very grumpy doctors on Harley Street, which sounds a lot more important than it actually is, and I have some new friends, which, post-holiday, seemed the best thing to do under the circumstances.

And I wanted a holiday. I hadn't been away for two years, apart from to visit friends who were working overseas which was less of a holiday (they never wanted to take you to the tourist attractions) and more of an extended piss-up. I'd been single for eighteen months. Eighteen months. I felt like a born-again virgin. It was a desert out there. Or at least it was if you didn't have tiny thighs and a modified nose, like the clients I saw every day. They seemed to do all right.

And it hadn't exactly been wine and roses before then. My last boyfriend, Bill, had . . . well, it had never really progressed to the right moment to go on holiday. There isn't really a right moment, sometimes. With Bill I always felt like I was saying, 'Fancy going on holiday?' and he'd hear, 'Fancy getting a mortgage and getting married tomorrow and having nine children and you're never allowed to go out ever again and I'm about to put on four stone?'

He once condescended to take me on a long weekend barge trip with his unpleasantly sporty friends. It was the most boring thing I've ever done in my life. Travelling at two miles an hour whilst getting up and down to open locks isn't a holiday, it's exercise for a sixty-year-old recovering from a heart attack.

Maybe it's me. Maybe holidays and me are just not destined to go together. Maybe I'm designed to spend the rest of my life waking up at 7.40 a.m. and eating Weetabix for breakfast, even though I hate it, because apparently it means I won't feel hungry again until lunch, even though I always do and have a KitKat at eleven. With four fingers if it's raining. I'm not allowed to eat them in front of the clients though, we do a lot of liposuction, and they might turn wild and tear the wrapper out of my hands.

Back in the bar I toyed with my white wine. The rain was lashing down outside. I wasn't sure it was just about a holiday. I think I need more excitement in my life. I shouldn't get so excited, for example, when a new flavour of Pringles comes out. I'm twenty-seven. I feel I should be exploring the world; having mad passionate love affairs; dancing in the surf.

The city is fine, but it's hard to feel truly free with an Oyster Card. There must be more to life than magazine day (Tuesday – my favourite day. I especially like it when the stars tell you their diet and exercise secrets when we've had them in two weeks before).

'What if . . .' I said to Lydia. She really is intimidatingly beautiful, which makes the clients think they'll end up looking like her. I'm 'approachable-looking' according to Dr Bennet, which I think means they hired me so that even if an operation goes horribly wrong, the patient will still come out thinking, Well, at least I still look better than the receptionist. 'What if I organised a holiday so fantastic, you came back totally relaxed and had the best time you'd ever had and it was in paradise?'

Lydia looked at me sceptically. 'What, and it's free?' she said.

'No, of course it's not free. What are you talking about?'

'Oh. The way you're talking about it made it sound like it would be free.'

'No. But I'd organise it and do all the legwork.'

'Who's going? It'll have to be somewhere fancy.'

'Like all the really fashionable places,' I said casually, as if I was totally au fait with where those might be.

'They don't have to be fashionable.' She sniffed. 'They just need to have rich people in them.'

'Which makes them expensive,' I said.

'Well, duh.'

'OK, so do you have a secret trust fund I've never heard of? Are you not really a receptionist, but actually an heiress slumming it for a reality TV show?'

She shrugged. 'You asked what it would take to make me go on holiday with you, when it's a given that all holidays suck. And I'm telling you – somewhere posh and full of rich blokes but not too expensive for us.' She looked at me. 'Actually, I'm not sure we should go together after all.'

'What's wrong with me?'

Lydia didn't say anything, just played with her glass. 'Nothing. Oh, I don't know. Maybe I should take a busty blonde, you know? For contrast? Enhance my prospects?'

And she wasn't even joking. Proximity makes you some funny friends.

I wasn't downhearted. Yet. Next stop Bailey. I've known Bailey for ever. We grew up on the same street, and spent a lot of time hiding from my brothers.

His mother, in the manner of a zookeeper feeding fish to sharks, kept throwing him together with the beasts in the hope that they'd all become friends, rather than Bailey becoming Chump.

I think of Bailey as my backup. He's not gorgeous, but he

is funny, well off and really smart. Lydia keeps going on about wanting to meet him. I do my absolute best to keep them apart; I don't want her getting her talons into him.

It didn't help that he was very small and very clever and absolutely refused to know when he was beaten – even the time John Jr buried him headfirst in the sandpit he still came out spitting mud and threatening to curse them unto the third generation (he was going through a *Lord of the Rings* period at the time).

To escape the sheer brute force he took to hanging about with me, even when I made him spend an entire summer as a patient whilst my girlfriends and I played *Casualty*. I was always fascinated with medicine. It was one of the biggest disappointments of my life when I entered my third year of physics, chemistry and biology, hoping to romp into a fabulous career as an emergency doctor (this was pre-*ER*, but nonetheless I think I already had George Clooney in mind before he was even invented), only to discover to my shock and horror that I didn't understand a word of it. Not wave forms, not Boyle's law, not photosynthesis.

How I was ever going to perform emergency transplant surgery when I couldn't even remember the parts of the flower I did not know, so I switched to business administration instead. Mind you, there's not a lot I don't know about healing times for bhleroplasty (that's your upper eyelid). Sometimes I think if I work at the Saint Harley Clinic for long enough I'll become a plastic surgeon by osmosis, another scientific concept Mr Gahery failed to explain adequately to me in Year Nine.

Still, I do get to do quite a lot of interesting stuff at work – I've sat in on various ops, so I'm not the least bit squeamish, even for pus. And I run the back office too, all the paperwork. Well, most of it; Dr Bennet has a secretive streak. It's a more prestigious job than Lydia's, which drives her crazy.

Bailey came and found me a couple of years ago when I was drowning in a hospital basement on this ludicrous temp job I'd picked up, coding people's injuries in their medical files. So: hit on head, 310. Hit on head with brick, 310-12; hit on head with fish, 310-96; hit on head by flying saucer, 310-977, etc. It was doing my brain in.

'I've found a job for you,' he'd said, observing me over the top of his lunchtime hummus sandwich. 'It's got windows and daylight and everything.'

I liked it when Bailey did things like this for me. Made me think he cared.

'Oh, yeah?'

'Harley Street.'

'I don't believe in private medicine,' I'd said snootily.

'Do you believe in . . .' and then he'd mentioned a figure nearly twice what I'd been gritting my eyes up for.

'I also have very flexible moral standards,' I added (unnecessarily), thinking about Top Shop's new collection. Bailey briefed me for the interview too, to make me appear a bit classier than I actually am, and I was in.

12

Anyway. Bailey, being a mini-genius – he really plays up this angle, too much I think – wears shirts with buttons on the collar that he gets in America, and John Lennon glasses, like he's in the Geek of the Month club. Anyway, he took to the summer of *Casualty* too, and is now head of development for a cutting-edge hospital design company who build really big things, and he's always flying all over the world with a briefcase chained to his hand and being extremely important and constructing the world's largest MRI scanner or something. I always make sure I mention it to the beasts at Christmas time. Patrick says, 'Well, it's no wonder he's building big things, he's such a tiny fellow,' and John Jr pretends not to remember who he is, even though he hit him with a spade every day for nine years.

I met Bailey near his office in Fitzrovia two nights after I saw Lydia. There were lots of other zippy people in the pub looking clever and explaining things to each other using rulers. I know it's nerdy, but I secretly think it's also quite cool. Plus, lots of blokes work for Bailey's company. I think it's very rude of him not to devote more time to finding a man for me.

'Let's go on holiday,' I said, almost before we sat down. Bailey looked up at me, blinking in surprise behind his glasses. When we were sixteen we snogged in Clissold Park. For four hours, even though up until then I'd only ever thought of him as the brother I could push around. It was a really mild night in early spring. The next day neither of us said a word about it. But it's nice to think it's there. I often think we should have one of those Julia Roberts 'if we get to thirty without meeting anyone . . .' pacts. Just to formalise things.

'Why?' he said. 'I'm always on a bloody plane and you hate holidays.'

'Well,' I explained patiently, 'I hated asparagus too, until someone made me some in butter sauce and told me not to eat the bottom bits.'

'So you think you'll like holidays if you just avoid the bottom bits?'

'Exactly!'

'Well,' he said. 'What kind of holiday are you going to have?'

'A *good* one,' I said emphatically. 'With lots of nice people all having fun together.'

'Are your brothers coming?'

'Are you listening to me or what? I said nice people. People we like.'

'Is it going to be a sun, sea, sand, paperbacks kind of holiday? They're quite boring.'

'No, they're not! That's my dream!'

'Sounds boring.'

'OK, well, what if it were a sun, sea, sand and lots of interesting activities holiday?'

'Hmm. Cambodia's very interesting right now.'

'The place with all the skulls?'

'It's interesting. It's a country in transition.'

'I don't want a country in transition! I want a completely stable country with sun, sea, sand and cocktails.'

'Wouldn't you rather do something that helps indigenous peoples and increases your cultural understanding of our planet?'

'No, because that would be annoying and make me feel guilty and I spend my life being annoyed and feeling guilty. That's why I need a holiday.'

'So you're going to spend a lot of money on the holiday of a lifetime but endeavour to make it as banal as possible? Where are you going? Does it matter?'

'Not to you,' I said grumpily. 'You're not coming.'

'Oh, come on, Evie!' he said. 'I'm only teasing. Anyway, I know what this is about.'

'What do you mean?'

'This sudden push for a holiday.'

'What?'

'You're jealous.'

'Of what?'

Bailey just drummed his fingers on the table and waited for me to catch up. 'Well, all your brothers got married in the last two years . . . you're just feeling left out, in need of adventure.'

I stuck my lip out.

'Well, it's not fair, is it? John Jr is a big fat bastard, Patrick thinks he's God's gift . . .'

15

'Well, his marriage only lasted four months.'

'Yes, and that bronze bridesmaid's dress monstrosity will take twenty-four thousand years to decompose on a land-fill . . . I can't believe he chatted up the lady vicar.'

'Mmm.'

'And Cassandro . . . I mean, he's younger than me.'

He'd married a girl from my year at school. They'd disappeared to the Caribbean on holiday and called us when the deed was done.

But I'd seen the photos – the pink, clear sky, the soft yellow sand and Jilly and Cassandro looking so absolutely blissed out and beautiful and tanned. Jilly had a simple white cotton shift on and a huge flower tucked behind her sun-bleached hair, and she looked radiant. Cassandro had pale trousers rolled up over bare feet which made him look not quite as much a dick as it might have done. They looked like they were part of a perfect, romantic world, miles away from the grey streets and the everyday and the commute and the dirt I had to put up with. Why couldn't I get a bit of that?

I was jealous. I was jealous of their obvious, sun-kissed happiness. They looked part of a scene straight out of a movie, and I wanted a bit of it.

'Is that the rain again?' said Bailey, sighing heavily and staring out of the window.

'What happened to this drought we're supposed to be having?' I asked moodily.

'Well, no, it still rains, but it all runs off people's decking because nobody can be bothered to cut grass any more, so it doesn't soak into the soil and therefore people use more water to . . .'

'Yawn, yawn, yawn,' I said. 'Glad you're not coming on my luxury holiday. I'd say it was girls only, but that wouldn't necessarily rule you out.'

'Doesn't matter,' he said infuriatingly. 'I'm off on a big luxury secret junket anyway, and it's all paid for, and it's somewhere gorgeous. So there.'

I walked into work the next day downhearted but determined not to be put off by a few negative reactions and, well, the fact that my credit card statement had just arrived.

I'd left it on the mat, jumping over it quietly as if it were a poisonous snake I was praying hadn't noticed me. It's my fault, of course: in a moment of impassioned clarity I decided to transfer my balance onto one of those zero interest credit cards, the way you're meant to. Then, of course, I didn't either pay it back or transfer it onto *another* credit card, which meant 3000 per cent interest or something kicked in and I realised I'm the sucker who's funding everyone else's free credit cards. Which I wouldn't be, I suppose, if I didn't leap over my credit card statement as if it were a poisonous snake.

Anyway, I'm not exactly sure what's in there, but I know it's not pretty. So the absolute last thing I should be doing at the moment is planning luxury holidays. Or planning any-thing, in fact, apart from, obviously, getting a night job and moving into a shed until I've paid the damn credit card off, which I suspect, unless I win the lotto/marry a millionaire (not likely until I, at the very least, get my roots touched up) or invent something great (like, for example, the way to tell the difference between black and navy tights when it's dark and cold in your bedroom first thing in the morning and you've still got sleep in your eyes), is a very, very long way off.

So, I thought, heading into the office. Just to recap. I want to go on a fabulous holiday with my friends, except nobody wants to go with me and I don't have any money.

'Good morning,' said Dr Bennet. He's very handsome and smooth and he makes all the ladies fizzy. Doesn't do much for me; I've seen his toupee flap in a high wind and met his ter-rifying wife, but he smells nice.

'Dr Bennet, where would you go on holiday if you wanted to go somewhere nice?' I said.

He tried to wrinkle his brow thoughtfully, even though he can't: it's shot full of dead cow stuff and doesn't move.

'A nice holiday?'

'A fabulous holiday.'

'Aha. Well, you don't have a private jet, do you?'

'I do actually,' I said. 'I just park it in the mews.'

'Well, you should fly with British Airways first or Virgin upper class. Obviously you would think first would be better, but, you know, I don't always like the stewardesses, and the food is a little frilly for my taste. And, in fact, now you mention it, somewhere I visited for a wedding, Necker. You know, Richard Branson's island? He has a private island in the Caribbean; nobody there except people to look after you. Oh, it's beautiful. It's in the Balinese style, and it's so quiet, and the food, oh my God, I can't even begin to tell you about the food . . .'

His large brown eyes looked a bit melty as he stared out of the window into the grey and red-brick surroundings of Harley Street.

'Of course, it's expensive, you know? It's forty-five thousand dollars a day.'

'OK.' I said, sitting down at my desk. I did some quick addition in my head. 'Uhm. Can I have a raise of three hundred and fifteen dollars?'

Dr Bennet smiled. 'Well, OK. But you did ask me for fabulous. That is fabulous. Maybe I should be a plastic surgeon in America. It annoys me that I can't afford Necker myself.'

'I'm really, really sorry too,' I said as sincerely as I could manage. He can't be that far off, anyway, the amount of loaded old bruisers that march through the doors. And I'm not calling them that to be mean. Well, I am, but trust me, they are *really*, *really* mean to me first.

'Yes,' he said, picking up his case list for the day. 'Well, anyway, if you have not got much money, Venice is always nice.'

'Oh, yes?' I said, but without enthusiasm. I did want to go

to Venice, madly, but I had a secret life plan for Venice which involved, ideally, a flashing-eyed lover who would call me *cara* and we would run over picturesque bridges together and fall madly in love and feed each other spaghetti, like in *Lady and the Tramp*. So Venice was out. For now.

'Spain?' he said.

'Oh, no.' I shuddered, remembering my teenage Spanish experience.

His mouth twitched. 'Really? You have seen all of Spain? Much of it is very beautiful, don't you think? Have you been to Bilbao?'

'I don't like Spain,' I said firmly.

'Oh, well. There is only one place. The South of France, huh? Beautiful, warm sunshine, expensive Orangina . . . you would like it.'

The bell pinged, and one of our regulars, Zephyr, an ageing model (she calls herself a supermodel in the press, but I don't think there's anything terribly super about getting your tits out for *Nuts* magazine twice a week), came in for a top-up of fillers. It's not Dr Bennet's fault, he only does what she demands, but she's getting very weird-looking. Her top lip is now so pronounced she has to drink through a straw, and the very top touches her nostril, which can be extremely off-putting while she's talking to you.

'Hello, my dear!' Dr Bennet launched himself at her, charm personified. 'I'm terribly sorry, we don't treat under-eighteens here.'

Zephyr attempted what might have been a smile, but, hampered by the thick layer of plastic that now made up her face, came out more like a twitch.

'Hello, Yuri,' she hissed in a bad transatlantic lisp. Really, knowing your plastic surgeon by his first name. Is that sad or what? 'I need you to get to work.'

'Indeed, my dear. Although I am weak in the presence of beauty,' said Dr Bennet. I rolled my eyes. 'My dear, why don't you come through for a cup of herbal tea?'

'Got any champagne?' said Zephyr. It was ten past nine in the morning.

'But of course. Evie,' said Dr Bennet, 'see to our guest, will you?'

Zephyr didn't even bother glancing at me as I led her into Dr Bennet's office and made her comfortable with a copy of French *Vogue* on an armchair that cost more than my annual salary. I didn't think much of her shiny tight skin, but I couldn't help myself admiringly glancing at her long giraffe legs, carelessly clad in skinny white designer trousers. What must it be like to be able to wear tight white trousers? If you had legs like that did you think about them, or did you not even notice the elegant way they folded up under you without spilling out at the sides? The first and last time I tried on a pair of 'skinny' jeans, my legs looked like parsnips.

'There you go,' I said cheerily. A sniff came from Zephyr's suspiciously hollowed-out nostrils.

'Tell me,' she said as I reached the doorknob, 'what's Dr Bennet's wife like?'

I considered telling her she was ninety and had no teeth, just to see if she would try to seduce him, but I'm not a horrible person. Well, I have horrible thoughts, but I don't *think* that's the same thing, is it?

'She's absolutely bloody terrifying,' I said kindly.

Zephyr nodded her head a fraction – gratefully, I think – and went back to her magazine, as Dr Bennet entered the room.

'Now, my beauty. How can I improve on perfection today?'

Zephyr sighed. 'Oh, God, I have to fly to Barbados *again*. Sort me out, they don't even run Concorde there any more.'

'It's a scandal,' said Dr Bennet seriously. And I think he meant it.

I knew I hadn't got long to check holidays online, because Fanny Eleanor Moncrieff was coming in at 9.30, and she always brought her four tiny yappy dogs. Naturally dogs aren't allowed in a health centre, even one as lax as ours, so guess who has to take them out and round the block regardless of the weather? I wouldn't mind, I like dogs, but these aren't dogs, they're rats wearing coats, and they hate me, and each other, and spend their time getting their Chanel dog leads wrapped up with one another. Fanny Eleanor Moncrieff is ninety but, thanks to the wonders of Dr Bennet, looks eighty-five.

The door pinged as Dr Maitland marched in, head down as usual. He's not one for good mornings. In fact, I've worked here for three years and Dr Maitland's lack of interest in the niceties borders on the completely weird. He's not interested in charm, but he's unbelievably good at what he does. I can tell the difference between his work and Dr Bennet's in a minute – not that Dr Bennet is bad, but he gives a definite plastic surgery 'look'. Which, weirdly, some women actually prefer, in the same way platinum blondes don't really expect you to think their hair is that colour.

Anyway, if I needed anything done (ha ha, ha ha! More like, if I decided to start to tackle, over a period of some years, the pug-nosed freckle factory that is my face), it would be to Dr Maitland I'd go. Which is why he annoys me so much. It's OK for Dr Bennet, he's got family to support (as well as a sports car habit). But I don't understand why Dr Maitland is wasting his time, and his talent, injecting goo into stupid women who park their SUVs in the middle of the street then shout at me when they get a parking ticket. Why isn't he at Great Ormond Street repairing burns victims, or working in a plastics unit for people who get their faces eaten by dogs or something? Even helping kids who get teased at school for their huge ears would be more worthwhile than this. Which is just my opinion, obviously. And I realise the money is good – for all I know he's supporting ten thousand orphans through university. I just can't help feeling it's a bit of a waste of a very good doctor.

Anyway, he walked through the outer office, grunting as usual, and taking off his hat. He isn't old – not older than forty anyway – but he dresses like he's about a hundred. He always wears a hat and a bow tie. I asked Dr Bennet about the bow tie and he said it's so your tie doesn't drop into the mucky stuff when you're operating, which makes sense I suppose. Despite Dr Maitland's complete lack of personal charm, he's always busy because he's so good. In fact, he gets more celebrity clients than Dr Bennet, because you can hardly notice his work and because he's extremely discreet, or, possibly, lost his tongue in a climbing accident (I imagined once in a dull moment).

'Morning, Dr Maitland!' I said in a friendly way. Technically, you were meant to call him and Dr Bennet 'Mister' as they were so eminent, but I always called them doctor (secretly, I think they preferred it. What's the point of swotting for all those years if you can't impress total strangers on the street). I know to make him a cup of very strong coffee very quickly. That's one thing we've all caught off Dr Bennet – I can only drink coffee now if it comes in a tiny cup with the spoon standing straight up out of it.

'Hello,' said Dr Maitland, rustling his *Telegraph*, grabbing his coffee and rustling past as quickly as possible. He makes the ladies fizzy too, actually – God, what is it about women and doctors? They've seen your guts, for goodness' sake. Do you really want to sleep with a man who spent his formative training years sticking his fingers up old ladies' bottoms?

'Ocean Consortium rang again,' I said, reading off from his messages list.

'Oh, bloody hell,' he muttered, almost to himself. 'This thing just doesn't quit . . .'

I had no idea who Ocean Consortium were, except that they kept phoning, that it was secret, and that Dr Bennet was always delighted to hear from them, and Dr Maitland was always pissed off. Sometimes I heard them arguing about it in the consulting suites.

'Who are these people?' I said. 'They're incredibly persistent.'

'Don't ask,' said Dr Maitland, disappearing into his office. 'Nothing good.'

That sounded interesting. I was just about to look them up on the Internet when I realised Fanny Eleanor Moncrieff, with dog entourage, was already standing right in front of me, and I hadn't even helped her up the steps.

God, it was freezing out there walking those bloody rats. I stomped around the block, calling in on Lydia to see if she wanted to join me. She laughed, pointing out that she was sitting in a nice, cosy, centrally heated office. Her place is much posher than mine; she works for three brothers from Tripoli who specialise in lunchtime lipo. But she has less to do – they have a practice manager for the docs; she just smiles and answers the phones. She's always pretending to be sympathetic about my horrible workload though. Plus, she added, she was getting her sneer ready for when the new girl band turned up in five minutes' time.

'Do they get a discount for doing all five at once?'

'Yeah, course. That producer sends all of them here. The only thing is, they don't get to choose what they get done, he does.'

'Yuk.'

'Oh, they're so desperate. You could say, "OK, we're just going to graft an extra ear on, here, over your tits," and they'd say, "Awesome! That's hot!"'

'You're very harsh.'

'I'm just a bit stressed out.'

'You need a holiday.'

She narrowed her eyes at me. 'I NEED you to close the door and stop letting the heat out. What are those things you're walking anyway? They look like mops.'

'Psychotic mops.'

'OK. That's enough. Shoo. Shoo!'

Back at the office Fanny Eleanor Moncrieff was being ushered out by our nurse, and I took over pronto to make sure her driver was outside to pick her up.

'Thank you, my dear,' she croaked through the white bandages. She peered at me suddenly, her eyes sharp, even though she must have been well under the cosh of the painkillers Dr Bennet doled out with a liberal paw.

'You know, you really are very helpful. Are you looking

forward to Cannes . . . ?' Her voice trailed off as her long-suffering driver opened the back door for the dogs, firstly, then helped her in.

'Am I looking forward to what?' I said. You never know, sometimes people get a bit woozy and think they have to tip me. Dr Bennet's warned me very seriously about it, but I don't see the harm.

'I love the place, you know,' she said, going a bit misty eyed. 'Lost two husbands' fortunes on the Riviera. Great days. Life on the ocean blue . . .'

And before she had the chance to go any further, the big black doors of the Mercedes had closed behind her, and the huge vehicle simply slipped away.

Chapter Two

'That's strange,' I said, pulling my cardigan tightly around me as I bounced back into the welcome warmth of the office. Dr Bennet was ticking off the charts.

'What?' he said. 'You weren't soliciting for cash again, were you?'

'I do not "solicit for cash",' I said. 'One time that Arab princess offered me a small gratuity just for mentioning you couldn't even tell she'd had surgery.'

'While she was wearing her veil.'

I tried to look contrite. 'Well. That wasn't it. Miss Moncrieff mentioned something.'

'Did she indeed?' Dr Bennet raised one of his perfectly plucked eyebrows.

'About Cannes.' I pouted. 'Are you going on yet another jolly and not taking me?' It wouldn't be the first time.

Dr Maitland entered the office, silently as ever.

'The FDA turned it down again,' he announced gruffly. 'Now there's a surprise. A sensible decision.'

'Wilf, come here a second,' said Dr Bennet. 'I was just thinking about discussing Cannes with Evie here.'

Dr Maitland barely raised an eyebrow.

'Well, she'll have to know sometime.'

'What do you think? We could divert the phones, have a bit of a human face. And she was just telling me how much she needs a holiday.'

'I was.' I nodded emphatically. I didn't know what they were talking about, but it sounded promising.

'What would you think about her joining us in Cannes? We could do with the help on the paperwork.'

'That's hardly a holiday,' said Dr Maitland, running his hand through his thick hair. 'There's masses to do.'

'Well,' said Dr Bennet. 'It could be time we got some extra help involved, don't you think? For "Operation Sunshine"?'

Dr Maitland squinted a bit and lowered his voice. 'Whatever you think. Won't everyone else be taking those daft model dolly birds though?' He looked at me apologetically. 'I wouldn't want you to feel out of place.'

I was slightly insulted that he didn't think I'd be mistaken for a six-foot dolly bird, despite evidence to the contrary.

OK, so I don't look like Lydia and most of the other girls up and down Harley Street. But I'm not a gargoyle; if you saw me coming you wouldn't throw your hands up and shout, 'For the love of heaven, cover it up!' then light torches and come and burn me out of my house.

In fact, boyfriends have on occasion called me pretty. It's not my fault that at some point in the last five years freckles went from being cute to being considered a vile mark of global warming, or that curls are out and all hair must be straightened and ironed until it's as flat as a sheet of metal.

But this was just insulting. I knew that the docs didn't really see faces as faces per se – just as problems to be looked at, imperfections to be fixed. They had a picture in their minds of a woman's face: long, high of cheekbone, pointed of chin, tiny of nose, peculiarly flat of forehead, and anything that deviated from this presented itself as a series of problems to be fixed. *But I was standing right here.*

Dr Bennet leaped in, anxious to pour oil on troubled waters, as usual.

'No, we don't need any slutty types,' he said. 'Just someone friendly-looking to help people if they're feeling nervous.'

Dr Maitland raised an eyebrow. 'I don't think anyone in Cannes is ever nervous.'

My heart, which had been beating too fast at the insult, suddenly skipped a beat. Cannes? South of France?

'Well, I think it's a good idea. You know this thing is about to go huge.'

'I suppose,' said Dr Maitland grudgingly. Gee, thanks boss.

Dr Bennet turned round to face me squarely.

'OK, Evie. Would you like to help us with Operation Sunshine and come with us to Cannes?'

Would I? My head filled immediately with visions of palm trees; red carpets; great big yachts; beautiful actresses dancing on the sand; sunshine and blue skies.

Dr Bennet smiled as he noticed my reverie.

'Now,' he said, 'it's not a holiday.'

'Of course not,' I said, shaking my head seriously. Dr Maitland rolled his eyes and went back to his office.

'It's this practice's latest project. We'll be working with and talking to some of the best doctors and richest financiers in the world.'

I nodded, but my brain was doing a little dance to 'holiday holiday holiday holiday'!

'I was going to use the admin company from the conference organisers, but Miss Moncrieff might just be right . . . why shouldn't it be you? You could make sure everything runs smoothly . . . book the flights, the hotels . . . take minutes.'

Ooh. Business-class seats were de rigueur when the docs travelled . . . I wonder, maybe we should book a private jet? And as for hotels, wasn't there a really famous one there?

Where George Clooney always stayed and you had to pay in cash even though it was a million pounds.

'I think separate accommodation for doctors and administrative staff,' said Dr Bennet hurriedly.

I nodded.

'Good. It's settled. We're quiet in July anyway. We'll just divert the phones. Now, come here.'

Dr Bennet handed me a thick file. On it was a picture of a beautiful woman in a striped bathing suit. TOP SECRET was stamped on the cover. Ooh! In big letters across the bottom it said: OPERATION SUNSHINE.

'Looks exciting,' I said. Then I opened it and saw it was full of boring-looking legal documents. Hmm, maybe later.

Anyway, just then the door pinged to admit Hank, an American actor who always comes by whenever he's in London, despite the fact that he thinks, correctly, getting stuff to make his face freeze is doing absolutely nothing for his emotional range (bloody doctor/patient confidentiality kills me; if my friends knew who I'd been having cosy little chit-chats with, and how gay he was, no way would they keep blowing me off for holidays). Dr Bennet slipped off to his consulting room, before I even had a chance to say thank you.

'Aha ha ha,' I messaged Lydia, who I could see was online. 'You know what you were saying about free luxury holidays? Well . . .'

Infuriatingly, the message came back almost immediately.

'Oh, that. Yes, my docs are going. I didn't want to mention it in case you weren't invited.'

I couldn't believe this. What kind of a work-based acquaintance was she, not filling me in on all the juicy trips? What else was I missing out on?

'So you're going then?' I messaged. 'Business class?'

This time it was my turn to receive the laughing smiley.

'I booked my ticket two months ago,' the message read. 'All the seats have probably gone by now. But the coach only takes thirty-six hours.'

Wow, Lydia really does kid around a lot.

'So, anyway, I won't be able to come to the all-night horror show at the NFT,' I casually dropped into the conversation, as Bailey and I sat with our noses in the trough at Wagamama. I didn't really like horror films, but Bailey liked someone to grab at creepy moments, and I didn't mind.

'I'm going to be in . . . oh, let me see, where was it again? Oh, yes, the South of France!'

Bailey looked up from his udon noodles. His glasses were steamed up.

'No way! Yuri's taking you?'

Yuri is Dr Bennet. Him and Bailey are thick as thieves; I've never really understood why.

'Don't sound so surprised,' I said. 'Can I have the last dumpling while you're staring at me with your mouth open?'

'You know I'm going to be there?' he said. 'It's my project.'

'Operation Sunshine?' I said, to make myself look in the know.

'Yes! What do you think?'

'Oh, fabulous.' I must read the brief. 'Amazing.'

I changed the subject as quickly as I could.

'So, everyone's going. It's going to be a proper jolly. Lydia's coming too. There you go, I asked for a holiday and look what's arrived. I think Noel Edmonds is right about that cosmic ordering.'

'Is Lydia the one who wants to meet me?'

'Oh, yes, I forgot.' I frowned. 'I think she wants to do it with you like they do on the Discovery Channel.'

'Charming.'

'I mean it. I think beneath her elegant exterior lies a sex-crazed maniac.'

Hang on, wasn't I meant to be putting him off her?

'You can see the tension in her ten-inch fingernails.'

This was a high-risk strategy to keep him away, all right. I wondered if it would work.

'This isn't a jolly, you know,' said Bailey. 'It's a big serious development.'

'Yes,' I said, slurping the last of my apple and ginger juice. 'Do you think polka dots are still in this year?'

'Who am I, your gay BF?' said Bailey crossly. 'Talk sensibly or I'm taking out *Practical Mechanic* and reading at the table again.'

*

I'd tried – and failed – not to eat too much as Mum and Dad had invited me round for tea – I'd agreed to go only if the beasts weren't invited too. I called in on them and told them about the trip. At least Mum sounded genuinely pleased, even if she thought that meant I might be getting a promotion of some kind. I don't know how to tell her there's not much in the way of promotion in the medical reception field unless, like Lydia's evil plans, you get lucky and marry the boss and/or a client.

'I'll look out your old French book,' she said. Oh, yes. Suddenly something that had been niggling at the back of my mind jumped to the forefront. Well, have you ever met anyone who *doesn't* put 'French' on their CV? No, you haven't, have you? So maybe, just maybe, under 'other languages' on my application form, I'd written 'French' quite proudly because, 1) how often was I going to have to use that in Harley Street and, 2) if required I could order a cup of coffee with pretty much no problem at all. (Although was it *un* or *une* café? I could never quite remember.)

'So, the boys are coming round . . .'

'They're not, are they?' I said, looking around our beige sitting room like a caged animal. Mum and Dad got so used to all their nice things being destroyed or broken that they'd never got out of the habit of buying the absolutely cheapest of everything, and the room looks like it's been entirely furnished from the back of the Sunday supplements.

'Evie Esme, don't be silly. You've got to stop thinking like you're nine again.'

35

'That's like saying to a victim of torture that they can't go through life looking over their shoulder,' I grumbled, picking up a fruit scone and removing all the raisins from it in one practised move. 'I've got post-traumatic stress disorder.'

Sure enough, as I was doing this my mum quickly set eight places at the table. Why I hadn't noticed the size of the stew pot she was stirring I don't know. And then the doorbell rang.

'I can't believe this,' I said. 'You lured me here under false pretences.'

'We've got to welcome Cassandro's new wife,' said Mum. 'It was the only way I knew you'd turn up.'

'By telling lies to your only daughter?'

'Hello, hello.' John Jr's loud tones rang through the house. His horrible bullying ringleader ways when we were children have made him a highly successful manager of a car show-room, and he's got the trophy wife, Kelly, to prove it. Kelly's thirty-one and weighs about six stone, most of that gold jewellery and lip gloss.

'Just parked the new Lexus outside. Hope it won't get stolen, huh huh. Evie. How's it going? What are you driving these days.'

John Jr knows fine well I can't afford a car in London, but he always asks people what they're driving the second he meets them. It's like some knee-jerk thing he can't help, if I'm being charitable. If anyone (a man, usually) is foolish enough to venture an answer he will suck in his teeth and go,

'Oh. Happy with it?' Then, if they say yes, he'll raise his eyebrows, as if he can't believe they're such an idiot for driving that car, but he wouldn't like to mention it in polite company. Usually he'll work his way round to bragging about Lexuses (Lexi?) for hours. I don't know anything about cars but I do know that if I ever buy one it will never ever, ever be a Lexus, not even if it was free and delivered by George Clooney carrying a year's supply of jam.

'Hello,' said Kelly. Despite being incredibly pretty (if you like the bleached-blonde aerobicised look, and in my experience blokes really, really do, even if sometimes the girls are a *teensy* bit difficult to tell apart), she was incredibly insecure about her looks. She was always on at me to find out the latest procedures and peels, then went home and got her unqualified beautician to do them for her. I really wished she wouldn't, but she won't be told. 'What's new?'

I thought for a bit.

'Well, there's Radoflux 9000. Gives you baby skin apparently. But it keeps getting turned down by the FDA in America, and the BMA won't look at it. That means you can't use it. It's driving Dr Bennet demented. *Don't* try and buy some off a dodgy website.'

'Would I?'

'Remember that chemical peel?'

'It smelled like Cillit Bang.'

'Remember what we said? If it looks like Cillit Bang, and smells like Cillit Bang . . .'

'Don't use in the under-eye area.'

'Don't use in the under-eye area, that's right.'

She was all right Kelly. I don't know why she was so insecure; John Jr was unbelievably lucky to have pulled her in the first place. It would never strike twice.

'Ooh, what's for dinner, Anne? Smells gorgeous.' Kelly always says this, but never eats anything, and we all pretend not to notice.

'Stew,' said Mum. 'How are you doing, JJ?'

John Jr sat down on the best armchair and spread out his big beefy legs, like a visiting king.

'Yeah, great, Mum. We're thinking of building a swimming pool onto our conservatoire extension, ain't we, Kell?'

Kelly looked pleased. I wasn't surprised: wow, a swimming pool.

'Well, we thought what's the point, right? What's the point of even *having* a conservatoire if it ain't got a pool? Doncha think?'

As soon as John Jr made some money they moved out to Essex, and they live on a gated executive estate, or, as I like to think of them, wanker zoos. My mum blinked. Her and Dad have struggled all their lives – he's only a cabinetmaker, a good trade nobody wants any more, and she spent her life bringing us up, but they wouldn't dream of asking John Jr for a helping hand now and again, and he wouldn't dream of offering. Or me, of course, not that I give a shit. I just wish he wouldn't keep pointing out exactly how much money he makes, and asking me about my salary all the time.

The door crashed open and Patrick burst in, without a girl in tow for once. He's extremely good-looking, or so my female friends have always insisted. At least, he doesn't have a face like a burst pudding, like John Jr. He has a bad-boy swagger that's made the girls go all wobbly since I was twelve – he's also got a motorbike, wears leathers and sneers. It's amazing that still works these days, but it does. Anyway, by night he drinks cider and plays the bad boy, by day he goes to work in a surveyor's office with his hair combed down.

'All right,' he said sulkily, throwing himself down.

'Hiya, Patrick,' Kelly said. Patrick ignored her like he does all women, which usually makes them worse. I rolled my eyes and pointedly asked Mum if she'd like any help in the kitchen.

'Where's Mr Ball and Chain then?' said Patrick. 'I can't believe he got caught by a bird like that. Is she up the duff?'

'Patrick,' said Mum. 'It was very romantic, that's all. They just got carried away on a beach.'

'Yeah,' said Patrick. 'And then they had to get married.' He and John Jr sniggered. 'Got any beer, Mum?'

'Are you on that motorbike?' asked my mother. 'Because if so, no.'

Patrick tutted as my father came in and patted me

39

comfortably on the head. He's at least a head shorter than the boys and always looks slightly puzzled as to how on earth he could have produced them.

'All right, boys?' he murmured.

'Yeah,' said Patrick. 'Mum was just getting me a beer.'

'Dad, you going to get that wreck through its MOT?' said John Jr. 'You really want to think about upgrading, you know.'

My father muttered something and took his seat at the head of the table, looking around for his stew. My mother looked at the brown clock on the kitchen wall – it has birds that are meant to chirp every hour but they haven't chimed since 1978, when John Jr had a spectacularly high-reaching tantrum. In this case, I'm glad.

'I wonder where they are,' she said nervously. It can't be helped; Cassandro, by virtue of his being as slippery as a snake and not actually evil, is her favourite, and I could tell how nervous she was about meeting his new bride, even though she'd known Jilly since her knees were permanently skinned.

'Probably still at it,' sniggered Patrick.

'Stop that!' said Mum. 'I won't have that kind of chat at the dinner table.'

'Well, I'm not sitting down at the table yet, am I?' said Patrick.

'It's romantic though, innit?' said Kelly. 'A beach wedding. Just you and the one you love. Simple and gorgeous.'

Which is a bit rich, because they had three hundred

people to a sit-down in the world's most floral hotel and Kelly wore a dress so wide people had to brace their feet and heave to get her into the toilet.

'And cheap,' said John Jr. 'Nice one.' He heaved his fat bottom onto one of the creaking kitchen chairs. Because Kelly isn't interested in food, she doesn't much care about John Jr's diet, and I think everything that enters his body has to come wrapped in pastry. I sometimes think Kelly wants him fat and lethargic so that he won't have the energy to chase other women; and possibly so he'll have a heart attack.

My mother sighed and started dishing out stew and dumplings. Patrick tried Cassandro's mobile, but didn't get an answer. He then started texting someone at the table, until Dad gave him a very hard look.

'So,' said Mum. 'Anyone else got any news then?'

'Best February sales in three years,' said John Jr through a thick mouthful of stew. 'I'll be getting some kind of prize.'

'Oh, JJ, that's wonderful,' said my mum, genuinely pleased.

'Yeah, well,' said John Jr. 'Takes bloody thirteen-hour days, but it's worth it.'

'I've got news too,' I said. Everyone turned to me with concerned-looking expressions on their faces. Oh, for goodness' sake. Why do they assume my news is automatically going to be terrible, like I've been arrested or something?

'I'm being sent abroad on a business trip,' I said. That sounded pretty good, actually.

'Where they sending you then?' said John Jr. 'Timbuktu? Is it a one-way ticket?'

'No. The Côte d'Azure actually. That's in France.'

'"That's in France",' mimicked Patrick. 'Why are they sending *you* to France?'

'To administer to a major conference, *actually*.'

'Why, have doctors medically discovered a cure for farting, Evie?'

'No, it's about how to make surveyors more interesting. No cure's been discovered yet, sadly.'

Patrick went back to stuffing his face. I was just about to elaborate on my glamorous trip, now I'd got a word in edgeways, when the doorbell rang.

'Here they are!' sang my mother, her face lighting up. And in swanned Cassandro and Jilly. Even on this dull rainy evening, they seemed to emit a glow – not just their light tans; their happiness and love seemed to light up the whole house. As they chatted excitedly about dolphin-spotting, barbecues on the beach and yacht parties, I felt my mood get lower and lower. Everything I wanted – excitement, change, adventure, sunshine. It was right here at the table, and none of it was mine. I got quieter and quieter and, as soon as I politely could, left to catch the tube, after swallowing a Battenberg cake that tasted like ashes in my mouth.

'Everything booked?' said Dr Bennet, bowling into the office the next morning. I'd got in early too. Three business-class seats (not for me, sadly – Dr Bennet's scary wife was accompanying him) was going to cost over two thousand pounds. For a two-hour flight and a sandwich! Despite my gloom, it felt fun to spend that much money. Yes, those were the circles I was in now. Two thousand pounds? No problem! Now, hotels. Christ, there were thousands. I didn't trust myself not to stick them in some underground dungeon by mistake, and decided to ask my supportive friend and colleague for advice.

'Oh, for goodness' sake. Just as well I didn't want to go on holiday with you. We'd have ended up at the Birmingham Novotel, but paying five times the rack rate.'

'What's rack rate?' I said to be annoying. Lydia was bringing me back down to earth.

'If I tell you, do you promise not to follow me around like a little puppy dog when we get to Cannes?'

'Well, I thought I could be your wingman.' I had, actually. I didn't mind pulling the good-looking guy's best friend; they're normally more fun anyway. Just call me Ms Brightside.

'Is that what you thought?'

'Yeah, you know, pinpoint the hot young docs . . . check out wedding rings . . .'

Lydia sighed and named two hotels.

'One for them, posh, lots of other docs there. One for you, not quite so posh, lots of PAs there so I won't be the only person you turn to when you need your shoelaces tied.'

Wow, Lydia was lucky my brothers had already softened

43

me up for lots of insults. Anyway, I'd already started dreaming about suntan lotion . . . large oversized sunglasses (except they didn't make me look all weeny and young and fragile, like an Olsen sister, they made me look legally blind), acres of white sand and young Frenchmen with pert bottoms and a widespread knowledge of history, art, literature and the erotic arts.

Chapter Three

The Saturday before we left I went to the drawer under my bed where I keep clothes I've bought by mistake, or for a special occasion, or that don't fit quite as well as I thought they might when I bought them. It's a big drawer. Normally I stay away from it as it just serves to remind me of stuff I've spent money on but haven't got around to wearing. Yet.

I pulled everything out one by one. OK, the ethnicy kaftan might be a bit last season (and made me look like one big square box from my shoulders to my thighs, where it cut off at a ridiculously high point) but surely it would be just the thing for pulling on after, let's say, a swim to the pool bar?

So yes, the kaftan was in. Now, swimwear. In my knickers drawer I had my swimming costume, which I'd had since school, and although it gave me a bit of hungry bum these days, it was still wearable. It was also, however, a plain black Speedo and did make me look like I was about to cover myself with goose fat and have a shot at the Channel, whilst wearing a nude-coloured skullcap.

This was no good. I needed at least one fancy bikini – Coleen McLoughlin always looks like she takes about fifteen on holiday. Mind you, her job is going on holiday. Why didn't I fall in love with a footballer?

I added to the pile an ill-conceived bright orange skirt, bought during that peasant frills fiasco we all went through a couple of years ago – maybe in Cannes they'd think it was retro chic. Anyway, from what I remembered from our school exchange, all French people wore skin-tight white denim and those women that didn't all wore black suits whilst smoking furiously and talking about pudding, and I wasn't going to be able to manage any of that.

Buying bikinis is such a hideous affair but it was either that or spend my weekend reading the briefing notes, and I didn't think I could take it. Also, I had forgotten it was half term and thus found myself in a department store with about a million unbelievably skinny teenagers moaning to their mothers. I wish my mum had taken *me* shopping for clothes when I was a teenager. But no, she was taking the boys to casualty while I was working in a handbag shop. Why didn't these moony whingers work? Then I wouldn't have to wait two hours to get into a changing room and feel sweaty and hot before I even tried anything on, then wondering how sweaty other people had been whilst trying on bikinis. Yikes. I was *not* in the holiday mood.

'Oh, for goodness' sake,' I exclaimed to myself, trying to turn around in the minuscule cubicle. I felt like a dog chasing its tail.

That reminded me, it was one of the few conversations Dr Maitland and I had had. Geneva Pitt, a horrid society stick woman who calls everyone 'girls' and pretends she's some kind of a dizzy lassie but is actually the most ruthless witch ever, had come in howling. Her face is so stretched and shiny it looks like she's made of pink chewing gum.

'Wilf!' she'd hollered, ignoring my greeting. For goodness' sake. He's your doctor. Just call him 'Doctor'. What, you think we're impressed that we bill your poor husband for tens of thousands of pounds a year?

'I've got cellulite!' she screamed. 'My life is over!'

Seriously, she was in tears. Must have nicked them off a spare crocodile she'd passed on Wimpole Street. Then, right in the middle of the waiting room (there was no one else there except me, and I'm invisible), she pulled down her incredibly tight leather trousers to reveal, just under her absurdly tight bum, one tiny, tiny bump which was only visible when she scrunched up her arse. Honestly, sometimes I realise how men can be completely confounded by women.

'There, there,' he'd said gruffly. 'Follow me, err. Mrs . . .'

He'd forgotten her name! What a boor. I quickly jotted it down in big letters on a piece of paper and held it up behind her back.

'. . . Pitt,' he finished. 'Come right in.'

Afterwards, he came up to me whilst picking up his hat.

'Thank you,' he said quietly, in his dignified way. He was right to thank me; the whole business relies on making women feel pampered and special, and it's hard to feel special when someone is calling you Thingy.

'That's OK,' I said. Then I added, 'Can I ask? Cellulite . . . What is it? I mean, really. Will it go away if you stop drinking coffee?'

'Oh, God,' he said. 'Professional ethics forbid me from talking about it.'

'OK,' I said, trying not to sound sniffy. Professional ethics seemed to stop him from talking about a lot of things, up to and including a 'How are you, Evie?' once in a while.

'Well,' he said. Then he looked around again. 'Can you keep a secret?'

I nodded heartily, regardless of the fact that this wasn't perhaps 100 per cent true.

'It doesn't exist,' he whispered.

I almost jumped. 'What do you mean it doesn't exist?' I said. 'I've got bloody masses of the stuff.'

He shrugged. 'Well, it's simply an aesthetic term. What you've got is fat deposits on your bottom and hips.'

'Thanks very much.'

'That's where fat deposits in females. And that's what it looks like. End of story.'

'But . . . aren't we supposed to be able to get rid of it with brushes and stuff.'

'You can get rid of it by stripping all the fat out of your body. Paula Radcliffe doesn't have any. Nor does Ms, ahem, Pitt, once you suck it out. Otherwise, well, that's it.'

'But all those creams, and potions . . .'

Dr Maitland shook his head. 'You think a cream can penetrate your skin and specifically dissolve fat?'

'I would like to think that.'

He almost patted me on the head.

'Bless you,' he said. 'I don't think you'd like liquid-permeable skin. Certainly not after the first time you took a bath. And, I promise, there are many, many more important things in the world to worry about than cellulite, a made-up money-spinner for the beauty industry.'

Then why, I thought, for the nine thousandth time, as he left to hop into his little MG, quietly closing the door behind him, don't you worry about any of them?

Reassuring though this had been at the time, well, it wasn't bloody helping me *now*, was it? I wrestled myself into another pair of 'boy cut' bikini bottoms. I'd asked all the men I knew (apart from the beasts) what they thought about cellulite and none of them knew what the hell I was talking about, except for Bailey and he said it didn't bother him, though what would he know about it seeing as he only dates supermodels? Or, at least, better-looking girls than I'd think he'd get without the platinum corporate Amex and the access to cheap boob jobs.

Then I turned around and saw 'it'. It was just hanging there, on the shelf full of stuff to be taken back into the store. Obviously one of the Keira Knightley-esque teens had tried it on and nearly drowned in it . . . but for me . . .

It was a dark red dress: not an in-your-face tomato juice colour, but a deep, shimmering silk that slipped on like a second skin. I wondered for a moment if it might look a bit like a nightie but, when I tried it on, it didn't. It looked like someone had sat down and designed a beautiful red summer dress, just for me.

Shopping moments like this almost never happen. When they do, your only choice is to grab them and run with it. Terrified in case the person who'd orginally tried it on realised they'd made a terrible mistake and came running back, I whipped it off, grabbed the first bikini that came to hand and charged to the checkout.

It's not that I didn't have anything to do that Saturday night *at all*. I would have had loads of offers, probably. It's just I happen to really, really like my mum's cooking, especially when she's doing lamb, that's all. My mother's roast lamb is so good it makes it worth sitting next to a bunch of disgusting animals in a zoo. Which is just as well.

I'd spent the afternoon curled up in my old bedroom with the pictures of ponies still on the wall, immersing myself in a guidebook on the Côte d'Azure and occasionally jumping up to try on my new dress again. I didn't want to show Mum; she had conniptions about anything that cost over £15.99, and this had cost quite a lot over £15.99.

Cannes looked incredibly thrilling. Miles of palm trees and golden beach, huge yachts tied up in the harbour at sunset; pictures of Chanel and Louis Vuitton shops. It wasn't actually that crucial for me to know the whereabouts of the Louis Vuitton shop. I suspected I may have bought the wrong guidebook – *The Côte d'Azure Guide For the Skint and Non-Beautiful* wasn't in stock, but *The Glamour Guide to Cannes* was.

Don't miss, it enthused, *the many glamorous parties and premieres of the film festival. Some prefer the Splendid to the Eden-Roc, overrun as the latter is at this time with movie stars and wannabes.*

Movie stars and wannabes sounded all right to me. And I would be delighted not to miss the many glamorous parties, if someone would only tell me where and when they were; I had the dress for it.

Or of course just moor the yacht (but make sure you've got mooring sorted well in advance – tel: 06 55 43 32 10).

I had definitely bought the wrong guidebook. Although I was tempted to call the number. 'Hello, *bonjour*, yes, I just need to reserve my yacht parking space. For the film festival, yes. My name . . . uh, it's Jennifer Aniston. A-N-I . . .'

Dressing for dinner in Cannes is very dressy indeed – now is the time to wear your couture, and break out your family jewels. View the setting sun from the terrace of the Hotel Belles Rives, which shimmers nightly with crystal champagne glasses and diamonds.

'Evie!' my mother yelled up the stairs. 'I need a hand chopping cabbage.'

I sighed.

'OK!' I shouted down. 'I'll just back up the yacht,' I added to myself.

Downstairs, sitting *right there* was John Jr, watching the sport.

'Oh, it's all right,' I said. 'You've already got John Jr to chop the cabbage.'

'Yeah, yeah,' said John Jr. 'Some of us are actually recovering from a hard week's work where you don't just sit behind a desk reading magazines.'

'I would do it, Anne,' said Kelly. 'But, you know. Fingernails.' She held up her hands apologetically. Her nails must have been three centimetres long.

'You do that on purpose!' I said.

'It's just grooming!'

'It's chore avoidance!'

'Because she's a lady,' said John Jr proudly.

I wielded the knife grumpily, wondering if he'd fancy the cabbage if I stuck some lipgloss on it.

'So, Anne,' Kelly was saying, examining her cuticles. 'Apparently in Cannes the champagne glasses and the diamonds shimmer in the setting sun.'

'That sounds lovely,' said my mum, who was sweating slightly, pulling huge trays from the oven. 'You're going to have such a lovely time.'

I turned round, shocked.

'What are you talking about?'

'In Cannes, you know?'

'Yes, I do know. Are you going there?'

'Why?' said Kelly in a teasing voice. She knew how I felt about John Jr. 'Scared we'll show you up?'

'Other way round more likely,' said John Jr.

Thing is, I do like Kelly – it was her choice to marry an unmitigated baboon, but she has to share an en suite with him, so it's her that's suffering. But I really, really didn't want them barging in on my holiday. This was my trip; my chance to be whoever I wanted to be. I didn't need someone creeping up behind me making farting noises while I was talking to Dr Maitland or, well, anyone really.

'I thought you said the French had arseholes for mouths, hated fighting wars and ate their own shit,' I accused John Jr, whose sentiments on the peoples of the world were often expressed.

'What my darling wants she gets,' he said, not taking his eyes off the television.

'Apparently it's really, really classy and lovely,' said Kelly. 'Chanel shops everywhere and that.'

'Yeah,' I said.

'Evie don't know what that is,' said John Jr.

'It's clothes,' said Kelly. 'And they do skis, like what Posh Spice has.'

'I *know* what Chanel is,' I said.

'Don't worry,' said John Jr. 'We're going high style, so I don't think we'll see much of you.'

Then he leaned over.

'But Kelly wants you to introduce us to all your doctor friends,' he said.

I looked at Kelly. 'No way. Really?'

She shrugged. 'Well, I was thinking of getting some more serious work done . . . I am nearly thirty-two.'

'Don't do it,' I advised immediately. 'I could tell you some stories that would curl your GHDs.' Actually, most of what we do is pretty safe, but even so, it's still a bit dumb that someone as pretty as Kelly would submit herself to the knife. And I can always tell.

'Not your guys, though,' said Kelly.

'No,' I conceded. 'My guys are very good. But you're gorgeous, Kell. What do you want to go messing with that for?'

Kelly leaned back, looking mollified. But she didn't take her eyes off the French brochure I'd noticed earlier in her lap.

'Any news from Cassandro?' I asked loudly, trying to change the subject. My mother's brow furrowed.

'Yes,' she said. 'He called to tell us they loved Antigua so much they're thinking of going back and opening a beach bar and living happily ever after.'

Oh, God, that sounded blissful. I could just imagine it – clear blue skies, soft blue seas, rum punch every day. Oh, God, I so needed to get away.

'Lazy bastard,' said John Jr. 'He should come back and get a job. In the rain,' he added.

'You never tell John Jr off for swearing,' I immediately pointed out to Mum.

'Cos I'm not a lonely spinster like you,' said John Jr.

I mouthed 'bastard' in the direction of his beefy shoulders but carefully, so Mum didn't see.

Heathrow early in the morning is a fearsome sight. The airport was so huge, mobbed with people and slightly imposing, what with the policemen carrying machine guns and everything. I looked at my scruffy green rucksack. It was inherited from the boys' turns at the Scouts, and smelled like it too. And it hardly had anything in it: a couple of suits and my orange skirt; my not-bad bikini, which wasn't too disastrous if you half closed your eyes and repeated very loudly 'cellulite doesn't exist' three times whilst tapping your heels together (it also struck me that the South of France might be somewhere you'd be expected to wear high heels with your bikini so I'd thrown in my party shoes too); one sun dress, slightly faded, bought the year I said I really was sick of never going on holiday and was going to go and tour India all by myself, then I'd crapped out at the last minute; and of course the new red dress. I'd caressed the material packing it. It felt so full of possibility. It was a pulling dress, if you were being vulgar. A romantic dress, if you weren't.

Lydia came striding towards me. She looked chic and striking in a black trouser suit and white shirt that you could tell was really well cut and expensive, rather than the white shirt I own, which make me look like a pregnant man painting a house. She was also wearing a positively gigantic pair of sunglasses.

'Did you know you've got two coffee cups stuck to the front of your eyes?' I asked by way of greeting.

'Nice jeans,' she replied. 'Are they those loss leader ones they do for five pounds in Tesco?'

'No.'

'Oh, how funny. I could have sworn the waist was elasticated.'

'OK, OK, truce,' I muttered. 'Shall we go and check in?'

She sniffed loudly as we made our way across the concourse. She was trailing a chic black bag with a completely indiscreet large gilt label on the top, just in case it got mistaken for the million other identical black bags out there.

I wouldn't have minded but, looking round the queue, there were certainly a lot of very slim-limbed women, and none of them was wearing jeans. They were wearing Gillian McKeith-style trouser suits in pale shades, or, occasionally, mini skirts. There was one girl in 501s, but as soon as a smart mother shouted, 'Magda! Toilet the children, please!' it became patently obvious she was the hired help.

'Well, this isn't right.'

I tuned in from my sulk to hear Lydia remonstrating with the check-in woman, who looked scared.

'I send a lot of business your way, and I have to say, it doesn't seem too much to ask.'

'Yes, but we have to keep those seats . . .'

'Yes, but I checked in online six weeks ago.'

The woman looked pink. Honestly, sometimes I don't know why Lydia's working on reception. She should be marshalling troops somewhere.

'I'll just go talk to . . .' the woman scuttled off. I forgot I was meant to be sulking.

'What's up?' I said. In reply Lydia looked at me like I wasn't there.

The woman came back from her secret office at the back. 'I'm going to be able to upgrade this ticket,' said the woman. Lydia bestowed a beatific smile.

'*Thank* you.'

'If you'd just follow me.'

Fantastic! Upgrade! Lydia was bloody marvellous! I'd never travelled swish class before. I looked at the rest of the queue with pity. So long, suckers! Enjoy the cheap seats! I picked up my bag to follow them. At that precise instant, they both turned to look at me and the expression on their faces was almost identical. It said, 'Not you, you moose.'

Crushed, I put my bag back down slowly.

'Well, nice to run into you, Evie,' said Lydia casually. 'See you later, yeah?'

I think it was at this point that it started to occur to me that Lydia maybe wasn't all that great a friend.

'Magda! Tell Jacintha to stop kicking,' came the voice behind me for the millionth time.

'Stop keecking, pleece, Jacintha,' said a low, tentative voice that I could already tell would have no effect on Jacintha, because Jacintha was right behind me and it was me she was kicking, and had been for an hour and forty-five minutes.

'NOOOOOOOO!'

When I'd seen the family group I'd wondered why on earth you'd take your nanny on holiday. Having become well acquainted with the feet of Jacintha, it was no longer such a mystery. Certainly didn't help me focus on the briefing notes, anyway. I couldn't read a thing.

Sighing I turned towards the window. We were descending – I'd had my breath taken away earlier, both by a Jacintha boot to the kidneys and the sight of the snow-topped Alps just below us, continuing on for miles. Now, though, I was looking at a long swathe of bright buildings lining the shore and glistening in the bright sunlight, framed by dark forbidding mountains rising up above.

As I watched, looking for the airport, we continued on past the beach and out into sea. This was odd, as we were definitely getting lower and lower. I could see the white wakes of the boats out on the open sea . . . now I could see their sails. Uh, I didn't want to cause panic, but was no one else aware that we were about to all crash into the water and drown?

I looked around for a stewardess but there was none to be found. Oh, no! They must all be up the front, huddling! Or maybe they'd all bailed out already. I found my fingers making a clawing shape as the wings tilted and nearly hit the water. Bugger! I was going to die before I had the chance to go to Cannes! I was going to be a terrible loss just as my life was beginning! I couldn't help it; even though my heart was pounding, I had a momentarily satisfying flash of my brothers all crying and being miserable and wishing they'd been nicer to me, and my mother would say, 'I knew we should have bought her that pony,' and they'd all be very sorry I was dead and would think about me all the time. I hoped I'd get to come back like that girl in *The Lovely Bones* and watch them all being sad and talking about how fantastic I was and how they wished they'd told me when they had the chance, and Bailey would throw himself onto my coffin and say I was the only girl he'd ever loved and now his life was practically over too.

I was just closing my eyes to prepare for impact – and hoping it was quick – when the plane wheels bumped down onto something solid. I realised, with a sense of mild disappointment, that we'd landed, and that the airport seemed to be in the middle of the sea.

My spirits perked up, however, when I heard the captain say, 'Welcome to Nice, Côte d'Azure, ladies and gentlemen . . . where the temperature is twenty-seven degrees Celsius.'

The terminal building looked, frankly, too clean for my manky old bag. It was last out too – maybe they'd temporarily mistaken it for a duster of some kind. God, Lydia better have waited for me. She would know how to get to Cannes, surely? Otherwise, if she'd left me on my own . . . well, maybe I should have prepared slightly better for when I got here, but obviously I'd had a lot of very difficult bikini issues to work out and simply hadn't had the time.

Oh, thank God, there she was, standing with her gigantic sunglasses on, next to a short man. A man with sticky-up hair. A man who looked incredibly familiar, in fact.

'Oh, there you are,' she said. 'I thought you'd got completely lost. Anyway, I just wanted to tell you, I'm getting a lift in this lovely gentleman's helicopter, OK? So I suggest you get the train or a taxi, if you can afford it. *Adieu!*'

'Hello, Bailey,' I said. Lydia's eyebrows shot up.

'*You're* Bailey?' she said, as Bailey came up and gave me a hug. '*Bienvenue*,' he said. It didn't seem fair to be annoyed with him because a) he'd not yet thrown himself on my grave in the event of my imaginary death, and b) he'd not got to know Lydia yet.

'I certainly do,' I said. 'What's this about a helicopter?'

'They've sent a helicopter for me,' said Bailey, half apologetically, half obviously unbelievably delighted. 'I am the chief designer, I suppose.'

'Oh, how boring. Helicopters again,' I said. 'Why don't you ask for the space shuttle like all the fashionable people?'

'Shall I see if there's room for you, too?' he asked.

'They do have quite strict weight limits,' said Lydia. Then she turned round. 'We were sitting next to each other. In business.'

'Oh, did you go business?' I said, trying to sound airy. 'I thought they'd led you off to put you in the hold.'

'Well, this is going to be fun,' said Bailey. He turned to a smartly dressed man and spoke a few words to him in rapid French. Lydia made a big show of widening her eyes and nodding her head along to show she understood, though I bet she didn't.

'OK, no problem,' said Bailey to me. 'I promise not to throw your horrible kit bag into the sea either.'

'Yes, I must swap it for a handbag, like you have,' I said. In fact, it was a man bag, but I smiled to show him I was genuinely pleased to see him.

Ooh, and I was. What a thrill. I instantly realised that this was the way I was born to live. The speed from which I could get from a manky high street changing room to going *flip flip flip flip flip* (helicopter noise, as experienced first hand by me) over the deep blue Mediterranean sea must mean something. It must register a change in my life; a fresh start, a new beginning. As I sat back in the (not very comfortable) seat and stared into the sun, it certainly felt like it.

Chapter Four

Well, this wasn't exactly what I'd been dreaming of. A huge black car had been waiting at the helicopter pad (hurrah!) and, after whisking us through busy traffic, it had dropped Bailey off at some huge five-star joint on the front, where three little flunkies, actually wearing hats and white gloves, hopped down to take his luggage.

Then the car had dropped Lydia off at a nice smart white-washed place that looked more house than hotel, with bright green shutters, wisteria growing up the walls, overflowing window boxes, a lawn, a pool and a nice fat lady who'd greeted Lydia by name and with a kiss. 'Why didn't you recommend I book here?' I'd asked. 'Well, I can't give the name and address out to just anyone, can I?' said Lydia, as if this were reasonable.

Anyway, it was now forty minutes later and the driver was circling what looked like a housing estate in the back end of nowhere, looking grumpy and muttering to himself under his breath. I hope I wasn't meant to tip this guy. Well, even if I was, I only had twenty-euro notes, and not that many of those, and he certainly wasn't getting one.

The driver said something which sounded like 'vlah vlah GarRUMPH' and stopped the car, pointing towards a grimy-looking apartment block. I thanked him, considered offering him a pound coin but then scarpered before he had the chance to say anything to me I wouldn't understand. Hmm, maybe my French wasn't just 'rusty'. Maybe it was more like 'non-existent'.

This couldn't be right, though. It was just a big block of flats, and all the windows were covered in metal grilles. I turned round, but the driver had already whizzed off, obviously affronted that his beautiful car had had to pass through such upsetting surroundings.

Hoisting up my rucksack, the sun suddenly felt like it was beating very warmly on my head – I looked at my watch. It was noon, the hottest time of day. I moved to what had to be the front door. Sure enough, there written next to a bell was *Hôtel de Cannes (deux)*.

I sighed. Well, Hôtel de Cannes had sounded such a good bet. You know, like the best hotel in Cannes, thus the title. The fact that it was so cheap in the middle of conference season was simply a bonus. Now I suspected that the *deux*

might actually be quite important, some kind of legal require-
ment from somewhere. I rang the buzzer, which sounded deep
inside the building, and sighed.

There was no answer. Actually, after a couple of minutes
my heart lifted a bit. If the hotel was shut I'd just have to
move – maybe to that place Lydia was in, that looked nice. Or
maybe Bailey would have a spare bedroom in his luxury
bloody hotel or something. But just as I was wondering where
I could get a cab, the door creaked open. A small woman stood
there. Very slender and with her hair fiercely tied back she did
not look a single bit like the friendly woman with the rolled-
up sleeves who had greeted Lydia.

'*Oui? Qu'est-ce que c'est?*' she barked at me, and various
other sentences stuck on the end. I looked at her blankly.

'Uh, *bonjour*,' I said, my brain searching for the set phrase
I'd learnt off by heart to ask for my room. But I wasn't going
to get that far.

'Ah,' she said. 'Hell-OH.' She said it in a deliberately slow
and simple way, I reckoned, as if by not being French it was
clear that I was mentally retarded. 'Yes? What do you want?'

'Uh . . . the hotel?' I said, as if *she* wouldn't be able to
understand more than a few simple nouns.

She raised her eyes to heaven and then pointed out some
numbers under the sign, which I'd assumed were the address
or something.

'*Fermé 12–14h*,' it said.

'*Fermé*,' she said. 'Closed. Until two o'clock.'

65

Closed? I didn't know hotels could close. I thought that was the entire point of why something was known as a hotel rather than, say, a youth hostel where you had to do chores.

'I can't get in till two o'clock?' I said.

'No,' she said. Then she turned her back on me and clip-clopped off down the road.

I love it. France. I do. I love travelling and going away and visiting new countries and having holidays in lovely places such as France.

These are a few of the thoughts that did NOT go through my head for the next two hours, as I sat on my gigantic bag. I thought about trying to go somewhere – anywhere – but I couldn't move the damn thing and I could only see apartment blocks in both directions. I called Bailey but got no answer and I couldn't bear to phone Lydia – after that little conversation about the hotel I didn't really trust her to help me, rather than, say, come and run me over with her hired car.

So I had to stick it out, listlessly reading *Heat* magazine for the ninth time and trying to work out what horrible thing I could do to this hotel room to get my own back. By the time I'd got to jamming up the plug sockets with egg sandwiches (a favourite trick of Patrick's, particularly when I had friends round at that awkward stage in my early teens, who very quickly became not my friends when they realised my room smelt funny) I was ready to scream.

Nobody passed me in the street at all, apart from a curious

fat woman who stared at me rudely. Where was everybody? Were they all getting ready for super-fancy cocktail parties? Asleep? I was in the middle of the buzzy Côte d'Azure. Puff Daddy comes here to throw Beyoncé into the sea. I'd arrived by bloody helicopter, for goodness' sake, didn't that stand for anything?

Nineteen hours later, at two minutes to two precisely, there came a clip-clopping up the road. I regarded the woman through narrow slits for eyes.

'*D'accord*,' she said. She didn't ask if I'd had lunch or been for a swim or even had a glass of water, simply eyed me as I heaved my enormous, stupid, smelly bag and traipsed wearily after her.

The Hôtel de Cannes (deux) was . . . well, it was cheap. It was up a flight of stairs and seemed to be built around an apartment block, which was a new concept in hotelling to me – I'd expected a swimming pool. It smelled of disinfectant, which failed to mask the odour of old cigarette smoke and cheap coffee. The walls were a horrible brown, with mirrors reflecting back more dismal brown.

The woman checked me in grudgingly, as if my sit-in outside her hotel was some kind of ruse to scam her out of a room. Finally, after laboriously photocopying my passport, and amidst many weary sighs – how could she possibly be expected to fill out these forms after a mere two-hour lunch break? – she handed me a slightly sticky key card and nodded me up to the third floor.

Here was a long corridor of brown once again. There wasn't another soul in sight. I stomped along, pulling the bag behind me like an errant dog. At room 317 I stopped and inserted the card. The cheap, brown Formica door swung open. It really did look quite a lot like the kind of room someone would get murdered in in an exploitation movie from the seventies.

Brown, stained lino. Shutters closed on a small window, rendering the place wreathed in gloom. Chipped cabinet with yet another brown-reflecting mirror.

I figured I'd have a shower and that would make me feel a bit better, but the water was brown and dribbly and lukewarm. I had to get out of here.

The hotel woman grudgingly pointed me in the direction of the promenade ('It is water. You just go *downhill*.' '*Merci*,' I said. We really were talking to each other like idiots) and I headed out into the bright afternoon light.

It was lovely. Fresh and clean under the bright blue sky and I slipped on my sunglasses as I walked down towards the harbour. The air felt warm on my skin and I began to forget all the indignities of the last couple of hours. There was street after street of apartment blocks, painted yellow and blue, with wrought-iron balconies draped with swimming trunks hanging out to dry, mixed with the high gates and walls of white-washed villas whose driveways curled up into the hills. Coming further into the town there were indeed the promised lines of shops: Louis Vuitton, Chanel, Gucci. Here it was absolutely thronging with people; emaciated women of a certain age, with huge powdered hairdos and tiny little dogs, picking their way through the cobbles on heels. Suave, Italian-looking men with slicked-back hair and pink shirts took telephone calls as sullen-looking model-y girls with Russian accents looked at incredibly over-the-top dresses in Nancy Dell'Olio colours.

Baby girls in big puffs of pink fluff were being pushed around in baby carriages that looked more like small convertibles, and gorgeous, tanned teenage girls showed off flat stomachs over low-slung jeans and Hi-Top Converse, chattering loudly all the while. Quite obviously set apart from the colourful locals mooched groups of tourists: Brits, Dutch, German, all made obvious by their sloppy sports gear and bad posture.

At last I emerged at the water's edge. The soft Mediterranean waves – now with a hint of early evening pinkness on them – shimmered into the endless distance, whilst the boats bobbed up and down along the quay. There were huge white boats; huge blue boats; little boats that would look grand if they weren't tied up next to the huge boats. There was a massive grey boat that looked like a warship but, judging by the chandeliers, it was a big gin palace too. There was the easyJet cruise ship, stuck out in the bay miles from shore, looking like a big orange blob. Young, hunky men cleaned the sides of the boats while others carried crates of champagne on board. Huge Bentleys and BMWs purred up and down the road. I liked it. A lot.

I watched the most absurd little yellow sports car with a million-decibel engine roar by. People were congregating at pavement cafés and ordering carafes of wine and I suddenly felt a distinct desire to be one of them. I decided to go and get Bailey. I could do with a friendly face to go with the rosé.

Bailey's hotel was set right on the palm-lined seafront, past carousels and ice-cream stands and immaculate-looking couples strolling hand in hand, accompanied by their clean and beautiful children. It didn't remind me much of home.

The hotel looked like a cake that had been spun out of icing sugar for some ridiculous billionaire's wedding – layer upon layer of scallops and frills which resolved themselves, as you got closer, into balconies and crenulations. It was wildly over the top, there were turrets everywhere. I loved it.

As I clopped up the stairs into the huge lobby I started to wonder if I should have just thrown on the red dress straight away. That, actually, it was a little subtle. If the women on the street had been dressed up, the ones here were positively festive. Millions of sparkling lights from the chandeliers bounced off huge mirrors and onto glinting ear lobes, huge rings and heavy necklaces.

This was serious jewellery, and it all looked real. I tried not to stare too much, but I couldn't help it, and anyway, why would you wear this stuff if you didn't want people to stare at it? And they were all so thin. This wasn't just in shape, or gently toned, Coleen McLoughlin style. This was full on I-will-never-not-ever-eat-a-meal style. It was amazing their tiny wrists and necks could even take the weight of the precious stones. It looked like just wearing them would be all the exercise they would need that day. I saw some pretty high-glamour women at the practice, but even they weren't like this. This was a different realm altogether; it wasn't millionaire's wives looking for bigger tits. It was billionaire's wives looking to float away, and only the rocks were keeping them tethered to earth.

'Oh, my,' I said, out loud.

'Can ah 'elp you?'

I did find it mildly dispiriting that the beautiful young man in the smart designer uniform could tell I was English before I'd even opened my mouth or glanced in his direction. Damn you, Topshop, for making us all so completely identi-fiable from thirty metres or more.

The receptionist was beautiful, though he had a look in his eye that implied that if I was only in here for a quick sniff around, he'd rather I left.

'Bailey Arnold, please,' I said in my best imperious tones, which aren't that imperious, frankly, and make me sound con-stipated.

'Ah, Monsieur Arnold. Of course.'

He nodded his head and made a quick call.

'Go right up – room 801, on the top floor.' I wondered if that was penthouse good or servant's quarters bad as I got into the incredible panelled lift, which had a small red chair and a small red man who pushed the button to '*numéro huit*', as deftly rehearsed by me.

The lift slid smoothly up and deposited me on a bright landing, with large windows at either end and thick, lush carpet spreading out in both directions. There were only two doors visible on the entire floor, which went on for miles: 801 and 802. I figured it probably wasn't the servant's quarters.

There was a proper old-fashioned bell outside the door so I pushed that. Bailey opened it immediately as if he'd been waiting for me.

'Come in!' he said. 'Come in! Learn why it was, in fact, worth getting my head kicked in by the beasts every day because they knew to lie in wait for me outside the technical library! Learn why, yes, CAD physics is worth giving up every Tuesday night for a year for. Yes, why—'

'Shut up, boffin-oh,' I said. I wanted to take in my surroundings in peace because, quite frankly, I'd never been anywhere so nice in my entire life.

You entered the suite via a parquet-floored hall in which stood a coat rack and various large pieces of marble art, until the room opened out into a vast living area. It had a vast, spotless cream carpet that felt like it could curl up to my ankles; it was like walking in moss. Three huge windows overlooked the pale blue sea, sails bobbing up and down in the distance. A huge fireplace had a fire dancing in it, even though it was hot outside, but the room still felt temperate. There was a glass table set for dinner with an enormous bowl of fruit on it, and several huge and comfortable-looking jewel-coloured sofas. In the corner was a fully stocked drinks cabinet with proper-sized bottles, none of your minibar nonsense (I didn't even have a minibar in my 'hotel'). Panelled doors led off either side of the living area, presumably into more rooms.

'*Mon dieu*,' I expostulated.

'*Mais oui*,' said Bailey.

'Fuck a duck,' I said.

'*Exactement*,' replied Bailey.

'I don't understand,' I said, looking round again. Bailey? Here? It was just amazing. 'I mean, this is for rock stars, or royalty, or . . . or . . . you know, VIPs. Not swots from St Michaels' whose hobby was "getting their head kicked in".'

Bailey sank happily into one of the other sofas.

'My dear,' he said. 'In the world of dynamic changing environments in healthcare, I *am* a rock star.'

I'd always known Bailey was a brainiac with a brainiac job, but this was something else. I'd clearly completely underestimated him. No wonder he went out with supermodels all the time. Imagine, a man in undying love with me having all this.

'Where's your robot butler? Can you have him bring me a gin and tonic?' I said looking round and trying to be casual.

'*Mademoiselle?*' and from one of the panelled doors came, I promise, a man dressed in a black frock coat. For a second I thought he really was a robot and nearly screamed. Bailey looked embarrassed.

'He comes with the room,' he whispered to me. 'I don't know how to make him go away.'

'Uh, a gin and tonic, please,' I said hesitatingly.

The butler glided over to the bar and started mixing drinks, the sound of which made me very happy indeed.

'I knew I should have copied off you at GCSE,' I said. 'Bugger. What have you actually done?'

'Well, you've read the brief?'

'Oh, yes, of course.' Well, I would. I'd hate to look unprofessional.

I opened the balcony doors, to be greeted with a sudden yell that sounded like it was coming from next door.

'You'd think they'd soundproof this place,' said Bailey. 'Seeing as it's a royal palace and everything.'

'Yeah,' I said. 'Can't the robot butler . . .'

Bugger, what was I thinking? I'd completely forgotten he was a real live man, standing there.

'*Immédiatement, mademoiselle,*' he said, and shimmied out of the room as if on wheels.

'That butler thing gives me the creeps,' I announced.

'He's a real person,' said Bailey. 'Do try and treat him like, you know, a humanoid. Now, do you want to see the rest of this place? I have to say, it's the nicest . . .'

But before he could beckon me over, the butler came hurtling back into the suite, looking terrified for his life, closely followed by a leering, menacing – why, it was none other than John Jr.

'Oh, for crying out loud,' I said, almost stamping my feet. John Jr was in full flow.

'So if I say best room in town oi MEAN best room in town and that means, buster, if oi want to have a bust up with the old trouble and strife you better keep your big nose aht of it, know wharra mean?'

The butler had recovered his composure somewhat and gave John Jr a look that said 'You will never order another dish in any restaurant bar or café in this town without someone I know personally peeing in it,' but he said nothing.

'John Jr, for God's sake.'

John Jr turned round at that. He got the shock of his life when he saw me; his already red face turned puce.

'Evie . . . Evie, for fuck's sake. Are you staying here?'

I sighed. 'If I say I am will you move?'

Kelly came out of the suite to see what the commotion was. Now I understood the noise; there'd obviously been some sort of incident with the hair straighteners. A large chunk of her hair looked distinctly singed.

'Ow, hello, Evie,' she sniffed, smiling bravely. 'I hoped we'd run into you.'

'Yup,' I said. 'Well, this was quick.'

'Now, I don't want to push in . . .'

'Uh huh . . .'

Kelly looked towards Bailey. 'But is this one of your fabulous doctors?'

I looked round at Bailey, who was retreating towards the

windows of his huge suite, away from John Jr. It was almost comical to see. He probably didn't realise he was doing it, just vestigial habit.

John Jr narrowed his piggy eyes. 'Hey. I recognise you.'

Bailey's lips twitched and he fussed with his glasses. I'd never mentioned at home that I still saw Bailey. Mum would have wanted us to get married and the beasts would never have let me hear the end of it.

'It's Bailey boy, innit? Ol' Bailey boy, Snaily Bailey.'

I could see the colour rise in Bailey's cheeks. I forgot sometimes, encased as he was in his great job and nice lifestyle, that it had been pretty bad for him too.

'Mnnff,' said Bailey.

John Jr's face broke into a huge smile. 'Well! Fantastic to see you! We had some great times back then, didn't we? Some right laughs. Kelly, this is Bailey, one of the old gang from Leadbetter Road. Come here.'

And he marched up to Bailey and gave him a great bear hug. I don't think I've seen a man so surprised since Will Young won *Pop Idol*. Bailey took a step back as soon as he reasonably could.

'John Jr,' he said stiffly. 'It's been a long time.'

I instantly felt sorry for him; it sounded like he was saying it in a James Bond/*Goldfinger*-type fashion and should be stroking a pussycat and dreaming up shark-related tortures for his lifelong foe. Instead John Jr clearly thought he'd stumbled on a long-lost 'homie' from back in the 'hood'.

'Kelly, Kelly, come meet Bail the Snail. Oh, we had some times in those days, didn't we, Bailey boy?'

'I don't know,' said Bailey stiffly. 'It was quite hard to hear because you kept dunking my head in a bucket of water.'

John Jr guffawed mightily. 'Right laugh, so it was.'

'Hello,' said Kelly. 'Now I don't want to bother you, but I wanted to talk to someone about this freckle.'

She pointed to something invisible perched on top of her cleavage.

'Getting someone to feel your knockers again?' roared John Jr. 'She's a right tart, my wife, eh?'

'I'm not a doctor,' said Bailey. 'I'm an engineering specialist.'

'Pff. That sounds boring,' said John Jr. 'Mind you, you always were a speccy get. Any money in it?'

There was a short silence as we waited for the penny to drop.

'Oh! You're stayin' here, are you? Well, well done, my son, well done. Looks like it wasn't a waste getting all those swot levels after all. Course, I went to the university of life . . . oy, gar-*SON*!'

Oh, no. Once John Jr got started on the university of life diatribe the evening was well and truly done for. And he didn't go to the university of life at all. He went to the university of misbehaving at school, causing teachers to have nervous breakdowns, then leaving at sixteen and hanging around amusement arcades before falling into second-hand car dealing and borrowing money off Dad to open his own garage, a loan I'm sure he's never paid back. John Jr went to the university of being a complete arse. And now he was hollering at the butler for drinks – we had to do something! And fast!

'Uh, Bailey,' I said meaningfully. 'We're going to be late for dinner. You remember. That *very* important dinner.'

Bailey was still trapped, looking like a rabbit hypnotised by a snake.

'Right. Dinner,' said John Jr. 'That sounds great.'

'It's a private dinner,' I said. 'There won't be any room for you.'

'Oh, we'll see about that,' said John Jr. 'Little lesson, Evie. Money can open a lot of doors. Come on, Kelly, get yourself dressed up.'

As Kelly was already wearing a bustier twinkling with Swarovski crystals, spray on black trousers and five-inch heels, and her hair resembled the crest of a tidal wave, I couldn't imagine exactly what he meant by 'get dressed up', but she instantly shuffled off.

'Right,' said John Jr. 'Where we going? Hope it's not too fucking Frog. They eat horse, you know. Did you know that? Filthy fuckers. Are we going to a horse restaurant? Hope not. *GarSON*. What does horse taste like?'

Defeated, as if taking part in some horrible zombie movie, we headed for the lift. I pressed the polished brass lift button; it pinged, the lift already there.

'Oh, fabulous, you're all ready,' said Lydia, stepping daintily out of the lift and taking Bailey by the arm as if he were her personal property. She was wearing a beautiful, understated, swinging navy and cream cotton-knit dress that I swear I've seen on Sarah Jessica Parker, with a dinky navy handbag to match. As soon as I saw it I knew that instead of buying half a dozen cheapy high-store outfits I should have saved up for something like that and just worn it every day.

'Dinner time? I'm totally ready to go.'

She lowered her voice by about half a decibel and pouted her mouth in the direction of Bailey's ear. 'Didn't realise we were taking the Addams family, though. Ah huh huh huh!'

Chapter Five

I had had a fantasy of how my first night in the South of France would be. The evening light would be soft and sweet-smelling (that at least was true) as we strolled down to the Croisette, home to every film star of the last fifty years, including the porny ones.

Bailey would be handing me a cocktail as we stood on a balcony watching the sun go down; he'd tell me how much he'd loved me all these years and I, looking elegant and graceful and like something out of the twenties, would touch my elegant hand to the top of the balcony, accept the cocktail with sadness and say, in perfect French, 'I'm sorry, Bailey. I can never love you,' as my gaze lingered on the extraordinarily hunky doctor who was waving at me from the beach, where he was running, shirtless, with his black Labrador. A single crystal tear dropped from my eyes with the exquisite pain of *les affaires de la coeur* and . . .

'Steak fwites, that's what it's called,' John Jr was saying loudly, stomping out into the road without looking (the Ferrari swerved to avoid him, worse luck. Mind you, in a fight between John Jr and a small lightweight sports car, my money was on JJ). 'Oh, right, not to worry, we'll just find somewhere with pictures in the window. *Comprendez?*'

We were all marching in a long line across the Croisette, the street which ran parallel to the sea. It was covered in palm trees, and the hand- and footprints of European film stars were embedded in bronze in the concrete, just like in my fantasy. The place was absolutely mobbed with people, none of whom looked anything like as British as us. Bailey and Lydia were behind me, deep in conversation, Kelly was bringing up the rear in very high heels that made her look as if she was trying to perform a circus act by balancing on tiny knives.

'I was thinking maybe somewhere nice and traditional,' I said timidly, holding up my guidebook. 'Somewhere that . . . *"brings alive the freshness of the Mediterranean and the gentleness of the soft Côte d'Azure breezes, wrapped up in the tastes of the Provençal hills and grated with the zest of—"'*

'Steak fwites,' said John Jr.

And so it was that we found ourselves sitting outside a restaurant with plastic flowers on the table, surrounded by several other tables full of lost English people looking at the laminated plastic menus with pictures on them and trying to ignore their badly behaved children. John Jr thinks he likes the finer things in life but when it comes to his stomach he's pretty straightforward.

'Oi! *Garson!*' shouted John Jr. 'How many of us are there? Five? Right. Five bottles of white wine. Sweet.'

The waiter gave John Jr a look he absolutely deserved but one, sadly, he was incapable of noticing.

Bailey sidled in next to me. 'Em, I think we have to—'

'Kill him,' I whispered. 'I know. I thought maybe we could drop his body in the bay.'

Bailey's brow furrowed. 'Um. I was thinking, maybe try and lose him.'

'Oh,' I said, trying not to look too disappointed.

'Obviously, you know, death would have been a good option too.'

'It would,' I said. 'One down, two to go.'

'But really, I just meant . . . please don't think I want to hang out with your brother all week.'

I was shocked by the injustice of this. 'What do you mean? You think I do? I didn't invite him! You're the one that's all "Oh, great to see you John Jr, let's catch up," kiss kiss.'

'I was not,' said Bailey hotly. 'I didn't say anything.'

'Well, maybe you should have,' I said. 'I tried to save you with the whole "fake dinner" thing and you just stood there, wobbling.'

Bailey looked at me and suddenly I had a flashback to him aged eight. Nobody likes being reminded of how embarrassing their childhood was. Also, telling men they're cowards is hardly a guaranteed banker either. I saw he was really hurt, and I felt really bad.

'OK,' he said, and left the seat, heading to the other end of the table where Lydia had saved him a seat. Oh, good. I'd sent him into the arms of Cruella de Vil. I poured myself a very large glass of wine. This was going to be a long night.

'I said a hey-a ho-a wibble-a wobble and a hammy and a bullet to beat.'

Oh, God. Oh, God. How had everything gone so terribly wrong? It was several hours and many, many bottles of wine later. I'd reached that horrible point where I was too afraid to move, convinced that my legs no longer possessed the power to lift me. The wine had definitely seemed to improve the more of it I'd drank. I wondered if this was because it had had time to breathe. Or maybe because it had stripped the taste-buds from my mouth – I wasn't sure.

Bailey and Lydia were buried in conversation down the other end, which pissed me off big time. I didn't know why; normally when Bailey introduced me to some gorgeous girl I could hold off getting jealous for about ten minutes, waiting until she said something idiotic like, 'Isn't it amazing how every sheep born has its own baa? Do you know what I'd really love to do? Go on *Big Brother*,' and then I could relax again. But this was Lydia, whom he'd already seen being not very nice to me. And every time I tried to casually sidle up to their conversation Lydia shot me a look that very clearly said, 'You, go away,' in monkey language.

Meanwhile, Kelly was talking to me about face cream at the most extraordinary length. I was ready to knock myself out with the pepper grinder. Every time I thought Kelly was my ally in the war against John Jr, she'd start doing this; banging on about pentapeptides or fruit acid till I wanted to cry.

John Jr, who I'd been trying to ignore as he snurfed his way through what seemed like several bottles of nasty wine, had decided to get up, lift his polo shirt and expose his pork-red body (no wonder Kelly was always crying). Using the wine bottle as a microphone he started singing along to the piped music whilst the waiters appeared to be entering a superciliousness competition, leaning against the flapping canvas with their arms folded. Oh, God. This couldn't get any worse.

'Hello, Evie.'

There was a funny noise behind me, beyond the plastic covering, and it sounded like it was calling my name. Half nervous, half pleased to be temporarily distracted I slowly turned round.

Oh, God, of course it was. Of course. After all, who else did I know in the entire country?

'A hibby-hobey-hibb,' yelled John Jr, oblivious to Dr Maitland standing on the other side of the plastic, immaculately dressed in a pastel shirt and a pale linen suit which as usual was ludicrously old-fashioned, but somehow looked rather dashing here.

I smiled wanly. Both docs weren't due in till the morning; I was going to collect them from the airport, for goodness' sake. I thought it was a bit rude of Dr Maitland to turn up and witness my embarrassing family before I could safely get rid of them.

'Hello,' I said, jumping out of my chair and barrelling towards him in an attempt to distance myself from everyone behind me and thus render them not even acquaintances. John Jr had taken off his shirt entirely and was hurling it round his head as he came to the emotive finale of the song.

'So, you know everyone in Cannes already!' said Dr Maitland. 'Good networking skills.' Oh, God, please tell me he had another dinner to go on to. Please. I tried to keep him out of Kelly's sight line; she'd ask him to eat with us immediately.

I shrugged and tried to look nonchalant and businesslike and not at all tanked up on cheap wine.

'Was your flight OK? I'd have arranged transport.'

'Yes, I decided to come early. Little bit of groundwork. Big week ahead for us, don't you think?'

I agreed heartily.

'HE-llo,' came a voice. Oh, bugger. I'd only considered

the risk from my end of the table, but Lydia had spotted an opening.

'It's Dr Maitland, isn't it? Want to join us for a drink?'

'Hi.' Bailey waved hello.

'Well, er . . .' Dr Maitland looked at me enquiringly, which was nice of him. Suddenly, John Jr's glazed vision gained focus.

'Oi! Oo are you? You're not after our Evie, are you?'

Oh, Christ on a bike. How mortifying. Dr Maitland went a little pink, which was quite cute.

'No, no . . . we work together.'

'Yeah, didn't think so . . . you're definitely out of her league, ain't he, Eve?'

'Shut UP,' I said. I was used to crap like this from JJ, though, so it didn't harm me that much. But Dr Maitland's head snapped up.

'Excuse me?'

'Don't listen to him,' I said. 'It's just my . . . um, brother. He's a bit pissed.'

'Not as pissed as he'd have to be,' shouted John Jr jovially.

'Don't speak to her like that.'

I had to admit, I was quite impressed. Dr Maitland was tall, but John Jr weighed about three of him.

'Yeah, and oo are you?'

'JJ,' shouted Kelly. 'It's the *doctor*!'

Now I was even more embarrassed. Doctors, lawyers – any professionals – get automatic 'respect' in my family. A bit outdated, forelock-tugging, I'd always thought, but thank goodness, because it worked.

'Doctor?' said JJ, as Kelly pulled at him to sit down and handed him another full glass of wine, perhaps unwisely. All the tables in the restaurant were watching us extremely closely. Dr Maitland took off his glasses and started to rub them with a handkerchief. I bet he was glad he'd stopped by.

'I think I'll get on,' he said. I was burning up with mortification. He must have thought I was a real guttersnipe.

'OK,' I managed to stutter. 'Uh, see you tomorrow.'

'Uh, OK then,' he said.

'Lovely family,' Lydia had smirked, as she'd departed into the night – in the same direction as Bailey, I couldn't help but notice.

'He was just pissed,' I said stiffly. Kelly and John Jr had already departed, John Jr drunkenly insisting on splitting the bill exactly, which then took hours. I mean, I could slag JJ off, because he was mine, but nobody else could. Then I'd trudged the long way up the hill in the dark, conscious that I'd drunk too much, not had any fun and now had to get up at the crack of dawn to fetch bloody Dr Bennet from the airport.

Nice airport was cool and white in the early morning glare as I held up my printed sign. Obviously Dr Bennet knew who I was, but he thought this looked smarter.

I looked around at the women passing through the airport. Oh, they were good-looking all right. But in such a boring way (it seemed to me – of course I know men are relatively simple in their tastes for these things). Tiny bottoms, long legs, tits hoisted up to clavicle level, hair bleached to straw, huge sunglasses balanced on augmented cheekbones – it looked so relentlessly dull, so uniform. We got quite a lot of desperate divorcees at the surgery. Often, their husbands had left them for someone who looked absolutely identical to them but was twenty years younger. Why bother? I often wondered. If you kept trying to look the same way you would get gradually more grotesque, and if your tit perkiness was all your man was after, well, there would always be someone perkier.

Not a single woman looked remotely happy. I bought a croissant to eat at the little coffee bar outside Arrivals and could almost feel them sneering behind me as I tucked in to the refined carbs and sugar.

OK, so I was a midget with curly brown hair next to this lot. But hey! At least I was getting a yummy croissant for breakfast.

The gate started to flood with people – many of them men with that unmistakeable patina of plastic surgeon about them. Maybe I've become a bit of an expert. But their skin is always a little smoother than yours, as if they know about a secret bar of soap you're barred from, and their stubble is always non-existent, as if they've given themselves electrolysis instead of shaving. There was a clattering of different languages – it sounded like German and Dutch – and I got quite engrossed looking at the expensive luggage and loafers and silk ties and . . .

'Hello!' said a friendly voice. Shaken out of my reverie I turned around. There was a man standing in front of me. He had a cheerful face with freckles, and russety hair. He looked very young. I hoped he didn't want money for something.

'*Non, merci,*' I said loudly.

His face looked a little crestfallen at my obvious confusion.

'Uh, you're here for me?' he said. I was what? He looked a bit nervous. 'I know, I look a bit young to be a doctor, everyone says that, ha ha ha.'

I blinked.

'Oh, shit, are you French? I mean, *merde*. Eh, eh. *BON JOUR. Je m'appelle doc-TEUR Bennet.*'

'I'm not French,' I said.

'Oh. OK.' There was a pause. 'Uh . . . are you *special*?'

'What do you *want*?' I said crossly.

'I'm Dr Bennet. Are you picking me up?'

Oh, for goodness' sake, how could I have been so dense?

'Sorry,' I said. 'Um. There's another Dr Bennet. It's not you.'

Freckle face looked puzzled. 'Oh. Right.'

'Are you here for the conference?'

'Yes,' he said. 'I'm a junior. I don't know why they sent me really. So that's why I thought you were picking me up. I'm not used to all this.'

'Me neither,' I said. 'It's my first time too.'

'As a driver?'

'No. I'm a medical receptionist.'

'Really? Where are the dragon claws and fire coming out of your mouth?'

'Ah, I'm private,' I said. 'If you pay money you get a smile and maybe even a cappuccino. Maybe.'

'Well, that does sound like it's worth thousands and thousands of pounds,' he said, his face looking slightly cross suddenly. 'I'm Tom Bennet.'

'Evie Kennedy,' I said. 'Hi.'

'Hi. I don't suppose you know where the bus stop is, do you?'

'I'd offer you a lift,' I said, 'but . . .'

Just then I saw my Dr Bennet and his wife emerge from Arrivals. As usual, he looked poised, and she looked furious. He'd mentioned looking forward to having a romantic time in Cannes. In my head, the idea of having a romantic time with Mrs Bennet seemed akin to trying to clamber on top of an unwieldy metal chair, but I nodded and smiled hello to her nonetheless. In response she sighed at me.

The effect on Tom was immediate; he got very nervous, glancing from the Bennets to me. I thought he was very embarrassed.

'Not to worry yourself,' Tom said. 'See you around. Is it a big place,' Cannes?'

'Not really.' I watched him go. Under other circumstances, bumping accidentally into a young doctor at Côte d'Azure airport might be construed as rather romantic. This one though had skin that looked like it might burn up in direct sunlight. How disappointing. Still, compared to everyone else I'd seen come off the plane, he was definitely number one.

The Bennets weren't chatty in the cab, which made me think that perhaps I shouldn't have bothered coming and instead kept the probably hundred extra euros it had cost to keep the driver handy in the car park, for all the thanks I got.

They seemed oblivious to the sun glancing off the waves, the girls rollerblading in bikinis on Nice promenade, the real French families unfolding picnic baskets containing golden, sticky-looking roast chickens and whole cheeses and baguettes. I don't know why I got a little thrill when I saw French people with baguettes. I suppose it would be like coming to London and seeing everyone dressed up as pearly kings and queens and saying lor, luv a duck.

When I'd checked the itinerary I'd drawn up earlier my heart had sank – they were in the same hotel as Bailey and my idiot brother. Oh, good, I was so glad everyone was in the very height of comfort and luxury whilst my bed smelled of someone else's deodorant.

'Do you want me to talk you through the schedule?' I said

when we drew up in front of the hotel. Once again the chap with the white gloves was out doing his stuff. I wondered if every so often some plutocrat just dropped him ten thousand euros for no reason.

'Yes,' nodded Dr Bennet. 'I've lost mine,' he added. That was strange. Dr Bennet never lost anything.

The beautiful boy on reception had given me even more of a curled lip today, as if I was some prostitute that followed men up to their bedrooms. Mind you, from what I'd heard that didn't exactly faze people who worked in posh hotels. Maybe he just thought I was a really cheap prostitute. Dr Maitland joined us in the lobby. I was embarrassed to see him again, but he looked even more so, so I didn't mention anything.

'OK,' I announced. 'The backers want to see you first, then there's the Ocean Consortium meeting – does that make sense to you?'

They nodded mutely.

'It's in the DeVere rooms, then the introductory session, then at five it's cocktails for everyone in the Belles Rives American bar, then dinner . . . my God, just as well you're not in surgery this week. You'll all be completely wombated.'

For the first time Dr Maitland looked like he might be about to smile. 'Not everyone,' he said, 'gets falling over drunk just because there's free drink available.'

'Why not?' I said. 'How can you help it?'

His eyebrows twitched. 'Well, you know your limits, so you're careful with top-ups.'

'But it's *free*,' I explained again, just in case he hadn't got it the first time.

'It's free,' he said, 'it's not compulsory.'

'Do you do any operating?' I asked. 'At this expo? I wondered if there might be . . . you know, like competitions.'

'Competitions,' said Dr Bennet gravely. The two doctors looked at each other. 'Like, races?'

Oh, God, I MUST read the brief.

Dr Maitland looked at me sternly over his spectacles. 'Evie Kennedy, is there anything else?'

'No, sir,' I said.

'Are you coming to the introduction?'

'Can I?' I nearly squeaked. There was a free bar! Not, of course, that I would be conducting myself with anything other than total decorum at all times.

'Well, you're taking notes, aren't you?'

Curses.

The first person I saw when I arrived at the venue – which was completely gorgeous, I could see why people liked this South of France malarkey so much – was Lydia.

There was the cheering sound of clinking glasses as I approached, trying to look as if I dropped in on these occasions all the time and was thus completely blasé about the whole thing even though I was the only woman in the entire place who wasn't wearing a rope of pearls big enough to drown you if you fell into the sea whilst you were wearing them.

I decided to take the sophisticated adult stance and give Lydia a Kennedy 'cool nod', as I tried to flounce past with my notebook.

'Hey, you.'

Well, it didn't work with my brothers either. They just gave me Chinese burns until I eventually let out some kind of sound.

'Uh-huh?' I said snootily. 'I'm very busy with my important conference.'

'Forget about that,' said Lydia. She looked me up and down. 'You look good,' she said.

I smelt a rat immediately. Lydia never thought I looked good. Lydia usually said things like, 'Don't you need tits to wear those wrapover tops?' and 'Platform soles? How hilarious,' about my new boots, and things like that.

'Uh-huh,' I said. 'How's your luxury B and B?'

'Oh, it's not all that,' said Lydia. 'All that freshly baked patisserie, it's havoc on the figure. *Why French Women Don't Get Fat*; by ignoring the white flour their country is drowning in, that's how.'

I just stood there.

'So,' Lydia leaned over conspiratorally, as we walked into the beautiful room, which overlooked a perfectly manicured garden. She swiped two glasses of champagne from a black-and-white-dressed waitress; I was quite impressed by how smoothly.

'We've been such great friends for *ever*, and I can't

believe you've never told me about your wonderful friend.'

'Kelly?' I said to be annoying. The champagne was delicious. 'Yeah, she's great.'

Lydia did this funny laugh thing. 'Darling,' she said. 'The fascinating Bailey.'

'Bailey isn't fascinating,' I said. 'He's a dork. Although I did think there was something up—'

'Yes?' said Lydia, her eyes lighting up.

'When he sat seven A levels. I thought he was just showing off.'

'Geniuses don't have to show off,' said Lydia knowingly.

'Short-arses do,' I said.

'So is he . . . you know?'

'Quite annoying?'

'Married? Gay? He is terribly fascinating.'

'Do you mean rich?' I asked suddenly, looking suspiciously at Lydia's necklace. Yup. Pearls. 'Because let me tell you one thing. He may be a bit of a know-it-all, but when it comes to women he's a bit of a divot, so if you dare mess him about, you'll have me to answer to.'

'Wooo,' said Lydia, her face changing. 'Ooh, sorry. I didn't realise. Do you want me to back off?'

'Didn't realise what?' I said, suddenly feeling slightly daft for my outburst. Maybe I'd gone in a bit strong.

'That you're, you know . . . in love with him.'

I felt my face go all hot suddenly, the way you do when

you're six stops from home and you remember you've forgotten your wallet. It all suddenly went quiet. I wasn't in love with Bailey. *Was I?*

Lydia gave me a meaningful look and backed away towards a large group of doctors, who all smiled at her and widened their circle to let her in. That would never happen to me. I was left completely alone in the middle of the room, my head in a whirl.

Chapter Six

'Evie? You look like you are a whole world away. Are you dreaming of London, huh? How much you miss its rubbish-soaked streets and shouting young men in hoodies?'

I spun around. Dr Bennet was standing there, immaculate as ever, looking at me kindly.

'No, I . . .' I looked round for inspiration. 'I don't know anyone.'

Dr Bennet looked round. He obviously didn't want to introduce me to anyone himself; it was tantamount to him saying, 'Look everyone, here's the assistant I'm having an affair with,' and even if he dared to have an affair, which I very much doubted, I assumed he'd like people to think it would be with someone a bit more impressive than me.

'Don't you have some kind of secret international secretary's cabal?' he said. Well, I knew one witch, I thought.

I shrugged. 'I'm fine, Dr Bennet, honestly. I'm just ready to take my notes, that's all.'

As I said this my eye was irresistibly drawn to a bright red beacon that seemed to be glowing above the rest of the crowd. It rotated to face me and I realised I was looking at that other Dr Bennet bloke I'd met at the airport. His hair was glinting in the sunlight bouncing off the chandeliers. Our eyes met.

'Hello?' said the other Dr Bennet – Tom, that was his name. He said it tentatively, as if he was prepared for me to completely blank him. Maybe he still thought I had a learning disability.

'There we are,' said the original Dr Bennet, pleased. 'You young folk have a good time.' And he shot off towards the sleekest-looking doctor with the most expensive-looking loafers.

'Hi there,' I said. 'Having fun?'

'Not sure,' he said, looking around. 'I mean, it seems like I should be having fun, doesn't it? Champagne, sunset, lots of shop talk . . . but somehow it's just not coming together.'

'I know how you feel,' I said. 'But they seem to be getting very agitated over there.' I pointed to where a large group of Germans were gesticulating wildly. One did a particularly graphic arm movement, he appeared to be pulling on his vest underneath his shirt.

'What's he doing?' I asked.

'I don't know. Tummy tuck?'

'You really are a doctor,' I said, impressed.

'Hmm,' he said. 'Med student really.'

'Oh, yes? How come you get sent off to five star . . .' I waved my hand expansively, just as a waitress appeared with a tray of caviar things. I've only tried caviar once, at John Jr's wedding, and I'd absolutely hated it, but I didn't want to look unsophisticated in front of Tom, so I grabbed a canapé and stuffed it in my mouth. Yes, just as I thought – revolting. I took a huge slug of champagne to compensate, then choked a bit. I hate it when I do that.

'Are you all right?' said Tom, looking at my red face with concern. I was a bit miffed by that.

'It's OK, no medical assistance required,' I said, when I finally got my breath back. Tears had sprung to my eyes.

'I didn't think so,' he said. 'But, you know. If your lips had gone blue I'd have been right in there.'

'Glad to hear it,' I said. 'It would be very embarrassing to be saved from death, you know. *Too early.*'

He smiled.

'So what are you here for then?'

Tom looked slightly unsettled. 'Well, um. It came up in the department and nobody wanted to go, so they let me go.'

'Although you're only a student?'

'Well, yes. We don't normally get sent on things like this.'

'So they must think you're a scalpel whizz?'

'Mmm,' said Tom. He stuffed about nine canapés in his mouth and didn't choke on any of them. 'God, I'm starving. I don't speak any French and when I point at stuff in shops they just keep raising eyebrows at me and offering me Chanel handbags and things. Which serves me right, I suppose.'

'It does,' I said. 'What were you doing at school?'

' Physics . . . chemistry . . . biology, that kind of stuff.'

'Oh, yeah,' I said.

'Anyway, I deal with burns mostly. I'm not really interested in this end of things. What about you? Do you work for . . .' He nodded at Dr Bennet, who was laughing outrageously at a joke that couldn't possibly be that funny, bless him. He was the world's best schmoozer. Nobody had better introduce him to their clients. Dr Maitland was standing in the circle too, looking miserable. Honestly, if he didn't like the clients and he didn't like his colleagues and he couldn't fake either it was more of a mystery than ever why he was in this line of work in the first place. I waved to him tentatively, and he waved back in, I suppose, a way that didn't scream, 'Get away from me, you of the unbelievably tacky family.'

'Yes,' I said. 'And I know Bailey Arnold, who's giving the talk.'

And who, apparently, I might be in love with, I didn't add. Bailey wasn't here; I suppose they kept him hidden behind a curtain backstage until his time came to be revealed. I bet he pretended to be annoyed by all the fuss but secretly loved it.

I wondered if he still wanted to get off with me. Ten years was a long time. Too long?

Tom looked around. He didn't seem terribly interested. 'Oh. Right. So, you're like the best-connected person here.'

I laughed, which he immediately looked offended by, and I realised I sounded like I was saying, 'Ha ha, yes, if I was well connected do you think I'd be standing here talking to you?' which wasn't what I meant at all.

'I think we're going in,' I said. 'Shall we grab a couple more glasses just in case the speech is very boring?'

'That's not very flattering for your friend,' said Tom.

'He's my friend, that doesn't mean I have to understand *everything* he says,' I pointed out, lifting four glasses from a passing waiter with almost as much élan as Lydia had shown before.

On a stage that had been erected at the side of the room were several orange-backed chairs, as well as pitchers of water and little mikes. Worryingly, it all looked rather like we might be about to have a bit of a lecture.

'This doesn't feel like a holiday,' I grumbled to Tom as we found two seats near the back. I approved of his choice, much easier to snicker and pass notes unseen.

'You're on *holiday*?' he said, with some surprise.

'Not a very good one,' I said, as I picked up the information pack that had been left on our seats.

'You can say that again.'

'But still,' I mused, 'better than most.'

Tom looked as if he felt extremely sorry for me. I leafed through the pack that was given out to everyone. It was full of groovy drawings of palm trees and beaches, none of which made a lot of sense, and phrases like 'facing the future' and 'a brand-new paradigm', which didn't mean much to me either. I'd better concentrate on the speech.

I was about to ask Tom what it was all about when the lights dimmed dramatically and Dr Bennet, followed by Bailey, walked on the stage. My heart beat a little faster when I saw Bailey, standing there with his button-down collar and glasses, a large sheaf of paper clutched in his hands. Something to the side caught my eye. I glanced across, and Lydia was staring at me, arching an eyebrow in a meaningful manner. Immediately I felt myself flushing. She twitched in a 'I thought as much' kind of a way and turned back, looking satisfied. Damnit. And I'd missed Dr Bennet's intro.

Then a distinguished-looking man stood up and, in French, thanked everyone for coming, and then, thankfully, he switched to English and started talking about a great new opportunity for plastic surgery, blah blah blah. I slightly tuned out at this point, and found my thoughts, and my eyes, creeping towards Tom and wondering if he had red chest hair, and if he did, was that really, really disgusting? Or mildly interesting? After all, Damien Lewis had red hair, and he was gorgeous.

Then I looked at Bailey. He looked so sweet and vulnerable on stage, his glasses reflecting the spotlight as he sipped his water, looking hardly older than eight. I blinked a few times. I mean, I felt so much for him – and you were always hearing about people realising that in fact they were really in love with their best friends. I mean, look at Ross and Rachel, and Chandler and Monica. OK, they were fictional people, and I was never that convinced by Chandler and Monica anyway, but still . . . people said you should settle with someone whose company you really enjoyed . . . who you could spend a lot of time with, who never bored you, and all those things were true about Bailey. Plus, I suppose, he was really successful, and although I didn't like to think of myself as someone who cared much about stuff like that – mostly because I'd seen an awful lot of the girls who did, and I didn't think much of them – it was nice, nonetheless, and fun, to feel proud of him. Which I was, so much. I hadn't realised until I'd got here just how well he was doing.

I snapped out of my reverie, realising I'd missed the entire speech, as someone – something – marched on the stage. It was a woman (I was reasonably sure), about six foot tall, and she looked as close to a human Barbie as it was possible to look.

Her hair was huge – surely a wig – and blonde, back-combed miles into the air and flowing back over her broad shoulders, with which her tits were nearly level, narrowing to a waist the size of a pin, amply outlined by the skintight pink leopard-skin jacket she was wearing at least two sizes too small.

A pierced belly button was visible above a pelmet skirt that only just covered her hips – I think if we'd been sitting any lower we'd have seen something one wouldn't ordinarily wish to see – and she had the skinniest pair of mile-long stick legs I'd ever seen, ending in fuschia pink stilettos with needle-sharp heels. I looked at Tom and he made an extremely comical face at me.

The woman approached the lectern and picked up the mike.

'My name is Cindy Linklater,' she said. The voice was a shock. I looked around in case it was booming out from somewhere else. It was the voice of an old lady; an old lady who'd smoked a lot.

'And I am sixty-two years old.'

Amazingly, a huge round of applause broke out through-out the hall. But this women was scary! She was grotesque! She looked like a horrible Frankenstein-esque monster some-one had stuck together from Jordan's spare parts!

Holding the mike she marched down the steps from the stage and paraded up and down the aisles so we could all have a good look at her.

'And I'm widely believed to have had the most plastic surgery in the world,' she said. No kidding. On the back of the stage appeared a photograph of a normal, completely pleasant-looking woman with worried eyes and a nice smile, if slightly crooked teeth.

'That,' she said, in a sneering tone, 'was me.'

She was closer now. Close up, she appeared even more frightening. Her face was a pulled-back mask, weighed down with pots and pots of bright orange make-up. Her throat was so tight it looked like she'd have difficulty swallowing with it. I shrank back as she came past in case she invited me to come and take a look inside her gingerbread house.

'And I'm just showing the beginning of what we can do. Growing old is a choice.'

She said this with a curl of her huge synthetic lips and it was eerie to look at. I glanced at Bailey to see if he would say something along the lines of growing old not being a choice if you were born in Sierra Leone or something, like he normally would, but he was watching in silence. That didn't seem right.

'Which is why I'm going to be the perfect face for the opening of New Horizons. Tax free. Offshore. Completely private. And a place for new experimental technologies to begin. To keep us beautiful. For ever.'

All the doctors started to applaud. I looked around. What was this? It sounded like some evil James Bond master plan to take over the world. Why hadn't I read the brief? Were they going to create a race of crone-faced super-zombies? Would it be compulsory?

'So I'd now like to hand over to our elite team of creative construction engineers . . .'

Bailey stood up on the stage. The crone retreated. 'Must be time for her to eat another baby,' I whispered to Tom, who was scribbling stuff on a piece of paper, in true student style, and didn't reply.

'Stay beautiful!' croaked the crone, and opened her mouth widely in what I suppose her withered brain had once considered to be a smile. Her teeth were absurdly white and straight and looked like she kept them in a glass by her bed. 'For ever!' Then she tottered off.

Bailey came to the front of the stage and started talking about timescales, engineering difficulties, water tables and stuff I had no idea what he was talking about. I wish I'd listened to Dr Bennet's intro. Although, I couldn't have listened even if I had understood, I don't think. I was concentrating on him so hard, about seeing him in a different light. Not as nerdy little Bailey, complaining about everything again, or getting his head kicked in, but as a confident if quiet speaker talking about a large project, and clean lines, and vertical-suspended stabilisers and things. I risked a glance at Lydia again. She was watching, purportedly with rapt attention. Well, it was certainly food for thought.

The thing is, I don't want to care about what people do. That's the point of democracy and stuff, right? So when I see people like Cindy, I do think, well, it's her choice. But then when I talk to some of our clients – I mean, they're not all rich. Some save up for years, or take out loans. They're usually the more talkative ones. And it's always the same – their husbands have left them, or they never knew their dads, or they're lonely, or scared of something. And I always want to say that I see rich beautiful women all the time and they're miserable too – maybe even worse. And really, they'd probably be better off keeping their money and taking the kids to Euro Disney or something.

A couple of times – and he doesn't know I know this – Dr Maitland has talked people out of surgery. Maybe they don't need it, or patently can't afford it, or have wildly unrealistic ideas of what it's going to do to their lives. I don't know what he says to them, but they come out of his surgery sniffing hopeful tears, and head off, looking happier than a lot of our ladies.

Dr Bennet never turns anyone away, not even the skinny girls with the hollow eyes who come in asking about spot lipo.

After the speech was over, I glanced at my notes and realised I'd forgotten to take any at all. Oh, no, the docs would be expecting this written up shortly, and I'd been miles away.

'Can I borrow your notes?' I said to Tom as we got up to file over for drinks. He looked a bit uncomfortable.

'Didn't you take your own?' he said.

'Why, are yours covered in pictures of willies and things?'

I asked. 'And doodles of the AC/DC logo, and women's boobies?'

'No,' he said. 'It's just I promised I'd fax them back to my consultant.'

'Right,' I said. 'And the little fax pixies take the paper away and curl it up really small and you never see it again.'

He smiled. 'Let me fax it first. Then maybe you can have them. If you're good.'

'I'm always good!' I protested, following him towards the bar.

'Except at note-taking and paying attention when you're being paid for it?'

'That's a quibble,' I said.

Bailey was standing next to the bar, surrounded by intense-looking docs chatting to him. I caught his eye, and immediately felt weird.

'Good speech,' I said with my nicest smile. I felt nervous suddenly, my hands felt a little sweaty. I felt like I was talking to someone I didn't know at all.

He gave me a very characteristic Bailey grin though. 'Did you understand it all?'

'Yes!' I said indignantly.

'Even the stuff about sea vectors?'

He made his way over to me. I felt inwardly triumphant.

'You're creating a race of terrifying blonde zombies to take over the world from your secret, evil, underwater lair,' I said. 'What's hard to understand about that?'

Bailey's brow furrowed a bit. 'You weren't listening at all, were you?' he said.

'It's true, isn't it?'

'No! It's a creative project. It's very exciting.'

'Until all the evil starts.'

'It's a huge challenge. It's going to be amazing.'

'Well, whatever it is, I bet you'll kill a lot of fish.' I think my mind was on undersea villain's lairs.

Bailey looked a little uncomfortable at that, though, and sipped his drink deliberately. He liked to think of himself as a person with values, I knew that.

'I eat fish,' he said finally, just as Lydia dashed over and, with a completely uncharacteristic show of enthusiasm, started to gush madly about what a genius he was.

'That was amazing,' said Lydia. 'You know, I have a lot of project management in my background.'

'Really?' said Bailey to her. I must have let the surprise show on my face, because Lydia said, 'Oh, *sorry*,' in the most exaggeratedly concerned fashion. 'I forgot Evie wanted to get you *alone*.'

And she shot me a look and flounced off to where Dr Bennet was standing. He didn't seem to have quite the same problems making small talk with her as he did with me.

'What did she mean by that?' said Bailey, turning round to face me. His earnest grey eyes blinked, magnified behind his spectacles. We must be, I estimated, almost exactly the same height. I looked at him closely, stared him right in the eye.

My romantic history has been nothing to write home about, much like my holidays. I used to get horrible crushes on my brothers' friends, which they would always manage to find out about (which wasn't hard even for lard brains like them; I would just possibly conspire to be hanging around whenever Miles or Fraser or Mark or whoever it was that day was round kicking a football, playing Tekken or discussing how to pull the trampy-looking girl that worked at the local HMV), and then tease me absolutely mercilessly, including telling the boy, shouting his name in supposed fits of passion whenever I passed by and searching my bedroom for evidence of me writing my first name with said boy's surname.

They made such a good job of destroying my confidence it took a lot of reasonably comprehensive cider drinking and copping off with the easiest, grottiest boys in the neighbourhood (starter snogs I liked to think of them) to work my way up to an actual boyfriend, one who could cope with the reality that he would never ever get invited back to my house.

There was Greg, who already had a girlfriend, which, even though I knew this, didn't stop me making a complete fool of myself; Danny, who I went out with for three years, more for the novelty factor of having a real, live boyfriend rather than any huge love bond on either side; Bill, who was too old for me; and Jingo, of whom – well, I don't want to talk about Jingo. Let's never talk about Jingo. If I were to give advice, though, which I hate to do, it would be to try not to date men who live in trees. And are called Jingo.

Anyway. The older I got the more I was beginning to believe that the difference between the desperate, yearning way I'd felt about my crushes – those tall lanky boys with white grins and feet so big they looked like boats on the end of their legs – and the boys I'd actually ended up with, was a simple fact of life. And at the back of my mind I always liked to think, Well, there's Bailey. My mother would be delighted. And it would be nice to be with someone who liked me for a change, rather than someone who liked racing bicycles with a side order of me.

Even though it was ten years ago – a little more – that we'd had our clumsy attempt at a snog, I'd always considered that it meant he was there for me, and the amount of time we spent together was an indication of that.

And here he was, grown up, successful – so successful I was finding it hard to believe – standing, with a glass of champagne, in a beautiful room overlooking a stunning sunset on the Côte d'Azure. Right in front of me, all mine. Was it time to grasp the nettle?

'What?' he said, looking slightly amused and nervous all at once. I felt reckless, attractive in this room full of men, and suddenly decisive. People always said, didn't they, that you should end up with a friend, with someone you could talk to? That looks fade, but companionship is for ever, blah blah

blah? And we'd grown up together, Bailey and me. Maybe we were meant to be together.

'Uh, come out to the balcony with me. I want to look at the view,' I said. Bailey shrugged and acquiesced.

It took a long time, though, to cross the room. Everyone wanted to stop and ask Bailey something or congratulate him on the speech. My heart was beating fast – what was going to happen? What was I going to do? Should I say something? Just lean over and snog him? Should I take his glasses off first? Should I take my high heels off? My stomach was incredibly nervous. Did I have some gum in my bag? Oh, no. Well, I'd only been drinking champagne – and all that caviar, gah, yuk. I'd have to get rid of that. I did find a mint, and my hands were shaking so much I almost couldn't get it out of the wrapper.

Bailey was speaking to someone near the French doors – but he kept glancing at me to check where I was, so he obviously knew something was up. His face looked a little concerned. He must be wondering what was going on. I was slightly wondering myself. I took another gulp of champagne, which didn't mix well with the mint at all. But maybe tonight was meant to be . . .

I smiled at him in what I hoped was a slightly encouraging, come-hither manner (though it might have looked freaky, or a bit frightening), and stepped out onto the balcony alone. The sun was setting over the mild-looking blue sea, and everything looked tinted with roses in the soft, warm evening air that seemed to caress my skin like a shawl. The breeze smelled of flowers and lemons, with an undercurrent of car fumes on hot road, from the busy route behind the hotel, and out in the harbour, white and blue boats bobbed up and down; some huge, some just pottering about, one whisking a water-skier behind it, the wake a paper-cut of white in the blue. It was beautiful. I sipped my drink and sighed. This was more like it.

My attention was drawn to the beautifully tended garden that led towards the cliffs. It was laid out with perfectly straight flowerbeds, and topiary lined the immaculate sheets of lawn – but there was somebody down there. No, two people. No, make that one person and one dog. Oh, goodness. It was Tom, and a red setter. Heaven knows where he'd found the dog, but the huge beautiful creature was bouncing about gloriously, its russet hair streaming in the breeze – and that was just Tom. They were having a wonderful time, running about on the perfect lawns, wrestling with a stick and rolling about together before leaping up to tear across the green.

I couldn't help but smile; Tom looked about nine years old. There was a gracious lack of self-consciousness to his movements that had been entirely lacking in the slightly nervous, studious demeanour I'd noticed when we'd talked. He looked graceful too, even lolloping around with a dog; his legs and arms were long and sporty-looking.

It felt like I watched him for a long time. It's very rarely, especially if you live in a city, that you get to study somebody. Everyone is nervous, everyone is so ready to believe you're a mugger or a terrorist; and there's never any space, you're never so far away from everyone that you're not conscious of being watched, of the proximity of millions and millions of other people all around, cramming into every nook and cranny. But here, despite the roomful of people behind me, there was space, and calm, and peace and quiet. So this was what money bought. The money I saw every day on Harley Street was pushy, trashy and flashy, desperate to get itself noticed, but I saw now that it could be tranquillity, and beauty. I felt very happy, for some reason, and no longer nervous at all.

At that moment, Tom turned round. I thought he was about to see me and nearly ducked behind the stone balustrade, but he was looking up behind me, further up into the hotel. He seemed to wave and then, suddenly, caught my eye. He looked surprised – so did I, I imagine. Then, after a split second, he grinned, showing white healthy-looking teeth, and I grinned back. He came bounding up to the balcony, the dog a little way behind. His head was level with my feet, so I crouched down.

'Is this your girlfriend?' I said, reaching to pet the dog. Why did I say that? What a terrible thing to say. At worst, I'd just accused him of bestiality, ugly-looking girlfriends at best.

'Second cousin,' he said, smiling at me. 'What are you doing out here?'

'I came to give you this,' I found myself saying, and passed over the glass of champagne I'd originally picked up for Bailey. What was the matter with me? I felt like some kind of wild tramp.

'Thank you,' he said, giving me a direct look. There was a tiny bead of sweat just visible at the top of his hairless chest. I suddenly wanted to lick it.

That wasn't right. I mean, I was just about to see my oldest friend, the person who'd been with me through thick and thin . . . I couldn't possibly be thinking about licking other people's chests. That was just ridiculous. I mean . . .

'What are you thinking about?' said Tom. 'You look like you're trying to do quadratic equations in your head.'

'Are those the extra-tricky ones?' I asked.

'I'm good at them though,' he said. I looked at him. He had the same jokey-looking smile on his face, but it was impossible to read what was in his eyes.

'Did you bring this dog all the way to France?' I asked.

'No.' He smiled, 'He's . . .uh. I don't know, I just met him in the garden.'

Tom rubbed the creature's head with a hard but tender stroke. The dog closed its eyes in pleasure. I suddenly found myself jealous of the dog.

No! This wasn't right! This wasn't right at all! I must just be carried away with the champagne, and the sunset, and the beautiful surroundings and the romance of it all. But sod romance. You should settle down with your best friend, everyone said it. Courteney Cox said it, lots of my romance novels said it, bloody Dr Miriam Stoppard said it. You should end up with your best friend. That was the way to build something enduring, something wonderful.

'What about,' said Tom, 'if you scramble up on top of the banister and I lift you down and we can play in the garden?'

I eyed up the slightly crumbling balustrade, considering it. Considering what it would feel like to have a pair of strong arms around me, his long body . . . oh, God, was I drunk again?

'Hi, there,' said Bailey, arriving on the balcony in a flurry of papers. 'Sorry I took so long. Now, what was it you wanted to talk about?'

Chapter Seven

It wasn't Bailey's fault that he was caught at such an unfortunate angle. It wasn't his fault at all that I was crouched down by his feet – not a position he usually found me in. And it wasn't his fault that before I straightened up, I couldn't help noticing what he was wearing on his feet.

I never normally noticed what Bailey wore. He hadn't gone through a big teenage transformation, dying his hair one week and dressing entirely in black the other, like I had. In fact he'd pretty much gone from school uniform to tidy, button-down preppy-looking shirts without changing noticeably at all. He didn't wear a tie to work, which, for ages, I'd taken to mean that he was just a backroom boy but in fact, as I was discovering, just meant he was too big a cheese for anyone to have any say in what he wore at all. And dressing exactly the same your entire life has the huge advantage of never making you look any older.

Anyway, here I was, crouched on the stone floor of a balcony for the most ridiculous reason – i.e. I wanted to go play with another man, and his dog – when I noticed something. Bailey's shoes.

Well, I call them shoes. They were a bit more difficult to pin down than that. The sole was thick rubber, as, perhaps, in a climbing boot or snowboarding shoe. But the top was brown suede, like in a pair of Hush Puppies. But there were thick black laces like in – well, like I'd never seen. The entire effect was ghastly, a horrible mishmash that suggested someone trying to buy built-up shoes but who couldn't quite bring themselves to go the whole hog.

I glanced upwards. Bailey was glancing down at me, blinking through his thick glasses.

'What's going on? Did you find a glass slipper in the garden?'

'No,' I said, scrabbling up. I could feel my face go red hot. And I sensed Tom watching us closely from down below.

'Well, what is it then?'

He looked at me intensely. I stared at his shoes. Was it likely, really, that I was in love with someone who was just a friend? That I could make myself in love with someone that I really just liked, just because I was lonely?

Or was I just getting desperate and going for anything with a pulse, because people said we'd be 'good together'?

'I've forgotten,' I mumbled. 'I think I just wanted to say well done.'

'Out here?' He frowned. 'I should probably get back in. I don't like unprotected UV rays on my scalp.'

'No,' I said. 'You wouldn't.'

He turned to go then paused for just a moment and looked back at me. I didn't quite know what to make of that look. Had he guessed? Did he know? Was he really still into me after all these years (as I liked to think)?

He stopped. 'Are you having a good time?' he said.

'I . . . I think so,' I replied, finding my voice had gone a bit strange.

'Good,' he said. 'Well, I suppose I'm going to head on out to dinner with Lydia . . .'

Lydia! Oh for Christ's sake. OK, maybe I didn't want to snog – at this particular moment in time – someone who wore schizophrenic shoes, but the last thing I wanted was that evil princess getting her mitts on him.

'Oh, yeah,' I said. 'I'll call you . . . to catch up.'

This was a complete lie, I had no intention of calling anyone out here. I'd got the cheapest price plan at the available time, which meant to call overseas was effectively the same cost as the interplanetary conversation in the old hit song 'Clouds Across the Moon', when she can only afford to call her boyfriend for three minutes once a year.

Bailey nodded, turned round and headed back into the

room, where I could already see groups of people opening up to welcome him in.

Turning back I realised that, stupidly, by turning down dinner with Bailey and the rest I'd made it look completely like I was up for, well, something else. If I'd been doing what the books tell you, I should have immediately left with Bailey – arm in arm probably – thus rendering Tom mad with jealousy and willing to lay jewels at my feet until I capitulated etc. etc. (By the way, has anyone ever met any of these guys? Where are they? The ones I meet all just tend to be . . . well, drunk, I suppose, now I think about.) On the other hand, if I wanted to be with Bailey, I suppose I'd just done exactly the right thing. It was very confusing.

Sure enough, as I turned round I swear I could see a bit of a smirk in Tom's eyes. Bugger it! But then if I pretended I had other plans now he might believe me and I'd be all on my own without dinner with *anyone*, which really *would* be disappointing, and the waste of a beautiful evening, on my holiday.

'So . . .' said Tom casually, still rubbing the dog. God, I don't think I'd found a redhead so attractive since David Caruso. And the sunlight made his hair more gold than red anyway, I told myself. Disliking redheads was a ridiculous prejudice, like making preferences on the colour of skin and totally not based on fact at all. *And* I liked his freckles too.

I realised I was drooling a bit when he added, 'Do you have plans for the evening?'

'Well, I thought I might have a quiet night in, you know . . .'

I thought of what a quiet night in would be like in my tomb-like hotel room with no air conditioning and the tiny window completely covered to keep out the noise. Like being buried alive in a coffin, I supposed. Well, think positive.

Tom raised his eyebrows. 'Oh, that's a shame,' he said. 'Because I still have to walk this dog, and I wondered if you'd like to join me.'

I tried to look calm and collected.

'Well, I suppose it's on the way back,' I said. (Coolly, I thought.)

Tom looked confused. 'Actually, walks can go pretty much either way. Are you along the beach?'

'Well, kind of in a beach-hill type of direction, I suppose,' I muttered.

'Good idea,' said Tom. 'Come on.'

And we walked through the most lovely rose garden, which led down a secret flight of stone steps to a wrought-iron gate that opened directly out onto the sand. The dog bounced on joyously ahead.

'Seriously, whose dog is it?' I said, taking off my shoes as we hit the sand. 'We're not going to get done for dogknapping, are we?'

'No,' said Tom. 'I just ran into someone I knew and offered to borrow their dog. He's called Cachou.'

'I thought you didn't know anyone here,' I said. 'I thought that's why you had to follow me about.'

'I have to follow *you* about,' said Tom, 'otherwise you won't have a clue what's going on.'

'Yeah, yeah, yeah,' I said.

The cool water felt absolutely delicious on my bare feet and I stood in the lilac-coloured waves enjoying the calm in the air.

'Ta dah!' said Tom, as if out of nowhere producing a clearly pinched bottle of champagne from behind his back, and we swigged from it happily as we wandered up the beach that ran alongside the Croisette, looking at the fancy cars and hotels which seemed a long way away from the quiet peace of the water's edge. It was so easy to talk to Tom, he was so likeable and funny. For the first time since I'd got to France I felt unstressed and properly relaxed, like I was having a real holiday. Cachou bounded joyfully around as we tossed him the occasional stick, and sometimes our hands brushed together, but neither of us pulled away. I was trying to catch sight of Tom out of-the corner of my eye as he told me a very funny story about old ladies falling over in Norwich (it was funnier than it sounds). Deep in my stomach, I couldn't quite believe it. Come to France, meet a handsome (if ginger, nothing wrong with that) young doctor, have romantic strolls along the beach . . . coupled with all the champagne I felt entirely light-headed; daring and dramatic and not my normal moany self at all.

I mean, things like this just didn't usually happen to me. But why shouldn't they? Why should Paris Hilton get every bloody bit of romance on earth? How come Girls Aloud got all the lush blokes? Statistically, it had to happen to someone, didn't it? So why shouldn't it happen to me?

'You're miles away,' said Tom, and I realised he was looking at me. My hair whipped around my face – it felt heavy, and not too frizzy. Salt water was actually quite good for my hair, it made it look thicker. The champagne and the evening air made me feel heady and free. I looked at him.

'I'm not, actually,' I said, quite boldly for me. 'I'm right here.'

And, as we turned back to walking up the beach again, he tentatively took my hand, and I let him. I hoped my hand didn't feel clammy – his felt big and warm and reassuring. Oooh! Ooh! Holiday romance alert!

We were reaching the end of the beach, or rather, a big piece of land was in the way of the next beach. The beaches just go on and on and on, all the way to Spain and Italy. Cachou was having a splash around in the water. Since Tom had taken my hand conversation had slowed and now it stopped completely. He led me gently towards an overhang of rock, looking at me questioningly to make sure I knew what he meant. I looked back at him, making it clear that I did.

I love the moment before the first time you kiss someone, but after you know you're going to. It feels like everything slows down as you come into the orbit of someone else's body; it's like there are sparks that jump from your skin to his as you get closer and closer together. And it was like that with Tom. A delicious sense of anticipation followed by his putting his big hand on my face, which I liked very much. Then he leant closer and closer and I tipped my head up towards him and we kissed. And somehow I'd already known that he'd be a good kisser. As I gave myself up to him completely, I knew that this was the best holiday I'd ever had.

Minutes, hours later – it must have been hours, it was dark and there was even a chill in the air – we reluctantly pulled apart. Cachou had started to howl piteously and it was really getting late. The bottle of champagne was empty, but I was more drunk on lust; Tom's eyes were glazed too, and we clung to one another a little desperately.

'I have to go,' I said. Frankly that was the last thing I felt like doing, but lusty as I felt, I didn't want to go too far on our first date . . . oh, all right. Honestly, I just didn't want to get sand in my pants. I really liked this man, and I wanted it to be special and, frankly, the risk of having a jellyfish sting me on the bum made me feel it would be anything but.

'Really?' said Tom, looking wickedly at me.

'Really,' I said, trying to look like I was a modest picture of chastity, rather than someone frightened of getting bitten by a crab in a sensitive area. 'We could . . .'

I trailed off, hoping he'd immediately say, 'Hey, let's take the day off together tomorrow and run through the sand and eat ice cream and do all sorts of things that if you saw them in a film would make a bit of a montage,' but he didn't. He said, 'Well, *you* may not have to go to lots of boring lectures tomorrow, but I do.'

'Oh, who'd know?' I said. 'Just write down, "*Tighten skin with Sellotape*" and send it in. That's all they'll be saying anyway. "Chop into skin with great big knife."'

'They're doing a seminar on vaginal modification,' said Tom musingly, caressing my back.

'Anyone who lets a scalpel anywhere near there needs therapy, not bloody plastic surgery,' I grumbled, and suddenly, the moment was gone. Amazing how just one little mention of designer vaginas was enough to ruin the mood. Tom twitched his eyebrows.

'Well . . .' I said.

'We should get back,' he said. And I felt low. But then he added, 'Or maybe . . .' and pulled me back into his arms. Just a little while longer.

Chapter Eight

I opened my eyes, feeling a burst of unaccustomed happiness. What was it again? Oh, yes! I was on holiday in France with a gorgeous, if slightly freckly bloke after me! Joy, joy, joy! I bounced up. It was going to be a perfect day on the Côte d'Azure. I figured I'd go out for breakfast – I had some time off! There was some assessment thing, but I was free to go and finish up reading the briefing (or, in my case, start) and make sure everything was ready for the party tonight – which I'd already done! Well, I'd phoned the number of the party organisers, and they'd said, '*Oui*, madame, everything is ready,' so you couldn't do much more than that, could you?

The sky was clear with a few perky-looking clouds bouncing around in the ether, but it was early enough that there was still a cool breeze flowing through the streets as I bounced down in my new espadrilles, heading for the shore. The restaurants were sloshing out and getting ready for the day, and the little shops were busy.

Now this is how life should be, I thought, looking at the bustling street market as I approached the beach, clutching gigantic almond croissants in my hands. I had *meant* to go in and ask for '*un croissant aux amandes, s'il vous plait,*' and had been practising it under my breath until I actually got to the boulangerie. There was a huge queue and everyone was yelling and chatting at a ridiculous speed, all at once, and I lost my place in the queue about nine times and by the time I got to the front I was so flustered and nervous I just stabbed my finger in the direction of the biggest ones they had and grunted, like I was a helper monkey that had been trained to do the shopping. Still, I'd accidentally bought two.

I decided to forgo the umbrella option when I found out that to hire one for the day would cost fifteen euros, which, frankly, was my wine money. So I found a nice spot down by the water's edge, where the sand was deliciously cool, and took a sunbed. I dabbled my hand in the water as it lapped around my toes and let my mind drift to seeing Tom at the party tonight. I'd wear my new red dress – or would it clash with his hair? No, it would be fine. The dress was THAT good. So, I'd walk on to the yacht, and . . .

*

AARGH! Oh, God! Where was I? What time was it? Why couldn't I move? I felt pinned to the sunbed. Trying to move was agony. Checking my watch – which, I noticed, had an ominously white patch of skin underneath it – I saw it was afternoon. Oh, God, I'd fallen asleep on the beach! In the middle of the day! The sea had receded and I was stranded, spreadeagled on the sunbed in full view. Gingerly I tried to raise myself up. Ow ow ow ow. This was *not* in the holiday plan.

I trudged painfully up the beach. It had taken ten minutes to stand up. My back was on fire. So much for my morning off. The strap of my beach bag was agony across my shoulders, and I'd have to find a shop to buy some aftersun. I didn't know what that was in French. *Après soleil?* That would surely be too obvious. It was probably called something like *Oui, c'est moi, le complet idiot.* I sighed and traipsed on, feeling entirely sorry for myself, and a little sick.

Picking its way gingerly down the promenade steps was a bizarre-looking figure, even for here. I'd already been amazed by the women on the beach. I'd always thought that beachwear meant a bikini or swimsuit, flip-flops and a sarong for chubby moments. And I'd assumed that those articles in magazines that told you which jewellery to wear with which bikini and how to take your beach look into your evening look were just made up bollocks to sell suncream (and which therefore, in retrospect, I ought to have paid attention to).

But no, here, for the first time in my life I was witnessing women – gorgeous, tanned, young women, or scrawny, liver-spotted older women – actually wearing high heels. On the sand. High heels, on the sand. Really, it should be an Olympic sport, or a circus act. 'Come watch the amazing ladies – who can walk in stilettos *on the sand*!'

Not only this but they were indeed bedecked in jew-ellery – and not just any jewellery, or a couple of beaded necklaces picked up from the local market. Oh, no. This was full diamond earrings, gold necklaces and bracelets (the gold, I noticed, had the unfortunate effect of making old brown skin look even older than it was; the smooth surface of the precious metal only pointing out the crêpe-paper effect of the skin beside it.

And it didn't stop there. There were turbans, with jewels in the middle of them, like a maharajah, or Elizabeth Taylor in the seventies. There were ankle bracelets and toe rings. There were bikinis made of gold, or sequins, or what looked like two pieces of cheese wire. Having always thought of the beach as a place to relax, I now realised how wrong I had been. These women couldn't lie down or get wet. It was very very strange.

And the woman in front of me – unless I was becoming delirious, not entirely out of the question – was the strangest of all. Her hair was sprayed into a huge puff at the front which gave it the texture of candyfloss. She was wear-ing full make-up, including bright blue eyeshadow and pale pink lipstick, even though it was incredibly hot. Her bikini was entirely studded with what looked like Swarovski crystals, which glistened and caught the sun. The top half was simply two triangles which actually perched on top of the pointy breasts rather than supported them – the breasts were so solid they didn't look in the slightest need of support. And the bottoms were so narrowly cut you could tell exactly what explicit instructions she'd had to give her waxer.

'EVIE!' shouted the vision. Oh, God, now I really was hallucinating. Where were five hundred doctors when I needed them?

The figure tottered over on the ridiculously high shoes, and lifted up the humongous pair of sunglasses it was wearing.

'It's me! Kelly!'

Christ on a bike, so it was.

'I was just going to the beach!' she squealed.

'What – while dressed for church?'

Kelly lifted up her huge sunglasses (with some effort) and peered at me. 'Oh, ma Gawd, Evie, what happened to you?'

'What, this? Oh, nothing,' I said. 'I got attacked by a bear.'

'Getting too much sun on the first day is *very dangerous*,' she scolded. 'You should have been going to three sunbeds a week, like I do.'

'Well, I'm done now,' I said.

'Your back's done,' said Kelly.

'Thanks.'

She examined me closely. 'You know, I think that's going to come up nicely brown.'

'I've got second-degree burns, Kell. I'm on my way to hospital.'

'Yes, but it'll be worth it now, won't it?'

'No, it won't. I'm a div. Where's JJ?'

'John Jr . . . he said he had some business to do.' She looked a bit embarrassed. 'He was a bit . . . OTT last night.'

'I'm used to it.' I thought back, wincing at the memory, as well as my back.

'In front of that nice doc too. He was a bit of a hunk.'

'Dr Maitland? You are joking. He wears three-piece suits.'

She raised her eyebrows. 'Oh, Evie, you have to introduce me to your docs. I have to do something about these wrinkles.'

'You're saying this as you prepare to baste yourself in cooking oil and lie in the sun?'

'You're one to talk,' she said. 'I know. You've got to struggle to be beautiful.'

I laughed. It really wasn't Kelly's fault she'd promised herself to John Jr 'for fatter, for thinner'.

'OK,' I said. 'There's a yacht party tonight. Wall to wall docs. Fancy it?'

Her eyes went wide. 'Yeah!'

I gave her the details. 'OK. I'm just off to call an ambulance.'

'And I'm off to self-baste like a chicken. Mwah!'

*

I paused only to stumble into a pharmacy, where I simply showed them my back and got exceedingly worried at the look of terrified shock on the sales assistant's face (*Mon dieu!*). They piled me up with creams and ointments that took a ridiculously large chunk out of my holiday budget, but by now I was feeling a bit shaky so I just nodded. They offered me some pills too but I'd heard that in France you had to take all pills up the arse, so I shook my head.

At least my hotel room was dark. Very dark, in fact, and stuffy too, but I didn't care about that right now. I examined myself in the bathroom mirror. There wasn't even a proper bath there, just one of those crappy half-baths.

Oh, God. I looked . . . well, I looked like two halves of a person stuck together. My face was half milk-white, with a few unavoidable freckles popping up here and there, and half bright red. Plus some really obvious 'I was snogging for four hours down the beach on holiday' stubble rash all over my face and chin. From the back I looked like I'd been tied to a mast of a pirate ship and whipped solidly for six hours. I groaned, running my wrists under the cold water. I felt kind of fine just as long as no portion of my back touched anything.

My arms felt like big plump sausages that needed pricking, to let all the juice ooze out – wow, that was disgusting. For a second I thought I was going to be sick. Then I fell onto the bed face first and, thankfully, into a deep sleep.

*

If there's anything worse than waking up in the middle of the day when you don't know what time it is, sticky, sore and headachey in a hot airless little room, I don't know what it is. How could I have gone from cheerful to cross in such a short time? I felt sweaty and horrible.

I found my pharmacy bag, which I'd forgotten about, and took it in the shower, which made me feel a bit more human and a bit less like a dirty, old, stuffed toy full of gunk. In fact, I had just groaned – perhaps a little too graphically – when, after the briefest of knocks, the door was pushed open and Lydia stormed in. Why did I give her the address?

'Oh, *sorry*,' she announced, in a way that clearly meant she wasn't sorry in the slightest. 'I didn't realise you were . . .uh, busy. Oh, my God, look at you.'

I'd turned round to put on some clothes and of course she'd caught sight of me.

'Your neck . . . your back . . . it's *everywhere*.'

She sounded absolutely delighted.

'Yes, I know,' I said. 'Good, isn't it?'

'Is that what you think?' her voice took on a very fake concerned tone. 'But, Evie, you know, burning your skin can lead to all sorts of unpleasant consequences.'

'Oh, it's not burnt,' I said. 'It just goes that colour.' I finished putting my bra on, with difficulty. 'Doesn't hurt a bit.'

When she saw I plainly wasn't going to get in to it with her, she changed her tack.

'Well, anyway, I just came over to see where you've been all day. The reception is in twenty minutes.'

I couldn't believe I'd slept the entire day. No wonder I felt groggy and thick in the head.

'Oh, *God*,' I wailed. 'But I've got a date! Shit! Shit!'

Lydia's face took on a look of consternation. As it did so I realised a little something about our relationship – normally, I would go round to her office, complain about my shitty life and she'd smile superciliously and let me yabber on. I'd thought this was because she was nice and a good listener. In fact, I now realised, my moaning made her feel superior about herself. It did neither of us any good. She could sit and polish her nails whilst listening to a stream of consciousness from me that reassured her that although she was only working in reception and not yet the wife of a billionaire, she was nonetheless still winning in some hypothetical life competition. Meanwhile I just got whingier and whingier. Ugh.

'*You?*' she said now. 'Who with? Did you hook up with a waiter? You want to watch the waiters round here, Evie. They're infamous for loving and leaving . . .'

'With one of the doctors, actually,' I said. I hadn't really meant to say anything about it at all – for once, I was going to be a quietly dignified person who was reticent about her private life, damnit! – but I couldn't help myself. Anything to get that smug look off her face. 'The young one, you know.'

'The ginger?' she said, but I could tell I'd got to her. Tom was by far the youngest and best-looking doc there. Well, Dr Bennet was probably better looking, and Dr Maitland wasn't as old as he looked, but apart from that there wasn't much in it; most of the docs were over forty and either looked like stereotypical doctors on television – white hair, little round glasses, concerned expressions (trade secret: they do it on purpose to look reassuring) – or like they were using too much of their own product.

'Mmm,' I sniffed. 'Strawberry blonde, actually.'

'Ever heard you shouldn't crap on your own doorstep?' Lydia asked sweetly. 'It's so unprofessional.'

Well, that was rich coming from a woman who had already registered the website www.huntandtrapyourdoctorhusband.com.

'Aren't you supposed to be working?' Lydia asked suspiciously.

'Yes, well . . . Dr Maitland decided I should be in more of an advisory capacity after the whole profiterole incident.'

I turned to my suitcase. What the hell was I going to wear that wasn't going to cause me terrible agony? My lovely red dress would just make me look like a burns victim. Alas, I ended up in a black vest to go with my pretty, if outdated, orange skirt. The orange was about the same hue as my skin, and the vest felt painful already, but what else could I do?

I looked at myself properly in the mirror. Oh, God. Oh, God. Oh, God. I was a monster from the black lagoon.

'So Dr McCarrots loves the way you tan, does he?' said Lydia sweetly. 'Wow, you two sound really compatible.'

I must have been sleeping on the lounger with the right side of my face down, because the left side was completely red and the right completely white. I looked like Janus. The effect was startling; there was practically a line down the middle of my nose.

'Oh, Christ, I can't go,' I said, not even caring that Lydia was there. 'I'm not going. I'll stay in and play hard to get.'

'But you can't,' said Lydia. 'It's the yacht, remember?'

Oh, God. I couldn't miss it. And I had to tell my mum I'd been on a yacht.

'They can do it without me,' I moaned. 'Say I'm sick.'

Lydia sniffed. 'But what about your sister?' she said suddenly. 'I saw her at the beach. You couldn't miss her.'

'She's not my sister,' I said.

'She was really looking forward to meeting up tonight. Seemed really excited.'

She glanced out of the tiny window.

'And you don't want to play *too* hard to get. After all, the conference is only on another two days, and there's lots of models round here. Although of course I know what a great advocate you are of inner beauty. I'm sure thingy – whatever his name is – will see yours.'

Her mouth twitched.

'OK, OK, OK. All right, let's get this over with,' I said, and we headed for the door.

*

The lights of the harbour gleamed, bobbing up and down on the scented airy breeze, which felt good on my overheated body. Maybe with a couple of cocktails I'd feel all right. We passed by the little boats, the fishing boats and pleasure cruisers, which had names like *The Office* (ha ha! I'm just at 'the office' etc.) and *The Other Woman*, I reckoned they were owned by idiot accountants from Surrey – or the foreign equivalent – with more money than sense who frankly didn't deserve them.

Then we went past the slightly larger yachts, with tables and chairs placed out on the rear deck, and vases of flowers stuck on top of them. Slightly stiff middle-aged couples sat there, drinking gin and tonics and looking awkward, even though they were obviously there to be looked at by the promenaders strolling up and down having a sticky beak before their evening meal.

'They should wave,' I said. 'Like the queen.'

'They're all too drunk,' said Lydia in a haughty voice. 'If they stood up to wave they'd fall in the sea.'

'Know lots of yachting types, do you?' I asked her. I was horribly nervous. I hadn't heard from Tom all day, and he had my number. I mean, he could at least have texted me or something . . . maybe he'd woken up this morning and thought it had all been a terrible mistake? And let's face it, I was hardly going to change his mind looking like this now, was I?

'A few,' said Lydia, looking contemptuously at a boat emblazoned with gold curlicues everywhere and entitled *Paradise IV*.

'Well, you do get around a bit, don't you?' I said, betraying my nerves.

We passed on by the medium-sized boats and came up to a gated area manned by a man wearing very smart shiny boots and a cap. I felt a bit nervous; there wasn't anyone else around and it didn't entirely look like we were meant to be there. Lydia, however, flounced up to the bouncer and rattled something out in loud French. I was impressed despite myself.

'I do not understand you,' said the guard. 'Speek more slowly, pliz.'

Excellent! Looking furious Lydia held out her card.

'Invitation,' she hissed. 'Party. *Comprendez?*'

'Of course, madame,' said the guard, raising the barrier with a slightly supercilious smile.

Now we were in a completely different world.

'It's called the *Quai des Milliardaires*,' said Lydia, obviously anxious to maintain her French superiority. 'That means . . .'

'Millionaire's Quay?' I said.

'No, actually,' said Lydia, delighted. '"Milliardaire" actually means "billionaire".'

But I couldn't listen. I could hardly speak; I was just gazing at the sights before me. The yachts here . . . well, they weren't like boats at all. They looked, to me, like huge shimmering palaces. Strung with lights and gleaming; their hulls, white and blue, shone like they'd been polished with toothbrushes, which they probably had been. I could see helicopters sitting on top of the boats; huge salons stretching onto goodness knows where; what looked like jacuzzis on huge decks.

What must it be like, I wondered, to have one of these. One of these great, huge, luxurious toys to play with. What would you do? I supposed you would just pay someone to take it anywhere in the world you wanted to go. Or you could just go out into the middle of the sea, and stop, and dive into the clear water with no one around you for miles and miles and miles.

You could have parties and invite hundreds of friends. Mind you, I didn't have hundreds of friends. Maybe if you were rich enough to have a yacht you automatically got loads of friends thrown in as a job lot. It would have to work like that, because presumably to earn enough money to buy one of these things you wouldn't have time to make your own.

'Wow,' I said. 'I can't believe we're going on one of these.'

'Oh, they're all pretty much the same,' said Lydia, trying to look blasé. Oh, for goodness' sake. I know she desperately wanted to pass herself off as good rich-man fodder and everything but this was ridiculous.

'So you're a yacht-hopper, are you?' I said, using a term I'd picked up from *Hello!* magazine. 'You've been on loads of boats as big as this?' I indicated the boat in front of us, which was four storeys high and looked more like a luxury hotel than anything actually built for the high seas.

Lydia shrugged. 'I've been on boats.'

'Boats. Big boats. Just as big as this one?'

'Well, not quite *that* one.'

I pointed to another, slightly smaller sleek-looking white craft. 'OK, as big as that one then?'

'I wasn't measuring.'

'Come off it,' I said. 'You've never been on a yacht, have you? Your dad's fishing trip to the Isle of Wight? The car ferry? Have you been on a booze cruise? Did you get two hundred Regal King Size and stock up on bottles of Malibu?'

'Stop it,' said Lydia.

'Did you roll on, roll off?' I said.

Lydia stuck her nose in the air and tried to walk in front of me like she wasn't with me at all. But I was perking up.

She pulled up, finally, in front of one of the largest boats in the marina. It was a ship, really, and towered over us, level after level. It was lit up entirely with tiny lights illuminating its lines, with a huge ornate staircase at the back. People were everywhere and we could hear the tinkling of glasses and polite chit-chat in the air. I felt excited and nervous all at once; I'd never been anywhere like this before (though I'd seen *Titanic* a few times). It was so glamorous and elegant and . . . I swallowed hard. Well, they'd just have to deal with me too. I could be glamorous and elegant. When half my face wasn't hanging off, obviously. But I could manage it. I was going to shimmy onto this boat and wave to Tom like I came to parties on yachts every day of my life. We were going to drink champagne and dance the night away. I saw us, dreamily, in each other's arms as he whisked me about to romantic orchestral music. Of course, in my mind's eye I was wearing a big *Strictly Come Dancing* dress and could actually dance – as could he – but it perked me up nonetheless. I felt slightly better when I saw the name of the boat was *Let's Have a Party*. Something that naff couldn't be that scary, surely?

Lydia looked like she was making her mind up about something too.

'OK,' she said, looking around at me. With the lights reflected off the water behind us she looked wonderful: enchanting and mysterious. I'm about as mysterious as a chicken pie but hopefully the romance of the evening would do something for all of us.

'Let's go,' she said. 'That's a billionaire's yacht full of doctors and free champagne. Frankly, if we can't pull in that we don't deserve the title "doctor's receptionist".'

And she stalked off towards the gangplank.

After removing our shoes (de rigueur apparently) and flashing our invites at a young, terrifyingly hearty-looking young man in a pure white uniform, we scampered aboard. The deck was thronged with people, and waitresses carrying canapés and champagne were circulating amongst the crowd. I relaxed: obviously they'd been fine sorting things out without me. You'd think these folk having spent all their time together would be short of things to talk about, but no. I looked out for Bailey, which was quite difficult amongst the tall women and loud men. The noise levels were increasing. I noticed there was a band; a jazz band with men playing clarinets and trombones, and wearing interestingly patterned ties. Nobody was dancing yet, though, and it made things very cramped and incredibly noisy. Heavy perfume fell on the air and without my high heels on I felt squat and invisible, especially next to all the glamorous women in their peacock dresses; turquoise, green and yellow, shimmering over taut, nut-brown bodies.

'Hello!' came a familiar voice at my elbow. Then, as I turned round to greet him, 'Christ on a bike, what happened to you?'

Suddenly, I noticed lots of people looking at me and making murmuring remarks to one another. There was almost a gap in the crowd opening up for us. I felt extremely red and hot all of a sudden.

'Nothing,' I replied sulkily.

'Did you fall asleep in the sun?' asked Bailey, with his PhD in stating the bloody obvious. 'Don't you realise it's dangerous?'

'Really?' I said. I guessed I was going to have to answer these kinds of questions all night. I'd hoped the soft lighting and heavy make-up would have covered me up sufficiently, but obviously not. 'I had no idea. You'd think they'd give out some kind of warning about a fiery ball of molten gas.'

'OK, OK,' said Bailey. 'You're being very sensitive about it.'

'That's because it's very sensitive, but there's absolutely nothing I can do about it now.'

'Oh,' said a large doctor from Ghana. 'Look at this. You should have kept your skin out of the sun.'

Another doctor leant in to have a look. 'Yes, you should protect your skin in the sun . . . there are these things called UVA, you know, they're like rays.'

'All right, all right,' I said, grabbing a glass of wine off a passing waitress. 'Wow, what amazing geniuses you've gathered here.'

'Oh, come back, Evie,' said Bailey, turning round to the doctors apologetically. 'She's always so moody.'

But I was pushing my way through the throng to a narrow set of stairs set in the side of the ship. I could see through the window a completely over-the-top salon, filled with gold antiques and an indoor waterfall. It looked dreadful and quite good fun, but the lighting was even brighter, and I didn't really feel like being a medical specimen.

Upstairs there was a formal dining room, with a huge buffet table being set out with seafood and fruit and fresh bread. But I kept on climbing the stairs. Finally, I was on the top deck – the entire top of the ship. There was a large jacuzzi, covered over with an awning, though I wouldn't take bets on that remaining on for long.

I crept along the side of the boat, holding the railings. I could hear the murmur of voices. One, French-accented, was saying, 'But how much then?'

The other, to my surprise, was Dr Bennet.

'Look, it doesn't matter, OK? Once we're at sea, the sky is the limit.'

'The limit. That is not the exact figure I'm looking for from my British partners, *n'est-ce pas*? It's sloppy.'

I didn't have a clue what they were talking about, but cleared my throat loudly so I wasn't sneaking up on them.

'Uh, hello,' said Dr Bennet, looking startled. The other man made a quick farewell and vanished into the shadows on the other side of the boat. 'What are you doing here?'

'I just came to get some fresh air.'

'Well, I hope . . . yes. Have a good party. I must go.'

And he turned on his heel and walked off. It wasn't like him to be so abrupt. Had I done something wrong?

Worried, I headed to the very front of the boat (I know there's a name for it but I don't know what it is) where there was a cluster of seating; moulded plastic benches with plump blue- and yellow-striped cushions over them. They were, thankfully, completely deserted, which, after the cluster and clamour of downstairs, was a huge relief. I padded over to them and sank down in the deep plush cushions with a sigh of relief. I'd wait here, remarshal my forces and . . .

'Owww! Get off!' came a voice.

Shocked, I stumbled and found myself rolling right off the cushions and onto the deck of the boat with a thud.

'Who the hell's that?' I said.

'Well, I could ask the same question, seeing as an elephant

just dropped out of the sky,' came a cross, familiar voice. I sat up.

'Tom?'

'Uh . . .'

He sat bolt upright in the cushions with an almost comical look of disbelief on his face.

'Evie?'

I saw myself through his eyes. Sprawled, dishevelled and completely red in the face. I compared myself to all the elegant girls flitting about downstairs like they were born to yachts and inwardly cursed.

'Hi,' I said.

Tom looked just as discombobulated as I felt.

'Uh . . . uh . . . sorry I called you an elephant.'

'Yeah,' I said, 'you should be.'

'But it felt like you fell from the sky.'

'I gracefully jetéd from over *here*.'

'Oh.' He looked down.

'What are you doing?'

'Uh, nothing,' he said guiltily. I saw his hand grab his mobile phone.

'Who are you calling?'

He still looked unsettled. 'Uh . . . you?'

I grinned at him and he smiled shyly back at me.

'You look . . .'

Then his eyes must have adjusted to the light. 'Well . . . Christ, were you out in the sun?'

'Yes, yes, yes, blah blah blah,' I said. 'Do you kiss burns victims?'

'I don't know . . . are you crispy?' He looked anxious suddenly. 'But shouldn't we also be getting down to the party?'

'You looked like you were up here hiding from the party.'

'I was, but I was only . . . waiting for you.'

Well, obviously he wasn't, but I figured I'd take it anyway.

'Well, lucky I threw myself on you then.'

'Yes, I was thinking that.'

And then he drew me close and gave me a kiss.

Magazines say that you should just be confident then you'll give off an inner beauty that will make you shine far more than some boring model or something. I have never for even a millisecond thought that that might be true. Most men will take a brain-dead slug who looks like Cameron Diaz over a pig-faced personality a hundred times out of a hundred. Nonetheless I definitely felt a little taller and a little better as we headed back into the crowd, me with good-looking Tom at my side.

'Hey!' I said cheerily to Lydia, who was in intense conversation with a dark-haired chap. She waved to me wearily as if I was someone she'd met six years ago and couldn't remember the name of. Bailey, as usual, was surrounded by people wanting to talk to him. He was like a mini-celebrity. Personally, I'd rather have stayed upstairs with Tom, a bit of peace and quiet, a bottle of champagne and those very deep and comfortable-looking cushions, but here we were, doing our bit.

'Can you introduce me to your friend Bailey?' said Tom.

'I thought you didn't know who anybody was,' I said, slightly miffed.

'I heard him speak though. He's very interesting.'

'He's not really,' I assured him. 'He's a geek.'

But we made our way across anyway.

'Hey, Freddy Krueger,' said Bailey, handing me a glass.

'Ha ha. That is just so funny,' I said, taking it. 'This is . . . Tom.'

Tom shook Bailey's hand. 'I really enjoyed your speech. I was wondering if I could ask you a few things about it.'

This was good. Maybe he was trying to impress me by taking an interest in my friends.

I couldn't help comparing Bailey with Tom when I saw them standing side by side. A ridiculous thing to do, I knew. Tom was a sandy hunk, frankly. Bailey was not. But Tom was bent over, listening intently to Bailey like a little boy, and asking him esoteric questions I didn't even understand, about supply chains and scarcity values. Ooh, my boyfriend was so smart, I mooned.

After a while, Tom went to find us both a drink, and I tried to keep the smug smile off of my face. After all, Bailey must be feeling a bit usurped.

'You know,' I said, 'I think I could just about get used to this.'

I looked out over the dark water, as the lights reflected in it shimmered. It was so beautiful I wanted to hug myself. I looked up at the candles dancing in the light breeze.

'You'd think the candles would blow out,' I said to Bailey.

'They're windproof candles,' he said absent-mindedly. 'You get them for boats.'

'*Do* you?' How did that work then? Why didn't they make all candles like that.

Bailey looked a little nervous suddenly. 'So, Tom is . . .'

Oh, Bailey. This must be hard for him.

'So you two are . . .' Bailey took off his glasses.

' What?' I said nervously.

Ah, poor Bailey, he couldn't help being a bit jealous I supposed.

Dr Maitland sidled past our group, suddenly, in his normal dour way. He shrugged, though, looking as if he wanted to talk to us but not quite knowing how normal conversation was actually started.

'Hello,' I said, thinking I'd better be the one to take responsibility for the social niceties. 'Yes, ha ha, half my face is peeling off in a terrible radiation accident. Yes, I'm an idiot that doesn't understand even the rudimentaries of skincare. Yes, that makes me a terrible liability at a plastic surgery conference.'

Dr Maitland held up his hands. 'It's all right,' he said quietly. 'I saw you and I just wanted to give you this. I had it in my sample case.' And he handed me a small tub of cream. 'Stick this on tonight, you'll feel fine in the morning.'

And he nodded awkwardly then moved away towards Bailey, as I looked at him, speechless.

'Uh, Dr Arnold, can I have a word?'

'Sure,' said Bailey, and they wandered off into a huddle.

Tom sidled back up to me. He took the cream out of my hand and stuck out his bottom lip, impressed.

'Wow, this is the stuff . . . costs a fortune.'

'Does it?' I said. 'Will I wake up with the skin of a new-born baby?'

'Maybe one with severe colic,' he said. 'Shall we . . . go and explore a little?' And he shook the cream at me in a suggestive fashion.

The party was getting increasingly loud and excitable – champagne and noise was flowing. The lights of Cannes were glistening all the way up into the hills, and I could see the smart villas that perched over the bay. The water lapped at the bow of the boat and the band were playing something romantic and dreamy. I let myself almost casually sink into Tom's arms. Or rather, I kept leaning in his general direction until he took the hint. To his credit, he didn't say 'oof'.

'Come on,' he whispered.

He led me downstairs to the lower decks. Sporadic giggles and expostulations could be heard but it was much quieter than elsewhere. There was a lower salon where a vast plasma screen was showing what looked like fashion catwalk shows. Couples were dotted around the place, smoking and drinking and generally looking pretty relaxed as they reclined on huge squashy sofas.

'And that's me at Milan,' I heard someone say. I rolled my eyes – model alert! – and we beat a hasty retreat.

Pushing back into the ship I marvelled at the sheer wanton weirdness of the whole thing. The doorknobs were gold, inlaid with what looked like real jewels. The wood was panelled in intricate shapes. There were mosaics on the floor. It was as if someone had said, 'This isn't quite expensive enough in one piece. I want it all broken up into tiny pieces because I think that will probably be more expensive.'

Logos were everywhere – Versace, Gucci. I'd always thought logos were for people who couldn't actually afford to buy designer items, so you'd wear a cheap T-shirt that said Chanel on it, or buy some knock-off Louis Vuitton bag. But apparently if you could afford to buy every last piece of nasty designer tat on earth, down to the Chanel skis (which I could see parked in a corner), you still wanted the brand. Kelly would love it. Personally I'd have thought having the fuck-off boat would be evidence enough that you had all the money in the world, but maybe not.

'Who owns this place?' I said, breathless.

'A schizophrenic with a platinum Amex?' said Tom, looking at the carpet, which appeared to be a priceless Persian rug trimmed with Burberry.

'With *class*,' I said, nodding to a huge oil painting of a grotesque nude women painted entirely in different shades of burnt orange. Hung next to it were large blown-up photos from magazines from around the globe, showing what had to be the same woman, but it was the naked painting that truly drew the eye.

Tom smiled at me. 'You know, I was in the mood, but somehow, now . . .' he trailed off, and I grinned back, but started to feel really nervous. This obviously wasn't just a nosy about, this was, well, Tom meant business. Yikes!

And I thought about it. After all, here I was. And I wanted him, didn't I? I mean, guys like Tom . . . they just didn't pop by every day. I mean, I did really fancy him and everything. But at a party? It felt a little . . . teenage.

On the other hand, this wasn't every party, was it? I suddenly pictured us, in ten years' time, telling people, why, yes, we got it together on a party on a yacht and everyone laughing at how hilarious and cute we were.

And what alternative did I have? I didn't fancy my hotel room much . . . and the conference would be over in a couple of days and he'd be gone, and then I'd be miserable and regret it horribly for the rest of my life and end up having to take the veil and enter a convent.

Gah, it was all so difficult.

Tom slung an arm casually around my shoulders.

'Your heart,' he said. 'It's beating really fast.'

He looked at me, his lovely strong face open and sexy looking.

'Is it because of me?' he said softly.

I nodded. 'Yes.'

*

He was gorgeous. Oh, it was lovely. I felt like a rusty old bike, unused for years but suddenly getting oiled up, getting a paint job; setting off to ride again . . . I couldn't not enjoy it. Even the satin sheets we'd found in the surprisingly small but eminently luxurious room. (The carpet went right up the walls! Why going up walls was a feature particularly to be treasured in a carpet I had absolutely no idea but obviously it was just all part of the mega-luxury – 'Get the carpet up the walls, goddamnit, the floor alone is not enough for a jillionaire like me!') Anyway, even the satin sheets felt oddly romantic and wonderful and I forgot all about my silly sunburn and my crappy job and low-level simmering feuds and practically everything apart from my young, muscular, radiant redhead.

Afterwards I crept into the bathroom. They had a huge triangular bath there with jacuzzi jets poking out of it. Oh, goodness.

Well, I'd already done a few unpredictable things this evening, and I wasn't going to pass up on this one.

'Mmm, lover boy,' I purred seductively, tilting the paler side of my face round the bedroom door.

'Mmhmm,' said Tom sleepily.

'There's a jacuzzi in here . . .' I said.

'Wow,' he said. 'Maybe you should use it to try and seduce me . . . oh no, hang on, we already managed that . . .'

'Don't you think it would be fun?'

'We've just had fun,' he said, but heaved himself off the bed nonetheless.

The jacuzzi filled in two seconds flat and I poured some of the expensively packaged potions indiscriminately from the side of the bath.

'I hope none of these react with each other,' said Tom, but leant over to kiss my shoulder to show he didn't really mean it.

I slithered into the water. Oh, it was absolutely blissful on my poor ravaged back.

'Ahh,' I said.

'Better than sex?' asked Tom with a twinkle in his eye.

'*No*. But nearly as good at making me forget my sunburn. Are you coming in?'

'I thought I'd stay here and rub your back.'

'Well, don't. I don't want any of it to come off in your hand.'

It was blissful in there in the soft lights of the bathroom. Tom found something which brought up an iPod – a full iPod, in the bathroom! – and he'd managed to find Prince on it. He was gently playing with the hair at the back of my neck and I was idly wondering how long we could stay there without getting into trouble – personally I liked the idea of about nine or ten years – and whether anyone had ever died from falling asleep in the bath and then drowning when he leaned over next to my ear.

'So,' he breathed. 'Your friend Bailey?'

I felt my brow furrow. What did he mean? He couldn't think Bailey was my boyfriend, could he?

'What about him?'

'You're close, aren't you?'

I smiled. 'Oh, darling, not like that. I mean, once, years ago, but really, we're just friends.'

'Oh, not *that*,' he said, a bit insultingly I thought. 'I mean, do you know lots about his plans and stuff?'

'Why?' I said. 'I mean, he yabbers on, but I don't really listen or anything. But why are you asking?'

'Oh, I just wondered,' said Tom, nuzzling my neck in the most amazing way. 'I'm just interested in what he's doing. And Dr Bennett. Just to show I've been paying attention.'

'You want me to be your spy?' I said, giggling.

'Yes,' he said, tickling me. 'That's what I want. I need you to be a super spy.'

'So you can get extra kudos?'

'That kind of thing. And rapid advancement and international fame and glory.'

'I thought you were just a humble med student.'

'A humble med student with big dreams.'

'How big?'

'*Very* big,' said Tom and he jumped into the jacuzzi with me, splashing the water everywhere.

'The roof-to-roof carpeting!' I gasped.

'I think whoever owns this behemoth can probably afford to get the carpets cleaned, don't you?' he said. And then he started kissing me again.

Just as I was getting into it he surfaced and winked at me.

'So,' he said. 'Bailey and Yuri's ship is ready . . .'

I drew back. 'What on *earth* are you talking about? What ship? Why do you keep asking me this stuff?'

Tom looked a bit confused then, as if he knew he'd gone too far. He backed up onto the side of the bath.

'Why? I mean it, Tom.'

I was a bit peeved now; he looked really guilty, like a boy who'd been caught out doing something naughty.

'Eh, just, you know . . . making conversation . . .'

'We were *snogging*! You can't chat and snog. Spit gets everywhere, it just doesn't work!'

I was getting a little upset now and looked around for a towel so I could get out of the bath.

Suddenly, from the other room, Tom's mobile telephone went off. He froze. I stared at him. He looked . . . well, he absolutely did *not* look like a man making love to his new girlfriend for the first time who'd suddenly been mildly irritated to hear the phone ring. He looked shocked.

Tom grabbed the first towel that came to hand – it was huge, hot pink and had the Versace logo emblazoned on it nine thousand times – and backed out of the bathroom.

'I'm just . . . I'll just go see who that is . . .'

'Why?' I asked, quite sharply, but he'd already retreated into the other room.

'You just stay in the bath and I'll be through in a minute!'

'OK,' I said cheerily, making some splashing noises. Then using my very best Nancy Drew girl detective skills, I turned on the tap then crept to the door where he was crouching – actually crouching – right at the other side of the room behind the bed, whispering into the phone.

I held my breath and took the little water glass off the sink. Did this actually work? I couldn't remember. The boys used to use it on my door if I ever had a friend round, but they always gave themselves away by grunting and snorting by accident. Still, I leaned in closely to the crack, placing the glass against the door.

'Yeah,' he was saying. My heart was now beating danger- ously fast but for very different reasons than before. Was it his wife? Girlfriend? Gay lover?

'Yeah. I know. But she doesn't . . . she doesn't really seem to know much.'

Who was he talking about? Me? Know much about what? What did he mean?

'No, I know she's friends with B but I don't think she's got much info.'

B? Did he mean Bailey? What was he talking about? Was he some kind of *spy*?

'I know, she's pretty useless.' Then, there was a smirk in his voice that I hadn't heard before. 'Well . . . not *completely* . . .'

I took a sharp intake of breath. A red mist descended. A fury grew behind my eyes and I felt like I was going to burst. What was going on? Was Tom . . .? What was he doing? Was he doing something bad and had pumped me – literally – for information. I couldn't believe it. I couldn't . . . what the FUCK was this shit doing?

'What the FUCK are you doing, you shit?' I howled, throwing myself out of the bathroom, only another hot pink Versace towel protecting me. Tom jumped up, a vicious flush spreading over his freckled face. 'Are you talking about me?'

'Uh, no, of course not . . .'

'Give me the phone then! Who are you talking to?'

'Nobody . . .'

'GIVE ME THE PHONE!'

'NO!'

He snapped the phone shut and held it above his head, just like John Jr used to do with my Tiny Tears. Nothing was more guaranteed to send me into a rage. I tore at him.

'GIVE IT!'

I caught a flash of panic cross his face just before he turned on his heel and bombed through the door, with nothing more than the towel round his waist. I was half crazy with fury, but not so crazy that I didn't quickly grab up the nearest thing that came to hand – his boxer shorts, in fact, and his grey T-shirt. I threw them on as quickly as I could and charged towards the door, howling in rage.

He had obviously gone upstairs; there were wet footprints on the wooden decking. Also, as I ascended at full speed I could hear people starting to mutter and giggle, which meant there was obviously a six-foot, freckly, practically naked man ploughing through them. But I HAD to catch up with him – if he ran off and escaped, well, I just didn't know. What was he doing? What was he after? Had I just . . . I mean, was he like a spy? Had I just been Mata Haried? The idea made me absolutely crazy. Pretty useless? *Pretty useless??*

'Stop that naked man!' I screeched as I reached the top of the stairs. This didn't have quite the desired effect, however, as all the beautifully dressed party guests immediately turned to look at me rather than trying to catch Tom's skinny arse, which I now saw was trying to push its way through the throng to the exit.

'Oh, look, he's stolen her honour,' said one supercilious voice.

'Do you think she's one of those lady boys and he got a shock?' said another.

'With those hips? Don't think so.'

'Catch him for God's sake!' I screamed. 'He's a SPY!'

'Where's he hiding his gun, then?' shouted someone else, to general merriment. Tom was nearly at the gangplank now, having given me a cursory backward glance. There was no way I was going to reach him across the crowd of people and even if I did, what was I going to do? Wrestle him to the ground?

He must have been thinking the same thing because he made it to the gangway and – the bastard – gave me a quick, but obvious wink. Then he turned back, only, suddenly, to find his way blocked.

I gasped in amazement. Standing right there, all eight-foot

square of him, looking pink and fat and out of place, was none other than John Junior. Truly, I had never been so pleased to see him in all my life. He was implacably huge, hanging onto the ropes on either side of the gangway. There was no way for Tom to get past him.

John Jr grunted with satisfaction. I could tell that even though he didn't know what was going on, it looked like there was whomping to be done, and whomping was what John Jr liked to do best. Behind him I could see Kelly, teetering in her spiky high heels going, 'Leave it, John, he just isn't worth it.' But John was oblivious to all that now. I waved hard at JJ and made a punching motion with my hand.

'What you doing with my little sister?' he growled menacingly, in his best *EastEnders* voice.

'Nothing,' said Tom, sounding offended. 'Can I get past here?'

'You can,' said John Jr, 'if you give me that towel.'

The entire deck had gone silent. Even the jazz band had stopped playing.

'He, um, snogged me under false pretences,' I squealed. 'He's a spy! He tried to get information out of me.'

There was a rustle among the crowd now. Obviously having a big fat bloke on my side made my word much more reliable.

'Is that true?' said John Jr.

'Get out of my way,' said Tom, sounding a lot less sure of

himself. 'If you do anything to me there's lots of witnesses.'

'Neh, we're on the sea,' said John Jr (dubiously, I thought). 'Law of the briny deep, innit? Now, were you spying on my sister?'

'I'm not *spying*,' said Tom, suddenly looking extremely exasperated. He looked around realising the game was up. He turned to face the crowd.

'I'm information gathering, that's all.'

There was a shocked intake of breath from everyone there, including me. He *was* a spy. Some kind of industrial spy. Which meant that all the romance . . . all the kissing . . . even the bloody stubble rash . . . was, oh, God, nothing at all. I'd been taking in by a tall good-looking idiot. Not for the first time, admittedly, but this was even worse than normal. This was completely awful.

I noticed Bailey stepping up to face him.

'Why? What for?'

'Let me explain . . .' said Tom, looking slightly wild-eyed. Thank goodness he was naked, at least he couldn't possibly be concealing a bomb, unless it was a really tiny one, and even then, I think I'd have probably come across it earlier.

Tom, however, did not get his chance to explain. To widespread cheering from the assembled throng, John Jr hoisted him up over his shoulder in a fireman's lift, marched to the side of the yacht and threw him into the dark oily water below.

There was a gasp from everyone as we all dashed to the side to see what had happened. I hoped he could swim – oh,

God, what if he drowned. There weren't sharks round here, were there? John Jr came up to me.

'What did you do that for?' I yelled. 'What if you've killed him.'

John Jr grunted. 'Then you could thank me,' he said. 'Hanging's too good for 'em.'

John Jr says this about anyone who commits any crime of any sort at all.

'OK,' I said. Then before I could think about it, I gave him a huge hug. 'Thank you. You're not all bad.'

'Family, innit?' said JJ, but he seemed pleased.

I pored over the side. I could just make out the sandy head above the water, splashing and choking, but striking out towards the quay.

'What on *earth*?' Bailey said.

I sighed. 'It's a long story,' I said.

'Oh, well done,' said Lydia. 'It looks like the party's over. And you ruined it.'

On the contrary, actually, it looked like somebody being thrown into the water might have been exactly what the party needed. The excited chatter was reaching fever pitch. Four burly bodyguards wearing dark glasses, at eleven at night, with wires coming out of their ears were humming and hawing around looking grumpy. Lots of people were staring at me – again. Bailey and John Jr were heading for the gang-plank, along with Dr Bennet and a few other people. I followed them as Tom clambered up the metal bars that served as a rough staircase out of the docks. Several fisher-men and crowds of passers-by watched him in amazement. As he stood up you could see by the lights of the nearest boat – all the crew was leaning over the top – that he was absolutely filthy, covered in black patches of oil and seaweed and goodness knows what. And – oh, joy, oh, joy, it became clear as he turned around – the towel had got lost some-where in transit.

Bailey and John Jr, looking like Little and Large, had reached him. The whole party followed, heading down the gangplank carefully. I was still in Tom's T-shirt and boxers which, I noticed, smelled just like him.

'Well?' John Jr was shouting. 'What were you doing to my little sister?'

Tom's face was a picture of consternation. Hurrah for JJ!

'No . . . nothing,' he said, both hands still covering his crotch. I could have gone back and got his clothes, but I didn't want to miss anything.

'Who do you work for?' said Bailey. 'Are you even a doctor?'

The four big bodyguards had come out. I'd forgotten there were various rich people from around the globe here – investors and so on – who actually needed, or at least had, people like bodyguards. Wow. How annoying must that be? Did they stand outside the loo when you needed to go for a poo? Did they time you? Did they bitch you up between themselves? They must do. Anyway, the bodyguards were standing behind Bailey and you could see Tom looking really frightened.

'Not exactly,' said Tom. My skin bristled. Oh, God, I'd been taken in completely and utterly. Any old idiot could fool me. Completely fooled. Stupid self-obsessed Evie. Half my face was peeling off and I was such a pointless conversation alist that I didn't even know about Bailey's big plastic surgery plans. Tom wasn't even looking up, he couldn't even look at me. Although to be fair he was also trying to keep his goolies out of the way of some rather burly men who looked like they might want to kick them.

'I'm a vet.'

Oh, God.

'But that's not important.'

Well, it was quite important to me. Given that I'd inadvertently slept with someone who stuck his hand up dog's arses.

'I'm part of Earth Friends,' he said. 'We don't like what you're doing.'

'Well, you don't know what we're doing,' said Bailey. 'Presumably that's why you're here.'

'You want to use untested material.'

'We want to give people options.'

'What about giving animals options?'

'Didn't I see you eating the caviar?' said Dr Bennet.

Hang on, hang on, what on earth where they talking about?

'You have to stop,' said Tom. 'It has to be stopped.'

'By a naked ginger man trying to shag my sister?' said John Jr. 'I don't think so.'

'I was *information gathering*,' said Tom. Then he caught sight of me, hiding behind the bodyguards. 'Sorry,' he said.

'SORRY?' I yelled. I'd thought my anger had dissipated when he'd fallen into the sea, but it turned out I was wrong. Everyone turned to face me. 'I'll give you SORRY.'

And I raced towards him. He saw his chance, with everyone looking at me he turned round and legged it back to the bright lights of Cannes.

'Oh, let him go,' I heard Bailey say to the bouncers. 'He didn't get anything.'

I stopped running after I lost sight of his body, fleeing in and out of the excited crowds. On the pier all I could catch was the occasional glimpse of pale white buttocks, like the bobbing lights of the boats on the bay.

'The gendarmes will probably pick him up,' said Bailey, coming up behind me. 'God, a spy. Wow, I had no idea.'

I turned round, all my anger gone and just a huge sadness and embarrassment settling on me.

'Neither did I,' I said, and burst into tears.

Everyone was very solicitous, bringing me drinks, and Bailey wrapped me up in a blanket (I don't know why, it was still about twenty-five degrees outside) whilst listing all the hideous and deadly diseases Tom had certainly caught from swimming in the harbour. I said that I hadn't slept with him, but I don't think anyone believed me.

'I don't even understand *why*,' I said to Bailey, choking through my sobs.

'Because you're an irresistible creature,' he said encouragingly, but his face was distracted. 'You're sure you didn't tell him anything?'

'Anything what?'

Bailey shook his head. 'Well, from your private briefing paper.'

'But I'm on *holiday*. I haven't . . . exactly . . .' I noticed Dr Bennet hovering awkwardly and stopped.

'Evie, you seem, by virtue of your ignorance . . . to have helped us out.'

'Is that good?' I said. 'What's going on?'

Bailey and Dr Bennet glanced at each other.

'Tell me, then.'

'Well,' Dr Bennet started. 'You know Bailey designs hospital facilities?'

I nodded. Someone had handed me an Irish coffee, and I was suddenly very grateful to have something to hang on to.

'Well, we're launching a new one. And launching is the operative word . . .'

'It's on a yacht,' said Bailey. 'Not this one. A really big one. Brand new. It's coming into port tomorrow for the first time. Yuri is finding investors, and we're showing it off here so that doctors will tell their clients, and money men will want to invest. Selected surgeons will be able to operate on board.'

I must have looked confused.

'So,' went on Bailey. 'To hide people from the paparazzi . . . to ensure complete and utter confidentiality—'

'Very important for celebrities,' said Dr Bennet.

'And to give an all-round surgery experience which is—'

'A cut above,' said Dr Bennet. Bailey winced slightly.

'A slightly different experience. Anyway,' Bailey's eyes lit up excitedly, 'it's like a cruise, or chartering a yacht – but with surgery. Hundreds of miles out at sea away from prying eyes. First-class care and a luxury cruise to boot.'

'Are you joking? That sounds like the set-up for the new *Die Hard* film.'

'Not at all,' bristled Bailey. 'Our security procedures are excellent.'

'Yes, I could tell that by the way nobody's managed to infiltrate your defences or anything,' I said.

'And we'll be in international waters,' said Dr Bennet dreamily. 'So we can use the most up-to-date and cutting-edge procedures. Tax free.'

I took a long sip of my coffee.

'I don't understand. Why would some Earth Friends vet be against that?'

Bailey shrugged. 'Craziness?'

'They don't like the cutting-edge procedures,' said Dr Bennet. 'They're against science and progress.'

'Oh,' I said, not really understanding.

'You've had a very tiring day,' said Bailey, looking concerned.

'No, I haven't! I slept all day! Now tell me about these cutting-edge procedures.'

'That's more your department,' said Bailey, looking at Dr Bennet. 'I'm off to bed.'

Bailey was right, though. I was tired. It had been a long night, and really I wanted to get back to my hotel room, throw myself on my pillow and have a good bawl. It wasn't too bad talking to the guys but I knew as soon as I was on my own and the memories of what I'd done started to hit, I wouldn't be able to control myself.

'So, we're not calling the police?' said Bailey.

'I think he'll probably have to call us when he needs bail,' sniffed Dr Bennet. 'Useless cretin.'

Suddenly there was a knock at the cabin door and Dr Maitland put his head round.

'How's our little Mata Hari?' he said stiffly.

'Mata Hari was the other one,' I said sulkily. 'I'm the rube.'

Dr Maitland patted me gently on the shoulder. 'Well, it sounds like you didn't let him get away with anything.'

'Mmm,' I said.

'Opposition, though,' said Dr Maitland, looking at Dr Bennet. 'Interesting. I can't believe he stole your name. That's quite ballsy.'

'It's unacceptable,' said Dr Bennet, turning on his heel and walking out.

I remembered the conversation I'd overheard earlier that evening and wondered now who Dr Bennet had been talking to. I felt a faint chill in the air.

Chapter Nine

The next morning I woke up feeling horribly alone on the lumpy bed. At first I felt kind of all right, before I was properly awake, then suddenly I remembered everything and let out a heartfelt groan. I had cried myself to sleep, which had worked, but now it was a new day, the sun was trying to push against the grimy window and I, God help me, was supposed to spend all day working at the conference. What did they do with the bits they chopped off on a hospital boat? I wondered. Maybe there were sharks following all the way from shore. Why had everything good turned so bad?

Still, maybe everything would look better after breakfast. I couldn't be feeling that suicidal if I still felt hungry. The worst of it was, after everything, I still found Tom residually attractive. How stupid was that? But it had been so romantic and lovely. I wondered if James Bond's abandoned ladies felt like this. Betrayed . . . yet seduced. And a little bit hungry. I should take this as a positive sign. Then I remembered the conference.

I couldn't believe I'd forgotten. Oh, God, why had I thought this was a holiday masquerading as a couple of minor annoyances? Today, they were having a team-building day. Team-building day? The schedule was 'fun' exercises in the morning followed by a golf game in the afternoon, which of course I was going to be able to do seeing as I knew as much about golf as I did mitochondrial enhancement. But that morning I'd been instructed to turn up, hand out briefings and generally look helpful.

It took two coffees, two croissants and a croque-monsieur before I managed to pluck up the courage to walk into the room. Today the venue was a large marquee parked next to the beach. Dress code was 'smart but casual', which meant that every single male was wearing chinos, loafers and a blue chambray shirt. They looked like a line of prison inmates from a particularly swanky jail.

Dr Bennet grabbed me by the entrance.

'You read French, don't you?'

Uh-oh. I'd been dreading this moment.

'Well, according to my CV . . .' I said timidly. He ignored

this and thrust a *Cannes Matin* into my hands. Right on the front page was a picture of Tom's rather foxy – no, no, evil – behind.

Étranger mystérieux, said the headline. Well, you didn't need to be a translating genius to figure that one out. 'Mysterious stranger,' I said confidently.

'Yes, yes, I'd got that far,' said Dr Bennet impatiently. I forget all the time that he is already perfectly fluent in a second language: English.

'Well,' I said. 'Well, that's it, isn't it? They obviously have no further information, otherwise they'd be calling him the "we've found out everything stranger".'

Dr Bennet sniffed. 'You seem to be bringing a certain notoriety to our launch.'

'I'm just efficient,' I said, and immediately grabbed a handful of folders to give out to people as they came in.

Lydia drifted up, wearing very red lipstick, which made her face look pointy.

'Ah, it's the talk of the town,' she said, and not in a nice way, if there is a nice way to say that. 'You're such a dark horse! Who else have you been sleeping with, huh? We need to know if any other secrets are being bandied about.' Then she laughed as if she was actually just joking.

'Here, take these,' I said, handing over a pile of the brochures. She picked them up and wrinkled her very small nose.

'Love in medicine?' she read aloud, then gave me a very sharp look. 'Is this a joke?'

'What?' I said, and glanced down. Yet again my lack of preparedness in everything except bikini choice was showing through; I'd scarcely glanced at what this team building would contain (though this time I had an excuse). But sure enough, there it was: 'The Healing Hand – bringing love and spirituality to medicine.'

'Oh, for goodness' sake,' I exclaimed loudly. 'What the hell is this bollocks? I don't think there should be love in medicine. I think love and medicine should be as far apart as possible. You don't want some surgeon all shaky with love and his heart pounding every time he chops into some old girl's carcass.'

I realised suddenly, with that horrible sixth sense, that there was someone standing right behind me. Lydia's face took on its favourite mocking expression. I turned around as slowly as I could. It was Dr Maitland, and his mouth was twitching.

'Actually,' he said. 'I couldn't agree more. In fact I'm only here because you terrified me so much with your skin damage yesterday that I didn't want to go out in the sun.'

I smiled at him. 'Brochure?'

He took it. 'Is this going to be what they call "touchy feely"?'

'You can bet on that with Evie around, sir,' said Lydia unctuously.

A commotion at the entrance hall caught our attention. As we turned round, I saw it was a tiny woman, tight as a drum from head to toe, wearing a hot-cerise suit over her small rump.

'Is this it? Is this the space?' She had a huge voice for such a little person. It came howling forth like an annoyed cheese grater, harsh American tones bouncing off the walls like hailstones.

'I'm not feeling it, Judy,' she said warningly. Next to her was a woman about the same height but twice the weight; much older-looking and slightly depressed. I guessed this must be Judy. I know you're not meant to judge by first impressions, but my heart went out to her in about ten seconds flat.

'If it's not a heart space I'm not sure I can work it . . . I specifically said a *heart space.*'

'It's a marquee,' said Judy.

'I can *see* it's a marquee, Judy. I can *smell* it's a marquee. But is it a *heart* marquee?'

Dr Maitland and I looked at one another in some bewilderment. Maybe I could see the wisdom of his constant customer avoidance.

The little woman stalked into the room. Huge arrays of flowers had been placed on plinths around the outskirts of the chairs. They must have cost tons of money. The lady sniffed.

'Pink roses. Not carmine. For goodness' sake, I thought we were dealing with professionals. *Wrongly*, obviously.'

Judy wrote something down on a clipboard which doubtless meant bad news for somebody. As she did so, Dr Bennet came bustling over from the coffee machine where he'd been fussing.

'And you must be Jal-Vita?'

Jal-Vita? 'What is that, a name or a snack?' I whispered to Lydia.

The woman's demeanour immediately changed, and she actually started to simper.

'Why, hello,' she said, putting out her hand. 'I am indeed. Of course, Jal-Vita is just my spiritual name. My real name is Janey.'

'And which do you prefer?' said Dr Bennet in full smoothness mode, as he picked up her hand and kissed it. Yuk! He had no idea where it'd been!

'Whatever you like!' she tinkled as if it was hilarious that she had a real name and a completely made-up bullshit name.

'And you're our star attraction,' went on Dr Bennet, purring like a vintage car, which was rubbish, as even I'd picked up by now that unveiling the boat was going to be the star attraction, and everyone knew it. Dr Bennet seemed to have his mojo back, though.

'I don't think of it like that,' said *Janey*, although she obviously totally did. 'I think of it as a spiritual journey for everyone . . . as they career down the heady highway of surgical success, to stop for a while and smell the roses. That's me.'

'You're indeed a rose,' said Dr Bennet pukily.

Janey smiled, equally pukily. 'Oh, no, I wouldn't say that.'

Well, she just did say that, I thought mutinously. I leafed through the brochure. An airbrushed picture of Janey, looking like she'd been entirely moulded out of Barbie doll material, complete with a coat hanger smile, beamed out from the page.

'Welcome,' it said, 'to a safe space to leave all your worries and cares behind.'

Great, a carefree non-worrier with a scalpel in his hands; just what the world needed.

Lydia had put her super-positive face on and gone bounding up to meet the new girl. This should be interesting, I thought. Two evil witches in a smiling competition.

'Jal-Vita, I'm a great fan of your work,' said Lydia, holding out her hand, which was graciously shaken. 'I really enjoyed *Spirituality in the Workplace – why love is there for everyone 9–5.*'

She had? I turned over a page in the brochure. The book had a full-page advertisement. The cunning fink! All she'd read was the blurb!

'Why, *thank you*,' gushed Janey. 'Which bit did you feel spoke to you the most?'

Ha ha. Take that, you gobshite.

'Well, I found it really spoke to my inner soul?' said Lydia, in an upturned inflection that matched Janey's. 'Or does that sound stupid?'

'Yes,' I said quietly, forgetting once again that Dr Maitland was right behind me.

'Not at all,' said Janey. 'Releasing your inner soul-ness is very much a part of what I'm trying to share with the world. Thank you for sharing your insight with me. What's your name?'

'Lydia.'

'And what's your heritage, Lydia?'

Lydia is *not* one of those people who likes discussing her heritage. I think she would just like everyone to assume she's an exotic Eastern princess of some kind, who descended to earth on a gold-tinted cloud.

'My parents are from Malaysia,' she said, almost grudgingly.

'Wow,' said Janey, taking Lydia's hands in hers. 'That's an amazing thing. An amazing heritage to have.'

'Yeah, whatever,' said Lydia. (For once, rightly, in my opinion. Why congratulate someone on their random genetics? You might as well say, 'God, you're left-handed; that's *amazing*.' Which is the kind of thing Janey probably did say.)

'Now, I know this is just going to be the most wonderful day,' said Janey. 'When do they all arrive?'

Dr Bennet looked slightly worried, but as he turned to face the entrance of the marquee – which was huge, with row after row of those gilt-edged, red-seated chairs lined up around it – the docs, looking a bit hungover and slightly sheepish, started to sidle in.

Janey prepared her razor-toothed American grin in welcome, but to her – and my – surprise, they all headed towards me.

'Hey, what happened to you last night? Are you all right?' asked one.

'You were really brave, chasing a spy like that,' said another. 'Amazing really. You probably saved the whole project. Under torture, too.'

Out of the corner of my eye I caught sight of Bailey grinning. Oh, bless him! He must have spun some story about me where I didn't look like a hapless slut after all!

Another one was nodding. 'Yeah,' they said. Then they turned to Dr Maitland. 'You must be really proud of her.'

And Dr Maitland said the most surprising thing; he replied, 'Yes. Yes I am.'

I was so taken aback, I nearly started crying again. Fortunately there must be some kind of term limit on tears, or I'd just dried up, I didn't know. Tom had knocked my confidence so hard I was just amazed they didn't all want me to lie on the floor so they could take turns kicking me.

'*Hello*,' said Janey very loudly. The doctors slowly turned round to face her. She looked annoyed that her attempt to get all the attention had failed. Near me, her little runt Judy looked a bit shaky.

'If I can just ask for your attention for two minutes . . .'

The docs smiled at me, and chuntered their way towards the chairs. I stayed standing at the back.

'My name is Jal-Vita and I am lucky enough to have been blessed in my life enough to now pass on the secrets of love and spirituality in business that I have learned along the way.'

There was a little bit of noise from the audience at this, and the latecomers looked somewhat wistfully towards the coffee machine.

'Today, through some *fun* games and exercises I hope we're going to find a way to take forward a little bit of the love and spirituality that we can carry around with us all the time – even when faced with that difficult patient or tricky operation. But first, a little bit about me . . .'

'Oh, Christ,' said Dr Maitland. I realised he hadn't gone and sat down but was still standing beside me. 'I knew this would suck. You know she negotiated it with Yuri in return for some free filler.'

'She did not!' I said. 'That's . . . corrupt.'

'Well, she is a professional . . .'

'Professional what?'

'. . . and then that's when I started what I call my *whole life journey*,' emphasised Janey.

'Will you help me out with the "exercises"?' said Dr Maitland. 'I don't think I can bear it. And if she says the word "diversity" I'm out of here.'

'. . . that brings a whole new paradigm of love and diversity into the workplace,' said Janey. I looked at Dr Maitland pointedly.

'Oh, I can't leave,' he said, fumbling with his bow tie. 'I promised Yuri.'

'Wimp!' I whispered back and, amazingly, he smiled. He had a rather lovely smile, I couldn't help noticing. Like the sun coming out from behind a cloud.

After about another forty minutes of Janey wittering on about how being a nurse in a casualty unit had taught her more than she'd ever dreamed of about love in the workplace, which was news to me, because one of Patrick's girlfriends had been a nurse in a casualty unit and she said it had taught her more than she'd ever dreamed of about drunks, Janey finally stepped forward off the podium, her beady eyes sweeping the room.

'OK, guys and gals,' she said, in a horrible attempt to appear playful – pointless anyway, there was only one gal there, Miss Hodgkiss, who specialised in bum implants and herself had a massive one (which I guess was reassuring to her clientele).

'Now, the first thing we're going to do is find a partner so we can all relax with a trust game.'

I swear you could almost here a groan go through the room. Was this worth getting up early for? The shiny new career on the ocean blue?

'We can't expect to *spread* love if we don't at first *love ourselves*,' said Janey severely. 'And we do that by finding trust in others.'

'I think I've got to go outside and check the ticket

stand,' I lied suddenly, getting up. Let's face it, I was probably the least trustworthy person in this entire room. I'd probably get dropped if we had to do that 'fall back into somebody's arms' thing. From the corner of my eye I saw Lydia immediately grab Bailey's elbow. Well, but of course she would. I stood up.

'No!' said Dr Maitland suddenly.

I turned round.

'I mean . . .' His face looked stricken. 'I mean, I thought you were going to stay and be my partner.'

Janey was now chivvying people into position and hollering, 'Now, don't worry! This is going to be lots of fun! JUDY!'

Judy instantly stepped forward with a huge box full of blindfolds.

'Now, cover up your partner's eyes.'

Dr Maitland and I looked at each other. This was bizarrely uncomfortable. Judy waddled up to us awkwardly and handed the blindfold to Dr Maitland. He took it, looking at it as if it was a big black eel he'd just accidentally pulled out of the water.

'Um,' he said.

'There's still time to set the tent on fire and make a run for it under cover of all the smoke,' I said.

'Come on, you two at the back!' came a wild American screech. 'Get with the PROG-ramme.'

'*So* much love and spirituality,' I murmured, as Dr

Maitland tentatively approached me. I stopped talking as he draped the blindfold over my eyes. Suddenly I was so conscious of his body very close to mine. Perhaps because I'd had sex so recently, my senses and pheromones were up. I could feel my skin prickle.

Dr Maitland was quiet, but I could hear him breathing as he carefully, but with a steady hand, tied the blindfold at the back, not too loosely or tightly. I nearly asked him if he'd done it before, but already felt awkward enough.

'Now, you're going to guide your partner around the room using just your fingers and your voice . . . gently touch them from behind . . .'

It is to several medical professionals' complete credit that they didn't immediately start sniggering when they heard this, which I would certainly have done had I not been sad and very close to my boss. Instead, I felt a finger quite gently but firmly poking me in the back and a voice saying, 'I'm terribly sorry about all this.'

'Don't give it a second thought,' I said, stepping forwards in the pitch black and immediately falling over a chair.

'Whoops!' I shouted, as Dr Maitland made a grab for me and fetched me up with my bra strap, which he dropped as if it had bitten him.

'I'm sorry,' he said again.

'Now you two,' came the loud voice, sounding right next to my ear. 'You're not trusting each other.'

'She marched off!' said Dr Maitland.

'I thought you were pushing me in that direction.'

'Why would I push you over a chair?'

'So that I'd hurt myself and require expensive reconstructive surgery?'

There was a silence and I really wanted to pull up my blindfold and see what was going on, but a tiny claw came down on my arm and gripped it in a steely embrace.

'You,' said Janey, without as much love in her voice as I could have done with at this particular instant. 'Come here.' And she yanked me back round the chair.

'Stand here.'

And she shoved me into a large pair of tweedy arms.

'OK, *you*,' she said, and I knew it wasn't me she meant this time. 'Guide her.'

'Where?' said Dr Maitland.

'It doesn't matter where. It just matters that she trusts you.'

We were both silent then. And I realised, suddenly, with a flashing instant of clarity, that after last night I wasn't actually sure if I did trust him.

'Do you trust me?' said Dr Maitland suddenly, as if he was thinking the same thing. It seemed a very odd thing for a boss to ask his receptionist.

'Don't ask like that!' said Janey, trust expert extraordinaire. 'Just get moving!'

'Left,' murmured Dr Maitland in my ear then, and I took a little step that way. His finger moved down my back a little bit as he whispered, 'Forwards. Slowly.' And we gradually tiptoed out of Janey's orbit. Being in the dark in the huge marquee – I could barely hear the other pairs rustling about in the distance – was a very odd experience. I felt we could walk for ever, or straight into the sea.

'The project . . .' began Dr Maitland, but it was like he didn't know how to go on. 'The ship . . . I mean.'

He nudged me to the right. It felt a little like we were dancing. I was incredibly aware of him behind me. Oh, God, what was the matter with me? One whiff of testosterone and I was all over the place. This was my boss we were talking about.

'Uh, yes?'

He paused then as if sensing something. Oh, God, I was probably giving off some weird hormonal thing. I couldn't help it, though; as I felt his sure, strong fingers gently guiding me, it was hard to concentrate.

'You know, not all of us are as gung-ho as Yuri and Bailey . . . I mean, we're not all so determined.'

'What *is* it?' I said, as he prodded me again, lightly in the small of my back and I nearly shivered. 'What's getting everyone so riled up? So bad that someone sent a *spy*?'

He sighed. 'Well, in law, once you're out of sight of land . . . well, once you're in international waters, you can do . . . you can do pretty much anything.'

I spun round to face him. 'What do you mean, *anything*?'

'Well, new techniques. Face transplants. Anonymous work. Some women, you know . . . they'll stop at nothing to look better. And some doctors don't feel the pace of ratification by drugs bodies is quite fast enough. And then there's Radoflux 9000.'

I screwed up my eyes trying to remember where I'd heard that name.

'The drug that keeps failing its FDA?' I said.

'Yes,' said Dr Maitland. 'Side-effect issues.'

'Isn't it made out of something really dodgy?'

'Seal foetuses.'

'Urgh.'

'Everything's made out of something.'

'So what's the problem with that? You can't use it, end of story.'

'Well, some people aren't so sure about that . . .'

I didn't say anything and waited for him to continue. I wasn't sure but I thought we were near the corner of the marquee by now. I pulled up my blindfold and looked at him in disbelief. 'You want to use an unratified drug.'

Dr Maitland looked at the floor. 'Well, maybe. Yes.'

I couldn't believe it.

'So Tom was right! This *is* a bad idea.'

'Shh,' said Dr Maitland. He looked around. Various twosomes were hopping along or running into each other. They all looked very innocent.

'And these guys . . . they could use the boat to do, basically, anything they wanted?'

'And SWITCH!' yelled Janey.

'Look normal,' said Dr Maitland. 'I shouldn't really be talking to you about this.'

'So why are you?'

'Maybe I'm having doubts, I said that already,' he growled.

I had to get right up on my tiptoes to tie the blindfold around him. He had very clean ears, I noticed. Probably doctors knew quite a lot about terrible ear diseases.

'Is that too tight?' I said.

'It doesn't matter,' he said. 'We're having a conversation, not actually playing this stupid game.'

He sounded completely different; much less tentative than normal. He'd obviously crossed a line; he wanted to talk to me and talk about this. I prodded at his back reluctantly.

'It would be easier,' he said, 'if you just held onto my braces.'

It was.

He heaved a sigh. 'Well, you've proven you can keep a secret – even under the *deadliest* torture.'

'Could we not mention that, please?' I said. 'Just from, like, a basic standard of human dignity? And I think maybe Bailey slightly embroidered the torture thing anyway.'

He nodded his head. His back, as I studied it, was much more muscular than I'd have divined from those ridiculous tweed jackets.

'Sorry,' he said. 'The thing is. That holiday boyfriend of yours . . .'

I rolled my eyes, but he couldn't tell.

'He made me think. Or think more. What do you think, Evie?'

I thought about it as we negotiated a couple of the gilt chairs someone else had knocked over earlier.

'Why should I care what a couple of really rich cows do to themselves?' I said, considering it. 'If they want to shoot themselves full of monkey bollocks so that their face is rendered completely immoveable even in tornadoes, why should I care? Why should I care if they get swept overboard? You know, hypothetically.'

'Thanks for adding "hypothetically" on at the end there,' said Dr Maitland. 'Otherwise it might have sounded, you know, a bit twisted and bitter.'

'I'm just saying,' I said, realising I was getting quite het up, 'for most people in this world what some stupid rich person wants to get up to in her own spare time is miles away from anything even vaguely useful, like how you're going to pay your council tax or getting your landlord to fix that ridiculous drip that's been coming in from the roof for years. It's all bollocks. And I can't imagine why a good doctor would waste his training and his life on it, quite frankly. It's immoral. I mean, it's OK for idiots like me, but to go to medical school, learn how to help people, learn how to fix people, get trained up by the NHS and then piss it all down the drain for a six-figure salary . . . it's pathetic, really.'

'And stop!' shouted Janey. 'Now, is that all better? Do you really feel you're starting to trust one another now?'

Dr Maitland looked at me, blinking his big eyes in the light.

'Well, just as well you know everything,' he said.

'What did we learn?' shouted Janey at the group.

'I know, because I'm only a receptionist,' I said. My blood was up now. I was probably no, make that definitely – going to lose my job, but I didn't care. Who were these people who thought they could take people out into the middle of the ocean and gut baby seals for money? Maybe I just didn't want to be anywhere near them any more.

'I'm not rich, I'm not willing to throw thousands of pounds at you so you can hack me open and make me look like I've been caught in a wind tunnel. Amazing, I know. If I made any money – which I *don't*, by the way, you lot all act like I should feel unbelievably privileged to be working for you and should be doing it for the love of it – I'd spend it . . . well, I'd spend it on a home, and on beautiful things around me and hopefully, one day, someone I loved and who loved me, and it wouldn't be about how small a nose I had or how tight my bottom was. It would be because it was fun, and warm, and happy and we liked spending time together and spending our lives together. And do you know how many of those stupid people you think are so great have that? Hardly any. Hardly any of them at all. They're all bloody miserable. That's why they come and see you. And with all your bloody money and qualifications – you're bloody miserable too. And that's moral, is it?

Along with all the other bullshit, this boat is literally a drop in the ocean.'

'God, you don't stop when you get going, do you?' said Dr Maitland. He just stood there.

'I've stopped now,' I said. And I had. It was like all the anger drained out of my feet and I changed from red to white. I knew what I'd done. I'd buggered up my job – a job, as Bailey would point out, that I was lucky to get – and wouldn't get a look in at another one once word got round about the crazy girl at the Cannes conference, as I'd be known for evermore. I hoped they'd let me keep my ticket stub to get home.

'Good,' he said.

'You, girl! With the frizzy hair.'

To my horror, I realised that Janey was pointing at me.

'Were you volunteering to tell us what you've learned?'

I shook my head mutely but it was too late. She was advancing down on me, her red talons outstretched.

'Come on! It's a safe space here! Share what you're feeling about love and spirituality in the workplace!'

I opened my mouth. I'd already pissed on my chips, it wasn't going to hurt telling a few more people and I quite liked the idea of Lydia getting the smile wiped off her face.

'Well,' I said, 'I've learned that . . .'

Suddenly I felt a pressure on my arm. Dr Maitland had grabbed me, quite hard.

'She's overcome,' he said loudly. 'She's been so

overwhelmed by all the, uh, love and spirituality in the room that . . . that I have to take her outside for a sit down.'

'You do no—' I started, but his hand only clamped down even harder.

'So, we're just popping out,' he announced, pushing me backwards firmly towards the exit.

'Now, I do find it amazing when the power of love and trust just *fills* the room,' said Janey loudly. 'Look at that! And next, it's going to get even *more* intense.'

A quiet groan went up from the group as Dr Maitland manhandled me backwards. I caught sight of Lydia looking at me with narrowed eyes.

'What are you doing?' I yelled, as Dr Maitland got me out and took me to sit on the sea wall. 'What? I've learned too much about your evil plans and now you're going to have me killed? That's it, isn't it? I've stumbled on your evil secrets and now you're going to make me pay.'

'Are you getting hysterical?'

A small group of teenagers rollerbladed past under the palm trees. It is difficult to feel hysterical when there are teenagers and palm trees about.

'No,' I said sullenly.

'OK. Well, I wanted to think for a bit.'

'About whether to strangle me or just push me off the sea wall?'

'You are very, very annoying, you know?'

'Only when faced with certain death.'

Dr Maitland sighed and looked out to sea. 'Look, everything you said . . . calm down. I've been having doubts about this the whole time. Not unlike your friend.'

'He's not my . . . never mind.'

'Dr Bennet, you know. He's very keen. To push the boundaries. Try new things. He likes the money, yes, but you know, he's a very committed doctor too.'

'He's a very committed schmoozer, you mean.'

'That's part of it.'

I looked over the sea wall. Someone had carved a great sand sculpture of a mermaid. It was absolutely beautiful, I couldn't imagine how it was done. It must have taken someone ages. All that work to make something beautiful that would be washed out by the tide. It reminded me of something but I couldn't think what. Oh, yeah. Life. I pointed it out to Dr Maitland.

'Well, just because time and the tide wash everything away eventually . . . is that a good reason not to at least try to create something beautiful?' he said.

'Beauty is one thing,' I said. 'Health is quite another. And better, in my opinion.'

'Science is beautiful,' he said, looking mournful. I looked around in case I should be planning my escape but I reckoned the worst of the danger had passed.

'Where's the beauty in tearing a baby seal from its mother?'

'I don't know,' said Dr Bennet, his eyes on the far horizon. 'I just don't know.'

We sat there, side by side, for about ten minutes. It was oddly restful. Then, finally, Dr Maitland turned to face me. His eyes had a spark to them I'd never seen before.

'OK,' he said. 'Well . . . if you were serious about what you said . . . if we want to stop this ship, we'll need a plan.'

Chapter Ten

Lunch was a buffet sponsored by a wrinkle-plumping company. I was staying away from the cold chicken. Actually I was staying away from anything that looked like it might have been injected to plump it up before hitting the table.

'Does this food look *smooth* to you?' I asked Bailey. I'd timed it properly, so we were hitting the table at the same time.

'How are you getting on, Captain Catastrophe?'

I smiled at him. 'I've had worse holidays.'

Bailey looked around. We were in a dim room that seemed to be attached to a car park. 'You're joking.'

'No, I'm not. Remember that year we went to the Borders and I couldn't talk about it?'

'Oh, yeah. The trauma trip.'

'John Jr buried me in the sand.'

'That doesn't sound so bad.'

'The wet sand. Actually, it was clay. In the rain. Vertically. It was like *Merry Christmas Mr Lawrence*. But with more rain.'

'So you went on a holiday that was actually worse than a Japanese internment camp?'

I nodded vehemently.

'Oh, Evie.'

He put his hand on my arm affectionately. 'Have you heard of the calamity theory?'

'No.'

He bit his lip.

'You'd better tell me. Not everyone gets *Supergeek Monthly*.'

Actually, I was meant to be pumping him for information – step one of the plan – before turning him over to our side – step two.

'Oh, it's nothing. Silly really. There are some studies that show that certain circumstances will almost always attract adverse conditions. So, for example, if you have an earthquake then you'll probably get a flood, then cholera then . . . you know, just bad things attracting other bad things.'

'That's what you think about me?' When someone says something to your face that you've always secretly thought about yourself, it can take your breath away.

'No, of course not,' said Bailey.

'Oh, right. You were talking about parallel universe Evie.'
I poked my crackers, feeling sorry for myself and cross with
him and not quite sure what to say.

'It was meant to be a humorous analogy,' said Bailey.

'That turned out deeply hurtful,' I pointed out.

'Sorry,' he said. 'You can call me short if you want to.'

'It's OK.'

Bailey played with his three-bean salad. 'I'm sorry,' he
said, again. 'Sometimes I'm not sure that this "mixing friends
and work" thing is going as well as I'd hoped . . .'

I figured this was my chance – whilst it was quiet and he
was feeling on the back foot – to get him on side.

'Bailey,' I said. 'This project.'

He arched an eyebrow at me. 'Yes.'

'Well . . . can you fill me in?'

'The project you said you didn't care about as long as you
got to go somewhere sunny for a week?'

'Yes.'

'The project that I tried to explain and you said, "Be
quiet, I can't listen and eat pancakes with maple syrup at the
same time?" The secret briefing you never read . . .'

'All right, all right.'

'OK,' said Bailey. He sat back. 'Well, yes. Technically.
The boat can go into international waters and do anything. It's
not the one we were on last night – it's not here yet. They're
just finishing her up in the shipyard. She arrives tomorrow.
The hospital is a totally new design – it's beautiful. Do you

know, however much the boat moves, the operating theatre remains totally stable. It's got four pivoting stabilisers, and is suspended from above . . .'

'OK, forget the technical details,' I said.

'Pancakes?' said Bailey.

'OK, OK. Who commissioned it? I mean, I know Dr Bennet's running the show. But it's not his money, is it? I mean, he's always complaining that he can't afford his own private island and stuff.'

Bailey looked uncomfortable.

'Well, we just work through Dr Bennet, on behalf of a holding company.'

'What? You mean, you don't know?'

Bailey shook his head.

'You don't know who the holding company is? So it could be anyone. It could be, like, Mafia Associates plc.'

'I don't think the Mafia is a publicly listed company.'

'Bad Guys inc? Drug Runners International. Don't you see, though? That this whole place . . . I mean, it could be really, really wrong.'

'Look, Evie, people build prisons and things. They design guns. I mean, bad things happen out of design, and I'm just a designer. And we don't even know it's going to happen here. Don't you think your imagination is running away with you?'

'I would have done, if I hadn't been caught in a SPY SET-UP HONEY TRAP.'

We both looked around, then, nervously, in case we were overheard.

'OK,' said Bailey, leaning forward with an intense look on his face. 'That guy was a nut job, OK?'

'But if he was right?' I said, persistently. 'If it is bad. Don't you think we should stop it?'

Bailey's eyebrows crept together. 'Oh, Evie,' he said. 'When would things be that simple?'

'*Hello!*' Lydia pushed herself between us. Her entire buffet lunch consisted of three strips of peppers and two prawns. 'Mmm, prawn and pepper salad, delicious,' she said. 'What are you having, Evie? Are those deep-fried cheese balls again?' Without waiting for an answer she beamed her full attention towards Bailey. 'How are you doing today, Dr Millionaire Smartie Pants?' she asked perkily.

'Actually, we were having a conversation,' I said. I'd rather Bailey had said it, but needs must.

'Ooh, gossip?' she said. 'Dish, dish, dish! It's Evie again, isn't it? I saw her throwing herself over Dr Maitland at the love and spirituality workshop this morning.'

At that point, I decided. I was going to have to get Lydia out of the way. I didn't want to do it, but I was going to have to bring out my big guns – I needed a secret weapon.

Oh, crap. Lydia was now laying into Bailey with a whole bunch of bollocks she'd obviously picked up by scanning Janey's book.

'Don't you feel, when it comes to exciting new ventures

like yours that the most important thing to get right is the soul-space?'

'The what now?'

Maybe Bailey had already started to get tired of her. Well, that would help.

I excused myself and went outside.

I took a walk along the beach to try and clear my head. This was all happening so fast. I looked out to sea, at the big boats bobbing up and down in the harbour. Who knew what was happening out there? Could be anything. I felt my head had turned round 360 degrees. First, meeting Tom. Then, finding out he was using me. Then, finding out he may have a point . . . argh. My head hurt, and for once it wasn't just from too much champagne.

And Dr Maitland being against it too . . . it was too weird.

Along the beach I spied a stocky figure rubbing sun-cream on a skinny one. Not exactly an unusual sight round here.

'Hello, Evie!' Kelly shouted cheerfully, as if nothing had happened the night before. 'Great yacht.'

I half smiled. John Jr looked uncomfortable. His belly was going pink. Family skin.

'Hi, JJ,' I said. I felt shy too. 'Thanks again for everything last night.'

It just felt so odd to be saying something nice.

'No probs, sis,' said JJ. Kelly kicked him with a French-manicured toe. 'Oh . . . and . . . sorry. For ruining things at dinner with that doc.'

'You didn't,' I said. 'Don't worry about it.'

And we half smiled at each other.

'Great,' said John Jr. 'Because Patrick's coming out.'

'WHAT?'

'He heard the chicks here are amazing. He's on his way.'

'No chance! I can cope with one of you, but . . .'

'Maybe we'll find him a nice girl,' said Kelly, who honestly thinks Patrick is just misunderstood, rather than an indiscriminate shag beast.

'No way.'

'Gets here tonight, just in time for your casino night.'

I'd forgotten all about casino time. God, there wasn't a second off.

'Boys on the town,' said JJ.

Although it had given me an idea. Usually I let Patrick's glands do their own thing . . . but this might just work . . . was he really as irresistible as he liked to think? I steeled myself for the wildly expensive mobile call.

'Yeah?'

The voice was surly, like I'd just got him out of bed. Except I knew I hadn't, because he still worked nine-to-five, however much he liked to pretend he was a good-looking bad boy who obeyed nobody's rules but his own.

'Patrick?'

'Who is this?'

I sighed. 'It's your one and only sister, Evie.'

'Oh. What do you want?'

'When are you coming to Cannes? All the booze is free, the sun is shining and it's absolutely crawling with . . .'

I hated to say it, but I was going to have to.

'What?'

'Muff.'

'Yeah. Today. Right. Didn't think you'd be so happy about it. JJ says you've been right slapping it up.'

'JJ says a lot of things. Anyway . . . I've got a really pretty friend here who'll be happy to show you around.'

Patrick snorted. 'Is she as pretty as Jilly?'

It was true; pre-Cassandro, Jilly had mooned around Patrick endlessly when we were growing up, eating cheese strings whilst conspiring to be constantly in the corridor outside his bedroom. His bedroom was next to the bathroom; he must have thought she had a terrible bladder problem.

'Miles better looking. In fact, are you in front of your computer?'

This was unfair. I know Patrick would have preferred me to imagine he was out on the open road somewhere on a Harley, chatting up a waitress in a truck-stop café on Route 66.

'Hnn,' he said grudgingly.

'OK, go to www.yourperfectface.co.uk.'

I knew they used Lydia on the home page of the surgery she worked for. It was a pouty, Posh Spice-style photograph, which I had always thought gave off the message, 'Piss off, you could never look like me, you fat losers.' But this hadn't seemed to deter people.

'Is that her?' he said admiringly.

'Uh-huh!'

'For real?'

'And John Jr has a huge suite and would be delighted to see you' – I crossed my fingers – 'and, tonight we're all going to the casino and you get free money to play with.'

'And you can get me in?'

'Sure, the security's rubbish.'

Well, it was.

'Yeah. I'm on my way.'

That was Lydia taken care of. He may be an arse, but I haven't met a woman yet with the power to resist Patrick, at least on first glance till they find out what a tit he is – and not always then.

But I still had to get Bailey on our side. I headed back to the marquee, but he was *still* deep in conversation with Lydia, who was on full power, so that would have to wait. At least I'd sown the seeds. The next plan on my list, whilst Dr Maitland went off to spy on the docs, was the one I was least looking forward to. But it had to be done.

I found a quiet Internet café, took out Dr Maitland's mobile phone (mine is pay as you go and lasts for about one second overseas, as I'd just discovered phoning Patrick), and sat down with Google.

I had to find Tom. He presumably had access to all sorts of documentation about the project, hence his motivation for why it was wrong. He could help us stop this thing. Even if he was a horrible, sexy, nasty, sexy man.

I couldn't help it – suddenly, even though I was nervous about finding Tom, I was a little bit excited. This was like a proper adventure! And we were the good guys! Fighting for seals and against bad people getting new faces! Yeah!

OK. Obviously the mobile phone number he'd originally given me no longer worked. I'd taken that as a given; it wasn't even the first time in my life that that had happened to me, so ha ha ha, meanie pants.

But he had said he came from Cumbria. I think I'd have to assume from the slightly posh Northern accent that he was telling the truth. Cumbria wasn't a large place, was it? OK, lots of sheep maybe, but how many vets?

I didn't know how to divide sheep by vets, so I searched for Cumbrian vets and got a website listing all UK vets. (Wow, I mean, really, have you ever met someone who designs vet websites for a living? Is it for pigs that can use the phone?)

I started dialling, then stopped. Was Tom his real name? Bennet certainly wasn't. Well, you know, I think I'd just have to assume it was because he'd turned round when people were shouting it as he was running naked across a pier, when presumably your mind would be on other things apart from remembering your fake name. Plus James Bond always called himself James. It was all I had to go on.

I'd just have to try and be casual.

'Hi, is Tom there?'

'Tom who?'

'Oh, you know, just Tom.'

'Tom the carthorse Tom?'

'Uh, no.'

'The cat? Or I think we have a python ... no, that's Tomasina ...'

OK, maybe another approach.

'I'm trying to track down a vet called Tom. He's got bright ginger hair and his ears stick out.'

Responses varied from, 'We've got a ferret that fits that description' to 'Are you *sure*, luv?'

But finally, on the twenty-fourth call, I hit it.

'Tom Livingstone? Yes, he's not in today. He's away at a veterinary conference.'

Oh, was he now?

'Oh well ... it's quite urgent I get in touch with him. He was advising me about ... a hamster.'

'Was he indeed?' the voice sounded amused. Maybe they were used to getting phone calls from desperate girls with imaginary hamsters.

'Is it anything someone else could help you with? Tom's not really a ... hamster specialist.'

'No,' I said hotly. 'Gingerbread is very important to me and he's happy with Tom.'

'OK,' said the receptionist. I'm usually quite good at getting round receptionists, being one and everything.

'Is there any way I could get in touch with him . . . ?' I tried to make my voice sound pathetic. 'It's just . . . Gingerbread's got the most persistent cough. I couldn't bear to lose him. Maybe Tom could reassure me over the phone.'

'Mobiles are really just for emergencies,' said the voice.

'I understand,' I said in my smallest voice. 'I hope he lasts the night . . . when's he coming back?'

'Not till the end of the week.'

I sniffed loudly and didn't say anything.

'OK,' said the receptionist finally. 'Here's his mobile number. Just to set your mind at rest. I'm sure it's nothing.'

'Or TB,' I said. I was getting quite worked up about Gingerbread my imaginary hamster. But as she gave me the number and I hung up, I punched the air. I could be good at this!

My euphoria was short-lived, as I realised I was now actually going to have to make the call. Call the man who, just the night before, had humiliated me in front of everyone. Who I had had sex with. Not just with a man I hardly knew but with a man I knew all the wrong things about. Ugh. Oh well. Spies have to be very brave. I would just have to pretend that I was undercover too.

A thought struck me. What if he thought I was only calling him to get back together? Like he'd just been so absolutely amazing in bed that I didn't care that he was using me, I was just desperate for it? Oh, God, that would be awful. I should have got Dr Maitland to do this bit. But I wanted to show him I could handle it, that I was cool. Who was I kidding? I wasn't cool. Not even a tiny bit. With shaking fingers I dialled the number. At least he wouldn't recognise this phone number.

'Hello?' The voice sounded gruff and business-like, not the easy-going charmer I'd met. I steeled myself and hoped my voice wasn't about to wobble too much.

'Tom?'

'Who is this?'

I rolled my eyes. Torture me, why don't you?

'It's Evie.'

I could hear his brain gears tick over – he obviously wasn't expecting this. I prayed he wouldn't hang up.

'Uh,' he said. 'Look, I have to go . . .'

'No!' I said desperately. 'Don't hang up. It's nothing to do with last night.'

'How did you track me down?'

'You're helping me with my sick hamster.'

'Well, that's a new way of putting it.'

'Look, this is nothing to do with last night,' I repeated.

'Nothing at all? Are you sure?'

'Did you get arrested?'

He sucked in his breath. 'Not for want of you lot trying, no.'

'Uh, tell me you're not trying to *blame me* for last night. Please tell me that, before I have you arrested for indecent exposure.'

'You nicked my boxers and chased me like a loon!'

'Well, then . . . sex under false pretences.'

'It's hardly my fault if you refuse to see what's right under your nose, is it?' he said suddenly. 'I mean, I know you work in beauty so you hardly give a damn, but they're extracting live foetuses from seals to make some stupid fucking face juice and you think it's OK? They're going to completely ignore international protocol and do anything they like out on the high seas, but you don't mind?'

'I mind being taken advantage of,' I said softly.

He paused for a long time. Then his voice lowered. 'Actually,' he said. 'I'd already realised you didn't know anything. The day before, really, when we were walking along the beach. I mean, it was obvious.'

That winded me a bit. 'What do you mean?'

'I mean . . . you know, I still liked you.'

'That's not what you mean,' I said. 'I mean, you were sent to do a job and saw an opportunity. What was I, just another piece of meat like your dead bloody seals? Just something to take advantage of, even though I wasn't any *use* to you?'

'No . . . it wasn't like that,' he said.

'It sounds exactly the fuck like that,' I said. I was getting wound up again. Then I tried my best, my absolute best to get a grip on myself. I took in a huge breath and tried to blow it out through my nose, like yoga teachers tell you to do.

'Are you being sick?' asked Tom.

'No!' I said. But oddly, his remark made it a bit easier to get a hold of myself.

'Look,' I said. 'Forget all this. Me and Dr Maitland have been talking.'

'Uh-huh?'

'And . . . well, he has doubts . . . we have doubts about the project.'

'Do you now? What gave it away, the amount of businessmen around wearing sunglasses indoors and surrounded by goons carrying walkie-talkies?'

'They aren't . . . Oh,' I said, thinking about some of the larger men at the conference. 'I thought those were just really old-fashioned mobile phones.'

'We got some really bad intelligence, picking on you,' said Tom, but he said it with a smile in his voice.

'Shut up,' I said. 'You're not allowed to mention that ever again.'

'I won't,' he said, immediately sounding chastened. 'And . . . I'm sorry. I'm really sorry.'

'So you should be,' I said.

'Um, could you stop punishing me? Remember, you did make me run through Cannes in the nuddie.'

'What did you do?' I said. 'We thought you'd get arrested.'

'Lucky I didn't. I found a wine cellar and hid down there.'

'Don't tell me – you put a cork in it.'

'*No.* I improvised with a couple of aprons and made it back.'

I half smiled at the thought. 'Can we meet?' I asked. 'Dr Maitland and I have some questions.'

'OK, Nancy Drew,' said Tom. 'Do you know the Metropole hotel?'

'Yes,' I said.

'OK. There's a little ice-cream shop next to it. I'll see you in there.'

I couldn't help feeling a little excited as I pushed my way through the crowds on the Croisette. After all, they were just silly sheep on holiday. *I* on the other hand was on an exciting secret mission. With ice cream. So it was like a bonus holiday.

When I found the place, though, I didn't see Tom. I was slightly curious to see him again, just in case I wanted to accidentally kick him in the face, but he didn't appear to be there. Perhaps I'd just sit down, order a Knickerbocker Glory and wait for . . .

'Psst,' came a voice. I looked behind me. 'Psst,' again.

It was coming from the corner of the restaurant. Sitting there was a man with dark hair and a baseball cap, behind a Russian newspaper. I moved closer.

'*Tom?*'

'Shhh!'

He pulled me down by the arm to sit next to him. I could hardly contain myself.

'I am Rudi. Russian engineer,' he announced loudly.

'You *are* joking.'

'Shh.'

'You're in disguise.'

'Well, seeing as my face and arse are all over *Cannes Matin* and everyone that was at that bash knows it was infiltrated, it seemed wise, don't you think?'

'To cover your head in boot polish and jam your ears together? I'm not sure.'

'Did anyone follow you?'

'*What?*'

'I should have told them NEVER to hand out my number . . . my phone's probably been tapped.'

'Aren't you taking this a little too seriously?'

'Well, we're trying to derail a fifty-million-euro project – what do you think?'

I hadn't really thought of it like that. 'You mean, we could be in danger?'

'Sometimes it's hard to do the right thing,' said Tom pompously.

'You know, that would sound a lot more manly and impressive if you didn't have a smudge of raspberry sauce on your cheek. Where's my ice cream?'

'I wasn't sure you were coming.'

'What, you thought I'd get kidnapped on the way? Or double-cross you?'

He looked at me strangely then.

'What do you mean, double-cross me?'

'I don't mean anything. I mean, can I have some chocolate ice cream, please?'

'It would be a very quick change of tune for you,' he mused. 'From know-nothing receptionist to suddenly being interested in finding out everything I know.'

'Yes,' I said. 'Plus, they said if I screwed you over they'd throw in a free boob job made from starving baby elephants. Stop being an idiot.'

He lowered the paper.

'OK,' he said. 'It's hard to trust sometimes.'

'It certainly is when your job is screwing people over,' I said. *'Une glace, s'il vous plaît? Chocolat, oui.'* At times, my French is fine. 'Now. Who do you work for again?'

'Earth Friends,' he mumbled. 'It's a loose collective that tries to argues against the more . . . evil extremes of capitalism.'

'What, like those people who throw stones at Starbucks? I hate those people.'

'*No*, we're a bit more subtle than that. Why do you hate those people?'

'Because a cup of coffee is not that evil. Compared to . . . I don't know. Men that set women on fire if they've been raped. Or send people to fight in pointless wars. Or, you know, commit genocide.'

'Do you protest against those things?'

'Not *as such*. But I disapprove of them. A lot more than some stupid cup of coffee.'

'Well, I'm glad you're managing to provide such a vital stance against things you disapprove of in society by doing absolutely nothing at all.'

'Right, I'd be much better off taking a brick and throwing it through a shop window of a business someone's actually spent time building up and . . .'

'Can we get off the whole coffee thing for a minute? That's not my point. Earth Friends is more . . . think of a charity you do approve of.'

'Uh.' I couldn't think. 'The RSPB?'

'The *RSPB*?'

'Yes?'

He sighed. 'OK. Well, we're more like the RSPB. We campaign against grossly dangerous environmental projects and things we feel mark a really bad direction for society. And we make examples of specific things. Like, for example, a practically completely illegal boat where they're going to carry out dangerous medical procedures whilst getting through, incidentally, twenty thousand litres of fuel a week, whilst they experiment with God knows what.'

'So what did you want out of me?'

'Where it was headed . . . itinerary . . . whether Bailey knew, or whether you controlled Dr Bennet's diary . . . celebrity clients . . .'

'What, after you'd shagged me so spectacularly that the names of show business clients had come out of my mouth?'

Tom shrugged a little uncomfortably.

'Well. Maybe if you'd had dark hair and a Russian accent,' I said.

'It was just an idea,' said Tom sulkily.

'Has it ever worked before in the history of mankind?'

'Yes, all the time,' he said. 'Admittedly, mostly the other way around. Girls seducing boys, that kind of thing. Or boys seducing boys.'

'Well, at least it kept you off the letter writing campaign.'

I picked up a large spoonful of chocolate ice cream and devoured it. 'What I don't understand is why you didn't just ask me? Look, I'm here now, ready to come over on your side and fight the good fight.'

'How could I ask you? What would you think if some lunatic came up to you and suggested that you went against your friends and your employers and everyone you know on some crazed scheme?'

'I'm very open-minded,' I said.

'True,' said Tom, getting a faraway look in his eyes.

I ignored him and kept eating my ice cream. 'So,' I said. 'What's the plan?'

'Well, the original plan was to go to the papers with all the blueprints and celebrities and things,' said Tom. 'Can I have some of your ice cream?'

'NO! Dr Maitland and I think we should have a better plan. One that involves talking to Dr Bennet.'

'*Talking* to him? Talking him out of ten million euros? How are you going to do that?'

'*Ten million euros?*' This was ridiculous. It couldn't be true, could it? Who had that much money?

'Or, well, you know. Something like that. Lots and lots of money from his boat, all offshore.'

'Oh,' I said. 'So you don't know how much money he stands to make. You meant –' and I did the Dr Evil pinky lip – 'ten *meelion* euros.'

Tom didn't answer. He was too busy stealing a bit of my ice cream.

'So even if you could talk him out of it, they'll just get somebody else,' said Tom.

'OK, well, if we talk *everyone* out of it.'

'Everyone on earth? I still think getting agitation in the press is a better idea. Get them to stake out the place with paparazzi. Get some of our youth members along to demonstrate.'

'*Youth* members?'

'Yes. You know, some politically switched-on types have even heard of us.'

'Stop stealing my ice cream, you communist.'

We discussed lots of things. To me, it seemed crucial to get to Dr Bennet and get him on side. If Bailey couldn't give us valuable information about who exactly had commissioned the ship and was behind the job, Dr Bennet ought to be able to. Then the next stage was to threaten them with exposure or . . . well, we weren't sure about the 'or'.

'Couldn't they take all the money and build a children's hospital or something?' I said.

'What, for baby nose jobs? Anyway, look around you: you're in France. They're up to their eyeballs in totally perfect children's hospitals. Mind you, it's one up on what I thought you'd say.'

'What's that?'

'That you thought they should donate all the money to the RSPB . . .'

'Ha ha ha. Birds are very important, you know.'

'I know. Look, Earth Friends has the contacts, the press – we can lobby against this kind of thing once we know who's doing it.'

He looked up at me. 'So we're in this together, right? You can get me a pass to this casino shindig tonight?'

'I guess so,' I said.

Tom sat back on the banquette, looking pleased with himself.

'But don't smirk.'

'I'm not smirking! It's the drawn-on moustache.'

'You look like you're smirking to yourself. You look like you're thinking, Ah, my shagging plan worked. But I'm telling you it didn't.'

'OK.'

'Dr Maitland convinced me.'

'OK.'

'It was nothing to do with you.'

'Not at all.'

'And you're paying for the ice cream.'

I called Dr Maitland on his other phone. He'd gone to find Dr Bennet but hadn't managed to locate him.

'That's unusual, isn't it?' I asked. 'He's usually schmoozing up all over the place.'

'That's what I thought,' he said. 'Maybe he's headed up to the casino to sort things out for tonight. Or maybe he's back in his hotel room?'

We decided his room might be a good place to tackle him. Just a chat – a staff meeting between the three of us. Just to get a bit more clarity on the direction the practice was going (out to sea by the looks of things) and so on . . . nothing heavy.

The afternoon sun beamed down strongly on the beach and I stopped off and bought a large floppy hat. My redness was retreating somewhat, but I didn't want to risk round two; I already had freckles popping up over every available surface. Plus it might come in handy for a disguise.

Dr Maitland almost smiled at me as I met him in the cool marble lobby of the Metropole.

'Is that you in disguise?' he said. 'The big hat and sunglasses?'

'No! This is totally normal!'

'OK,' he said. 'You know, there's a new laser pen for freckles that . . .'

I shushed him. 'You know, some people *like* freckles.'

He frowned. 'Do they?'

'Yes. They think they're cute.'

He came closer and gave my face that penetrating clinical doctory stare thing straight at my face.

'Oh,' he said eventually, straightening up. 'You know they're marks of skin damage?'

I rolled my eyes.

'But yes,' he said. 'They are quite cute. OK, shall we tell the desk to call Yuri?'

Ugh, it was the same snotty pretty man on the desk as before. Did he ever go off duty? Was this whole place staffed by robots? He looked at me, quite convincingly managing to indicate that he had X-ray eyes that could look into my soul and see if I was wanting in the 'being served in a posh hotel' department. Obviously I was as he actually looked around to see if there was anyone else he could help before us.

'Let's not bother,' I said. 'Do you know the room number? We can just go up.'

'OK,' shrugged Dr Maitland.

I've always felt slightly odd in a lift with a man, I don't

215

know why. Probably just so many silly films and dumb Black Lace books, but there's something about being in that enclosed space . . . I suppose that's why everyone just ignores each other and stares straight ahead. Because there's always that ridiculous idea that creeps into your head along the lines of, Wouldn't it be *awful* if I suddenly just leapt cougar-like onto this near-stranger and gave them a big . . .

'I think we're here,' said Dr Maitland.

The door pinged open to reveal, waiting for the lift to go back down, a somewhat dishevelled-looking Janey reapplying her lipstick!

'Hello!' I said cheerfully. I didn't move to get out of the lift; this was (or could be) too good to be true! 'Are you staying here too?'

Janey looked at me with absolutely no recognition in her eyes, but perked up when she saw Dr Maitland.

'Hello, Doctor . . . I mean, well, what a coincidence seeing you here.'

'Is it?' said Dr Maitland gruffly.

'I was just . . .' She gave a self-conscious giggle. 'Uh, going over some paperwork with Dr Bennet.'

'Is that what they're calling it these days?' I wondered aloud. After all, she was already ignoring me. Dr Maitland trod heavily on my foot to shut me up.

'Of *course*,' he said. 'There's so much to go through, isn't there? Health and safety, disclaimers . . . it ties us all up in knots, red tape.'

He gently but firmly started manoeuvring us out of the lift so Janey could step in.

Janey had regained her composure fully now.

'Oh, abso*lutely*,' she said. 'As I was just saying to Dr Bennet . . . so ridiculous. Plus what *must* I look like coming out of his room in the middle of the day! People will talk. Mind you –' she regarded us frankly – 'you could say that about you two! Ha ha!'

My eyebrows shot up in surprise. Turning it round! Boy, she was good!

'Didn't mean to make you blush,' she said to me merrily, convinced now she had the upper hand. 'Well, buh bye!'

And the lift door pinged, and she was gone.

Dr Maitland and I looked at each other speechlessly.

'Well, it could have been innocent,' he said.

'She was putting lipstick on!' I yelled. 'How did her lipstick come off?'

'But . . . you know, women like her wear a lot of lipstick.'

This is indubitably true. They slather it on like they're about to be filmed for high-definition IMAX.

We headed up the corridor.

'Well, if Dr Bennet's naked from the waist up,' I suggested, 'this could be a useful bargaining tool. Where is Mrs Bennet again?'

'Shopping for teeth sharpeners,' said Dr Maitland, preparing to knock on the door.

'What?' he said as I stopped short.

'That is the first time I've ever heard you make a joke,' I said. 'I thought it just wasn't possible for you. That humour had been surgically removed or something, like an appendix.'

Dr Maitland sighed. 'Well, we all know what a good judge of character you are, Evie,' he said. Then he knocked the door, and we entered.

Alas, Dr Bennet was not, as I had hoped (and partly feared), picking up a pair of stockings with his teeth whilst singing, 'Hurray, hurray, it's adultery today,' to himself and sipping the last of the champagne from a glass stiletto.

He did, however, look quite surprised to see us, given that we were his right-hand men. Or so I thought.

'Wilf . . . Evie. Hello, my dears. Um . . .'

Was that a sneaky checking round the room in case of tell-tale signs? Mind you, I would have had to check around my hotel room too if someone turned up unexpectedly, just in case I'd left any of my *own* knickers draped over the chair or whatnot.

'To what do I owe the honour . . . Janey was just here dropping off some paperwork, so it's like Piccadilly Circus round here today!'

Curses! Still he didn't get away so easily – he must have guessed we'd have run into her by the lift.

'What papers?' I said. 'Why don't I take them away with me so I can file them promptly.'

Dr Bennet looked at me, then fumbled on the table for his reading glasses.

'Well, aren't *you* efficient? Here you are then – the course recommendations, the assessment forms . . . here, you can take all these ones from the other seminars too.'

He started loading down my arms with folders.

'And the extra-curricular sign-ups – actually, if you could input those on the database and cross-reference to the original attendance that would be extremely helpful to us . . . start sorting out the wheat from the chaff.'

'Yuri,' said Dr Maitland. 'Can we talk?'

'Of course, of course.'

Dr Bennet looked at us, beaming.

'So nice to have the team together, yes? How do you think it's going? I think it's going very well, very well indeed. Well, apart from a couple of minor . . .' He came over to me and patted my arm. 'How *are* you, my dear? Did you file charges?'

This wasn't like him. He must be worried I had come here to sue the firm.

'No, it's all right,' I said. 'I don't want to get prosecuted for being an idiot.'

'That's the spirit,' said Dr Bennet, as if that actually was the spirit. 'Janey says that you have to be bigger than the set-backs in your life.'

'Does she?' I said. 'But she's three-foot six.'

'Don't be personal,' said Dr Bennet.

'Yuri,' said Dr Maitland heavily. 'We need to talk. We've got some concerns about Operation Sunshine.'

Dr Bennet stopped moving about. 'What. Both of you?' he said, all business suddenly. He poured us all glasses of water. 'Together?'

We both nodded.

'Go on then. Out with it.'

Dr Bennet listened while we explained everything that didn't add up about the project; the lax laws, open access to goodness knows who; the environmental impact. He didn't say anything, just looked at us as we talked – it felt like presenting something to your form teacher, who listened to you indulgently as you told him, wide-eyed, that God didn't exist.

After we'd finished we kind of tailed off with a few 'So's . . .' and 'So that's whys . . .' and then sat back. Dr Bennet still didn't say anything, he just sat there, cradling his fingers in that way they teach them at Being a Doctor college. His brow nearly furrowed.

'Wilf,' he said. 'Wilf. Didn't we discuss this?'

Dr Maitland looked uneasy. He took off his glasses.

'I didn't realise it was such a big deal, Yuri. I thought it was a side project, an offshoot that would bring us in some extra income and provide an interesting diversion . . .'

'A diversion, eh?' Dr Bennet looked a little nasty. 'So the research opportunities were of absolutely no interest to you?'

'Well, yes, obviously, but now I'm feeling . . . conflicted.'

'Conflicted?'

Suddenly the smooth calmness of Dr Bennet – the only mode I'd ever seen him in, Mr Charming – vanished, and he stood to his feet.

'*Conflicted?*' We have a fifty-million-euro boat out there that's just been refitted and you're saying you're *conflicted*?'

Dr Maitland shuffled uncomfortably. Suddenly this felt horribly serious.

'Don't tell me you don't have a vested interest in this.'

I looked at him. He looked haunted.

'So maybe I'd go against my own interests.'

'Would you?' said Dr Bennet. 'Look, you two. Obviously *you* –' and he pointed to me – 'have been completely compromised by that lanky ginger idiot.'

'Lanky ginger idiot . . . with a point,' I said.

But he'd already turned his attention back to Dr Maitland. Now his voice went back to its normal, encouraging, wheedling tone.

'Come on, Wilf. Don't be daft, it's just progress. If we don't do it somebody else will.'

'So let's not do it,' said Wilf. 'That's not a good argument for anything. Plus if you get wrapped up in anything illegal it might be dangerous.'

Dr Bennet harrumphed at this. 'Science is not legal or illegal, Wilf. You know this.'

'I don't,' said Wilf. 'In fact, I think the practice should pull out.'

Dr Bennet set his glass down with a thump.

221

'Pull out! After all this money spent and the engineers employed and the doctors and the bankers lined up begging to get let in? Are you *crazy*?'

'No,' said Wilf. He stood up suddenly and took a deep breath. 'But I'm out.'

'You're what . . . you're resigning?'

Dr Bennet was trying to keep his cool, but I could see he was furious.

'I don't have to resign,' said Dr Maitland. 'You're not my boss. I'm your partner. I'm dissolving our partnership.'

Dr Bennet's mouth was open. So was mine. Oh my God! This wasn't a little holiday flirtation with activism! This was really serious! I knew, you see. Dr Maitland was miles better than Dr Bennet. Dr Maitland was what kept us on Harley Street, and in the celebrities' secret notebooks, and on the recommended lists. Dr Bennet could do the schmooze and the charm, but Dr Maitland was the one who wielded the knife; who could give nose jobs that don't even look like nose jobs (and believe me, when you've seen as many as I have you realise how rare that is).

'Wilf,' said Dr Bennet. 'You don't mean that.'

'I've been sleepwalking,' said Dr Maitland. He sat down, and didn't look at either of us. 'All this time, thinking chopping open stupid dumb blondes was fine, it was just training till I could take my skills somewhere else, somewhere useful. Go work in a war zone, or with burns victims in India. That was my plan. But then what happened? I got

222

used to the easy money, coming in at ten every morning, not having to talk to anyone if I didn't want to, living a nice life.'

I didn't think it sounded that nice, apart from the money part, but I didn't want to interrupt.

'So I never did any of that . . . all the big plans I had at medical school. The good life I'd mapped out for myself. I didn't want to go to Africa and get bitten by bugs and have to sleep in tents. I didn't want to go and work in dirty hopeless conditions in the Third World. I *liked* being comfortable.'

He stood up and walked over to Dr Bennet.

'But this *is* dirty. This is dirtier than . . . one of those countries where dogs eat dead dogs in the street. This smells worse than somewhere I'd have to wipe my scalpel on the long grass. Because this is what happens when you get complacent, when you get comfortable. Bad things happen. And bad things are going to happen here. And I'm not doing it.'

'Fine,' said Dr Bennet. 'Then we'll do it without you.'

And *then* he punched Wilf on the nose.

I knelt next to Dr Maitland, whose nose was discharging thick gouts of blood, while Dr Bennet, whistling slightly, washed his hands and picked up his briefcase. I was shocked, and breathing hard. I mean, obviously I'd seen plenty of blood, but usually people were anaesthetised.

'So I guess this is goodbye, Evie,' he said chirpily. 'I won't be paying you compensation . . . I'm sure you'll understand.'

'What, after you let me be assaulted at your conference? We'll see about that,' I said, white-hot with fury. 'You'll be hearing from my lawyers.'

'Who are your lawyers again?' he asked, looking amused. 'Ambulance chasers dot com? Well, I wish you good luck with that – there are very few extradition treaties between the UK and . . . the middle of the sea.'

He stood, looking impatient.

'Could you move now, please . . . I have an important session to run. And a new staff to recruit.'

I looked at Dr Maitland, but he still seemed too stunned to say anything. Dr Bennet didn't even look a tiny bit perturbed; simply ushering us out in his usual charming manner as if on his way to a hairdresser's appointment.

I drew myself up to my full height (five foot five) and tried to look him straight in the eye.

'You won't get away with this,' I said, voice trembling.

'What is this, *Scooby Doo*?' he said. 'What's to get away with? I'm pursuing a legitimate business interest without my partner. Big deal.'

'So why did you just punch him on the nose?'

'Are you joking? Six years without so much as a "good morning"? Do you know what it's like working with someone like that? I wish I'd done it years ago, the rude bastard.'

Hmm. He almost had a point there.

Chapter Eleven

'It's true,' Wilf – as he'd now suggested I called him – was saying, as we sat in the lobby drinking a restorative *citron* as he held a tissue to his nose. 'But I'm just shy, that's all. Shy and . . . I was slightly ashamed of my job.'

'I've always wondered,' I said, figuring it was now or never, 'why you wouldn't take your obvious skills somewhere more useful.'

He looked defensive, as if he wanted to avoid the question.

'Plenty of good doctors just work for the cash.'

'Yes, well, there's a difference between a good doctor and a good person.'

'Hmm,' said Wilf, looking uncomfortable. He dabbed at his nose some more. Then he turned to face me.

'You always tell the truth, don't you, Evie?' he said. 'It's an unusual habit.'

I looked into his grey-blue eyes. '*Good* unusual?' I found myself asking, a little short of breath.

Suddenly there was a huge commotion in the lobby.

'Hey, look, it's my half-naked slutbag sister,' came the cheery voice booming across the lobby. The concierge raised his eyebrows nastily. Obviously JJ had got over our touching family reunion.

'Hello, John Jr,' I said, trying to insinuate that I had much better things to be going on with. 'Is Patrick here yet?'

'I'm just going to get him, in I?'

He stared rudely at Wilf. 'Ooh, the doc again. You don't mess around, do you?'

'Hello, again,' said Wilf, a little stiffly. Oh, crap. Just when Wilf and I were getting along he'd be reminded that, technically, I was related to an orang-utan. Bugger. Though what was I being so snotty about – my GCSE in general studies?

'You know they've got brandies here for two 'undred euro a glass?' said John Jr. He paused to allow us to take in the impressiveness of his statement. 'I didn't like mine much. Only 'ad four. Ah well, all goes on the company credit card, eh, Doc? Eh? Eh?'

Wilf smiled nicely, which I liked.

'Gawd, if I had to add up the time I've spent waiting for

the missus to get her slap on . . . Stupid cow. 'Ere she is now.'

Kelly tottered towards us, her face in the widest smile I'd ever seen.

''Ello!' she said. 'Feeling better?'

'I'm totally over it now actually,' I said.

'And you with that awful skin peel too. You know, you want to get some Crème de la Mer – it is expensive, but it's *so* worth it. Anyway,' she said, 'you won't *believe* what's happened!'

'What?' I asked. I wasn't quite up to telling her my news: sacked, in trouble, penniless, etc.

'Well, I ran into your gorgeous Dr Bennet at lunch . . . and he asked me to be his *inaugural* client when he launches his new venture!'

Wilf and I looked at each other in consternation.

'Bloody hell,' I said. 'What did they say they're going to do to you?'

She smiled. 'Oh, this is the exciting part. It's completely new. They've never done it before. Roxy – something. They inject it under my entire face, and it apparently looks like I have completely new skin! Like a baby's! I'll look twenty!'

'You're only thirty-one,' I said.

She pouted. 'Exactly. Nothing like twenty.'

'Why do you even care? You're married, you've got a big house . . . I mean, what's it to you?'

'Well,' said Kelly, 'it's just a matter of personal pride and self-esteem, that's all.' Then she realised she might have insulted me and looked apologetic.

Wilf was looking anxious.

'Mrs Kennedy... this treatment they described to you... is it called Radoflux 9000?'

Kelly's face lit up. 'Yeah, that's it!'

I looked at Wilf. 'It's those bloody seals again, isn't it?'

He nodded.

'Do you think it's dangerous?' I said.

'We don't know if it's dangerous yet,' said Wilf. 'Possibly. And the use of animal stem cells in plastic surgery – or at all – well, it's very controversial.'

'There you go,' I said to Kelly. 'It's dangerous. Possibly. You'd be mad to do it, it's not even legal.'

'Well, why would a doctor have recommended it if it wasn't legal?' said Kelly, pouting a bit.

'And there, in a nutshell, is the problem with this fucking boat,' said the odd-looking person waltzing through the circular door.

'Who are you?' said Kelly. 'Why is everyone ganging up on me?'

'Don't listen to them, sweetheart,' said John Jr. 'They're just jealous.'

'I'm not jealous,' I said. 'We're just trying to stop her from having a procedure that might harm her!'

'But it's just a minor procedure, Evie,' said Kelly. 'It'll be fine.'

'Yeah,' said John Jr. 'You're just jealous she's getting something for free that you really bloody need. Look at you lot.'

Sure enough, with me, Tom arriving with boot polish under his nose and Wilf with dried blood trickling on his face we did make quite a sight.

Kelly appeared to think about it.

'I'll see you lot later,' she said finally. 'I'll be the twenty-year-old in the corner.'

And they swept out, or rather Kelly swept; John Jr waddled after her.

Wilf let out a heavy sigh. 'This is not good,' he said. 'This is not good at all. And who the hell have you come as?'

Tom looked a little insulted.

'Uh, sorry,' I said. 'This is our mystery man in heavy disguise.'

'A mystery man, eh?' said Wilf, looking puzzled. Pretty much every eye in the foyer was on Tom. A bit of his hair dye had run down onto his ear, making it look smudged. His sunglasses were a little wonky. And he had salt stains on his shorts. Out of the corner of my eye I felt the evil concierge send a little death ray in our direction. I clutched at my drink to show I had the right to be there.

'Oh, wow,' said Tom. 'Did you get in a big ruckus with Dr Bennet?'

'Not so much a *big* ruckus,' said Wilf.

'He got biffed on the nose,' I added helpfully.

'Oh, good,' said Tom. 'Did you discover all his backers? When is the boat coming in? What other evil plans he has up his sleeve?'

'Not exactly,' I said.

Tom thought about this. 'You know, we really need to know when the boat is coming in, so we can intercept it.'

'Maybe it's a surprise,' I said.

'It's a fucking liberty,' snapped Tom.

'He doesn't seem to think he's being evil,' said Wilf.

'Well, he *is*,' said Tom. 'And that injection thing is completely out of the question.'

'It didn't . . . it didn't go quite as well as we'd hoped,' I said.

'You mean, you guys messed it up?'

'He didn't seem to want to talk to us much,' mumbled Wilf. He checked out his reflection in one of the big gilt mirrors hanging overhead.

'It's all right,' I said. 'I don't think you need stitches.'

'Thank you, doctor,' he muttered.

Tom threw his hands up. 'Well, this is great. Did he sack you?'

'Well, he can't sack me, I'm his partner,' said Wilf. 'I resigned.'

Tom put his hands over his eyes.

'He sacked me though,' I added helpfully.

'I have to make a phone call,' said Tom.

*

'But I thought you guys had a *plan*,' Tom was saying as the three of us walked down to the seafront.

'We did!' I said. 'We thought we'd explain the error of his ways and then everything would be all right. Now I think about it, not such a brilliant plan.'

'So . . . all your contacts and hope of getting on that boat . . . it's all gone.'

'And I lost my job,' I said. 'And I'll never get another one in the same field now they've all seen me in your boxers.'

'You can come work for me,' said Wilf.

'I thought you told Dr Bennet you were going to work in darkest Africa,' I said.

'Oh, yeah,' he said, looking a tad disconsolate. 'So I am.'

'No!' said Tom. 'What do you mean! We're not giving up!'

'Well, we kind of have to,' I explained. 'Because, you know. We're not a part of this any more. Dr Bennet is just going to run the boat and it's our tough luck, and, I don't know, Kelly will probably end up taking liquids through a straw for the rest of her life.'

'I can't believe you're taking it like that,' said Tom.

I turned to him seriously. 'What do you expect me to do? I'm sorry, Tom. The boat is horrible. So are lots of things. It's going to happen with or without us, that's perfectly clear. But we did try. We all did. Why don't we just go out and have a few glasses of wine and try and forget all about it . . .'

'That's a shit attitude and you know it,' said Tom.

He left our group and looked at the road.

'You say you want to help and then you do fuck all.'

'I got a bloody nose,' said Wilf, but this only seemed to enrage Tom all the more.

'Fucking dilettantes. Don't you care what happens to this planet?'

'Yes,' I said. 'Let's discuss it over a glass of rosé. Maybe Wilf could help your charity.'

'Yes,' said Wilf, brightening slightly. 'With, you know. A UK-based helping job. Where I could still use my skills . . . maybe in the London area . . . research perhaps.'

'Forget it,' said Tom. He backed away from us, and onto the open road, stepping off the narrow pavement. He obviously didn't want to be anywhere near us. 'Forget it. This whole thing . . . You guys were a complete waste of time. I should have known it from the start.'

'I'm sorry,' I said, and I was. But what else could we do?

'You're not,' said Tom. Scooters and cyclists were having to swerve to avoid him. 'You don't give a . . .'

Suddenly a car, which should have gone straight past us, screeched to a halt. It was a huge, heavy-looking silver thing – a big steely Mercedes. It had blacked-out windows, which gave it a sinister appearance. Completely without warning the back door opened and two sets of arms came out. They hauled Tom backwards into the car's dark maw.

Taken completely by surprise from behind, Tom didn't even make a sound as he disappeared. His big gangling feet were the last to go, kicking in the air. Even before they were fully in, the car sped off. It couldn't have stopped for more than four seconds; it had barely inconvenienced the cars behind it. But suddenly, Tom was gone.

'TOM!' I screamed into the air. I threw myself forward, but the car had already taken a left turn and disappeared into the swiftly moving traffic before speeding away on the four-lane raised motorway that cut through the heart of Cannes like a knife. 'TOM!'

Unbelievably, under the shady palm trees, it seemed like no one else had even noticed.

Chapter Twelve

We went to the only place I was sure nobody would find us – my horrible guest house. The landlady hadn't looked me in the face once since I'd arrived so I could be reasonably confident she wouldn't be able to pick me out in a line-up or betray me to mysterious goons.

We sat there awkwardly, on my bed.

'Oh, God,' I kept saying, although it didn't really help matters much. 'Oh, God.'

'We must go to the police,' said Wilf. 'We must.'

'But they're already looking for him! They want to arrest him for being naked! Plus, what on earth would we tell them?'

'That a man was pushed into a car!'

'What kind of car?'

'A big silver car.'

'And where was it going?'

Wilf looked really concerned. 'This is serious, isn't it? This is serious stuff with bad guys and everything. This isn't like a holiday adventure at all.'

'What if they kill him?'

'They can't kill him,' I said, realising I was shaking. 'They won't.'

'Who, though?' said Wilf. 'Who are we even talking about? *Bloody* Yuri. We need to get to him.'

He tried his phone again. Dr Bennet wasn't picking up.

I glanced at my watch. 'He'll be at the casino. That thing will be starting.'

'Well, we'd better get there, then. Once we finally find out who's responsible and where he is we can call the *gendarmes*.'

We were going to rush off to the casino straight away, but this was a posh night and presumably Dr Bennet had already taken us off the guest list. We didn't want to stand out more than we already did. I sent Wilf onwards and, finally, slipped into the bloody red dress. In my head I'd imagined myself taking a long time getting ready in my large marble bathroom before slipping it over my sun-drenched skin. Not shoving it on over my blistered shoulders before running out to try and find our friend who'd been *kidnapped*. My holiday dreams seemed long ago and far away. And what had seemed like a bit of excitement was suddenly careering out of control.

I looked at the high-heeled shoes I'd bought to go with

the dress. Well, they weren't going to work because I had to run all the way to the casino as it was. Which meant I had a choice between my boots that I'd worn from London, a pair of red Converse – which were the right colour but made me look as if I was trying to make a ridiculous Lily Allen style statement – or a pair of flip-flops. Flip-flops it would have to be. At least my skin seemed to be settling down a bit. Though I hardly had the chance to do more than glance at myself in the mirror and bung on some red lipstick before throwing myself out of the hotel and tearing down towards the seafront. My heart was pounding. OK, Tom was an idiot, but he didn't deserve this. I had a sudden horrible mental image of him cowering in a room somewhere, or being thrown into the sea. And I was *furious* with Dr Bennet. He was going to tell us where Tom was if I had to . . . bloody pluck out his bloody eyebrows.

Holding my skirt with both hands – and tripping over every two minutes in those bloody flip-flops – I finally made it. Completely breathless and with sweat dripping off my forehead, I pelted up to the front of the casino, chest heaving.

The casino was white and palatial with steps leading up to it. Outside was a cashpoint machine. This put me off somewhat. I mean, obviously, it's useful for people to be able to pick up cash, but I didn't like the idea of people desperately pushing cards into the machine in the middle of the night just to feed their gambling addiction.

Expensive cars were disgorging expensive-looking

occupants as tourists walked past rubbernecking. I looked for the silver car but couldn't see it. Stealthily dangerous-looking bouncers hovered round the entrances. And there, looking tall and smart and slightly concerned, his bow tie untied around his neck, out of breath like I was, was Wilf.

He didn't see me at first so I waved furiously. Then, when he did, his face changed. The anxiety drained out of it – not completely, but enough to soften up his features and give a spark to his eye. And for a second I forgot that our friend had disappeared; that I'd lost my job; that this was a really weird holiday; that we'd failed in our mission to stop the project; that, in fact, my life had gone from mundane to disastrous in the space of about three days (and I was probably going to die of skin cancer too). Just for a second.

'Hello,' he said, coming down the steps towards me.

'Hello,' I said. We looked round. There was nobody there that we knew. He grinned that lopsided smile at me.

'You look . . . you look nice.'

'That's impossible,' I said. 'I just threw it on in two seconds. Literally. I'm not wearing any make-up or anything.'

Wilf shrugged. 'I don't like overdone women.'

I stared at him.

'You are joking. That's what you do.'

'Haven't we already established that I'm not *exactly* over the moon about what I do?' said Wilf. Then, shyly, he leaned over and planted a kiss on my cheek.

I stepped back, feeling my heart beat.

'Uh,' I said. 'Uh . . . we'd better go and do this thing.'

'Absolutely,' said Wilf. 'Fortune favours the brave. Let's go find Yuri and, I don't know, *tickle* the answers out of him.'

'Er, yeah,' I said.

'Um,' said Wilf. 'Could you do up my bow tie first?'

Bow tie looking like a badly wrapped party gift (hey, it's not like I sent my brothers out to black tie dos very often), we vaulted up the steps, planning our strategy. If Dr Bennet didn't come clean we were going straight to the police – well, as strategies went it wasn't a bad one. As long as we were on time. But I also thought, I mean, they'd probably just take Tom somewhere and make him walk home naked again to get him back for ruining their yacht party, wouldn't they?

First we had to get past the bouncers. I hoped against hope that Dr Bennet would have been too busy or annoyed to waste time getting our names taken off the list. And the person he'd usually have ordered to do so was, of course, me. He couldn't really find his way around a sheet of A4 without me.

Clattering up the steps we were conscious that there was an aura of low-key elegance about the place. Beautiful waitresses glided about with cocktails on trays. Smart music was tinkling. Expensive-looking paintings lined the walls. Everything about the place seemed designed to make you completely forget that its sole purpose was to send you down the road to rack and ruin and end up owning your house and, ideally, wife.

'Just look like we fit in,' I whispered as we mounted the red-carpeted steps.

'You're the one in flip-flops,' Wilf whispered back, then he took my hand and squeezed it. I squeezed it back, then let it stay there. It felt comfortable. I felt – even though we'd been thoroughly bested so far – that if I was with him, then maybe we were going to be all right.

'Aha,' came the familiar voice, and the face peered quizzically down on us from the top of the stairs.

'*Quelle surprise!*'

Lydia.

'I wondered if you two would have the cheek to turn up,' she sneered. 'But here you are – waif man and the deep-fried tomato. Holding hands. How touching.'

Lydia was clutching a large clipboard with names on it. Witch with a clipboard – ominous.

'You know, you don't have to be nasty all the time,' I said. 'It's not in your job description. *Is* it?'

'*Me* being nasty?' said Lydia. 'I'm not the ones that tried to embarrass Dr Bennet and the entire bloody Harley Street community, am I? I'm not the ones who are having a cheap and tacky affair and had a big strop when it was discovered and then quit their jobs leaving poor Dr Bennet in the lurch.'

'Is *that* what he said?' I yelled, furious. 'He's lying.'

'So I can see by the fact that you're holding hands.'

'We really need to get in there, er, Lydia,' said Wilf. 'Do you mind?'

'Yes, I do actually,' said Lydia. 'Because your names aren't here on my clipboard. Which means you've been disinvested. Which means if you do try and get in I'll have to shout to the nearest two gigantic bouncers who, and I haven't seen it myself, but *apparently*, can kick your arse from here to doomsday.'

I looked at the stealthy bouncers again. Yup. It certainly looked possible, if not probable. As I was looking at them, one of them turned round to give me stink eye. Lydia made a little motion with her manicured hand which looked like it meant 'Come over here I think I'm about to have some trouble.' Sure enough, the goon touched his partner and the pair started to lumber towards us. Wilf and I looked at each other. Oh, God. This wasn't going well.

'Please, Lydia,' I said, resorting to begging. She liked this and looked at me regally.

'Well, the problem is . . .' she started officiously, traffic warden-style.

Oh, God, she was about to explain why she'd really, really *like* to help us out but couldn't because of her obsessive rule-following and unpleasant personality.

'The problem is . . .' But then she stopped talking altogether, and just stood there with her mouth hanging open. I stared at her, then turned around, following her gaze.

Striding up the hall in motorcycle leathers, five o'clock

stubble on his manly chin, a touch of engine oil on his cheekbone, which he must surely have contrived to do himself with something he found in an easyJet toilet, was Patrick.

I hadn't seen the Patrick effect in quite a while – I tended to avoid places he went as it got very tedious watching him fend off the women – but it was undeniably impressive. I knew my brother was a bit of a dick – partly, I suspected, because women had acted like complete idiots in front of him since he was eleven years old – but it absolutely didn't show. He looked fantastic; everyone else faded into the background as he stalked up, as usual looking like he was pretending to be in his own movie and that he was indubitably centre stage. I turned to face him.

'Hi, Patrick,' I said casually. Kelly and JJ must be behind him somewhere.

'Hi, sis,' he said, and even stooped to give me a kind of hug. 'You look shit. Did you steal that dress off a pig in a farmyard?'

'Pigs don't even wear dresses, though,' I said. 'So your comment makes no sense.' Mum told me that the boys and I wouldn't bicker like children for ever. I was still waiting. Wilf was watching closely, but not with a fraction as much concentration as Lydia was.

'Er. so, Evie, ha ha ha,' said Lydia. 'Aren't you going to introduce us?'

Patrick stood back to take a look at her.

'Is that her?' he whispered to me in his Neanderthal fashion. I nodded. 'Not bad, for once,' he said.

'Lydia, this is my brother Patrick. He was really looking forward to coming to the casino evening with us . . .'

Patrick roughly pushed past me and picked up Lydia's taloned hand.

'Who the hell are you?' he said. He always went for this crude approach, and his hit rate was extraordinary. 'You're fucking gorgeous.'

Lydia giggled. This was a new sound for her and she nearly choked on it before it came out, but she got there in the end.

'I'm Evie's friend Lydia.'

Patrick made it very clear that he was sizing her up.

'Normally Evie's friends are all dogs,' he said. 'But you . . . I mean, you're byoo-tee-full.'

'We're not that close,' said Lydia.

'You can say that again,' I said.

'Shh,' said Wilf, as we started sidling towards the door.

'Are you a doctor?' asked Lydia. She was trying to put up her favourite final line of defence, but I knew it wasn't going to get her anywhere. I think Patrick had that smell men are meant to secrete that makes women go into labour and things.

'Neah, fuck 'em,' said Patrick. 'Anywhere round here we can get a drink?'

And that was the last thing we heard as we slipped unnoticed inside the casino ballroom.

*

The private room was ridiculously over the top. Carved cherubs peered down from pink and eau-de-nil ceilings which were inlaid with gold, as if to suggest that angels were blessing you as you spunked the housekeeping on a puggy machine. Huge mirrors reflected back images of smartly dressed men and inappropriately dressed women, and overhead vast, multifaceted chandeliers glittered. The whole thing would have been lovely and classy-looking if it wasn't for the banks and banks of slot machines lining the walls, all beeping and flashing, looking as if they'd be much more at home in a pub with a sticky brown swirly carpet. In the middle of the room were roulette wheels and pontoon tables (I suppose it was vingt-et-un here), and a craps table which everybody was eyeing but nobody was playing at, presumably because nobody understood the rules except that you have to shout 'snake eyes' at various points. I couldn't see Dr Bennet, or Bailey.

'Good work,' said Wilf. 'Is that really your brother? We should get him to do some modelling for the clinic . . . Oh.'

'Oh, yes,' I said. 'We don't work there any more.'

'Yes.' He looked round. 'He should be here somewhere.'

Everywhere there were excited-looking men making squeaks of delight as they placed their 'money'. (There was free betting for an hour – a mean trick, I thought, getting everyone carried away with champagne and Monopoly money until they got into the habit of wagering huge sums and moved directly on to the whole rack and ruin thing.)

'Hang on,' I said. I thought I'd spotted Bailey. 'Stay here. Or look for Dr Bennet, but don't go far.'

Wilf squeezed me briefly on the hand and disappeared into the flurry.

'Bailey!' I hissed. He was hiding behind a curtain and making a pretty good job of it – if I hadn't spotted the laces of those horrible shoes poking out from under the thick red velvet I might have missed him altogether.

He poked his head out briefly. He looked haunted.

'Oh,' he said. 'It's you.'

'Who were you expecting, the cat's mother?' I said. I decided the curtain was actually a very good place to hide myself, before I got thrown out or kidnapped by goons, so shuffled myself into its luxuriant, smoky folds.

'I'm hiding,' said Bailey, unnecessarily I thought.

'Really? I thought you'd moved in here.'

'From Lydia.'

'From Lydia? You two have practically been smoochy smoochy icky poo since the second we arrived.'

'No, we haven't,' said Bailey, looking truly appalled. 'She's followed me around everywhere! I can't believe you didn't notice.'

'You're right, I've had very little on. Anyway, I've taken care of Lydia,' I said.

'What do you mean?'

'I've got rid of her. So I could get to you.'

'How?'

'I've Patricked her.'

'No way.'

'Way. He was coming here anyway, so it made perfect sense.'

'You're a marvel. You haven't Patricked anyone for years.'

'No. Because I try to be more moral than that. But thank you. Now. Listen. Things have got really serious.'

'What do you mean?'

'I mean, shit-hitting-the-fan serious. This boat – it *really* has to stop.'

'What do you mean?'

And I told him everything: about the threats and the resignation/sacking and the kidnapping of Tom.

'Oh, God,' he said when I'd finished. 'I heard you'd just quit because of a sex scandal.'

'Don't tell me you believed that.'

Bailey shrugged.

'Oh, for God's sake! It was a completely malicious rumour.'

'Yeah, uh, that's what I thought.'

'It *was*! Anyway, that doesn't matter. We need to find Tom. It's dangerous. Genuinely, seriously dangerous. We need to find out who's in charge here, when the boat's arriving, and then go straight to the police. I saw someone up on top of the party boat the other night, Bailey. Who was it? Who?'

Bailey looked unhappy. 'Oh, God. Well, it's a consortium, you know.'

'I don't know. What is that?'

'It's a holding company. Lots of middle men and so on, you know.'

'Well, are they here?'

Bailey poked his head out.

'No one I recognise . . . I suppose we could ask Yuri.'

'You know where he is?'

''Well, he's here somewhere.'

Bailey emerged from the curtain still looking a bit nervous.

'It's all right,' I whispered. 'Patrick'll be giving her tops by now.'

'Do you have to be so crude?' said Bailey.

'Well, seeing as Tom is being tortured to death *right now* then *yes*,' I said.

People bustled around us, moving between tables.

'That's a nice dress,' said Bailey. 'Shame about the flip-flops.'

'Shut up!'

The noise levels were rising and the cocktail waitresses were busy. I noticed that all the windows were covered in the same heavy drapes as the one we'd been hiding behind. I remembered how casinos liked to block out all natural light in the hopes of keeping you in there for forty-eight hours or something without you figuring it out. I liked the fact that the human brain was so easily fooled. 'Oooh . . . dark . . . must eat peanuts and stay out late . . .'

Bailey nodded and grunted to the people who were, as

usual, trying to get his attention. Most of them were asking when the boat was getting in and when they were going to get a look at it. He brushed off the questions.

'Don't you know?' I said.

'Yes,' he said, insulted. 'I mean, roughly. I mean, we've got a display on it tomorrow so it will have to be here by then.'

'But you don't know where it is now?'

'Not exactly.'

'So Tom could be on it, or at the bottom of the sea having been thrown off it?'

'Don't you think you're being a bit melodramatic?'

'He got pulled into a *car*! How is that being melodramatic?'

Finally we arrived at the far corner of the casino room. There, tucked well away behind the blackjack table, was Dr Bennet. He was concentrating hard, surrounded by a group of men. And, to my shock, just behind his left shoulder, was Janey. She was standing there, preening, like she was his lucky charm. I glared at her, but she merely smiled and looked back, waving her little fingers delicately.

There was nothing delicate about Dr Bennet, however, when he saw me again. 'You,' he said. 'You're like cranial fungus. You just won't go away.'

'Thank you,' I said. 'But . . .'

'But what?'

Bailey stepped forward. 'Yuri, look.'

'Oh, God, not you too. First Wilf, now you. What, does she give unbelievable head?'

Janey whispered something in his ear that made him grimace. I couldn't believe that the doc I'd always thought so smooth was actually as coarse as a sailor's armpit.

'No,' said Bailey. 'The young guy's gone missing.'

'What do you mean, "gone missing"? Who cares? He could fall off Brighton bloody pier for all I care.'

'He was bundled into a car,' I said. That got his attention. 'I saw it happen.'

'Don't be ridiculous.'

'I was right there. So was Wilf. Ask him if you don't believe me.'

Yuri was looking definitely flustered now. 'Well, he was asking for it.'

'What the hell do you mean by that? Asking for it? He could be dead for all you know.'

I was starting to make a scene. Again. Bailey touched my arm gently.

'Look,' he said. 'I know there's a lot of guys here who've been involved with the project and so on. I've met some of them, you know most of them, we've all been working together, right? But I really need to meet the top guy. The guy who signs the cheques, the guy no one meets. Because he's got to know what's going on.'

'Or she,' I added, out of habit.

Dr Bennet shook his head. 'Well, I don't know where he is. He's not here. Now if you'll excuse me, I want to get back to my card game.'

I looked around. Nobody was watching me. Janey, however, had both her hands round Dr Bennet's shoulders and was leaning in to give him a good-luck kiss on the hair. Quickly, I took my camera-phone out of my bag and snapped a shot. I hardly ever used the camera facility – I'd been talked into it by some spotty chap in the shop – but I was incredibly grateful for it now.

'What? What was that?' said Dr Bennet hearing the click.

'It's great I don't work for you now,' I said. 'I must delete your wife's telephone number off my phone. Just as soon as I've sent her this pic, of course.'

I held it up. It was incredibly compromising; I think Janey was licking something. Of course, I didn't have his wife's mobile number, but he didn't know that.

'Give me that!' said Dr Bennet.

'Tell us how to find Tom. Where's the guy in charge?'

'Give me that phone!'

'I'll give you the phone when you give us the information.'

'No!'

We glared at each other. It was a stand-off. Dr Bennett looked around. I wondered if he had henchmen too.

'You are nothing,' he hissed suddenly. 'The girl who can't even take a holiday on her own. I've seen you cowering about the place.'

I took a step backwards. As a full-on assault his comment

felt just as vicious as if he'd punched me (which, as I'd already seen, he was entirely capable of doing too).

'"Oh, poor me, my brothers are horrible, poor me, my life sucks, I can't get a boyfriend, boo hoo hoo, pass me a magazine and let me empathise with Kerry Katona."'

'My life is *not* like that.'

'"I don't even have the decisiveness to go travelling. I'm so pathetic I need to go on holiday with the people I work with."'

'Shut up! Just shut up!'

'Give me the phone, little girl. And stop messing about in things you don't understand.'

His hand was nearly at mine and I couldn't think of a thing to do. I felt blinded with the pain of his words, I wanted to curl up in a ball and lick my wounds. Almost hypnotised, I felt my hand moving out . . .

Suddenly, the phone was snatched away and disappeared . . . into Wilf's pocket. I felt shaken out of my reverie.

'Where have you been?'

Wilf raised one eyebrow mysteriously. It looked strange, what with him in his dinner jacket and everything.

'Yuri,' he said. 'No hard feelings.'

Yuri rolled his eyes.

'What about a couple of rounds of vingt-et-un, for old times' sake.'

'What do you mean, "for old times' sake"?' he growled.

Wilf sat up at the table and ordered a martini. Really.

'Well, forget old times.' He leant forward across the table and opened his hands in a reasonable fashion. 'How about, if you win, you get the phone, and if I win, you tell us where Philippe is.'

I stared at Wilf. Philippe must be the big boss. And Wilf knew his name!

'Philippe, that was it,' said Bailey behind me. Ha, so, I wasn't the only person who forgot important things.

Yuri sat back in his chair, eyeing Wilf's pocket. The other men clustered round the table, muttering to themselves. A challenge! Yuri had to take a challenge!

It was true. he was looking at the male faces around the table. Wilf looked calm and unbothered, but he'd sent out a true threat to Dr Bennet's honour. I hung on closely. Janey did too. Wilf had brought a pile of chips to the table, and it was roughly the same size as Dr Bennet's. Dr Bennet raised his hands as Wilf threw a couple onto the table. Then he threw his own on too.

The dealer flicked out the cards in lightning-flash time. He put one of his own cards face up on the table. One was a ten. I looked at Wilf's hand. He had sixteen.

'Hit,' he said. The dealer gave him an eight.

'Hmm,' said Wilf.

After that, the game moved incredibly fast. Sometimes they'd double up the cards, and there'd be a flurry of cards on the table. Sometimes the dealer would fold without even looking at the other card. I was slightly bamboozled by everything that was going on, but one thing was certain: Wilf's pile of chips was getting smaller and smaller. Dr Bennet's expresssion was beginning to return to its normal self-satisfied look, and I felt my hand tightening its grip on the phone – Wilf had given it to me for safe keeping. Maybe I should make a dash for it – but so many people had come over to watch the game, and were now pressing up against me, I didn't know if I could fight my way out.

Finally Wilf was left with only a few red chips. He'd managed to make the wrong decision on practically every hand he'd had. He'd folded too early, he'd bust too high. He obviously had no clue what he was doing. I was wildly disappointed.

He looked at his hand, sighing, then threw them all into the centre of the table, as the dealer threw out a hand of cards, face down except for one of his own.

'All or nothing,' said Wilf. Dr Bennet smirked and took a long sip of his drink. The dealer was holding a four. 'All or nothing,' said Dr Bennet, pushing all his chips into the centre of the table. He'd had a run of winning on fifteens; he looked like he could afford to be generous. His eyes flicked to where I was holding the mobile phone. The dealer rapidly counted the chips and added an equal number from the bank.

Dr Bennet flipped over his hand. A ten and a queen. A gasp went up from the assembled crowd. The dealer turned his other card over. A ten. He had to hit. He did so, and got a jack – busted.

Then it was Wilf's turn. He flipped the first – yet *another* ten. The room, which had been so noisy for so long, now went completely silent. I realised I was holding my breath. Dr Bennet still looked quite nonchalant; what was going to beat his twenty? Then Wilf turned over his other card. It was the ace of spades.

The room erupted. I yelled out loud. Dr Bennet swore loudly and looked about to storm off as the dealer pushed the huge mountain of chips towards our seat. I couldn't believe Wilf had got this lucky. I looked at him, he hadn't even broken a sweat.

'Well done!' I whispered.

'Yuri?' Wilf was saying, getting down from his seat. 'Don't you have something to tell us? About the whereabouts of Philippe?'

There was a rustle of agreement from the crowd as Dr Bennet got up heavily from the table.

'Of course, you'll keep your side of the bargain?'

Dr Bennet muttered something, and Bailey, Wilf and I pushed our way through the crowd to get to him; Janey had already taken his arm.

'OK, OK, OK,' he said furiously as we surrounded him. 'Come with me. You don't want to make Philippe unhappy, though, you really don't.'

'Well, he's making us very unhappy,' I said. 'With *kidnapping*.'

Dr Bennet led us out of the main casino area and into a dark-panelled room off the main foyer. Out of the corner of my eye I could see Lydia and Patrick. He appeared to be unhooking her bra. I looked around for John Jr but I couldn't see him. It would have been very handy to have had some muscular back-up at this point.

I didn't see what he did, but suddenly Dr Bennet had opened a panel on the wall and was pressing in a key code. In front of us, a door slid open. Oh my God!

A short, dark corridor, lit with an illuminated cherub lamp, ended at another wooden door. Dr Bennet knocked gently. Someone grunted on the other side of the door, and Yuri said, 'Lysander.' A hand felt for mine and squeezed it. I didn't know whose it was.

Inside was a room so softly lit it looked like it was illuminated by gas lighting. It took a few moments for my eyes to adjust. Then I noticed that along one wall was a bank of monitors, showing every room in the casino, and the cars outside. This must be for security. Some of the monitors showed overhead views of the tables in the casino, I supposed to see if the dealers were cheating.

But then my attention moved to the shadowy figures in the room. There were three or four big men, who I supposed must be goons. Then, sitting down, with his head bent, was a figure I recognised, even though it was no longer sporting the moustache of the day before.

'Tom,' I shouted. He raised his head and peered through

a very black eye. Oh my God. He'd been beaten up. And what he said next shocked me to the core.

'Janey?' he said.

What? My eyes shot round to where Janey had inconspicuously followed us in.

'Darling,' she said, running forwards. 'What have they done to you?'

My brain couldn't take it in as she knelt down next to him.

'Are you all right?' She smothered him in kisses. 'Cachou misses you.'

'WHAT?'

I stepped forward, shaking off Wilf's restraining hand on my arm.

'What kind of a slut *are* you? Are both of you?'

'Evie,' said Tom, focusing on me suddenly. 'You found me.' He indicated his face. 'I told you it was serious.'

But I was looking at Janey. 'You were just in there trying to play suck face with Dr Bennet. Do you sleep with the dog too?'

'Information, darling,' she said to me, her American accent grating in my ears. 'And don't talk to the US head of Earth Friends like that, OK, sweetie?'

I stared at Tom. Oh, God, I felt I'd been betrayed twice. This was who he'd been calling; this was the person who owned the dog. My heart was pounding as a small man got up out of the swivel chair in front of the screens. I hadn't noticed him at all.

'Very interesting,' he said. 'But, Yuri, would you mind telling me what the *fuck* is going on?'

We all stared at Dr Bennet as he tried to explain he'd been blackmailed (which made me feel pretty good, I have to say; I didn't know I had it in me).

'But what do you want?' said Philippe – the little man – turning round to face us. His English was perfect, as was his suit. He didn't look threatening at all, he looked nice. If he was your doctor you'd feel reassured that he would never lose his cool or make a mistake. As soon as I heard his voice I knew it was the man I'd heard on top of the boat, talking to Dr Bennet.

We all began talking at once. He raised his hand for calm.

'You are activists, yes? I've heard as much from Tom.'

'Did you stand up under torture?' said Janey fondly, stroking his head.

'No,' said Tom, looking ashamed of himself. 'One of the goons elbowed me in the eye, and that was it. I pretty much told him everything. I hadn't realised torture would be quite so unpleasant.'

I rolled my eyes at this, which was cheeky because if anyone were to even so much as mention the word torture to me I'm sure I'd immediately start crying and betray everyone I'd ever met. But I was so furious that this pair had used us so ruthlessly. Earth Friends indeed. They could start by being actual normal human friends.

'Now, look,' said Philippe. 'The boat is going ahead, I'm afraid. There is really nothing wrong with it. There are millions of boats and millions of hospital procedures, and the two things are going to merge.'

'But Radoflux 9000 . . .' said Wilf.

'Radoflux 9000 will be *fine*,' snarled Philippe, suddenly cross. 'One or two minor flaws in the trials, that's all.'

'And stupid women who inject that stuff deserve all they get,' said Janey. 'Using animal products for their own vanity. It's disgusting.'

'You really are the queen of love and spirituality, aren't you?' I said.

She looked me straight in the eye. 'I think the time has come to get over Tom,' she said sincerely. 'I know some books that might help. *How to Stop Loving a Man That's Too Good for You*, that kind of thing.'

If I hadn't been wearing flip-flops, I'd have kicked her.

'Now I know what's up,' said Philippe, 'I think we have a solution. I'm sorry my men were a little heavy-handed, Tom – we're very afraid of terrorism, as you can imagine, and they had your picture on the CCTV from the other evening . . . we thought you were going to blow up the boat.'

'S'OK,' said Tom. That was the annoying thing about Philippe, I suddenly realised: he sounded so incredibly reasonable and spoke so gently it was hard not to believe what he was saying. He reached towards the desk and picked up a piece of paper.

'Here we are,' he said. When he held it up to the light we saw he was brandishing a cheque. A cheque for a huge amount, made out to Earth Friends. When they peered through the gloom to read the noughts on the end, Tom and Janey's faces both contorted.

'This is the precise sum of money that will carbon zero the ship,' said Philippe. 'It's for you. I want you to take it, plant trees, form a seal sanctuary. After all, it is the first rule of medicine, is it not: "Do no harm"?'

Tom and Janey were looking at each other. Janey had her stupid over-painted mouth open.

'Of course, this is annual,' said Philippe. 'We would hate to leave our footprint on the beautiful oceans of the world, even as we wish to render a service to make our world more beautiful through making its women more beautiful.'

They couldn't be swallowing this, could they?

Janey gulped and stepped forwards. 'Well, that's incredibly generous.'

Philippe shrugged. 'I am sorry we had such a misunderstanding. I agree; we should have thought more about saving the planet before we started our work. A little oversight, perhaps, Dr Bailey?'

Bailey stuttered, but didn't say anything.

'Well, then,' said Tom. He reached out and took the cheque. 'We can do a lot of good with this.'

'No, you can't!' I burst out suddenly. 'They're just buying you off! It's corrupt.'

Tom looked at Philippe as if they were both men of the world.

'No, they're balancing things out. We can do so much good with this money, Evie. Invest in saving millions of animals' lives.'

'Whilst they just sail around using illegal drugs and giving new faces to serial killers?' I yelled. Philippe and his henchmen laughed, and I felt really stupid and awkward.

'Don't be ridiculous,' said Philippe. 'This is a holiday cruise ship, that's all. Nothing for you to worry your . . . "average" little head about.'

Silence fell. Tom and Janey looked at each other and clearly passed a private message between them – to scarper.

'Well, thanks, Philippe . . . sorry for the trouble we caused,' said Tom. Oh, God, what a pathetic specimen.

'Not at all,' said Philippe. 'We'll all just keep quiet about it, *n'est-ce pas?*'

'And, *bye*, Yuri,' said Janey seductively. 'Give my love to your wife.' And she got up and prepared to sashay out. Tom got up to follow her. As she turned away, he turned to me. His face looked just a little regretful.

'Evie,' he said, 'I . . . I . . .'

I wanted to say something dramatic; a proper exit line. But all I could think of was 'you're a crap shag', and that wasn't even true, plus I didn't want to say it in a roomful of men. I didn't want to look pathetic.

'Bye,' I said. 'And stop pestering me with all those phone calls and flowers and things, please.'

He looked a bit confused for a second then shook his head. 'Right. OK. I'll stop.'

Dr Bennet was looking profoundly uncomfortable and staring at his feet as Tom and Janey left the room.

Chapter Thirteen

'Are you still here?' said Philippe, who'd turned back to look at the monitors. You could see Tom and Janey running across the foyer. I couldn't tell, but I thought they might be grinning like Cheshire cats. And Lydia's shoe seemed to be peering out from under a curtain. Well well well.

'Yes,' I said. 'You can't buy us off that easily.'

'Oh, can't I?'

Philippe looked at his watch and yawned.

'This is getting very boring,' he said. 'OK, here's the deal. If you' – he pointed at Wilf – 'want to work in plastic surgery again, keep your head down and shut up like a good boy. And if *you* –' this time it was Bailey – 'want to work in hospital design, do likewise.'

'What about me?' I said. He ignored me.

'You go to the papers, they won't be interested. You go to the police – we haven't done anything wrong, and the boat will be in at five in the morning and back in international waters this time tomorrow night. You have nothing on us, nothing at all. We, on the other hand – and it is regrettable, in international business – have absolutely no compunction at all about giving you a smack for wasting so much of our bloody time and making Dr Bennet look an idiot.'

One of the huge goons grunted in agreement, and Dr Bennet looked like he was going to say something about whether or not he was an idiot, then thought better of it.

'So. Fuck off now – no smack. Do you understand me?'

Both Wilf and Bailey looked really constipated. I suppose this is what it comes down to in boy world – whether or not you can handle a whupping. All the school bitching they avoid; all the body facism they get to skip; all the daft girlie hair removal stuff they don't have to spend money on, but it still comes down to this. Can they handle a whupping? Suddenly I wished John Jr were here.

Bailey looked at Wilf. 'The thing is,' he said. 'I was brutalised as a child, and I'm a terrible physical coward.'

Wilf nodded, looking relieved. Come on, wimps! My blood was up. Fight! Wilf held up his hands. 'I would, but . . . my hands are insured for half a million . . .'

'Yeah,' said Bailey.

'Come *on*, you cowards!' I yelled. 'Are you just going to let him get away with it?'

Philippe was already on the phone. 'Hi, yes . . . I'd like the saddle of lamb, with braised cabbage . . .'

The goons were moving towards us. God, they really were big. Big and fierce-looking.

Wilf and Bailey looked at one another. 'OK, RUN!' they shouted, and, pushing me ahead of them, we all tumbled forward through the secret passageway and into the bright lights of the chandeliered foyer.

'I'm not sure I'm cut out for this crime-fighting lark,' said Bailey, as we'd paced our weary way home along the seafront. The bars and restaurants were open and lively, and it was still warm as we found an empty beach-side table and took a seat. Wilf ordered '*trois grand* . . .' then looked at us expectantly. Whisky would have felt appropriate, but I hate the stuff, so I had a large Bacardi and Coke, which wasn't quite as world weary. The tie I'd tied on so badly for Wilf had undone itself and was lying open round his neck. The effect was quite sexy actually.

'No,' said Wilf. 'I'm much better at the job I've given up with no hope of getting another one.'

'You'll get another one,' said Bailey. 'Philippe can't know everyone who wants plastic surgery on earth.'

'Can't he?' said Wilf. 'Surely that's why he started this project.'

'Oh, yeah,' said Bailey, taking a large sip of his double advocaat (he's even worse at spirits than me).

Wilf sighed. 'Well, I suppose we should chalk it up to experience and adventure . . .'

'What are you talking about?' I said, spluttering through my drink. 'My sister-in-law is still getting on that boat tomorrow for a free shot of Radoflux 9000!'

Wilf's face fell and he took another sip of his whisky (at least he was drinking a man's drink).

'Oh, crap, I'd forgotten about that.'

'Well, I haven't.'

'At least your friend's safe,' offered Bailey. I harrumphed.

'I wish they'd thrown him off something just one more time for luck,' I said.

'Ah, a woman scorned,' said Bailey, and got up to go to the bathroom. I was about to take up my cause again on Kelly's behalf when Wilf leaned forward.

'Uh, can I ask you something?' he said.

'Sure.'

'Is that your . . . is Bailey your boyfriend?'

I blinked in disbelief. 'My *what*?' I said stupidly.

'Your other half . . . uh, partner . . . I mean . . .'

'Wilf, didn't you realise I, em, made out with Tom?'

'Well, yes,' said Wilf. 'I thought maybe that had caused a few problems.'

'Well, it would, wouldn't it?'

I sipped my drink again.

'Look. Bailey is . . . he's my friend. We grew up together. And, sometimes, I think, maybe we should be together, you know? Neither of us is getting any younger, and I really like him, and well, I could do a lot worse, and it's not like there's anyone else on the horizon, so maybe I should just settle down with him.'

'Wow,' said Wilf, obviously a little surprised by how much I'd told him. 'Nothing like aiming high in life.'

'Well, I aimed high for a holiday and ended up embroiled in some death boat, so maybe the time has come to stop trying.'

'And what does Bailey think of all this?'

'Oh, he's always had a thing for me. I know my face isn't a hundred per cent symmetrical but some men do, you know, think I'm all right looking.'

Wilf's face softened. 'Do they?'

'Do they?' echoed another voice, right by the table. Bailey pointed up above our heads.

'Toilet window. Right there. Er, Evie, do you mind if we have a word?'

We walked a little way along the beach, to where the sounds of the bars and the music of Cannes faded behind us and the noise of the sea was louder than anything else. Bailey seemed to be struggling with something. I couldn't believe myself. What had I said? If I hadn't been so keyed up and hysterical, I wouldn't have said nearly so much. There was just something about bloody Wilf being so quiet that made me talk too much. And I didn't know how to explain this to

Bailey. Or how great I thought he was, or how impressive – and not just because all the docs thought he was amazing, or Lydia was desperately trying to pull him, before I'd Patricked her.

'So,' said Bailey finally, as if he were pulling the words out. 'I'm your safety, am I? Your back-up plan?'

I couldn't possibly have let him see on my face how accurate those words were so I picked up a stone and threw it out to sea.

'Don't be stupid,' I said. 'I was a bit het up. I just told Wilf what I thought he wanted to hear.'

'That I'm your back-up plan that you don't really fancy but think would be better than nothing?'

I could hear the fury in his voice now.

'I mean, where the fuck do you get off? Who do you think you are, Scarlett fucking Johansson?'

I shook my head. I was mortified. It must be a horrible thing to hear about yourself; that someone thinks you're a lapdog, ready at your bidding to devote their life to you.

'Has it escaped your notice that my life is going completely fine without having you on my arm?'

'Yes, I *know* that,' I said.

'Do you really think I'm so pathetic that if I fancied you I wouldn't ask you out?'

'OK, OK,' I said. 'I'm sorry. I got it wrong. Obviously.'

'Obviously,' said Bailey. 'Look, Evie. I'm sorry you're single and that all your boyfriends have been dicks.'

'Not all of them,' I protested, then thought about it. 'Oh, yes. All of them.'

'But I'm not your knight in shining bloody armour, OK? I'm not your "make do". I'm not anybody's "make do".'

'I know,' I said.

'I know you still think of me as a six-year-old who's just wet his trousers, but it's just not like that any more. So get over it.'

'OK,' I said, feeling thoroughly chastised.

'Can we forget about this?'

I nodded.

'And you won't . . . I don't know, be expecting a ring on your thirtieth birthday or something equally cretinous?'

I shook my head.

'OK. Come here.'

And he gave me a hug. We didn't hug very often. As we did so I realised something; that some people have a smell. A smell you click with. Tom, alas, had it. It's something to do with pheromones, something below consciousness.

Bailey didn't have it. The chemistry wasn't there. Not because we were working too hard, or waiting for the right moment, or sowing our wild oats before we headed into the sunset together. But because it would never have worked out.

I squeezed him hard for helping me realise this.

'Oof,' he said.

I grinned. 'Come on. Admit it. I was your safety too.'

'You were not!'

'Was too!'

'Were not! Your mate Jilly was my safety and she went and married your bloody brother Cassandro.'

'Whereupon, you switched to me.'

We drew apart.

'Well, maybe a little,' he said.

'I knew it,' I said.

He gave me a half smile. The moonlight glinted off his glasses.

'Goodnight,' he said. And he turned and marched on up the beach.

I headed back to the café table. Wilf was still there, holding out a large gin and tonic.

'Everything OK?' he said, looking alarmed and standing up. 'Have you broken his heart?'

'No,' I said. 'I don't think so. Definitely not.'

'Has he broken yours?'

I smiled weakly at him. 'No. My heart is pretty used to being punched around.'

Wilf smiled at me. 'That's a shame.'

'Yeah, well, what can you do? Us lonely crime fighters, too busy saving the world . . .'

Suddenly, Wilf took my hand. An electric shock ran up my arm. What was this – friendly advice or something more?

'You don't need to make a joke out of everything, you know,' he said gently.

I swallowed hard, thinking over my many humiliations.

'Yes, I do,' I said. 'Anyway. What are we going to do about Kelly? I don't give a shit about what Tom and Janey are doing: this isn't over.'

Wilf removed his hand and sighed.

'Evie. You've met Philippe. He's a serious thug. What can we do?'

'I don't know,' I said. 'Something. To show we're not cowards and we're not giving up. We even know when the boat's coming in.'

'You're not a coward, Evie,' said Wilf. 'Not like me. But I think the time has come to give it up.'

We sipped our drinks quietly as we stared out to sea.

'It is beautiful, isn't it?' said Wilf.

The lights of the yachts on the far quay were still twinkling in the water. I thought of a cold, harsh operating theatre, out there on the water somewhere, all ready to perform God knows what kinds of things.

'Sort of,' I said. 'What's that famous quote about the Riviera?'

'A sunny place for shady people,' said Wilf.

'Yes,' I said. 'Like that.'

I headed back alone, bidding a quiet goodnight to Wilf. I didn't want him to walk me back to the hotel. I didn't think there was anything left to say.

After the evening's events I doubted I'd be able to fall asleep. By the side of my bed were some postcards I'd bought to send Mum and Dad but I couldn't think what to write on them.

Dear Mum and Dad. Wish you were here. Slept with a yellow-bellied eco-terrorist. Got burnt. Lost chance of marrying that nice bloke who lived down the road. JJ not quite as bad as we always thought. Sorry about the disfigured daughter-in-law, having a lovely time, E.

Instead, and to my surprise, I pitched forwards onto the bed, still fully dressed, then didn't wake up for five hours. I wouldn't even have woken up then if it hadn't been for my phone going off. Utterly confused as to where I was, I blearily stretched out a hand to the night table. It was still dark outside.

'Uh-huh?'

'Sis?'

'Who is this?'

The voice was whispering and sounded very agitated.

'Sis, it's me. Patrick.'

'Patrick? Where the hell are you?'

'That friend of yours, sis.'

He sounded hoarse, almost as if he'd been crying.

'She's a *maniac*.'

'Oh,' I said. I was becoming more awake now. 'Who, Lydia?'

'Keep your voice down! I don't know where she is.'

'Where are you?'

'That's the problem. I don't know. She took me back to her hotel and tied me up and . . . did *things* to me.'

'Patrick. Have you been interfered with? Did somebody touch your special area?'

'Well, I liked it to start with, but . . . she just went on and on. And *on*.'

'She's been holding herself back for the right person. I think it's all coming out in a flood.' I thought for a second. 'God, *that* explains the unchannelled aggression.'

'She said she's just going to get some whipped cream . . .' Patrick's voice was almost a sob. 'How do I get out of here? She's going at it with an egg beater right now.'

'Just creep out very quietly,' I said. 'Forget about your pants. Then go through the courtyard, and just start down the hill. Everything here goes downhill. When you get to the seafront go to the Metropole hotel and ask for JJ. He can look after you after that.'

'If I turn up at JJ's without my clothes he'll rip the piss.'

'Well, it sounds like someone's going to rip something.'

There was a gulp on the line.

'Bye.'

I couldn't get back to sleep after that. The sun was starting to creep over the horizon, I could tell, even in my dank little room. I felt a little buzzy still, the way you do when you've had adrenalin running round your system, no dinner and not enough sleep. So I ran a bath. It was that horrible French bath, but as long as I threw both my legs over the side I could just about lie back. What could I do? Today was the last chance to have a shot at it – my flight home was tomorrow. Without a job, without a friend, without anything. And that bloodstained boat would be sailing straight out to sea.

Well, not if I could help it. If I only had one day, I could give it my best shot. I leaned out of the uncomfortable bath and grabbed my phone. One last shot.

'Did I wake you?'

'Oddly enough, no,' said Wilf, who did actually sound wide awake.

'Good,' I said. 'What were you doing?'

'Just thinking about things.'

'What things?'

There was a pause.

'You ask a lot of questions, Evie.'

'I know,' I said. 'You'd think I'd be a better spy than I am.'

I could hear him smile down the phone. 'Don't tell me. This isn't a good news phone call. Or have you called me to tell me you *don't* want to do something completely stupid?'

'What do we have to lose?' I said. 'We've already lost our jobs, our trip . . .'

'Our dignity . . .'

'Dignity's overrated,' I said.

'Right,' he said. 'And what's with the "we"?'

'Listen,' I said. 'You don't have to go near the boat, or Philippe. You just need to talk to Kelly. Put on your best serious doctor voice,' I said. 'You know you can do it. Pretend you're breaking bad news. It will be, to her.'

It felt oddly intimate, lying in the bath naked, talking to Wilf. He didn't even know where I was.

'Are you splashing?' came the voice. 'Are you in the bath?'

'No!' I said, inadvertently making an even bigger splash in surprise.

'You are! You're calling me from in the bath!'

'Shh,' I said. 'We've got important plans to discuss.'

'Well, it's hard to discuss them when I'm picturing you in the bath.'

'Well, don't then. Picture me wearing a snow suit or something.'

There was a pause.

'Break the bad news,' I said.

'Uh-huh,' said Wilf reluctantly.

There was a silence on the end of the phone. I could hear him breathing. The room was still dark, with only the solitary tap dripping at the end of the bath. I felt like we were the only two people on earth. Sometimes things are more intimate over the telephone.

He took a deep breath. 'I don't like breaking bad news,' he said. There was another long pause. Then it all came out.

'When I was a young surgeon – well, hardly a surgeon at all, a senior house officer, I had to tell two parents that their six-month-old baby— The child had been shot. Drive by. No reason. I was assisting. Anyway. It doesn't matter. They . . .

she . . . didn't make it. The consultant had a six-month-old himself. He couldn't face it. He got me to do it because "I had to learn sometime", and I didn't have children.'

There was a long pause after that. I wasn't sure, but I think from the tenor of his breaths he was crying.

'Well, I can tell you it doesn't matter if you have children or not.'

There was another long pause as he got control of himself.

'And that was it for me, really. I mean, I finished my training and everything . . . but telling people that their life – their world, everything they had ever had – was completely fucked, as from today . . . I mean, that's not a job. Or, it wasn't a job I could do.'

'All doctors learn to, though, don't they?' I said timidly. 'They just have to get on with the job.'

'I know,' he said. 'But not me. I couldn't. I just couldn't.'

'So you went somewhere where you wouldn't have to,' I said.

Finally I understood. All the skills, wasted in the wrong place.

'Because I'm a wimp,' said Wilf. He half laughed. 'I'm not up to the job.'

'But you're a wonderful doctor,' I told him simply. 'Wonderful.'

'And a coward,' he said.

'You're not a coward, are you?' I said. 'Look at you, up at all hours, preparing to help me. A coward wouldn't have decided to make a stand, would he? A coward wouldn't have confronted Dr Bennet. A coward wouldn't have fronted up to him with that card game the way you did. You were even going to take on my brother.'

'Oh, yes,' said Wilf, remembering. 'I wasn't, really. If he'd raised a hand I was going to run for it.'

'Shh!' I said. I was on a roll. 'A coward wouldn't be going down right now to talk Kelly out of this dangerous surgery, not with John Jr on the loose. You're a lion! A lion! Grr.'

'Am I?' he asked faintly.

'Of course you are.' I reached over for a towel. 'You've got over your fears without even trying! Watch you go! Grr!'

'Of course I am!' he said. I heard some warmth come back into his voice, and the sound of him jumping up. 'What are you doing?'

'Me?' I said. 'Well, once I get out of the bath—'

'Aha,' he said. 'I knew it.'

Busted.

'Uh, I mean . . .'

I was about to explain the plan I'd come up with walking home the night before. Then I figured that he'd try and stop me, particularly in his newly invigorated state, so I didn't.

'I think you'll manage it all fine by yourself,' I said. 'Nothing. I'm going to stay here and order breakfast in bed.'

I took a look round my grubby cell and laughed hollowly to myself.

'OK,' said Wilf. 'I'll come and get you when I know what's happening. If we can get your sister—'

'Sister-in-law.'

'Off that boat . . . well, I think that's as much as we can do.'

'I agree,' I said, and hung up the phone. I didn't agree in the slightest.

Chapter Fourteen

Even at first light, when the whole of Cannes looked like an army of pixies had been up all night scrubbing it clean (hey, maybe they had, they're all rich round here), there were lots of people down by the docks – some early fishermen, coming in with the morning's catch, then there were bakers' shops open for early trade, and lots of yachties. I'd learned to recognise them; young men and women with very clean polo shirts, identical shorts, brown legs and nice teeth, who looked after the ships that lined the shore. They looked like their lives were pretty fun, as they loped on and off the gangplank, hailing their friends on other boats. The girls were getting on with shopping, the men were washing down the blue and white sides of the boats, or hosing the decks. I idly wondered if they had better lives than mine. Hey, who was I kidding? One of those lab rats that gets given electric shocks all day has a better life than mine.

I marched down to the big quay again; the one reserved for the largest boats. Behemoth after behemoth loomed out of the oily depths. Near the end I drew to a halt. *Operation Sunshine*. Here she was.

This boat wasn't a shimmering city of lights, like the party boat had been. It wasn't full of fun people having a fun time. It was sleek, and grey – grey all over, like pewter. The portholes were small, and the front of the boat sharpened to a point, as if it was designed for cutting through something. It was huge, but looked like it had more in common with a warship than a pleasure boat. She looked sinister, even at dawn with the golden rays of another perfect day breaking over her bow.

I didn't have a good plan about sneaking on board. I realised I had imagined something out of an old Laurel and Hardy movie, like a laundry van driving up that I could jump into, so I tried to hover inconspicuously.

Suddenly a friendly-looking girl was standing in front of me.

'G'day!' she said cheerfully. 'Are you looking for die work?'

I was so shocked for a second I couldn't speak, until I realised she was Antipodean, and had actually said 'day work'.

I had no idea what day work was either, but it sounded a lot better than 'die' work, and she was wearing a polo shirt with 'Operation Sunshine' embroidered on the pocket, so I decided to say yes, in lieu of a better idea, and see what happened.

'You're first,' she said. 'Die workers normally don't start queuing till seven.'

'Actually, this is my first day-work job,' I said, hoping she'd give me at least the tiniest clue as to what a day worker was.

'Oh, will done you,' she said. 'Will, you're just in time for breakfast if you like.'

And she turned round and indicated that I follow her on board. It was as simple as that.

Having been in two minds about this 'day work' charade, suddenly, from the bottom of a very steep set of stairs I smelt bacon frying . . . with tomatoes, and was that mushrooms? And that was definitely toast. I hadn't eaten since my plate of ice cream yesterday about lunchtime.

'Great!' I said truthfully.

'I'm Dibs, by the way.'

'Hiya, Debs . . . I'm . . .'

I couldn't think of a fake name straight away. 'Wow, I'm Debs too,' I said.

'*Wow!*' said Debs. She was quite smiley. 'That's *amazing*.'

She led me down the steep staircase. At the bottom was a large, low room with lots of doors leading off it. A large TV played in the corner, next to other screens that monitored locations around the ship. Around two large tables sat a host of healthy-looking boys and girls – well, in their early twenties, I supposed – who had the sheen of people who eat a lot of good food and get plenty of fresh air and sunshine. They just looked gleamy. I felt shockingly haggard in comparison.

'Hey, everyone,' said Dibs. 'This is Dibs – amazing, eh? I'm going to put her on as a day worker. Remember it's a big day today.'

There was general muttering. Obviously getting a day worker wasn't a particularly unusual occurrence, and a few of the boys (mostly good-looking) rather annoyingly tilted up their heads then went straight back to their bacon sandwiches. I ordered myself sternly to keep my mind on the task. It was *good* that no one was looking at me. I was a top secret agent.

I squeezed myself round the table and found space for my vast plate of food and, despite my nerves, managed to eat every scrap, keeping my ears open for gossip. Debs was mentioning the large party of people who were coming on board that day and how everyone had to stay away from the basement. My ears pricked up. The basement, huh? I filed that away as extremely useful information. I suppose it would make more sense to put an operating theatre in the basement, rather than, say, an upper-floor conservatory.

She also warned everyone again to keep security tight on the gates. I loved the fact that I didn't look like I needed security. Hooray for James Bond and her out of *Alias*; everyone obviously thought infiltrators would arrive looking attractive and well dressed.

Dibs passed me a clean polo shirt and shorts of my very own and ordered me to go and get changed. I was delighted. As soon as I did so (if I put my hair in a very perky pony tail), I would look just like one of these guys. Effectively, I hoped, I'd become invisible.

Just as I'd finished changing, a young guy pushed past the curtain. He was thin and bald and had a friendly face.

'Excuse me,' I said.

He stared at me. 'Who are you?' he said rudely.

'I'm the new day worker.'

'Day worker? Bloody Debs; nobody's allowed on the boat today.'

My heart started to pound. I was about to be unmasked and thrown off – or worse. I thought of Tom's black eye, and gulped.

The man gave me an appraising look then furtively glanced outside. He leant towards me.

'You don't look like a yachtie,' he said.

'Well, that's where you're wrong.'

'Which side is port, then?'

Shit. Shit. Shit. Rumbled.

The man took a deep breath. 'Earth Friends?' he whispered.

My heart leapt in shock. 'What do you mean?'

'Are you Earth Friends?'

'Why?'

Was he going to dob me in?

He winked and held out his hand. 'Kizza. Earth Friends' man on the inside.'

Oh my God. As I looked at his open face I realised that word obviously hadn't yet filtered down to the rank and file that Earth Friends had, in fact, turned.

'I'm here to help you any way I can,' said Kizza. For a second I thought he was going to salute. 'But whatever you're doing . . . it's got to be *fast*. We have to leave the port tonight.'

I found my voice again. 'Can you get me to the operating theatre? When the docs come?'

He nodded. 'Yes.' Then he slipped behind the curtain as fast as he'd appeared.

First, I followed Dibs. The thrill of being undercover lasted about as long as it took to comb out the first rug so that all the woollen strands were facing the same way. It's true. This is the kind of job people do on yachts.

'You wouldn't *think* pipple would notice,' said Dibs. 'But they rilly, rilly do.'

So here I was, bent over, combing through tiny strands of presumably priceless Persian rugs along miles and miles of corridor, constantly looking at my phone to see if Wilf had called. He hadn't, and I didn't want to call him in case he was in the middle of something. I knew he'd get in touch the second anything was happening. I thought back to our conversation this morning. I'd been touched by how much he'd confided in me. The more I got to know him, the more I liked him. Not that history had proven my skills in that department.

Once I'd finished with the rugs, Dibs set me to polishing

anything brass I came across. I wondered how much I'd get paid for this then remembered that, actually, as soon as word came from Wilf that he'd talked Kelly out of it I was scarpering, so it didn't actually matter. But still. This certainly felt far more like work than sitting behind a nice warm desk in London. If the air con hadn't been so fierce I'd have been on the verge of sweating.

Finally, after what seemed like hours and hours, I heard a bit of general kerfuffle going on outside. Dibs poked her head into the main cabin, where I'd just finished up. It had been bedecked by the other girls with huge, towering flower arrangements that gave the air a heady scent.

'Let me look at you,' she said. 'OK. Grab a pair of white slip-ons and come and join us.'

There was a big box of very clean white shoes by the crew door and I found a pair that fitted. But then, I didn't really have any choice in the matter as I was drafted in, with all the others, to the back of the boat near the gangplank. Half of the crew – the senior half, I assumed, including Kizza – had changed into formal naval-looking uniforms, complete with epaulettes and hats. The rest of us were in our polo shirt outfits. Dibs got us all into position so that we fanned out from the gangplank on either side, uniforms in front, polo shirts in the back, to welcome the visitors on board.

My heart sank into my shoes. Oh my God. Now I realised. We were going to stand here like some royal-receiving line whilst Philippe, Dr Bennet and, Christ, probably Lydia as well, all marched past. At least I was in the second row, but oh my GOD.

'I have to go to the bathroom,' I muttered to Dibs.

'You cin't,' she muttered back, resplendent in her crisp white shirt. 'They're arriving. Stand still.'

And she pushed me into line, shaking, as the huge shiny cars drew up on the jetty.

If my heart could have stopped, it would have. Every cell in my body was flattened with the mental effort of me trying to turn myself into a two-dimensional object, as close to the far side of the ship as possible. I took a deep breath. Sure enough, first to emerge was Philippe, looking as smooth as he had the previous evening, with two of his omnipresent goons. Then from the second car slithered Dr Bennet, next to him, Lydia. So, she had taken my place after all. Well, it was what she'd always wanted.

Lydia looked, and I suppose was, utterly shagged out. It was mesmerising; for a second I almost forgot to be frightened for my life. Her normally shiny straight hair was mussed and a complete fright at the back. Her eyes were ringed with dark shadows and her normally pale and perfect skin was flushed, like the blood vessels had expanded in her face. If this was what *she* was like, I really didn't want to see Patrick. Then, to my complete and utter horror, out of the other side of the car, got Wilf.

I felt like someone had punched me in the chest and I involuntarily took a step backward, then steadied myself in case I drew attention. Both doctors wore their white coats, which somehow removed them from being normal people; it was like a suit of armour. If you wanted to look stern and responsible – stick the white coats on.

They mounted the gangplank. Dr Bennet's and Wilf's – Dr Maitland's – heads were close together. He must have sought him out last night after I'd gone. No. Not after our conversation, surely? After everything we'd said – he must have thought he was a coward after all; that a safe job and a cushy salary was good enough really. And why would he want to give it up, anyway? Not for me. Oh my God, the filthy, lying . . . I strained to hear their conversation.

'I'm just so sorry,' Wilf was saying.

'It's all right,' said Dr Bennet. 'These things happen. You got carried away with a girl. But *that* girl though . . .'

I bit my lip. Yuri shook his head.

'Anyway,' went on Dr Bennet. 'I'm very glad to have you with us today. It's a tricky operation, this.'

'Looking forward to it,' said Dr Maitland.

Inside I was boiling. I couldn't believe it. That rat had betrayed me. After our conversation this morning. He must have thought about it then decided that he absolutely wasn't going into charity medicine, or travelling abroad or anything he'd talked about after all, because he was still just a big crawling coward. He'd thought about it then scrambled back like a rat to his regular pay cheque. He probably thought I was still in my hotel room, waiting patiently for him like a dog. Well, was he going to get a shock . . .

I kept my head down, blushing furiously. I was sure that at any moment Philippe, who was at the front of the group, was going to lean over and grab me by the shoulders but, as I held my breath, he strode along the line of waiting staff with barely a grunt for the captain. Lydia followed, nose in the air, though I don't think she'd have looked quite so snotty if she'd known that it clearly displayed the stubble rash on her chin. Then I darted my eyes up just a little, in time to see Dr Bennet whispering in Dr Maitland's ear, close as you like. I wondered how much Dr Bennet had made him grovel. Loads, probably. Arse-licking extraordinaire. I thought of how much I'd started to like him, and sighed. Suddenly, I felt very, very alone. And furious with my stupid bloody sister-in-law.

I stayed stock still as it seemed to take them for ever to parade up the line, deep in conversation. At least Bailey wasn't coming on, he'd have cracked immediately. But finally they passed by into the main body of the ship and I could let out a sigh of relief.

Or could I? As I straightened up, my brain spinning from Dr Maitland's deception, I spied a whole group of people coming up the pier. It was the docs. They looked happy and excited to be finally witnessing what they'd come for. Real operating conditions, and a real boat to work on. They must all be seeing the pound signs in front of their eyes as they imagined flying out only their richest, their most *exclusive* clients for a week or so of sun, sea and surgery. They were like a group of overexcitable schoolboys. The money men were there too, looking graver. And behind them, another car was pulling up. This time, a pure white limo, the sun glinting off its roof like a mirror. Hmm. I wonder who was in that.

The doctors coalesced round the limo as it drew to a halt, and a chauffeur jumped out to open the back door. They actually started to applaud. I rolled my eyes. No way. Here was Kelly, a pretty girl who got lucky, or unlucky depending on your tolerance for JJ, stepping onto a Riviera yacht and being hailed as a conquering hero. The only time I'd ever had a round of applause was when I'd walked across that entire nightclub dance floor with my skirt tucked in my knickers.

Well, obviously Dr Maitland hadn't worked very hard to convince her. I wondered if he'd even tried. He'd thought about his mortgage, and his sports car, and what side his bread was buttered on, and he'd caved in like the yellow-bellied snake he was, crawling back to Dr Bennet, begging forgiveness. Which of course he'd gotten – Dr Bennet knew he needed him; knew he was the better surgeon by miles. Maitland would have spun some line about falling under my spell – ha – and they'd all have been big boy mates together again in no time. Men. All the bloody same.

Kelly was acknowledging the claps gracefully, which was good of her, then let JJ, who'd heaved himself out of the other side of the limo, and was looking particularly scarlet that morning, escort her up the gangplank, as if she were a fine piece of bone china. I couldn't help wishing for a second that someone treated me like that. They weren't such a bad couple, those two.

I steeled myself, ready for the inevitable howl of recognition – I was wondering if I could write it off as coincidence; tell them that this really was my new job. Philippe and Dr Bennet had already disappeared into the bowels of the ship. But, to my complete amazement, they stalked right past the line. Well, my goodness. That shows how long it takes to think you're better than everyone else – about two minutes, obviously. We might all have been mice living down a hole for all the attention JJ and Kelly gave us.

After the doctors had been herded on, them, too, not giving any of us a second glance, we were told to stand down and head back to work. I wasn't 100 per cent sure what to do. Being on the receiving line had proven that I had a very good disguise. But now Wilf had gone back to the enemy, I was on my own.

'DIBS!' shouted Dibs, interrupting my train of thought. 'Kizza says he needs you down in the garage to valet the cars.'

Valet the *what*? There were cars driving on here? But I didn't mind. I knew where the garage was; it was down. And that was the way I needed to go.

'So what's your plan then?' said Kizza. It was dark and warm in the garage, and it smelled (quite reassuringly) of petrol. His face looked amused in the half-light, but wary too. I didn't blame him.

'I don't know,' I said. 'I just know I've got to get my sister-in-law off this boat. And stop the operation.'

'Right,' said Kizza. Then he paused. 'But you know we're going out to sea.'

Suddenly I heard the ominous hum of the huge engines starting up. It wasn't a roar; just a low and very definite vibration.

'I left my second in the engine room,' said Kizza, which didn't mean a thing to me. I was suddenly terrified. Up until now it had all been a bit of a lark, but this was it, no turning back now. It was me against this entire boat. Bruce Willis in a polo shirt. What the hell was I going to do? I stared at the car I was meant to be polishing (something called a 'Maybach'; it looked like it weighed 95 tonnes) and wondered what it would be like to feel the clanging bars of a prison cell.

Chapter Fifteen

'The thing is,' Kizza was talking, but I could hardly hear him. 'Just so as you know . . . when we stop . . .'

I forced myself to look at him. My hands were all soapy, holding a large damp sponge. They were shaking.

Kizza looked uneasy.

'You know, the tender's at the back.'

'What?'

'The tender.'

I shook my head.

'A little boat. That goes inside the big boat,' he explained patiently. 'To take people into land when we're anchored at sea.'

'Oh,' I said.

'Anyway.' He looked around, as if there might be a goon

hiding behind a fire extinguisher. 'Well, it has to make a run to the coastguard's office. At two o'clock.'

'Uh-huh.'

Kizza scratched his head.

'I've seen a lot of things go on on board ship,' he said. 'I've been doing this for a long time. But *this*. Cutting people open at sea. I don't like it. I really don't like it. I wouldn't like it to happen to my sister.'

'Sister-in-law,' I murmured, but it didn't seem to matter any more.

'Anyway,' Kizza said again. 'It'll be out the back in about an hour. Probably. The tender can't wait, though, it has to leave on time. If someone wasn't there, well . . . it would have to leave without them.'

'Thanks,' I said.

Suddenly I heard a noise. It was a very distinctive noise. It was the ping of a lift.

'There's a lift on this ship?' I asked.

'There's three,' said Kizza.

'And one goes down to the operating theatre?'

He nodded. 'Do you know the way?'

I shook my head. Oh my God. This was it.

'Level minus four. Past the engine room on the right-hand side. Over the metal grille. I've unlocked the door. It leads to the back of the anaethetist's cupboard. It's a sterile area, OK? I could get shot for leaving it open.'

'Right,' I said.

'Then you're in the theatre.'

'As easy as that?'

My heart felt like a pack of galloping horses.

'As easy as that.'

Kizza patted me on the arm. 'You must be used to these undercover operations, eh? Must be pretty shit hot for Earth Friends to send you on your own. What do you do – karate? Ju-jitsu?'

'Something like that,' I muttered. I couldn't take my hand off the car door, I was shaking too much.

'Well, good luck! Better get a move on; I'll go lower the tender.'

I wiped my hands down once more on my new shorts as I crouched listening to the muffled voices. I could tell there was Dr Bennet, Dr Maitland, a couple of other people I didn't know, the anaesthetist, I supposed, a nurse. A growl that sounded like Philippe. And, squeaking excitedly, Kelly. If I was to get to Kelly before the anaesthetic did I was going to have to move now. I had to get going, however much my legs were telling me to run away as fast as I could. Oh, God. How could I do this? I had no idea what I was doing. This was just stupid, surely. I couldn't . . .

I looked around for something to take in with me – a weapon? Was that a good idea? What was I going to threaten them with? A pounding from a fire extinguisher? What if I hurt someone? What if they already had Kelly on the table? I thought about it, still wiping down my sweaty hands. Then I stopped.

What was it doctors hated and feared more than anything else? What was it they couldn't bear anywhere near them when they were working? What we had to watch for every second of every day? I looked around the basement. And here there was *loads* of it.

Dirt. Dirt and grime. Infection. MRSA. Septicaemia. The one thing that couldn't be tolerated under any circumstances.

Of course, this was probably the cleanest basement on earth. But it was still a basement.

I rushed over to the corner. Sure enough I found a pile of swept-up dirt and motor-oil spills. I took handfuls and rubbed the dirt liberally all over my face, arms and hands until I was black. I must have looked shocking, but I didn't care. I even ran bits through my hair, until I felt like I was camouflaged up for the jungle. Then I approached the door again. This was the best I could do. If I could just hold up the operation for long enough and make them have to sterilise their instruments again – well, if the boat had to leave at sundown, they wouldn't have long enough. I checked my watch. Twenty minutes till Kizza's tender left. It was now or never. I twisted open the handle of the watertight door. Well, I had wanted change in my life.

I was in a disinfected area. It looked like the pristine new bottles of steriliser had been opened and used. That meant that everyone was soaped up and ready to go. I read the big red sign on the door again, the one that said absolutely no entry except to authorised personnel. I was so not authorised personnel.

The voices were clearer now. I could hear the two doctors. They rarely operated together unless it was a big job, but their murmurings showed how practised they were at working together. A Frenchwoman's voice – she must be the anaesthetist.

I took a deep breath. OK. I may be rubbish at holidays, and family, and holding onto jobs and spotting what blokes were actually like. But I absolutely did not QUIT. And I knew when you had to fight dirty. I burst through the heavy door.

'Jesus Christ!' said Dr Maitland. He was the first to see me. Dr Bennet looked up and swore and dropped his scalpel. Good. Kelly was lying on the table, blinking warily. She'd obviously had her first injection to relax her, but not yet the second to knock her out cold.

'Who *is* this bitch?' yelled Philippe. Glancing above his head I could see a bank of windows with the doctors looking in. Some of them already had cocktails in their hands.

I ran to the bank of instruments and wiped my filthy fingers all over them.

'Don't do that!' squeaked Dr Bennet. 'You're contaminating the sterile area!'

'Am I?' I said, running over to Dr Bennet and touching his

face and hair. He jumped back like I was poisonous, which I was.

'Kelly!' I shouted. 'Wake up!'

'Whas going on?' she slurred.

I pulled the venflon out of her arm as gently as I could, careful not to touch her skin at any point.

'We need to go!'

'You do *not* need to go,' said Dr Bennet. 'What you're doing is dangerous and completely illegal.'

I danced out of his reach and spat on the operating table. The doctors now were all crowding round. I spotted Mrs Bennet.

'Hey, Mrs Bennet!' I shouted. 'Your husband knocked off the Earth Friends woman! I saw them!'

'*Stop this immediately*,' said Philippe. He grabbed me from behind, and his grip was strong and painful.

'Let her go!' shouted Dr Maitland. He'd pulled down his mask.

'I don't need help from you, jelly legs!' I shouted. I kicked out using Philippe as support and, amazing myself, managed to kick over a whole tray of instruments. They made a tremendous noise on the floor. 'Scared of losing your pension, were you?'

Thinking of Wilf's betrayal made me a wildcat. I stomped down on Philippe's foot (expensive loafers – nice soft leather) and he howled. 'Didn't want to give up the sports car?'

'No, it wasn't . . .' said Wilf, looking at me unhappily. Kelly was sitting up on the table.

'Wot's going on? Are you trying to ruin this for me?'

'Yes, I am,' I said. 'Now hurry up, we have to get a move on.'

'I don't want to get a move on. I want my operation.'

'You can't have it. I've contaminated the area. So come on, move, before they inject you with something that's been banned from every bloody country on earth.'

'Well, it hasn't been banned from France, 'as it?'

'We're not in France, you plank! We're nowhere! We're out in the middle of the ocean where you let them knock you unconscious so they can stuff you with bloody seals just to see what would happen! You pricks!'

Suddenly, Philippe released me, and I realised that he'd actually had my feet off the ground. I dropped heavily, winded. He pulled me round to face him.

'You're ruining my investment,' he said menacingly. 'Now I am going to ruin your life.'

'How?' I said. There was so much adrenalin coursing through me I didn't feel in the slightest bit afraid.

'I will find out where you live, where you work, where you sleep and I will make sure it becomes a living hell.'

'My life already sucks,' I said. 'And anyway, you won't. I'm not that pretty. You've never even looked me in the eye. You completely ignore anyone who isn't blown up like a big, blonde, inflatable doll. So I bet you –' and I pointed at him – 'don't even know my name. Because I look normal.'

He paused and caught his breath. Everyone went silent. The seconds passed like days. Finally Dr Bennet stepped forward.

'It's—' he started. I turned my face towards him, just as Dr Maitland grabbed his arm. He stared at me for one minute. Then he lowered his eyes and didn't say any more.

'*Evie!*' screamed Kelly. 'What the hell are you doing?'

'Oh, for fuck's sake!' I yelled. Then, as Philippe made a strange growling noise, and a lunge straight towards me, I grabbed her arm. 'RUN!'

I pulled her back through the door to the disinfected room, picking up a bottle of steriliser.

'BLEACH!' I yelled as Philippe pulled open the door behind us, squirting as much of it as I could over his Jermyn Street suit. He staggered backwards, covering his eyes, as I ran, half supporting Kelly, who was a little wobbly on her feet (probably because she wasn't wearing stilettos, like a Barbie doll), through the garage and towards the stairs.

We burst out onto the deck just as the doctors came swarming out of the salon towards us.

'Run!' I said. 'Don't touch us! Don't TOUCH US!'

Oh, God, I must have looked unbelievably crazy, because they all stood back! They must have remembered me from the other party as a dangerous maniac. We pounded down to the back of the boat where, sure enough, and thank God, Kizza was standing, his hand on the tiller of a beautiful wooden speedboat. I've never been so pleased to see

297

anything in my life. He helped Kelly down the stairs at the back and got her sitting down and comfortable. I prepared to follow her when I heard my name called again.

'Evie!'

It was Wilf. He was standing on the highest aft deck. He must have caught the lift all the way up. He looked immeasurably sad and was holding up two vials. It must have been the last of the Radoflux – well, bugger him. As I watched him, he threw both vials far, far away into the sea, as I threw myself into the tender.

Kizza was frantically untying ropes as Philippe pounded up the deck towards us, his handsome face completely transformed by a huge snarl. He was brandishing something at us. It couldn't be a gun, could it? Oh my God, was it a gun? I'd never seen a gun. Shit, was he going to shoot? Were we going to die? Was I going to die single without a man to throw himself onto my coffin, howling, 'It should have been me'?

Well, it wasn't to be my time to find out. With a grunting roar, John Jr leapt forward out of the crowd and did what John Jr does best – picking people up and throwing them in the water.

Philippe was swallowing, shouting and cursing us desperately as the rest of the doctors peered over the side, eyes wide. Some of them were laughing. Maybe they hadn't seen the gun. If it was a gun. Maybe it was just a very big syringe.

More importantly, as I clung onto Kelly, struggling to catch my breath as Kizza accelerated away, I could make out the bankers in their formal suits, huddled together, desperately trying to get signals on their mobile phones. And I don't think they were calling to increase their stakes.

Chapter Sixteen

It was morning. My bags were packed. I'd slipped out of the hotel without settling my bill – they could charge bloody Maitland and Bennet, I wasn't paying for it, those bastards. I'd dragged my bags down with me to the beach. My flight didn't leave for another six hours. Theoretically I supposed Philippe could track me down and come and find me there, but I didn't think he would. I'm not sure bad people really do go around killing people willy-nilly like they do on TV. I think they're as rational as the rest of us; they weigh up the best thing for them in any given circumstance and go ahead and do it. So storming the beach and knifing me just probably wasn't worth his time. I fervently hoped.

So I went back down to the beach – I had my bikini on under my clothes, but I was pretty well wrapped against the sun this time. I had the paperback I hadn't picked up the entire trip, and I had decided to sit, look at the sea and not let a single thought cloud my mind. Not one. Not the fact that we had left John Jr behind on the boat with an angry mob (though that had interesting possibilities) or that Kelly had actually been a bit pissed off with me, at least for a bit, till I explained what was really going on. Certainly not Wilf's betrayal – well, there was just too much betrayal going on at the moment even to consider it.

Nope, I was going to stare at the sea, maybe have a swim and a snooze and think about a big fat white nothing until it absolutely was time to go home and start picking up my life again with, I reckoned, a lot of help from my mum's shepherd's pie.

It was in this state of mind – not exactly made worse by buying an ice cream every time the seller came round – that I sat, gazing at the sun on the water. I didn't even notice two figures, slightly out of focus, appear in my peripheral vision.

'*There* you are,' said Lydia. 'Everyone's going nuts.'

She was dragging Patrick behind her. He looked a broken man. I think he'd lost weight in twenty-four hours. But weirdly, he was smiling.

'Go away,' I said. 'I never have to speak to you again. So, go away. You're horrible.'

She pouted. 'Well, you *might* have to speak to me again,' she said, 'if I become part of your family.'

301

Patrick whimpered a bit at that. Well, maybe it was time he was taken in hand.

'The boat's gone,' she said. 'It went last night. The bankers decided not to invest. They're going to dismantle the operating theatre and use it as a cinema. Too at risk from terrorism apparently.'

'I'm a terrorist?' I said. 'Cool.' Then I worried about the police. But I'd been invited on the boat. I hadn't really done anything wrong. I didn't think.

'They dumped us all off last night,' she said. 'They got us as pissed as farts on Cristal as long as we promised not to mention it.'

'Ah, plastic surgeons,' I said. 'Nature's incorruptibles.'

'Your "friend" Bailey pulled a supermodel they'd brought in for promotional pictures. Oh, *sorry*. Did I hurt your feelings?'

I shook my head. 'Not really.'

And I half watched as Lydia dragged Patrick up the beach, whispering something about love under the dunes.

After that I must have dozed off, because when I woke the sun was low in the sky. At least I was covered up this time. As I gradually opened my eyes I became aware that someone was standing over me; standing very still, as if they'd been there for some time. I jumped out of my skin, throwing myself upwards off the sunbed. My heart tried to get up before I did. I had to blink a hundred times before realising that it wasn't

Philippe and his henchmen come to kill me; it was Dr Maitland.

'Christ,' I said. 'I thought you'd come to kill me. Have you?'

'No!' said Dr Maitland. 'No.'

He shuffled and looked at the sand.

'Well, you can fuck off then,' I said. 'I'm fired, remember? I never have to talk to you again.'

I took a slug of Sprite to clear my sandy mouth. I wanted to tell him a thing or two. Then I realised I didn't. I was sick of being outraged and angry. I was tired of it all. I was relaxing, remember? And then I was going home.

'You were very brave on the boat,' he said. 'Very brave.'

'You weren't.'

'You looked very cute covered in engine oil.'

'I'm glad you think so. Now fuck off back to your MG, will you?'

His face looked pained. 'I wasn't going to tell you this . . .' He tailed off. 'Some idea of nobility, I don't know. Stupid. Anyway.'

He swallowed hard.

'I can't stop thinking about you, and I can't help it.'

I blinked in the sun.

'Your sister.'

'In law.'

'Yes . . . anyway. I, em, I did a bit of switching on board.'

'You did what?'

'I switched. I switched the Radoflux with saline. It

303

wouldn't have done anything at all. She'd probably have thought she looked better or something – crap, she's only thirty-one – but it would have been harmless. I thought that was the best way of helping.'

'But you made up with Dr Bennet!'

'I had to, didn't I? How else would he let me in the operating theatre?'

I thought about it.

'Why didn't you tell me?'

'I told you I was going to do what I could. I thought you'd trust me to come up with something. I didn't want you to worry until it was all over.'

I shrugged. 'You know, trusting men hasn't seemed to get me very far recently.'

He moved towards me. 'Your plan worked better anyway.'

'Yours would probably have been less messy.'

'Maybe life is messy.'

'Oh, it is,' I said.

'I know,' he said. 'I think I've been avoiding the messy bits of it for too long.'

'So what are you going to do?' I said.

He shrugged. 'I thought I might go look at hospital practice – maybe not abroad, but there's a lot of great reconstructive work going on in the UK. There's a face transplantation team that might be recruiting.'

'That'd be great,' I said. 'Good for you. I think I'm going to amass a private army and take over the world.'

'I bet you could too.'

He paused, and pushed his feet in the sand.

'You know . . . I think you've made me braver too.'

'Neh,' I said. 'It must have always been there.'

'Well, maybe . . .' he said. 'Uh, Evie . . . back in London. Do you want to get a cup of coffee sometime?'

I stared at him. 'You are joking.'

'What do you mean?'

'Well . . .'

Everything that had happened spun through my mind. Tom, Bailey, the boat, and now Wilf . . . I think I had trust issues.

'It won't work,' I said. 'I don't think so. I have men problems and you have . . . well, just general problems.'

'As solved by me being very brave,' he said. 'Haven't you seen *The Wizard of Oz*?'

I smiled. He really was lovely once you got to know him.

'I'm sorry,' I said. 'I think I need some R&R on my own for a while.'

'What the doctor ordered,' he said wryly, then came over and gave me a very sweet, very gentle kiss on the forehead. I almost changed my mind right there and then but for once was going for a bit of dignity.

'Bye,' I said. He looked defeated and a little clumsy, stomping up the beach. The sand must be getting in his brogues. I'd never asked him why he dressed like that. I think I'd got to like it, then stopped noticing. Oh, well.

*

The airport was mobbed again, but this time I strode through
it confidently. I didn't need a helicopter or a business-class
seat. I was Evie Kennedy, fighter for seal rights, and I didn't
need to be anyone else at all. In the queue I stood behind
Lydia and Patrick, but they were snogging too hard to notice
me and I didn't really feel like chatting. Bailey had squeezed
through too on his way to business class. He'd given me a
big hug and asked if I wanted to go to Wagamama when we
got back, as if nothing had ever happened. Typical. I told him
Wagamama was really no good for geeks like him, the soup
steamed up his glasses too much. He was also talking excitedly about some underground project in Dubai that I reckoned
I'd better keep a close eye on.

As we were chatting, Kelly and John Jr got out of their
chauffeur-driven limo. John Jr was shouting at the driver
about something. I looked at Bailey and he looked at me.

'Oh, no,' he said.

'He saved my life!' I said. 'We have to.'

And we hoisted our bags and went towards them.

'JJ,' I started. 'I know we think you're an oaf . . .'

'And you were really mean to me when I was small,'
added Bailey.

JJ's face contorted. 'And?'

'Thanks,' I said. 'Thank you for everything. You're a good
brother.'

'Better than Patrick?'

'Of course.'

'Better than Cassandro?'

'He bloody started all this,' I mused, briefly. 'Stupid over-romanticised holidays.'

'Aren't they all?' said Bailey.

I gave JJ a hug. 'See you at Mum's,' I said.

'I'm not hugging you,' said Bailey.

'I'd break your arms if you tried,' said JJ. But then he smiled.

Back in the queue, out of the corner of my eye, I noticed two familiar figures skulking in. They didn't see me. I was shocked as they headed for the first-class desk. Oooh, those charlatans! Someone was behind them, carrying all their bags. She saw me and broke away.

It was Janey's helper, poor old Judy. She ran across to me when she saw me and grabbed me by the hand.

'You saved those seals,' she said, as if I'd raised them from the dead. 'You did it!'

'Not really,' I said, trying to look modest. But it was too late. The noise had attracted attention.

'I love seals,' Judy was saying. 'That's why I work so hard to save them. I love seals.'

'Oh, it's you,' said Lydia, turning round in the queue. 'You'd better ask for extra rolls on the plane. Keep you going for a while now you're unemployed.'

I ignored her, tried to ignore everyone, and kept my head down.

*

'What do you mean, customs want to see me?' I'd just heard Lydia say. 'Well, yes, I do work for Dr Yuri Bennet . . . what do you mean, you're holding him? No, I don't want to answer any enquiries . . . Rado what?'

I realised that there were two security guards standing right next to her. Oh my God! Oh, they'd find out she was clueless, surely. Not before she spent a little time cooling her heels, though, I should think. And not in business class either.

Then there was a commotion across the departures hall. Someone was pushing their way through, with a bold, confident stride. I ignored it, until the tumult stopped right under my nose. I looked up. There, right in front of me, was Wilf.

'Courage,' he said, when he was as close as he could get. Then he grabbed my face in his hands and gave me the best kiss of my life.

I was gasping when we came up for air. Now there was a hubbub all around us.

'I'm sorry, ma'am, but you definitely cannot board this aircraft,' I heard the BA woman say to Lydia.

Then everything faded away as Wilf kissed me again. A few people even clapped, which shows you how much there is to do waiting in a long departure queue at an airport.

'Come on!' he said loudly.

'Where? I'm waiting for a flight.'

'I've got you a flight,' he said, brandishing two vouchers in his hand. I knew what they were. They were helicopter passes. Lydia gave me a filthy look. She knew what they were too.

'My darling girl. I'm not letting you go. Come with me. You haven't even had a holiday yet. You haven't seen anything of Cannes . . . or Antibes, or Mougins. There are art galleries, and walks, and bars, and sunsets and lots and lots of things for us to do with the money I won at the casino. But first, there's a helicopter taking us away to a quite appallingly decadent lunch. Absolutely no seal on the menu. Coming?'

'How did you win that money again?' I asked him. 'It's been bugging me.'

'Bored medical student,' he said. 'Docs have great memories. We can all count cards. I'm surprised Yuri didn't figure it out. Anyway. Lunch?'

I couldn't help it. I grinned a grin that threatened to burst my face, then stretched out my hand and put it in his.

'Well,' I said. 'I do believe I need a holiday . . .'

WEST END GIRLS
Jenny Colgan

The streets of London are paved with gold . . . allegedly.

They may be twin sisters, but Lizzie and Penny Berry are
complete opposites – Penny is blonde, thin and outrageous;
Lizzie quiet, thoughtful and, well, definitely not thin. The one
trait they share is a desire to *do* something with their lives, and
as far as they're concerned, the place to get noticed is London.

Out of the blue they discover they have a grandmother living in
Chelsea – and when she has to go into hospital, they find
themselves flat-sitting on the King's Road. But, as they discover,
it's not as easy to become It Girls as they'd imagined, and west
end boys aren't at all like Hugh Grant . . .

'Hugely entertaining and very funny' *Cosmopolitan*

'Fast-paced, funny, poignant and well observed' *Daily Mail*

'A delicious comedy' *Red*

978-0-7515-3763-5

Other bestselling titles available by mail

☐ West End Girls	Jenny Colgan	£6.99
☐ His Other Lover	Lucy Dawson	£6.99
☐ A Bad Bride's Tale	Polly Williams	£6.99

The prices shown above are correct at time of going to press. However, the publishers reserve the right to increase prices on covers from those previously advertised, without further notice.

──────────────── sphere ────────────────

Please allow for postage and packing: **Free UK delivery.**
Europe: add 25% of retail price; Rest of World: 45% of retail price.

To order any of the above or any other Sphere titles, please call our credit card orderline or fill in this coupon and send/fax it to:

Sphere, PO Box 121, Kettering, Northants NN14 4ZQ
Fax: 01832 733076   Tel: 01832 737526
Email: aspenhouse@FSBDial.co.uk

☐ I enclose a UK bank cheque made payable to Sphere for £ . . . .
☐ Please charge £ . . . . . . to my Visa/Delta/Maestro

Expiry Date ☐☐☐☐   Maestro Issue No. ☐☐

NAME (BLOCK LETTERS please) . . . .
ADDRESS . . . .

. . . .

. . . .

Postcode . . . . Telephone . . . .

Signature . . . .

Please allow 28 days for delivery within the UK. Offer subject to price and availability.

WIDEACRE

Philippa Gregory is an established writer and broadcaster for radio and television. She holds a PhD in eighteenth-century literature from the University of Edinburgh. She has been widely praised for her historical novels, including *Earthly Joys* and *A Respectable Trade* (which she adapted for BBC Television), as well as her works of contemporary suspense. *The Other Boleyn Girl* won the Parker Romantic Novel of the Year Award in 2002 and it has recently been adapted for television. Philippa Gregory lives in the North of England with her family.

Visit www.PhilippaGregory.com for more information and www.AuthorTracker.co.uk for exclusive updates about Philippa Gregory.

PHILIPPA GREGORY

Wideacre

HARPER

Harper
An imprint of HarperCollins*Publishers*
77–85 Fulham Palace Road,
Hammersmith, London W6 8JB

www.harpercollins.co.uk

This production 2013

First published in Great Britain by
Viking 1987

A catalogue record for this book is
available from the British Library

ISBN 978-0-00-793272-6

Printed and bound in Great Britain by
Clays Ltd, St Ives plc

I

Wideacre Hall faces due south and the sun shines all day on the yellow stone until it is warm and powdery to the touch. The sun travels from gable end to gable end so the front of the house is never in shadow. When I was a small child, collecting petals in the rose garden, or loitering at the back of the house in the stable yard, it seemed that Wideacre was the very centre of the world with the sun defining our boundaries in the east at dawn, until it sank over our hills in the west in the red and pink evening. The great arch it traced in the sky over Wideacre seemed to me a suitable boundary for our vertical influence. Behind the sun was God and the angels; beneath it, and far more significantly, ruled the Squire, my father.

I cannot remember a time before I loved him, the blond, red-faced, loud Englishman. I suppose there must have been a time when I was confined to a white-frilled crib in the nursery; I suppose I must have taken my first steps clinging tight to my mother's hand. But I have no childish memories of my mother at all. Wideacre filled my consciousness, and the Squire of Wideacre dominated me as he ruled the world.

My first, my earliest childhood memory is of someone lifting me up to my father as he towered above me in the saddle of his chestnut hunter. My little legs dangled helplessly in space as I rose up the yawning void to the great chestnut shoulder – a hot, red rockface to my surprised eyes – and up to the hard, greasy saddle. Then my father's arm was tight round my body and his hand tucked me securely before him. He let me grip the reins in one hand and the pommel in the other, and my gaze locked on the coarse russet mane and the shiny leather. Then the monster beneath me moved and I clutched in fright. His pace was erratic and rolling to me, and the long gap between each great stride caught me unawares. But my father's arm held tight and I

7

gradually raised my eyes from the muscled, steamy shoulder of the mountainous horse, up his long neck to his pointy signalling ears . . . and then the sweep of Wideacre burst upon me.

The horse was walking down the great avenue of beech and oak that leads to the house. The dappled shadows of the trees lay across the springing grass and the rutted mud tracks. In the banks glowed the pale yellow of spring primroses and the brighter sunshine yellow of celandine. The smell, the dark, damp smell of rain-wet earth filled the arch of the trees like birdsong.

A drainage ditch runs alongside the drive, its yellow stones and white sand rinsed clean by the trickle of water. From my rolling vantage point I could at last see a clear view of its length, even where the black leafmould at the banks carried the tiny, forked hoofprints of nighttime deer.

'All right, Beatrice?' My father's voice behind me was a rumble I could feel in my tense, skinny little body as well as hear. I nodded. To see the trees of Wideacre, to smell the earth of it, to be out among the breath of wind of Wideacre, bonnetless, carriageless and motherless, was beyond words.

'Like to try a trot?' he asked.

I nodded again, tightening my small hands on the saddle and reins. At once the giant strides altered and all around me the trees lurched and jigged as the horizon moved in great sickening leaps. I bobbed like a cork in a spring-flood river, sliding painfully to one side, and then, perilously, correcting. Then I heard my father click to the horse and the stride lengthened. Wonderfully, the horizon steadied, but the trees sped past. I regained my balance and, though the ground flashed by under the thudding hoofs, I could breathe and look around again. Your first canter is the fastest speed you will ever go. I clung like a louse to the saddle and felt the spring wind in my face, and saw the shadows of the trees flash light and shade across me as the chestnut mane streamed, and I could feel a great burble of delighted laughter and scream of fear gather in my throat.

On our left the woods were thinning and the steep bank dropped away, so I could see through the trees to the fields beyond, already brightening with the spring growth. In one a hare, large as a hound puppy, stood on its hind legs to watch us go by, its black-tipped ears pointed to hear the thud of the hoofs and the jingle of the bit. In the next field a line of women, drab against the deep black of the ploughed field, bent double over the furrows, picking, picking, picking, like sparrows on the broad back of a black cow, clearing the earth of flints before sowing.

Then the sliding scenery slowed and slowed as the hunter dropped into a teeth-chattering trot again, and then pulled up at the closed gates. A woman erupted from the open back door of the lodge house and scuttled through a scatter of hens to swing open a tall iron gate.

'A fine young lady you have to ride with you today,' she said smiling. 'Are you enjoying your ride, Miss Beatrice?'

My father's chuckle vibrated down my spine, but I was on my dignity, high on the hunter, and I merely bowed. A perfect copy, had I known it, of my mother's chill snobbery.

'Say good day to Mrs Hodgett,' my father said abruptly.

'Nay!' said Mrs Hodgett, chuckling. 'She's too grand for me today. I'll have a smile on baking day though, I know.'

The deep chuckle shook me again, and I relented and beamed down on Mrs Hodgett. Then my father clicked to the hunter and the smooth walk bore me away.

We did not turn left down the lane that leads to Acre village as I had expected, but went straight ahead, up a bridle track where I had never been before. My excursions until now had been in the carriage with Mama or in the pony-cart with Nurse, but never on horseback along the narrow green ways where no wheels could go. This path led us past the open fields where each man of the village could farm his own strip in a ragged, pretty patchwork. My father tutted under his breath at the ill-dug ditch and the thriving thistles in one patch and the horse, eager for a signal to canter, broke forward again. His easy strides took us higher and higher up the winding path, past deep banks dotted with wild flowers and with exciting-looking small holes, crowned with hedges of budding hawthorn and dogroses.

Then the banks fell away, and the fields and hedges with them, and we were riding, silent on thick leafmould, through the beech coppice that crowds the lower slopes of our downs. Tall, straight, grey trunks rose high as a cathedral nave. The nutty, woody smell of beech tickled my nose, and the sunlight at the end of the wood looked like the bright mouth of a cave, miles and miles away. The hunter, blowing now, rushed upon it, and in seconds we were out in the brilliant sunlight at the very tipmost-topmost point, the highest peak in the entire world, the pinnacle of the South Downs.

We turned to look back over the way we had come and the shape and the setting of Wideacre opened up to me, like a magical page in a picture book, seen for the first time.

Closest to us, and extending far below us, were the green, sweet slopes of the downs, steep at the top, but easy as soft shoulders lower down. The gentle wind that always blows steady and strong along the top of the downs brought the smell of new grass and of ploughing. It flattened the grass in patches like seaweed tossing under currents of water, first one way, then another.

Where the ground grew steep and broken, the beech coppices had taken hold and now I could look down on them, like a lark, and see the thick tops of the trees. The leaves were in their first emerald growth and chestnuts showed fat, mouth-watering buds. The silver birches shivered like streams of green light.

To our right lay the dozen cottages of Acre village, white-washed and snug. The vicarage, the church, the village green and the broad, spreading chestnut tree that dominates the heart of the village. Beyond them, in miniature size like crumpled boxes, were the shanties of the cottagers who claimed squatters' rights on the common land. Their little hovels, sometimes thatched with turf, sometimes only a roofed-in cart, were an eyesore even from here. But to the west of Acre, like a yellow pearl on green velvet, amid tall, proud trees and moist, soft parkland, was Wideacre Hall.

My father slipped the reins from my fingers and the great head of his horse dipped suddenly to crop the short turf.

'It's a fine place,' he said to himself. 'I shouldn't think there's a finer in the whole of Sussex.'

'There isn't finer in the whole world,' I said with the certainty of a four-year-old.

'Mmm,' he said softly, smiling at me. 'You may be right.'

On the way home, he let me ride alone in glorious solitude on top of the swaying mountain. He walked at my side, a restraining hand gripping the frills and flounces of my petticoats. Past the lodge gates and up into the cool quietness of the drive, he loosened his grip and walked before me, looking back to bawl instructions.

'Sit up! Chin up! Hands down! Heels in! Elbows in! Gentle with his mouth! You want to trot? Well, sit down, tighten the rein, and dig your heels in! Yes! Good!' And his beaming face dissolved in the heaving blur as I clung with all my small might to the leaping saddle and bit back shrieks of fear.

I rode alone up the last stretch of the drive and triumphantly brought the gentle great animal to a standstill before the terrace. But no applause greeted me. My mama watched me, unimpressed, from the window of her parlour, then came out slowly to the terrace.

'Get down at once, Beatrice,' she said, waving Nurse forward. 'You have been far too long. Nurse, take Miss Beatrice upstairs and change and bath her at once. All her clothes will have to be washed. She smells like a groom.'

They pulled me off my pinnacle and my father's eyes met mine in rueful regret. Then Nurse paused in her flight towards the house.

'Madam!' she said, her voice shocked.

She and my mother peeled back the layers of petticoats and found my lacy flounces stained with blood at the knees. Deftly Nurse stripped them off so she could see my legs. The stitching and the stirrup-leather flaps had rubbed my knees and calves raw and they had bled.

'Harold!' said my mother. It was the only sign of reproach she ever permitted herself. Papa came forward and took me into his arms.

'Why didn't you tell me you were hurt?' he asked, his blue eyes narrow with concern. 'I would have carried you home in my arms, little Beatrice. Why didn't you tell me?'

My knees burned as if stung by nettles but I managed a smile.

'I wanted to ride, Papa,' I said. 'And I want to go riding again.'

His eyes sparkled and his deep, happy laugh shouted out.

'That's my girl!' he said in delight. 'Want to go riding again, eh? Well, you shall. Tomorrow I shall go to Chichester and buy you a pony and you shall learn to ride at once. Riding till her knees bled at four years old, eh? That's my girl!'

Still laughing, he led his horse around to the stable yard at the rear of the house where we could hear him shouting for a stable lad. I was left alone with Mama.

'Miss Beatrice had better go straight to bed,' she told Nurse, ignoring my wide-awake face. 'She will be tired. She has done more than enough for one day. And she will not go riding again.'

Of course I went riding again. My mother was bound by all sorts of beliefs in wifely obedience and deference to the head of the household, and she never stood against my father for more than one self-forgetful second. A few days after my ride on the hunter and, alas, before the little scabs on the inside of my knees had healed, we heard a clatter of hoofs on the gravel and a 'Holloa!' from outside the front door.

On the gravel sweep outside the house stood my father's hunter with Father astride. He was leaning down to lead the tiniest pony I had ever seen. One of the new Dartmoor breed, with a coat as dark and smooth as brown velvet and a sweep of black mane covering her small face. In a second my arms were round her neck and I was whispering into her ear.

Only one day later and Nurse had cobbled together a tiny version of a tailored riding habit for me to wear for my daily lesson with Papa in the paddock. Never having taught anyone to ride, he taught me as he had learned from his father. Round and round the water-meadows so my falls were cushioned by the soft earth. Tumble after tumble I took into the wet grass – and I did not always come up smiling. But Papa, my wonderful, godlike papa, was patient, and Minnie, dear little Minnie, was sweet natured and gentle. And I was a born fighter.

Only two weeks later, and I rode out daily with Papa. Minnie was on a leading rein and beside the hunter she looked like a plump minnow on the end of a very long line.

A few weeks after those first expeditions and Papa released me from the apprenticeship of the leading rein and let me ride alone. 'I'd trust her anywhere,' he said briefly to Mama's murmured expostulations. 'She can learn embroidery any time. She'd better learn to have a seat on a horse while she's young.'

So Papa's great hunter strode ahead and Minnie bobbed behind in a rapid trot to keep up. In the lanes and fields of Wideacre, the Squire and the little Mistress became a familiar sight as our rides lengthened from the original half an hour to the whole of the afternoon. Then it became part of the routine of the day that I should go out morning and afternoon with Papa. In the summer of 1760 – an especially dry hot summer – I was out every day with the Squire, and I was all of five.

These were the golden years of my childhood and even at that age I knew it. My brother Harry's baby illnesses lingered on; they feared he had inherited Mama's weak heart. But I was as fit as a flea and never missed a day out with Papa. Harry stayed indoors almost all winter with colds and rheums and fevers, while Mama and Nurse fussed over him. Then when spring was coming and the warm winds brought the evocative smells of warming land, he was convalescent. At haymaking, when I would be out with Papa to watch them scything down the tall rippling grass in great green sweeps, Harry would be indoors with his sneezing malady which started every year at haytime. His miserable 'atchoo, 'atchoo, would go on all through the hot days of summer, so he missed harvesting, too. At the turn of the year, when Papa promised I could go fox-cubbing, Harry would be back in the nursery or, at the best, sitting by the parlour fire with his winter ailments again.

A year older than me he was taller and plumper, but no match for me. If I succeeded in teasing him into a fight, I could easily trip him up and wrestle with him until he called for Mama or Nurse. But there was much good nature in Harry's sweet placidity and he would never blame me for his bumps and bruises. He never earned me a beating.

But he would not romp with me, or wrestle with me, or even play a gentle game of hide-and-seek with me in the bedrooms and galleries of the Hall. He really enjoyed himself only when he was sitting with Mama in the parlour and reading with her. He liked to play little tunes on the pianoforte there, or read mournful poetry aloud to her. A few hours of Harry's life made me unaccountably ill and tired all over. One day in the quiet company of Harry and Mama made me feel as weary as a long day in the saddle riding over the downs with Papa.

When the weather was too bad for me to be allowed out, I would beg Harry to play, but we had no games in common. As I moped round the dark library room, cheered only by finding the breeding record of Papa's hunters, Harry would pile all the cushions he could find into the window seat and make himself a little nest like a plump wood pigeon. Book in one hand, box of comfits in the other, he was immovable. If the wind suddenly ripped a gap in the thunderclouds for the sun to pour through, he would look out at the dripping garden and say: 'It is too wet to go out, Beatrice. You will get your stockings and shoes soaked and Mama will scold you.'

So Harry stayed indoors sucking sweets, and I ran out alone through the rose garden where every leaf, dark and shiny as holly, extended a drop of rain on its luscious point for me to lick. Every dense, clustered flower had a drop like a diamond nestling among the petals and when you sniffed the sweetness, rainwater got up your nose and made it tickle. If it rained while I was roaming, I could dive for shelter in the little white latticed summerhouse in the centre of the rose garden and watch the rain splashing on the gravel paths. But more often I would take no notice at all and walk on, on and out through the streaming paddock, past the wet ponies, along the footpath through the sheltered beech wood down to the River Fenny which lay like a silver snake in the coppice at the end of the paddock.

So although we were so near in age, we were strangers for all of our childhood. And though a house with two children in it – and one of them a romp – can never be completely still, I think we were a quiet, isolated household. Papa's marriage to Mama had been arranged with a view to wealth rather than suitability and it was obvious to us, to the servants and even to the village, that they grated on each other. She found Papa loud and vulgar. And Papa would, too often, offend her sense of propriety by donning his Sussex drawl in her parlour, by his loud, easy laugh, and by his back-slapping chumminess with every man on our land from the poorest cottager to the plumpest tenant farmer.

Mama thought her town-bred airs and graces were an example to the county but they were despised in the village. Her disdainful, mincing walk down the aisle of the parish church every Sunday was parodied and mimicked in the taproom of the Bush by every lad who fancied himself a wit.

Our procession down the aisle, with Mama's disdainful saunter and Harry's wide-eyed waddle, made me blush with embarrassment for my family. Only inside our high-backed pew could I relax. While Mama and Harry stuck their heads in their hands and fervently prayed, I would sit up by Papa and slip one cold hand in his pocket.

Mama would recite prayers in a toneless murmur, but my little fingers would seek and find the private magic of my papa's pocket. His clasp knife, his handkerchief, a head of wheat or a special pebble I had given him – more potent than the bread and wine, more real than the catechism.

And after the service, when Papa and I lingered in the churchyard to learn the village news, Mama and Harry would hurry on to the carriage, impatient of the slow, drawling jokes and fearful of infections.

She tried to belong to the village, but she had no knack of free and easy speech with our people. When she asked them how they did, or when a baby was due, she sounded as if she did not really care (which was true) or as if she found their whole lives sordid and tedious (which was also true). So they mumbled like idiots, and the women twisted their aprons in their hands as they spoke, and kept their mob caps dipped low.

'I really fail to see what you see in them,' Mama complained languidly after one of these abortive attempts at conversation. 'They really are positively natural.'

They were natural. Oh, not in the sense she meant: that they were half-witted. They were natural in that they did as they felt and said what they thought. Of course they became tongue-tied and awkward in her chilly presence. What could you say to a lady who sat in a carriage high above you and asked you with every appearance of boredom what you were giving your husband for dinner that night? She might ask, but she did not care. And even more amazing to them, who believed the life of Widenore was well known throughout the length and breadth of England, was that the Squire's lady clearly did not know she was speaking to the wife of one of Acre's most successful poachers, and so a true answer to the question would have been: 'One of your pheasants, ma'am.'

Papa and I knew, of course. But there are some things that cannot be told, cannot be taught. Mama and Harry lived in a world that dealt in words. They read huge boxfuls of books delivered from London booksellers and libraries. Mama wrote long criss-crossed letters that went all over England: to her sisters and brothers in Cambridge and London, and to her aunt in Bristol. Always words, words, words. Chatter, gossip, books, plays, poetry and even songs with words that had to be memorized.

Papa and I lived in a world where words were very few. We felt our necks prickle when thunder threatened haymaking and it only needed a nod between us for me to ride to one corner of the field and Papa to ride away over to the other acres to tell the men to stack what they could and be ready for the rain. We smelled rain on the air at the start of harvesting and, without speaking, would wheel our horses round to stop the sickle gangs from cutting the standing corn with the storm coming. The important things I knew were never taught. The important things I was born knowing, because I was Wideacre born and Wideacre bred.

As for the wider world, it hardly existed. Mama would hold up a letter to Papa and say: 'Fancy . . .' And Papa would merely nod and repeat: 'Fancy.' Unless it affected the price of corn or wool, he had no interest.

We visited some county families, of course. Papa and Mama would attend evening parties in winter, and now and then Mama would take Harry and me to visit the children of neighbouring families: the Haverings at Havering Hall, ten miles to the west, and the de Courcey family in Chichester. But the roots of our lives were deep, deep into the Wideacre earth and our lives were lived in isolation behind the Wideacre park walls.

And after a day in the saddle, or a long afternoon watching the labourers ploughing, Papa liked nothing so much as a cigar in the rose garden while the stars came out in the pearly sky and the bats swooped and twittered overhead. Then Mama would turn from the windows of the parlour with a short sigh and write long letters to London. Even my childish eyes saw her unhappiness. But the power of the Squire, and the power of the land, kept her silent.

Her loneliness showed itself only in her continual letters, and in the way her disagreements with Papa were never won nor lost, but dragged on in indecisive pain.

The riding quarrel rumbled on throughout my childhood. My mama was bound to conventional obedience to the Master's word, but utterly free of any moral standard. Behind her respectability and her worship of the conventions she had the morality of the gutter. Without power, she had spent all her life seeking minuscule advantages in perpetual quest for the satisfaction of getting her own way in something, *anything*, however small.

Poor woman! She had no control of the housekeeping monies, which were submitted by butler and cook directly to Papa and paid for out of the estate accounts. She had no control over her dress allowance, which was paid direct to the Chichester dressmaker and milliner. Once a quarter she received a few pounds and shillings for spending money: for her church collection, for her charities and for the dizzy indulgence of buying a posy of flowers or a box of sweetmeats. And even that little purse was discreetly regulated by her behaviour. After a moment's lapse when she had spoken out to Papa shortly after my birth, the allowance had magically stopped – a seven-year-old secret that still rankled enough for Mama to whisper it to me in her enduring resentment.

I listened not at all and cared less. I was for the Squire. I was Papa's little girl, and I understood well enough that disloyal, resentful whispers like that were part of the same attack on me and my papa as her opposition to my riding. Mama was always in search of family life as it was depicted in her quarterly journals. That was the secret reason for her hatred of my father's uncompromising loudness, his bawdiness, his untamed joy. That was why she gloried in the quiet prettiness of her fair-haired boy. And that was why she would have done anything to get me off horseback and into the parlour where young girls, all young girls, whatever their talents and dispositions, belonged.

'Why don't you stay at home today, Beatrice?' she asked in her sweet plaintive voice one morning at breakfast. Papa had already eaten and gone, and my mama turned her eyes from his plate with the great knuckle bone of ham chewed clean and the scatter of crumbs from a crusty Wideacre loaf.

'I am riding with Papa,' I said, my words muffled by my own hearty portion of bread and ham.

'I know that is what you planned,' she corrected me sharply. 'But I am asking you to stay at home today. To stay at home with me. This morning I should like to pick some flowers and you could help me to arrange them in the blue vases. This afternoon we could go for a drive. We could even visit the Haverings. You would like that. You could chatter with Celia.'

'I am sorry, Mama,' I said with all the finality of an indulged seven-year-old, 'but I promised Papa I would check the sheep on the downs and I will need all day. I shall go to the west side this morning and then ride home for dinner. This afternoon I shall go to the east side and not be back till tea-time.'

Mama compressed her lips and looked down at the table. I barely noticed her rising irritation and her tone of anger and pain was a surprise to me when she burst out: 'Beatrice, I cannot think what is wrong with you! Time and time again I ask you to spend a day, or half a day with me, and every time you have something else you would rather do. It hurts me; it distresses me to be so rebuffed. You should not even be riding alone. It is outrageous, when I have specifically asked for your company indoors.'

I gazed blankly at her, a fork of ham halfway to my mouth.

'You look surprised, Beatrice,' she said crossly, 'but in any ordinary household you would not even have learned how to ride. It is only because your father is horse-mad and you are Wideacre-mad that you have such licence. But I will not tolerate it in my daughter. I will not permit it!'

That made me afraid. Mama's overt opposition to my daily rides could mean I was returned to the conventional pursuits of a young lady. A miserable enough fate for anyone, but if I was to be kept inside when the ploughing started, or when the reaping bands were out, or at harvest time, I should be in continual torment. Then I heard my papa's clatter in the hall and the door banged open. Mama winced at the noise and my head jerked up like a gun dog at the sound of game, to see his bright eyes and merry smile.

'Still feeding, little piglet?' he bellowed. 'Late to breakfast, late to leave and late in the fields. You have to be on the west slope and back in time for dinner, remember. You'll have to hurry.'

I hesitated and glanced at Mama. She said nothing and her eyes were downcast. I saw the game she was playing in one swift, acute second. She had put me in a position where my defiance of her would be absolute if I went now with my papa. On the other hand, my obedience and devotion could be transferred wholesale to her if I insisted on staying indoors. I was not going to be managed by such paltry parlour games. I swallowed my mouthful and cast Mama's secrets before my father.

'Mama says I must stay at home today,' I said innocently. 'What am I to do?'

I glanced from one to the other, the picture of childish obedience. I looked as if I sought only guidance, but in my heart I had staked a large gamble on my papa.

'Beatrice is needed out on the downs today,' he said baldly. 'She can stay at home tomorrow. I want her to look at the flocks today before we separate them for market and there is no one else free who can ride up there and whose judgement I can rely on.'

'Young ladies do not generally spend all day in the saddle. I am afraid for Beatrice's health,' Mama said.

Papa grinned. 'Oh stuff, ma'am,' he said rousingly. 'She's as lean and as fit as a racehorse. She's never had a day's illness in her life. Why don't you say what you mean?'

Mama bridled. Plain speaking is not the natural voice of ladies.

'It's not the proper upbringing for a girl,' she said. 'Spending all her time talking with such rough men. Knowing all the tenants and cottagers and galloping around the countryside without a chaperone.'

Papa's blue eyes sparkled with temper. 'Those rough men earn our bread and butter,' he said. 'Those tenants and cottagers pay for Beatrice's horse, aye and even the dress on her back and the boots on her feet. A fine little city-miss you would have on your hands if she did not know where the wealth is made and where the work is done.'

Mama, a city-miss in her girlhood, looked up from the table and came perilously close to defying the convention that Ladies Never Raise Their Voices, Never Disagree with Their Husbands, and Keep Their Tempers Under the Tightest of Wraps.

'Beatrice should be brought up in a manner befitting a young lady,' she said tremulously. 'She will not be a farm manager in later life; she will be a lady. She should be learning how a lady behaves.'

Papa was red to the ears – a sure sign of his temper. 'She is a Lacey of Wideacre,' he said, his voice firm and unnecessarily loud for the little breakfast parlour. The cups jumped and chinked as he bumped the table.

'She is a Lacey of Wideacre, and whatever she does, however she behaves, will *always* be fitting. Whether she checks the sheep or even digs ditches, she will always be a Lacey of Wideacre. On this land her behaviour is the pattern of Quality. And no damned mincing, citified, pretty-pretty gentility could change that. And nothing could improve that.'

Mama was white with fright and temper.

'Very well,' she said through her narrowed lips. 'It shall be as you order.'

She rose from the table and picked up her reticule, her shawl and the letters that lay by her plate. I could see her fingers tremble and her mouth working to hold back resentful, bitter tears. Papa detained her with a hand on her arm at the door and she looked up in his face with an expression of icy dislike.

'She is a Lacey of Wideacre,' he said again, trying to convey to this outsider what that meant on this, our land. 'Bearing that name, on this land she can do no wrong. You need have no fears for her, ma'am.'

Mama tipped her head in cold acquiescence and stood like a statue till he released her. Then she glided, in the short dainty steps of the perfect lady, from the room. Papa turned his attention to me, silent at my breakfast plate.

'You didn't want to stay at home, did you, Beatrice?' he asked, concerned. I beamed at him.

'I am a Lacey of Wideacre, and my place is on the land!' I said. He scooped me from my place in a great bear-hug and we went arm in arm to the stables, victors of a righteous battle. Mama watched me go from the parlour window, and when I was on my pony and safe from her detaining hand, I reined in by the terrace to see if she would come out. She opened the glass door and came out languidly, her perfumed skirts brushing the stones of the terrace, her eyes blinking in the bright sunshine. I stretched an apologetic hand out to her.

'I am sorry to grieve you, Mama,' I offered. 'I shall stay at home tomorrow.'

She did not move close to take my hand. She was always afraid of horses and perhaps she disliked being too close to the pony who was pulling against the bit and pawing at the gravel, keen to be off. Mama's pale eyes looked coldly up at me, sitting high, bright and straight backed on a glossy pony.

'I try and try with you, Beatrice,' she said and her voice was sad, but also flawed with self-righteous complaint. 'I sometimes think you do not know how to love properly. All you ever care for is the land. I think sometimes you only love your papa so much because he is the master of the land. Your heart is so full of Wideacre there scarcely seems room for anything else.'

The pony fidgeted and I smoothed her neck. There seemed little to say. What Mama said was probably true, and I felt a momentary sentimental sadness that I could not be the daughter she wanted.

'I am sorry, Mama,' I said awkwardly.

'Sorry!' she said and her voice was scornful. She turned and swept back through the door leaving me holding a restless pony on a tight rein and feeling somehow foolish. Then I loosened the rein and Minnie sprang forward and we clattered off down the gravel to the grassy track of the drive. Once in the shadow of the branches, which cast dappled bars of shade across my track while the early summer sunshine warmed my face, I forgot all about the disappointed woman I had left in her pale parlour and remembered only my freedom on the land and the work I had to do that day.

But Harry, her favourite, was a disappointment to her in another way. The high hills and the rolling chalk valleys and the sweet River Fenny flowing so cool and so green through our fields and woods were never enough for him. He seized at the chance of visits to our aunt in Bristol and said he preferred the rooftops and rows of tall town houses to our wide, empty horizon.

And when Papa broached the idea of a school, Mama turned

white and reached a hand for her only son. But Harry's blue eyes sparkled and he said he wanted to go. Against Papa's certainty that Harry would need a better education than his own to deal with an encroaching and slippery world, and Harry's quiet but effective determination to leave, Mama was helpless. All August, while Harry was ill again, Mama, Nurse, the housekeeper and every one of the four upstairs maids dashed around all day in a frenzy of preparation for the eleven-year-old hero's departure for school.

Papa and I avoided the worst of the fuss. In any case, there were the long days we had to spend on the open downland pastures collecting the sheep to separate lambs from ewes for slaughter. Harry, too, remained secluded in library or parlour choosing books to take to school with him, and scanning his newly purchased Latin and Greek grammars.

'You cannot want to go, Harry!' I said incredulously.

'Whyever not?' he said, frowning at the breeze that had blown in with me as I flung open the library door.

'To leave Wideacre!' I said and then stopped. Once again Harry's world of words defeated me. If he did not know that nothing outside Wideacre could match the smell of Wideacre's summer wind, or that a handful of Wideacre earth was worth an acre of any other land, then I had no way to tell him. We did not see the same sights.

We did not speak the same language. We did not share even the similarity of family resemblance. Harry took after my father in colouring, with his bright blond curls and his wide blue, honest eyes. From Mama he had inherited her delicate bone structure and the sweetness of her smile. Her smiles were rare enough, but Harry was a merry-faced golden cherub. All the petting and indulgence he had from Mama had been unable to spoil his sunny nature – and his smiling good looks reflected his sweet and loving spirit.

Beside him I was a throwback to our Norman ancestors and the founders of the line. Foxy-coloured, like those greedy and dangerous men who came in the train of the Norman conqueror and took one look at the lovely land of Wideacre and fought and cheated and lied until they got it. From those ancestors I had my chestnut hair, but my hazel-green eyes were all my own. No portrait in the gallery showed a set of eyes slantingly placed above high cheekbones like mine.

'She's a changeling,' Mama once said in despair.

'She's her own pattern,' my blond papa said consolingly. 'Maybe she'll grow into good looks.'

But Harry's golden curls could not last for ever. His head was cropped for his first wig as part of the preparation for school. Mama wept as the radiant springs fell all around him on the floor, but Harry's eyes were bright with excitement and pride as Papa's own wigmaker fitted a little bob-tailed wig on his head – as shorn as a lamb. Mama wept for his curls; she wept as she packed his linen; she wept as she packed a great box of sweetmeats to sustain her baby in the hard outside world. The week before his departure, she was in one continual flood of tears, which even Harry thought wearisome, and Papa and I found pressing business on the far side of the estate from breakfast to dinner.

When he finally departed – like a young lord in the family carriage with his bags strapped on the back, two outriders and Papa himself riding alongside for company for the first stage – Mama shut herself in her parlour for the afternoon. To my credit, I managed a few tears and I took good care to tell no one they were not for Harry's departure. My father had bought me my first grown-up mount to console me for the loss of my brother. She was an exquisite mare, Bella, with a coat the colour of my own chestnut hair, a black mane and tail and a stripe like starlight down her nose. But I would not be allowed to try her paces till Papa came home, and he would be gone overnight. My tears flowed easily enough, but they were all for me and white-nosed Bella. Once Harry turned the corner of the drive and was out of sight, I scarcely thought of him again.

Not so Mama. She spent long solitary hours in her front parlour fiddling with little pieces of sewing, sorting embroidery silks or tapestry wool into the ranges of shades; arranging flowers picked for her by me or one of the gardeners, or tinkling little tunes on the piano – absorbed by the little time-wasting tedious skills of a lady's life. But, unconsciously, the little tune would stop and her hands would fall into her lap, and she would gaze out of the window to the gentle shoulder of the green downs, seeing their rippled loveliness, yet all the time seeing the bright

23

face of Harry, her only son. Then she would sigh, very softly, and drop her head to her work, or take up the tune again.

The sunlight, so joyous in the garden and in the woods, seemed to beat cruelly on the pretty pastel colours of the ladies' parlour. It bleached the pink out of the carpets and the gold out of Mama's hair, and the lines into her face. While she faded in pale silence indoors, my father and I rode over the length and breadth of Wideacre land, chatting to the tenant farmers, checking the progress of their crops against those we farmed ourselves, watching the flow of the River Fenny over our turning millwheel, until it seemed that the whole world was ours and I might take a proprietary interest in every living thing that – one way or another – belonged to us.

Not a baby was born in our village but I knew of it and generally the child took one of our names: Harold or Harry for my father and brother, Beatrice for my mama and me. When one of our tenants died, we concerned ourselves in the packing and the leaving of their family, if they were going, or the succession of the oldest son and the co-operation of his brothers if they were staying. My father and I knew every blade of grass on our lands, from the weeds on the lazy Dells' farm (they would be looking for a new tenancy when their lease ran out) to the white-painted fence posts on the spick-and-span Home Farm we farmed ourselves.

Small wonder I was a little empress riding over our land on our horses, with Father – the greatest landlord for a hundred miles around – riding before me and nodding to our people who dropped a curtsy or pulled their forelocks as we passed.

Poor Harry missed all this. Not for him the pleasure of seeing our land under every daily light and in every season. The ploughed fields ringed with white hoarfrost and crunchy as fudge, or the swaying corn in the beating heat of summer. While I rode like a lord at a lord's side, Harry moped at school and sent sorrowful letters home to his mother, who replied in pale blue ink blotted with tears of sympathy.

His first year was miserable with longing for his mama and her quiet sunny parlour. The boys all belonged to gangs with fierce tribal loyalties, and little Harry was bullied and tormented by every child an inch taller or a month older. Not until his second year brought a new batch of victims into the arena did Harry's life improve. His third school year meant the dizzy heights of being nearly a big boy, and his cherub-like brightness and his undimmed sweetness brought him petting as well as occasional cruelty. More and more often, when he came home for the holidays, his great trunk was crammed with comfits and cakes given him by older boys.

'Harry is so popular,' Mama said proudly.

Each holiday, too, he would tell me tales of the courage and dash of his gang leader. How every term they would plan a campaign in the war against the apprentice lads of the town. How they marched from the school gates to spring upon the lads in glorious, epic battles. And how the hero of the day was always Staveley, Lord Staveley's youngest son, who gathered around himself the strongest, the meanest and the prettiest of all the boys in the school.

Harry's new-found zest for school could only widen the gulf between us. He had caught the schoolboy's tone of arrogance like a galloping infection and, apart from boring me to tears about the demigod Staveley, scarcely deigned to speak to me at all. Towards Papa he was always polite, but his unconcealed enthusiasm for his studies made Papa at first proud, and then irritated that Harry should so obviously prefer to spend his days in the library when the windows were open and the cuckoos calling to everyone to take a line and rod and try for some salmon.

Only with Mama was he totally unchanged, and those two spent long, intimate days in easy companionship, reading and writing together in library and parlour while Papa and I, intent on wider, freer pursuits, watched the land under every light, under every season and under every sort of weather. Harry could come and go as he pleased; he was always a visitor in his own home. He never belonged to Wideacre as I belonged. Only Papa, the land and I were the constant elements in my life. Papa, the land and I had been inseparable since the first time I had seen Wideacre in its wonderful wholeness from between the hunter's ears. Papa, the land and I would be here for ever.

2

'I don't know what I'll do without you when you leave,'
Papa said casually to me one day as we rode down the lane
to Acre village to see the blacksmith.

'I'll never go,' I said, my confidence unshaken. I was only half
attending for we were each of us leading one of the heavy plough
horses to be shod. That was easy for Papa, high on his hunter,
but my dainty mare only came up to the work-horse's shoulder,
so I had to keep her alert and wide awake to follow his great
strides.

'You'll have to go some day,' said Papa, looking over the
hedges to see the plough using the second team of horses starting
to turn over the sluggish winter earth. 'You will marry and leave
with your husband. Perhaps you'll be a fine lady at Court, not
that there's much of a Court left and all filled with ugly German
women, Hanover rats, they call 'em; but you'll be away and care
nothing for Wideacre.'

I laughed. The idea was so ludicrous and adulthood so far
away that nothing could shake my belief in the trinity of Papa,
and me, and the land.

'I won't marry,' I said. 'I shall stay here and work with you
and look after Wideacre, like you and I do now.'

'Aye,' Papa said tenderly. 'But Harry will be Master here
when I'm gone, and I would rather see you in your own home
than rubbing against him. Besides, Beatrice, the land is well
enough for you now, but in a few years you will want pretty
clothes and balls. Then who will watch the winter sowing?'

I laughed again with my childish confidence that good things
never change.

'Harry knows nothing about the land,' I said dismissively. 'If
you asked him what a short-horn was, he would think it was a
musical instrument. He's not been here for months – why, he

26

hasn't even seen the new plantation. Those trees were my idea, and you planted them just where I thought they should be. The man said I was a proper little forester – and you said I should have a stool made from the wood of my trees when I was an old lady! Harry cannot be Master here – he is always away.'

I still had not understood. Silly fool that I was. Though I had seen enough older sons inheriting the farms and enough younger sons working as day labourers or going into service before they could marry their patient sweethearts, I had never thought of them as landowners as we were.

I never imagined that the rule that favoured older sons to the exclusion of all others could ever, possibly, apply to us – to me. I had seen village girls of my age working as hard as adult women to earn money for the family coffers. I had seen their sisters, a few years older, on the look-out for older sons – always the eldest – to marry. But I never thought that the rigid, crazy rule that the first boy takes all could apply to us. It was a feature of the lives of the poor, like early death, poor health and starvation in winter. These things were not the same for us.

Oddly, I had never thought of Harry as the son and heir, just as I had never thought of Mama as the Mistress of Wideacre. They were simply private individuals, seldom seen outside the walls of the park. They were the background to the glory of the Squire and me. So my father's words had not disturbed me – they had passed me by.

I had much to learn, the little girl that I was then. I had never even heard of 'entail', the legal process of tying up a great estate so it is always handed to the next male heir – be he ever so distant, even if there are a hundred daughters loving the land before him. With childlike concentration I still had the ability to hear only what interested me – and speculation about the next Master of Wideacre was as remote as the music of the spheres.

While I dismissed the thoughts from my mind, my father had pulled up his hunter to chat with one of our tenants trimming his boundary hedge of blackthorn and dogroses.

'Good morning, Giles,' I said, my seat in the saddle, the tip of my head, a perfect copy of my father's friendly condescension.

'Mistress.' Giles touched an arthritic hand to his head. He was years younger than my father but bent double with the burden of poverty. A lifetime of waterlogged ditches, muddy fields and frozen pathways had permeated his bones with agonizing arthritis which no amount of dirty flannel wrapped round his skinny legs seemed to cure. His brown hand permanently ingrained with dirt (our dirt) was as knotted and as gnarled as a holly trunk.

'A grand little lady she's becoming,' he said to my father. ''Tis sad to think she'll have to leave us some day soon.' I stared at the old man. My father picked a sprig of clipped elder from the hedge with the butt of his whip.

'Aye,' he said slowly. 'But a man must run the land and maids must marry.' He paused. 'The young Master will be home soon when he's finished with his books. Time enough then to learn of country ways. The fields and the downs are good enough for a girl with the teaching her mother gives her, but these are bad times. The next Master of Wideacre will need to know his way in the world.'

I listened, silent. Even my mare seemed to freeze as my father spoke and the great shire-horses dropped their heads as if to listen while my father tore down the secure world of my childhood with his quiet, deadly words.

'Yes, she's a good girl and as sharp on the land as a bailiff for all she's so young. But she'll be off to marry some lord or other some day, and young Harry will take my place. He'll be all the better for his learning.'

Giles nodded. There was a silence. A long, country silence punctuated with the springtime birdsong. There was no hurry on that timeless afternoon which marked the end of my childhood. My father had said all he had to say and said nothing. Giles said nothing, thought nothing, gazed into space. And I said not a word for I had no words to deal with this pain. In a series of clicks, like the moving parts of some strange and cruel clock, all my pictures of the adult world were falling into place. The precious elder son always took the land – and the redundant girls could go where they could find a man to take them. My residence at Wideacre was not an exclusive favour, and Harry's departure an exile – but I was kept at home because I was not worth educating.

Harry's school was not an interruption of his Wideacre life but an essential preparation for it. While I had been revelling in the

28

land and the freedom of being the only child at home, Harry had been growing stronger and more skilled and would return to expel me from my home. Papa did not love me best. Papa did not love me best. Papa did not love me best.

I took a deep shuddering breath, softly, softly, so that no one could hear. And I looked at my father with a new, strange clarity. He might love me tenderly, but not enough to give me Wideacre. He might wish the best for me, but he could see no further than a good match and permanent exile from the one place in the world that was my home. He might plan ahead for Harry's future but he had forgotten me. Forgotten me.

So that was the end of my childhood; that warm spring day on the lane to Acre with the two great shire-horses beside my papa and me, and Giles, blank as chalk scree, staring at nothing. The absolute security of owning the land I loved left me, then, in that moment, and I never had it fully back. I left my childhood with my heart aching and my mind full of anger and resentment. I started adulthood with a bitter taste in my mouth and a formless determination that I would not go. I would not leave Wideacre. I would not surrender my place to Harry. If it was the way of the world that girls left home, then the world would have to change. I would never change.

'You'll have to hurry and change,' my mama said in her continual, unconscious contradiction of me. She held the hem of her green silk dress clear of the puddles in the stable yard as we clattered in. Always, she had this way of innocently opposing me, just as she continually opposed my father. From her I learned early that you do not have to argue or to state your beliefs to oppose someone. You can simply turn your head from them; from their ideas, from their loves and their enthusiasms. Without Papa, she might well have been a more direct, a sweeter-natured, woman. With him, her sense of her own purpose had soured into frustration. What should have been directness and honesty had become unspoken opposition.

'You must hurry and change into your pink silk,' she repeated with emphasis as I slid from the saddle and tossed the reins to a waiting stable lad. 'We've a special guest for dinner – Harry's headmaster.'

My father directed a long, silent look at her.

'Yes,' she said defensively. 'I did ask him to visit. I am worried about the boy. I'm sorry, Harold, I should have told you earlier, only it is some time since I wrote and I thought he was not coming at all. I would have mentioned it before . . .' She broke off and stopped. I understood my father's rising irritation. But his reply was checked, as a man all in black except for the white band of a clerical collar appeared at the rose-garden gate.

'Dr Yately!' my father said in a tone of convincing delight. 'How good to see you! And what a surprise! I should have been home to meet you had I known you were coming.'

The tall man nodded and smiled and I gained a quick impression of a cool, astute man of the world. I dipped my curtsy and shot another look at him as I rose. This was no social call. He had come for a purpose and he was anxious to complete his mission. I saw his wary eyes assessing Papa, and I wondered what he wanted of us.

He had come, it was clear, to do Mama's work for her. She still longed to have Harry home to fill the gap his absence had left in her life. Dr Yately, for reasons I could not yet guess, was ready to take the part of the pale wife against the Squire himself. For some reason, he was as anxious to be rid of Harry as Mama was to have him home.

I attended dinner in the girlish dress of maidenly pink and correctly said not a word except in reply to a direct question – and I had few of them. I sat facing my mother. It was one of my father's foibles that a male guest should take the foot of the table and he the head. So Mama and I – equally unimportant – sat in silence while the men talked over our heads.

Dr Yately had evidently come to persuade my father to remove Harry from his expensive, exclusive school. But if he succeeded, he stood to lose a pupil who had taken every costly extra, who was likely to need a tutor from the school to attend him to university, and who might well choose to take that tutor with him to Europe on the Grand Tour. With the disappearance of Harry, Dr Yately could say goodbye to thousands of pounds of fees. So why should he want to be rid of him? What could Harry have possibly done that was too gross a secret for a frank explanation to my father, and too shameful for Dr Yately simply to overlook and continue to pocket the fees?

The clever man knew his business. He kept off the subject of Harry but praised the roast beef and relished the wine (only our second-best claret I noticed). He clearly knew nothing about farming but he drew my father out to talk about some of the new techniques we might try. My father grew expansive, jovial. He even offered Dr Yately the chance of a few days' hunting ne..t season it he could take a holiday. Dr Yately was polite, but non-committal.

Once Papa started melting towards the visitor and broached another bottle, Mama was in a hurry to leave the gentlemen together. With the sharp regret of a fourteen-year-old girl who had been on horseback all day, I watched some apple charlotte returning untouched to the kitchen. But Mama rose from the table and Dr Yately and Papa politely bowed us from the room and settled down to their port and talk.

My mother's pale face was flushed with pleasure as she opened her workbox and handed me my embroidery.

'Your brother Harry will come home as soon as term ends, and never go to that dreadful place again, if only your papa agrees,' she said, elated.

'So early?' I asked, keenly defensive of my position. 'Why? What has he done?'

'Done?' Her eyes met mine directly, no subterfuge in their pale shadows. 'Nothing! Whatever could he do? It's what those brutes of boys have done to him.' She hesitated and chose a strand of silk.

'When he was last home for the holidays he needed a chest plaster, do you remember?' Of course I did not. But I nodded.

'Both Nurse and I saw marks on his poor body. He had been beaten, Beatrice. He begged me to say and do nothing, but the more I thought of it the more certain I was he should be taken away from that school. I wrote to Dr Yately and he replied that he would see what was happening. Then he arrived here today!' My mother's voice was full of pride that she had taken action that had produced results, and dramatic results. 'He tells me that Harry has been forced to join one of the boys' gangs, and that in their games they have some shocking rules and punishments.

31

The worst boy – the ringleader – is the son of . . .' She paused. 'Well, never mind who, precisely. But it is someone the Doctor simply must not offend. This boy has established some sort of hold over Harry. He made him sit next to him in class, have his bed next to him in the dormitory and has teased and bullied him all term. Dr Yately says he cannot separate them and he suggests – Oh! I hope your papa agrees – that Harry is of an age when he could pursue his studies at home and learn about the estate at the same time.'

Unseen by Mama, my head low over my embroidery, I raised ironic eyebrows. Harry learn about the estate, indeed! He had lived here all his life and did not even know the exact lie of our borders. He had driven through Wideacre wood every Sunday, and yet he did not know where in the wood there was a nightingale's nest, or where in the stream you could always find trout. If Harry was going to learn about the estate it was to be hoped he could find it in a book, for he had never even glanced from the library windows when he was last home.

But my confidence was undermined by a shiver of unease. All Harry knew about Wideacre at the moment could be written in a chapbook. But once he was home at the request of Mama, and not because Papa needed him, he might become the son my papa had wanted; had sought in me. He might become, in truth, the heir.

The gentlemen did not come to the drawing room for tea and Mama sent me early to bed. After my maid had twisted my chestnut hair into one fat plait down my back, I sent her away and climbed out of my bed to sit on the window seat. My bedroom was on the second floor, facing east, overlooking the fat sickle of the rose garden, which curves around the front and east of the house and with a glimpse of the peach trees and fruit cages of the kitchen garden. Not for me the larger bedrooms in the front of the house, like Harry's room, which faces south. Still, from where I sat I could see the garden in the moonlight and the wood pressing up to the garden gates. The cool night air carried countryside smells to me. The promising scent of growing meadows, damp with dew and the occasional warble of a restless blackbird. From the woods I heard the abrupt bark of a dog fox and from downstairs I could hear the rumble of my father's voice as he talked about horses. I knew then that the quiet man in black had got his way with Papa and Harry would be coming home.

A dark shadow crossing the lawn interrupted my thoughts. I recognized the gamekeeper's lad, a boy of my age, built like a young ox, with a lurcher dog – a poacher's dog to catch poachers – at his heels. He saw the candle in my window and came from the garden (where he had no business to be) to stand beneath my window (where he had no business to be), one hand casually on the warm sandstone wall. The silk shawl I had over my night-dress seemed too flimsy when I saw his warm eyes on me, and his smile as he gazed upwards.

We were friends, and yet not friends, Ralph and I. One summer, when Harry had been especially unwell and I had been left to run wild, I had found this unkempt boy in the rose garden and, with the haughtiness of a six-year-old, ordered him out of the gate. He tipped me into a rose bush with one hard shove as his reply, but when he saw my shocked, scratched face, he kindly offered to pull me out again. I took his proffered hand and, as soon as I was on my feet, I bit it as hard as I could and took to my heels – not to the Hall for shelter, but through the lychgate to the wood. This refuge was impenetrable to Mama and Nurse who were ignorant of the little animal pathways among the thickets, and were forced to stand at the gate, calling and calling, until I chose to reappear. But this stocky child wormed along the tracks as fast as I went, and arrived at a little hollow among brambles, roses and bushes on my heels.

His dirty little face was split in a broad grin and I grinned back. It was the start of a friendship that, childlike, lasted the summer and then stopped as quickly and as thoughtlessly as it had begun. Every day during that hot, dry summer I would escape from the busy parlourmaid, who had suddenly found my care added to her duties, and skip down to the woods. Ralph would meet me by the Fenny and all morning we would fish and splash in the stream, go on great expeditions all the way to Acre lane, climb trees, rob birds' nests, or catch butterflies.

I was free because Harry was watched night and day by Nurse and Mama. Ralph was free from the day he could walk because his mother, Meg, a slattern in a tumbledown cottage in the middle of the woods, had never troubled where he went or what he did. This made him a perfect playmate for me – and he taught me all the paths and trees of Wideacre woods in a great sweep around the Hall as far as my little legs could carry me in a morning.

We played like country children, speaking little and doing a lot. But the summer soon ended; Harry recovered, and Mama returned to her eagle-eyed scrutiny of the whiteness of my pinnies. Mornings were again given over to lessons, and if Ralph waited in the woods while the leaves turned yellow and red, he would not have waited for long. Very soon he had given up playing altogether and trailed around behind the gamekeeper, learning the skills of keeping game and killing vermin. Papa heard Ralph's name as the handiest lad in the village for pheasant chicks, and by the time he was eight he was paid a penny a day in the season.

By the time he was twelve he was earning half a man's pay but doing a man's job in and out of season. His mother had come from nowhere; his father had disappeared, but that meant he was free of the family loyalty that kept poachers safe in Acre village. And his tumbledown house in the woods was an advantage too. They put the pheasant breeding pens all around the dirty little cottage by the Fenny and Ralph's deepest sleep could always be broken by the crack of a twig near the game birds.

Eight years is a lifetime in childhood, and I had almost forgotten the summer when the dirty little urchin and I had been inseparable. But somehow, when I was mounted on my pretty mare, with my tailored habit and tricorn hat, I felt awkward riding past Ralph. When he pulled his forelock to Papa and nodded to me I did not feel easy and gracious as I said, 'Good day.' I did not enjoy stopping and talking with Ralph, especially if I was riding alone. And I did not like now the way he leaned, so self-possessed, against our wall and looked up at me, illuminated by my candle.

'You'll take cold,' he said. His voice was already deep. He had filled out in the past two years and had the solid strength of a young man.

'Yes,' I said, shortly. I did not withdraw from the window for that would somehow have been a concession to his advice . . . and an acknowledgement that I was conscious of his eyes on me.

34

'Are you out after poachers?' I asked, unnecessarily.

'Well, I'm not going courting with a dog and a gun,' he said in the slow drawl of the downs. 'A fine lass I'd get with a gun and a trap, don't you think, Miss Beatrice?'

'You're too young to think of courting,' I said dictatorially. 'You're no older than me.'

'Oh, but I do think of courting,' he said. 'I like to think of a warm, friendly lass when I wait alone in the woods on a cold night. I'm not too young for courting, Miss Beatrice. But you're right, we are the same age. Are girls of near fifteen too young to think of loving and kisses on warm summer nights?'

His dark eyes never left mine, and they seemed somehow to shine in the moonlight. I was very glad – and yet somehow sorry – that I was safe in the house, high above him.

'Ladies are,' I said firmly. 'And the village girls would know better than to think of you.'

'Ah.' He sighed. The country silence filled the pause. His dog yawned and stretched out on the gravel at Ralph's boots. Contradictorily, I wished with all my heart that he would look at me again in that shining, hot way, and that I had not called myself a lady and reminded him that he was nothing. His head dropped and his eyes no longer stared up at me, but were fixed on the ground. I could think of nothing to say; I felt awkward and foolish and also sorry, sorry, sorry, to have been arrogant to one of our people. Then he shifted his weight and hefted his gun over his shoulder. Despite the shadows I could see he was smiling, and that he needed my pity not at all.

'A lady is the same as a village girl in the cold, or in a quiet hayloft, or in a little hollow of the downs, I reckon,' he said. 'And if fifteen is old enough for me, I reckon it's old enough for you, too.' He paused. 'My lady,' he added, and his voice made it into an endearment.

I choked with shock, and while I said nothing like a fool, Ralph whistled to his dog, a black dog, his shadow, and left me without even a by-your-leave. He walked like a lord across his own acres, a dark shape in the shadowy garden, over our lawn and through the little gate to our woods. I was stunned at his impertinence. Then, with a sudden spurt of rage, I bounced from my window seat to go down to the Squire, who should have him whipped. Dragging on my wrapper, I was halfway to the door before I paused. For some reason, I could not think why, I did not want Ralph whipped – or thrown off Wideacre. He should certainly be punished, but not by my father, nor the gamekeeper either. I, alone, should find some way to wipe that insulting, warm smile from his face. I went to bed planning revenge. But I could not sleep. My heart was thudding so loud. I was surprised it should beat so .ast with rage.

In the morning, I had all but forgotten him. It meant nothing, nothing at all, that I chose to ride in the direction of his home. I knew he would have been watching for poachers in the woods all night, and so would be home till noon at least in the horrid, damp cottage near the disused mill on the River Fenny. The flow had never been reliable there, and my father's father had built a new mill to grind our corn further upstream. The old mill had fallen into disrepair and the tiny worker's cottage alongside seemed to be sinking into the boggy ground. The woods grew close to the back door of the low-roofed shack, and as Ralph grew taller I believe he must have stooped all the time indoors. It was a two-roomed place, more a hovel than a cottage.

His mother was a dark, large-boned woman with wild, dangerous looks like his. 'A gypsy of a woman,' my father called her with relish.

'Really?' said my fair-haired mother coldly.

We often rode this way, my father and I. He would stop outside the poor cottage and Meg would come out to him, stooping under the low eaves, her skirt held high above the mud, barefoot, her strong brown ankles splashed and dirty. But she met my father's eyes with a proud, bright smile like an equal, and brought him home-brewed ale in a rough cup. When he tossed her a coin she caught it as if it were her due, and sometimes I saw the hint of a smile of understanding between them.

There could not be secrets between this wild and lonely woman and the Squire, my father. But once or twice when he had ridden fast from home, full of impatience with my mother and her small, fiddling ways, we had seemed naturally to drift towards the Fenny and the little cottage in the woods where Meg, the gypsy woman, swayed towards us with her barefoot dancing step and her eyes bright with knowledge.

She was supposed to be a widow. Ralph's father, the black sheep of one of the oldest families in Acre, had been pressed into the Navy and disappeared: dead, or missing, or run away. The other men of the village followed her with their eyes like hungry dogs but she looked neither to right nor left. Only my father, the Squire, brought a smile to her eyes, and those dark eyes to his face. No other man was ever worth a second glance. So, although she had offers, oh, many, she and Ralph never moved from the dark little house by the river.

'A hundred years ago she would have been burned for a witch,' said my father.

'Oh, really?' said my unbewitching mother.

She did not seem surprised to see me at her garden gate alone, but then nothing surprised her. She nodded and brought me a cup of milk in the way of country hospitality. I drank, still sitting sidesaddle on my mare and, as I drained the cup, Ralph came like a midnight shadow from the woods. He had a pair of dead rabbits hanging from one hand and his dog, as ever, at his heels.

'Miss Beatrice,' he said in a slow greeting.

'Hello, Ralph,' I said graciously. In the bright daylight his night-time power had gone. His mother took my cup and we were alone in the sunlight.

'I knew you would come,' he said confidently. It was as if the sun had gone out. Like a mesmerized rabbit I gazed straight into his dark black eyes and could see nothing, nothing, but his eyes fixed on mine and the slow smile of his mouth, and the way a small pulse was beating quick under the tanned skin of his throat. The tall youth had all the power of last night. He carried it with him. He stood at my mare's head and I was glad to be seated above him, at shoulder height in the saddle.

'Oh, really?' I said, in unconscious imitation of my mother's frigid tones. Abruptly, he turned, and walked away from me, through the purple willowherb to the Fenny. Without thinking what I was doing, I slid from the saddle, hitched my horse's reins to Meg's ramshackle fence and followed him. He never glanced behind, he never waited for me. He walked as if he were quite alone, down to the riverbank, and then turned upstream to where the ruins of the mill stood, the deep millpond dark behind it.

The wide, arched door where they used to load the wagons stood open. Ralph never looked back and I followed him without a word inside. A half-floor for storing sacks stretched across the room, a rickety ladder leading up to it. In the warm gloom of the old building I could smell the fusty, safe odour of old straw and feel the thick softness of dusty chaff underfoot.

'Want to see a swallow's nest?' Ralph offered nonchalantly.

I nodded. Swallows are lucky and their little mud and grass cup-shaped nests on beams or ledges under the eaves always pleased me. He led the way up the ladder and I followed unhesitatingly. When he reached the top he stretched out a hand to pull me up, and when I stood beside him, he did not let my hand go. His eyes met mine in a long, measuring stare.

'There they are,' he said. He pointed to the nest being built on a low beam under the roof. As we watched, a parent bird swooped into the barn with a tiny beakful of mud to add to the growing sides and swooped away. We watched in silence. Ralph let my hand go and slid his hand around my waist, drawing me closer. We stood side by side and his hand smoothed over the velvet of my gown up to the curve of my small breast. Without speaking a word, we turned together and he dipped his head to kiss me. The kiss was as gentle as the flight of the swallow.

His mouth brushed mine with soft, gentle touches. As he repeated them, I felt him tense, and the grip on my waist grew tighter. Swoony with pleasure, I found my knees giving way beneath me and I sank on to the dusty straw-strewn floor with my arms around him.

We were half children, half adult. I knew everything about mating animals, but nothing of kisses and lovemaking. But Ralph was a country lad and had been drawing a man's wage and drinking with men for two years. My hat fell off as I tipped my head back to meet his kisses, and it was my hands that opened the neck of my gown to his exploring, clumsy fingers, and opened his shirt so I could press my forehead to his chest and rub my burning face against him.

Somewhere in the back of my mind a voice said: 'Fever. I must have a fever.' For my legs were too weak to rise and somehow I was trembling, trembling all over. In the core of my body, under my ribcage, was a fluttering, painful feeling. Down my spine was a long, long shiver. Ralph's smallest move made me shudder. When his forefinger drew a line from under my ear to the base of my neck, he could feel me tremble all over. 'I must be ill,' said my drowning consciousness. 'I must be very, very ill.'

Ralph eased back from me and leaned on an elbow looking down into my face. 'You should go,' he said. 'It's getting late.'

'Not yet,' I said. 'It can't be two o'clock yet.'

I fumbled in my pocket for my silver watch, a miniature copy of my father's, and opened it.

'Three!' I exclaimed. 'I shall be late!' I jumped to my feet, reaching for my hat and shaking the straw from my skirt. Ralph made no effort to help me, but leaned back against an old stook of straw. I buttoned the front of my gown, watching him covertly under my eyelashes. He pulled a straw from the stook and chewed on it, watching me, impassive. His dark eyes showed nothing. He seemed as content to be left as to be visited, as still as a secret pagan god left neglected in old woods.

I was ready to go and should have been hurrying away, yet the flutter under my ribcage had become some sort of ache. I did not want to leave just yet. I sat down again beside him and laid my head prettily on his shoulder.

'Say you love me before I go,' I whispered.

'Oh, no,' he said without heat. 'I'll have none of that.'

In surprise I jerked my head back to stare at him.

'You don't love me?' I asked, astounded.

'No,' said Ralph. 'You don't love me, do you?'

I paused, a cry of outrage on my lips. But I could not say I did love him. I liked the kissing very much, oh, so very much, and I would like to meet him again, here in the darkness of the old mill. Perhaps the next time I would slide my dress off and feel his hands and lips all over me. But he was, after all, Meg's son. And he lived in such a dirty little cottage. And he was only the gamekeeper's lad and one of our people. And we let him and Meg live in the cottage for practically nothing; it was almost charity.

'No,' I said slowly. 'I don't suppose I do.'

'There are those who love and there are those who are loved,' he said thoughtfully. 'I've seen grown men weep like babies for my mother, and she never look at them. Gentlemen, too. I'll never be like that for a woman. I'll never love and pine and fall sick for someone. I shall be the one who is loved, and gets the presents and the loving and the pleasure . . . and then moves on.'

I thought swiftly of my father, bluff and heart-whole, and of my mother's stifled sighs and pining for the love of her son. Then I thought of the girls I had seen in the village follow a lad with their eyes and blush scarlet and grow pale. Of the village girl who drowned herself in Fenny pool when her lover went into service in Kent. Of the constant pain there is for a woman in loving, and wedding, and childbirth and the loss of looks and then the loss of love.

'I shan't be the one who loves either,' I said firmly.

He laughed aloud.

'You!' he said. 'Oh, you are like all the Quality. All you care for is your own pleasure and owning the land.'

Our pleasure and owning the land. It is true. His kisses had been pleasure; wonderful swoony pleasure. Good food, a taste of wine, hunting on a frosty morning; these things are pleasure. But to own Wideacre is not pleasure; it is the only way to be alive. I smiled at the thought. He smiled kindly in return.

'Oh,' he said longingly, 'you'll be a proper little heartbreaker when you are ready. With those slanty green eyes of yours and your beechnut hair, you'll get all the pleasure you want, and all the land, too.'

Something in his voice convinced me he was telling the truth. I would have all the pleasure, and all the land as well. My misfortune of being born a girl would not be my destiny. I could take pleasure, and I would take land, too, just like a man. And the pleasure I would have in courting would be far more than any man would have. Ralph had enjoyed our kissing, I knew, but his pleasure had been nothing to mine. I had been faint with delight at the feelings of my silky skin. My body was a perfect animal, so lithe and slim and sweet. I would get pleasure with any man I wanted. I would get the land, too. I wanted Wideacre with every waking thought, and breath, and dream. And I deserved Wideacre, too. No one cared for it as I did, or loved it as I did, or knew it as well as I.

But I looked at Ralph speculatively. I had heard something

else in his voice, and his eyes were no longer impassive; they were warm and sensuous again.

'You could love me!' I said. 'You nearly do already.'

He threw out a hand in the way the lads do when they wrestle and want to surrender.

'Oh, yes,' he said, as if it hardly mattered. 'And perhaps I could make you love me. But there would be no place for us. You belong at the Hall and I belong in Meg's cottage in the woods. We can meet in secret and take our pleasure in dark and dirty places, but you will marry a lord and I will marry some slut from the village. If you want love, you must find someone else. I will take you only for pleasure.'

'For pleasure then,' I agreed, as seriously as swearing to a covenant. I turned my face to him and he kissed me solemnly as a binding pledge. I scrambled to my feet, but then I paused to look at him. Leaning against the stook of straw, he looked like some dangerous harvest deity. I smiled at him, almost shyly, and went back to stand before him. Lazily, he reached up a hand to me and pulled me down to him. I was in his arms once more; we smiled into each other's eyes like equals, as if there were no Hall and no cottage. Then his hard mouth came down on mine and my hat fell off again.

I did not get any dinner that day.

But I was not hungry.

3

For three unbearable days, Mama, in a flutter of excitement over Harry's promised return, had the landau out every day to take us into Chichester to buy new wallpaper for his room. The journal she read was full of the craze for the Chinese style, and Mama and I leafed through prints of dragons until my head spun with weariness and boredom. Three long days, while the early summer sun grew hotter and, somewhere, by the river, Ralph waited. Yet I spent every one of them in the drapers of Chichester choosing a new bedspread for Harry, selecting new brocades for the curtains and hangings in his room.

It was all for Harry, all for Harry's return. When I asked if I might also have new curtains and hangings for my room, I met with one of Mama's most hurtful rebuffs.

'It hardly seems worth it,' she said vaguely. She said no more. She needed to say no more. It was not worth the expense for the second child, in second place. It was not worth the expense to please a girl. It was not worth the expense to decorate a room for one who was merely passing through on her way to a marriage and another home.

I said nothing; but I begrudged Harry every penny. I said nothing; but I begrudged him every fraction of his unearned status. I said nothing; but I ill-wished him every morning of those three long days.

If I knew my brother at all, he would enjoy them for the first week, then forget them. But I knew also his sweetness, and that Mama would be repaid for her trouble in full by one of his tender, gentle smiles. Nothing would repay me for my trouble because I loathed days in Chichester, sitting idly in a shop while Mama played princess and hesitated between one shade of colour and another. Worse than all of this, for some reason I was ill.

I did not tell Mama, for I dreaded her concern, and for some

42

reason I did not want to be touched by anyone. When I stretched out my kid-gloved hands and spread the fingers, I could see they trembled. Worse, my belly gave great, unaccountable leaps in swoops like fear or dread. I was not hungry. Only Mama's obsession with the redecorating distracted her from the fact that for the past three days I had eaten only at breakfast.

Stroking the pile of some printed velvet in one shop, I thought suddenly of the smoothness of the skin of Ralph's shoulders and my knees buckled suddenly. I sank into a chair and found my heart racing and I could not catch my breath. 'I must be ill,' I thought.

On the evening of the third day we followed the sun home. It was setting over the downs in a gold and rosy glow. Mama was a fulfilled woman. In the bandboxes of the landau we had silks and satins for new cushion covers, quilting and new patterns. Following us tomorrow would be brocades, wallpapers and several pieces of extremely ugly furniture which were to convert Harry's lovely old English bedroom into something as like a pagoda as the Chichester merchants and Mama could imagine.

Mama was at peace with her purchases all around us, and I was smiling like a madonna to be driving home through the mild evening air of a Wideacre spring. The smells of the roadside flowers blew towards us as the weary horses trotted home, ears pricked for their stable. In the banks I could see the greeny yellow of the last primroses and in the little coppices the bluebells shimmered in a watery haze. Blackbirds singing for their loves trickled out notes so sad and lovely, and as we turned through the tall lodge gates, I could hear the insistent call of the cuckoo.

In the shadow of a great yew tree by the lodge gate stood Ralph. The horses were walking and I was carried slowly past him. His eyes were fixed on mine as if neither of us could see anything else. All around me the wood grew dim as if I were suddenly blinded. My belly gave a great lurch as if in mortal terror and then the terror turned to joy and I smiled at Ralph as if he himself had brought the spring, the bluebells and the cuckoo. He tipped his head at the landau – but he did not tug his forelock in the usual way of our people – and his eyes never left mine. His face warmed and his eyes crinkled in a slow intimate smile. The carriage went past at walking pace, but oh! far too fast. I did not look back, but I felt his eyes, warm, desiring, on the back of my neck all the way up the drive until the sweep around the great copper beech hid me from him.

The next day, God bless them, the carters lost a wheel from the wagons and could not bring the goods. Mama was in a fidget to set me to work hemming curtains but she had to wait. Tomorrow, I might be indoors labouring over Harry's damned dragons, but today I was free. The day stretched before me like a reprieve from a death sentence. I changed out of my morning dress into my new green riding habit – back from Papa's tailor only that week – and twisted my hair under the matching green hat with especial care. Then I was off on pretty Bella, down the drive and across the stone bridge over the Fenny. I turned her to the right to let her canter down the track that runs alongside the river.

The Fenny was swollen with the spring rains and was brown and boiling like clear soup. Its swirlings and splashings over new-formed waterfalls matched my mood and I rode at an easy canter beside the river, smiling. The beech trees were in their early haze of green over my head and between the rustling leaves of last autumn new straight shoots were poking through, miraculously slender and strong. Every bird in the world was calling, calling for a mate. The universe of Wideacre was alive with the urgency of love and springtime, and I was dressed in green like life itself.

Ralph was sitting beside the river, a rod in his hands, his back against a fallen pine. He looked up at the sound of my horse's hoofs and smiled without surprise. He seemed as much part of my beloved Wideacre as the trees themselves. We had not planned this meeting but it was as natural as the birdsong that we should meet whenever we wished. Ralph by the river drew me to him as surely as hidden water draws a forked willow stick to point downwards.

I tied Bella to an elder bush and she drooped her head in recognition that we were here for the afternoon. My steps rustled in the leaves as I walked towards him and stood, waiting, before him.

He smiled up at me, squinting against the brightness of the springtime sky behind me.

'I've missed you,' he said suddenly and my heart jumped as if I had taken a tumble from one of Papa's hunters.

'I could not get away,' I said. I put my hands behind my back so he should not see them tremble but, absurdly, my eyes seemed to be filling with tears and I could not keep my lips from quivering. I could hide my hands and no one could tell under the smooth skirts of my green gown that my knees were weak, but my face seemed naked as if I had been caught in sleep or in a second of shameful fear. I risked a glance at his face and caught his eyes upon me. I saw in that second his easy confidence had gone. Ralph, too, was as tense as a snare. I could see his breath was as fast as if he had been sprinting. In wonder, I stepped forward and put out a hand to touch his thick, black hair. In a swift, unpredictable movement he snatched my hand and tugged me down beside him. Both his hands on my shoulders he glared into my face as if torn between a desire to murder, and a desire to love me. I had no thoughts. I just gazed back as if I was famished for the look of him.

Then the dangerous, fiery look melted from his eyes and he smiled at me as warm as a summer day.

'Oh, Beatrice,' he said, lingeringly. His hands slid from my shoulders down the neat-cut jacket to my waist and he pulled me close and kissed my lips, my eyelids and my throat. Then we sat side by side, with his arm around me and my head on his shoulder, watching the river and the bob of his pine-cone float for a long, long time.

We spoke little, for we were still country children. When the float bobbed and Ralph jumped to pull the line in, I had his cap ready to catch the fish as neatly and surely as in our childhood summer. Dead leaves, bracken and old twigs made a little fire under the trees by the river, and Ralph cleaned the trout and spitted it on a twig while I fed the little flames. I had eaten little for three days and the burned skin of the trout was salty and good. It was part raw, but whoever cares for such things when it is your own trout from your own river cooked on a fire of your own twigs? I washed my fingers and mouth in the rushing water and drank some of the sweet flood. Then I leaned back against the log and Ralph's arms were around me.

Young ladies, girls of the Quality, are said to have painful

45

childbirths, difficulty monthly seasons, fearful loss of virginity. Without one direct, honest word, Mama had ensured I knew that wifely duties included the making and bearing of an heir, and had convinced me that the task would be disagreeable and painful. Perhaps it is. Perhaps mating the man of your parents' choice in the great wooden family bed, with the plans of two families on you, and your duty clear before you, is a painful insult to your body. All I know for certain is that to lie with the lad of your choice, like any free maid, under the Wideacre trees and sky is to become part of the old magic of the land, to hear the great heart of Wideacre thud in your ears, to feel the pulse of the earth.

We rolled together as inexpert, yet as graceful, as otter cubs; then the inexplicable, unexpected, unplanned sensations added and added and added up to a sudden crisis of delight that left me gasping and weeping into Ralph's shoulder while he said, 'Oh,' as if he were extraordinarily surprised.

Then we lay in silence, clasped together as close as interlaced hands. And then, like the children we were, we fell asleep.

We woke, cold, cramped and uncomfortable. My back was patchy with the impress of twigs and leaves and Ralph had a red line across his forehead from pitching forward against the bark of the log. We huddled into our clothes and hugged for warmth as the quick springtime twilight lengthened the shadows of the bushes and the trees. Then Ralph cupped his hands for my foot and tossed me into the saddle. There was one wordless, warm look between us and then I turned my horse's head and trotted for home. I felt badly in need of a hot bath and a huge meal. I felt like a goddess.

Those first wordless meetings set a pattern of pleasure that grew and grew all spring and early summer as the days warmed and the crops greened the dark fields. The lambs, the cows in calf and the sowing kept me out of Mama's way with an excuse for absence almost every day. Once I had looked over the animals, or helped move the flocks up to the sweet grass of the spring downs, I could do as I pleased. Ralph knew some hidey-holes in the woods further afield than where we had played as six-year-olds, and on the few wet days we met at the old mill again. Above

46

our shifting bodies, the little swallows hatched and were fed. I knew we had been lovers for weeks when the little hungry squeaks from the nest of mud grew louder and louder, and then one day they had flown. It was the only sign I noticed of passing time.

The transition from spring to high summer seemed to stand still that year to allow Ralph and me endless warm secret afternoons. The land itself conspired to hide us as the bracken on the common grew taller, and the undergrowth in the woods thicker and more lush. The weather of that wonderful spring smiled and smiled until Papa said he had never known such a season – that it must be magic to make the hay so early.

Of course it was magic. Through every warm day and through every dream at night, Ralph strode like a dark god of the earth making all of Wideacre glow with growth while our passion and our loving made the days sunny and long and the night skies full of the clearest stars.

We grew more skilled at pleasing each other but we never lost some sense of awe at each other's mere presence. Just being there, under the swooping tall beech trees or curled up under the bracken, seemed a continual wonder to me. Anything we could imagine, any refinement of pleasure we could dream, we did with tenderness, with laughter, with breathless excitement. We would lie naked for hours touching each other all over, taking turns.

'Is it nice if I touch you like this? Like this? Like this?' I would ask while my fingers, face and tongue explored Ralph's outstretched body.

'Oh, yes. Oh, yes.'

We loved the excitement of near discovery as well. We met unplanned one afternoon when Ralph had come to the Hall with a hare and I was picking roses for Mama in the garden. He came from the kitchen at the back of the house and the gate clanged as he entered the garden. I turned, saw him and the basketful of roses dropped, instantly forgotten. Reckless of the windows of the house, which overlooked the garden, Ralph simply strode towards me, took my hand and led me to the summerhouse. He stood, back arched to carry my weight, and lifted me on to him, my silk dress creased and bunched between us, his head pressing down to kiss my breasts. We gasped in hasty incredulous pleasure, and Ralph set me down on my feet again. Then we laughed, and could not stop laughing at the sheer comic audacity of love-making in the garden in broad daylight before Mama's parlour, before every window in the front of the house.

On my birthday morning in May, when I woke early with excitement to hear the birds singing and singing at the rosy dawn, my first thought was not of the expensive presents I could expect from Papa and Mama, but what Ralph might bring me.

I did not have long to wonder. While I splashed water on my face I heard a low, long whistle under my window and, wearing only my shift, I swung open the casement window to lean out and see Ralph, smiling with joy at seeing me.

'Happy birthday,' he called in a hoarse whisper. 'I have brought you a present.'

I jumped down from the window seat and went to my dressing-table drawers for a ball of yarn. Like a fairy-tale princess, I dropped it from my window and Ralph tied a little withy basket carefully on the threads. I pulled it in as gently as if I were landing a salmon, and laid it on the window seat beside me.

'Is it alive?' I said in surprise when I heard a rustle of leaves inside the meshes.

'Alive and scratching,' said Ralph and held up a hand to show me a long red scratch along the back.

'A kitten?' I guessed.

'Not for you,' Ralph said dismissively. 'Something more exciting.'

'A lion cub,' I said promptly and smiled to hear Ralph's slow country chuckle.

'Open it and see,' he advised. 'But open it carefully.'

I unfastened the little catch on the lid and peeped inside. A deep blue gaze met mine, a glimpse of ruffled, fluffed-out, angry feathers – a baby owl, rolled on his back with his sharp taloned feet pointing up at me in defence, a hoarse, cross squeaking coming from his open, red-tongued beak.

'Oh, Ralph!' I said, entranced. I glanced down; Ralph's face was beaming with love and triumph.

'I climbed the pine tree right up to the top for that one,' he said proudly. 'I wanted to give you something no one else could give you. And something from Wideacre.'

'I shall call it Canny,' I said, 'because owls are wise.'

'Not very wise,' he said, teasing. 'We nearly fell out of the tree when it scratched me.'

'And I shall love it for ever because you gave it to me,' I said, gazing at its mad, deep blue eyes.

'Wisdom and love then,' said Ralph, 'and all earned by one little owl.'

'Thank you,' I said, with my heart in the words.

'Coming out later?' he asked casually.

'I might,' I said and beamed down at him. 'I'll be down at the mill straight after breakfast,' I promised. Then I turned my head to listen for the noise of a maid stoking the kitchen fire. 'I must go,' I said. 'See you at the mill, and thank you for my present.'

There was a small, disused store room among our outbuildings and there we decided to keep Canny. Ralph taught me how to feed the baby bird with raw meat wrapped in fur or feathers, and how to gently stroke its breast feathers so it hooded its blue eyes to doze.

That summer, Ralph would have climbed any tree, dared any risk for me. And I would have done anything for him. Or almost anything. One thing I would never do for him, and if he had been wiser, or less in love, he would have been warned by it. I would never take him into my papa's bed. Ralph had a longing to lie with me there, in the great master bed, under the dark, curved wooden roof upheld by the four pillars as thick as pine trunks. But I would not. However much I loved the gamekeeper's lad, he would never lie with me in the bed of the Squires of Wideacre. I evaded the question, but one day, when Papa and Mama were visiting in Chichester and the servants were on a half-day holiday, Ralph asked me directly to lie with him there, and was met with a direct refusal. His eyes went black with anger, but he said nothing and went alone to set snares in the woods instead. He soon forgot that one isolated refusal. A wiser man would have remembered and carried that reservation of mine through every day of that golden, timeless summer.

It was no timeless summer for Mama, who counted the days

until the return of her golden boy from his school. She even made a little calendar, which she hung on the parlour wall, marked with the days of his term. Indifferently, I saw one day ticked off every evening. With little enthusiasm, and even less skill, I hemmed curtains and helped embroider the dragon counterpane for Harry's new-style bedroom. And despite my ham-fisted efforts with the curly tail of the stupid beast, it was completed in time and spread on Harry's bed to await the arrival of the emperor himself.

The first day of July, too good a day to waste at the parlour window listening for Harry's carriage, saw us waiting for him. As soon as I heard hoofs on the drive I obeyed my instructions and called to Mama. She summoned Papa from his gun room and we stood on the steps as the carriage swept around the bend in the drive and drew up before the front door. Papa greeted Harry, who jumped boyishly from the carriage, without waiting for the steps to be let down. Mama surged forward. I held back, resentment, jealousy and some sort of fear in my heart.

Harry had changed in this last term. He had lost his rounded, puppy-fat face and looked like a clear, lean youth rather than a golden baby. He was taller. He greeted Papa with a frank smile of affection and beamed at Papa's great bear-hug. He kissed Mama's hand and cheeks with tenderness, but he did not cling to her. Then, and this was the greatest surprise of all, he looked around for me and his bright blue eyes lit up when he saw me.

'Beatrice!' he said, and jumped up the front steps in two long-legged strides. 'How pretty you have grown! How grown up you are! Do we still kiss?'

I lifted my face to him with an easy smile in reply, but I felt my colour rise at the touch of his lips on my cheek and the soft prickle of the little growing hairs of his upper lip.

Then Mama swept upon him and took him into the house, and Papa talked loudly over her fluttering inquiries about the roads and the inns and when he had last dined, and they all left me alone on the sunny front door steps as if I had left the house and belonged nowhere at all.

But it was Harry who paused at the parlour door and looked back through the open front door and called to me. 'Come in, Beatrice!' he said. 'I have a present for you in my bags.'

And my heart suddenly lightened to see his smile and the hand he held out to me. And I went with quick steps into the house and felt that perhaps Harry might not displace me, but could make my home a happier place for me.

However, as the days went on Harry's charm wore a little thin. Every housemaid, every tenant's daughter, had a smile for the good-looking young Master. His new confidence and awareness of himself won him friends everywhere he chose to ride. He was charming, and he knew it. He was handsome, and he knew it. We laughed that now I had to look up to him, for he was a head taller than me.

'You will not bully me any more, Beatrice,' he said.

He was still bookish: two of his trunks from school were filled with nothing but writings on philosophy, poems, plays and stories. But he had outgrown his childish illnesses and was no longer forced to spend all days indoors reading. He even made me feel ashamed that I had read so little. I might know more about the land than Harry ever could know, for I had spent years out on Wideacre and my heart was in it, as his never was. But that counted for little when Harry would toss off a reference to a book and say, 'Oh, Beatrice! You must have read it! Why it's in our library. I found it when I was about six.'

Some of his books were about farming, too, and not all of them were foolish.

This new Harry was the product of the natural growth of a boy nearing manhood. The ill health of his childhood was forgotten. Only Mama still worried about his heart. Everyone else saw his slimmer body, the strength in his arms, the brightness of his blue eyes and his conscious, sly charm with the pretty housemaids. But the principal influence was still Staveley. Staveley's name was once more heard daily in Mama's parlour and at the dinner table. Mama had her own opinions about Staveley and his gang. But she kept her head down, her tongue still and let her adored son talk and talk. He boasted about his role as Staveley's right-hand man. The gang had grown more and more daring and its discipline more and more strict. Harry was second in command, but that had saved him no beatings from the demigod Staveley. Staveley's swift rages, his harsh punishments, his tender forgiveness, were retailed to me in many confidences.

Harry missed his hero terribly, of course. Throughout his first weeks at home he wrote every day, asking for news of the school and Staveley's gang. Staveley himself replied once or twice in an ill-formed and misspelled scrawl Harry treasured. And another boy wrote once or twice. His last letter told Harry he was now Staveley's second in command. On that day Harry looked gloomy, took his horse out in the morning, and was late for dinner.

Yet however pleasant Harry could now be as a companion, with him at my side I was no longer free to slip away to meet Ralph by the river, on the common land or on the downs. As the days went on, I grew more and more impatient with Harry always at my side. I could not get rid of him. Mama wanted him to sing to her; Papa needed him to ride to Chichester, but Harry chose to go with me, while Ralph waited and waited and I burned up with desire.

'Every time I order my horse from the stables, he has to go riding, too,' I complained to Ralph in a snatched moment as we met by accident on the drive. 'Every time I go into a room in the house he trails around after me.'

Ralph's bright dark eyes shone with interest.

'Why does he follow you so close? I thought he was tied to your mother's apron strings?'

'I don't know,' I said. 'He's never paid much heed to me before. Now I can't shake him off.'

'Maybe he wants you,' said Ralph outrageously.

'Don't be silly,' I said. 'He's my brother.'

'Maybe he's learned something at that school of his,' Ralph persisted. 'Perhaps he's had a wench at school and learned to look at a girl. Maybe he sees, like I saw, that you are young and burning and ready for pleasure. Maybe he's been away from home so long he's forgotten he should think of you as a sister and just knows he's in the same house as a girl who is warmer and lovelier every day and looks just about ready for all that a man could offer.'

'Nonsense,' I said. 'I just wish he would leave me alone.'

'Is this him?' Ralph asked, nodding to an approaching horseman. My brother, in a riding coat of warm brown, which set off his broadening shoulders, was trotting towards us. He looked, surprisingly, like a young copy of my father, mounted on one of the high Wideacre hunters. He had my father's proud, easy way and his ready smile. But Harry's sweetness was all his own and his lithe slimness showed no sign of Papa's broad solidity.

'It's him,' I confirmed. 'Be careful.'

Ralph stood a little back from my horse's head, and pulled his forelock respectfully to my brother.

'Sir,' he said.

Harry nodded at him with a sweet smile

'I thought I'd ride with you, Beatrice,' he said. 'We could go up on the downs for a gallop.'

'Certainly,' I said. 'This is Ralph, Meg's son, the gamekeeper's lad.' Some devil prompted me to make them face each other, but my brother barely glanced at him. Ralph said nothing, but watched my brother intently. Harry simply did not realize Ralph was there.

'Shall we go?' he said, smiling. With a sudden shock I remembered the gulf between Ralph and me, which I had forgotten in the days of sensuality under the equal sky. Harry, of my blood and my Quality, ignored Ralph because Ralph was a servant. People like us, my brother and me, were surrounded by hundreds and thousands of our people who meant nothing; whose opinions, loves, fears and hopes never could mean anything to us. We might take an interest in their lives, or we might ignore them completely. It depended wholly on ourselves. They had no choice in the matter. For the first time, seeing Ralph beside my graceful, princely, high-riding brother, I blushed in a horror of shame, and the dreams of those spring days seemed a nightmare.

We turned our horses and moved off. I felt Ralph's eyes on us as he watched us ride away, but this time they did not fill me with joy but with dread. I rode stiff-backed, and my mare felt my unease and pricked her ears and was wary.

I was proud, but I was young and sensual and it had been many days since I had been alone with Ralph. The track up to the downs was where I had ridden with my father on the first day I had seen the sweep of Wideacre from horseback, and it was a favourite meeting place for Ralph and me. As we rode through the beech coppice I could remember a long lazy afternoon of teasing each other's desire in a deep shady hollow, and as the horses climbed to the highest point of the downs they passed one of our little nests of ferns. My shame faded in the memory of pleasure.

In that spot, only a few yards from the hoofs of my brother's horse, I had insisted that Ralph lie as still as a statue while I undressed him and ran my tongue and the long tresses of my hair all over his body. He had groaned with desire and with the conflicting pain of the struggle to lie still. In sweet revenge, he had laid me on the grass and kissed me lingeringly all over, in every unexplored sensitive crevice of my naked body. Only when I was actually weeping with longing did he slide into me.

Remembering that pleasure made me burn with a wet heat and I glanced sideways at my brother in sudden dislike that he should interrupt my summer with Ralph now the bracken stood high to hide us, and only a soaring peregrine falcon could see with his sharp black eyes our secret nakedness.

I said suddenly, 'I have to go, Harry. I am not well. It is one of my headaches.'

He looked at me with quick concern. I felt a passing pity at his tender gullibility.

'Beatrice! Let me take you home.'

'No, no,' I said, maintaining the pretence. 'You enjoy your ride. I shall go to Meg's house and have some of her feverfew tea. That always cures them.'

I cut short his protests and anxiety by turning my horse back down the way we had come. I felt his eyes upon me and drooped in the saddle as if every step jolted my aching head. But once I was under the shelter of the beech trees, and out of sight, I sat up and swung along at a good pace back down the track. I took the short cut to Meg's cottage – not up the drive but a neat little jump over the park wall – and then a brisk canter alongside the Fenny to where the little heap of a house slumbered in the sunshine. Ralph was sitting outside, his dog outstretched beside him, knotting a cord into a snare. At the very sight of him my heart twisted inside me. He heard the horse's hoofbeats and laid his work aside. His smile as he walked to the gate to meet me was warm and easy.

'Shaken off your high and mighty brother then?' he asked. 'I felt I was dirt on the road compared to him.'

54

I had no answering smile. The contrast between the two of them was too painful.

'We rode on the downs,' I said. 'Near our places. I missed you too much. Let's go to the mill.'

He nodded as if accepting an order and the smile had gone from his eyes. I tied the mare to the gate and followed him along the little path. As soon as he was inside the door he turned, took me in his arms and started to say something, but I dragged him down to the straw and said urgently, 'Just do it, Ralph.'

Then my anger and my sadness melted as I felt the familiar, ever new pleasure starting to warm me. He kissed me hard with an anger and sorrow of his own, and then opened the front of my gown at the neck. With shaking fingers I untied the leather thongs at the front lap of his breeches while he fumbled among the layers of petticoats under my riding habit. I said impatiently, 'Let me!' and swept the habit and petticoats off over my head.

Naked, I spread myself under him and shivered with pleasure as his weight came down on me. We were panting like hounds, hard-pressed. My hands gripped his buttocks forcing him into me, and in some distant recess in my head I could hear my sobbing whimper of pleasure settle into a rhythm of sighs that matched the rocking of our loving bodies. Then the great half-door swung wide open and a white wall of brilliant sunshine fell on us like a physical blow. For a second we were frozen with shock and terror, Ralph twisting round and me peeping white-faced over his shoulder.

In the sunlit archway stood my brother, his eyes blinking in the gloom, peering at the sight of his naked sister impaled by lust on a dirty threshing floor. For a split second nothing moved, like an obscene tableau, then Ralph leaped off me. I rolled to one side, crouching for my clothes and Ralph hitched his leather breeches over his hard nakedness. Still no one spoke. The silence lasted a lifetime. I stood, my new riding habit clutched to my naked breasts, staring at my brother in a sort of terror.

Then Harry gave a choking cry and rushed at Ralph with his riding whip upraised. Ralph was heavier and taller, and had been fighting village lads since he could walk. He fended Harry off and Harry's wild blows with the whip fell only on his arms and shoulders. But then a cut across his cheek slashed him into anger and he jerked the whip from Harry, thumped him hard in the belly and tripped him roughly to the floor. Harry thudded down on his back and a sharp kick from Ralph's foot into the crutch made him scissor together in a ball. He cried out, I thought in pain, and I called urgently, 'Ralph. No!'

But then my brother's face lifted from the dusty straw and I saw his angelic smile and the haze of his blue eyes. My blood ran cold as I recognized Harry's blissful expression of happiness as he lay in the dirt at Ralph's feet and gazed slavishly up the length of his tall body and at the whip in his hand. He shifted his body in the dust and crawled towards Ralph's bare feet.

'Beat me,' he said in a begging, childish voice. 'Oh please, beat me.'

As Ralph's incredulous eyes met mine in the dawning realization that we would escape scot-free, I knew at last why my brother had been expelled and the mark Dr Yately's school had left on him for life.

Ralph's light flicks of the whip slapped Harry's well-cut jacket and breeches and Harry tightened his grip on Ralph's naked foot and gave a sharp cry then a shuddering sigh of pleasure. The future Master of Wideacre sobbed like a baby with his face buried in dirty straw, his hands cupping a labourer's foot. Ralph and I looked at each other in utter silence.

That silence lasted, it seemed, all summer. My brother no longer dogged my footsteps, walked in my shadow, hung around the stables while I watched my horse being groomed, trailed behind me when I walked in the garden, sat at my side in the parlour in the evening. Now he followed Ralph. My father was pleased that Harry should be out on our land and not wandering around the house or sitting indoors. Slowly Harry learned the fields, the woods and the River Fenny as he followed in Ralph's footsteps as faithfully as Ralph's new black spaniel puppy. As Ralph checked the coverts, scattered grain for the game birds, set wire-noose traps and noted the fox holes and the badgers' dens Harry shadowed him, learning, in the course of his faithful pursuits, the secrets of Wideacre I had learned as a child.

I was free of him at last, but Ralph and I were impossibly awkward when we met in my brother's silent, sharp-eyed presence. Even on the few days when I rode out early to see Ralph before Harry was up, we did not embrace with the old passion. I felt chilly and tense and Ralph was stoical and silent. I felt as if at any moment my brother might come upon us and might again crawl to Ralph's feet for a beating. I could not even ask Ralph if he and my brother . . .? If on their long wanderings around the estate they, too, paused in sheltered hollows and . . .? Whether when Ralph's untrained puppy rolled on its back after a beating, Ralph turned to Harry with the whip still raised and . . .? I could not. I could not picture the two of them together; I could not find words for the questions I longed to ask, but did not dare.

Perhaps I should have felt jealous, but I felt nothing. The magical summer of Ralph, the dark god, seemed to be over. It had ended like the magic it was, as soon as it had begun. It ended for me on the drive on that hot day when Ralph pulled his forelock to my brother and my brother had not even noticed. Ralph had taught me about pleasure, and to keep my heart well guarded, but there could be no future for us. He was one of our people, a servant, and I was a lady of Wideacre. When I rode to hounds on a hunter of my own, or took the carriage to church, or walked over our fields, I should not want to see Ralph slouching beside a hedge smiling at me with his secret, knowing smile. It was not jealousy but a sharp sense of caste that made me hate that smile when I saw it directed at my brother; when I saw the gamekeeper's lad with the next Master at his beck and call.

So I saw little of Ralph in the following weeks and he did not seek me. He smiled that secret smile at me once when I was driving down the lane to Acre beside Mama in the carriage, and I thought I saw behind his velvety black eyes some message. It was as if he were waiting for something. For a chance to speak freely with me, for an opportunity to turn a long-considered idea into words. But he was a country boy and believed in waiting for the right season.

In any case, his time was taken up with a sudden increase in poaching. The price of mutton had soared sky high after an epidemic of foot rot in the spring, and even our own tenants were not respecting our coverts. Pheasant after pheasant went missing and at every meal Harry spoke of Ralph's plans to catch the poachers and praised Ralph's determination and daring.

57

It was a dangerous job. The penalty for poaching is death by hanging and the men driven to it are desperate men. Many a poacher has added murder to his crimes – clubbing down a gamekeeper who had recognized him. Ralph kept his guns constantly primed and carried a heavy stick. His two dogs – the black lurcher and the black spaniel puppy – scouted before and behind him, as much to protect their master as the pheasants.

At breakfast, dinner and tea we had enthusiastic accounts from Harry as to how the war against the poachers was going, and how Ralph's assistance to the gamekeeper was making all the difference. Then when Bellings, the keeper, fell sick with the flux, Harry was urgent that Ralph be paid an extra two shillings a week and given the job until the older man was well again.

'He's very young,' said my papa cautiously. 'I think it might be wiser to bring in an older man until Bellings is well.'

'No one knows the estate better than Ralph, Papa,' said Harry confidently. 'And although he is young he is fully grown and as strong as an ox. You should see how easily he throws me when we wrestle! I don't think any other person could do the job better.'

'Well,' said my papa tolerantly, his eyes on Harry's bright face, 'you'll be the Master here when I am gone. Appoint a young keeper like Ralph and you will work with him for all your lives probably. I'm happy to take your advice on this.'

My eyes flickered to Papa's face and then back to my plate. Only a few weeks ago Papa would have asked me what I thought. Then I would have praised Ralph to the skies, for I adored him. Now I was not so sure. He had my brother in utter thrall, and my ears had pricked up at the mention of their wrestling bouts. It sounded like Staveley all over again. And for some reason, I could not have said why, I feared the idea of Ralph having such a hold on Harry's impulsive heart.

'I need someone to check the sheep today,' said Papa, looking down the table with his eyes equally on Harry and me.

'I'll go,' said Harry, 'but I must be done by dinner. Ralph has found a kestrel's nest and I am going after it this afternoon before the hen lays a second brood.'

'I'll go,' I said. 'They'll need to be checked for foot rot and you will not recognize the signs, Harry.'

Papa beamed, unconscious of the latent jealousy in my voice.

'It seems I have two bailiffs then!' he said, pleased. 'What d'you say, ma'am?'

Mama smiled, too. At last everything was falling into what she saw as its proper place. Only I was still intractable.

'Harry should go,' she said sweetly. 'I need Beatrice to cut some flowers this morning, and this afternoon she may come with me and pay some calls.'

My eyes flew to Papa's face in an instinctive, silent appeal. But he was not looking at me. Now his son was home our easy, loving comradeship had taken second place. He was watching Harry learning his way around the land with as much love and interest as he had shown when he had been teaching me. There was pride as well as love in his eyes when he looked at his tall, golden son. He saw Harry growing, broadening and developing from the milksop mother's boy into a young man. And he saw in him the future Master of Wideacre.

'Harry can go then,' he said with careless cruelty. 'I'll ride out with you, Harry, and show you what foot rot looks like. If Beatrice is right and you do not know, then it's high time you learned. Wideacre is not all play, you know!'

'I wanted to ride today,' I said, my voice small and my face mutinous.

Papa looked at me and he laughed as if my disappointment and pain were funny.

'Ah, Beatrice!' he said with casual, worthless affection. 'You must learn to be a young lady now. I have taught you all I know on the land. Your mama must teach you all you need to know in the house. Then you can rule your husband in and out of doors!' He laughed again and Mama's little tinkling laugh told me I had been beaten.

Harry learned to spot foot rot from Papa and he also used the time to persuade Papa that Ralph and Meg should be rehoused. When I heard him mention it at tea, I could not keep a still tongue in my head.

'Nonsense,' I exclaimed. 'Ralph and Meg do very well in their little cottage. It's practically rent-free as it is, and Meg is a sluttish housekeeper. The straw roof is blowing away because Ralph is too lazy to glean straw to rethatch it and Meg is too idle to care. They've no call to be rehoused. Meg would not know what to do with a good house.'

My father nodded his agreement, but he looked to Harry. The way his eyes strayed from me cut me to the bone. He was looking at his successor, his heir, measuring his judgement. My opinion as the daughter of the house might be right or wrong, it hardly mattered. But Harry's judgement mattered very much, for on him the future would depend. He was the male heir.

Papa had not ceased to love me. I knew that. But I had lost his attention. He had broken the thread of our constant companionship that had held me ever since he first took my pony on a leading rein and that had kept my mare to his horse's shoulder ever after. Now there was another horse riding beside my papa: the future Squire's.

I might ride my mare, or practise the piano, or paint little pictures, it hardly mattered. I was the daughter of the house. I was just passing through. My future lay elsewhere.

And while Harry had Papa's ear, Ralph had Harry's. And if I knew Ralph he would use that influence for his own ends. Only I could see clearly into Ralph's mind. Only I knew the longing for the land. Only I knew how it felt to be an outsider in your own home, on your own land. Forever longing to belong and to be secure. Forever denied.

'Ralph's a first-rate man,' Harry said firmly. He had lost most of his quiet diffidence but still had his gentle voice and manners. He was openly disagreeing with me, without a thought in the world that I might be irritated or angry. 'It would be a shame to lose him and there are many landlords who would pay him more and house him better, too. I think he should have the Tyacke cottage when the old man dies. It's a handy cottage and near to the coverts.'

I nearly exploded with anger at my brother's stupidity. 'Nonsense! Tyacke's cottage is worth £150 a year and the entry fee to a new tenant is £100. We can't throw money like that away on Ralph's convenience. We could repair his old cottage or move him into a small cottage in the village, but the Tyacke cottage is out of the question. Why, it's practically a house! What would Ralph or Meg want with a front parlour – they'd only use it to keep the pheasant chicks in.'

My mother, stone-deaf to the discussion, heard only the tone of my voice and it roused her from her habitual indifference.

'Beatrice, decorum,' she said automatically. 'And don't interfere with business, dear.'

I ignored the caution, but my father nodded at me to be silent.

'I'll consider it, Harry,' he said. 'Ralph is a good man, you're right. I'll look into it. He's reliable with pheasants and foxes and we need to keep him on the estate. Beatrice is right that the Tyacke property is a handsome cottage, but Ralph does need something more than that shack by the stream. Full of ideas Ralph is. Why, he's even got one of those mantraps for the woods. He knows his job and he works hard. I'll consider it.'

My brother nodded and smiled at me. There was no malice or triumph in his smile. His friendship with Ralph had brought him a new confidence but no arrogance. His smile was still that of a cherubic schoolboy, his eyes still the clear blue of a happy child.

'He will be pleased,' he said serenely.

I realized then that this was Ralph's idea, Ralph's arguments, Ralph's very words. He had given me pleasure and possessed me, but he held my brother in the palm of his hand. Through my brother he could influence my father and I knew, because I knew Ralph, that he was after more than the pretty little Tyacke cottage to rent. He was after land, and then more land. More to the point, he was after our land. Few people ever move more than five miles from the village where they are born. Ralph was born on Wideacre land; he would die here. If he wanted land, it was our land he was after. The cottage was just a first step for him and I could not imagine where his hunger would end. I understood it as clearly as I understood myself. I would have done anything, committed any crime, any sin, to own our fields and woods. With a growing fear I wondered if Ralph also had the same desire, and how my besotted brother would ever stand against him.

I excused myself from the table and slipped out to the stables, ignoring my mother's murmured instructions. I needed to see Ralph, no longer as a lover needs to see the man she loves, but to see if I could feel in him the passion for the land that he had seen in me. If he wanted Wideacre as much as I wanted it – the serene and lovely house, the warm gardens, the folds of the hills and the rich, peaty earth with the silver traces of sand – then my family was lost. Harry's enthusiasm would admit a cuckoo that would throw us mercilessly to one side and claim the golden kingdom for himself. My mare trotted swiftly down the track to the cottage that was suddenly not good enough for Ralph, and then shied, nearly unseating me, as a bush near the path swayed and rustled.

'Ralph!' I said. 'You nearly had me off!'

He grinned. 'You should ride on a tighter rein, Beatrice.'

I turned the head of my horse and urged her forward so I could see what Ralph was doing. He was pegging out the jaws of a huge mantrap, a vicious weapon, on to the ground. It yawned like a great clam, custom-made in a London workshop for the protection of the gentry's sport. Nearly four feet wide, made of sharpened, spiky iron with a spring as quick as the crack of a whip.

'What a horrid thing,' I said. 'Why aren't you putting it on the path?'

'I can see the path from the cottage,' said Ralph. 'They know that. Just here, before the path bends, they creep through the bushes to get to the pheasants roosting. I've seen the prints of their boots. I reckon this will give them a welcome they weren't expecting.'

'Does it kill a man?' I asked, visualizing the jaws snapping shut.

'Can do,' said Ralph, unconcerned. 'Depends on his luck. In the great estates in the north they stake them out round the walls and check them once a week. If a man is caught, he may bleed to death before the keeper comes round. Your father wouldn't allow such a thing here. If the man is lucky, he has two broken legs; if he is unlucky and it has cut a vital path of blood, he bleeds to death.'

'Won't you be there quick enough to save him?' I asked, repelled by the weapon spread like a deadly invitation in the leaves.

'Nay,' Ralph drawled, unconcerned. 'You've seen me cut a deer's throat. You know how quick an animal dies when the blood is gushing. It's the same with a man. But chances are they'll just walk a little slowly for the rest of their days.'

'You'd better warn your mother,' I cautioned.

Ralph laughed. 'She was away as soon as she saw it,' he said. 'She's fey, you know. Said it smelled of death. Begged me to have nothing to do with it.' He glanced at me sideways. 'I sleep alone here during the afternoons and I watch at night.'

I ignored the unspoken invitation, though a prickling on my skin reminded me of what a long afternoon in Ralph's cottage would have meant in the time that had gone.

'You're very thick with Master Harry,' I said.

He nodded. 'He's learning his way round the woods,' he said. 'He's got no feeling for the land like you, but he'll make a good enough Squire in time with the right bailiff.'

'We've never had a bailiff,' I said swiftly. 'We don't have bailiffs at Wideacre.'

Ralph, still kneeling, gave me a long, cool look. His eyes were as bright and sharp as the teeth of the trap.

'Maybe the next Squire will have a bailiff,' he said slowly. 'Maybe that bailiff will know the land well, better than the Master even. Maybe that bailiff will love the land and be a good Master to it, better than the Squire himself. Isn't that the Master the land should have? Isn't that the sort of man you'd like to see here, at your side?'

I slid off my mare and hitched the reins to a low branch, carefully away from the trap.

'Let's walk to the river,' I said. 'Leave that.'

Ralph kicked a few more concealing leaves over the trap and turned to follow me. I swayed towards him as we walked and my cheek brushed his shoulder. We walked in silence. The River Fenny, our river, is a sweet clean trout stream you can drink in safety over every inch of our land. The salmon reach this far in summer, and you can always have a trout or a bowlful of eels for half an hour's netting. The pebbles here are golden and the river is a streak of silver in the sunlight with mysterious amber pools under the shades of the trees. We watched the endless flow of water over the stones and said in unison, 'Look! A trout!' and smiled that we should speak together. Our eyes met in a shared love of the trout, the river and the sweet Sussex earth. The days of absence slid away from us, and we smiled.

'I was born and bred here,' Ralph said suddenly. 'My father

and his parents and their parents have been working this land for as long as we can trace back. That gives me some rights.'

The river babbled quietly.

A fallen tree trunk spanned the river. I stepped on to it and sat, my legs dangling over the water. Ralph balanced down the trunk and leaned against one of the branches looking at me.

'I can see my way clear now,' he said quietly. 'I can see my way clear through to the land and the pleasure. D'you remember, Beatrice, when we spoke that first time? The land and the pleasure for both of us.'

A trout plopped in the river behind him, but he didn't turn his head. He watched me as close as my owl watched me at night, as if to read my thoughts. I looked up, a slanting, sliding glance out of the corner of my tilted eyes.

'The same land and the same pleasure. We share them both?'

He nodded. 'You'd do anything to be Mistress of Wideacre, wouldn't you, Beatrice? You'd give anything you owned, make any sacrifice there was, to be the Mistress in the Hall and be able to ride over the land every day of your life and say, "This is mine."'

'Yes,' I said.

'But you'll be sent away,' he said. 'You're not a child any more. You can tell what your future will be – sent to London and married to a stranger who will take you far away, perhaps to a different county. The land, the weather and the farming will be all different. The hay won't smell the same; the earth won't be the same colour. The milk and cheese will taste different. Harry will marry some high-bred girl who will come and queen it here and take your mother's place. You'll be lucky if you're allowed a visit once a year at Christmas.'

I said nothing. The picture was too clear, all too likely. Ralph had been planning while I had been dreaming. Everything he said was right. I would be sent away. Harry would marry. Wideacre would not be my home for ever; I would be far away in some unknown part of the country. Perhaps, even worse, I would have to live with some fashionable husband in London and never smell new-mown hay again. I said nothing, but I hurt inside and I was afraid.

The bedroom my mama would not redecorate for me, the

warning my papa had given me, the love they both showed for Harry all told me, as clear as a tolling bell, where I was going. I was on my way to exile, and all my will and all my passion could not save me.

Ralph turned his head from my shocked face and watched the stream. The slim, silver trout was finning gently, nose pointing upstream as the sweet water flowed all over him.

'There is a way to stay here and be the Lady of Wideacre,' he said slowly. 'It is a long and crooked way, but we win the land and the pleasure.'

'How?' I said. The ache of loneliness in my belly made my voice as quiet and as low as his. He turned back to me and sat beside me, our heads together like conspirators.

'When Harry inherits you stay beside him. He trusts you and he trusts me,' Ralph said. 'We cheat him, you and I. As his bailiff, I can cheat him on his rents, on his land, on his harvests. I tell him we have to pay more taxes and I bank the difference. I tell him we need special seed corn, special animals, and I bank the difference. You cheat him on his accounting. In his wages for the house servants, the house management, the home farm, the stables, the dairy, the brewery. You know how it could be done better than I.' He waited and I nodded. I knew. I had been involved in the running of the estate since my earliest years when Harry was away at school or staying with relatives. I knew I could cheat him of a fortune in the household accounts alone. With Ralph acting with me I calculated that Harry would be bankrupt inside three years.

'We ruin him.' Ralph's voice was a whisper, mingling with the clatter of the stream. 'You'll have a jointure protected, or probably a dower house protected, or funds. Your income is safe, but we make him bankrupt. With the money we've saved I buy the estate from him. And then I'm the Master here and you're what you deserve to be, the Mistress of the finest estate and house in England, the Squire's Lady, the Mistress of Wideacre.'

'And Harry?' I asked, my voice cold.

Ralph spat contemptuously to the riverbank. 'He's clay to anyone's moulding,' he said. 'He'll fall in love with a pretty girl, or maybe a pretty boy. He could hang himself or become a poet.

He could live in London or go to Paris. He'll have some money from the sale; he won't starve.' He smiled. 'He can visit us if you like. I don't think of Harry.'

I smiled in return, but my heart was beating faster with mingled hope and anger.

'It could work,' I said, neutrally.

'It would,' he said. 'I have been many nights planning.'

I thought of him, hidden among the ferns in the woods, his dark eyes staring brightly into the darkness, watching for poachers and yet looking beyond the shadows to the future when there would be no cold, uncomfortable nights. When other men, paid men, would do his watching for him, and he could drink and dine and stand before a roaring fire and speak of the slackness of servants and the problems with rent rolls, and the state of the crops, and the incompetence of the government; and gentlemen would listen to him and agree.

'It would work, except for one thing,' I said.

Ralph waited.

'My father's healthy, strong as an ox. He could sire another son tomorrow and provide the child with trustees and guardians. Apart from that possibility, Harry may be fascinated with you now, but I doubt you'll hold him for twenty years. My father's forty-nine. He could live another forty years. By the time he's dead, I'll have been married thirty-five years to some fat old Scottish nobleman with a pack of barefoot children, maybe future dukes and duchesses, and probably grandchildren on the way too. Harry's wife, whoever she may be, will have settled in nicely, growing fat and comfortable with two new heirs out of short clothes. The most you can hope for is Tyacke's cottage. And the most I can hope for', my voice quavered on a sob, 'is exile.'

Ralph nodded. 'Aye,' he said. 'That's the difficulty. It would work, but it would only work now, this summer. If it's to happen it's got to be done while Harry's at a loose end, trailing around after me, or mooning around after you. In love with both of us and afraid of both of us. It has to be now while we are land-hungry and love-hungry. I don't want to wait, Beatrice.'

His eyes on my face were bright. He was in love with me and with my land, a heady mixture for a labourer, the son of a labouring man. But the bleak reality of my life away from Wideacre as it must be, as it was bound to be, was a stark contrast to this dream future that Ralph saw, that Ralph thought we could win: as Lady of Wideacre.

'My father looks well,' I said drily.

There was a long pause as our eyes met in clear mutual knowledge of how far we were prepared to go to achieve Ralph's dream, my dream.

'There are accidents.' Ralph's words fell into a silence as ominous and deep as the still millpond. Like a stone tossed in deep water the idea spread widening ripples in my mind. I measured the appalling loss of my beloved, my delightful, papa against the certainty of my loss of Wideacre.

The precious, essential presence of my vital, noisy papa against the certain loneliness and coldness of my exile, which would come as surely as my sixteenth birthday would come, and at much the same time. I looked at Ralph unsmiling.

'Accidents,' I said flatly.

'It could happen tomorrow,' he said, as cold as me.

I nodded. My mind searched like a skilled spinner over a tangled skein of wool to find the ideas and threads of ideas that would lead me through a maze of sin and crime, and out of the maze into the broad sunshine of my home. I measured in silence how much I needed my papa against how much I needed that security; considered Harry's infatuation with Ralph and how far it would lead him. Thought of my mama and how the loss of my father would make me more vulnerable to her, but ever and again came back to that picture of me in a comfortless northern castle far away from the land where I belonged, pining my heart out for the sound of a Wideacre morning. Always seeing my papa's profile as he turned his face from me to watch his son. He had betrayed me before I ever dreamed of betraying him. I sighed. There could only ever have been one answer.

'It could work,' I said again.

'It would work now,' Ralph corrected me. 'Harry could change in a year, in a couple of months. If he is sent away to prepare for university we will both lose our hold on him. It would work only this summer. It would work tomorrow.'

'Tomorrow?' I said with a flash of irritation. 'You say tomorrow. Do you really mean tomorrow?'

Ralph's dark eyes were black with the knowledge of what we were saying.

'Yes,' he said. 'I do.'

I gave a gasp. 'Why so soon?' I said in instinctive fear. Yet my heart had leapt at the thought of moving quickly, of securing my future in an instant; of making something happen at once.

'Why wait?' said Ralph with cruel logic. 'Nothing will change for me. I trust your mettle, Beatrice. If you are for Wideacre, if you wish to live there, if you are as determined as I think you are – why wait?' His eyes were narrowed, measuring me, and I knew that together we were an explosive combination of elements. Without me this plan would never have been in his mind. Without me it could not have worked. Without his urgent pressure I could not have gone ahead. We led each other on like a pair of falling angels spinning down into hell. I breathed a deep sigh to slow the pace of my heart. The river bubbled neutrally beneath us.

~ 4 ~

I woke with a jolt in the pearl-grey light of a summer dawn and knew that today I had to do something – that I had woken myself early because I had something to do. But for a few dozy, sleep-drenched moments I could not for the life of me recall what it was. Then I gave a little gasp as yesterday came back to me – bright as an enamelled picture – Ralph and me sitting with the Fenny flowing beneath us, talking madness, talking death, talking treason.

Ralph had caught me while I was off balance; he had touched me on the raw of my jealous, exclusive heart, which says – which always said – 'Love me. Love me only.' The sight of my papa loving someone else, choosing another to ride with him, to chat with him, to run the land with him, had thrown me into such churning rage that I simply wanted to lash out – to hurt everyone as much as I was hurt. If I could have dropped Harry dead to the ground with a wish, I would have done so, for usurping my place with Papa. But the deep core of my resentful grief was directed against the father who had turned against me, the fickle and worthless man, after I had loved him without fail and without faltering for all of my life. It was his lack of fidelity to me that laid me open to any alliance. It was his failure to honour the love and trust between us that sent me spinning, rootless, amoral, into the world where any chance thought or vengeful plan could catch and hold me. It was as if I had sworn him fealty and he had broken his oath as liege lord. Disappointment and grief were the least of it – I had been betrayed.

And Ralph had made my counter-attack sound so easy. Ralph had made it sound so gentle. Ralph had made it sound so sensible. A well-schemed, cool-headed plan anyone would be wise to undertake. So logical that I could not fault it. It would work. It

69

would give me what I needed – Wideacre – and it would revenge me for the pain my papa had caused me.

I shook my head on the pillow in the grey light of my white-washed bedroom. I had been mad for a few seconds there, back on the tree trunk with Ralph's persuasive voice gentle in my ear. I had been mad to listen and doubly mad to appear to consent. The thought of my papa in pain and realizing at last that he needed me was a sweet picture. The thought of him magically gone, and Harry magically gone, leaving me alone, in sole control, was another fine picture. But I was not fool enough to think such things could happen because I willed them. They were the dreams of a hurt child. I had been dangerously close to believing them.

To set such a course in motion was madness, and yesterday I had been mad with my jealousy and fear of the future. But today, with the dew falling and the sun not yet hot and the birds not yet singing, was another day. As soon as the servants were up and had unbolted the kitchen doors I should slip down to Meg's cottage in the woods and tap on Ralph's window and tell him I did not mean it. I would not have long to wait for they work long hours in the kitchen and the youngest maid would be stoking the kitchen fire and bringing in the logs in less than an hour. Until she opened the back door I could not get out without leaving an unbolted door behind me, and that would lead to questions that might take some answering. I had only to wait a few minutes, slip on some clothes, tiptoe downstairs and slide out while her back was turned. If Ralph had been out for poachers last night I might even meet him on his way home.

I snuggled a little lower under the covers, relishing the warmth in the knowledge that in a few moments I would have to leave the cosy softness of my bed and get dressed in a cold room and washed in cold water. I would set things right with Ralph and we would think of some other way. Perhaps things would come right of their own accord. If Harry left early for university, or even went to stay with some of Mama's family for a few weeks, I would have the time to win back Papa's attention. He might turn from me now, but I knew in his heart he loved me. He would tire of Harry; he would tire of teaching him. He would want the wordless instinctive companionship he and I had developed over years of riding the land together. Then he would look for me, and I would be at his side, and Harry would be the one who was left out and unwanted. Comforted by the thought I dozed and woke to check the brightness of the window. I listened for the kitchen maid but there was no sound. It was too early. If I fell asleep I would wake the moment I heard the back door open or the girl bring the logs in. I dozed, then I slid into a deeper sleep.

I awoke with a jump to see my window bright with early morning sunshine and my bedroom door opening as my maid brought in hot water for me to wash and an early morning cup of chocolate.

'You slept late, Miss Beatrice,' she said cheerily and clattered the cup at my bedside table. I threw back the covers and ran to the window. It was full day.

'What time is it, Lucy?' I asked urgently, splashing water on my face and throwing off my shift.

'Eight o'clock,' she said, as if it did not matter. As if it did not matter at all.

I gasped. Pointless to reproach myself for oversleeping on this one vital morning. 'Help me,' I said peremptorily. 'I'm in a dreadful hurry.'

She moved like a dolt but I was dressed in minutes and racing down the stairs to the hall. No need for the kitchen door; the front door stood wide open. I caught sight of my papa eating his breakfast as I dashed past. He called good morning to me and I called back but did not stop. There still might be time to catch Ralph.

There still might be time, I thought as I ran, through the rose garden, through the little gate, across the paddock, the burrs catching at my long skirt, which I held bunched up in one hand. Then I was in the wood and settled down to a steady pace along the riverbank. A hundred things could delay Ralph at home and make him late setting out today. If he had been out late last night he might oversleep as I had. If he had stayed out all night he might now be having breakfast before going out again. He might still be out and on his way home. Or – and I had some faith in this – he might know, as lovers and young people often do know, that I was desperate and anxious; he might be waiting for me because he could somehow sense my urgency to see him, to tell him I had changed my mind, that I had been mad for a few moments – for an afternoon and a night only! – and that I knew now, as I had always known really, that of course my papa was sacred. On his own land he was the Squire and could not be touched. As my papa he was my dearest love – dearer to me than my own life I thought. What I said against him was spoken out of grief and hurt. I had never meant it for more than one foolish afternoon and one night.

My breath was coming in gasps and my tight-fitted dress was soaked with sweat under my arms and down my back but I did not dare stop. I thought I was as fit as a hunter in training but I was hampered by my skirts and by the rough ground under my boots. And it is a long way. But I did not dare stop. At this very moment Ralph might be pulling a jacket on, reaching for his cap and going out into the woods where I could not find him.

I had not asked him for a plan so I did not know, had no idea where he would then go. How he planned to meet my father, how he planned to do the act to which I consented – but did not mean. So I gasped at the burning pain under my ribs and panted for breath but ran on. It was like one of those nightmares when you run faster and faster but can get no purchase on the earth. My beloved Wideacre earth seemed to be turning to clay underneath my boots and though my legs were running I could feel that I was slowing, slowing; that my strides were not so long, that they were not so quick. I was losing time because I could not run, because I could not fly, and every second that passed might make the difference between seeing Ralph at the edge of the wood at the back of his cottage – or not seeing him at all.

I burst into the sunlight by the little cottage, speechless with lack of breath, banged through the garden gate and staggered, half drunkenly, up to the front door. I thumped on it with both clenched fists, then doubled up on the threshold whooping for breath, near sick with the strain of running so hard and so far. I heard footsteps inside and I felt dizzy with relief that I was in time. It would be all right. I had caught him, and the madness of yesterday's conversation would be something we would both laugh about in a few moments. When he would say, 'You did not think I really would have?' and I would be able to laugh and laugh and say, 'No, of course not.' The door opened, and there was Meg.

'Meg!' I said, my face aghast, peering past her into the gloom. 'Where's Ralph?'

'Gone out,' she said, her dark eyes blank to conceal her curiosity, her face impassive at the sight of the Squire's daughter, wet with sweat, hair down her back, gasping on the doorstep.

I gaped at her as if she had signed my death warrant. Death indeed. Death I thought it was.

'Where?' I asked. I was still panting and could say only one or two words.

She shrugged, still carefully incurious. 'Into the woods,' she said. 'Towards the common, I think.'

I put my face in my hands. I could not think. I had been so sure that if I had run without pausing, had punished myself with such a merciless pace, I would certainly catch him. Or that he would somehow know. That, in any case, the dream of a vengeful child does not become reality. That I could count on the world's not being such that if I wished something it would happen.

Meg left me abruptly and came back with an earthenware beaker filled with water in her hand. I took it and drank it without seeing or tasting. I had overslept. I had run as fast as I could. But Ralph had gone.

The sun was hot on the side of my face; I could feel sweat on my scalp and my face was wet with it. I sat numb and unmoving and cold with horror.

'Did he take his gun?' I asked, my voice bleak.

'No, nor the dogs,' Meg replied, nodding towards the two of them tied up by a shack that was their kennel.

No gun. My mind seized on that like a hopeful omen. Perhaps it meant he had known when he woke this morning, as I had known, that it was all madness, all folly. That we had been talking, as children will talk, about what they would like to do. Or what they would do if they could. He had not taken his gun. Perhaps he had just gone out to check the traps. Perhaps my father was safe.

My father.

I suddenly realized that my father could be perfectly safe. Ralph was somewhere out there, but inside the house my papa was utterly secure. With me, he was absolutely safe. Indeed, if he was with anyone Ralph would not touch him, but leave the

73

execution of the plan for another day. Ralph would certainly come home this afternoon or evening. I could see him then and tell him that I had changed my mind. All I had to do was to ensure that my papa did not ride alone today. And I could do it by merely asking if I might ride with him. He was safe. And I could save him.

'Tell Ralph I want to see him urgently,' I said peremptorily to Meg. I got to my feet and found I swayed a little with dizziness. I ignored it and went through the garden and back to the path along the riverbank where I had dashed in such terror only a few minutes before. My breathing was back to normal and I walked briskly, the sun shining in my face. I walked a little faster. Worry snapped at my heels like a black dog. I had left my papa at breakfast and he had the morning papers; the post had not yet come. I could be fairly sure he would not have finished his meal by the time I got back to the Hall. Or could I? I quickened my pace a little, my heart thudding faster again, not at the speed but at the dawning of fear.

He would almost certainly wait for his letters. He might even be waiting for me to return. With a little luck I should walk up the path through the rose garden and see him standing on the terrace, sniffing at the air and smoking a cigar with the morning paper under his arm. The thought of him there was so clear in my mind I could almost smell the blue cigar smoke drifting on the air. I dropped into a trot. He was there, I had a certainty he was there. Looking at the roses, wondering what took me out of the house in such a tearing hurry, and waiting for the boy to come back with the mail from the early coach from London. The trot speeded into a run. I knew he was there, but I had been so frightened today that I wanted to see him. I wanted to race up to him, even hot and dishevelled and sweaty as I was, and feel his strong heavy arm around me in a hard hug, so I could know for certain, know for sure, he was safe. That I could not possibly harm him. Even if I had wanted to. I had a sharp pain under one of my ribs that made every breath a little gasp as a red-hot needle pricked me with each step. And I could feel an ominous tightening in my calf muscle. Although I knew, I *knew*, he was safe, it seemed some sort of magic that I should run as fast as I could. I was not in terror for him, but I would not feel easy until I saw him, until I could take his arm and say, 'Today, I shall ride with you all day.' Or even say to stupid Harry, 'If you are riding with Papa today you must be with him all the time, and you must promise that.' Harry would promise, and Harry would keep his word. So my papa was safe. I just needed to see him.

I was running as fast as I could again, and the bushes were tearing at my skirt and the noise from the Fenny, rippling beside the path, was as loud as the thudding of my heart, and the thundering of my boots on the soft earth. I raced over the fallen tree that made a bridge to the paddock gate, tore it open and banged it behind me. With sweat in my eyes I could not see the terrace clearly and the run had given me dancing flecks before my eyes as if I was looking through a veil. Papa was on the terrace, I was sure of it. I could not see him, but I felt he was there. There safe. And Ralph might wait in the woods all day and it would not matter.

At the gate to the rose garden I blinked to clear my eyes and scanned the front of the house. I could not see him, but the front door stood wide open; he might that moment have gone back inside for another cigar or another cup of chocolate. I trotted along the flagged path, looking towards the front door, expecting to see him at any moment, strolling out into the sunshine unfolding the paper and heading for one of the stone seats. I was up the steps and into the hall so quickly I was blinded by the darkness after the brightness of the sun outside.

'Where's Papa?' I asked one of the maids, a tray in her hands coming from the breakfast parlour.

'Gone, Miss Beatrice,' she said, dipping a curtsy. 'Gone out riding.'

I stared at her disbelievingly. This could not be happening. All there had been was one little rolling pebble of an idea and it was growing and growing into what threatened to become an avalanche.

'Gone riding?' I said incredulously.

She looked at me a little oddly. Since Papa rode every morning of his life my tone of horror must have sounded strange.

'Yes, Miss Beatrice,' she said. 'He left about a quarter of an hour ago.'

I turned on my heel then and went to the front door. I could have called for a horse from the stables and ridden desperately down the drive, or spent the day chasing round the estate looking for Ralph or for my papa, or for both of them. But I felt like a sailor must when he has been throwing ballast over the side, and pumping out water, and yet still the ship is sinking. The luck was all against me today. It might be the luck was all against my papa also. He had ridden out this sunny morning on to his land where a murderer might be waiting for him. And there was nothing I could do. Nothing. Nothing. Except protect myself. I slipped up the stairs to my room like a shadow. I wanted to wash and change before I met Mama or Harry. What was happening out there in the woods was beyond my control, beyond my responsibility. I had helped in the germination of a deadly seed. But it might not grow. It might not grow.

That afternoon they brought my father home. Four men shuffled slowly and stiffly at the four corners of one of the withy fences we use for penning sheep. It was bowed in the middle under his weight, and the weave was splitting. He lay on his back. His face was crumpled like a ball of parchment. The real person, my beloved, vigorous, spirited papa was gone. All they brought home to Wideacre was a heavy bundle.

They carried him through the front door and across the hall, their dirty boots marking the polished floorboards and the rich carpet. The door to the kitchens banged and half-a-dozen white faces peered. I stood motionless, holding the door as they carried him past me. There was a great crater of a wound on the side of his skull. The father I had adored was gone.

I stood like a tree frozen in mid-winter as they shuffled past me so slowly. They crept past as if it were a dream and they were wading thigh-deep in thick water. They dragged their feet as if we were locked in a nightmare and they wanted me to see the dreadful wound in my papa's head. The great, deep gash half into his skull, and inside the great hole some grainy mess of bones and blood.

And his face! His face was not like my lovely papa at all! His face was a mask of horror. His brave, bright, laughing face had gone. He had died with his teeth, yellowish, bared on a scream, and his blue eyes popping at the sight of his murderer. The colour had gone from him and he was as yellow as the sandstone of the Hall. He was a statue of horror in Wideacre stone, and the withy fence bowed under him as if the very wood could not bear the burden of this death.

The slow, clumsy march of the men passed me at last and my father's unseeing, staring blue eyes passed by me and were gone, no longer meeting my blank gaze of terror. Every step of the great staircase creaked as they humped their burden up to the master bedroom, and somewhere in the house I could hear the nagging noise of someone crying. I wished I might cry. I stood unmoving in the brightness, still holding the door, staring unseeingly at the shaft of sunlight shining on the polished floor where the mud from their boots was drying. Outside, waiting, were half-a-dozen of our tenants, the men bare-headed, the women with their aprons to their eyes.

They said his horse must have thrown him. He was found dead beside the little wall separating the park from the farmland on the northern boundary. The horse, unhurt, was grazing near by and the saddle was pulled round as if the girth had been too loose. He had set the horse at the wall and then tumbled off on the Wideacre side. The unwanted, inescapable picture of Ralph hiding in the lee of the wall and then reaching up to grab the horse's reins and to club my father with one of the stones from the wall came to my mind unbidden. The only comfort I could find was the idea that my father had died on the park side of the wall, under the trees he loved, on the land he loved. But there was no other comfort for me.

Ralph had done this. Ralph had committed this assault. This filthy attack. This dark wicked sin. While my mama wept and wept easy tears that cost her little, and Harry wandered round the house in a haze of shock, I found my mind clearing and sharpening to a point of utter hatred. Ralph had done this thing. He alone was responsible.

Aye, I had been there, on the tree trunk spanning the river. My lips had met his. I had said, 'Accident', and 'It would work', but I had not known it would be like this. I had agreed. But I had not known what I was setting in train. Ralph had known. Ralph had knifed deer, skinned hares, hand-chopped rabbits. Ralph knew all about death and he invited my consent to his dark plots while I was a mere child. I had not known. I had not understood. And when I did, it was too late. *It was not my fault*.

I did not wish my father dead! I wanted him to turn to me again with his blue eyes bright with love. I wanted him to insist once more on my company when he was rounding up sheep. I wanted him to call for me as easily and naturally as whistling his dogs. I wanted him to forget Harry and Harry's claims to the land. I wanted Harry to slip from his mind again, as Harry had gone once before. I wanted to be first in his heart again and first on Wideacre, and safe in his love and safe in the land.

Now Ralph had killed him and my papa would never love me again.

But Ralph had done worse. He had forgotten the divide. There was a gulf between Ralph and me he had forgotten. I never took him to my papa's bed; I never took him inside the Hall. He was not Quality; he was not fit to wear linen. Homespun, Ralph was, and his mother wore rags. And this lad had dared, he had *dared* to lie in wait for my bright-brave Squire papa and leap on him like a thief and bring him down. And my papa had died in pain and terror at the hands of his false servant.

Ralph should pay.

While Harry's grief and sense of loss grew, and he daily came to me for instructions and advice, and while Mama's slight tears dried and she busied herself with ordering gloves, mourning favours, mourning clothes, and funeral plans, I stayed dry-eyed and burning with hatred.

Ralph should pay.

No man touches a Lacey of Wideacre and escapes. No Lacey of Wideacre ever fell without a sword to defend him. If I could have had Ralph arrested and hanged I would have done so. But he might have accused me and I could not bear to have such horrors spoken aloud. The death of my papa was not my plan. The murder was not my act. I did *not* order it. Ralph carried me along towards it because I did not know what it meant. Now every day the memory of my father's silently screaming face would come before my eyes and the only way I could blot out that horror was to say silently, reassuringly, to myself, 'Ralph will pay.'

At the funeral service my eyes behind my dark veil were black

78

with hatred for the murderer and I said not one prayer. No Christian God could play any part in this blood that called for revenge. The Furies were after Ralph, and I was coming for him as deadly as any vengeful, thirsty goddess, hot with hatred, riding a wave of dark will.

My hatred made me sharp and cunning and nothing of my thoughts showed in my face. When the earth thudded on the lid of the coffin I drooped against Harry as if I were not rigid with anger and strong with hatred. We held hands in the coach on the way home and my grip was gentle and tender. I was saving Harry too when I wiped out this killer, this deadly parasite on our land.

Mama was weeping again and I took her hand in mine. She was cold and she did not return the squeeze I gave her. She had been withdrawn ever since the slow shuffle of feet of four men bringing Papa home, and now and then I would feel her eyes fixed on me as if she did not see me, or as if she was looking through me to some speculation of her own. Now, through the black mesh of her veil, her eyes met mine with an unusual sharpness.

'You know your papa's hunter, Beatrice,' she said suddenly in a clear voice, quite unlike her usual tentative murmur. 'How could it have thrown him so? He never fell in year after year of riding. How could he have fallen, and fallen so badly, at such a little jump?'

My hatred of Ralph kept my own conscience clear, and I met her eyes directly.

'I do not know, Mama,' I said. 'I suppose it may have been his saddle slipping. I have thought of nothing else, and of the pain he suffered. If it were the horse at fault I should order it to be shot. I would not suffer an animal to live which had injured my papa. But it was just a tragic accident.'

She nodded, her eyes still on my face.

'There will be many changes now,' she said. The carriage rocked as we turned right up the drive. 'The estate is entailed on Harry, of course. He will have to get a bailiff to run it for a while. Or do you propose to help Harry?'

'Of course I will help all I can,' I said delicately. 'We never have had a bailiff and Papa thought they were not a good idea. I

79

would prefer if we could manage without. But that is a decision for you, Mama . . . and Harry.'

She nodded. There was a pause. The horses' hoofs were muffled where the drive was carpeted with autumn leaves.

'The only thing Beatrice loved more than her father was his land,' said Mama, musingly, gazing out of the window. Harry and I exchanged a startled glance. This vague, seer-like voice was so unlike Mama. 'There never was a girl who loved her father as much as Beatrice, but she loved the land, Wideacre, even more. If she had been forced to choose between them I think she would have chosen the land. It will be a great consolation to Beatrice to think that although she has lost her papa she still has Wideacre.'

Harry's shocked blue eyes met mine.

'There, there,' he said feebly, patting Mama's black-gloved hand. 'You are upset, Mama. We all loved Papa and we all love Wideacre.'

Mama turned her gaze from the tall trunks of the trees and the fields and stared at me as if she would read the very depths of my soul. I met her eyes look for look. It was not my crime. I need take no blame for it.

'I shall help Harry as much as I can,' I repeated steadily. 'My papa will not seem so very far away. I shall do what he would wish. I shall be the daughter he deserved.'

'There, there,' said Harry, deaf to all meaning, but catching the tone of my voice. He reached out his hand to me and his other to Mama. Handfast we arrived outside the Hall and sat for a moment in silence. I swore once more, before I let their hands go, that Ralph would pay for the injury he had done us all. He would pay at once. He would pay that night.

My papa's will was read that afternoon. It was the straightforward work of an honest man. My mama had the dower house and a fair income from the estate for her life. I had a substantial dowry in money invested in the City, a home on Wideacre until my brother married, and then with my mother wherever she might choose to live. I kept my eyes on the table at this easy disposition of me and my love for the land, but my colour rose.

Harry inherited, by unquestioned right, all the fertile fields, the rich woodland and rolling downs. And if he died before providing an heir, the whole lovely land would go intact to the nearest male relation, as if I had never been born. My entire family, Papa, Mama and Harry, could all die in pain and horror and still I would be no nearer to the ownership of the land. There was a barrier against me no skill of mine could overleap. Generations of men had built defences against women like me, against all women. They had ensured we would never know the power and the pleasure of owning the earth beneath our feet and growing the food that went on our tables. They had built a great chain of male control, of male power and beastly male violence between me and my need for the land. And there was no way, enforced by male-dominated laws and male-established tradition, that I could overthrow them.

His father had served him well. Harry took the land, the produce of the land and the joy of ownership. His to enjoy, to use, to exploit or to abuse as the whim took him. There were no surprises in such an inheritance, and no sense in any heart (except mine) that what seemed so fair on the surface was part of a conspiracy to defraud me of my beloved home and to exile me from the one place on earth to which I could ever belong. My home was given away to the male newcomer, to the male stranger; he neither knew the land nor loved it, and yet it was his.

I heard the will read in a haze of hatred. Not towards Harry, who benefited despite his doltish silliness, but towards Ralph who had cost me my papa in return for this pittance of a dowry and this treasure for Harry. Harry had everything. I had lost the love of my papa, who would never have let me go, unhappy, into exile. And Ralph's foul scheming had benefited only Harry.

After the petty bequests and little gifts, there was a personal message from Papa to Harry, exhorting him to care for the poor of the parish: standard rhetoric that no one would take seriously. But then Papa had written, 'And I commend you, Harry, to take care of your mother, and my beloved daughter Beatrice – most dear to my heart.'

Most dear to his heart. Most dear. The tears, the first since his death, stung in my eyes and I choked on a great sob of grief that seemed to be tearing its way out of my chest.

'Excuse me,' I whispered to Mama and rose from the table and hurried from the room. In the open air on the front steps my sobs were stilled. He had called me 'beloved'; he had told them all I was 'most dear'. I breathed the smells of a late summer twilight and felt an ache like an illness, which was my longing for him. Then I walked bare-headed through the rose garden, through the little gate into the paddock and towards the wood down to the Fenny. My papa had loved me. He had died in pain. And the man who had killed him still lived on our land.

Ralph was waiting for me at the old mill. He lacked his mother's gypsy second sight and he did not see his death when it walked towards him, smiling. He held out his arms to me and I went into his embrace and let him hold me and kiss me in the dark shadows of the barn.

'I have been longing for you,' he whispered in my ear as his hands moved quickly over my body, opening the front of my dress. I sighed as he smoothed my breasts and he bent his head and kissed me. His stubbled chin scratched my cheek and then my throat as his head dropped down the open gown. I shivered as I felt his warm breath on my neck.

Above us the last late swallows lined up on the old beam. I saw and heard nothing but the dark outline of his head and the steady, rapid sound of his breath.

'Oh, it is so good to touch you,' Ralph said earnestly, as if there could be any doubt. He pressed me backwards to a heap of straw and lifted my skirts and petticoats.

'When we have each other and Wideacre, that will be a pleasure, eh, Beatrice? When we make love as man and wife in the great master bedroom at Wideacre? When I come to you like this, in the great carved bed under embroidered quilted covers and between fresh linen sheets like I was gentry born and bred?'

We closed together, and his words went unanswered as I clung to him, begging him to move faster and faster, harder and harder. I groaned like a dying man as easy passion overwhelmed our destiny and the world grew dark and still as if a great wave had washed over me and drowned me. Alone, I was yet enveloped and held by Ralph as he thrashed, and he groaned too and lay still. Then the feelings drained from me, and left me weak but clear-headed and cold as ice. I had a sense of deep, sudden sorrow for the pleasure that had gone so fast and left me so empty. And because that moment, that precise moment, would never come again.

'That's a good, dutiful wife,' Ralph said, teasingly. 'That is how it will be in the master bedroom. I shall sleep between linen sheets every night of my life, and you may bring me coffee in bed every morning.'

I smiled at him under my half-closed eyelids.

'Shall we spend all our time here?' I asked. 'Or shall we go to London for the season?'

Ralph sighed luxuriously and lay back beside me, hands behind his head, his breeches still around his ankles.

'I'm not sure,' he said deliberately. 'I'll have to decide. Winter in town would be nice, but there's the fox hunting and shooting here. I wouldn't want to miss that.'

My lips curled in a smile, but no trace of sarcasm crept into my voice.

'Do you think you can take my father's place?' I asked. 'D'you think the county gentry will accept you when they've know you as Ralph, the gamekeeper's lad, the son of Meg the gypsy and a runaway father?'

Ralph was unmoved. Nothing could penetrate his contentment. 'I don't see why not,' he said. 'I'm no worse than they were a dozen generations ago. I'll have earned my place at Wideacre, which is more than they have done to gain theirs.'

'Earned it!' I could scarcely keep the disdain from my voice, but I kept my tone sweet. 'Odd work you have done this day, Ralph! Murder and unchastity!'

'Ah, hard words,' Ralph said negligently. 'A sin is a sin. I'll take my chance at the Day of Judgement with this on my conscience. Any man in the country would have done the same. I'm prepared to stand alone. I don't share the blame with you, Beatrice. I planned it. I'll take the guilt and the consequences. I did the act – I did it partly for you and partly for our future together – but I'll take the blame alone in this world or the next.'

The tension sloughed off me like a snake's skin. It was his crime. I was innocent.

'You did it quite alone?' I questioned. 'You had no one to help you at all? You spoke of it with no one but me?'

He tightened his grip on me and touched my face in a gentle

83

caress. He had no idea his life hung on a thread. He had no idea when he had snapped that thread in two.

'I work alone,' he said proudly. 'There'll be no gossip in the village, no tongues wagging, no fingers pointing. I would not risk that for myself, and I would especially not risk it for you, Beatrice. I did it alone. No one but you and I know.'

He touched my face with his fingertips in one of his rare, precious caresses. I saw in his eyes and in his gentle smile his tenderness for me, and the slow and steady growth of a love that would last as long as our two hearts were beating in time with Wideacre. Despite my anger, I felt tears prickle behind my eyes and my mouth quivered when I tried to smile back at his loving face. How could I help but love him – whatever he was? He was my first love and had risked everything to give me the greatest gift any man would ever be able to give me: Wideacre.

I lost my childhood on the road on that damp spring day when my papa spoke of my banishment. I lost my contented, easy childhood in the moment when I realized he would take Wideacre from me, would take it to favour Harry, with no thought of me and my pain at all. But that hurt was healed when I lay in Ralph's arms and knew he had gambled everything to have me and Wideacre. And my tears rose at the thought of the reckless, gallant gamble he had so utterly lost.

Ralph had a dream, a hopeless, impossible dream, that only a very young lover could have. The two of us, married despite the conventions, as if the world were some paradise from romance where people may marry the love of their hearts and live where they wish. As if all that truly matters is love and passion and loyalty to the land.

It was a dream of the future that could never have been, and the only stupid mistake I ever saw Ralph make was to forget that however often we tumbled in straw, grass or bracken, or whatever I called out in my fainting pleasure at the strength and skill of his hard force, he was just a servant, the son of a slattern. And I was a Lacey of Wideacre. If it had been any other land I swear I would have sacrificed it for Ralph. If it had been any other house I believe I would have schemed to put him into it. Any other house in the land and Ralph should have slept in the master bed and sat at the head of the table. Any other land in the country could not have hoped for a better master than Ralph.

But it was not any land or any house. It was my beloved Wideacre. And no damned gypsy's brat would ever rule there.

The gulf between Ralph and me was as wide as the Fenny in flood, and as deep as the green millpond. I might take Ralph for pleasure, but I would never be his woman, his wife. The moment Ralph thought to rule me, he made our end certain.

Besides – how could he have forgotten? – he was of gypsy stock; he understood he was my father's assassin. And I would never, ever forgive him.

In my mind was a vivid, angry picture of my father, the brave, bright Squire, being pulled down and clubbed to death like a brawling common man in a back-street fight. The man with Lacey blood on his hand would never live on Wideacre. The poor man who attacked the gentry would never hide here. The upstart who planned to climb the ladder to the master bedroom through lust and bedding and blood should be destroyed, like any vermin on the land, at once.

When one says *at once* at fifteen one means *at once*. That meant my father died the day after Ralph's ugly egg of a plan hatched its nightmare brood. That meant Ralph must die with my father's blood still wet on his hands.

'It is our secret then,' I said. 'And it dies when we die. And now, I must be going.' He helped me to my feet and dusted my black mourning dress. The straws clung to it and he knelt and with meticulous care picked off every incriminating speck.

'It will be better when I have Tyacke's cottage,' he said impatiently. 'See to it that your brother expels the Tyackes first thing in the morning. I can't wait for the old man to die. He can die in the poorhouse if he wishes. I'd like to move in there this quarter day, and there's no cause to wait now. See to it in the morning, Beatrice.'

'Of course,' I said submissively. 'Is there anything else while I'm speaking with Harry?'

'Well, I'll need a horse soon,' he said thoughtfully. 'Perhaps one of your father's hunters? I suppose brother Harry won't be riding out for a while, and your mother can hardly want to keep your father's favourite in the stables after the accident? He's a good animal. I made sure he wasn't hurt. You could tell Harry he should be given to me.'

The thought of Ralph riding one of my father's high-bred horses made me flush with anger and an icy cold rage was steady behind my eyes, but my smile did not flicker. It was only words and plans.

'Of course, Ralph,' I said gently. 'There will be many changes you will want to make.'

'Aye,' he said thoughtfully. 'And when I'm master here, even more.'

The word 'master' on his lips made my skin crawl, but my eyes stayed fixed on his face and their green hazel gaze never wavered.

'I must go,' I said again and he held out his arms to me in farewell. We kissed goodbye, a long sweet kiss, and I broke from it with a sob to turn my face into his shoulder. His rough fustian jacket smelled so good – of woodsmoke and clean sweat and the inimitable heart-wrenching smell of his skin. The familiar pain of first love mounted inexorably and ached at my heart. My arms tightened around his waist in a fierce hard hug of farewell to the strong, lovely body I had known so well and loved so much.

With my head against his chest I heard his quickened breath, and his heart speeding, as his desire for me rose again at my closeness. He kissed the top of my head hard, and turned my face up with a pinch on my chin.

'What's this?' he said tenderly. 'Tears?' He dropped his head and, gently as a mother cat, licked each wet eyelid in turn. 'There's no need for tears now, my bonny Beatrice. No need for your tears ever again. Everything is going to be different from now on.'

'I know,' I said, speaking from a heart so full of pain I could believe it might break. 'I know everything will be different. That's what made me sad. My love, my darling Ralph. Nothing will ever be the same again.'

'But it will be better, Beatrice!' He looked questioningly at me. 'You surely regret nothing?'

I smiled then. 'I regret nothing,' I confirmed. 'Now or later. What has been done you did for me and for Wideacre. What is going to happen is also going to happen for Wideacre. I have no regrets.' But my voice quavered as I spoke and Ralph's grip on me tightened.

'Wait, Beatrice,' he said. 'Don't go while you are so sad. Tell me what is wrong.'

I smiled again to reassure him, but the ache under my ribs was growing into such a pain of grief I was afraid I might weep.

'Nothing is wrong. Everything is as it should be, as it has to be,' I said. 'Now goodbye. Goodbye. Goodbye, my darling.'

I really thought I should never find the courage to leave as he looked at me so tenderly, so concerned and so trusting in my love for him. I kissed him once more – a gentle, final kiss on the lips – and then I pulled myself from his arms. I felt as if I had left half my soul with him. I walked away and then turned to see him. He raised a hand to me and I whispered, 'Goodbye, my love, my only love,' so low he could not hear me.

Then I saw him turn into his cottage and stoop his dark head under the low door. I drew into the thick bushes at the side of the track and counted a slow and careful three hundred. Three hundred in counted seconds. Then I waited. My love and my anger were one mesh of pain and rage in my head. I was half blind with the conflict. It was as if the Furies were in my head – not after Ralph at all – but tearing me apart with two loyalties, two loves, two hatreds. I gave a little silent groan of physical pain and then saw on my closed eyelids once again the stare of my murdered papa carried past me into the darkness of the Hall. Then I took two deep shuddering breaths, opened my mouth and screamed as loud, as shrill, as panic-stricken as I could:

'Ralph! Ralph! Help me! Ralph!'

The door of the cottage exploded open and I heard the noise of his sprinting feet up the track. I screamed again and heard him swerve from the track towards my guiding voice. I heard his feet pounding through the deep leaves and then the deep and dreadful twang of the mantrap's forged iron spring, and simultaneously the sound of his legs breaking – a clear and unmistakable snap! snap! like chopping wood – and Ralph's hoarse, incredulous scream of pain. I dropped to the ground as my knees buckled under me and waited for another scream. My head against a tree trunk I waited and waited. None came. My own legs were useless, but I had to see him. I had to know I had done it. I clawed my way up the beech tree's comforting grey trunk, clinging to it for support and so that its rough bark pressed against my face would keep me from fainting before I had seen – because I had to see.

There was still no sound.

For long minutes I clung to the tree, feeling, but not aware of, the reassuring sun-warmed bark under my fingers, and the familiar, safe smell of dry leaves. The silence seemed as if the world that had been cracked apart by Ralph's shriek was quietly rebuilding itself.

Somewhere, a blackbird started to sing.

Then I ceased to take comfort from Ralph's long quietness and was filled with a horrid senseless fear. What was happening only yards away from me, hidden in the bushes? My legs moved as stiff as a cripple. As I left the beech tree I staggered and nearly fell, but I had to see him.

I parted the bushes and gave a whimper of horror as I saw my lover caught like a rat in the trap I had baited with love. He was slumped over the upright jaws. He had fainted from the pain of his crushed knee bones, and the teeth of the trap held his legs as stiff as a marionette's, while the top half of his body slumped like a doll's. One of the sharpened teeth of the trap seemed to have severed a vein and the steady flow of blood darkened his breeches and soaked down his leg into the black earth.

Faced with the wreck of my lover, my knees buckled again and I put out my hands to save myself as I collapsed before him. My hands clenched on the dark peaty earth as if I was hanging to a rope to pull me from a crevasse of horror. Gritting my teeth, I got to my feet again, and then, as quietly and as carefully as I had come, as if I feared to wake a beloved, weary husband, I walked backwards, one stiff, courtly step at a time, with my eyes never moving from his crumpled body while his lifeblood drained into the earth; left to die like vermin.

I crept home like a criminal and slipped in by the open kitchen door. Then, remembering, I went back to the little store room and fetched the owl, Canny, and carried him up the back stairs to the landing outside my room. I met no one. I glanced out of my window at the rising moon, a sad thin sickle of a waning moon with a little rejected teardrop of a star beside it. Ten lifetimes ago I had sat at the window and felt Ralph's eyes shining on me, laughing at me. Now I could not face starlight. I wondered with one sharp corner of my mind if he was dead yet, or if he was lingering, like a rat in a gintrap, in unrelieved pain. If he had recovered consciousness and was crying my name, hoping I would come and help him, or if he guessed it was my trap and was facing his death, staring grim-faced into the darkness.

Canny was perched, wide-eyed, alert on the top of the wardrobe. He was fully fledged, nearly ready to fly. Ralph had promised to hack him back to a wild life in the woods, to feed him little by little until he had learned to hunt. Now he would have to fend for himself. In this new harsh world lit by the sickly yellow moon, we all had to learn how to survive, and there was no help. Trust I had felt for my papa in the golden summer of my childhood, or Ralph had in my smiles, for my lying direct eyes, trust and keeping faith had gone. So I lifted him down, his talons gentle and feathery on my bare hand, and untied the jesses on his bony legs. His foot, which had been up inside his fluffed-out feathers, was endearingly hot. I opened the window and held him out. The night breeze ruffled his feathers.

'Go then, Canny,' I said. 'For I do not know love and wisdom any more.'

His grip tightened as the wind rocked him, and his head bobbed as his body moved, but he stayed quiet, looking around him.

'Go!' I said, and I cruelly tossed him, aiming him direct at the moon as if he could fly away and take all the pain and sorrow with him. Instead he fell, tumbling like a feather duster over and over down from my second-floor window and I gasped to see him fall. But even as I gripped the sill I hardened myself. I had learned one thing in this painful struggle into adulthood: that everything you do, and everything you say, *everything* has a consequence. That if I threw a newly fledged bird into the night he might fall and break his neck. If I nodded to a killer then bloody murder would follow. If I called my lover into a trap he would be caught by his legs and bleed and bleed.

The owl tumbled over and over but spread his wings before he hit the ground. He glided down towards the kitchen garden and clattered into a currant bush. His feathers were pale in the moon-light and I watched him as he sat still, perhaps surprised to find himself free. Slowly I relaxed the hand that was gripping on to my window sill. But my other hand held something. I could not think what it was. The cramped fingers unfolded and showed me a handful of earth and leaves. I had clenched my hand on it when I had gripped the forest floor in my mindless vigil waiting for a second cry from Ralph. Now I still held tight to it as Canny spread his wings and flew low over the kitchen garden towards the waiting wood like a message of my loss of wisdom, of my loss of love.

I slept with that handful of leaves and earth under my pillow, still gripped in my cold hand, soiling the clean Irish linen Ralph had coveted so. I slept easily, like a good child, and dreamed no dreams. In the morning, I wrapped it in curl-paper and put it in my jewel box. An odd thing to do. But that morning I felt odd: light-headed and unreal as if the previous night and all the days of the summer had been a strange dream I was still dreaming. At first it seemed to me like a talisman, to ward off the fear that followed me home like a black dog. It is all I have left of Ralph; the only thing I have from him now his owl has flown. A handful of earth from the place of his death. A handful of our land, Wideacre.

The next day I waited for the news of Ralph's death. I was certain it would be brought to the Hall by some gossip from the village and waited for my mother or for Harry to repeat the story of the dreadful accident at breakfast. I waited for the story at dinner. I waited for the story at tea. I waited for the story as we sat in Mama's parlour in the evening . . . Nothing.

'You've not eaten a thing all day, Beatrice,' my mother said gently. 'You must try, my dear. And you seem so overwrought.'

Harry looked up, his attention now drawn to my evident paleness and strain.

'She is grieving, Mama,' he said. He got up from his chair on the other side of the parlour fire to cross to me and sit beside me on the sofa. He took my hand gently in his own. 'Poor Beatrice, you must try not to be so sad. Papa would not wish it.'

I smiled, but my heart was cold. Then the thought flashed

through my head that Harry knew Ralph was dead, and was keeping the news from me, to protect me.

'I just have this feeling that something awful is going to happen,' I said. I shrugged. 'I don't know why. I think I should feel better if an accident did happen, and then I could believe the bad luck had passed.'

'Like happenings in threes.' My mother spoke foolishly, but her eyes were sharp. 'But nothing has happened, has it, Harry.'

Harry patted my hand; his sympathy and gentleness could not reach my cold isolation. 'No, Mama. No, Beatrice. What could happen? Beatrice is just overtired, and you, Mama, are full of fairy tales. We shall all feel better in the morning.'

I did not feel better in the morning. Nor the next morning, nor the morning after. Surely someone had found him by now? His mother, Meg, must have come home and found the cottage empty, the front door banging. She would call his name and then follow the track along and then back. Surely she would call someone to help her search for her boy, and surely they would find him soon, doubled up over his trapped legs. Dead? I sat in the window seat of my room looking out over the garden unconsciously kneading my hands until my wrists showed red marks. What could they be doing, so slow and so lazy that they had not found him now? How could Meg pretend to be a loving mother with her fey fears for her son if she had not yet sensed that something was wrong and found him?

Over and over my mind pictured the scene: the message to the village, and the village carpenter making the coffin. The gossip brought to the Hall by a friend or relation of one of the servants. Told to my brother, or even my mother, or perhaps whispered to me by Lucy, my maid. Surely the story even now was the talk of the kitchen and one of the servants would tell one of us soon. I had to be patient. And I had to watch myself with every care so that not a flicker of this turmoil showed. But surely they had found him by now!

I rose to leave my bedroom and join Harry and Mama for breakfast. Another day – the fifth day – and still no news. It had to be today. I had to be ready. My hand on the door of my room, I turned and looked at myself in the glass. My eyes were an opaque green that showed nothing of my distress. My skin was pale, pale cream against the blackness of my dress. I was a beautiful daughter grieving for her dearly loved papa, no trace of the vengeful goddess showed in my face. No trace of the secret strain showed, although my skin felt too tight on my head and around my eyes. I missed my papa; I missed him so badly that tears rolled down my cheeks when I was alone. And I missed Ralph, too, with a feeling of physical sickness. Always, beneath my ribs, I carried this deep gulf of longing and desire, and always my heart ached for the two men who had made that golden summer perfect. That easy summer world when my papa had loved and protected me, and when Ralph had loved me, and teased me, and lay beside me every long lazy afternoon.

So what if a few years had brought me exile and misery? If I could have wakened this morning and had breakfast with my beloved papa, and ridden out in the afternoon to hide in the woods with my dark and clever lover, I should have wakened happy. And I should have been free of this pain of emptiness and longing and grieving and lost love.

I smoothed the skin of my forehead in the unconscious gesture of an older, tired woman; then I turned and went downstairs. Even my light steps on the wooden stairtreads sounded lonely, and there was no laughter floating up the stairs from the breakfast room.

There was no news. We sat in silence while Harry ate a hearty breakfast at the top of the table and Mama crunched toast at the foot. I drank tea and said nothing. We were a picture of domestic peace. When Harry had finished eating and my mother had left the room, Harry looked at me tentatively and said, 'I have some odd news for you, Beatrice, that I hope will not upset you.'

I had half risen and I sank back on my chair. My face was calm but my head was dizzy with fright.

'Ralph, the gamekeeper's lad, seems to have gone missing,' my brother said uncertainly.

'Missing!' I exclaimed. My head jerked up to stare disbelievingly at Harry. 'He can't be missing!' The picture of Ralph anchored so securely by his broken legs in the mantrap was so bright that I feared Harry would see two little reflections of it in my staring eyes. 'How could he get away?' I said, betraying myself.

'What do you mean, Beatrice?' Harry asked gently, shocked at my outburst. 'Here,' he said and handed me my cup of tea. I found my hands were shaking so badly I could not hold it and when I put it down on the saucer there was a click and the delicate porcelain had cracked. I must control myself; I must not break down. Aware of Harry's eyes upon me I took a deep breath and tried to force myself to appear calm. This could be Harry's way of breaking the news to me gently, but to hear that Ralph was missing rather than dead was like a flowering of the nightmare of the past four nights when I dreamed Ralph was crawling behind me, as fast as I could run, with the mantrap clanking at his bloody knees. I gave a gasp of fear and Harry turned with an exclamation and fetched the brandy from the dining room.

'Drink this,' he said. 'Go on, Beatrice.' I swallowed and felt the warmth spreading through me. I cleared my throat. 'I am sorry, Harry. My wretched nerves. Were you saying something about Ralph?'

'Another time, Beatrice, it doesn't matter.' Harry was patting my hand again. 'I had no idea you were so distressed still, my poor sister.'

I stilled his hand and tried to keep my voice steady. 'I'm not really distressed, Harry dear,' I said gently. 'My nerves are bad, as you know. And I have had a premonition that Ralph is dead. I don't know why. But please tell me if that is so?'

'No, my dear, no,' said Harry soothingly. 'It's not as bad as all that. He just seems to have gone missing. A loss for the estate, and for me especially because he was as good as a manager for me. But we will survive without him.'

'Harry, I must know,' I said. 'How did he leave? Why did he leave?'

'Well, that's the mystery,' said Harry, seating himself beside me and still holding my hand. 'My man tells me that someone from the village called at Meg's cottage and found their few things strewn around, their clothes gone and Ralph's two dogs missing. No message, no word. They just seem to have vanished.'

The nightmare was slowly becoming real. Somewhere, beyond the walls of the Hall, Ralph was alive and free. He would know, as no one else would, that I had planned his death, that I had left him in his agony to die. He would know that I had let him kill my father and then tried to destroy him. And now, outside the walls of the house, Ralph would be waiting for me. Waiting and waiting and never, for a second in all my life, would I be free from fear again.

'What sort of state did they leave the cottage in?' I asked. I could scarcely believe the coolness of my voice. It was as if I were thinking of re-letting the miserable heap.

'Well, we'll never get a local tenant for it again,' said Harry. 'There's all sorts of nonsense about blood sacrifice and Meg's witchcraft. Gossip I won't repeat to you, my dear.'

My mind shrank in fright, but I had to know. 'Oh, I'm all right now, Harry,' I said reassuringly. 'Please tell me what people are saying. I would rather hear it from you than from my maid or someone in the village.'

Harry needed little encouragement: the schoolboy in him was bursting with the news.

'Well, it is odd,' he said with ill-concealed relish. 'Mrs Tyacke called to see what furniture Ralph wanted in her cottage. Ralph had told her he would be taking the place over. First she noticed the door open, and then she saw bloodstains on the step.' Every fraction of my body froze rock still. 'There were marks on the floor as if someone had dragged a kill into the kitchen. But what is equally odd is that there were bowls and buckets of bloodstained water all around, and Meg's only sheet was all torn and bloody.'

I could see the scene too well in my mind. Meg, warned by her second sight, coming home early, hunting for her son, perhaps guided by his cries of pain. Finding some lever and using all her strength to prise the jaws of the dreadful trap apart. Ralph tumbling to the ground and Meg picking him up and dragging him with all the strength of a passionate mother into the cottage, blood draining across the floor. Then her desperate attempts to staunch the flow, ripping up the one sheet and pressing cold cloths into the wound, and then . . . and then . . . and then . . .? Was Ralph dead? Had Meg hidden the body? She would not know it was not an accident. Perhaps even now she was mourning him in some quiet part of the wood and I was safe. I clung to that hope and turned an untroubled face to my brother.

94

'Is that all?' I asked.

'Well, I should think it was enough!' he said with the gossip's relish for bad news. 'But there is more actually. Although they left their furniture, they took an old handcart. Old Betty swears she saw someone who looked like Meg pushing the handcart with a body in it and two black dogs following up the London road three mornings ago. She never said anything before because she thought she was mistaken. But with the handcart missing and all, the village has put two and two together.'

I nodded and kept my eyes and face down so my brother should not see my despair and my fear. It had all gone wrong. It sounded very, very likely that Meg had managed to save Ralph's life, though he was too weak to walk. Ralph must have been able to tell her who set the trap, and who had baited it. If he had not told her, she would have instantly brought him to the Hall. But she did not! She had taken him away, far away from the Hall and out of my reach; away to her people, to her untamed gypsy tribe. Away to heal him so that he could get fit and strong and able to come back and confront me. Away from our lands and our influence, so he could move and plot and scheme and forever threaten my life and my future. Every waking moment from now on I would half expect to see him as I already did in every night's dreams. Limping, or horribly mutilated, coming after me for revenge. The picture in my mind was so bright, so vivid, so inescapable, that it seemed to me Ralph was at that second heaving his legless body up the steps to the door of the Hall. I could control myself no longer.

'I am ill, Harry. Call my maid,' I said, and I dropped my head on the breakfast table in a swoon of terror.

My mourning now looked real enough and I smiled no more at my mirror. I could not eat my food for fear that Ralph had been in the kitchen with one of Meg's gypsy brews to poison me. I dared not even walk as far as the rose garden in case he was waiting for me in the summerhouse, or at the gate to the wood. Even in the house I was on the precipice of a collapse every second of the day, but especially when the early winter darkness came and the curtains were drawn, and there were dark shadows on the stairs and in the hall where he could hide unseen, and wait for me to pass. I slept little at night and awoke with screams of terror. My mother called the local apothecary and then a London surgeon and they gave me draughts to make me sleep. But the deeper the sleep, the worse the dreams, and for three, nearly four, months of cold, hard, iron season I endured, like a captured wild animal, inescapable days and nights of terror.

But slowly, mercifully, it dawned on my panic-stricken imagination that nothing ɪ ad happened. In my terror, in my anticipation of fear, I had missed that saving point: nothing had happened. No one knew that my father had been torn from his horse and clubbed like a dying rabbit. No one knew that the blood from Ralph's sweet, hard thighs had poured into our dark earth in a trap baited with betrayal. Those two events had happened at the freezing of the year, and since then everything had iced up. All through the dark winter months everything, except my dashing brain and thudding heart, had been still.

The winter softened and one morning I woke, not to the song of the one solitary robin, but to a burble of birdsong and to the distant sound of the ice on the Fenny giving way to a rush of melt-water. I threw a thick shawl on over my dark woollen dress and walked in the garden. The pane of glass that had been between me and the land seemed to be dissolving like the ice in the chalk of the frozen downs. Everywhere I looked there were little green shoots, brave slight spikes pressing through the earth. And no Ralph. Thank God, no Ralph.

When I looked towards the wood where his home had been all I could see was the innocent haze of the first buds of leaves which made a halo of green around every black-branched tree. The wood was not blighted by his blood or by my treacherous death-kiss. Our love and his blood had been absorbed into the earth – the good neutral earth – as easily as the death of a rabbit or the spitting of a snake. The land had not hardened for ever into a season of revenge; it was growing moist and warm and full of the promise of spring like any other year. And whoever won the land, and whatever sins they crawled through to claim it for their own, the snowdrops would still flower in an icy carpet under the bare trees where the sap was secretly rising.

Whatever had happened had happened in the past. And it had happened in autumn when it is natural for things to die and blood to be spilled. Autumn is a time of challenge and killing; winter a time of rest and recovery, and spring means new plans, new movement and new life.

I walked faster, down to the end of the rose garden, with my old swinging stride. I went through the gate where the new lichen was growing, wet and smeary to the touch, into the wood and under the dripping trees without a second thought. I put one hand on the damp bark and felt the thudding heartbeat of my beloved Wideacre in the sweet urgency of the new season. The spring had come with the speed of a damp wind blowing, and the wet earth was warming to a new, a yellow, sun. I sniffed the wind like a pointing dog and smelled the promise of more rain, the scent of the growing earth, and even the tang of the salt sea from southerly over the downs. And I had a sudden real, glad delight in the fact that although Papa and Ralph might be dead, I had survived, and my body was stronger and more curved and lovelier than ever. I came home humming a tune and realized that for the first time in months I was sharply hungry for dinner.

Harry cantered up the drive and waved to me. I strolled through the rose garden and noticed the weeds growing through the gravel. I should speak to Riley. Harry dismounted and waited for me at the gate and I realized with an inner smile as I glanced at his strong, lithe body – broadened and stronger with his riding and maturity – that there was even a little flicker of desire somewhere deep inside me. I was alive, I was young, and I could once more see myself as lovely – the Wideacre goddess renewed by the spring, leaping up from the deaths of old pains and old sorrows.

So I smiled sweetly at my brother, and put my fingertips lightly on his arm and let him lead me into the hallway of our house.

It was a measure of my recovery that Harry raised the question of Ralph again, and I did not flinch at the mention of his name. We had stayed up late to finish reading a novel together, which Mama had declared too silly to cost her sleep. But I had begged Harry to read to the end. We were alone in Mama's parlour in front of the dying embers of the log fire.

'I suppose we need a new gamekeeper's lad,' Harry said tentatively, watching my reaction.

'Good heavens, haven't you found one yet!' I exclaimed, naturally horrified. 'Bellings can't do it all, and if you don't get someone young and fit the villagers will be all over the coverts. You won't hope to hunt this autumn unless you stop them shooting foxes now. As for venison, you must get another keeper for the young deer, Harry, or there will be no sport and no meat.'

'No hunting anyway,' he reminded me. 'We'll still be in mourning at the start of the season. But I'll get a young keeper. I miss Ralph rather.' His eyes were bright with curiosity, and something deeper, some anxiety. 'He was very able, very agreeable. He helped me with the estate.' He paused. I understood in a flash what Harry wanted to know. 'I quite liked him,' he said, denying with an easy lie his infatuation with Ralph. 'I think you did too?'

The incongruous picture of Ralph and me naked while Harry crawled towards us, his face in the dusty straw, laying his cheek against Ralph's bare foot, flashed into my mind, but I still said nothing until I was certain what Harry was thinking.

'He had a very strong, not to say forceful, personality,' Harry continued, picking his words with care. I took my cue and raised my tear-filled eyes to his open and anxious young face.

'Oh, Harry,' I said, my voice breaking on a sob. 'He made me do such dreadful things. I was so afraid of him. He said he would lie in wait for me and tell, oh, such dreadful lies about me if I didn't obey him. He terrified me and if you hadn't come in that one time, I don't know what would have happened.'

'I . . . saved you?' asked Harry hopefully.

'He would have dishonoured me and our family name,' I said firmly. 'Thank God you came in time, and since that day he was too afraid of you to pursue me any more.'

The truth of the scene was fading from Harry's malleable mind to be replaced with a rosier picture of his heroic rescue of his virtuous sister.

'My dearest sister,' he said tenderly. 'I have been so worried, but I scarcely liked to ask . . . He did not complete his dreadful act? I came in time?'

My cheeks flushed pink with maidenly embarrassment, but my sincerity and honesty gave me courage to speak.

'I am a virgin, Harry,' I said demurely. 'You saved me. And the man who threatened me has gone for ever; exiled, no doubt, by the hand of God. My honour is yours.'

Darling Harry, such a growing, broadening man, yet such a baby. And so like Mama in his preference for the easy lie rather than dreadful truths. My smile to him was warm and convincing while the outrageous lies went on.

'You saved my most precious honour, Harry, and I will never forget that I am under your protection. You are the head of the house now, and the head of the family. I am proud and confident to put myself in your care.'

He stretched out his hand to me and I moved into a chaste and affectionate embrace. A flicker of desire again stirred in me as I felt a man's arms around me, and half consciously I could feel the muscles in my legs and buttocks tense as Harry's hands gently spanned my waist. Some tiny demon of childlike mischief made me turn in his fraternal hold so one hand slid accidentally up the smooth warm silk to the swelling curve of my breast.

'Unreservedly,' I said.

He left his hand where it chanced to lie.

~ 5 ~

That night my mind played a strange trick on me in my dreams. I dreamed of Ralph, not the Ralph of my nightmares but the old Ralph of our loving summer. I was drifting through the rose garden, my feet skimming over the gravel paths. The gate opened before me and I made the same ghostly progress down to the river. By the bank stood a figure. I knew it was my lover and we slid together. His body entered mine with piercing sweetness and I moaned with pleasure. The high note of pleasure and pain disturbed my sleep and I awoke, full of regret. The dream faded fast as I opened my eyes, but the face of my lover as he lifted his head from our deep kiss was Harry's.

I suppose I should have been shocked, but instead I merely smiled and sat up in bed. To dream of Harry while the spring was stirring seemed natural and right. We were constantly in each other's company and I gained more and more pleasure from our comradeship. It was pleasant to walk in the gardens with him. We were planning a shrubbery, and we would take a stake and map out the shape of the paths on the newly turned earth. Then, when the carter came loaded high with swaying trees and shrubs, we spent a glorious couple of days ordering their planting by the three gardeners, and even treading them in, tying and staking out the branches ourselves.

Sometimes we drove up to the downs together. Although I was still forbidden to ride outside the grounds, I had hunted out an old governess cart and broke my mare to driving so I could range all around the estate and drive as far as the foothills of the downs with Harry riding alongside. I thought sometimes how pleased Papa would have been to see us in such unity on the land he loved.

'Are you not tired, Beatrice?' Harry would ask solicitously.
And I would smile without replying and we would stroll to-

gether to the top of the downs to look down on the surrounding greening fields and woods; or turn our backs and look southwards to where the sea gleamed like a blue slab in the distance.

I started to lose my fear of Harry's superior education, especially when I saw how little he still knew about the land. And I started to enjoy hearing about his books and the ideas that interested him. I could never see what actual difference it made whether one had an agreement called a Social Contract or not, but when Harry spoke of the struggle for the ownership of land, and whether land could be owned by an élite of a people, I found my interest suddenly sharpened.

He would laugh at me then and say, 'Oh, Beatrice, you care for nothing at all unless it relates to Wideacre. What a little heathen you are! What a little peasant!'

And I would laugh back and accuse him of being so full of ideas that he could not recognize wild oats in a wheat crop – which was shockingly true.

If there had been more young people in the neighbourhood we would have spent far less time together. Or if Harry had known more about the land he would not have needed my company daily. If we had not been in heavy mourning, Harry would probably have spent the previous winter in London for the season, and even I might have been taken to town for a few days. But as things were, we were very much on our own. My returning spirits showed themselves in my better health and I became once more buoyantly fit, restrained only by Mama who tried to keep me eternally stitching embroidery by her side in the pale parlour. There was no Papa to come banging in from the stables and rescue me from the tyranny of conventional behaviour now, but I could generally rely on Harry to need my advice for some work on the land.

The land missed Papa. Harry was inexperienced and slow to learn how to control the tenants who poached and thieved outrageously. Nor could he organize the villagers' sowing and weeding of our crops. But beside his ignorance my status grew, and it was very pleasant to be able to order this thing or that thing to be done without confirming an order with the Master. I kept thinking how good it would have been if I could have had the land wholly to myself, but it was only ever a passing thought.

It was also good to drive down the lanes to the fields with Harry riding alongside, and to look up in the evening and find his eyes smiling upon me.

He was no longer the schoolboy home early. He was a man in the first broadening and strengthening of his youth. As for me, every day made me a shade more golden, my eyes brighter hazel, my hair a tinge redder from the sun. Every day as I bloomed in the warmth of that especially fine spring, I felt a greater longing for a lover. I pressed my lips together remembering Ralph's rough biting kisses, and my body warmed and tingled under the black silk of my mourning dress when I remembered his intimate, shameless probing. Harry once caught my eye in one of these erotic daydreams as we sat alone beside the library fire one evening, supposedly doing accounts. I blushed at once to the roots of my hair.

Harry, oddly, said nothing, but he looked at me as if he were somehow bemused and blushed too.

We were so delightfully strange to each other. My pleasure with Ralph had been in confirming the person I was, the things that were important. With Ralph I hardly needed to speak. We both knew if the day would be fair or if it would rain. We both knew that the villagers would be planting the fields on the bottom slopes of the downs so we would have to hide in the woods that day. We both knew that passion and the land are the most important things in anyone's life, and that any other interests are secondary and slight.

But Harry knew none of these things, and while I could not help despising his ignorance, I felt also a great curiosity about the things he did know, and the things he did care for. Harry was a great intriguing mystery to me, and as the warm spring days became reassuringly hot summer ones I found my interest in him growing and growing while the corn turned silver-green. The only distraction from this growing affection and intimacy was Mama, who would intermittently insist that I behave as a normal young lady and not as a farm manager. But even she could not ignore Harry's real need for me on the land. One day when she insisted that I stay at home to receive a call from the ladies from Havering Hall, we lost something like fifty pounds on one day's work! Harry could not control the reaping gang and their families following behind to glean robbed us of one stook in every three.

The ladies – Lady Havering and little mousey Celia – had chatted politely with Mama as I watched the sun stream through the window, and knew in impotent rage that Harry would not be watching the reapers. When he came in for afternoon tea my fears were confirmed. He reported with great pride that they had finished the Manor Farm fields already. Properly cut they should not have been finished until the following day. Harry sat beside Celia Havering and nibbled seed cake like a sun-kissed cupid without a care in the world, while I could hardly sit still for anxiety.

He chatted away like a caged songbird to Celia, who actually spoke back in a voice a fraction clearer than her habitual whisper. Half an hour he spent talking of the lovely weather and the latest novel, before a hard look from me reminded him that he had workers in the field who were, I knew, taking an equally lengthy break. He took himself off with much flowery bowing and kissing of hands and seemed almost sorry to leave. The mysterious tastes of my beautiful brother were not always a delight.

'You seem very anxious about the harvest, Miss Lacey,' said Celia softly. I looked sharply at her to see if she was being impertinent, but the soft brown eyes were guileless and her face pale and quite without a spark of malice.

'It is the first harvest Harry has had to supervise,' I replied absent-mindedly. 'He had been away from home and does not know our country ways. I am afraid I am needed out in the fields.'

'If you would like –' she paused delicately. 'If you would enjoy a drive –' She broke off again. 'We came in Mama's carriage and you and I could . . . I am sure . . .' Her flutter of words came to a total standstill but her meaning finally penetrated my ears. I had been watching some rain clouds on the horizon that would have ruined everything if they had come to anything, but they seemed to be breaking up.

'A drive?' I said. 'I should love it!'

'Mama's carriage' turned out to be a large old-fashioned open landau, and after much fussing with parasols to protect our delicate complexions, we drove towards the fields. Celia tilted her sunshade precisely at the sky to cast a shadow over her face. She was milk compared with honey sitting beside me. Her skin looked as if she had been reared in a cellar she was so beautifully pale, while I was a clear honey colour on face, hands and throat, and had even a disastrous dusting of freckles on my nose. Even in my dark mourning clothes I was bright beside Celia, with flushed cheeks from the warmth of my heavy dress in the sun. She was pale and cool, her shy brown eyes scarcely daring to look over the hedges as we drove. She had a little trembly face and a quivering rosebud mouth. She seemed so young beside me. Five years older but such a sweet baby.

She showed no signs of anxiety at the plight of being ill-loved and unmarried at twenty-one. Her pale prettiness had not taken in London during her one cut-price season. Lord Havering had opened Havering House for her coming-out ball and had stood her the price of a court gown. But all of Lady Havering's fortune at marriage had been squandered on betting and gambling, and there was little to spare for her daughter. Celia's own substantial fortune, secure from her step-papa by sensible settlements, had guaranteed her one or two proposals. But Celia had demurred, and Lady Havering had not insisted, and she had come home to her restricted and hard-working life at the Hall with little idea that life for a young girl could include pleasure, or liveliness or joy.

She had little enough joy in her life. When her mama accepted Lord Havering and moved into the Hall little Celia went too, more like an extra bandbox than a person whose wants might be consulted. Aged eleven, she had been put in charge of the jolly, noisy Havering children for day after long crowded day, while Lord Havering recouped his gambling debts by dismissing house-keeper, governess and nurse, leaving his new wife and step-daughter to share the work of running house and nursery between them.

The nobly born, ill-bred Havering children cared not a rap for their quiet-voiced, subdued new sister, and Celia, in silent mourning for her papa and their quiet, invalid's routine, lived a life of loneliness and solitude in the very heart of one of the biggest houses in the county.

Enough in that situation to make any girl nervous. Celia was fortunate only in that her dowry, which was a handsome parcel of land adjoining ours, a good half-dozen farms tied up by her mother's lawyers, was safe from her spendthrift stepfather as part of the marriage settlement. I knew her from childhood when our mamas would call on each other and I would be taken to the nursery to romp with the small Haverings and attend Celia's solemn dolls' tea parties. But when I grew old enough to ride with my father, I saw little of her. We sometimes took our hounds over to Havering Hall, and I would wave to her as I rode beside my father in my smart dark green or navy riding habit, and see her watching, a fragile flower in white satin, from an upstairs window. She never rode, of course; she never even came to greet us from the front door. I think the major expeditions in her week were the two church services on a Sunday, and the occasional social visit like this one. What can have prompted the idea of a drive, the Lord only knew. I would have driven with the devil himself to see the fields; what Celia hoped to gain I neither knew nor cared.

As soon as we came in sight of the field I saw that I had been right. A dozen men were cutting in the line with their wives and children coming behind to collect the corn and set it in stooks. By rights, when the corn had been cut, the women and children and the men could then glean, picking up the broken straw for bedding or fodder for their animals, and picking up the dropped heads of corn for themselves. Harry had been letting them cut so carelessly that whole patches of the crop would be left standing for the convenience of the gleaners, and they were trying the old cheat of slicing the corn so short it would not bind into a stook and would be dropped for the families to collect.

Instead of supervising this shambles, Harry was stripped down to shirtsleeves himself and playing around with a sickle at the end of the line. Even in my temper I could not ignore his dazzling looks. Wig off, his own hair shone like pure gold in the bright sunshine and his loose white shirt billowed around him. He was taller than the men around him and slim. His dark breeches were cut close to his strong legs and back. I swear a saint would have felt desire on seeing him. Celia's eyes, like mine, were glued to him, and he glanced up and saw her and waved and came to the gate.

'It's to be hoped you don't cut your feet off,' I said acidly. I was hot and irritable draped in my heavy black mourning clothes. Celia beside me was the picture of cool perfection in white silk under a cherry parasol.

Harry laughed in delight. 'I dare say I will!' he said happily. 'It's splendid fun! When I think of all the harvests I've missed! Do you know this is my first-ever harvest at Wideacre?'

Celia widened her brown eyes sympathetically. She could not drag her gaze from him. His open shirt revealed the glint of a few hairs at the top of his chest, and his skin was as pale as creamy milk with a pink tinge where he was catching the sun.

'They should be closer together,' I said. 'They're missing more than a yard every time they move forward.'

Harry smiled at Celia. 'I'm such a beginner,' he said help-lessly.

'I know nothing of such things,' Celia said in her soft voice. 'But I do love to see the men working.'

'Working!' I said impatiently. 'That lot are on holiday! Help me down, Harry.' I left the two of them admiring the beauty of the scene and stalked across the stubble (or rather through it, because it was a good foot high) to sort the men out.

'Watch out,' said one, loud enough for me to hear. 'Here comes the Master.' The slow chuckle of country humour spread among them and I grinned too.

'Enough of this,' I said, loud enough for the whole reaper gang to hear. 'You close up, all of you. John Simon, I don't plan to keep your family in corn for free all winter! Move closer to William there. You, Thomas, you cut nearer to the hedge. Don't think I don't know what game you're all playing! Any more of this nonsense I'll have you all out at Michaelmas!'

Grumbling and chuckling, they closed the ranks and started the process again, scything their way in a line up the field, this time leaving no part of the swathe uncut. I smiled in pleasure at the sight of our corn rippling and falling in great pale golden heaps in our fields, and turned and made my way back to the landau.

Celia's laugh trilled out, as happy as a mistle-thrush, and I saw my brother smiling warmly at her. I paid no attention at all.

'D'you see now, Harry, how they're closer together and there's less waste?' I asked.

'Yes, I do,' said Harry. 'I did tell them but they just seemed to straggle apart again.'

'They're hoodwinking you,' I said severely. 'You must show them that you're the Master.'

Harry grinned at Celia and I saw her smile shyly in reply.

'I'm a worthless fellow,' he said to Celia, begging for a contradiction.

'You are indeed,' I said before she could disagree. 'Now get back to the men and don't let them stop for more than ten minutes for tea, and they're not to go home till sunset.'

He stuck to his job and the labourers did not trudge home to their cottages until long after sunset. Harry rode home whistling under a round golden harvest moon. I heard him as I dressed for dinner, and for some silly reason I felt my heart lift as his horse clattered up the drive and around to the stables. I paused in twisting my hair into a knot on the top of my head, and looked more carefully at myself in the glass. I wondered how I looked beside Celia. I was beautiful, there was no doubt, thank God, about that, but I wondered how my clear, bright looks compared to Celia's sweet loveliness. And when I remembered the scene at the field it struck me, for the first time, that Harry might not relish being reprimanded by his sister in front of the men. Perhaps his heart did not lift at the sight of me, and certainly I knew he did not watch my body and my movements as I had watched his when he bent and stretched in the cornfield.

I slipped down to Mama's room where she had a long pier glass so I could see my full-length reflection. The sight reassured me. Black suited me – better than the pale pinks and blues I had been forced to wear before. The gown was tight-waisted with black stomacher and square neck, showing me as slim as a whip. The shorter hair around my face twisted into natural curls (with a little help from the tongs) and my eyes in the candle-light were as inscrutable as a cat's.

Behind the image of my dark figure the room was reflected in shades of shadow. The deep green curtains of the old four-poster bed were dark as pine needles in the light from my single candle and, as I moved, my shadow leaped, huge as a giant's, on the dim wall behind me. Some trick of light, some nervous fancy, made me suddenly certain I was not alone in the room. I did not turn to look quickly behind me as normally I would have done. I stayed facing the mirror with my unprotected back to the room, my eyes trying to pierce the shadowy corners of the dark room reflected in the darker glass to see who was there.

It was Ralph.

He lay, where he had longed to be, on the master bed. His face was warmed with that familiar, that beloved smile that always lighted him when he turned to me. A look part confident, part male pride, part tenderness, and the anticipation of rough as well as gentle pleasure.

I froze. I could not see his legs.

I neither moved nor breathed.

I could not see his legs.

If they were whole, then the last months had been a nightmare and this was sweet reality. If they were gone, then the nightmare was with me and I was in its grip, but a million times worse than I had dreamed in my bed. The curtains of the bed cast deep slabs of shadow across the counterpane. I could not see his legs.

I knew I must turn and face him.

My face in the glass was the only bright thing in the dark room and it glowed like a ghost. I bit the inside of my cheeks for courage, and like a doomed man turned slowly, slowly, around.

There was nothing there.

The bed was empty.

I croaked, 'Ralph?' out of my tightening throat and only the candle flame moved. I took three stiff steps and held the candle high to see every inch of the bed. There was no one there. The pillows and the embroidered silk counterpane were smooth and undented. I put a shaking hand out to touch the pillows and they were cool.

No one had been there.

I staggered to Mama's dressing table, set the candlestick carefully down, and crumpled on to the stool, my head in my hands.

'Oh, God,' I said miserably. 'Don't let me go mad. Don't send me mad now. Oh, don't let it end in madness when I am so nearly at peace at last.'

Long minutes passed in utter silence except for the steady ticking of the grandfather clock in the corridor. I took a deep breath and took my hands from my face. My face was as serene and lovely as ever and I gazed at it in the glass as if it belonged to someone else, a stranger's beauty. Even I could not penetrate its calm looks or imagine what terrors were hidden behind that green cat-like gaze.

Then a floorboard outside the door creaked and the door opened. I jumped with a scream in my throat, but only Mama stood there. For a second she did not move and I read her concern for me, and some hint of a darker thought in her expression.

'It's not like you to be preening in front of a mirror, Beatrice,' she said gently. 'Did I startle you? What were you thinking of, I wonder, that you should be so pale?'

I smiled a strained smile and turned away from the glass. She said nothing but crossed the room and opened her top drawer and took out a handkerchief. The silence lengthened and I felt a familiar drumming of blood in my head as I became anxious, wondering what would come next.

'You must have missed your pretty dresses when you saw Miss Havering this afternoon,' my mother said, wrong as usual. 'How lovely she looked, didn't she? I thought Harry was most struck.'

'Harry?' I said mechanically.

'There could scarcely be a better match,' my mother said, spraying eau-de-cologne on the lace handkerchief. 'Her dowry lands lie so convenient for our own – your papa always had his eye on them – and she is such a dear, charming girl. I understand she is accustomed to very difficult circumstances at home, and the poor thing is well used to adapting herself. Lady Havering assured me that, should there be a match of it, you and I would stay here as long as we wished. Celia would expect no alteration. I do not think that one could plan better.'

I felt a growing chill inside me. Mama could not be talking about a match for Harry. Harry was my friend, my companion. We farmed Wideacre together. We belonged together, alone on Wideacre.

'A match for Harry?' I asked incredulously.

'Of course,' Mama said, not meeting my eyes. 'Naturally. Did you think he would stay a bachelor all his life? Did you think Harry would forget his duty to his name and die childless?'

I gaped at her. I had never thought of the matter at all. I never thought beyond this easy summer of my growing intimacy with Harry. Of the happiness I felt when he was so sweet to me. Of the warmth of his smile. Of the tenderness in his voice when he spoke to me.

'I never thought of the future at all,' I said, speaking truly of my youthful, feckless half-planning.

'I have,' said Mama, and I realized that she was watching me intently and that my face was unguarded before her. I had thought of her for so long as an unimportant pawn on the great chessboard of our fields that it came as a shock to recall that she had been watching me for all my life, watching me closely even now. She knew me as no other person could. She had given birth to me and watched me walk away from her, watched my growing passion for the land and my growing pleasure in running it. If she knew . . .! But I could take that thought no further. It was impossible to consider what she might think if she had dared to go beyond the barriers I had placed on my own mind.

But she had been uneasy about me for years. Her little plaintive, nagging contradictions added up to a great suspicion that I was not a child of proper feelings. While my father had insisted that a Lacey of Wideacre could do no wrong, she had been forced to acquiesce and had assumed, as he had insisted, that her complaints about me stemmed merely from her town-bred conventionality. But now no rowdy, careless Papa was there to overbear her judgement and she could see me ever more clearly. She did not merely object that I did not behave in a conventional way – that would have been easily mended. She objected, she suspected, that I did not feel in my private heart as a young girl should do.

'Mama . . .' I said, and it was a half-conscious appeal to her to protect me, as a parent should, from my fear. Even though what I most feared were the thoughts behind her suddenly sharp eyes.

She ceased her fiddly tidying of her chest of drawers and turned towards me, leaning back against the chest, her blue eyes scanning my face with anxiety.

'What is it, Beatrice?' she said. 'I cannot guess what is in your mind. You are my own child, and yet sometimes I cannot even approach a guess at what you are thinking.'

I stammered. I had no words to hand. My heart was still hammering from my foolish vision of Ralph. It was too much to have to deal with Mama, to have to face her only minutes later.

'There is something wrong,' she said with certainty. 'I have been treated as a fool in this house, but I am not a fool. I know when there is something wrong, and there is something wrong now.'

I put my hands out, half to stretch towards her, half to ward off the words and the thoughts I feared she had in her mind. She did not take my hands. She made no move towards me. She was not grateful for a caress; she stayed cold and questioning, and her eyes drained me of courage.

'You loved your papa not as an ordinary child loves its father,' she said definitely. 'I have watched you all your life. You loved him because he was the Squire and because he owned Wideacre. I know that. No one cared what I knew, nor what I thought. But I knew that your sort of love is, somehow . . . dangerous.'

My breath hissed in a gasp as she searched and then found that dreadful, illuminating word.

My hands were back in my lap loosely clasped to hide their trembling. My face upturned to my mama felt as white as a sheet. If I had been a murderer on trial in the dock I could not have seemed more aghast, more guilty.

'Mama . . .' I half whispered. It was a plea to her to stop this remorseless progress of ideas which could lead her all the way into the deep secret maze of the truth.

She moved from the chest of drawers and came towards me. I nearly shrank away, but something, some pride, some strength, kept me rock-still. I looked into her face with my brave, lying eyes, and matched her gaze.

'Beatrice, I am preparing for Harry's marriage to Celia,' she said, and I saw her eyes glisten with a hint of tears. 'No woman welcomes the arrival of another into her home. No woman looks forward to seeing her son turn away from her to his bride. But I am doing this for Harry.' She paused. 'I am doing this for you,' she said deliberately. 'You must, you shall be freed from your

fascination with this land and with its master,' she said urgently.
'With another girl a little older than you in the house, you will go
out more. You can visit the Haverings, perhaps go to London
with them. And Harry will be absorbed in Celia and he will have
less time for you.'

'You wish to come between Harry and me?' I said in impulsive
resentment.

'Yes,' said my mother baldly. 'There is something in this
house. What it is I cannot say, but I can feel it. Some hint of
danger. I feel as if I can smell it in every room where you and
Harry are working together. You are both my children. I love
you both. I should guard you both. I will save you both from
whatever danger it is that threatens us all.'

I found, in the deepest reserves of my courage, a confident
smile, and I held it on my face.

'Mama, you are sad and still grieving for Papa. We are all of us
still mourning. There is no danger, no threat. There is only a
brother and sister trying to get the work done that only their
papa knew and understood. It is just work, Mama. And Celia
will help us and soon Wideacre will be straight again.'

She sighed at that and her shoulders trembled in a nervous
shudder, and then straightened.

'I wish I could be sure,' she said. 'I sometimes think I must be
mad to think of danger, danger everywhere. I suppose you are
right, Beatrice. It is only grief letting in foolish thoughts. Forgive
me, my dear, if I alarmed you with my silliness. And yet, remember what I said. Now your papa has gone you are in my
charge and you will have to lead a more normal life. While Harry
needs your help you may indeed aid him, but when he has a wife
you will be less important on Wideacre, Beatrice. And I expect
you to accept that change with good grace.'

I bowed my head, my eyes smiling under the lowered eyelids.
'Yes, indeed, Mama,' I said submissively. And at the same time
I thought, 'You won't keep me stitching in the drawing room
when the sun is hot and the reapers need watching in the fields.'
And I knew she could not.

But the betrothal exposed once more my vulnerability. I had
no plan. Ralph had been the planner and Ralph had paid for his
upstart wickedness. I had only let the sunshiny days slip by me,

resting like a child in the pleasure of the day. I was not even the principal person on the land that summer. I still knew more than Harry could ever learn. I still knew the needs of the lands, the needs of our people and the additional, slightly special Wideacre ways. But that summer Harry's star was in the ascendant and while I might give orders, the sun came out when he came into a cornfield.

He could never control a reaper gang as I could. He was both too friendly – with his eccentric insistence on using a scythe very badly himself – and too distant – leaving them at dinner break to come back to the Hall. They preferred to have me overseeing, knowing that I would do my job well – watching the line, checking the yield and planning the work – and leave them to do theirs. Then when the girls came through the stubble with great flasks of cider and home-brewed beer and huge crusty loaves of yellow bread, they knew I would sit in the prickly field beside them and eat as hungrily as any of them.

But that year they were not my people. They were Harry's.

I could not hate Harry for it. I hated with every fibre in my spiteful, resentful body the old men, the male lawyers, the male Parliament, the male judiciary and the male landowners who had constructed a system of laws expressly designed to ensure that their mothers, their wives and even their own little daughters should forever be excluded from everything that makes life worth living: the ownership of land. But I could not hate Harry. No one could. His ready smile, his sweetness of temper, his quick humour and his dazzling good looks earned him favour wherever he went. The men of the reaper gang might prefer working in the field where I was watching, but their women blushed as red as cherries if Harry so much as rode down the lane. He was the harvest deity that summer. All I could be was priestess at the shrine.

No one was immune to the high summer appeal of the new young Master of Wideacre. I think I was the only person on Wideacre who remembered the previous Master with continual regret. For everyone else, Harry was the rising sun; and his good looks – enhanced by hard work and radiant health – and his joyous energy clearly identified him as the summertime prince of Wideacre. Only I, dark in my black mourning, sour in my temper, worked in that golden summer with relentless efficiency but with little joy.

The cream of the year at Wideacre is the harvest supper when the last of the wheat is in. No one on the estate escapes the drudgery of the final days of the harvest when every man, woman and child is racing against the weather and the coming of the autumn rain to get the golden corn under cover before the dark clouds build up and demolish the year's profit in one wicked night.

You work half consciously to that end from the first winter ploughing and spring sowing of seed. All the long year you watch the earth and the sky. Not too cold for the new seeds at the end of spring. Not too dry for the little shoots. Plenty of sun to ripen the grain but enough rain to make it green and lush. Then no rain – oh, you pray – no rain when the corn is standing proud and high but so vulnerable to storm and disease. Then the sense of triumph when the reaper gang go swish, swish, into the first field, which is as ripply as a vast, golden inland sea. Then the race starts between people and the wanton and unpredictable gods of the weather. And this year, the year of the harvest god Harry, the weather held and held and held until the people said they had never known such a summer, and everyone forgot the hot summer Ralph and I had made last year, a lifetime ago.

On the last day of harvesting, I watched the work in the morning and Harry rode out to the last field in the afternoon. When I judged they would be nearly finished, I rode down to the great granary and barn behind the new mill to watch the carts come in. Only the miller – Bill Green – and his wife were at home. Their two labourers and three sons had all gone off to bring the harvest home. Mrs Green herself was in a flurry of preparation for the evening harvest supper and her kitchen was crowded with the staff from the Hall, unpacking great hampers and flagons from our kitchens.

I sat alone in the courtyard, listening to the tumble of the water into the millpond and the rhythmic slap, slap, of the millwheel, and watching the flock of doves leaving and returning to the dovecote built into the point of the roof.

A solitary cat stretched out in the sun, too hot and too lazy to wash her crackling, dusty fur. When I moved, her eyes, as green

114

and inscrutable as my own, snapped open and gave me gaze for gaze. By the river, the tallest beech trees rustled in the breeze but the lower branches never stirred. The wood birds were silent in the heat; only the doves cooed in a continual purr of courtship. Courtyard, cat, doves and I were all motionless in the heat of the afternoon, baked into silence by the August sun.

Unbidden, into my dozy, daydreaming mind, came thoughts of my brother. Not Harry my brother the schoolboy, nor Harry the incompetent farmer. But Harry the harvest demigod at whose bidding and on whose land the corn stood tall. At the Harry that Celia saw when she found the courage to order out her mama's landau to drive down the lanes under the pretext of obliging me, but really to see him stripped down to shirtsleeves and riding breeches. Of the Harry that I saw growing in authority and power. Of the Harry who was daily becoming a true Master of Wideacre, whom I could never shift.

And then I thought, with dawning clarity, that I did not *want* to shift Harry. That I liked seeing him learning about the land, that I liked seeing the earth growing to his bidding. That I liked seeing him at the head of the table smiling down the length of it to me. That every second of this hot summer I had spent with Harry had been delight and pleasure. And the long periods of dull time without him had been spent in thinking of him, and remembering his smile, his special tone of laughter, or just hearing again in my mind snatches of our conversation.

In the distance I heard the rumble of the carts and the sound of people singing. I hardly knew what to do, I had been so enwrapped in this revelation of the rightness of Harry at Wideacre. I crossed the yard and entered the barn as Mr and Mrs Green exploded from the house and ran to open the yard gate. I could clearly hear the harvest songs as they rounded the track to the mill – even distinguish different voices and Harry's clear tenor ringing out.

The beam across the great curved barn door was heavy and I had to go to the furthest end to lever it up. Then it jerked and tilted away from me and I could drag it from its mountings. As the carts rumbled into the yard in a great triumphant procession of proven fertility, I swung the great double doors open and faced the Wideacre harvest.

The first cart was a swaying wall of golden stooks with Harry perched high up to the sky on top of them all. The heavy shire-horses halted before me at the door and the load rocked as the wheels stilled. Harry leaped to his feet and stood framed against the hot, blue sky looking down at me. My head tipped back to see him; I gazed up at him on his mountain of wheat. He was in his gentry clothes stripped for work, an outfit both impractical and indecent. A fine linen shirt, already torn on one shoulder and opened wide at the throat, showed the brown column of his neck and a glimpse of hard smooth collarbone. His riding breeches fitted snugly to his body and emphasized the muscles of his thighs. His knee-high leather riding boots were scratched beyond repair by his walking through the stubble. He looked exactly what he was: Quality playing peasant, the worst sort of landlord one could have. And I looked at him with naked delight on my face.

His spring down to the carter's seat and to the ground was stopped short by the look on my face. He paused and his eyes suddenly darted to mine. The careless, hedonistic, laughing look vanished and he looked deeply shocked as if someone had suddenly slapped his smiling face. His eyes never left mine, as if he were about to ask me some question of enormous importance – but had never guessed before that I would know the answer. I stared back at him, my lips half open as if to answer, but able only to take shallow fast breaths. Harry's gaze slowly ranged from the top of my glinting chestnut hair to the black hem of my skirt and returned again to my face. All he said, very low, was, 'Beatrice', as if he had never known my name before.

The carter waited for me to step to one side, then clicked to the team who ambled past me into the barn. Other carts drew into line behind and the men sprang up beside Harry to help throw the stooks down, while others below caught and stacked them in a great spreading and growing mountain of Wideacre wealth. I don't think Harry even saw them. He stood in the middle of the flying stooks, his eyes on mine, and his look had the intensity and the disbelief of a man drowning.

We exchanged not one word all the rest of that long hard-working day, though we worked near each other until every stook of corn was piled in the barn and every scrap of straw either in the barn or lashed under covered stacks. When the great trestle tables were laid in the yard in the twilight, Harry took the head and I the foot and we smiled when they drank our healths and cheered us. We even danced a little jig, first with each other in a breathless, dreamlike circle, and then with the handful of the wealthiest tenants who had turned out to work on the harvest that day.

As it grew darker and the moon rose, the respectable villagers said their goodnights and rode the carts homeward. The young men and girls stayed behind to dance and to court, and the wilder, single men and bad husbands started to circulate little flasks of the powerful gin they buy from the London carters. Harry fetched my mare from the mill stables and his own hunter, and we rode home under a harvest moon as round and as golden as a guinea. I was so weak with desire that I could scarcely hold the reins or keep straight in the saddle. The merest glance from Harry set me trembling, and when our horses brushed together and our shoulders touched, I jumped as if I had been scorched.

In the stable yard luck favoured me for there was no groom to lift me from the saddle. I kept my seat until Harry came towards me and then I put out both hands on his shoulders. He lifted me down and I swear he held me close to him. I shuddered as I slid down every inch of his hot, weary body, and smelled the open-air smell and the warm maleness of him. As his gripping hands gently set me on my feet I swayed slightly towards him and lifted my face. In the magical moonlight his clear hard-boned face was an invitation to swift, gentle kisses all over his eyes, forehead and scratchy cheeks. His eyes were hazy as he looked down at my face.

'Goodnight, Beatrice,' he said with an undertone of huskiness in his voice. His face came down to mine in a gentle, dry, chaste kiss on my cheek. I hardly stirred. I let him kiss me as he would and I let him release me. I let him step back and take his hands from my waist. Then I slid away, consciously graceful, towards the stable door and up the back stairs to my bedroom. The golden moon lit my way like a promise of paradise.

It was a painful paradise, that autumn and winter. Harry's courtship of Celia and his growing maturity meant he was away from home often, dining or drinking with new friends, or visiting Celia at Havering Hall. While my power on the land grew in his absence, my power over myself diminished, and I longed for him every second of every dull day that he was away.

I watched him secretly at breakfast, watched him read the paper and comment with assured knowledge on political developments and the news of London society. I watched his quick stride out of the room and listened for the bang of the front door as he went out. At dinner I was by the window to see him ride home, his head full of ideas about his agricultural books. I sat at his right hand and made him laugh with gossip about Mama's afternoon callers. At tea in the evening I poured his cup and my hand trembled as I gave it to him. I was hopelessly, desperately in love, and I rejoiced in every painful, delightful moment of it.

When he spoke of Celia I cared not at all. Her pretty manners, the fresh flowers of her parlour, her marvellous needlework and her tasteful sketches meant nothing to me. My brother's genteel courtship of the angelic Celia was not what I wanted. The little songs and pretty presents, the odd bouquet and the weekly visit – she could keep them. I wanted my brother to feel for me the passion I felt for him, which Ralph and I had shared. Instead of shying away from the memory of Harry burying his face against Ralph's foot and his groans of pleasure at the feel of Ralph using the riding whip on his back, I recalled it with hope. He could feel abject desire; he could be fascinated and overwhelmed. I had seen him with Ralph; I had seen him infatuated and helpless with love. I longed for him to be infatuated again – this time with me.

I knew also – a woman always knows though she may conceal her knowledge even from herself – that Harry desired me in return. When he knew I was in the room his face was schooled and his voice neutral, but if he came upon me unexpectedly, or if I walked into the library when he had thought I was out, his eyes would light up and his hands would tremble. The long discussions we shared over the planting of next year's crops and Harry's new theories on crop rotation were spiced and lightened by this unspoken exchange of excitement, and when my hair brushed his cheek as we both leaned over a column of figures, I felt him stiffen. Disappointingly, he did not move forward, but nor did he draw away.

All the long autumn and winter I hardly noticed the chill and the dreary rain, I burned so inside. In the early months, when the chrysanthemums and the thick Michaelmas daisies bloomed, I carried them in to fill the house with their peppery smell and shuddered at the flaring colours. The hunting season came and I had to trail around in my heavy black dress on mornings when the sun rose like a red ball over the hoar-frosted fields and I could hear the hysterical yelp of hounds rushing like mad things in the first runs of the year. By some erratic social ruling, Harry was allowed to attend the meet, dressed in dark colours, and follow the hounds over the first few fields, but was not allowed to be in at the kill. The same inflexible social code ruled that I could not ride in company, and was thus banned from hunting for the whole of the frosty bright season. Only my secret rides about the estate were allowed, as long as none of the gentry saw me.

So there were no wild gallops for me to burn off the energy I felt. There was little work to do on the land, so I was much indoors. As the damp and the rain lifted, and the frost took hold, I longed for Harry with sharper and sharper need. My desire grew so strong that the pleasure curdled into pain on some days. Once, waiting for his return in the stable yard, I broke the ice on the drinking trough and crushed the splinters in my hand to still my impatience. But then, when he came riding in like a warrior high on a steed, and his face lit up to see me, every icy bit of pain melted into joy.

Christmas and New Year passed quietly for we were in second mourning. When a sudden frost made the roads usable, Harry took the coach to town for a week to transact some business. He came home full of the new fashions and plays of the season.

His absence gave me an opportunity to note, with ironic self-knowledge, that although I missed him, I relished the absolute power over the land that was mine when he was away. Our tenants, our labourers and the Acre craftsmen knew well enough who was the master, and would always consult me first before taking a plan or request to Harry. But merchants or dealers who did not know the county well sometimes made the mistake, that first year, of asking to see the Squire. I was always piqued when they entertained me with social gossip but then paused, waiting for me to leave the room before they started business talk. And Harry, with one half of my knowledge and experience, would always be flattered and would sometimes say, with a smile to me, 'Don't let us detain you, Beatrice, if you have something to do elsewhere. I am sure I can manage this alone and I will discuss it with you later.' At which I was supposed to take my leave. Sometimes I went. But sometimes I committed the social solecism of smiliᵤg back and saying, 'I have no business elsewhere, Harry. I would rather stay.'

Then the merchant and Harry would exchange the rueful grin of two men with a recalcitrant female, and discuss the deal for wool or wheat or meat. Wideacre always had the best of it when I was there, but I was unfailingly offended at the assumption that my business could be elsewhere when wealth was on the table.

While Harry was away, however, the merchants, the traders, the lawyers and the bankers had perforce to recognize my ability to give and honour my word. The law, the eternal male law, did not recognize my signature, any more than if I were a bankrupt, a criminal, or a lunatic. But a business man generally needed only one hard look from me before he realized that if he wanted a contract with Wideacre he had better not suggest awaiting Harry's return. In Harry's absence my power on the land shed its concealment and everyone, from the poorest tinker or shanty dweller to the leaders of county society, could see that I ruled the land.

We had a week of cold, clammy fogs after Christmas but in mid-January the hills shed their grey and became clear and frosty and bright. Every morning I awoke from a night of confused hot dreams and got up from my bed to throw my window open and breathe in the sharp freezing air. A few hard gasps would send me shivering back into the room to wash and dress before my log fire.

The weather took its toll in Acre. Bill Green, the miller, slipped on some ice in his mill yard and broke a leg and I had to send for the Chichester surgeon to come and set it for him. Mrs Hodgett, the lodge-keeper's mother, took to her bed when the snow started falling and complained of pains in her chest. They could not root her out. After a week of this nonsense, Hodgett held the gate for me one morning and confessed that he was sure she was in bed only out of pure spite, and that his wife, Sarah, was exhausted with the extra cooking and washing and tired by two walks a day to Acre village to take the old crone her meals.

I nodded and gave him a smile and the next day took my roan hunter down to Acre village and tied him to old Mrs Hodgett's wooden gate. I could see no face at the window of the little cottage but I knew the old witch would have been peeping. By the time I had swept up her snowy garden and burst into her house, stamping the snow off my boots and pulling my gauntlets off, she had skipped back into her sick bed, covers up to her chin, her bright healthy eyes shifty with deceit.

'Good day, Mrs Hodgett,' I sang out. 'I am sorry to see you abed.'

'Good day, Miss Beatrice,' she quavered. 'It is kind of you to visit a poor old lady.'

'I can do better than a visit,' I said encouragingly. 'I have come to tell you that I am sending for the new Scottish physician, Dr MacAndrew, to come and see you. I hear he is wonderful with chest complaints.'

Her eyes were bright with eagerness.

'That would be grand,' she said. 'I've heard tell on him. They speak well of him indeed.'

'But have you heard of his special treatment?' I asked. 'He has a wonderful reducing diet which they say never fails.'

'No. What is that?' she asked, walking unsuspecting into the trap.

'He calls it starving out the infection,' I said, lying through my teeth with a candid gaze. 'The first day you take nothing but hot water, and the second day you have hot water with one spoonful, no more, of gruel. The third day you have plain hot water again and the fourth you have a spoonful of gruel. That goes on until you are cured. They say it never fails.'

I smiled encouragingly at her and inwardly apologized to the young doctor whose reputation I was traducing so wilfully. I had not yet met him, but I heard he was excellent. His practice was mainly with the Quality families, of course, but he had a growing name for caring for the poor, and in some very hard cases he was giving his services for free. He would survive this faradiddle. No one but a very foolish old lady would believe such nonsense. But

Mrs Hodgett was aghast. She stared incredulously at my face and plucked at the bedding with her plump fingers.

'I don't know, Miss Beatrice, I'm sure,' she said hesitantly. 'It can't be right to eat so little when you're poorly.'

'Oh, yes,' I said blithely, and turned as the door opened. It was Sarah Hodgett, who had walked from the gatehouse with an earthenware bowl of stew in her hands and a crusty new-baked loaf of bread wrapped in a spotless towel balancing on the lid. The smell of rich rabbit stew filled the frowsy little room and I saw the old lady's eyes gleam.

'Miss Beatrice!' said Sarah with a courteous half-bob and a warm smile for me, her favourite. 'It's good of you to call on Mother while she's poorly.'

'She'll be better soon,' I said with certainty. 'She's going on Dr MacAndrew's special reducing diet. You might as well start now, had you not, Mrs Hodgett? So you can take your rabbit stew home again, Sarah. I dare say that it won't go to waste there!'

'I could start the treatment tomorrow!' Mrs Hodgett intervened despairingly, fearing the disappearance of Sarah's hot dinner.

'No, today is best,' I said firmly. 'Unless you are already feeling better?'

She seized on the way out with an audible gasp of relief.

'I am a bit stouter,' she said. 'I think I might well be on the mend.'

'Exercise then,' I said, firmly putting out an imperious hand and hauling the old lady out of her bed. 'Sarah can pop home and lay an extra place, and you can walk up to the lodge for your dinner today.'

'Out in the snow?' she squawked, as if its touch would poison her. I glanced to the door and saw the pair of stout leather boots and the warm shawl and bonnet hanging on a peg.

'Yes,' I said inexorably. 'It's either exercise or the special diet for you, Mrs Hodgett. You are too important to us all for us to take any chances with your health.'

She smiled at the compliment but scowled at the options and then, grudgingly, complied. I left Sarah bundling up the old devil in layers of flannel for her outing and went to untie Sorrel, well satisfied. I had done the Hodgetts a favour that they would not forget, and I had given the village a joke that would last them until spring. My swinging stride into the cottage and my starvation diet would be mimicked and laughed over in every taproom in a hundred miles' radius. And the toast, when the long country guffaws had died down, would be the joking tribute: 'The Master of Wideacre – Miss Beatrice!'

I called to one of the Tyacke boys, who was making snowballs in the lane, to come and hold Sorrel while I climbed awkwardly on the wall to reach the saddle, and then tossed him a penny for his help, and then another one because I liked his gap-toothed smile of hero worship as he looked up at me.

'Gaffer Cooper is poorly, too,' he volunteered, turning the coins in his hand and planning a feast of buns and toffee.

'Bad?' I asked, and the lad nodded. I could call on my way home. He was one of the cottagers who patched together a living on the fringe of the village where it merges with the common. In summer he had the odd day's work harvesting or reaping in the Wideacre gang, in winter he would help someone kill a pig and be paid with a good measure of bacon. He had a couple of scrawny hens that sometimes laid an egg or two. He had a thin old cow that gave him a little milk. His cottage was built from wood scrounged and stolen from our woods, and from branches legitimately cut on common land. His roof was made of branches and sods of turf. His wood fire burned turves and wood from the common and filled the little room with smoke. He sat on a three-legged stool carved years ago, and he ate from a wooden bowl with a tin spoon. He cooked in a three-legged pot set in the embers of his fire, which burned on a stone in the middle of the room and smoked the room as well as the bacon hung from the rafters.

It was not a life I would choose to lead, but Gaffer Cooper had never had different and never settled to regular work and called no one master. In his dirty little shanty, sleeping on a bed of bracken, rolled up in rags, Gaffer Cooper called himself a free man; Papa, who had a sensitive eye for other men's pride, always called him Gaffer Cooper and never John. And so did I.

Sorrel was tired of standing still, and chilled, so I gave him a brief canter down the snowy lane and back before turning right down the track that leads towards the cottages. The wood was silent, magical in the snow. The deep green pine trees and firs each held a thick line of snow along their branches and pointy fingers. Even the tiniest pine needles were capped with a sliver of ice. The silver birches looked grey instead of white against the icy brightness, and the beech trees' grey trunks were pewter-coloured. As I rode I could hear the Fenny clattering louder around the ice-floes and I went closer to see the green water sliding secretly under little silver skins of ice to make silent pools under the white ceiling.

The snow in the woods was pockmarked with animal tracks. I saw the two round two long prints of a rabbit and the little dots of a weasel or stoat following close behind it. There were fox tracks, like a little dog's, and even the scuffed trail of a badger whose low belly brushed the thicker drifts.

Looking up through the tracery of snow-laden branches, I could see from the sky that we would have more snow later in the day and I put Sorrel into a canter to get home before dinner. Someone had been down the track before me. A stout pair of boots and a pair of wooden clogs, so Gaffer must be ill indeed if he was being visited.

As we rounded the bend to his cottage I guessed I was too late. The door of his cottage stood wide open, something that happened generally only on the most scorching of summer days, and coming out was Mrs Merry, midwife and layer-out in Acre parish – and owner, as befitted her rank, of a good pair of boots.

'Good day, Miss Beatrice. Gaffer's gone.' She greeted me matter-of-factly.

I drew rein beside the fence of hazel sticks.

'Old age?' I asked.

'Aye,' she said. 'And the winter takes them.'

'He had enough to eat, and enough clothes?' I asked. Gaffer was not one of our people. He was neither tenant, labourer nor pensioner, but he had scraped his living on our land and I should feel to blame if he had died in want.

'He ate one of his hens only last night,' said Mrs Merry. 'And he had survived many winters in those clothes and in that bed. You need have no fears, Miss Beatrice. Gaffer's time was come and he went peacefully. Would you care to see him?'

I shook my head. There was no family in Acre who would be offended by my refusal. I could please myself.

'Did he leave any savings?' I asked. 'Enough for a funeral?'

'Nay,' she said. 'It'll be a pauper's grave for him. We have found nothing.'

I nodded. 'I'll stand the coffin and the service,' I said briefly. 'Set it in hand, Mrs Merry. I won't have Wideacre folk buried in shame.'

Mrs Merry measured me with her eyes and smiled.

'Eh, but you're so like your papa!' she said, and I smiled in return at the compliment: the best that could be paid me.

'I hope so,' I said and nodded my farewell.

In a day or two the plain whitewood coffin would take Gaffer's remains to the churchyard and he would be buried in the far corner where the water pump is and the tools are kept. I would pay for a plain wooden cross with his name on it. The service would be read by the curate to whoever was there, idling from work, for Gaffer had few friends. A couple of the other cottagers might attend to pay their respects to one of their own from the village within a village, but Acre itself would be little touched. I would pay the extra penny necessary to toll the funeral bell for him, and at the sound the men ploughing in the fields, or trimming the hedges and digging ditches, would stop their work and pull off their caps to be bare-headed for the passing of the old man who never earned such a mark of respect in his life.

Then the bell would cease and the caps would go back on to the quickly chilled heads. The men digging would spit on their cold hands, grasp the spades again and curse the life that forced them to stand knee-deep in icy water in mid-January with no break until dinner, and no chance of being warm and dry until dusk.

The freezing weather was hard enough on the labourers but this winter it was a nightmare for the shepherds. It was especially hard because the snow fell so thick and so early that the sheep had not been gathered off the downs in time for them to lamb on the lower, more accessible hills. Day after grey snowy day we toiled up that blocked track to the top of the downs to poke about with long sticks in the snow to try to find the firm white lump that meant a buried sheep, and then set to the miserable job of digging the thing out.

We lost remarkably few because I made sure the men were out from dawn to dusk and they cursed me with language that should have dropped me faint with horror from the saddle, but that instead made me laugh.

They learned a great, if grudging, respect for me that winter. Unlike the labourers and tenants who saw me almost daily, the shepherds worked alone. Only at a time of crisis like this one when most of the flock was buried under six-foot drifts did they work in a gang commanded by me. They noted the advantage the horse gave me and cursed me roundly when I trotted past them up the track, or when they slipped and fell into great deceiving hills of snow while I rode dry-shod. But they knew also that not even the oldest, wisest one of them could match me for sensing where a sheep was buried or guessing where a little flock would have huddled. Then, when they were digging, more often than not I would be side by side with them in the snow, probing for the buried animal, and feeling for its head.

And when it came to rounding up the chilled and silly things to move them downhill, the shepherds knew that although I was tired and cold I would ride behind the stragglers and bawl at the dogs until we had them all safe in a lower meadow.

Only then, when the gate was pulled shut and hay thrown on the snow, would our ways diverge. The men would go home to their little cottages to dig out potatoes, or swedes, or turnips for their dinner, or reluctantly go to work their tract on the common fields. Or they would go out to set a snare for a rabbit or mend a leaking roof. Working, even in the dark, working, working, working, until they fell into their beds and slept, sometimes still in their wet clothes.

But I would trot home and toss the reins to a stable lad, climb the stairs to my room and sink into a tub before the fire while Lucy poured ewer after ewer of hot water over me and said, 'Miss Beatrice! You will scald! You are all pink!'

Only when my skin was stinging with the heat would I heave myself out and wrap up in a linen towel while Lucy brushed my hair and piled it up and powdered it ready for the evening.

I found I could chat to Mama at dinner, and she showed some

interest in my day, although the weight of her disapproval curbed my tongue. She disliked what I was doing, but even she could see that when a fortune of wool and meat lay buried in the snow one could not leave it to paid labourers to dig out, when and how they fancied.

But once the covers were removed I became quiet, and by the time the tea tray came into the parlour I was weak with sleepiness.

'Really, Beatrice, you are good for nothing these days,' Mama said, looking pointedly at a spoiled piece of embroidery which had been in and out of the work basket every night for a sennight. 'It is hardly like having a daughter at all,' she said.

'I am sorry, Mama,' I said in sudden sympathy. 'I know it seems odd. But we have had such bad luck with the sheep. Another couple of days and they will all be in, and then Harry will be home in time for lambing.'

'In my girlhood I did not even know the word lambing,' said Mama, her tone plaintive.

I smiled. I was simply too tired to try to restore her to good humour.

'Well, as Papa used to say, I am a Lacey of Wideacre,' I said lightly. 'And while I am the only one, I have to be Squire and daughter, all at once.'

I tossed the stitchery back into the workbox and rose to my feet.

'Forgive me, Mama. I know it is early and I am no company for you, but I am too tired to stay awake.'

I bent down for her goodnight kiss, a cool resentful one, and left her.

Every night was the same. As I climbed each stair my tiredness fell away and my thoughts turned to Harry. His smile, the sweetness and tenderness of his expression, his blue eyes and the set of his coat became more and more vivid with every step I took up to my room. By the time I was undressed and lying on my back in bed, I could almost feel his body on mine and his arms around me. With a moan I would roll on my side and try to put the insane, senseless picture from my mind. I was sure that I longed for the touch, for the pleasure of Ralph. But the thought of Ralph was a nightmare to me, so my mind had played this trick on me and made me dream of Harry. Once he was home, and we were working side by side again, I might enjoy his company and this strange, fevered dreaminess would be gone. I tossed and turned, and dozed and woke with a jump until midnight. Then I sank into sleep and dreamed only of golden curls and a sweet, honest smile . . . and acres and acres of snow hiding precious sheep.

Harry came home the second week of February, later than he had promised. His lateness meant I had the first week of lambing to manage alone. The shepherds and I spent each long dark evening, after every long cold morning, finding sheep in lamb, checking the lambs and moving the sickly ones indoors to barns where they could be watched. Some of the flock, the less hardy ones, were to lamb indoors anyway.

I loved going into the barn when it was full of sheep. They rippled like a woolly river away from me as I walked through them. Outside the wind howled and the beams of the barn creaked like a ship at sea; but inside it was snug and sweet-smelling. The oil lantern cast a yellow glow when I checked the newborn lambs early in the morning, or last thing at night, and the smell of the oil on their fleeces lingered on my greasy hands when I rode home.

I was tired and chilled and smelling of lanolin one night riding home, when I noticed fresh hoof marks in the snow of the drive and, absurdly, my heart sprang up like a winter robin. 'Perhaps Harry is home,' I said to myself and spurred Sorrel on to a faster canter, sliding on the icy snow.

His horse was standing at the front door and Harry, gross in a caped cloak, was in the doorway, hugging Mama and answering her babble of questions with a laugh. The sound of Sorrel's hoofs on the icy gravel made him turn and come back out to me, though I saw Mama's detaining hand on his cape.

'Beatrice!' he said and his voice was full of joy.

'Oh, Harry!' I said and blushed as scarlet as a holly berry.

He reached his arms up to me and I slid from the saddle towards him. The capes of his riding cloak billowed round and half drowned me in the smell of wet wool, of cigar smoke and horse sweat. He held me in a hard hug before he released me and I sensed, with the sureness of my leaping heart, that his heart was pounding too, as he held my slim body in his arms.

'Come along, you two,' called Mama from the doorway. 'You will both catch your deaths of cold out there in the snow.'

Then Harry's arm was round my waist and he swept me indoors like some buffeting winter wind, so we arrived in the parlour breathless and laughing.

Harry was full of town gossip – the snippets of political news he had heard from old friends of Papa's, the family news of our cousins and a bundle of little presents. He had the playbill of the theatre he had visited and the programme from a concert.

'Wonderful music,' he said enthusiastically.

He had visited the sights of London, too; Astley's amphitheatre and the Tower of London. He had not been to Court but he had been to several private parties and met so many people he could not remember half their names.

'But it's fine to be home,' he said. 'My word, I thought I should never get here at all. The roads were shocking. I planned to come post but I left my baggage at Petworth and rode the rest of the way. If I had waited for the road to be cleared for carriages, I think I should have been there for Easter! What a winter it has been! You must have been busy with the sheep, Beatrice!'

'Oh! Do not ask her!' Mama threw her hands up with sudden vivacity at the return of her lovely boy. 'Beatrice has become a full-time shepherdess and she smells of sheep, and talks sheep and thinks sheep until she can barely speak at all but only bleat.'

Harry roared. 'I can see it's high time I came home,' he said. 'You two would have been pulling caps in another week. Poor Beatrice, you will have had hard work to do in this weather! And poor Mama, with no company!'

Then I saw the clock and hurried to my room to change. My bath was even more scalding than usual that night and my scrubbing with the perfumed soap even more meticulous. I chose a deep blue gown of velvet with wide swaying loops of material over the paniers at the side. My maid powdered my hair with extra care and placed among the white curls deep blue bows that echoed the colour of the gown. Against the powder, my skin was clear, pale honey, my eyes hazel rather than green. I doubted if there were lovelier girls even in London, and after Lucy left me I stayed seated before my mirror gazing blankly at my reflection.

The gong roused me from my daze and I hurried downstairs in a rustle of silk petticoats and rich velvet.

'Very nice, dear,' Mama said approvingly, noting my unusually thorough powdering and the new gown.

Harry frankly gaped at me and I stared back at him.

In half-mourning, like Mama and me, he had to wear dark clothes, but his waistcoat was a deep, deep blue embroidered with intricate black thread. His long coat with the dandified wide cuffs and lapels was deep blue also – a sheeny satin that caught the light when he moved. His hair was tied back with a bow of matching blue material, and his satin evening breeches were blue also.

'You match,' Mama said unnecessarily. 'How very fine you both look.'

Harry smiled, but his eyes had a confused, transfixed expression in them. With jesting ceremony he bowed to Mama and me, and offered us both an arm, but behind the smile and the ready courtesy I knew him to be keenly aware of my every move. I smiled back as if I was at ease, too, but the hand I put on his arm trembled, and when I sat in my chair the table swam before my eyes as if I was going to faint.

Harry and Mama exchanged family news over the dinner table and I concentrated on schooling my voice to make normal, laughing replies when one or other of them turned to me. After dinner Harry refused port and said he preferred to come at once with us to the parlour.

'For I have brought home the family jewels from the bank, Mama,' he said. 'And I am longing to see them. Such a great weight! I had them tucked under my arm on the horse for I feared to leave them with the rest of my baggage. I was certain I should be robbed!'

'There was no need to carry them,' Mama said apologetically. 'You could have left them with your valet. But you shall certainly see them.'

She went to her room for the key and then opened up the little chest and lifted out the three fitting trays.

'Celia shall have these on her wedding day,' she said, picking out the family heirloom, the Lacey diamonds: a set of gold and diamond rings, bracelets, a collar of diamonds, eardrops and a tiara.

'I should think they would bring her to her knees,' said Harry laughing. 'They must weigh a ton. Have you ever worn them all, Mama?'

'Good heavens, no!' she said. 'We only had one season in town after our marriage and I looked behind the times enough without being draped in old-fashioned jewels. These were given to me on my wedding day, as is the custom, and then stored at the bank. But Celia should at least see them in October.'

'October?' I said. The eternal piece of embroidery slipped in my hands and the needle jabbed into my thumb.

'Oh, poor Beatrice!' said Harry. 'I must have this embroidered kerchief when it's done. There are more blood spots on it than thread. What tortures you put her through, Mama!'

'The torture is in trying to teach her,' Mama said, laughing with her beloved son. 'After a day out with your sheep she can barely see to put a stitch in its place. And she was always clumsy with a needle.'

She packed the jewels back into the box and took them up to her room. Harry took my hand in his and inspected the welling spot of blood on the ball of the left thumb.

'Poor Beatrice!' he said again and kissed the thumb. His lips opened and he sucked the little spot of blood. In my nervous, passionate state I trembled like a high-bred mare. The ball of my thumb was pressed against his teeth, and I could feel his tongue, wet and warm, sliding over the ridges of the thumbprint. His mouth was hot, and fascinatingly wet. I held my hand up to his face and scarcely breathed.

'Poor Beatrice,' he repeated. He raised his eyes and looked at me. I hardly dared move. There was such pleasure in having him touch me, such delight in a tiny gesture. I could not have taken my hand away had my life depended on it. But somewhere in the back of my mind was a growing awareness that he had kept hold of my hand for some time. The casual gesture was turning into a caress. There was silence.

He took the thumb from his mouth and inspected it with playful seriousness.

'Do you think you will survive this wound?' he asked.

'I'm scarred from a thousand similar battles,' I said, trying to keep my voice light, but I could not help it quivering. I noticed that he was breathing slightly faster and his eyes had that absorbed, incredulous look again.

'Poor Beatrice,' he said, as if he had forgotten any other words. He still held my hand and I rose from my seat to stand beside him. We were nearly the same height and if I had moved half a step closer my breasts would have rubbed his chest and our bellies brushed.

'I hope you will always care for my wounds and sorrows so tenderly, Harry,' I said.

'My dear sister,' he said sweetly. 'I will always care for you. You must promise to tell me if ever you are unhappy or unwell. I am sorry I left you with so much work to do, and I was sorry to see you so pale.'

'My heart flutters so, Harry,' I whispered. It was hammering like a drum at the closeness of him. He put his hand against my ribs as if to feel for the pulse and I covered it with my own, pressing his palm against me. Scarcely knowing what I was doing, I slid it towards the curve of my breasts, very soft under the blue velvet.

Harry gave a gasp and his other hand came around my waist to draw me towards him. We stood like two statues scarce believing that our hearts were hammering hot blood round our bodies and that we were moving closer and closer together. I felt his leg press forward, then closed my eyes at the blissful moment of contact as our bodies touched down the quivering length. With my eyes still closed I blindly lifted my face and felt the warmth of his breath as his head bent down to me.

His lips touched mine as gently and as chastely as any brother's could. Instinctively I opened my mouth in pleasure and felt his whole body flinch in surprise. He would have pulled away but my hand was behind his neck and held his face to me. Then my tongue slid into his virginal mouth and I licked him in a thoughtless fit of passion.

He jerked back, and I came to my senses and let him go.

'That was a brotherly kiss,' he said gently. 'I am so glad to be home and to see you again that I wanted to give you a hug and a brotherly kiss.' Then with cruel suddenness he turned on his heel and left me. Left me with a sweet smile and a sweet unconvincing lie.

He had lied to spare us both the knowledge of our mutual desire. He had lied because he knew nothing of passion between a man and a woman. He lied because he had two irreconcilable pictures of me in his mind. One his dear pretty sister, and the other the irresistible beauty who greeted the wheat carts with her head tipped back and the glory of a goddess of the harvest in her eyes.

So he left me with a lie and I stood, one hand on the mantelpiece of my mama's parlour and my feet on the hearthstone of my home, and shuddered with longing for him. And looked that longing, at last, in the face.

Nothing could stop us or divert us from the road down which we were travelling, Harry and I. No word of mine or act of will could have kept us from each other. We were both like driftwood on the Fenny's springtime floods, and our passion and our love grew as remorselessly as the buds on the trees and the spring flowers in the hedgerows.

If I had wanted to escape this destiny I do not know where I could have gone. I was as driven to Harry as the birds were driven to build nests and lay eggs; my heart and my body called to him as wilfully as the cuckoos called in the greening woods. He was the Master of Wideacre; of course I wanted him for my own.

The first days of the warm spring weather passed for me in a haze of sensual daydreaming. The lambs were fit and we transferred the flock back to the spring grass on the downs and I was suddenly at leisure. I rode around the woods; I even made myself a little line and spent one morning fishing in the high fast river. I took myself up to the downs and lay on damp grass gazing up into the blue sky where a few early larks were climbing. The spring sun warmed my cheeks, my closed eyelids, but inside I was scorching. And there was nothing I could do to stop it.

My nonchalant dismissal of the courtship Celia enjoyed was now past history. When Harry and Mama spoke of the October wedding, I felt nauseous with envy. Harry's every other sentence was of Celia and her likes and dislikes and I could scarcely school my face to remain smiling and serene when I heard her name. She was no longer something off Wideacre, as distant and unimportant as the London scene; she was a threat to me that was coming ever closer. She held my brother's heart in her little hands. She would be coming into my home; she would sit at the foot of the great Wideacre table and Harry would smile down the length of it to her. Worse, most nightmarish picture of all, every night of our lives she and Harry would climb the stairs together and shut the bedroom door, and he would hold her and possess her while I lay in my single bed and trembled with longing.

I did not dream now; I started to think. In the back of my mind a plan was forming to give me the land, and to give me Harry. To forge out of these demented, unlikely elements some stability, some basis for my future. But I could not be certain that it could be done. It depended so much on Celia, and I knew her only slightly. Next time she was due for a visit my eyes were sharp upon her.

Harry met the Havering landau at the steps of the Hall with Mama at his side and me in polite and reticent attendance a few steps behind. I had a perfect view of Celia's face as Harry greeted them, and I saw with amazement that she was nervous with him. Her pale pink parasol trembled over her little head as Harry brushed the footman aside to open the carriage door. He handed Lady Havering out, then turned to Celia. He bowed low and took her gloved hand. The colour flowed from her face and then rushed back as he kissed her hand, but I knew – with the keen insight of a woman in love – that it was not the nervous heat of passion I felt for Harry. What was the silly thing blushing for? Why was she trembling?

I had to understand what went on behind those soft brown eyes, so this time it was I who suggested a drive while our mamas gossiped over the teacups.

We went through the lanes to see Harry's new turnip field. Harry rode politely behind, at a distance to avoid the white chalky dust of the high lanes. So I had her to myself. It was a warm spring day, almost as hot as last summer when we had gone to see the harvest, when I had cared nothing for either of them. Now I knew they could either wreck or make my life.

'Celia,' I said sweetly, 'I am so glad that we shall be sisters. I have been so lonely with just Mama and Harry and I always wanted you as a friend.'

The colour mounted to her face in one of her easy blushes. 'Oh, Beatrice,' she said, 'I should be so glad if you and I were to become special friends. There is so much that will be new to me and strange. And I feel so awkward coming into your mama's house.'

I smiled and pressed her little hand.

'You always seem so grown up and confident,' she said shyly. 'I used to watch you and your papa setting off hunting, and wished so much that I could know you better. And the great horses you rode! When I think now of living in Wideacre Hall, I feel' – she gave a little gasp – 'quite frightened.'

I smiled gently at her. Although she had lived all of her adult life in Havering Hall, as the unwanted stepdaughter and step-sister, she had seen little of country society, and had played no great part in the life of the Hall. She was nervous, of course, and it occurred to me that she might want Harry merely as the lesser of two evils.

'Harry will be beside you,' I said comfortingly.

'Oh, yes,' she agreed. 'But gentlemen can be so . . .' She paused. 'Marriage is so . . .' and she stopped again.

'It's a big step for a girl,' I said helpfully.

'Oh, yes!' she said with such emphasis in her soft voice that I racked my brains to think what was behind all this flutter.

'There is the new position – as the Lady of Wideacre,' I said, biting my tongue on the pain that the title would go to this baby.

'Yes,' she said. 'That is rather frightening, but . . .' There was something more, something else.

'Harry seldom drinks to excess,' I said at random thinking of her stepfather.

'Oh, no!' she said quickly, and I had drawn a blank there, too.

'I am sure he loves you very, very much,' I said. Envy made me faint as if I had an illness. But it was true. I was sure he did, damn her.

'Yes,' she said. 'That's the trouble really.'

I recovered rapidly. The trouble? *What* trouble? 'The trouble?' I repeated.

Her head with the pretty little bonnet bowed low. I saw a tear drop on her figured satin and one gloved finger covered the spot.

'He's so . . .' She couldn't find the word and Lord help me I couldn't think what could be wrong.

'He's so . . .' She tried again, and I was dumb.

'He's so . . . unrestrained . . .' she got out. 'I suppose it is because he is interested in farming . . . but really . . .'

I nearly gasped aloud at this revelation. While I had been aching and longing for Harry and trembling at his touch, this little ice maiden had been refusing his kisses and shrinking from an arm around her waist. Envy made me physically queasy, but my face must not show it.

'I expect men always are,' I said, imitating her awed whisper. 'Is he always like that?'

'Oh, no!' she said. The deep brown eyes flickered to my face. 'The last two Sundays, he changed. He tried to kiss me . . .' – her voice dropped even lower – 'on the mouth! Oh, it was horrid.' She broke off again. 'Something else, too.'

I remembered with every cell of my sensuous body the warmth of Harry's body against mine, my lips opening beneath his and my tongue seeking his mouth. His hand tightening and pressing my breast. That had caused the change.

'He forgot himself,' said Celia with some little determination. 'He forgot who I am. Young ladies do not . . .' She paused. 'And certainly they do not let gentlemen touch them . . . in that way.'

I caught my breath in a hissing sigh. It had to have been the evening in Mama's parlour that had made the difference. I had pressed his hand to my breast. I had opened my mouth to him. He had gone from me to Celia hot with desire and tingling with the touch of his first woman – and cold, unloving little Celia had rebuffed him.

'Did you tell him so?' I asked.

'Of course,' she said. The brown eyes opened wider and she stole another glance at me. 'He seemed angry,' she said. Her lower lip trembled. 'It made me rather afraid . . . for later.'

'Don't you want him to kiss you?' I burst out.

'Not like that! I don't like kisses like that! I don't think I ever will! I don't see how I can learn to bear them. Mama and Step-Papa don't behave like that; they . . . they have an arrangement.'

The whole world knew that Lord Havering's arrangement was a ballet dancer in one of the London theatres when Lady

Havering put her foot down after two children and four miscarriages.

'You would like that with Harry?' I asked. I couldn't believe my ears.

'Oh, no,' she said miserably. 'I know one cannot, until there is an heir. I know there is nothing to be done. I shall just have to . . . I shall just have to . . .' She gave a piteous little sob. 'I shall just have to endure it, I suppose.'

I took her hand in my firm clasp.

'Celia, listen to me,' I said. 'I will be a sister to you in October, and I will be a friend to you now. Harry and I are very, very close – you know how we run the estate together – he will always listen to me because he knows I have his interests at heart. I will be a friend to you, too. I shall help you with Harry. I can talk to Harry and no one but you and I need ever know what you have told me. I can make it all right between the two of you.'

Celia raised her eyes to my face.

'Oh, if you would!' she said. 'But won't Harry mind?'

'Leave it to me,' I said. 'I make only one condition.' I paused and the cherries on her little bonnet trembled. I realized that to escape Harry's embraces she would promise me anything.

'The condition is that you always tell me everything about you and Harry, everything.'

The cherries bobbed as she nodded vigorously.

'Should you change in your feelings to him, or should he change to you, you will tell me at once.'

The cherries bobbed again and she held out her hand.

'Oh, yes, Beatrice. Let's shake hands on the bargain. I promise you shall always be my best and closest of friends. I will always confide in you and you shall have thousands of favours from me. Anything you want that I can give shall be yours.'

I smiled and kissed her cheek to seal the agreement. She had only one thing that I wanted – that I would ever want – and she was far along the road to giving it me, my heart's desire, my brother Harry.

6

I came home from that drive my head full of anything but turnips. Celia's inarticulate murmurs about Harry's courting had made my head throb with jealousy and longing. She might be happy to hand over to me the control of her married life, but it was still her downcast eyes that Harry watched, even when I was near by. And when we stood side by side looking at the turnip field, he had bent his head low to see her pale prettiness under her parasol.

I left her in the parlour and went to my room to take off my bonnet. I looked at myself in the little mirror but my reflection gave me scant joy. If Harry preferred sugar and cream then my clear strong beauty would help me little. My green eyes looked blankly back at me, dark with desire. I could not believe, I could not make my mind believe, that any man would refuse me if I set my heart on him. I sighed and pressed my forehead against the cool glass and longed and longed for Harry.

My skirts hissed as I turned from my room and went downstairs. Celia might not want his love, but she had it. And while I flinched at the sight of his courtesy to her and his gentle words to her as she sat sipping tea, it was worse to be in my room alone, knowing that downstairs he was beside her on the sofa. I might spend more hours with him but never, never could I sit, my eyes downcast, and feel his gaze scanning my face. Never could I look up in the delicious certainty that my eyes would meet his. We were much together, but our magical moments were few. We were always interrupted; Mama was always coming in and out and her eyes were sharp on her beloved son.

At the turn of the stairs I paused. Some careless maid must have left the back-stair door open and one of the stable cats had sauntered in and was sitting, proud as punch, in the first-floor corridor. Mama was ill whenever she was in a room with a cat and it was a house rule that all the stable cats were locked firmly out. I should have to rush this one back to the yard and then air the corridor, or she would have one of her painful gasping attacks when she could not breathe and her face went from white to yellow. Her heart was delicate and last time she had suffered an attack the London specialist had warned her most strongly against risking another. So the rule against cats was rigidly enforced and I should save someone a dismissal if I got the animal away before Mama came up to change.

But as I went towards it something made me pause. And then I stopped stock still. I had no idea in my head, nor the shadow of a plan. But my passion for Harry moved me as if I had no will of my own. I was in the grip of such a longing to be alone with him that my aching sensuous body moved as if of its own volition. I feared Mama's sharp eyes, her instinctive knowledge of me. The way she could almost smell my warm sighs. The cat's eyes met mine, green to green, with a key to Mama's absence as clear as a spoken word between us. Then my hand was on the latch of her bedroom door and the door yielded to my half-conscious touch. Like some obedient familiar the cat stretched and walked, tail proudly high, into the master bedroom and I shut the door behind it. I still could not be sure what I had done. I still could not have said whether I had let the cat in, or if the cat had let itself in with my hand only opening the door. Cat, Mama, Harry and I seemed caught in a web of someone else's spinning. I was as unthinking as the cat itself. I went down to the parlour with my face as clear and calm as the Fenny on a summer's day, and my eyes as opaque as the cat in my delicate mama's bedroom.

I sat beside Celia and even accompanied her on the piano and sang a little duet with her, her thin warble keeping my richer voice more or less in key. Then Harry and she sang a folk song and I took the moment to excuse myself from the parlour and go back upstairs.

The blessed thing had made puddles all over the floor which I had to wipe up. But it had curled up on Mama's bed and sunned itself on the pillow where her head would lie that night. I picked it up by the scruff of its neck and swept down the back stairs with it and set it on its feet outside the stable door. It gazed at me unwinkingly as if it knew we shared a secret — a discreet conspirator.

139

We retired early that night but I was disturbed around midnight by the sound of a door banging and running feet. Mama's maid was probably carrying her a hot posset from the kitchen and a warming pan for her chilled feet. I half thought about getting up to see if I could help her, but my bed was too warm and I was too sleepy to move. Even as I thought I really should go to her, I fell asleep.

When I visited her in the morning the blinds were down and the room reeked of camphor and lavender water. She lay absolutely still on the great bed, her face white on the pillows where the cat had slept and licked its matted dirty fur.

'I am so sorry, dear, but I cannot speak. I feel so ill, so very ill,' said Mama in a thread of a voice. 'Please tell Harry not to be concerned. I shall be better soon.'

I gave a small murmur of sympathy and bent over and kissed her. Her face was strained with pain and she was as white as her sheets. My own head ached in sympathy when I saw the skin drawn tight across her forehead, and my own heart thudded in fear when I heard how her breath rasped and saw her lips tremble. But my eyes gave away nothing, like the cat's. I had planned nothing. I was guilty of no premeditated crime. The deceiving, unreliable old gods of the land had set magic at work on Wideacre and all I could do was to follow blindly wherever they were leading me. The insistent pull of my longing for Harry had brought the cat to wait for me outside my mother's bedroom. Now she struggled for breath in a darkened room. Her pain made me ill. Ill with sympathy for her, and ill with anxiety on my own account.

'Mama,' I said weakly. I needed a smile from her to reassure me that this was only a passing illness. That although she looked as white as death she was still breathing, her fluttering heart was still working. She would be recovered in a few days, she would still have time to love me. She might still turn from her adoration of Harry and learn to value me. I might still become her beloved, her perfect child.

She opened her eyes wearily and saw my anxious face.

'It is all right, Beatrice,' she said with a hint of impatience. 'Go to your breakfast and go out if you wish. I only need rest.'

I heard her tone of dismissal and it hurt me, as she was still able to hurt me. She turned her face away from me without the smile that I was waiting for. There was no need for me to stay. I closed her bedroom door behind me with the slightest of clicks and turned my thoughts from her all that day.

In her absence that afternoon, Harry led me into dinner and for the first time in our lives we faced each other at the head and foot of the candle-lit dinner table and dined alone. We spoke in hushed voices. Although Mama's room was too far away to be disturbed by our talk, the murmur emphasized our privacy in the quiet house, the glow of the room a little island of peace and contentment in the darkened house on the dark land. I sat with Harry as he drank his port, and when he had finished we went to the parlour together. We played cards until Stride brought the tea table in. When I passed Harry his teacup our fingers touched, and I smiled at his touch but I did not tremble. Then we sat in companionable silence before the fire. When he glanced up from watching the burning logs in the grate, he smiled at me and I smiled back without a shadow of need.

It was an evening like an island of peace in a fast-flowing river of desire. We were tired and quiet like two children at the end of a happy, busy day. With no other person calling Harry's attention from me, with no other person frightening me with the prospect of a loss of love, I was able to sit and smile and dream. And I was free at last from need. I went to bed with a chaste, fraternal kiss on my forehead and wanted nothing more. I slept soundly that night with no ache of desire and no confusing dreams of longing. I was secure at last in his affection and undivided attention and that seemed to me then so much. It even, for that one magic, easy night, seemed enough.

The next day was so lovely we decided to make a holiday of it and we rode out together up to the downs. My mourning was at last reduced and I had ordered a pale grey riding habit which suited me well. The underskirt was a soft grey worsted and the smart little jacket was grey velvet. With a matching grey velvet cap on my head, I felt I could stay in second mourning for years. Nothing in bright colours could set off my figure better.

On the top of the downs the wind was stronger and howled my cap away so Harry and I rode a race for it. He won. In truth I reined in and let him win, and he leaned low in his saddle and scooped it up on his riding crop. He cantered back to me and presented it with a flourish. I smiled with all my heart in my eyes.

The horses walked shoulder to shoulder on a long rein along the old drovers' way across the top of the downs and we looked south to glimpse the sea. Larks struggled up and up and up, singing out their achievement, then closed their tiny wings and plummeted to the earth. In the woods a pair of cuckoos called amorously, irresponsibly, to each other, and everywhere there was the lazy rasp-rasp of grasshoppers and the whirring drone of bees.

I was alone on my land with the man I needed, and he had eyes only for me. Today Harry was nobody's son and nobody's fiancé. He was alone with me and my jealous, hungry heart could be still, knowing that all day and all evening we should see no one else. No one would come into the rooms when I was longing to be alone with him. His head would lift and his eyes would smile for no one but me.

The horses rubbed shoulders as they walked, and we talked together of Harry's latest book about farming and my comments on what might work and what would not. We spoke of the house and of the changes that would come in October. Then, without prompting, Harry spoke of Celia.

'She is so pure, Beatrice, so innocent. I respect her so much,' he began. 'A man would be a brute indeed to try to force her in any way. She is like a beautiful piece of Dresden china. Don't you think so?'

'Oh, yes,' I said with ready sympathy. 'She's as beautiful as an angel and so sweet. A little shy perhaps?' I let my voice make a gentle question of the statement.

'And nervous,' Harry agreed. 'With that brute of a stepfather she can have no idea of what a loving marriage can be.'

'Such a shame,' I said carefully. 'Such a shame that such a lovely girl, that your future wife, should be so cool.'

Harry looked quickly at me, his blue eyes piercing.

'It's what I fear,' he said frankly. The horses ambled into a sheltered little dell and stopped to crop the springy downs turf. At our backs the ground rose steeply and below us a hazel coppice shielded us from the north. Sitting there we were screened from everyone and yet could see half of England looking west. Harry jumped down from the saddle and tied his horse. I made no move, but sat idly in the saddle and let my horse graze on a loosened rein.

There was a singing in my ears as sweet and insistent as the lark, and I knew it was the magic of Wideacre and the hum of the spinning wheel spinning the thread of our lives together.

'You are a man of strong passions,' I said.

Harry's profile, as he stood at my horse's head and looked away from me over our land, was as clear and as strong as a Greek statue. My body ached for him, but I kept my voice steady and low.

'I can't help it,' he said and his cheeks flushed red under the golden colour of his skin.

'I understand,' I said. 'It is the same for me. It is in our blood, I think.'

Harry turned quickly to look at me. I was sweating with nervousness like a mare put to the stallion. I could feel the grey gown damp under my arms. But my face was calm and clear.

'A lady can be a perfect lady,' I said. 'Her public behaviour can be meticulous, and yet she can feel desire when she loves and when she has chosen well.'

Harry was staring at me. I could find no words to go on. I merely looked back at him with my passion and longing written all over my face certain that he would see the truth of what was between us.

'You have a fiancé?' he asked in amazement.

'No!' I exploded. 'And I never wish to have one!'

I sprang from the saddle and reached out my arms to him. He caught me as I slid down and I grasped the lapels of his coat and nearly wept in anger and frustration.

'Oh, Harry!' I said, and my voice broke on a sob and then I could not stop crying. The ache in my heart was too strong, the singing in my ears was deafening. 'Oh, Harry! Oh, Harry, my love!'

He froze as if my words had turned him to stone. But I could not stop weeping. I was ruined and he would never love me, but I could not contain myself. I had watched and waited for his touch so long that now his arms were around me I could not play the pretty maiden like Celia. I could not stop myself from clinging to his jacket as if I were drowning. I banged my forehead against the muscled strength of his chest and moaned aloud. He still did not move, but his arms around my waist were as tight as a vice. My sobs quietened and I bit my cheeks to force myself to silence. Slowly, painfully, I pulled a little away from him and raised my eyes to see his face.

Harry's eyes were dark with desire and his heart under my hands was thudding. His mouth was trembling, just slightly, and he gazed into my face as if he would eat me alive.

'It is a sin,' he said in a low voice.

The world was spinning around me. I could hardly hear him; I could hardly find words to reply to him.

'It is not,' I said immediately. 'It is not, Harry. It is right. You can feel it is right. It is no sin. It is no sin. It is not.'

His head came down to me and my eyes half shut in expectation of his kiss. He was so close I could feel his breath on my face and I opened my mouth and breathed in the air from his mouth in a little shudder of longing. But still he would not kiss me.

'It is a sin,' he said softly.

'Worse sin to be married for ever to a woman who is as cold as ice,' I murmured. 'Worse to live with a wife who cannot love you, who does not know how to love, while I wear out my days in yearning for you. Oh, pity me, Harry! If you cannot love me, then pity me.'

'I can love you,' he contradicted me, his voice a husky rumble. 'Oh, Beatrice, if you knew! But it is a sin.'

He was holding on to those four words as a talisman to keep his lovely head from coming down that fraction lower to crush his mouth on mine. I could feel his body was taut with desire and yet he had himself under control. He loved me, he desired me, and yet he would not touch me. I could bear his closeness and the half-inch between our mouths no more. I lunged up to him and bit him, as hard as I could, on his teasing, tormenting mouth. My riding whip was still looped on my wrist and I slid my hand from his chest and caught it dagger-like and stabbed it into his thigh.

'Harry, I will kill you,' I said and I meant it.

His mouth was bleeding and he took one hand from my waist

to put the back of his fingers to his lips. He brought his hand away and saw it was stained with blood. Then he gave a great groan and flung his full weight on top of me. He ripped at my riding habit and as the buttons at the neck parted he moaned and buried his face in my breasts, kissing hard, and biting without mercy. I dragged his breeches down to his knees and he pushed up my skirts and petticoats.

Still half dressed and too desperate to care we rolled together on the grass as Harry thrust with impatient, unskilled stabs at my body, thumping his hardness into my thighs, at my back, against my wet softness until there was that one second of terrifying pleasure as frightening as falling from a tree, as painful as a knife blow and he found the sweet hidden secret place and pushed in, like a fist through curtains. For a split second we both froze still, stunned by the sensation, then he shook my body like a terrier holding a rat, and in seconds I was screaming. My legs and arms grabbed him to me and we writhed like frantic adders. With a great bellow Harry collapsed and lay still and I, hungry, greedy, insatiable, arched my back on the soft downs turf and rubbed and rubbed against him till I gave a great sigh of release and lay still.

Slowly I opened my eyes and saw Harry's head against our blue sky and our larks singing up and up and up. The Squire of Wideacre lay heavily on me. His seed was in my body, his land beneath our coupled bodies; our grass was in one of my clenched hands, and the little meadow flowers and herbs drenched with my wetness beneath me. At last, at last, I had Wideacre and the Master. Our land beneath me, the Squire inside me. I gave a shuddering sob. The ache of longing I had carried with me all my life was gone, and my jealous anxiety had finally released me.

Harry tensed at the sound of my sob and rolled off me, his face a picture of guilt and misery.

'My God, Beatrice, what can I say?' he said helplessly. He sat up and buried his face in his hands. His shoulders sagged, his head bowed. I sat beside him and pulled my gown together at the neck, but not too close. I put a gentle hand on his shoulder. My body was still trembling with the shock of Harry's rough loving; my mind was too dazed with delight to be able to think what was wrong with him.

Harry lifted his sad face at the touch of my hand and looked at me in abject misery.

'My God, Beatrice! I must have hurt you so badly! And I love you so! What can I say? I am so ashamed!'

For a moment I gazed at him blankly, and then his words penetrated my dazed mind and I realized he was full of guilt at what seemed to him some kind of rape.

'It is my fault,' he said. 'I have longed for you ever since the day when I rescued you from that brute. But God forgive me, Beatrice, I have kept seeing you in my mind as I saw you then, naked on the floor. Oh, that I should have saved you from him to ruin you myself!' He dropped his head into his hands again in despair. 'Beatrice, before heaven I never meant to,' he said muffled. 'I am a villain, but God knows not such a villain as to plan this thing. I did not dream such a thing could happen between brother and sister. I am totally to blame and I do not shirk my guilt. But, Beatrice, I did not know such a thing was possible.'

I put my hand tenderly on his silly head.

'You are not totally to blame,' I said gently. 'And there is no blame. You have been dreaming of me, and I have been dreaming of you. There is no need for guilt.'

Harry raised his tear-filled eyes to my face with a glimmer of hope.

'It is a sin though,' he said uncertainly.

I shrugged, and at the movement my dress parted and one silky shoulder and the curve of my breast caught Harry's gaze.

'I cannot feel it is a sin,' I said. 'I know when I am doing wrong and this does not seem to me wrong. It seems to me where I should be, where I have been going towards all my life. I cannot see this as something wrong.'

'It is wrong though,' said Harry. He could not take his eyes from the gap in my gown. 'It is wrong,' he repeated. 'And one cannot say something is not a sin just because it feels right . . .'

His voice, the voice of the authoritative know-all male tailed off as I lay back and shut my eyes. Harry leaned beside me, supported on one elbow. 'You are not thinking logically, Beatrice . . .' he said, and he said no more. He leaned forward and kissed my eyelids as gently as a downland butterfly alighting on a flower.

I made not a move; I barely sighed. I lay as still as a leaf as he traced a line of gentle kisses down my cheek, down my throat, and down the smooth flatness between my breasts. He pushed at the gown with his forehead and rubbed his face, as gentle now as he had been rough before, along the swell of my breasts and then took the crowning nipple in his mouth.

'It is a sin,' he said muffled.

His eyes were shut so he could not see me smile.

I lay still with the sun on my eyelids and felt Harry's weight shift over to come on me again, and felt his insistent hardness. He might have all the resources of education in rhetoric but I had the high singing magic of Widacre, and the easy pull of two young bodies. We moved together and there was a spark of pleasure like lightning before a storm as we touched, but came no closer. We rubbed like courting otters; face to face, body to body, legs entwined, biding our time.

'It is a sin and I will not do it,' said Harry. His denial was exciting to both of us.

'I will not,' he said again as he did. We rocked together and he slid inside me like an otter entering deep water.

'Beatrice, my darling,' he said. I opened my eyes and smiled at him.

'Harry, my love,' I said. 'My only love.'

He groaned and fell on my mouth, and his tongue and his body stirred me at once. This time we were slower, more sensuous. I slithered down on him and twisted to give him as much awareness of me as I could. Harry's ignorant bumpings on me had me shuddering with delight. Then we moved faster and faster till a great explosion of feeling when Harry reared up and banged my head and shoulders on the soft turf of the downs in ecstasy and triumph.

Then we were still for a long, long time.

We rolled apart and dressed. I was quiet in my mind and sore in my body. From a saddlebag I unpacked ham, floury bread still warm from the baking, beer for Harry in a stone jug with a glass stopper, and a broad withy basket of Wideacre strawberries. We sat side by side looking out over our lands and wolfed the food. I was as hungry as if I had been fasting for a week. Harry fetched me a glass of water from the spring further down the hill at the start of the beech coppice and I drank in silence. It wells out of the chalk here as pure as filtered rain. It was icy cold and tasted green and sweet.

After the last strawberry we still had said nothing. I rolled on my back and gazed up at the sky and after a little hesitation Harry lay down beside me, then raised himself to look at my face. He rested his head on one hand and touched my face gently, nervously, with the other hand. As I smiled he took one tress of my loosened chestnut hair and wound it around his finger.

'It pleased you,' he said. It was not a question. He had seen and felt my delight, and it was with relief that I saw there was no need to lie.

'Yes,' I said, rolling to lie on my side as we faced each other mirror fashion.

'Does it seem wrong to you?' Harry's moral certainties had been overthrown by his body, but always he would need words. Even now, sticky with pleasure and worn out from lovemaking, he needed to talk, to put into words the speechless magic that was in the air and the earth all around us.

'We are the Laceys of Wideacre,' I said simply. That statement of family pride still seemed to me the only explanation I would ever need for my behaviour, even though the man who had said it was dead and his son, my brother, had lain in my arms.

'We are the Laceys of Wideacre,' I said again. Harry was blank. He needed words and complicated explanations. Nothing simple would ever do for him. 'Who else could there be for me?' I asked. 'Who else could there be for you? On our own land, where we rule. Who else could there ever be?'

Harry smiled. 'You are as proud as a peacock, Beatrice,' he said. 'It's only a little estate, you know. There are bigger places and older names.'

I stared as blankly at him as he sometimes did at me. I scrutinized his face to see if he was joking, but to my amazement he really meant it. He really could compare Wideacre to other estates as if anywhere else would ever do for a Lacey, as if anywhere else could exist for a Lacey.

'Maybe,' I said. 'But they mean nothing. Here on this land there is only one master and mistress and they are always Laceys of Wideacre.'

148

Harry nodded. 'Aye, it sounds well,' he said. 'And what takes place between you and me is a private matter which no one need ever know. As you say, on our land it is our affair. But we will need to be careful at home.'

My eyes widened. I had meant to explain to Harry that it was inevitable that we should be lovers, as surely as one season follows another. I was myself the heart of Wideacre and he had been the demigod of the harvest. The moment I had opened the barn doors to him I had opened my heart to him. The moment the earth grew for him, he was mine. I took him as easily and as naturally as the chalk soaks up rain. But Harry understood none of this. What he had heard, and what he was now thinking, was that on our own land we could meet and make love in secrecy. He was right. And to be able to love in secret and security would require some planning. But the picture in my mind of the chalk-blue butterfly coming to the flower was not the one Harry had, of hiding from the neighbours and deceiving the servants. I had thought no further than my insistent need for Harry, of the magic that had brought us to this little cup of land as naturally as one kingfisher finds another, though there be only two on the whole length of the river. But Harry had his man's mind on loving me and he wanted to establish ways and means.

'How could we meet in the house in private?' he asked. 'My bedroom is beside Mama's and she is always listening for me. And yours is on the second floor where I could have no excuse to be. Yet I will need to see you, Beatrice.'

'What about the west wing?' I suggested, thinking aloud. 'We hardly ever use the guest bedrooms, and the scullery and breakfast parlour downstairs are closed up. Why don't we convert the parlour into an office for the estate work and I could move into the guest bedroom above?'

Harry frowned, trying to visualize the change.

'The guest bedroom?' he queried.

'It adjoins your room,' I said with half a smile. 'Indeed there was a connecting door which was closed to make two shallow cupboards in each room. But we could easily have it opened up again. Then we could be together in perfect privacy at any time – day or night.'

Harry beamed, like a child promised a treat. 'Oh, Beatrice,' he said, 'that would be so good.'

'We'll do it then,' I said briskly, the dreamy sense of magic gone from me. 'I'll set the work in hand tomorrow, and I'll tell Mama only that we are making an office for the estate work.'

Harry nodded but his face was shadowed again.

'Mama,' he said thoughtfully. 'The faintest shadow of the idea would kill her. I could never forgive myself if we grieved her so. I could not live with myself if she knew. And then there's Celia. And there's your future to think about too, Beatrice.'

I could feel the wall of words building up inside Harry again and I sighed for my own easy, instinctive wordless loving. My eyelids flickered down so he could not see the rueful gleam that showed in them when I thought how I had made love one long hot summer with Ralph and never exchanged more than a dozen words at any meeting. But Harry was so clever.

I gave him a gentle push that laid him flat on his back in the sweet-smelling grass again. He smiled at my playfulness but then his eyes darkened with desire as I leaned over on top of him. The muscles in his body tensed in anticipation of a caress . . . but none came. I put my face close to his throat and pursed my lips but did not kiss him. Instead I blew gently and watched his muscles ripple at the feeling of the tiny cool breaths. In the sudden tense silence I slid down the length of his chest, touching him nowhere but letting him feel my cool blowing in a straight line from his tanned throat to the dimple of his navel and the coarse hairs that pointed like an arrow down to his untied breeches. When the cool promise of my breath stirred the hairs between his straddled legs I reared up and smiled at him. My curls were tumbled, my face flushed, my green eyes gleamed with pleasure – pleasure at the feeling in every inch of my smooth supple body, and in the excitement at this exercise of my natural good power.

'Never mind worrying, Harry,' I urged him with my easy sensuality. 'Just think about what you would like to do now.'

It did not take him long to decide.

At home, Mama was still unwell but she had lost the blueness around her mouth and her breath was coming more easily. One of the under-parlourmaids had confessed to Stride the butler that she had left the stable door open and she was afraid that it had been her fault if a cat had come into the house. Stride had threatened her with dismissal and was waiting for me in the hall before dinner for me to confirm his decision. I was sleepy with pleasure and in a haze of satisfaction.

'She must go,' I said. I had almost forgotten that it had been my hand on the latch of Mama's door. The girl was sent home to Acre village without wages or a character. My mind was too full of my own happiness to contrive better for her.

Stride nodded and summoned us in to dinner. Harry sat at one end of the long polished dining table and I at the other. We glowed like a pair of angels in the candle-light and the room was golden with our happiness.

We talked casually about the land. We spoke of Mama's health and whether she would like to go to the sea for a few days' rest or whether it would be good for her to see one of the best doctors in London. Then Stride left fruit and ratafia before me, and cheese and port before Harry and went out, closing the door behind him. We listened to the sound of his steps down the hall to the kitchen quarters, the swish of the door as he pushed through, and then silence. We were alone.

Harry filled his glass to the brim with the plum-coloured wine and raised it to me in a toast.

'Beatrice,' he said. I formally raised my glass to him in return, in smiling silence.

We gazed at each other down the length of the table in mutual easy appreciation. There was real pleasure to be had in the formality of the room after our rumpled passion on the downs. It was good to see Harry dressed so elegantly for dinner, so like my papa in my papa's chair, while I glowed in a gown of deep violet silk.

Harry broke the spell.

'What of my marriage to Celia?' he asked. 'What shall we do?'

I shook myself alert. I had almost forgotten Celia. I was in no mood for planning and thinking; I felt languorous like a stable cat after a rough mating with a scratchy tom. But Harry was right; we had to decide about Celia. And I noted with pleasure that the decision was to be ours: his and mine.

Not again would Mama announce to me something that

concerned Wideacre and concerned me. I should be part of that decision. Indeed, the decision would be mine.

'She has asked me to speak to you,' I said. Remembering Celia's fear of Harry's sexuality I could not keep the smile out of my voice and Harry's eyes crinkled in amusement as I reported the conversation. 'Apparently, though she wishes to leave her home and become the Mistress of Wideacre, she does not fully wish to be a wife.'

Harry nodded.

'Cold, as I thought,' he said. Like all converts, Harry was an enthusiast. Celia's virginity was no longer a delightful asset; her frigidity was something he now despised.

'Is she proposing a bargain where she takes everything and gives nothing in return?' he asked meanly.

'She is actually rather afraid,' I said fairly. 'It seems that she experienced some rough wooing.'

'Rough!' exclaimed Harry. 'Beatrice, I swear I only kissed her on the lips and held her in my arms. I may have pressed . . .' He broke off. 'But I would hardly call that rough. Would you?' His reasonable tone of argument died on his lips as he recalled exactly what would seem rough between us and he grinned with re-membered pleasure. With one accord we rose from the table and stood side by side at the fireplace looking down at the smoul-dering logs. In the mirror above the fireplace I could see how the dark violet gown enhanced the colour of my smiling sun-rosy face. How my hazel eyes gleamed more cat-like and satisfied than ever. The sun had placed copper lights in my hair and they gleamed through the light powder. I stood at arm's length from Harry, teasing myself with his nearness.

'She would like an arrangement,' I said.

'She means this?' Harry asked incredulously.

'I believe so,' I said honestly. 'She knows Wideacre must have an heir and she's prepared for that. But I think at heart she's a cold woman who prefers to be alone. She's a quiet girl, and shy, and it isn't hard to guess that her home must be a torment to her. What she wants is the position and peace of Wideacre without having to pay for it more than once in the shape of a son.'

'How would this suit us, Beatrice?' Harry asked and my heart warmed at this reassurance that it was my word now at Wideacre.

It would be I who decided whether the wedding went ahead or not. Celia could be the pawn I moved on the chessboard of my desires. My mama, too, could be present or absent as I desired. I held the Master of Wideacre in the palm of my hand, and his land, and his power, and his wealth, were mine as they should be.

I shrugged negligently.

'It is your choice, Harry,' I said, as if I did not plan to make the decision. 'You have to marry to come into full ownership of the estate and to take control of the capital from the lawyers. Otherwise we will have to wait until you are of age. It might as well be Celia as any other. The plans have gone ahead and it would be difficult to withdraw. Besides, a wife who does not seek your company too often will make it easy for us to be together.'

Harry glanced up quickly from watching the fire to look at me, tantalizingly out of reach.

'Do you find me rough, Beatrice?' he asked thickly.

A denial and reassurance in case he was afraid he had hurt me was on the tip of my tongue, but some wise instinct made me pause. There was some flaw in Harry that mingled pleasure and pain in his mind and that I never would understand. The thought of hurting me was making him breathe a little faster, was making his cheeks flush. I did not dislike it, for his arousal made me shiver inside. Harry's way would never be my way. Yet I could satisfy him.

'Yes, you hurt me,' I breathed.

'Are you in pain?' he asked, as taut as an animal ready to spring.

'I am bruised,' I said. 'You hammered my head on the ground and you bit my lips till they bled.'

We were both breathing faster but still I stayed just out of his reach.

'Were you afraid of me?' Harry asked.

My eyes met his and I could see our family likeness. Brother and sister, our darkened eyes of desire were the same. In that frozen hot second we were more than siblings, we were like twins.

'Yes,' I said. 'But I shall have my revenge when I hurt you.'

I had the key to Harry. The statues moved. His arm pinned me to him for a hard biting kiss and his other hand smoothed down the silk of my back and then clenched my buttocks with his fingernails digging in. My mouth opened wide under his and he forced me down on the dining-room floor and took me as roughly as an enemy. One of his hands clasped mine above my head so that I was helpless beneath him, while the other hand pulled up my skirts and petticoats. But when I struggled he instantly released me and checked his inexpert heavy thrusts. But I freed my hands only to hold him closer and guide him inside me.

'My love,' I said. Perverse. Wordy. Pompous. He was still the Squire of Wideacre and I wanted him inside me.

'My love,' I said.

I slept in my own bed, the first sweet sleep I had had since the death of my father and the crippling of Ralph. My darling Harry had taken from me the dreadful tension and I felt I could rest. Not once in the night did I hear the snap then the thud of a closing mantrap and the sharp crack of breaking bones. Not once did I jerk into wakefulness, thinking I heard a clank outside my door as some hideous cripple clawed into my room, dragging his legs in the mouth of a monstrous trap behind him. Harry had set me free. The golden boy had released me from my darkness, and I no longer ached with pain and fear, nor with longing for those I had loved whom I would never see again.

And their loss now seemed to me to be part of the natural order of things. In farming you have to break the earth and drain ditches to make the land flower and fruit. I had done some breaking; I had ordered a culling. But now the new life was in the earth; there was a new young master, and the proof that I had done right was that the future was very bright and sunny, and that I was safe on the land where I belonged.

I stood before the little mirror on my dressing table and tilted it to see how I must look to Harry. I saw a bruise mouth-shaped on my left breast and I touched it with wondering fingers that I should have been bitten so hard, and yet remembered no pain. In the morning sunshine my skin had the bloom of a ripe peach, ready for picking. From my feet, so white with such high-arched insteps, to the copper curls that framed my face and warmed and tickled the curve of my bare back, I was made for loving. I fell back on the bed, my hair fanned out on the pillow, and craned my neck to see in the mirror how I had appeared to Harry when he took me on grass or on wooden floor, wide-eyed and wide-legged. Watching myself I became luxuriously certain that Harry would soon come to me. It was early; my maid would not call me for an hour; my mother was still safe in her drugged sleep. Harry and I could lie together now and steal off to a hollow in the downs or in the woods after breakfast.

I did not move when I heard the step outside my door but simply turned a lazy head to the opening door and smiled my welcome to Harry. Instead – I jumped as if I had been scalded – there was my mother!

'Good heavens, child,' Mama said calmly. 'You'll catch your death of cold. Whatever are you doing?'

I held my tongue and blinked lazily at her. The only thing I could do.

'Have you just woken?' she asked. I yawned and carelessly reached for my shift.

'Yes,' I said. 'I must have thrown off my clothes in the night as it was so hot.' I felt better with my shift on, but underneath my relief I was prickly with irritation – at myself for that guilty start, and at my mother who walked so calmly into my room as if she owned it.

'How lovely to see you up and about again,' I said smiling. 'Are you sure you are well enough? Hadn't you better go back to your room after breakfast?'

'Oh, no,' said Mama as if she never had a day's illness in her life. She crossed the room, her morning dress rustling, and made herself at home on the window seat.

'I am feeling so much better! You know how it is with me after these attacks. Once they are over I feel as if I should never be ill again. But you, Beatrice,' – she narrowed her gaze and looked at me closely as I sat up in bed – 'you are looking so well, so glowing! Has something pleasant happened?'

I smiled and shrugged my shoulders.

'Oh, nothing really,' I said dismissively. 'Harry took me for a ride on the downs yesterday, and I felt so happy again to be out and about in the lovely weather.'

Mama nodded.

'You must go out more,' she said. 'If we could only spare a lad from the stables it would be all right for him to ride behind you and then you could go out more. But I doubt if there is one to spare with the horses wanted out on the land. Still once Harry is married you will have Celia for company. You can teach her to ride and take her out.'

'Lovely,' I said absently and turned the subject. Mama spoke about clothes and said how glad she was to be out of the heavy mourning black we had been wearing.

'You can have something pretty for Harry's wedding, but not too bright,' she said. 'And while they are away we can plan for a little party to welcome them home and that can be your coming-out party, Beatrice. That way you will be able to make more calls with Celia, and if the Haverings take her to London, you will be able to go too.'

I stopped stock-still in the act of pouring water from my ewer into the basin. 'Going away?' I said blankly.

'Yes,' said Mama lightly. 'Celia and Harry are to have one of these new-fangled wedding tours. They are planning to go all the way to France and Italy – did no one mention it to you? Celia wants to sketch and Harry wants to visit some farms he has read about. I should hate such a marathon and, I dare say, so would you. But if the two of them wish to go they may enjoy it. You and I can keep each other company here, my dear. You will be busy overseeing the winter sowing for Harry, I suppose.'

I bent my head over the basin and splashed the cold water in my face, keeping my head down so that Mama could not see me. I reached blindly for a towel. Mama would not be able to tell I could not control a grimace of pain and fear. I buried my face in the towel and held its softness to my eyes where tears of anger and fear were stinging hot. I did not feel unhappy; I felt murderous. I wanted to strike Celia, to smash her pretty face and scratch her soft brown eyes. I wanted Harry to suffer the torments of the damned and crawl to me for forgiveness. I simply could not bear the thought of those two alone together, travelling in a post-chaise and staying at hotels. Dining together without family or friends around them, able to slip away for kisses and caresses any time they wished, while I ached with desire and

156

loneliness and waited for Harry's return like an old spinster, unwanted at home.

And I was angry, for it had only been last night that I had drawn such pleasure from the knowledge that never again would I be the one whose life was planned for her, whose days were made to revolve around another's. I was certain that with Harry's heart in my hands and my secret key to Harry's sensuality, I should have Wideacre. Now, mere hours after I had lain with Harry on the hard wooden floor, my mama was telling me news as if I was of no more importance than the young daughter of any house.

'Is this Harry's idea?' I asked, coming out of the towel and dressing with my back to Mama in the window seat.

'He and Celia dreamed it up together when they were always singing Italian songs,' she said complacently. 'He thought she would like to hear them sung by Italians or some such nonsense. They won't be gone long, only two or three months. They will be home for Christmas.'

I gasped, but she did not hear me, and as I turned to brush my hair at the mirror she did not notice that my face was white. All my old pain of longing for a safe arm to hold me and a promise of love I could trust was flooding back over me. It was even worse now I had lain with Harry and knew what it was to be loved by him. I could perhaps live without his loving. Or I could live without being the first person on Wideacre. But I could not live with neither. And I could not bear the prospect of another woman having both the love and the power. If Celia was a beloved wife there was nothing to stand between me and the dominance of my mama. Nothing to save me from the emptiness of dutiful daughter days. Nothing to prevent me from being married off to the first likely suitor who chanced our way. If I lost Harry now, I would lose everything I had ever wanted – my pleasure and land. Just as Ralph had said.

This trip had to be prevented. I knew, because I knew Harry, that if he were all alone with Celia for two months he would come to love her. And who could resist him? I had seen him with a frightened foal or an injured hound, and I knew how he prided himself on his gentle understanding, on winning a shy creature's confidence. He would see Celia's coldness as a result of her cruel treatment at home and set himself the task of becoming her friend. Once he came to know her he would realize she was indeed the best bride he could have found.

Under her shy and cool defences, Celia was warm and loving. She even had a little bud of humour, and Harry would learn to make those brown eyes twinkle and he would hear her girl's ripple of laughter. It would be inevitable that they would warm to each other, and equally inevitable that one night, after the opera or the theatre, or some peaceful dinner for two, Celia would be smiling with wine and new confidence. Harry would turn to her for a kiss and she would give him one. He would touch her breast and she would not push his hand away. He would stroke her narrow pliant back and whisper endearments, and she would smile and twine her arms around his neck. And I? I would be forgotten.

Nothing of these panicky thoughts showed in my face as Mama and I went downstairs, but when we entered the break-fast parlour some hours later I had a second shock of pain at Harry's delighted greeting to Mama and his warm smile to me was as sunny and open as his delight in seeing her. I drank tea and ate a little toast, while Harry wolfed down cold ham, cold beef, some new bread and honey, some toast and butter and finally a peach. Mama ate heartily too and laughed and joked with Harry as if she had never been ill. Only I sat silent. I was back in my old place at the side of the table rather than at the end. The outsider again.

'Beatrice looks so well and so happy I think she should have some more riding,' Mama remarked as Harry carved himself one more slice of meat. He picked at the white fat with his fingers and ate it first. 'Perhaps you could make a point of seeing she goes out daily,' Mama said, as if I were a lapdog that needed walking.

'Rather,' said Harry unhelpfully.

'Could she ride today in the morning or in the afternoon?' she asked. I looked up from my plate and my eyes sent an urgent message to Harry. 'Now! Now! Say now, and let us race up to the downs and tumble into our little hollow and I will forget this jealousy and pain and give you such pleasure that you will never want to come home and never want another woman in your life.'

Harry smiled at me, his open, brotherly smile.

'If you don't mind, Beatrice, I will see to it tomorrow. I promised Lord Havering I would look at his coverts with him today and I dare not be late.'

He took out his watch and pushed back his chair to go.

'I'll not be back till late tonight, Mama. I shall stay to dinner if I'm asked. I have not been there for three days and I shall have to make my apologies!'

He bent and kissed her hand and smiled at me in farewell and strolled out of the room as if he had not a care in the world. I heard his footsteps cross the hall, then the front door open and close. In the silence I could hear the clatter of his horse as the groom led it round from the stable and then the clip-clop as he rode away. He rode away as if love and passion meant nothing. He rode away because he was a fool. I had put my heart in the keeping of a fool.

My mama looked at me.

'You must not mind, Beatrice,' she said. 'A young man is bound to be thoughtless of his family when he is engaged to be married. You cannot blame him for preferring Celia's company to ours. We will all be more settled when this time of waiting is over. I am sure he will find time to ride with you tomorrow.'

I nodded and moved my face muscles into a semblance of a smile.

I held that smile all the long day.

In the afternoon Mama was going calling, but she had enough sympathy with my forlorn state not to force me to go with her. As soon as her carriage had vanished, I took my horse out and rode down to the River Fenny – not near the old cottage where Ralph used to live – but upstream to a deep, clear pool where Harry sometimes tried to catch fish. I tied the horse to a bush and lay face down on the ground.

I did not weep or sob. I lay silent and let the great waves of jealousy and misery wash over me. Harry did not love me as I loved him. Sensuality for him was an occasional pleasure – necessary in that second of desire, but swiftly enjoyed and forgotten. To me it was a way of life, the very kernel of myself. Harry had his outside life: his newspapers, his journals, his books, his men friends, his engagement to Celia and his visits to the Haverings. All I had to dream of, to fill my life, to keep me alive and glowing, was Wideacre. Wideacre and Harry.

And at this moment I had only Wideacre. My cheek lay on the damp, dark leafmould of the forest floor, and when I opened my eyes I could see small, spindly plants with heart-shaped leaves pushing their narrow stems up through the dark peat. Beyond their bowed little heads was the sheen of the Fenny, gleaming like pewter. It flows almost silently here between deep banks, overhung with maidenhair fern and lit by brilliant lanterns of kingcups – as bright above the water as their reflections on the shiny surface.

In the centre of the river one can see two worlds. The reflected world of air and winds, the tossing trees and cloudy sky, and the underworld of the riverbed, a mixture of pure white sand and stones as yellow as gold. In the dark curves of the river where ponds have formed the filtered scraps of peat make the hollows black and ominous, but in the main stream the riverbed glows like sunshine. The bright green weed tossing in the current hides young trout, baby eels and a few salmon. The green ferns at the bank mask the holes of water shrews and otters.

I lay in silence until the thud of my own angry and resentful heart had stilled and until I could hear the safe steady beat of the heart of Wideacre. Deep, deep in the earth, so deep most people never hear it, beats the great heart, steady and true. It spoke to me of endurance and courage. Of setting my heart on the land and staying with the land. Of being full of sin and blood to get thus far, and of other sins which would take me steadily further.

I saw them pass before me without blinking. The death's head of my father's agonized face; the scream from Ralph; even the fluttering fall from my window of the owl we had called Canny. Wideacre spoke to me in my loneliness and my longing for love and the beat of its heart said, 'Trust no one. There is only the land.' And I remembered Ralph's advice – which he himself had fatally forgotten – to be the one who is loved. Never to make the mistake of being the one who does the loving.

I listened to that secret beat, that hard wise secret, for a long, long time, until my cheek took the impress of the dead leaves and the front of my grey habit was darkened with the damp of the soil. The chill cooled me and hardened me, like a new-forged weapon of iron. Then I mounted my horse and trotted at a ladylike pace for home.

We dined early for there was no point in waiting for Harry. I poured Mama's tea for her in the parlour and she told me about her calls and the latest women's tittle-tattle of the neighbourhood. I took care to nod and look interested. When she rose to go to bed, I threw another log on the fire and said I would stay and read for a few minutes longer. She kissed me goodnight and left. I sat stock-still, like an enchantress in a fairy story, my eyes on the burning log in the grate.

The front door opened quietly. Harry made no noise crossing the hall, thinking the whole house was asleep. He saw the light under the parlour door and came in. I saw at a glance that it was as I had hoped. He had been drinking and was unsatisfied. His walk had a quickness and an alertness. His blue eyes sparkled.

'Beatrice!' He said my name as a thirsty man might say, 'Water!'

I smiled and, more like an enchantress than ever, said nothing, but let the magic of my body and face draw him from the doorway across the room to kneel at my feet before the fire.

'I felt we should be apart today,' he said hesitantly, apologetically. 'I needed to think.'

My face showed no sign of my impatience at his silly lie. Harry *think* indeed! I knew he had lost his nerve and – afraid of my sensuality, afraid of his own, afraid of the sin, afraid of the consequences – had fled to Celia's coolness to escape the heat of home. And I knew well enough what had happened there. Celia and her pretty young sisters had petted and teased him all afternoon; Lord Havering's good wine and generous glasses of port had made him bold again. He had begged a moonlit walk in the garden with Celia and her frightened, struggling refusal of a kiss had set him on fire again with unsatisfied desire and brought him back to my feet. But it was not love with Harry. And it should not be love with me.

'I hope you did not mind,' he asked tentatively. He looked up at me and took one still, unresponsive hand. I looked as if I had no idea why I should mind. My hazel eyes fixed on the fire were wide open with detached and polite interest in Harry's conversation.

'I was afraid of us as lovers,' he confessed honestly, his eyes fixed on my face. Still I said nothing. My confidence was growing but I was still chilled inside from my sad vigil in the wood. And I would never love a man who did not love me more.

He fell silent and I let the silence stretch.

'Beatrice,' he said again. 'I will do anything . . .'

It was a clear plea. I had won.

'I must go to bed,' I said, standing. 'I promised Mama I would not stay up late. We did not expect you back so soon.'

'Beatrice,' he said again, looking up at me.

If I had slackened my control and allowed so much as one of my fingers to touch one of the curls of his head, I should have been lost. I would have collapsed to the hearth rug with him and he would have taken me that night and left me the following morning for Celia on a pendulum that would have swung every day of a miserable life. I had to win this struggle with Harry. If once I lost him, I lost not only the love of the one man I wanted, but I also lost Wideacre. I had staked my life's happiness on this indecisive, conscience-ridden creature and I had to win. Against his own good conscience and against his own good, sweet betrothed, I had set his passionate nature and the taste of perverse pleasure he had with me – my whip on his thigh, the taste of blood when I bit his lips, which he would never have with gentle Celia.

I smiled down at him but took care not to touch him.

'Goodnight, Harry,' I said. 'Perhaps we will ride on the downs together tomorrow.'

I undressed slowly in a dream by candle-light, hardly knowing whether my desperate gamble had won me security or whether I had lost everything. Was Harry even now on his knees at his bedside praying like a good child for God to keep him pure? Or was he still kneeling by my chair in the parlour burning with desire? I slid between the sheets and blew out the candle. In the dark I could hear the house settle in the silence but I lay wakeful, reliving the scene downstairs and aching for my lover. I waited for sleep but I expected to lie awake. My aroused heart beat fast and every muscle in my body quivered in expectation.

In the silence of the night I heard an odd, soft noise and I held my breath to listen. I heard it a second time – the creak of a board in the passage outside my door and then – the most welcome sound in the whole world – a soft sad moan as Harry pressed his forehead to the unyielding wood of my door and kneeled on the floorboards outside my room.

He did not dare to try the handle of the door; he did not dare even to tap on the door to see if I would let him in. He was like a whipped dog in the passageway and knew his master at last. He knelt in longing and in remorse and silence on my threshold. And I let him wait there.

I turned over in bed, smiled in silent delight . . . and slept like a baby.

My mother teased Harry about the dark shadows under his eyes at breakfast and said she did not know what to blame – Celia's pretty face or Lord Havering's port. Harry smiled with an effort and said with careful nonchalance, 'A morning's gallop on the downs will soon blow the cobwebs away, Mama! Will you come riding with me today, Beatrice?'

I smiled and said, 'Yes,' and his face lightened. I said not another word at breakfast, nor did I speak until we had ridden up past our fields where the corn was ripening to the downs. Harry led the way like a practised lover to our little hollow among the ferns, dismounted and turned to help me.

I kept my seat and looked steadily down until I saw his confidence waver.

'You promised me a gallop,' I said lightly.

'I have been a fool,' he said. 'I have been mad, Beatrice, and you must forgive me. Forget yesterday, remember only the day before. Don't give me that pleasure and then rob me of it. Punish me another way, be as cruel to me as you like but don't teach me of the loveliness of your body and then take it from me. Don't condemn me to live in the house with you, to see you every day and yet never be able to hold you again! Don't condemn me to a living death, Beatrice!'

He stumbled to a halt on what was nearly a sob and as he raised his face I saw his mouth trembling. I reached out to him and let him hold me as I slid down from the saddle. But I freed myself when my feet touched the turf and stepped back so we did not touch. His eyes were hazy blue with desire and I knew mine were dark. The slow, warm heat of arousal was beating in my body and my control over myself and over this scene was slipping fast. My anger at Harry and my conflicting desire to be under him again fused into one passion of love and hatred. With my full force I slapped him as hard as I could on the right cheek and then struck him a violent back-handed blow on his left cheek.

Instinctively, he jerked back and lost his footing over a tussock of grass. I followed, and still guided by wordless anger, kicked him as hard as I could in the ribs. With a great groan of pleasure he doubled up on the grass and kissed the toe of my riding boot. I tore off my dress as he ripped his breeches away and flung myself like a wildcat on him. Both of us screamed as I rode him astride, like a stable lad breaking a stallion. I pounded his chest, his neck and his face with my gloved fists until the climax of pleasure felled me like a pine tree to lie beside him. We lay as still as corpses under our sky for hours. I had won.

The following day I went to call on Celia. Mama chose to come too and she and Lady Havering closeted themselves in the parlour with wedding-dress patterns and tea and cakes while Celia and I were free to wander in the garden.

Havering Hall is a bigger house than Wideacre – built on a different scale as a great showpiece, while Wideacre has always been a manor house extended and improved, but firstly a beloved home. Havering is large, rebuilt in the last century in the baroque style, which was popular then, with plenty of stone garlands and statuary niches and swags of stone ribbons over the windows. If you like that sort of thing it is said to be a fine example. I think it fussy and overdone. I prefer the plain clean lines of my home with the windows set honest and straight in the sand-coloured walls and no fancy pillars blocking the sunlight from the front rooms.

The gardens were laid out at the same time and they show the neglect even worse than the house. The paths were planned with a ruler and compass to follow straight lines around square and rectangular flower beds leading one, like a bored pawn on a gravel and grass chessboard, to the square ornamental pond in the centre of the garden where the carp are supposed to fin among flowering water lilies, and the fountains play.

In practice, the pond is dried out because it sprang a leak and no one had the wit to find the hole and have it mended. The fountains never played well because of low water pressure, and when the pump broke they stopped for ever. The carp benefited the herons but no one else.

The ornamental flower beds may still preserve their soldier-straight rows of flowering plants and the centre crowns of roses, but it is hard to tell for the towering weeds. They are the friendly wild flowers of my Wideacre childhood – rosebay willowherb, gypsy's lace, wild foxgloves. But they look like a sign of the end of the world in these formal gardens. The ladies of Havering – Celia's mama, herself and her four stepsisters – can see no solution but to wander around the garden saying, 'Dear, dear' at the greenfly and the suckers and the crumbling flower-bed edges. A week's hard work by two sensible men would reverse the decay, and anyone but a fool would set them to it. But the ladies of Havering prefer to endure, with sad acceptance, the rack and ruin of garden and, more seriously, of farmland.

'It is a shame,' Celia concurred. 'But the house is worse. It is so gloomy with the furniture under dust sheets and bowls out to catch the drips of water when it rains. And in winter it is really very cold.'

I nodded. I could sympathize with Celia's position as a stepdaughter from a previous marriage brought into a home both overpoweringly grand and unnecessarily uncomfortable. But for Celia our lands and our position were not just enviable for themselves – they were her refuge from the discomforts and humiliations of her home. With good management, a lot could have been done with the Havering estate; Harry and I expected a handsome profit from Celia's dowry lands. After all, we shared the same good soil and easy weather. There was no God-given reason that Wideacre cattle should be twice the size of the Havering beasts, or that Wideacre fields should offer double the yield. Except, of course, for the crucial ingredient of the Master's boot. Wideacre had never been neglected by an absentee landlord spending the profits faster than they grew.

Wideacre Hall might be plain and unfashionable. The rose garden might be modest and too like simple gardens of cottages and small farmhouses. But that was because when the land yielded a good golden profit, the money went back into the land, repairing buildings, fences and gates; buying time so fields could be rested between sowings; carting mulch from the stables to make the earth yield in greater and greater abundance. But Lord Havering cared nothing for the land except as a source of gambling money, and his wife and his daughters could live in a broken-down barn for all he cared as long as he had an income from his rack-rents to gamble away at White's or Brooks's in London.

'You will be glad to get to Wideacre,' I said sympathetically.

'I will,' she said. 'Especially with you there, dearest Beatrice. And your mama too, of course.'

'I am surprised, then, that you are going on a wedding tour,' I said carefully. 'Was it your idea?'

'It was,' she said dolefully. 'It was. Oh, Beatrice!' She glanced guiltily back at the house as if her mama's stern face was looking out of the windows, or as if her four stepsisters might at any moment creep out and eavesdrop. Abruptly she guided us into an overgrown arbour and sat down. I sat down beside her and put a sisterly arm around her.

'It was my idea when Harry was so sweet and gentle,' she said. 'I thought we would go to Paris and Rome and hear the lovely concerts, and make visits and things . . .' Her voice tailed off. 'But now when I think of marriage and the things one has to do, I wish I had never suggested it! Just think of being quite alone for weeks!' My body melted at the very thought of being alone with Harry for weeks, but I kept a proper face of sisterly concern.

'If only your mama could come with us,' Celia said wildly. 'Or Beatrice . . . or . . . or . . . or you!'

I was genuinely surprised.

'Me?' I said. I had thought only of stopping the tour but this was a new development.

'Yes,' she said quickly. 'You can come and keep me company while Harry is visiting his farms and lectures, and then when I am sketching you can keep Harry company in Rome.'

The idea of keeping Harry company in Rome made my head spin with imagined pleasure.

'Oh, Beatrice, say you will!' she said quickly. 'It is quite customary. Last year Lady Alverstoke took her sister on her wedding tour, and Sarah Vere did so too. Beatrice, do come with us as a favour to me. Your company would make all the difference in the world to me, and I'm sure Harry would like it too. We could all have such fun.'

'We could,' I said slowly. In my mind's eye were hot, sunlit afternoons with Celia sketching with her maid, or making calls, while Harry and I lay luxuriously together in the sunlight. Or in the evening while Celia attended a concert, Harry and I in a little discreet house dining together, and then retiring to a private room with a bottle of champagne. Of the long, sensuous hours while Celia was fitted with Paris clothes, of the snatched moments while Celia wrote letters to her mama. Of daily rides together in foreign scenes, of little secret places we would find to hide and embrace.

'Promise you will come!' Celia said desperately. 'It is yet another favour I ask of you, I know. But promise me you will!'

I took her fingers that trembled so pitifully in a comforting sisterly grasp.

'I promise I will come,' I said reassuringly. 'As a special favour to you, dear Celia, I will come.'

She held my hand as a drowning man might clutch at a branch. And I let her cling to me. Celia's hero worship of me might be tedious, but it gave me a strong hold on her and on Harry through her. We were sitting, hand-clasped, when her stepbrother George came running out to find us.

'Good afternoon, Miss Lacey,' he said, blushing the rosy red of a coltish fourteen-year-old boy. 'Mama sent me to find you to tell you that your mama is ready to leave.'

Celia fluttered ahead of us up the weed-strewn path to the house while George offered me his arm with elaborate courtesy.

'They have been talking about the bread riots,' he said with an awkward attempt at conversation with the lovely Miss Beatrice, the toast of the county.

'Oh, yes,' I said with polite interest. 'Bread riots where?'

'In Portsmouth, Mama said, I think,' he said vaguely. 'Apparently a mob broke into two bakers' claiming the bread was made with adulterated flour. They were led by a legless gypsy on horseback. Fancy that!'

'Fancy,' I repeated slowly, uneasy with a feeling of dread I could not properly understand.

'Fancy a mob being led by a man on a horse,' George said with youthful scorn. 'Why, next they'll be looting with a curricle and pair.'

'When was this?' I asked sharply, some premonition drawing a cold fingernail down my spine.

'I don't know,' said George. 'Some weeks ago, I think. They've probably all been caught by now. I say, Miss Lacey, will you dance at Celia's wedding?'

I found a smile to meet his open admiration. 'No, George,' I said kindly. 'I shan't be fully out of mourning. But when I am, at the first party I shall dance with you.'

He coloured up to his ears and escorted me up the steps to the Hall in breathless silence. Mama and Lady Havering were not speaking of the Portsmouth bread riots when we entered the drawing room, and there was no opportunity to ask more about it. It remained a faint shadow on my mind, like the cold shiver that country people say is someone walking over your grave. I did not like to hear of angry men on horses, of legless men leading mobs. But I could hardly have said why.

In any case, the most pressing problem before me was to seize my God-given chance to join the wedding tour. Some wise instinct made me delay telling Harry that his bride had asked me along for company until we were at tea: Mama, Harry and myself. I wanted to make sure that Harry could not refuse me as a lover what he could be forced to grant me as a brother.

I stressed that it was Celia's invitation to me, and said that I had told her I could give her no answer without mama's consent. I watched Harry's face carefully and saw the brief leap of anticipation and pleasure at the news, succeeded by the more permanent expression of doubt. Harry's good conscience had the upper hand again and I realized, with a pang of jealousy and pain, that he was looking forward to being alone with Celia, far away from her overbearing mother, far away from his stultifying, smothering, loving mama. Far away, even, from his desirable, mysterious sister.

'It would be a marvellous opportunity for you,' Mama said, glancing towards Harry to guess what her darling boy would prefer. 'And so like Celia to think of giving you pleasure. But perhaps Harry feels he needs you here while he is away? There is always a lot of work to do on the land in autumn, I know your papa used to say so.'

She turned to Harry, having prepared the ground so he could merely indicate his wishes and we would all rush to satisfy them. Everything in this house went to Harry. I curbed my impatience.

'Celia was actually begging me to come,' I said, a smile on my face. I looked directly at Harry down the walnut table. 'She rather dreads, I think, being left in a strange town while Harry seeks out some experimental farmer.' My eyes held his and I knew he would read my secret message. 'She does not yet share your tastes, as I do.'

He knew what I meant. Mama glanced curiously from his face to mine.

'Celia has many years ahead of her to learn to share Harry's tastes,' she said gently. 'I am sure she will do her very best to please him and make him happy.'

'Oh, yes,' I said in ready agreement. 'I am sure she will make us all happy. She is such a sweet good girl; she will be a marvellous wife.'

The thought of a lifetime with a 'marvellous wife' cast a shadow over Harry's face. I took a gamble on Mama's innocence and rose from my seat and walked to the head of the table. To Mama's view from the foot I was prettily coaxing my dear brother, but he and I knew as I came near him the speed of his pulse was raised and, at my touch and at the smell of my warm perfumed skin, his breathing became faster. I kept my back to Mama and put my cheek against his face. I felt his skin grow hot under mine and I knew that my touch, the glimpse of my breasts at the top of my gown, were winning the battle for me against Harry's weathercock feelings. There was never any need to argue with Harry. He was lost at the first reminder of pleasure.

'Do take me with you, Harry,' I pleaded, in a low coaxing tone. 'I promise I will be good.' Hidden from our mother, I breathed a kiss high on his cheek near his ear. He could stand no more and gently pushed me from him. I saw the muscles around his eyes were tense with self-control.

'Of course, Beatrice,' he said courteously. 'If that is what Celia desires, I can think of no more agreeable arrangement. I shall write her a note and join you and Mama in the parlour for tea.'

He got himself quickly out of the room to cool off and left me alone with Mama. She was peeling a peach and did not look at me. I slipped back into my seat and cut a few grapes from the fat cluster with a pair of delicate silver scissors.

'Are you sure you should go?' Mama asked evenly. She kept her eyes on her neat hands.

'Why not?' I asked idly. But my nerves were alert.

She groped for a good reason and could not answer me at once.

'Are you anxious at being left alone?' I asked. 'We shall not be gone very long.'

'I do think it would be easier if you stayed,' she concurred. 'But I dare say I can manage for six or eight weeks. It is not Wideacre . . .' She let the sentence hang, and I did not help her to complete it.

'Perhaps they need time to be alone together . . .' she started tentatively.

'Whatever for?' I said coolly, gambling on her belief in my virginal innocence. Gambling also on her own experience of marriage, which had not included courtship as a preliminary, nor a honeymoon as an introduction, but had been a business arrangement contracted for profit and concluded without emotion, except mutual dislike.

'Perhaps you and Harry would do well to be apart . . .' she said, even more hesitantly.

'Mama,' I said challengingly with my brave courage high. 'Whatever are you saying?'

Her head jerked up at the strength in my voice and her pale eyes looked half frightened.

'Nothing,' she said, almost whispering. 'Nothing, child. Nothing. It is just that sometimes I am so afraid for you – for your extreme passions. First you adored your father to such a height of feeling, and then you transferred that affection to Harry. All the time you will do nothing but roam around Wideacre as if you were a ghost haunting the place. It frightens me to see you so obsessed with Wideacre, so constantly with Harry. I just want you to have a normal, ordinary girlhood.'

I hesitated. 'My girlhood is normal and ordinary, Mama,' I said mildly. 'It is not like yours because times are changing. But even more so because you were reared in town whereas I have had a country childhood. But I am no different from girls of my own age.'

She remained uneasy, but she would never have the courage to look into the pictures she had of Harry and me, to see clearly what was taking place before her frightened half-shut eyes.

'I dare say you are not . . .' she said. 'I cannot judge. We see so few young people. Your papa had little time for county society and we live so withdrawn . . . I can hardly judge.'

'Don't be distressed, Mama,' I said soothingly, my voice warm with assumed affection. 'I am not obsessed with Wideacre, for, see, I am leaving in mid-autumn, one of the loveliest seasons. I am not possessive of Harry for I am happy at his marriage and I am making close friends with Celia. There is nothing to fear.'

Mama had neither wits sharp enough nor instincts true enough to filter truth from lies. In any case, if the truth of my relationship with Harry had stared her in the face she would have died rather than see it. So she swallowed her last slice of peach and gave me an apologetic smile.

'I am foolish to worry so,' she said. 'But I do feel the responsibility of you and Harry heavily on me. Without your papa you two have only me to guide you and I am anxious that ours shall be a truly happy home.'

'Indeed it is,' I said firmly. 'And when Celia lives here with us all it will be even happier.'

Mama rose to her feet and we walked together to the door. I opened it for her in a pretty gesture of courtesy and she paused to give me a gentle kiss on the cheek.

'God bless you, my dear, and keep you safe,' she said tenderly, and I knew she was reproaching herself for her lack of warmth towards me, and for the unease she felt when she saw me with my arms around my brother's neck.

'Thank you, Mama,' I said, and the gratitude in my voice was not assumed. I was truly moved by her attempt to do her duty by me, and to love me into the bargain. She had hurt me, and her preference for Harry turned my heart to ice towards her. But I could recognize her honest, honourable attempt to care for Harry and me equally.

'I'll order tea,' she said and left the room.

She left me beside the dining table, turning over a conflict of feelings. If only life was as my mama perceived it, how simple it would be. If Harry and I had an easy, sinless working partnership, if Harry's marriage was a real one of love, if my future could be a happy one in a new home with a loving husband – how easy it would be to live without sin. Then the door opened and Harry came in, his letter to Celia half finished in his hand.

'Beatrice,' he murmured. We faced each other at the foot of the polished table, our faces reflected in the dark wood. He had the face of an angel, and the shadowy reflection only made his clear-cut features more luminous. As I glanced down at the table I saw my own face, pale as a ghost with my white powdered hair piled on my head, regal as a queen. But my eyes were large and serious, and my mouth was sad. We appeared what we were: a weak boy and a proud and passionate young woman. But for that moment we could have halted the process we had, half consciously, started. I was filled with a sense of peace at my mother's gentle blessing, at her humility and at her own confused quest for proper behaviour in a world where sin was in every corner of her house, half sensed, half understood, but secretly threatening. Watching her struggle to find the courage to confront the truth, her struggle to love me, I saw the pattern of another sort of life, one where people might choose renunciation rather than grabbing for pleasure. Where one might count the cost in moral terms, and decide it was too high. Where one might search for goodness rather than gratification.

But the vision was a brief one.

'I'll come to your room tonight,' said Harry urgently. Then he paused and glanced curiously at my face. 'You *do* wish it?'

I hesitated. The refusal was on my lips and I believe that the first refusal would have been the hardest. Then perhaps we could have left those two evil days behind us. But then I caught sight of the letter to Celia. The page was open and I could see the first words written in Harry's boyish hand. 'My good angel,' it said. He called her his good angel even when he was hot with desire for me. And she would come into our house – my house – and be the angel of Wideacre while I would be married off and banished.

Not only Harry but Celia, Mama and I were all trapped in the roles we had to play. A second's hesitation from me and Celia would win Harry and Wideacre for ever, as surely as if she had plotted and schemed against me. She could take Wideacre from me without exertion, as a tribute to her sweetness and kindness. While I could hold it only by striving and planning and struggling. She was his good angel, and I, in the battle for ownership, was forced to be Lucifer.

I shrugged. My passion for Wideacre had brought me this far. It might take me further yet. In any case, it was not in my nature to say no to Harry when he stood there with a love letter to my rival in his hand, and his eyes dark with desire for me.

I walked through the doorway and let my body brush briefly against him as I passed. 'At midnight,' I said. 'Come to my room.'

I heard a sigh, almost like a growl, as my hair touched his cheek and then he followed me like an obedient puppy to the brightly lit parlour, to the cheerful fire, and to Mama with her loving smile for both of us, her good children.

That night I lay in Harry's arms and let him love me as if we could hold back the morning. My willingness and passion excited him and kept him from sleep for hour after heady hour. And after he had loved me we dozed and then woke, and loved again. He did not creep back to his own chill bedroom until the first notes of the chorus of summer birdsong were starting in the rose garden, and when I could hear, muffled by the servants' door, the clatter of water jugs and milk pails and the kitchen fire being lit.

When I was alone in my narrow bed I did not sleep but propped myself up on the pillows to look out over the garden. I felt physically sated, even physically exhausted, for we had kissed and rolled and embraced and loved all night. But I did not feel the deep calmness that I used to feel after as little as ten minutes with Ralph. Harry might fill me with desire, he might give me hours of pleasure, but he never left me at peace. With Harry I always had a lingering sense that I had to stay alert. With Ralph, the gypsy's son, I had been a sensual equal. But Harry owned the land, and I could never sleep easy beside him.

Now my plans seemed to have brought me to some secure harbour. The wedding would go ahead and both bride and groom counted on me as their main friend and ally. With them using me as confidante and messenger, I would be able to keep them estranged for ever. The only danger to my future I could foresee was the possibility of Harry having a son and heir. I could tolerate sharing the estate with Harry, but I could not have borne the sight of Celia's brat growing up on my land. While Harry fecklessly passed over to me all the management and power on the estate I could feel myself a joint owner, but once he had a son he would start planning for the future on his account – and I could not have borne that.

But it seemed so unlikely. Celia, who already trembled and turned pale at the very thought of the nightmare of marital duties, seemed unlikely to be a lusty breeder. I could not imagine them making love more than a few token occasions. I could not imagine Celia conceiving easily, like healthy peasant stock.

And I was not now jealous of Celia. I should not mind when she preceded me into the drawing room and into dinner as, following the conventions, I stepped back for her and then for Mama. I should not mind because I would know, and everyone would know, who was the true power on Wideacre. Ours is a small county and everyone knows everyone else's business. All our workers had long acknowledged me as the real force on the estate and all our tenants habitually consulted me first. While Harry had spent much time at Havering Hall this spring I had ordered fences to be repaired, entire cottages to be rebuilt, without his even noticing. The whole county knew that I ruled.

It would not take them long to realize that I would not release my control over the house to the new bride either. I controlled the purse strings at Wideacre and cook, butler and chief groom all brought their monthly accounts to me. There would be no extra expenditure made in the house or stables which was not first agreed by Miss Beatrice. If Celia tried to do so much as plan a dinner party without my knowledge she would find the cook apologetic, but reluctant. The wine could not be brought from the cellar, the lamb could not be butchered on the Home Farm without Miss Beatrice's say-so. Celia would discover – if she did not guess already – that her role in the household would be a very limited one.

What she might do, with my blessing, was to take from me the tedious time-wasting business of ladies' social calls and tea parties. No work on the land was so urgent that I could escape my duty as the daughter of the house to accompany Mama on one of these 'treats' at least once a week. We were 'at home' to callers every Wednesday afternoon, and my week seemed punctuated by those dreary afternoons when, dressed in silk or velvet, depending on the season, I sat behind the tea urn and poured tea and smiled and talked of the weather or the new play at Chichester, or the vicar's sermon, or a pending marriage.

Every Wednesday was overshadowed by the prospect of an afternoon that made my idle legs ache with boredom, as if I had the ague.

'Sit down, Beatrice, you are so restless,' Mama would say to me when the last nodding bonnet had driven away down the drive.

'I am stiff with sitting, I am aching with sitting,' I would reply desperately. And she would sigh, and look at me with irritated incomprehension. And I would throw on a shawl and walk until I was under the cover of the wood, and then I would lift my skirts and pelt along the woodland paths until the blood was back in my cheeks and the clean air back in my lungs and my legs no longer felt like lead. Then I would saunter home, my bonnet swinging on its ribbons in my hand, my head tipped back to watch the interlaced branches over my head, and my ears rinsed clean of the chatter and full of birdsong.

Celia could have Wednesday afternoons with my blessing. She could have Sunday afternoons, too. After we had attended Matins and eaten a substantial Sunday dinner, it was Harry's privilege to go to the library and supposedly read serious books – actually he used to put his feet up on the desk and doze in his chair, while in the parlour I sat ramrod-backed in a straight chair and read to Mama from a book of sermons. Celia could have the sermons, and much good might they do her.

All I cared for in county social life were impromptu occasions which happened when there were enough young people to roll back the rugs, and beg an aunt or an indulgent mother to let them dance. I liked the assemblies at Chichester we attended when lambing was done and the roads became easier. And I loved the easy male camaraderie out hunting, and the dances after dinner in winter. But outside those times, when my feet would tap and I would dance with anyone, anyone at all, for the sheer pleasure of swirling round the room, I could do without a social life. I followed my papa. My home was all I needed, and Wideacre could be represented by quiet, pretty little Celia at every county tea party from now till Doomsday with my blessing.

I should have been less easy at the promotion Celia would gain on marriage if I had not seen, without vanity but with clear eyes, that I was far the prettier. Celia was a lovely girl, brown eyes as soft as pansies, skin like cream. But set beside me she became invisible. That summer I glowed with beauty and sensuality. I never walked down a Chichester street but I felt people watching me – women as well as men – and watching me with pleasure in my easy swift stride, in the way my copper hair caught the light in its dancing, wavy ripple, and in my bright face and easy laugh.

If I had lived the life my mama wanted, I should have been as proud as any silly peacock in a dry aviary, for I should have had nothing to think about but how I looked and what colours best became me. But leading the life I had chosen, it mattered less to me whether my hair was right or my eyes bright or my skin clear than whether I could keep a gang of reapers in line. And I prized my eyes less for their clear lovely greenness, and more because one hard look from them could have a lazy ploughboy turned around and speeded up in one second.

But I should have been a saint in heaven if I had not watched Celia narrowly, for she was my rival. And I should have been an angel indeed if I had not looked forward to her wedding day when I was to stand beside her as bride's attendant, at a time when we would be side by side and I would shine her down.

I would look well in the grey silk Celia had chosen. My hair would be piled high except for one negligent curl, which would trail over my bare shoulder. It would be powdered with white, white powder, which set off the bright green of my eyes and the warm living tints of my skin. The cross old dressmaker, brought from London to Havering Hall for the final fittings, actually gasped when I came out of Celia's dressing room to stand before the glass in the dress.

'Miss Lacey, you will be the loveliest lady there,' she said.

I gazed at the pier glass in Celia's bedroom. The gown was watered silk, catching the light as I moved, yet as dully smooth as pewter. You could not look at it and not want to touch me. It clung to me – and as I was mother-naked underneath every movement I made let the rich fabric shout, 'Look! Look! Look!' I really was very, very lovely. And I was glad to be so lovely.

The grey stomacher was embroidered with tiny seed pearls

and tied so tight that I could scarcely breathe. Its pressure on my breasts made them flat so they overflowed in two warm curves at the low neck line. The silk overskirt parted to show the under-skirt, which was not of the usual thick quilt. I had deliberately chosen a silk of fine light weaving and I could feel its smooth, satiny texture against my bare legs as I walked.

But my complacent smile was wiped off my face as the door to the closet at the side of Celia's bedroom opened and she came out to stand beside me at the pier glass. In her wedding dress of white silk with a silver thread of pattern, she looked like a fairy-tale princess. No man could look at me and not feel hot desire. But no man or woman could look at Celia and not love her. Her waist, as slim as my own, was enhanced by the pointed triangle of the stomacher, and her slim back was hinted by the straight fall of silk at the back of the gown that swayed, tantalizingly, when she moved. Her soft brown hair was piled above her face. She had not powdered it today, but I could imagine that when she was powdered and curled she would set any man's heart racing, not only with desire, but with tenderness, too.

She smiled in unaffected pleasure at the sight of me and said generously, 'Why, Beatrice! You look lovelier than ever. You should be the bride, not me!'

I smiled back, but wondered if she was right, and which of us – with a free choice – Harry would prefer.

'Is anything the matter, Beatrice?' she said, turning to me. 'What are you thinking about to make you look so grave?'

'I was thinking about your husband-to-be,' I said, hoping to wipe the happiness from her face. I succeeded better than I meant. Her very heart seemed to stop and her face blanched.

'You can go, Miss Hokey,' she said to the dressmaker, and then sank down into the window seat, disregarding the fine silk of the dress, crushing it and creasing it under her twisting hands.

'Can you come on the wedding tour?' she asked, her brown eyes wide with fright. 'He wrote me a note to thank me for asking you but it was not clear if you could come, or no. Can you, Beatrice? For the more I think about it, the more certain I am I cannot face going away with him alone.'

'I can,' I said triumphantly and watched her face light up.

'Oh! What a relief!' she exclaimed and she turned her face and leaned her forehead against the cool of the window pane. She heaved a shuddery sigh but I saw her face was still strained.

'Is there something more troubling you, Celia?'

'It is wrong of me, I know,' she said. 'But it is the thought of the . . . bridal night. The plans are that we drive from the wedding breakfast to the Golden Fleece at Portsmouth, you know, and take a boat to France the following morning. I cannot bear the thought . . .' She paused and I could see the play of anxiety on her young face. 'If I should be hurt,' she said softly, 'or very much afraid, I should prefer it not to be in a small hotel, especially in England and especially so near home.'

I nodded. This might be meaningless to me. To me it was nonsense, of course, and all to my good. But I can recognize delicacy when I see it.

'You are thinking that if someone gossiped then people might say things about you,' I said understandingly.

'Oh, no!' she said surprisingly. 'Not about me, but Harry. I should not like him to be distressed by gossip, especially if it was because of my foolish inability to . . .' – she gasped – '. . . behave as I must.'

She really was a little darling! To be in such fear and yet think first of us. And it was good to know that the future Lady of Wideacre had a keen appreciation of our good name.

'I am sure Harry would excuse you the first night,' I said, and thought gleefully that his first night as a married man should be spent where most of his married life would be spent – with me. 'With the journey to Portsmouth and then France, perhaps we should agree to travel as friends until we are comfortably installed in Paris.'

Her eyes looked down and she nodded. In that assent she gave me another foothold in Harry's life. I smiled encouragingly at her and hugged her. Her waist was slim and pliant and I felt the warmth of her body through the gown. She turned her sad face to me and leaned her cheek against mine.

I felt the soft smooth skin just damp with the trace of a tear and could not avoid the thought that if she ever turned to Harry like this then all my passion and power would not hold him. Her lovely virginal body would be a potent attraction to a man like Harry, and her youth, her trust and her sensitivity would create in him the birth of a gentle and tender love. I gave her a little kiss on the lips and – coming as I did from Harry's hungry bites – she was soft and sweet. Then I got to my feet and slipped out of my bridesmaid gown and into my grey riding habit.

Lady Havering tapped at the door and came in as I was arranging my curls before Celia's mirror.

'Good gracious, Celia, get out of that gown immediately,' she said in her firm .oice. 'You will crush it and spoil it sitting around like that.' Celia dived for her closet. 'I suppose you girls have been dreaming of your trip,' said Lady Havering to me.

I smiled and bobbed her a decorous curtsy.

'It is so kind of Celia to invite me, and I'm so happy that Mama can spare me.'

Lady Havering nodded. She was an imposing woman, well fitted to her leading position in our county. Large-boned, well-made, she had a presence that totally overwhelmed her pretty daughter and everyone else, too. She settled into a chair and inspected me with the frank appraisal of a woman of the Quality in her own house. How she had fitted into the little Bath town house with her invalid first husband I could not imagine. Lord Havering had recognized in the rich widow someone who would overlook the poverty of his position for the pride, and who would never let down appearances however badly she was treated. He had chosen well; Lady Havering had done her duty, cared for the children of his first marriage and added to the nursery on her own account. She ran the Hall as well as she could for a woman who now had no money and no love for the land, and made no complaint either of her lord's frequent absences in London, nor at his frequent arrivals with a bunch of drunken friends who would roam about shooting pheasants, and riding down the corn.

'I see your mama lets you ride alone,' Lady Havering said abruptly. I glanced at my grey habit. 'Yes,' I said. 'I suppose I should have stayed inside the estate but I wanted to see Celia and I didn't think anyone would see me.'

'Lax,' said her ladyship, without meaning offence. 'But then you've always been allowed a lot of freedom for a young girl. In my young days no young lady would have ridden any distance, not even with her groom or her brother.'

So they knew at Havering Hall of my rides with Harry. I smiled neutrally and made no reply.

'You'll have to mend your ways when you come out,' she said. 'If you go to London you won't be able to range around town on one of Harry's hunters.'

'No,' I smiled. 'But I believe Mama has no plans to take me to London.'

'We might take you,' she said generously. 'If we open Havering House next season for Celia and Harry you could come along and be presented at Court. I will speak to your mama.'

I smiled and thanked her. It would take more than the promise of an opportunity to curtsy to the King to get me off Wideacre, but next season was far away. I might have my moments of vanity but I never lost my senses so totally as to prefer the larger audience of London when I could stay at home. The ripple of admiration when I entered one of the Chichester Assembly Rooms was the most extreme flattery I had ever had, and I was not such a fool as to want more.

'Shocking news of those bread riots in Kent,' said Lady Havering, conversationally.

'I haven't heard any news,' I said, suddenly alert. 'What has been happening?'

'I had a letter from a friend at Tunbridge Wells,' said her ladyship. 'There has been a riot and even some rick-burning. There was even talk of calling out the militia, but the Justices of the Peace arrested a few of the worst offenders.'

'Surely it's just the same as always,' I said. 'The harvest will not be a very good one this year. The price is going up already. The poor go hungry and a few bad 'uns get up a crowd and riot until some landlord comes to his senses and sells them cheap corn. It happens nearly every bad year.'

'No, this sounds worse than usual,' she said. 'I know one must expect insolence from the workers every time they have to do without, but this seems almost to have been a planned insurrection! Most dreadful! Let me see if I can find her letter.'

She felt in her pocket and I prepared myself for the twitterings of an old lady, scared half to death at the fanciful report of distant events. But as she started reading I listened more intently, with a seed of cold fear growing inside me.

'"Dear . . ." hmm, hmm, hmm, yes, here we are. "I hope your county is quiet for we have heard of the most dreadful events not twenty miles from Tunbridge Wells itself. I blame the Justices who have been so slack in punishing the disaffected in the past that the rabble think they have a licence to take whatever they want.

'"A certain Mr Wooler, a good honest tradesman, had secured a contract to send all his neighbour's corn to the London merchants, instead of having it ground locally, as is the custom. To further secure a return for his investment, he arranged that many other gentlemen in the neighbourhood should send their corn too in his wagons to London; a sensible and businesslike arrangement."'

I nodded. I understood perfectly. Mr Wooler had created a selling ring with his neighbours and they had secured a usurious price for their corn and were sending the harvest of the entire area out of the county, away from the local market to London. Mr Wooler would show a handsome profit. So would his neighbours. But his tenants and the poorer workers would have no locally grown, locally ground corn to buy. They would have to travel to the nearest market to get their corn and their demand would push the price sky high to the further advantage and profit of the landlords, the Mr Woolers of this unjust world. Those people who could not afford the inflated prices would have to do without. And those who could not fall back on a diet of potatoes, or on the charity of neighbours, would starve.

Lady Havering went on, '"Mr Wooler anticipated some problems with the rowdy element in the village, and took the precaution of protecting his wagons during their trip to London with five strong men riding alongside equipped with both firearms and cudgels."'

Mr Wooler seemed to me over-anxious. But only he would know how many families would be likely to die of hunger as a result of his profiteering, and how angry the parents of crying children would be in his part of the world.

'"He was prepared for trouble, but not for what took place,"' Lady Havering continued, and Celia slipped into the room and took a seat to listen.

'"As they entered an especially shady stretch of the track to the London road, where the thick wood makes the way twisting and narrow, Mr Wooler heard a long, low whistle. To his horror he saw some thirty men rise out of the ground, some armed with scythes and bill-hooks, some holding cudgels. Blocking the road ahead was a felled tree, and as he looked behind him he heard the crash of a tree falling across the road to cut off his retreat. In a dreadful bellow of a voice, which seemed to come from nowhere, the men with Mr Wooler were ordered to lay down their firearms, dismount from their horses and walk back to the village."'

I listened intently. It could have no application to us, nor to our land, for I would never, never make such a contract with London merchants – a practice my father had despised. Wideacre wheat was never sold while it was standing in the field. It always went to the local market where the poor could buy their pennyworths and the merchants could bid for it in a fair auction. Yet I felt a hint of unease, for any attack on property frightens its owners and this pitched assault was unlike anything I had ever heard. I never forgot, I think no member of the Quality ever forgets, that we live off the fat of the land and dress in silks and clean linen and live in warm, beautiful mansions – while all around us the majority of the people are in hunger and dirt. Within a two hundred mile radius there were perhaps only three wealthy families such as ourselves. And there were hundreds and thousands of poor people who worked at our beck and call.

So I felt an entirely reasonable fear at the thought of poor people organizing themselves into a pitched attack on property. But at the same time I felt a sneaking feeling of admiration for the men who stood up against this clever Mr Wooler to keep the corn they had grown in their own county, that they might buy at a fair price. They were against the law, and if they were caught they would be hanged. But they would be secret local heroes if they saved the village from a hungry winter, and if there was such a thing as natural justice, then no one could call them wrong. Celia's reaction was, predictably, more conventional.

'Dreadful,' she said.

Lady Havering read on, '"As the men hesitated and looked to Mr Wooler for guidance a voice shouted, 'Are you Wooler? If you move, you are a dead man!' And then a shot rang out and it knocked Mr Wooler's hat from his head!"' Lady Havering stopped reading to see if I was properly aghast and was satisfied at my suddenly appalled expression. Shooting with such accuracy takes years of training. I had only ever known one man, just one man, who could shoot so. Lady Havering turned a page.

'"Mr Wooler turned in the direction of the shot, seeking the leader of this dreadful assault, and saw a horse, a great black horse with two black dogs and a rider who called out, 'I have reloaded, Wooler, and the next is for you!' Mr Wooler could do nothing but obey the order and leave his horse and his whole fortune in the carts and walk back to the village. By the time the Squires had been alerted and the Justices called out the wagons had gone and were only found again four days later, empty."'

'Good gracious, how terrible,' said Celia calmly.

I said nothing. I had a picture very clear in my mind of the darkened wood and the ring of silent men, armed but quite still under orders. The leader on a great horse who could fire with such accuracy and reload so fast, on horseback. If I had not known Ralph I would not have believed such skill was possible. But it could be done; I had seen Ralph do it. Not even Harry with years of practice and the best pistols could do such a thing, but I had seen Ralph shoot and reload with one hand while his horse stood steady, in less time than it takes to count twenty. I found it hard to believe anyone else could have learned the skill, but my mind shied from the logical conclusion.

'"A few men were questioned by Mr Wooler and despite the most rigorous inquiries they said nothing. They will be hanged, of course, but they utterly refused to identify their evil band or their leader. Mr Wooler himself says he could not see the man clearly. He had a confused impression of a scarf around the man's face as a disguise."' Lady Havering glanced over the top of the page and broke off.

'Are you unwell, my dear?' she asked.

'No, no,' I said. I realized my hands were clamped on the window seat like a vice. I released my grip and tried to speak normally.

'What a terrible tale,' I said. 'Like a nightmare. Was there ...' I searched my mind for some way to frame the question. 'Was there nothing odd about the rider, nothing that would make him easy to identify?'

'No. Apparently not,' said Lady Havering. 'Mr Wooler has offered a huge reward but no one has betrayed this man. It seems he may get off scot-free. I am glad he is in Kent. It would be too dreadful if he were near Havering . . . or Wideacre,' she said as an afterthought.

I tried to smile and nod but I could not. I had lost control over the expression of my face and my teeth were chattering as if I had an ague. My hands, which had been gripping the edge of the seat, were clamped on it as if I were holding on to a spar while I was drowning. The legless man on the black horse in Portsmouth and the man on the black horse who could fire and reload with such accuracy in Kent could not be the same. It was foolish of me to feel such terror. It was dangerous to be out of control before Lady Havering and in front of Celia's concerned eyes. I tried to speak normally but I could only croak, my throat muscles rigidly holding the scream that was struggling to rip out. The Ralph of my nightmares seemed to be taking human shapes – many human faces. In Portsmouth, in Kent, everywhere. Leading men against property, always on a black horse, always coming closer and closer to me. Even as I fell into a faint I could feel myself struggling to keep my eyes open in case the darkness of the swoon let Ralph come for me. Ralph on a great black horse with thirty hungry, angry men at his back and his legs hacked off at the knees.

I don't remember how I got home. I'm told they sent me back in the Havering carriage with Lady Havering herself supporting me, but I remember nothing. I was not unconscious all the time, but I dropped into a faint twice, and the rest of the time I was in a daze of such fear that I could not speak or move. Whenever I closed my eyes I saw in my panicking imagination Ralph drooping like a broken doll over the sharp jaws of the mantrap and heard again the snap of his knee bones and his hoarse scream. When I opened my eyes in terror to escape this picture, I would catch a glimpse of a horseman from the carriage window and think in my fear that it was Ralph on his great black horse.

They called the new doctor from Chichester as soon as I was home, the clever young Dr MacAndrew whose reputation had survived my jest with old Mrs Hodgett. I barely saw him, I scarcely heard him ask some brief, pointed questions, and then I felt his arm around my shoulder and a glass to my lips, and the laudanum slid down my throat like an elixir of peace.

Dreams – thank God and laudanum – I had none. I slept like a child and no black shadow pursued me. I did not wake until the following day and then found Dr MacAndrew by my bedside. I did not smile or look at him. I spoke to him in a low voice, and said only, 'Please let me sleep again.'

He said, 'You'd best take my advice and face whatever it is that's frightening you. You've had your fill of sleep.'

I looked at him then, and at my maid standing by the bed and at my mama at the foot. I wondered if I had said anything in my drugged sleep that would ruin me later, and found that I hardly cared. His eyes met mine with a look of compassion and interest, but not like those of a man who has just heard a hanging secret. I believed he knew nothing.

'I expect you are right,' I said. 'But I know what is best for me. I beg you to give me that medicine again and let me sleep.'

His light blue-grey eyes looked into mine, gently appraising me.

'Well,' he said tolerantly, 'perhaps you know your own business best. You may take this to sleep now, and if you sleep through till tomorrow morning I shall call on you then.'

I drank the draught in silence and made no reply to my mama or my maid. I waited with my eyes shut for the merciful oblivion. Just as my terror started returning and my nervous frantic senses believed they could feel Ralph riding closer and closer to Wideacre, to me, I could feel the deep warm glow of the medicine and the sweet peaceful sleep steal over me. I relaxed, and smiled at the wavering image of the doctor in childlike gratitude. He was not especially handsome, but there was something in his square face, his pale blue eyes and his sandy hair that made me feel safe. Even the sound of his question to Mama – 'What do you think can have set off this nervous attack?' – failed to frighten me as I slid into sleep.

By the time I awoke the question had been answered and I had no need to frame some lie about nerves. My mama believed she saw in me her own severe reaction to cats and I had been sitting – bless the animal – on a cushion where Celia's spoiled Persian usually slept. The explanation was too persuasive to be resisted. Dr MacAndrew could look dubious but Mama and Lady Havering settled it between them and by the time I came downstairs on the third day I had no awkward questions. Harry, Mama and Celia, who was visiting for the day, were all quick to rush around and cosset me but no one thought to look beyond the explanation of the cat. The fateful letter from the gossipy friend of Tunbridge Wells had been forgotten by everyone but me.

Of course I could not forget it, and over the next few days it haunted me. I could remember every word of the description. The shady road in the overgrown wood, the brilliant ambush with the tree crashing down behind the wagons. The men coming slowly to their feet out of the bracken at the signal of the whistle – and most of all the leader's big black horse and his two circling dogs.

I did not need to hear one word of the story again; it was in my ears as I slept every night, and it was my first thought on waking. As the days went by no detail faded but I grew more and more hopeful that the gang would be caught and the public hangman would finish the job with Ralph that I had botched.

An attack of that size would provoke a huge reaction. The magistrates would search until the leader was found. Great rewards would bribe the loyalty of his followers, lengthy questionings and secret tortures would break the will of those who were captured. It would not be long before the leader was brought to trial, sentenced and hanged. So the gruelling game of waiting started again as I scanned the weekly papers for the news.

Nothing. Once there was a paragraph to say that Mr Wooler had increased the reward and that inquiries were proceeding. Once there was the story that half-a-dozen poor men, suspected of being in the gang, had been transported and three others hanged. The preparations for the wedding day went on, and I remained outwardly calm, but my old fears of the dark, of the noise of horses' hoofbeats, of the rattle of a chain or the clank of iron were back with me. I had a weapon against my night terrors thanks to that meticulous and careful young Dr MacAndrew. In a dark shelf, pushed well to the back near my bed, I had hidden a little bottle of laudanum and every night before I lay down to sleep, two or three pretty little drops slid down my throat and I lay in a golden haze of contentment.

Clever, keen, sandy-haired, sandy-eyelashed Dr MacAndrew gave me my first bottle – but my need quickly outstripped his meagre allowance. When I asked him for a second he made an anxious and disapproving face.

'I cannot agree to it, Miss Lacey,' he said in his soft accent. 'It may be the fashion for young ladies like yourself to take laudanum every night, but you forget, the young ladies forget, that this is not a bedtime drink of milk, but a medicine, a medicine based on opium. We know it is strong; it may be, for some people, addictive. You would not dream of drinking a bottle of brandy a week, Miss Lacey, and yet you are prepared to drink a bottle of laudanum in the same time.

'I gave it to you when you were overwrought, as a temporary measure to calm you. You are a strong-minded and upright young lady, Miss Lacey. Now your nerves are restored you must seek the solution to your anxieties and solve them – not escape them with laudanum.'

This was too uncomfortably perceptive of the young doctor and I closed the conversation. But his view of laudanum made no difference to me. It would take a stronger man than John MacAndrew to turn me from a course when my mind was set on it. In my life I had known only two such men and one they brought home on a stretcher with his horse limping behind, and the other I had left for dead in the dark. It was better that no one tried to cross or control me.

But Dr MacAndrew was not one to follow a polite shift in a conversation if he had something to say. He looked at me hard but his eyes were gentle.

'Miss Lacey,' he said. 'I attended you in your illness and you may think me too young or too newly qualified to be an expert but I do beg you to trust in my direction.'

I shot him a hard look. His pale northern complexion was flushed, even his ears were pink with embarrassment but his pale blue, honest eyes were steady.

'You are suffering under some anxiety,' he said steadily. 'Something you have imagined, or something real. I urge you to face it and overcome it. Whatever is threatening you, you have a loving family and, I am sure, many friends. You need not be afraid alone. Tell me if I am wrong, and rebuke me if I am impertinent, but I believe I am right in both diagnosis and cure. I think you are afraid of something and you will never escape this fear until you face it.'

Although the day was warm and the sun streamed into the parlour I shivered and drew my shawl around my shoulders. To face the fear would be to face the picture of Ralph sitting on his great black horse. To face the fear would be to imagine the changes in his expression from the smiling sensual confident face of my young, upstart lover, to the twisted grimace of a beggar, an outcast, a cripple unfit for any work. My imagination shied away from the idea, as it always would.

'You are mistaken,' I said, my voice low and my slanty eyelids down so he could not see my eyes dark with fear. 'I thank you for your kindness but I fear nothing. I am not yet fully out of mourning for my papa and I suppose I am still recovering from that shock.'

The young doctor's flush rose up again. He pulled his case towards him and opened it.

'I give you this against my better judgement,' he said, and placed in my hands a small phial of laudanum. 'It will help you to sleep but you *must* take it in moderation. Two drops only at night and never during the day. It will help you through this period of change while your brother is married and you prepare for your trip. Once you leave England you should give it up.'

'I shan't need to use it when I'm away from here,' I said.

'Oh?' he said, catching at the point too cleverly for my comfort. 'So your anxieties, like ghosts, cannot cross water – ?'

I dropped my eyes again. This young man had been trained to observe and he saw too much. 'I shall be seeing new sights and meeting new people. I shall forget my worries,' I said steadily.

'Well, I'll not question you further,' he said and rose to take his leave. I held out my hand and to my surprise he did not shake it but bent and kissed it, a gentle lingering kiss that left a warmth on my fingers after he had straightened up. He still held my hand in his.

'I would be your friend, Miss Lacey,' he said gently. 'I would keep your confidence since I am your medical adviser. But more than that I should like to feel that you can talk to me as a friend.' Then he gave a little bow, turned and walked from the room.

I plumped back down into my chair in genuine surprise. My spirits rose at the warmth in his voice, and I turned to the mirror over the fireplace to see my reflection. His kiss had brought the colour to my cheeks and the dark shadows under my eyes made me look fragile. Bright, reflected eyes met mine in dancing delight. I did not desire him, of course – he did not have Wideacre, nor could he help me hold it. But whoever disliked a man's eyes on her? I smiled at myself in simple vanity and joy at having been born with such looks. As my mother came into the room, I turned and smiled at her and she beamed back, pleased to see me well again.

'Was that Dr MacAndrew's curricle?' she asked, shaking out her petticoats and opening her sewing box.

'Yes,' I said.

'You should have called for me, Beatrice,' she said, gently reproving. 'You really should not see him alone.'

'He only came to inquire how I was,' I said casually. 'I never thought to send for you. He was only passing the house on the way to the Springhams; one of the little boys is ill.'

My mother pursed her mouth to thread her needle and nodded, unconvinced. 'I can't like the idea of a doctor who calls socially, anyway,' she said. 'In my younger days apothecaries only came when they were sent for, and then came in by the kitchen entrance.'

'Oh, Mama!' I said. 'Dr MacAndrew is hardly an apothecary! He is a doctor, qualified at the University of Edinburgh. We are indeed very lucky that he has chosen to stay in the neighbourhood. Now we shan't have to send to London every time someone is unwell. It can be nothing but an advantage. And besides, he is a gentleman and that makes it much easier to talk to him.'

'Oh, well,' my mother said equably. 'I suppose it's the new thing. It just seems so odd, that's all. But I'm glad he was here to look after you, dearest.' She paused and made a few stitches. 'But I shall not hear a word of his attending Celia when her time comes.'

'Good heavens!' I said, irritated. 'They're a fortnight from marriage and you are already looking for an *accoucheuse*!'

'Beatrice, really!' My mother sounded shocked but there was a smile in her eyes. 'If you talk so freely I shall have to start planning a marriage for you.'

'Oh, I've no taste for it, Mama,' I laughed. 'I couldn't bear to leave Wideacre and I couldn't be bothered with a husband. I've a fancy to stay here and be a sister to Celia and an aunt to all the dear little Celias and baby Harrys.'

'All girls say that before their marriage is arranged,' my mother said calmly. 'You will be glad enough to leave when you see your future before you.'

I smiled. It was a conversation that could have no conclusion. I sat down beside her and pulled the workbox towards me. We were engaged in the respectable task of hemming Harry's cravats. My sewing had improved and as I placed the neat, regular stitches I imagined this would be the very cravat he would wear on his wedding day and I would be the one – not shy little Celia – who would pull it from his throat on his wedding night.

'Harry is planning a surprise for you on your return from the wedding tour,' Mama said, interrupting my daydream. 'I mention it only because it would be such a waste to do all the work he is planning when it is not suitable.'

I raised my head and waited in silence.

'Harry is not just renovating some of the rooms in the west wing; he is converting them for your exclusive use,' she said. Her voice was unruffled but I thought I could detect a note of anxiety. 'I am sure that you will tell him it is not what you would like?'

She waited for my assent but I said nothing.

'Did you know of this scheme, Beatrice?'

'Harry suggested it some while ago,' I said. 'I thought it a good idea. I had no idea he had got so far forward as to have the work set in hand.'

'You both planned this, and neither of you consulted me?' Mama was becoming agitated. It was important to keep the whole discussion as calm as possible.

'Mama, it had gone wholly out of my head,' I said calmly. 'Harry thought it a good idea that while I am here I should have a suite of private rooms. Much as I love Celia it would be good for all of us to have our own drawing rooms for privacy. After all, Mama, you have your parlour and dressing room and bedroom upstairs, but I have only a bedroom.'

My mother's concern as usual was for appearances only.

'It will look so odd,' she complained. 'It is most unusual for a girl of your age even to think of her own rooms in such a way. You should have no need for privacy.'

'I know, Mama,' I said gently. 'But our situation is odd. Harry really does still need help on the land, and you know I keep the accounts of the estate. It will be some years before he is fully able to run the place alone and while he continues these improvements I think he will always need another person to check the figures and measure the yields. It is unusual for a young girl to have these responsibilities but since I do, I need somewhere where I can work without disturbing you or Celia. In any case the alterations are fairly minor. A small study and a dressing room where the old scullery and breakfast room were. I dare say no one will even notice.'

My mother bent her head over her stitching.

'I don't understand the estate,' she said. 'But I should have thought Harry could have managed it on his own. He is the Master. He ought to be able to run the place without his sister.'

I knew I had won, and the knowledge made me generous. I put my hand on hers.

'Why should he?' I asked in a warm, teasing voice. 'He cannot do without his lovely mother. He obviously needs a sister, too. You have spoiled him, Mama, and we are giving Celia a sultan for a husband who needs an entire harem in his house!'

Mama smiled and the worried look left her eyes.

'Oh, well,' she said. 'If that is what you and Harry and Celia want then I can have no objection. But all the work will have been wasted when you marry a lord and go off to live in Ireland or somewhere!'

'Oh, no, an Italian prince!' I said, relieved to be able to end the discussion in a light tone. 'I shan't be satisfied unless I come home a princess! Think of the opportunities I shall have in Paris and Italy!'

We laughed together and returned our attention to Harry's cravats with such industry that at the end of the fortnight he was able to pack fifty new ones in his trunk and see it safely stowed in the post-chaise along with Celia's four-trunk trousseau and my more modest two trunks and three boxes. The heavy carriage with Harry's man and my maid and Celia's maid, all crammed inside, would follow us through France and Italy. An odd trio they would be, and our post-chaise in front even odder, with an untouched wife, but a satisfied husband and an affectionate sister bowling along in the autumn sunshine.

'I can hardly wait,' I said and leaned on Harry's arm as we watched the grooms load the trunks and boxes in the stable yard. Harry's hand, out of sight, caressed the small of my back in silent agreement. His square hand straddled my spine and stroked me like a cat. Imperceptibly I swayed towards him.

'Two months of nights,' he said softly. 'Two months of nights and no one to notice us.' His hand rubbed up my spine sliding on the silk of my dress and I had to school my face not to shut my eyes and purr like a stable kitten. The muscles of my face I could keep still, but no control on earth could have stopped my eyes from growing green with desire. The servants were busy round the coaches and no one glanced at us.

'May I come to your room tonight?' Harry asked, his mouth so close to my ear I could feel the warmth of his breath. We had been together very seldom in the past few weeks of my illness and drugged sleeping and I could feel my old appetite rise in me. 'I am a bridegroom, remember,' Harry said.

I chuckled. 'Then you should be out carousing with your friends, enjoying your last night of freedom before your jealous, your passionate, wife claims you for ever.'

Harry laughed softly with me. 'Somehow I cannot see Celia in that role,' he said. 'But truly, Beatrice, I should like to lie with you tonight.'

'No,' I said, slowly relishing the pleasure of a short abstinence. I pulled myself away from him and turned to face him, my slanty eyes half closed from that secret, brief caress.

'No, I shall come to you as your bride tomorrow, on the night you are wed.' I swore it as a promise. 'Tomorrow we will stand together before the altar and every word you say, every "to have and to hold", shall be for me. And every reply you hear, every promise to love and honour, every "I do", shall be from me, although Celia's is the empty mouth that speaks. She is the

193

bride, but I shall be the wife. It can be her day tomorrow, for tomorrow night will be my night. And tomorrow night, not tonight, my darling. For tonight you can dream of me, and think of me. Tomorrow night the three of us will retire to our rooms and Celia may sleep the sleep of the good and stupid, while you and I will not sleep at all!'

Harry's blue eyes were bright. 'I agree!' he said quickly. 'This shall be our honeymoon, yours and mine. It is you I marry, and you I take away with me, and Celia can come as the servants or the luggage comes – to serve our convenience.'

I sighed with the pure pleasure of sensual anticipation and the pleasure of victory. 'Yes,' I said. 'Tomorrow we marry, and tomorrow night we mate.'

We did both. The magic tide that carried me along took me to Harry's side in the church. I stood before the altar in a dream and heard Harry's voice promising such pleasures of wedding and bedding that I could think of nothing but what was ahead of me that night.

Celia was, predictably, faint with nerves, and after Lord Havering had conducted her to her bridegroom and stepped back, I had to move forward to support her. Only her slight body stood between Harry and me, and as he spoke the promises of love and pleasures and loyalty he was able to meet my smiling eyes with his bright ones and make all the promises to me.

Celia whispered her responses, and then the service was over. The wedding breakfast was, as one would expect, an insipid affair with much simpering and weeping over Celia who looked flushed and shy and lovely. There was very little attention paid to me, or to Harry, who stood in a corner and drank heartily with Lord Havering. It was tedious. I had no one to talk to and was forced to endure Celia's silly sisters and sillier friends. Even Lord Havering's quick lecherous glances raking the length of my body in the grey silk dress did little to console me, for he took Harry off to the study and, apart from some elderly neighbours, we women were left on our own. That made the arrival of Dr MacAndrew all the more of a pleasure, and the ripple of interest as he crossed the room straight to my side made me raise my eyes and smile at him.

'I am very pleased to see you,' he said, taking a seat beside me. 'And on such a happy day, as well.'

I noted his tact in not referring to my health and I saw also, for the first time, what an attractive man he was. The other girls – the Havering sisters and Celia's two other bridesmaids – were watching him like sparrowhawks out of the corner of their eyes, and I turned my head to smile at them and rub their silly noses in their simpering vanity.

'Will you be away very long, Miss Lacey?' he asked in his gentle Scots voice.

'Just till Christmas,' I said. 'I could not bear to be away from home at Christmas and Harry and I both want to be back in plenty of time for the spring sowing.'

'I hear you are a keen agronomist?' He said it without a hint of the patronizing amusement I was used to from neighbours whose lands yielded half the profits of ours and yet thought my interest unbecoming.

'I am,' I said. 'My papa reared me to take an interest in our land and I love Wideacre and am glad to learn all I can about it.'

'It is a fine thing to have such a lovely home,' he said. 'I have not the advantage of a country seat. My family has always bought and sold property so frequently I never had a chance to put down roots.'

'You are an Edinburgh family?' I asked with interest.

'My father owns the MacAndrew Line,' he said diffidently. At once, pieces of information slipped into my head like the solution to a puzzle. His presence in the Haverings' house was explained at once. The MacAndrew Line was a highly successful line of trading ships plying from London, Scotland and India. This young doctor came from a family of fabulous wealth. Lady Havering would be swift to overlook his unusual profession in return for a chance at one of the greatest fortunes in Britain. She would have already earmarked him for one of the girls, and Lord Havering would already have tried to persuade the young doctor to invest in some sure enterprise that his lordship could set in motion if he only had the advantage of a few of the MacAndrew thousands.

'I am surprised he could spare you so far from home,' I said.

Dr MacAndrew laughed shortly. 'I'm afraid he was unhappy

when I left the family home and the family business,' he said. 'He wanted very much for me to work with him, but I have two older brothers and a younger one as well who will do that. I set my heart on medicine ever since I was a young boy and despite my father's objections I managed to get my training at the university.'

'I should not like to have much to do with sick people,' I said, speaking without reserve to this gentle young man with the warm eyes. 'I don't have the patience.'

'No, why should you?' he said sympathetically. 'I should like everyone in the world to be as fit and as strong as you. When I have seen you galloping your horse up to the downs, I have laughed with sheer pleasure at such a brilliant sight. You would not fit in a sickroom, Miss Lacey. I would always prefer to see such youth and loveliness in the open air.'

I was flattered. 'You should not have seen me galloping at all,' I said demurely. 'I was not supposed to go off the estate while we were in mourning, and I should never gallop in public. But when one has a good horse, and the wind is blowing just softly, I cannot bear not to.'

He smiled at my enthusiasm and fell to talking of horses. I had noticed, even in the period of my illness, that he had a good eye for a horse. The bays that pulled his curricle were a splendid pair: high-stepping, arch-necked, ruddy-bronze.

I had even wondered idly where a young doctor found the money to buy such beauties, but now he had explained that. I told him about the first pony Papa bought me, and he told me of his first hunting dog, and I forgot that half the eyes of the room were on us.

'Beatrice, dear . . .' my mother said hesitantly. I glanced up to see Lady Havering bearing down upon us. She swept Dr MacAndrew off like a competent hostess, to meet some of the other guests, and my mama reminded me that I must take Celia upstairs and help her change out of her wedding gown for the journey.

The extent of my help was gazing dreamily out of the window while Celia's maid bustled about, and making sure that my own cloak and bonnet were smooth and straight. I was miserable at leaving Wideacre. I could hardly bear to leave the familiar sight of the hills with the trees just starting to turn colour, and there were tears in my eyes as I kissed Mama goodbye and jumped into the carriage. She, silly dear, took them for herself, and kissed me warmly and blessed me. In the crowd of people around the post-chaise, kissing Celia's hand and calling out reminders and good wishes, I looked for Dr MacAndrew. He was standing at the back of the crowd and his eyes met mine. There was a little warm smile in them, especially for me, and I felt suddenly still. In the noise of the crowd I could not hear what he said, but his lips formed three words, 'Come back soon.'

I sat back in the chaise with a smile on my face and a certain warmth around me as we drove off on honeymoon.

8

The wedding night was all that Harry and I had planned, with the added excitement for me of deceiving Celia who was sleeping next door. Harry had to hold his hand over my mouth to smother my cries of pleasure, and that hint of his violence and my helplessness excited us even more. When his own time came he had to thrust his face into the soft pillows to muffle his long, low groans. Afterwards we lay in silence and peace and I did not trouble to creep back to my own room.

The Golden Fleece at Portsmouth is near the harbour walls and as we drifted into sleep I could hear the wash of the sea as the waves smacked the fortifications. The smell of the salt air made me feel that we were already on our journey and Wideacre hopes and Wideacre fears were far away from us. Harry sighed heavily and turned over, but I lay quiet in the strange room savouring the distance from home – while secure in the awareness that I had made it more my home than ever before. Unconsciously, my thoughts drifted to Ralph – the old Ralph of my girlhood – and his longing to lie with me between sheets in a clean bed. He was right to envy us. Land, and the wealth that land brings, is essential.

I lay on my back gazing clear-eyed into the darkness, listening to the waves wash against the harbour wall as if they were sighing for the touch of the land. I had Harry now, and next door Celia slept, secure in my friendship. The old nagging ache in my heart, my fear of not belonging, of not being loved, had eased. I was loved. My brother, the Squire, adored me and would come to me at the snap of my fingers. I was safe on the land. He owned the land outright and would do my bidding. But I gazed unseeing at the grey ceiling of the bedroom and knew it was not enough. I needed something beyond him, something more. I needed whatever magic had possessed him when he brought in the harvest like a living sheaf of corn himself, golden-headed, golden-skinned, tall on the mountain of wheat. When I had stepped out of the shadow of the barn I had greeted not only the man I desired but somehow something more: I greeted the god of the harvest, and when he gazed at me he saw the old dark goddess of the earth's green fertility. When he became a man in a nightshirt, snoring softly, I lost that vision and I lost my passion too.

Of course I thought of Ralph. In all our meetings and kisses in the sunny days of caresses in hiding, the magic never left Ralph. He was always something dark from the woods. He always breathed of the magic of Wideacre. But Harry, as he said himself, could live anywhere.

I rolled on my side and cupped my body around Harry's plump bottom ready for sleep. I could never have managed Ralph as I could control Harry. I could never have brooked a master, but I could not help a secret squirm of disdain for a man I could train as easily as a puppy. Every good rider likes a well-trained horse. But who does not enjoy the challenge of an animal whose spirit you cannot break? Harry always was, always would be, a domesticated pet. And I was something from further back, from wild days when magic still walked in the Wideacre woods. I smiled at the picture of myself as some lean, rare, green-eyed animal. Then I dozed. And then I slid deep, deep into sleep.

The bustle of the hotel woke me in plenty of time to slip through the adjoining door to my bedroom long before my maid had brought my morning cup of chocolate and hot water for washing. I could see the harbour from my bedroom and the water was a welcoming blue with fishing boats and yachts bobbing on the little waves. I was alive with anticipation and excitement, and Celia and I laughed like children as we boarded the ferry moored beside the high harbour wall.

The first few minutes were delightful. The little ship rocked so sweetly at its moorings, and the sights and smells were so new and strange. The harbourside was crowded with people selling goods to the travellers. Fruit and food to take on the journey in little baskets, little painted views of England for travellers going home to France, hundreds of little worthless pieces of trumpery made from shells or pretty pieces of glass.

Even the sight of a legless man – a wounded sailor – did not make me tremble with a sense of my danger coming closer and closer. Although I gazed in horror at the stumps of his thighs and saw how deft, how disgustingly skilful he was at swinging around on the ground – I had seen at the first sight that his hair was light-coloured and I was secure in the knowledge that in leaving Wideacre I was escaping Ralph and his slow, inexorable approach. I threw the beggar a superstitious penny, and he caught it and thanked me with a professional whine. The thought of Ralph, my lovely Ralph, reduced to poverty and squatting on pavements caught at my heart. But then I shrugged the idea aside as Celia called, 'Look! Look! We are setting sail!'

Lithe as monkeys, the sailors had swarmed up the double masts and unfurled sheets of canvas. They tightened the ropes as the sails flapped and billowed, and amid raucous shouts and curses the bystanders on the harbourside slipped the ropes free and threw them into the boat. Celia and I shrank out of the way as the men, as wild-looking as pirates, dashed from one rope to another heaving the sails up and tying the ropes tight. The harbour wall slid away from us and the people waving seemed very small, then the ship moved out to the harbour mouth where the arms of yellow stone seemed to try to hold us for one last second to England and home. Then we bounced through the boiling waters where river and ebbing tide meet the sea and scudded out.

The sails filled with wind and stretched and thumped and the men dashed around less, which Celia and I took to be a good sign. I went to the prow and, glancing around to ensure that no one was watching, stretched myself out along the bowsprit as far as I dared, to watch the waves rushing beneath me and the sharp prow cutting into the green waters. A good hour I spent there, fascinated by the rush of the waves, but then the rocking became more and more fierce, and although it was midday, the sky darkened with the deep clouds that mean a storm on land or sea. It started to rain, and I found I was weary. I had to sit in the cabin out of the rain and the rocking was no longer pleasant and it was very tiring to see the room going up and down.

Then it was not just tiring, but unbearably horrid. I felt sure I should be well if I could be up on the deck again, and I tried to hold to the memory of the pleasure of the prow cutting through the water. But it was no good. I hated the boat, and I hated the senseless rocking of the waves and I longed with all my heart to be back on the good solid earth.

I opened the cabin door and called for my maid who should have been in the cabin opposite mine. A sudden rush of nausea sent me to the basin in my room. I was sick alone and without help, and then a jerk and a dive of the ship sent me reeling into my bunk. Everything in the cabin swayed and rocked and the unsecured bags slid from side to side and crashed into one wall and then the other. I was miserably ill, too ill even to help myself. I clung to the side of the pitching bunk and wept aloud in fear and in sickness and for help. Then I was sick again and I dropped on to the pillows which bumped horridly up and down; then I slept.

When I woke the cabin was still shifting and heaving but someone had packed away all the bags so the cramped little room seemed less nightmarish. There was a pale smell of lilies and everything was clean. I looked around for my maid, but it was Celia sitting calmly in a heaving, pitching chair and smiling at me.

'I am so glad you are better,' she said. 'Do you feel well enough to take something? Some soup, or just tea?'

I could not puzzle out where I was, or what was happening. I just shook my head, my stomach churning at the thought of food.

'Well, sleep then,' said this strange, authoritative Celia. 'It is the best thing you can do, and we shall soon be safe and calm in port.'

I closed my eyes, too ill to care, and slept. I woke once more to be sick, and someone held a basin for me, and deftly washed my face and hands with warm water, dried me and laid me back on the turned pillow. I dreamed it was my mother, for I knew it was not my maid. Only in the night when I woke again did I realize it was Celia nursing me.

'Have you been here all the time?' I asked.

'Oh, yes,' she said, as if nothing could be more natural. 'Except when I was looking after Harry, of course.'

'Is he ill, too?' I asked wonderingly.

'Rather worse than you, I am afraid,' Celia said calmly. 'But you will both be perfectly well when we reach France.'

'Don't you mind it, Celia?'

She smiled, and her gentle voice seemed to come from a long way away as I slid back into sleep.

'Oh, no,' she said. 'I am stronger than I look.'

Next time I awoke the dreadful pitching and tossing had stopped. I felt light-headed and faint, but was no longer retching. I sat up and stretched my bare feet to the floor. I felt shaky, but better already, and tiptoed to the adjoining door to Harry's cabin without holding the chair for support. The door opened without a sound and I stood silently in the doorway.

Celia was standing by Harry's bunk with a bowl of soup in one hand, and her arm around Harry, around my Harry's shoulders. I watched as he sipped at the soup like a sickly infant, and then Celia settled him back on the pillow.

'Better?' she asked, and her voice was infinitely tender. Harry clasped her hand.

'My dear,' he said, 'you have been so kind, so sweet to me.'

Celia smiled and smoothed the hair from his forehead in an intimate, confident gesture.

'Oh, how silly you are, Harry,' she said. 'I am your wife. Of course I care for you when you are ill. I promised to love you in sickness and in health. I have been happy to care for you, and for dear Beatrice, too.'

I watched in horror as Harry took Celia's hand from his hair and held it gently to his lips. And she, the cold, shy Celia, bent and kissed him on the forehead. Then she drew the curtains around the bed. I stepped back, silent on my bare feet, and closed the door behind me. Celia's confidence, Celia's tenderness to Harry, amazed and alarmed me. I felt once more the knife thrust of jealousy, but also the fear of exclusion from the pale of the married state. For courage, for the reassurance of my beauty, I turned to the small mirror nailed on the wooden wall of the cabin. I was white and sickly looking, and my skin was like wax.

Any ideas I had of striding into Harry's cabin and raging at him or even of slinking into his bunk beside him were instantly dismissed. If he was feeling at all as I did, he would welcome neither a quarrel nor a passionate reconciliation.

I dressed, a puzzled frown still on my face. For the first time now we were unlike ourselves in illness, and unlike ourselves off our land. It struck me how little I shared with Harry. Away from Wideacre, away from my obsession, and too tired to be lovers, we were strangers. If I had gone into his cabin for anything other than a scene of passion, I should not have known what to say. It would never occur to me to order soup for him, or to feed him as if he was some disgusting, overgrown baby, or to draw his curtains so he could sleep. I had never nursed any invalid; I had never even played with dolls in my childhood, and I had neither instinct nor interest in the kind of lovemaking that consists of gentle caresses and kindly courtesies.

Celia blooming with a sense of her importance and Harry expansive and grateful for her nursing were an odd couple indeed, but I could not see there was any way to check their new relationship.

Nor did I, once I was up on deck watching a beautifully steady horizon, think it necessary to spoil Celia's moment of glory. If she liked to nurse Harry and me when we were hideous with seasickness, it was not a job I envied. And if Harry kissed her hand in gratitude, and thought of her drudgery kindly, well that did me no harm either. As the wind whipped my cheeks into a rosy colour, and my loose hair into curls, my hopes rose too. Here was France, and a long easy holiday with no eyes to watch us, no ears to listen to us, and only naive, silly, slavish Celia to deceive.

Harry and Celia joined me on deck, and I even forgave their interlaced arms – especially when I saw that my strong and healthy lover was leaning on Celia for support. He was pale and listless and smiled at me only when I assured him that we would be disembarked in under an hour. But I was no longer anxious. As soon as Harry was well and his appetite restored – for his dinner and for everything else – he would be mine for the taking.

We dined and slept that night in Cherbourg, and in the morning Harry was perfectly well. I did not complain, but I could not eat my breakfast for a renewed bout of seasickness.

The dizziness had gone, but as soon as I lifted my head from the pillow I felt sick and extremely unlike myself. The others breakfasted on coffee and rolls, while I strolled outside in the fresh air of the garden of the inn, and watched them loading up our post-chaise. I somehow dreaded the long road to Paris cooped up inside a swaying carriage, and could scarcely raise a smile in response to Harry when he handed me up the steps.

My seasickness stayed with me, far from the sight of the sea, far from the smell of the boat. Damn it, it stayed with me every morning along the road to Paris, every sunlit Parisian morning when Harry hammered on the door and called to me to come riding in the *bois*, every morning of our journey south.

I lifted my head from retching into the window box one morning and admitted miserably to myself the fact I had been avoiding. I was with child.

We were three days' journey from Paris, and in the heart of the French countryside and I stared out at a sea of roofs of a pretty old town and breathed air too hot for an English autumn. Then I smelled baking and some dreadful hint of spice or garlic too, and I retched again, but my belly was empty and nothing came.

Tears had squeezed from my swollen eyelids and I felt them cold on my cheeks as if I were weeping in sorrow. The pretty blue-slated roofs, the tall old church tower, the bluish horizon, all shimmering in a comfortable haze of heat, which had no power to warm me. I was with child. And I was afraid.

We were driving on that day; the others would be waiting for me below. I had lied and said I had forgotten something in my room to escape their eyes when I felt the flush coming to my face and my sickness start. Now I had to go downstairs, step into a post-chaise and spend nearly all day swaying and rocking on the rotten French roads and listen to Celia reading from her damned guidebook, and hear Harry snoring as he always, always did. And to no one could I reach out a quick hand of desperate need and say, 'Help me! I am in trouble!'

Every morning when I had felt so strange I had secretly known. When I had failed to bleed at the usual time, I had blamed the excitement of the wedding and the journey. But I had known in my heart for at least a week, perhaps two. I simply could not face the thought. And, more like Harry and Mama than my usual clear-headed self, I had hidden the idea from myself. But it came back to me. Every sunny morning when I woke ill and anxious. Through the day while I smiled at Harry and chatted to Celia, I could forget and reassure myself with an easy lie that it had all been a reaction to the travelling, that I was well again. And at night, when I was in Harry's bed and he thrust deep inside me, I could hope, in a little secret place in my head, that our clinging passion would make me bleed. But each morning was the same. And, more frightening, every morning was worse until I feared Celia's loving sharpness would notice and I would fail in my fatigue and loneliness to keep this secret well hidden. That my need for help and my need for love, for someone, anyone, to say, 'Do not fear. You need not face this alone,' would overcome my good sense.

For I was very much afraid, and very much alone, and I dared not think what was going to happen to me.

I took my handkerchief out of my reticule as my excuse and went downstairs. Celia was waiting in the hall while Harry paid the bill. She smiled when she saw me and I could feel my face muscles were too stiff to reply.

'Are you all right, Beatrice?' she asked, noting my pallor.

'Perfectly,' I said shortly, and she took my abruptness as a rebuff and said no more, although I was longing to weep and throw myself into her arms and ask for her help to save me from this threat over my future.

I had no idea what I was going to do.

I climbed into the coach as if I were going to my death, and stared blankly out of the window to discourage Celia's chatter. Counting on my fingers under the shield of my reticule I calculated that I was two months pregnant and that I could expect my confinement in May.

I stared in impotent hatred at the sunny French landscape, at the squat little houses and the dusty well-dug gardens. This foreign land, this strange place, seemed all part of the nightmare of my predicament. I was mortally afraid that the worst would happen and that I would die here in a shameful childbirth and never see my lovely home again. And my body would be buried in one of these horrid, crowded graveyards and not at Acre church where I belonged. A little sob escaped me and Celia looked up from her book. I felt her eyes on me but I did not turn my head. She put her little hand out and touched my shoulder with a gentle pat, like a caress one would make to an unhappy child. I did not respond but that token gesture comforted me a little and I blinked away the tears.

For two or three days of that miserable journey I rode silent in the carriage. Harry noticed nothing. When he was bored he rode on the box to see the view better, or hired a horse and rode for pleasure. Celia watched me with alert tenderness, ready to speak or be silent, but did not intrude on my brooding wretchedness. And I said nothing, kept my face serene when Harry was by, and gazed blankly out of the window when we were alone.

By the time we arrived at Bordeaux, I was over the first of the shock; my mind had stopped reeling like a drunkard. My first thought was to lose this little encumbrance and I told Harry I wanted a hard day's riding to shake the fidgets out of me. He looked doubtful at the stables when I picked out a wicked-looking stallion and insisted on a lady's saddle. They all advised against it. They all were right. Not even in the prime of health could I have stayed on that horse and he threw me in the first ten seconds in the stable yard. They rushed to help me to my feet and I was able to smile and say I was not hurt, I merely wanted to sit still. I sat and waited. Nothing seemed to have happened. I returned to my hotel room and waited for the rest of the day. The warm sunshine of the French autumn poured through the window and I scowled at it in an aversion for everything fruitful and strong. The pretty sunlit room was too small; the walls seemed to be closing in on me. The air was unbreathable and France itself stank. I snatched up my bonnet and ran downstairs. Harry had hired a landaulet for our stay in the town and I ordered it to be called to the door as Celia came slowly downstairs after me.

'Are you going to drive alone, Beatrice?' she asked, surprised.

'Yes,' I said tersely. 'I need some fresh air.'

'Shall I come with you?' she asked. This non-committal tone had irritated me excessively in the early weeks of the trip, but I had learned soon that it was not that Celia lacked opinions – she simply desired to please me.

Her questions – 'Shall I come to the theatre?' 'Shall I come to dinner with you and Harry?' – meant simply what they said – 'Would you prefer my company, or would you rather be alone?' – and Harry and I soon found out that it did not offend Celia whether we refused, or accepted.

'Don't come,' I said. 'Make tea for Harry when he comes in. You know how he likes it, and the servants here cannot make it. I shall not be long.'

Celia acquiesced with a smile and watched me leave. I kept my face calm as I passed the windows of the hotel but, once out of sight, I dropped the little veil on my bonnet and wept behind it.

I was lost, lost, lost. And I could not think, I could not make myself think, what to do. My first thought had been to tell Harry and, between the two of us, concoct some solution. But some wiser voice in my head cautioned me to wait and not to panic into a confession I could not retract.

If I had been at home, in the old days, my first visit would have been to Meg, Ralph's white witch of a mother. But I dismissed the memory of her with a shrug. I had known, as every country child knows, that girls gone into service, girls betrothed to the wrong man, or girls seduced by men already married, could rid themselves of their difficulties with the help of women like Meg and some secret, semi-poisonous plants. But never had I known what these were – nor would I have known how to use them.

Undoubtedly this sleepy French market town, like any other, would house a wise woman who could advise me. But I should not be able to find her without the whole inn, and thus every passing English visitor, hearing of the gossip. Short of a lucky, natural accident – and God knows I had terrified Harry and myself and been bumped and bruised but got no further forward – I was stuck with this growing weed.

I directed the coachman to drive on when he paused, waiting for instructions.

'Go on, go on,' I said fiercely. 'Out to the country, just keep driving.' He nodded his head and cracked his whip in obedience to the eccentric young Englishwoman. The carriage rolled out of the town and the houses gave way to little cottages surrounded by small gardens of dust. Then we were beyond the town limits, in the fields, the rows and rows of vines stretching for ever to the blue sky.

I stared miserably at the gentle, hilly landscape, so unlike the skyline of my lovely Wideacre. Whereas our hills roll up, part covered with beech coppices and crowned with caps of smooth sweet turf, these hills are terraced and walled every inch of the way with the monotonous vines broken only by peasant plots. It may be a pleasant country to visit, to bowl along a dusty road under a hot un-English sun, but I would not choose to be poor in France. Our people are far from wealthy – I would be over-paying them if they were – but they do not scrape and scratch a living from dry earth as the peasants do in France. Harry and I had learned much, driving round and talking to the leading landowners, though it was striking how few of them knew any-thing of their lands beyond the château gardens. But above all else we had reassured ourselves that the combination of new agricultural methods with a reliable labouring force was the way ahead for Wideacre.

A sudden bolt of homesickness shot through me and I thought with longing of my house and my land, and how I wished to be there now, and not in this strange and arid country with my dresses growing tighter around my breasts. Then the pain of homesickness suddenly crystallized into a thought in my mind so bright and so brilliant that I sat up with a yelp, and the driver reined in again to see if I was ready to go home. I waved him on and fell back in my seat, my hands instinctively clutching my slightly rounded belly. The child in there – this beloved baby that I had thought of only seconds ago as a growing weed – was the heir to Wideacre. If it were a boy – and I knew with certainty that it was a boy – then he was the future Master of Wideacre and my place there was assured for ever. Mistress in all but name of those most precious acres, and the mother of the son of the Squire. My baby would be the Master.

At once I felt different. My resentment melted away. I should hardly care for this discomfort, or even the pains, because these would be caused by the precious son growing and growing until he could be born into his rightful place.

Again I thought of telling Harry and gambling on his pride at the conception of a son and heir. But again, my instincts warned me to tread carefully. Harry was mine, very much mine, and this trip had proved it. Every evening as darkness fell and they brought candles to our rooms, or lanterns if we were dining outside, his eyes would turn to me and he would see nothing but the gleam of my hair in the flickering light, and the expression on my face. Then Celia would quietly excuse herself and leave us alone. The evenings and the nights were mine, and mine alone; and Harry and I pleasured each other for long hours and then fell asleep in each other's arms. The days, however, I had to share him with Celia, and I noted, but could not prevent, the birth of an easy, affectionate intimacy.

Ever since the time on that cursed boat, Celia and Harry had established a way of being easy together. She loved to be of use to Harry, to comfort him when he was tired, or to rearrange the rooms in our various hotels so they were elegant, yet comfortable. The painfully shy Celia, with her halting command of the French language, would sally down to the strange kitchens to confront the master chef with demands for tea. She would stay there, ignoring the outrage of the French domestics, until she had watched them make it exactly to Harry's liking.

She was amusingly protective of the man I knew to be all my own, and I permitted her this area of activity as a harmless hobby and one that freed me from the chores of housekeeping. It was Celia who packed and repacked the linen and the bedding every time we moved from one hotel to another. It was Celia who sought out tailors, laundries, bootmakers, florists and all the services we needed. It was Celia who repaired with exquisite small stitches a tear in Harry's embroidered waistcoat, and it was Celia's task to serve Harry like a maid while it was mine to amuse and delight him like an equal.

She was more confident after the tense night in Paris when they had become, finally, man and wife. Harry and I had jointly chosen the evening when he was to do his duty by her, and I had ensured that he regarded it as a disagreeable task. I had worn a low-cut dress for our outing to the opera and to supper afterwards. I had cast off my mourning with my first step on foreign soil, and that evening I shimmered in green like a young silver birch tree. My hair was thickly powdered white, and it showed my skin the colour of clear, dry wine. Not an eye in the hotel moved from me as Harry, Celia and I went to our table. Celia, beside me in pale pink, was eclipsed.

Harry drank heavily and roared with laughter at my witty talk. He was as tense as a wire and his nervousness took him to the edge of insensitivity towards Celia's feelings. She looked more like a prisoner on the way to the guillotine than a bride. She was sickly white in her girlish dress, spoke not a word and ate not a thing all evening. I sent Harry in to her bedroom certain that nothing could be done further to guarantee a pleasureless period of duty and pain for both.

He was even quicker than I expected. He came to my room in his dressing-gown with his night-shirt still stained with her blood. 'It is done,' he had said briefly and rolled into my bed. We slept together in warm companionship – as if I were comforting him for some secret sorrow. But in the morning, when the first grey light of the Paris dawn crept through my shutters, and the noise of the water-carts on the cobbles outside woke us both, we made love.

But it was a measure of Celia's new maturity – which I noted without comment – that not one word about that night of pain did I hear from her. Little confiding Celia told me nothing. Her intense loyalty to her husband – Harry the friend, Harry the invalid, and even Harry the legal rapist – kept her silent. She said nothing. She neither speculated, nor directly commented, on how long Harry and I sat together in the evening after she had retired. When she found Harry's bed untouched one careless morning when we had overslept, she said no words, assuming Harry had fallen asleep in his chair, or perhaps privately speculated that he was with a woman. She was the perfect wife for us. I expect she was deeply unhappy.

But it was Harry's response to her that made me pause. He had seen, as I had, Celia's unswerving loyalty to himself, to me, and to our family name. I saw his appreciation of her tentative services to his comfort. I noted his meticulous courtesy to her and the growth of confidence and trust between them. There was no way I could stop this short of a battle that could only expose me. But also there was no reason why I should. Celia could have the hand-kissing, and the courteous rising when she entered the room, Harry's sweet smile at breakfast, and his absent-minded politeness. I would have Harry's passion and Wideacre. And I knew from myself, and from Ralph, that sexuality and Wideacre were the most important things there could be in any person's life. As crucial as the keystone in the old Norman arch over the gate to the walled garden.

So though I was sure of Harry, the grey area of his feelings for little Celia made me pause before telling him I had conceived an heir. I shut my sunshade with a snap and poked the driver in the back. 'Drive home,' I said, ungraciously, and watched him clumsily back the pair into a dusty side road, and turn them for the hotel.

What I needed was some way of giving birth to the child and rearing it in absolute secrecy to give me time to bring Harry around to the idea of a son and heir conceived by me with him. I had to conceal the pregnancy, give birth in secret and find some trustworthy woman to care for the child until I could persuade Harry to produce the little boy before Celia as his son and heir and insist that she care for him.

I nibbled the end of my glove, and watched the vineyards slip past. The peasants were harvesting the grapes along the long rows of gnarled vines. Great, heavy black grapes that make the deep lovely Bordeaux wine. We would drink some this evening at dinner. They drink it young at this time of the year and the taste of it sparkles on your tongue. But there would be little pleasure for me at dinner, or at any other time, if I could not crack this kernel of conflict. First, Harry might simply refuse outright. Or he might agree and then be seized later by a fit of conscience and refuse to force his bastard on Celia. There were bastards in noble households up and down the land, but none that I knew had been imposed on the wife as an heir. Celia, alternatively, might refuse to accept the child, and she would certainly enjoy the support of my mother (not to mention her own family if she told tales). Then everyone would want to know where the baby had come from, and I could not trust Harry's abilities to sustain deception.

The problem of introducing a bouncing toddler into Wideacre as the new heir seemed insuperable, and while I worried at it a little flame of anger was lit within me again. It seemed that, like me, my son would find his way barred. But like me he would succeed. I should see him at the head of the Wideacre table, and with his foot on Wideacre land, whatever it cost.

In the meantime, I needed some kind, stupid, maternal woman who would care for a newborn baby and prepare him for the life he was to lead, and the place he had to fill. The landaulet stopped and I was handed down in a daydream. I had to find, in this strange land where I spoke not one word of the language, some gentle, stupid, loving woman to rear a cuckoo. I stood, poking the tip of my parasol into the ground at my feet and my sister-in-law, gentle, loving, stupid Celia, came down the steps of the hotel to greet me – and the solution to all my problems broke upon me like autumn sunshine in a thunderstorm.

'Are you feeling better?' she asked sweetly. I drew her hand under my arm as we walked up the steps.

'I am *so* much better,' I said, confidentially. 'And I have something to tell you, Celia, and I need your help. Come to my room and we can talk before dinner.'

'Of course,' said Celia, willing and flattered. 'But what do you need to tell me? You know I will help you in any way I can, Beatrice.'

I smiled lovingly at her, and stepped back gracefully to let her precede me into the hotel. After all, what was one gesture of precedence now, when I should, with her loyal and generous assistance, displace her, and any child of hers, for ever?

As soon as I had shut the door to my bedroom I composed my face into a solemn expression, drew Celia down beside me on a chaise-longue and put my hand in hers. I turned a sad, sweet gaze on her and felt my green cat's eyes fill with tears as I said, 'Celia, I am in the most dreadful trouble, and I know not which way to turn.'

Her brown eyes widened and the colour went from her cheeks.

'I am ruined, Celia,' I said with a sob, and I buried my face in her neck and felt the shudder that ran through her.

'I am,' I said, keeping my face down. 'Celia, I am with child.'

She gasped and froze. I could feel every muscle in her body tense with shock and horror. Then she determinedly turned my face up so she could look into my eyes.

'Beatrice, are you sure?' she asked.

'Yes,' I said, looking as aghast as she. 'Yes, I am sure. Oh, Celia! Whatever shall I do?'

Her lips trembled, and she put out her hands to cup my face. 'Whatever happens,' she said, 'I shall be your friend.'

Then we were silent while she digested the news.

'The baby's father . . .?' she said diffidently.

'I don't know,' I said, choosing the safest lie. 'Do you remember on the day I rode over to you to fit my gown I was taken ill at Havering Hall?'

Celia nodded, her honest eyes on my face.

'I felt faint on the ride over and had to dismount; I must have swooned and when I awoke, a gentleman was reviving me. My dress was disordered – you may remember a tear on my collar . . . but I did not know . . . I could not tell . . .' My voice was a strained whisper, almost silenced by tears and shame. 'He must have dishonoured me while I was unconscious.'

Celia clasped her hands around mine.

'Did you know him, Beatrice? Would you recognize him again?'

'No,' I said, disposing of the happy ending summarily. 'I had never seen him before. He was in a travelling curricle with luggage strapped on the back. Perhaps he was driving through Acre on his way to London.'

'Oh, God,' said Celia, despairingly. 'My poor darling.'

A sob stopped her from speaking, and we sat with our arms around each other, our wet cheeks touching. I reflected sourly that only a bride bred on tales from the romances and then raped once and left alone would swallow such a faradiddle. But by the time Celia was experienced enough to doubt conception while unconscious, she would be too well encased in my lie to be able to withdraw.

'What can we do, Beatrice?' she said, despairingly.

'I shall think of something,' I said bravely. 'Don't you grieve now, Celia. Go and change for dinner and we will talk more tomorrow when we have had time to think.'

Celia obediently went. But she paused by the door.

'Will you tell Harry?' she asked.

I shook my head slowly. 'He could not bear the thought of me sullied, Celia. You know how he is. He would hunt for that man, that devil, all around England, and not rest until he had killed him. I hope to find some way to keep this great trouble quite secret, between you and me alone. I put my honour in your hands, Celia, dear.'

She would not need telling twice. She came back into the room and kissed me, to assure me of her discretion. Then finally she took herself off, closing the door behind her as softly as if I was an invalid.

I sat up and smiled at my reflection in the glass of the pretty French-style dressing table. I had never looked better. The changes in my body might have made me feel ill, but had done nothing but good for my looks. My breasts were fuller and more voluptuous, and they pressed against my maiden gowns in a way that filled Harry with perpetual desire. My waist was thicker but still trim. My cheeks flushed with a new warmth, and my eyes shone. Now I was back in control of events I felt well. For now I was not a foolish whore encumbered with a bastard, but a proud woman carrying the future Master of Wideacre.

The following day, as we sat and sewed in the sunny parlour of the hotel, Celia wasted no time in returning to our problem. I was fiddling around, supposedly hemming lace that was to be sent home to Mama on the next packet – though I could not help suspecting she would have to wait a long time if she waited for my hemming. Celia was industriously busy: cutting broderie anglaise from a genuine Bordeaux pattern.

'I have worried all night, but I could think of only one solution,' Celia said. I glanced at her quickly. There were dark shadows under her eyes. I could believe she had hardly slept at all for worry at my pregnancy. I had hardly slept either, but that was because Harry had woken me at midnight with hard desire, and then again in the early hours of dawn. We could hardly have enough of each other, and I shuddered with perverse pleasure at the thought of Harry's seed and Harry's child inside me at once. And I smiled secretly at the thought of how I had gripped Harry's hips to prevent him plunging too hard inside me, guarding the child who deserved my protection.

And while I was lovemaking with her husband, Celia, dear Celia, was worrying over me.

'I can think of only one solution,' Celia said again. 'Unless you wish to confide in your mama – and I shall understand if you do not, my dear – then you will need to be away from home for the next few months.' I nodded. Celia's quick wits were saving me a lot of troublesome persuasion.

'I thought', Celia said tentatively, 'that if you were to say you were ill and needed my company, then we could go to some quiet town, perhaps by the sea, or perhaps one of the spa towns, and we could find some good woman there to care for you during your confinement, and to take the baby when it is born.'

I nodded, but without much enthusiasm.

'How kind you are, Celia,' I said gratefully. 'Would you really help me so?'

'Oh, yes,' she said generously. I noted with amusement that six weeks into marriage and she was ready to deceive and lie to her husband without a second's hesitation.

'One thing troubles me in that plan,' I said. 'That is the fate of the poor little innocent. I have heard that many of these women are not as kindly as they seem. I have heard that they ill-treat or even murder their charges. And although the child was conceived under such circumstances as to make me hate it, it is innocent, Celia. Think of the poor little thing, perhaps a pretty baby girl, a little English girl, growing up far away from any family or friends, quite alone and unprotected.'

Celia laid down her work with tears in her eyes.

'Oh, poor child! Yes!' she said. I knew the thought of a lonely childhood would distress her. It struck chords with her own experience.

'I can hardly bear to think of my child, your niece, Celia, growing up, perhaps among some rough, unkind people, without a friend in the world,' I said.

Celia's tears spilled over. 'Oh, it seems so wrong that she should not be with us!' she said impulsively. 'You are right, Beatrice, she should not be far away. She should be near so we can watch over her well-being. If only there was some way we could place her in the village.'

'Oh!' I threw up my hands in convincing horror. 'In that village! One might as well announce it in the newspapers. If we really wish to care for her, to bring her up as a lady, the only place for her would be at Wideacre. If only we could pretend she was an orphan relation of yours, or something.'

'Yes,' said Celia. 'Except that Mama would know that it was not true . . .' She fell silent and I gave her a few minutes to think around the idea. Then I planted the seed of my plan in her worrying little mind.

'If only it were you expecting a child, Celia!' I said longingly. 'Everyone would be so pleased with you, especially Harry! Harry would never trouble you with your . . . wifely duty . . . and the child could look forward to the best of lives. If only it were your little girl, Celia . . .'

She gasped, and I sighed silently with a flood of secret relief and joy. I had done it.

'Beatrice, I have had such an idea!' she said, half stammering with excitement. 'Why don't we say it is me who is expecting a baby, and then say it is my baby? The little dear can live safely with us, and I shall care for her as if she were my own. No one need ever know that she is not. I should be so happy to have a child to care for and you will be saved! What do you think? Could it work?'

I gasped in amazement at her daring. 'Celia! What an idea!' I said, stunned. 'I suppose it could work. We could stay here until the child is born and then bring her home. We could say she was conceived in Paris and born a month early! But would you really want the poor little thing? Perhaps it would be better to let some old woman take her?'

Celia was emphatic. 'No. I love babies and I should especially love yours, Beatrice. And when I have children of my own she shall be their playmate, my eldest child and as well loved as my own. And she will never, never know she is not my daughter.' Her voice quavered on a sob, and I knew she was thinking of her own girlhood as the outsider in the Havering nursery.

'I am sure we can do it,' she said. 'I shall take your child and love her and care for her as if she were my own little baby and no one will ever know she is not.'

I smiled as the great weight lifted from me. Now I could see my way clear.

'Very well then, I accept,' I said, and we leaned forward and kissed. Celia put her arms around my neck and her soft brown eyes looked trustingly into my opaque green ones. She wore her honesty, her modesty, her virtue, like a gown of purest silk.

Infinitely more clever, more powerful, and more cunning, I met her eyes with a smile as sweet as her own.

'Now,' she said excitedly, 'how shall we do it?'

I insisted that we do nothing, lay no more plans for a week. Celia could not understand the delay but accepted it as the whim of an expectant mother and did not press me. I needed nothing more than breathing space and time to consider my plans. I still had a massive hurdle ahead of me and that was to coach Celia into deceiving Harry. I did not immediately want to set her to the task of lying to the man to whom she had promised loyalty and love, because I knew she would lie extremely badly. The more she and Harry were together, the greater the bond between them grew. They were far from being lovers – however could they be with Celia's terrified frigidity and Harry's passionate absorption in me? But their friendship grew warmer and closer every day. I could not be sure of Celia's ability to lock her real self away from Harry, and I was not sure I could teach her to look her husband in the eye and tell him one bare-faced lie after another.

For myself, I had no doubts. When I lay in Harry's arms I was his, body and soul. But the possession lasted only as long as the pleasure. As soon as I lay beside him, our bodies green-barred by the hotel shutters closed against the afternoon sun, I was again myself. Even when Harry rolled his head on my hardening, swelling breasts, and exclaimed with delight, I felt no need to tell him that this new beauty was because of the forming of his child. He could see I was happy – anyone could see the glint in my eyes betokened deep secret satisfaction – but I felt no need to confide in Harry that every day brought me closer to an unchallenged place at Wideacre. Through Harry, I had assured myself of a place on the land, but to bear the next Master, and to know that all future Squires would be the blood of my blood and the bone of my bone, was a hard, secret delight.

When I sat at the hotel window in the morning and looked out along the wide, lovely avenue of slant-branched poplars, I daydreamed of other trees, of our lovely beeches. Then I smiled to think of myself an old lady, forever at the head of the Wideacre table: the Squire's autocratic aunt with more power than any other member of the family – ruling the Squire, his wife and his children with all the strength of blood and wit.

I sat so, dreaming, one morning, when I saw the cockade of the postman's hat coming down the street. A knock on the parlour door made me turn and smile to see some letters from home. There was one from Mama for me – I recognized the writing – and one for me in a strange, neat hand. I broke the seal and glanced first at the head of the letter, which started formally, 'Dear Miss Lacey', and then at the foot, where it was signed, 'John MacAndrew'. I believe I smiled. I believe I blushed. So Dr MacAndrew was entering into a clandestine correspondence, was he? Well, well, well. I smoothed the silk of my gown in an unconscious gesture of vanity, and turned again to the start of the letter. I could have saved my blushes. He was very businesslike.

Dear Miss Lacey,

I apologize for addressing you without your mother's permission, but I write to you concerning her health. She is not well, and I believe the responsibility for running the estate is causing her some worry.

She is in no danger; but I would advise you not to extend your trip beyond the promised limits.

I have attended her in a recent slight illness and my diagnosis is that she has a weak heart which should cause no major impairment of her health, provided that she can avoid anxiety.

I trust that you, Lady Lacey and Sir Harry are in good health and enjoying your trip.

Your obedient servant,
John MacAndrew.

My first instinct was one of intense irritation that John MacAndrew should be meddling in my affairs. Just when I needed to prolong my stay in France he was ordering me home like a child from school. I would not go, of course. But to escape this responsibility might cost me some trouble.

My second reaction was better. This problem with Mama's health could be the very thing to solve the pressing problem of keeping myself and Celia in France while Harry sped home. He could hold Mama's hand during her palpitations, or whatever ailment she was affecting to get her darling boy home. I put this suggestion – suitably embroidered – to Celia, and she fell on the idea.

'Oh, yes!' she said. We were in her room as she dressed to go out for our drive, and her eyes met mine in her long mirror. 'But you will be so anxious about your mama, Beatrice.'

'Yes,' I said sorrowfully. 'But until we have a solution, Celia, I could not go home. And at least I will have the comfort of knowing that Harry is at hand to care for her. Harry will be able to take the anxiety of running Wideacre off her shoulders.'

'Let us tell him at once,' said Celia decisively. So we tied our bonnets and adjusted our parasols and drove out to find him.

Harry was visiting a farm where they used seaweed for manure, as we planned to do at Wideacre. I believed that on chalk soil like our upland pastures you should use animal manure, and the seaweed is of use only in the sand and clay of the valley bottoms. But Harry believed it could be used on the slopes of chalk if it was properly rotted. He was visiting a farm where they dried and turned the seaweed in the sun and rain before ploughing it in, and we drove towards the farm expecting to see him riding home.

Celia's face lit up as we saw a horseman coming towards us. Under the influence of the French fashions in this little provincial town, Harry had taken to leaving off his wig and growing his hair. Under the tricorn, his golden curls glinted in the sunlight, and he rode his livery nag as if it were an Arab racer.

'Hallo!' he said, reining in alongside the carriage. 'This is a pleasant surprise.' His smile was impartially for both of us, but his eyes rested on me.

'We brought a picnic out for lunch,' said Celia. 'Have you seen a nice place?'

'Why, let us go back to the farm. They have a splendid river there. If only I had brought my rods with me, I could have tried for one of their trout.'

'I brought them!' said Celia triumphantly. 'I simply knew that if I brought a picnic you would have a trout stream at hand, and the first thing you would want would be your rods.'

Harry bent over her hand resting on the side of the carriage and kissed it.

'You are the best wife in all the world,' he told her lovingly. 'Excellent!'

He wheeled and called, 'Follow me!' to the driver and led us to the riverbank.

I did not mention Dr MacAndrew's letter until we had eaten and Harry had been sitting with his expensive rods and empty nets for a good half an hour. I showed him the letter and then Mama's lengthier, twice-crossed paper, which was full of anxieties about the winter sowing and confusion about which fields were to be sowed and which rested.

'We should return at once, I think,' said Harry when he had read Dr MacAndrew's brief note, and spent rather longer puzzling out Mama's spidery scrawl. 'Mama has always been susceptible to these attacks, I know, and I should hate her to be worried into illness.'

'I agree. We should get home as quickly as we can,' I said. 'Dr MacAndrew writes calmly so as not to alarm us, but he would not write at all if the situation were not serious. Which is the quickest way home?'

'We are lucky being in Bordeaux,' said Harry, thoughtfully. 'If this letter had caught us in Italy, or the middle of France, we would have taken weeks. As it is, we can get a packet ship home to Bristol and post-chaise from there.'

I smiled. Everything was well for me and I left the plan at that. When Celia glanced in surprise at me, I frowned at her, and she obediently said nothing.

Indeed, it was not until several hours later that I raised the problem of my seasickness and told Harry I feared I could not face a long sea trip.

'You will think me a very unloving daughter, I am sure,' I said smiling bravely. 'But, Harry, I dare not set foot on board for a long voyage, especially in November. I can barely face crossing the Channel again.'

We were in our private drawing room after dinner and Harry paused in his letter-writing, with the sailing times before him.

'Well, what is to be done, Beatrice?' he asked. He turned to me for a solution to problems just as he turned to Celia for little treats and comforts.

'Mama needs you,' I said bravely. 'So I think you should go. Celia and I can stay here until we hear how things are at home. If Mama is still ill once you have freed her from the cares of

Wideacre, then I shall simply have to find the courage to sail home. But if you are happy about her condition, and confident there is no danger, then we can travel post to the Channel and sail to Portsmouth.'

'Yes, or I could come and fetch you,' said Harry comfortingly. 'Or we could arrange for a courier to escort you. Of course you cannot travel alone. Does it seem the best plan to you, Beatrice?'

I smiled and nodded, trying to keep the satisfaction out of my face. Not only had Harry fallen in with my ideas to the letter, but noticeably he had not even glanced in Celia's direction for her opinion. She was to go home or stay in France as I pleased.

'What about the servants?' said Harry. 'I shall take my valet home, of course, but that leaves you with the maids and the two travelling coaches.'

'Oh, spare me!' I said in laughing consternation. 'We shall be following you in a few days! Celia and I are not so nice that we cannot manage with a French maid for a few days. Harry, pray do not leave me with a couple of servants and two carriages to transport home!'

Harry grinned. 'No, of course not,' he said. 'I can arrange for the carriages and all the heavy trunks to come with me, and if you wish it your maids can come with me too.'

'Yes please,' I said and turned to Celia. 'You do not mind being without a maid for that little while, do you, Celia?'

She kept her head down to her work, a poor liar and she knew it.

'Of course not,' she said, her voice steady.

'Very well then,' said Harry. 'It is decided. I shall see the landlord.' He paused at the door. 'I hope this is agreeable to you, Celia?' he asked politely.

'Of course,' she said generously. 'Whatever you and Beatrice wish.'

Harry went out and Celia held her tongue until the door had firmly shut behind him. Then she regarded me with awe.

'Beatrice, you did almost nothing, and yet everything came out as you wanted it,' she said.

I smiled and tried to keep the smugness from my voice.

'Yes,' I said. 'It always does.'

*

Harry sailed, but our last night together was one of lingering sweetness. He was ready to be sentimental at our parting. We had not spent one night apart since we landed in France, and we had slept every night under the same roof since we had become lovers. Now he was off to take responsibility for the running of a great estate, a full-grown man and a husband. I felt a glow of pride in him as I lay beside him, and smiled on him.

'My God, Beatrice. You grow lovelier every day,' he said, with pride of ownership in his voice. He leaned over me and buried his face in the warm valley between my newly plump breasts. 'I adore you, this bit fatter,' he said, his voice muffled as he kissed up one smooth slope and took a nipple in his mouth. I rumpled his hair and pushed his head down. Further down over the rounding curve of my newly hard belly so his tongue could trail a hot wet path lower, and lower and lower.

This was just playing at love – teasing each other's satisfied bodies after a long night of lovemaking. I sighed with pleasure, not only at the delightful little darts of sensation trailing hotly under my skin, but also at the knowledge that we had all this early morning alone, secure from interruption.

'When I come home,' I said idly, 'let's make sure that we spend afternoons and nights together like this. I shan't want to hide out on the downs or creep round the house like we did before.'

'No,' said Harry absently, rearing up to lay his head beside me on the pillow again. 'I have ordered them to open up the adjoining door from my dressing room into the west wing so I can be in your side of the house without anyone knowing it – and without having to cross the hall. I will be able to come while the others are asleep.'

'And at tea time,' I said smiling.

'And breakfast,' he said.

He rolled over and checked his watch lying on the bedside table.

'I must get dressed,' he said. 'Celia will soon be back from buying provisions for the voyage and I have to make sure she packs all my papers.'

I nodded but did not move.

'Write to me as soon as you get home,' I said. 'I shall want to hear about Wideacre. Remember to tell me which cows are in calf and how the winter wheat is looking, and if the hay will last.'

'And about Mama,' said Harry.

'Oh, yes, and about Mama,' I concurred.

'And you take care of yourself,' said Harry tenderly, reaching for a clean shirt. 'I wish you would come home with me now, Beatrice. I do hate the thought of leaving you all alone here.'

'Nonsense,' I said gently, and slid out of bed. 'Celia and I will be perfectly all right. We will enjoy a leisurely journey home and we can travel with Lady Davey and her daughters as soon as they arrive in town. Then you can come and meet us at Portsmouth, or even if you wish come over to France.'

'I may well do so,' said Harry, brightening. 'But only if I get my sea legs this time. I do dread the voyage, I must admit. You are well out of it, you little coward.'

'Chicken-hearted,' I agreed, smiling. I turned my back to him and swept up my long hair so he could fasten the little buttons I could not manage at the nape of my neck. His fingers fiddled with the little fastenings, and when he had done he bent his head to kiss me on the hairline, and tenderly grazed the strong muscles of my neck with his teeth. I leaned against him, enjoying the shivers that ran down my spine at the touch of his mouth. On the tip of my tongue was the confession that we were expecting a child. I thought for a moment that if only we were as we seemed to be – a mutually adoring married couple – how blissfully happy Harry would be at the news.

But my caution and my keen cool brain held me back from a confession grown out of the sweetness of love in the early morning. Harry's loyalties were already divided. I could not risk him protecting Celia from the injury that was coming to her. She might be too naive and silly to realize that in accepting my son as her own she would displace her own children for ever – but Harry was not. He would never consent to have my bastard son (even though fathered by himself) as his heir, when his wife could have other legitimate boys of her own.

My mood of relaxed love and trusting confidence passed. I would never trust anyone with all my secrets, not even my darling Harry. We had grown close and relaxed on this long easy journey, but there was a cutting edge in me, a sharpness of wit that Harry lacked. Harry was my lover, my desire, but he did not make me shudder as Ralph could, with one sideways glance. And I could not imagine Harry wading through sin and crime to come with bloody hands to me. With Harry I was the master; with Ralph we were sensual, passionate equals; equally sharp, equally wise. Good hard lust I had for Ralph; Harry gave me worship and kisses and cuddles like some lovesick youth.

I had two hanging crimes locked in my heart, and passing off a bastard was no light offence either. No one would ever again see fully into my heart as Ralph had done in the early days. No one ever again would hear a straight answer from me. Ralph was not the only one crippled in that dreadful trap – my honour, my honesty, was broken there, too. And I was right to be cautious with Harry. His next words proved it.

'Take care of Celia, Beatrice,' he said, tying a fresh cravat and eyeing it critically in the mirror. 'She has been such a little darling on this trip. I would not want her to miss me too much. Look after her and remind me to give you some spending money before I go, to buy whatever little things she wants.'

I nodded, and said not a word as he frittered away money from Wideacre, needed at Wideacre, on French trifles for a woman who already had enough.

'I shall miss you,' he said, turning from the mirror to hold me again. I slid into his arms and pressed my face against his clean starched shirt, sniffling with pleasure the clean smell of the linen and the warm smell of Harry underneath.

'Do you know,' he said in sudden surprise, 'I shall miss you both! Come home as quickly as you can, won't you, Beatrice?'

'Of course,' I said.

Of course I lied.

The circumstances made it easy for me to lie. But first I waited, waited a month in the old Bordeaux hotel until I heard from Harry in England. I smiled when I opened the letter because it was as I had expected. Our loving mama had her boy home again and she was not going to let him go. Harry – in a boyish anxious scrawl – wrote me that there were problems with the land, much poaching of the coverts, a field we had wanted to lie fallow had been mistakenly ploughed, and one of the tenants had had a fire in his barn and needed a loan.

'Mama seems quite overwhelmed by the work necessary to run the estate,' Harry wrote. 'I arrived to discover that she is suffering from very serious spells of breathlessness, which leave her quite weak. She had even concealed how bad they are from Dr MacAndrew. I think it impossible that I should leave her alone in charge again, so I beg you, poor darling Beatrice, to hire a courier and get your dear selves home either cross-country or sail.'

I nodded. I had known the estate would be too much for Mama. It was a full-time job for someone who knows and loves the land and a weak incompetent like Mama could be destroyed by the responsibility and the things that, naturally, are always going wrong. That was the risk I took when I could not bear to let Harry and Celia travel alone. Then I took another risk with Wideacre – leaving the estate in Mama's feeble hands. Now I had to trust to luck that Harry would wreak no great damage before I came home. For Harry had to stay in England, and I had to stay in France until our son was born.

I took up a pen and cut absently at the nib until I thought of the things I needed to say. I started my letter to Harry and confined myself entirely to business. The field should be planted with clover since it had already been ploughed. The tenant should be granted a loan at 2 per cent interest to be paid in cash or in produce from his farm, with his stock as security. The gamekeeper must either be made to work harder, more effectively, or dismissed. Lord Havering would know where Harry could find another. But then my tone grew more intimate. I told him I missed him badly – which was true – and that France gave me little pleasure without him – which was half true – and that I was longing to return home – which was not true at all. Then I nibbled the top of the pen and wondered how to break the news to him that Celia was carrying his child.

'However much I would wish it, my wishes come secondary for once!' I wrote with a sweet little jest. 'For Celia cannot travel, and the argument against her making the attempt is the only one that could stop me coming to you.' Sufficiently winsome for anyone this, I thought, well aware that Harry might read it aloud to Mama, or Lady Havering. 'I am deeply happy to be able to tell you that Celia is with child.'

I paused again. Celia's health had to be sufficiently difficult as to prevent her travelling entirely, and yet not so frail that Harry felt her needs more pressing than Mama's. I thought I could trust to Mama to keep Harry safe at home, but you never knew with my mama. She might be overwhelmed with tenderness for Celia and her unborn grandson and send Harry post-haste back to France in a spirit of inconvenient selflessness.

'She is extremely well,' I wrote, 'happy in her mind and fit. However, she finds any motion of carriage or boat brings on severe nausea. The local *accoucheuse* – who speaks excellent English and is most attentive and helpful – advises us that Celia should not attempt any journey until she is past the third month of her time, when she anticipates the symptoms will have abated and we can come home.'

I filled another page with assurances that I was caring for Celia and that Harry need have no concern whatsoever, and that we would be setting out on our journey home within two months. I threw in a caution that he should not think of coming to meet us or coming back to France without writing to me first: 'How unfortunate if our ships were to cross at sea, us coming home, you coming out!' I wrote, and thought that should keep him fixed at home.

I envisaged that at the end of the time I had allotted Celia's symptoms of nausea might improve, but then there would be the trouble of getting a ship. Then there would be the winter storms, and then we would be too near her time for us to consider a bumpy land journey or a slow sea voyage. I thought that if every letter sounded as if we were just about to set off, Harry would be happy to wait for us, and attract no blame from any friends and neighbours for lying snug at Wideacre while his wife and sister were in France. I knew I should have to do some clever lying in the letters – but I knew also that I could do it.

And all the time my body grew rounder and rounder until I scarce could believe the shape of it, as fat as a tulip on a slender stem. We had left the hotel as soon as Harry was safely away and had taken furnished rooms on the outskirts of Bordeaux, south of the Gironde river. Every day I woke to the sight of reflected ripples dancing on my ceiling and the noise of fishermen and boatmen calling across the water.

The widow who owned the house believed me to be a young married Englishwoman and Celia my sister-in-law. So any later gossip might be confused by the nearness to the truth of the lies we told.

The rhythm of the early winter days exactly suited my lazy mood in the middle of my pregnancy. And when I got heavier and tired, I was glad to draw up the sofa to a good wood fire and sit with my feet up, while Celia sewed and sewed an exquisite layette complete for a prince, for the heir to Wideacre.

Her face lit up when I said graciously, one day, 'He's kicking. You may feel him if you want.'

'Oh! May I?' she said eagerly, and rested her gentle hand on the curve of my belly and tensed with anticipation. Then a tender smile passed over her face as she felt the hard knobbly movements.

'Oh,' she sighed in delight, 'what a strong child she will be.' A shadow crossed her face. Silly fool that she was, she had taken this long to think of Wideacre. 'What if it is a boy?' she asked. 'An heir?'

My face was clear, my smile assured. I was ready for her. 'I know,' I said. 'I may have said "he" but I know it is a girl.' I was utterly certain in my lie, as I was utterly certain in my private conviction that I carried the heir to Wideacre in my belly. 'It is a girl,' I said again. 'I promise you, Celia, a mother always knows what her child will be.'

The cold wind that had blown all winter so strongly off the sea died down, and there was an easy, early spring. I pined for Wideacre like an exiled convict and could barely acknowledge the beauty of thi. warm French season. It seemed too hot too suddenly; there were no long days of anticipation. But then my heart leaped when I looked at the calendar and realized that, all being well and the new heir being prompt, I might yet get to home in time to see our wild daffodils still blooming under the trees in the wood.

Madame had arranged for a midwife well known to her who had a good record of successful births and was called often to attend ladies of Quality. We also had the name of a surgeon in case of complications. To my surprise, I found I had a secret longing for the cool, straightforward competence of Dr MacAndrew, and smiled at the thought of what his response would be if he knew that the lovely Miss Lacey was preparing for her confinement in France. But when the old midwife rubbed oils into my swelling belly, and Celia hung dried flowers and herbs over the door, and tossed special dust on the fire, I found myself heartily impatient with these superstitions. I would much have preferred Dr MacAndrew to look at me in that clear, honest way and tell me if it was to be an easy labour or not. In his absence, I had to rest on the belief that the stupidest women I know have packs of brats, so surely I could manage just one.

When the time came, it was surprisingly easy – a tribute, the midwife said, to my early hoydenish galloping about on horses – so unlike a good French girl. I woke in the night all wet and said drowsily, 'Good heavens, he's coming.' No more, but Celia had heard me even through the bedroom wall and was awake and with me in a second. She sent Madame for the midwife and got the little cradle and the swaddling bands ready, a pot boiling on the hearth and then sat calmly and helpfully at my head.

It was like heaving bales of hay, or pushing a great cart-horse round a stable. Hard work, and you know you are working, but for me there was no great pain. I screamed a few times, I think, but some part of my alert mind reminded me to keep any name off my lips.

Celia clung to my hand with a face as white as the baby's layette as I sat up in the bed, curved over my belly where the muscles stood up as square as a box. I could actually see the outline of my son, my darling son, the heir to Wideacre, pushing his way bravely and rightly down the long journey of my body, ready to be born.

'Poussez, madame!' yelled the midwife.

'Poussez!' shouted the widow.

'They say "push",' breathed Celia, overcome by all this noise and healthy physical activity. I choked on a laugh, then forgot the comedy of it as a great driving wave of feeling swept my body and the darling boy another inch downwards.

'Arrêtez! Arrêtez!' shouted the midwife, and she bent down with a corner of a dirty apron and wiped something that was no longer me. Celia's eyes filled with tears as we heard a tiny gurgling cry. My son, my heir, greeted the world with a yelp as with one last push and a wriggle and even a scrabble with his tiny feet, he swam free, and the midwife landed him like a beached fish on the bank of my suddenly flaccid belly.

I gazed at his eyes, so deep blue that even the whites of them were as blue as the early morning skies over Wideacre. I touched his wet head, dark but perhaps already with signs of a chestnut gleam from me. I looked at his tiny fingers, each one crowned with a perfect minute shell of a fingernail.

'Vous avez une jolie fille,' the midwife said approvingly, and busied herself with the sheets.

I gazed blankly from my tiny son to Celia's concerned face.

'She is a girl,' said Celia gently, in awe.

I could hear the words neither in English nor in French. The baby that I had carried so carefully and so long, this baby, for whom I had laboured all night, was my son, was Wideacre's heir. He was the end and triumph of my sinning and striving. This was my child, who would inherit by unquestioned right. This was my son, my son, my son.

'A lovely girl,' repeated Celia.

I turned on my side so roughly that the baby nearly fell but

Celia's hands were quick to catch her and hold her safe. The child set up a shriek as I jerked away and cried and cried in Celia's arms.

'Take the little brat away,' I said with hatred, and cared not who heard me. 'Take it away and keep it. You agreed. You wanted a girl all through. Now you have got one. Take her away.'

I did not repent all night, though I heard an insistent wail and the sound of Celia's footsteps as she walked the hungry baby backwards and forwards across the floor of her room. I heard her hushing it with little songs in a voice that grew more and more thin as the night went on. I dozed at the sound, and then woke to anger and bitter disappointment. All my life I had been denied my rights at Wideacre. I, who loved the land best of all of us, who served it better than any of us, who had schemed and plotted and crippled for it, was disappointed again. One stroke of luck could have placed me for life as the mother of the heir of Wideacre. Whether I had kept the secret in my heart for my own comfort and pleasure, whether I had used it, or whether I whispered it one day to my growing son, only time would have shown. But now I had a paltry insignificant girl who would be supplanted by Celia's first boy baby and who would be married away from Wideacre when grown, just as they still planned to marry me.

She was the death of my plans and I could not yet learn to bear the disappointment. The long, long wait for the birth and the struggle of labour to produce a miserable girl were too bitter a pill to swallow. In my vague, dozing dreams I grieved also with a strange sense of loss for the child that never was. The son I had made in my mind with pride and tenderness. And in my half-waking, confused thoughts I turned in need – not to the image of Harry, but to Ralph – and said indistinctly in my mind, 'I have lost something too now. You are not the only one who has suffered for Wideacre. You lost your legs, but I have lost a son.' There was comfort in this dream of telling Ralph of my pain, which only he would understand.

But into this dozing vision came the nightmare picture of a man on a big black horse and I sat bolt upright in my bed and shrieked myself into wakefulness.

It was daylight. Through the closed door I could hear the noise of breakfast being prepared and felt a sudden keen hunger for the hot croissants and strong black coffee Madame or Celia would bring to me. My body was sore: I felt as if I had been kicked in the groin by a stallion, and I was as tired as after a day's hunting. But my belly was as flat as a milk pudding – disagreeably wobbly but I should soon cure that. I pulled up my shift to enjoy the sight of my thighs and knees, which had disappeared from sight around the moon of my belly months ago. And then I thanked the gods in genuine gratitude that my navel had retreated to be a perfect little dimple again, instead of the little molehill that had formed as the baby grew.

Enwrapped in my mood of self-congratulation, I smiled with good humour as the door opened and Celia came in carrying my breakfast tray for me. Someone had gone to the garden and picked me white violets, and their cool, wet smell reminded me with piercing longing of the woods of Wideacre where the white and blue violets grow like pools at the roots of the trees. There also came the good smell of Madame's deadly strong coffee, and the sight of the flaky skins of golden croissants and the bland, unsalted butter. I felt as hungry as if I had been fasting for a year.

'Lovely,' I said, and took the tray on my knees and poured a deep black cup of bitter coffee and fell on the croissants. Only when I had polished the plate with a licked forefinger to get every trace of the flaky crumbs did I notice that Celia looked pale and tired.

'Are you unwell, Celia?' I asked in surprise.

'I am tired,' said Celia, her voice low but with some strength behind her tone that I did not yet understand. 'All night the baby cried. She is hungry but she will take neither pap nor goat's milk. The wet-nurse we were promised has gone dry and Madame is trying to find another this morning. I am afraid the child is hungry.'

I lay back on my pillows and watched Celia under my long eyelashes. My face was inscrutable.

'I think you should feed her yourself,' said Celia evenly. 'You will have to until we can find another wet-nurse. I am afraid you have no alternative.'

'I had hoped not to do so,' I said, affecting hesitation, and testing the strength of this strange, purposeful Celia. 'I wanted, for her sake and for all of us, to see as little as possible of her, especially in these early days when naturally I am rather distressed.' I let my voice quaver a little, and watched like a hawk for Celia's response.

'Oh, Beatrice, I am so sorry,' she said. 'I was thinking, wrongly, only of her. Of course I understand you will not wish to see her until you are more accustomed to the idea. I let my concern for her overcome my deeper concern for you. Do forgive me, my dear.'

I nodded my head and smiled at her kindly, and waved for her to remove the tray. She did so and I snuggled down into the pillows with a sigh of blissful contentment, which she took for tiredness.

'I will leave you to rest,' she said. 'Never fear about the little one. I shall find some way to feed her.' I nodded. I dare say she would. Had it been a boy – my son, my longed for son – I would never have let some poor French peasant near him with her milk and her dirt. But a girl baby could shift for herself. Hundreds of babies thrive on flour and water; this wrong-sex brat could do so too. Hundreds more die on the diet, and in many ways this would be the easiest solution to the problem of this crying girl. To force Celia to keep a life-long secret would take all my ability, and cost all my goodwill with her. That effort and struggle would have been a small enough price to pay to see my son as heir of Wideacre, but to do it to place a miserable girl in a poor secondary position was a high price to pay for no benefit at all. The girl was no good to me; girls are never any good to anyone. I shut my eyes on the disappointment and dozed again.

When I woke my pillow was wet with tears, which had slid down my cheeks in dreamless sleep. When I felt the wet linen against my cheek the tears sprung again to my eyes. Wideacre was so far away from this little overheated room in this strange town. There were long seas of grey waves between me and home. Wideacre was far from me, and my undisputed ownership as distant as ever. The place haunted me and my sleep like a Holy Grail that I could seek, and wear out my life in the seeking, but never attain. I turned my head on the pillow and said one sad word, the name of the man who would have won Wideacre for me, 'Ralph.'

Then I slept again.

Celia came in again at dinnertime with another pretty tray of delicious food. Artichoke hearts, breast of chicken, ragout of vegetables, a pastry, a milk trifle and some cheese. I ate everything with as good an appetite as if I had been walking the Wideacre fields all day. She waited until I had finished and then poured me a glass of ratafia. I raised my eyebrows in surprise but took the glass and sipped at it.

'The midwife says you are to have a glass a day, and stout or small-beer in the evening,' said Celia.

'What on earth for?' I said lazily, laying back against the pillows and enjoying the sweet taste against my tongue.

'To make the milk,' said Celia baldly.

I noticed for the first time that there were new lines of strain around her eyes, and a determined look in her face that I had never seen before. The flower-like face was no less pretty but the velvety brown eyes had a determination in them. I looked down to hide the gleam of amusement in my own green eyes. Celia was taking motherhood hard; at this rate she would loose her good looks by the time we were home, while I would be as sleek and relaxed as any pampered kitten.

'It is impossible to find a replacement wet-nurse locally and I have been forced to send to the curé who is in charge of the Magdalen house. Poor girls go there to have their babies and the children are taken away at birth,' said Celia. 'I have sent Madame's stable boy with a message, but it is unlikely we will find one immediately. Meanwhile the child cries and cries for your milk. She will accept neither cow's milk, goat's milk, flour and water or plain water.'

I stole a glance at Celia, still untouched by her news. But the look on her face disturbed me. I realized with a sudden shock that we had stumbled on an instance where she might be stronger than me. She was defending this troublesome brat as if it were, indeed, her own. Some reasons, perhaps the months of preparation and waiting, the anxiety to please Harry with the early arrival of the baby, her own tender loving nature and her need for something to love, had all combined to make her fall in love with the child as soon as it was born. She had held it newborn in her arms. Hers was the first voice it heard speaking in tones of love. Hers were the first arms that rocked it, the first lips that touched the wet, delicate little head. She felt all that a first-time mother should feel for her child. And now she was defending it. She was fighting for the life of her child and she looked ready to ride over anyone who threatened it. I watched her in open curiosity. This was not the easy biddable girl I had trained like a well-bred puppy. This was an adult woman with total commitment to another being – and that made her strong.

In this matter she was even stronger than me.

'Beatrice,' she said firmly. 'You have to feed this child. She will not trouble you. I shall bring her and take her away as soon as she is fed, and I ask nothing more than you do this every few hours until a wet-nurse is found.'

She paused. I still said nothing. I was ready to agree. Indeed, why not? It would not greatly spoil my figure, which I was certain would soon be as firm and lovely as ever. It would make me appear to be a sensitive woman. But I hesitated because I was curious to see how strong this new Celia was.

'It will be no more than a few days,' she said. 'But if it was a year, Beatrice, I would still ask, I would *insist* that you did this. The child is mine; I accept responsibility, so I must ensure that she is fed. And you alone can provide what she needs.'

I smiled an easy smile.

'Of course, Celia, if that is what you want,' I said generously. 'I did not offer only because I thought you and Madame had everything so well arranged.' I could have laughed aloud at the look of relief on Celia's face.

'You may bring her in,' I said graciously. 'But stay to take her away again. I shall want to sleep.'

Celia shot from the room like an arrow from the bow and returned with the little crying bundle. Her hair was deliciously soft and brown, formed into one peak of a curl on the top of her head – but, of course, that might change. Her deep, deep blue eyes would probably change, too. She gazed into my face as if she would see into my soul, and I amused myself by trying to outstare her. I have outstared cats and dogs and men. But these blue, blue eyes were impossible; they had the blank stare of madness and made me uncomfortable after a while, and a little afraid. Her hands were like shrivelled starfish, impossibly tiny; and her feet, like little crumpled leaves, peeked out from under the swaddling cloths. She smelled of a smell I recognized on myself – the sweet strong smell of birth. I controlled – with no great effort – a passing sense of our oneness, this tiny dot and I. But she was not a son. She would be of no use, and in any case I would have shrunk from a relationship which had already drawn lines of care and worry on Celia's face and put shadows under her eyes.

I put the little bundle to my breast and held her awkwardly. Celia's hands flew out from her sides involuntarily, but I saw her control the instinct to help, choosing to wait and see. Neither of us knew exactly what we were doing, but the baby was a fighter and at the first scent of my nipple she lunged forward. Her mouth made a sideways triangle of longing pointing at the nipple where a white drop already stood. I could feel a strange ache inside my breast and then a great ease and satisfaction as the baby took hold. She snuffled and huffed in a tiny sneeze, gave a brief, outraged cry of protest at the delay and then hurried on. Her eyes rolled and then lidded as she settled to a steady rhythm of sucking. My eyes met Celia's over the head of Celia's baby and we smiled.

'What shall you call her?' I asked casually.

Celia leaned forward to touch the tiny head and laid a finger on the little dent in the skull where one could see the pulse beating, strong and determined.

'This is my little Julia,' she said with calm certainty. 'Soon I shall take her to her home.'

I left it a week or two, and then I wrote the letter I had been planning in my mind:

Dearest Harry,
I am very proud and happy to tell you that your child has been born, prematurely, but safely. You have a girl and Celia is planning to call her Julia. Celia's delicate health has kept us anxious to the last, and when she felt her pains start two weeks early I was afraid. But we had a good midwife and help from our landlady here, and Celia was in labour for less than a day. The baby was small, of course, but she has gained weight

apace with her good wet-nurse, and by the time we are home you will not be able to tell the difference between her and a child carried full term.

That much at least was true, I thought, as I wryly added some persuasive details to the picture, and dictated a little note from Celia, supposedly recovering from childbirth, scribbled at the end of my letter.

I knew little enough of babies but I was fairly certain that if we were not home until Julia was a month or so old, no one would be able to swear an oath as to her age. Besides, the truth was too outrageous for anyone to guess. If anyone thought her a little plump, a little alert for a premature baby, the doubt would be cast on Celia and Harry – who would be assumed to have been early lovers – not on me. And Harry, who alone knew that he had not been in Celia's bed until that night in Paris, would hardly tell the age of a baby from looking. The dates I had offered tallied with that one, pleasureless night.

In a hurry, in a foreign land, under pressure, and certain that the child in my womb was the son and heir to Wideacre, I had contrived as best I could. I sealed the envelope and laid it on my bedside table for Celia to take to the post. I could do no more. I had to leave the rest to the old fickle gods of Wideacre, who so often blew good fortune my way, as my reward for fidelity to the land, and trust to Celia to play her part when we arrived, and get me safe home.

And she did. With an assurance that I had seen in her only once before – on that disastrous Channel crossing – Celia quietly organized the new wet-nurse, myself, squalling baby Julia and herself, on a packet sailing for England in a shorter time than seemed possible.

I was glad enough to be organized. I felt curiously exhausted. Although I had rested like a spoilt princess both before and after the birth, I still felt tired and moped in the little French *pension*. I could hear the baby crying at night through the wall, and although I relished the thought that it was not I who was having to light my candle in the darkness and blunder about to make the little thing comfortable, and it was not I who was walking, walking with it until it fell asleep, I still found that insistent, demanding little wail could call me out of the deepest sleep and set my breasts aching.

I was a divided woman. My body had always been in complete and harmonious tune with my mind. But now, still plump and flaccid at the waist, with disgusting pale pink lines at the hips where my skin had stretched – it did not seem like me at all. And the way my eyes opened and my muscles tensed when I heard the baby cry at night! And the way my tightly bound breasts ached to give milk! It was all wrong, all unlike me. It seemed all part of the tirelessly, tediously blue French sky, and the wrong-smelling land and the strange bread and the stinky cheeses, and all the things that should have been a Wideacre spring and yet were so unlike home.

The sea was reassuringly calm for most of the trip, and I enjoyed the salt smell and the breath of wind from the south and I even learned to bear the heaving of the ship. My body had slowly lost its rounded shape and started to regain its familiar smooth sleekness, which reassured me that I was also returning to my true self. The early bright sun put summertime gleams of copper into my chestnut hair and started to dust my nose with the slightest of freckles. I was still a trifle plump around the neck and my breasts were fuller and heavier, but when I stripped naked and gazed at myself in a little mirror in the heaving cabin I thought it unlikely that anyone would ever guess I had given birth – not even Harry when he explored every inch of my naked body with his eyes and hands and tongue.

As soon as Celia had found the wet-nurse I had turned the child over to her and bound my breasts. I told Celia that the milk had stopped at once and indicated my new slimness as evidence. It was only partly true. When I heard the hungry wail my breasts ached and the tight, tight bindings grew wet around the hard nipples. If Celia had so much as dreamed I had milk, she would have had the baby fed, and well and happy again. But even as I oozed milk in a warm, unstoppable richness, I met her eye blandly and swore I was dry.

The horrid pink scratches of stretch marks were fading to a near-invisible whiteness as Madame had promised they would, and the shadows under my eyes went as soon as I insisted that the baby, wet-nurse and Celia all move cabins to take them out of earshot of my best state room.

In fact, they slept little. While I strolled on deck, or sat in the sunshine watching the blue waves slide by under the prow, or leaned over the stern to watch the wake gleaming white and vanishing like a disappearing chalk lane in the distance, Celia, as often as not, was pacing with the baby in the hot cabin below.

Apparently the baby did not like the seafaring life, and the French girl hired as wet-nurse had temporarily dried up during her bout of seasickness. Her milk would flow again provided the baby was put often to the breast, but in the meantime it was once more hungry and once more turning its nose up at pap and water. When I saw Celia's face after a day of nursing the retching wet-nurse and a night of walking with a fretful baby, I nearly laughed aloud. If I had no other reason in the world to avoid motherhood, one glimpse of Celia's wan face would have convinced me. She looked years older than the shy bride who had left England nine months ago. She truly looked the part of a woman who had given birth prematurely. She looked as if she had born triplets at least.

'Rest, Celia. Rest,' I said, patting the seat beside me and stroking my skirts in to make a space for her.

'I can only sit for a minute while she sleeps,' Celia said, perched on the edge of the bench, her ears alert for any noise from below.

'What ails the child?' I asked casually.

'Nothing new, I think,' said Celia wearily. 'First the movement of the boat upset her. Then the milk began to fail and she grew hungry. Now I think the milk is coming through again and she did well at the last feed and then slept well.'

I nodded amiably, but with little interest. 'Wideacre air will soon set her to rights,' I said, thinking more of myself.

'Yes, indeed,' said Celia happily. 'And the sight of her papa and her home. I can hardly bear to wait, can you, Beatrice?'

My heart leaped at the thought of Harry and home.

'No,' I said. 'How very long it has been since we were at home. I wonder how everything is.'

Unconsciously I leaned forward to stare at the horizon as if to create a purple hump of land out of the flat line of sea meeting sky by sheer effort of will. My mind rolled over the problems and people I had left behind. First and foremost was Wideacre, but I already knew from Harry's detailed letters that the spring sowing had gone well, that it had been a mild winter and the winter forage had lasted out, so no animals had been killed because of lack of feed. The tenant farmers were convinced that turnips could be used as a winter-feed crop now we had proved on the Home Farm that the beasts could eat them through the winter. The French vines Harry had brought back from Bordeaux had been planted on our south-facing slopes of the downs, and seemed no more gnarled and dead-looking than they did in France, so perhaps they would take.

On the debit side, without me to restrain him, Harry had suffered from two bouts of his experimental madness. One mattered little: the ploughing up of some old fields that could soon return to grass. The loss there was the goodwill of the people who used the footpath across them, and of the neighbouring farmer whose lane was impassable after the ploughing. Harry had ignored the advice of the old labourers, and had planned to plant an orchard on Green Lane Meadow. He soon found out that the lush green grass was thriving there because of an unusual clay bed. His ploughshares stuck as if he were farming in Devon, his trees wilted and the sticky mud turned to rock in the sunshine. The entire hundred-acre meadow was ruined for that year and the investment in young trees, money and time would have to be written off as one of the prices paid for Harry's inexperience. It made me angry that I had not been there to prevent it, but glad, very glad, that the cost had been no higher. The wise old labourers, and even the young lads, would be shaking their heads over the young Squire's folly, and there would be many whispers wishing Miss Beatrice would hurry up and come home.

Harry's other nonsense could have cost lives, and that I found hard to forgive. He had some textbook clever ideas for controlling the flow of the Fenny, which, since time began, had been wide and fast and prone to flooding in springtime, and slow and sluggish in summer. Since everyone (everyone except Harry, of course) knows this, all the farmers whose lands run alongside the Fenny are ready for the spring floods and winter high water, too.

In the flatter fields they leave unploughed the great dried-out ox-bows where the flood waters can overspill and roar and loose their speed and power before rejoining the main torrent. In an average season we may lose a sheep or a silly calf, or once – I remember – an ill-guarded child, in the flood. But this is no mountain torrent. It is just the sweet Fenny. It can be managed; it can be watched in the old, sound ways.

But they were not good enough for Harry. He calculated that if the water level were to be regulated at its source in a little steep-sided downland valley with a wall to hold back the growing river, then all the extra field space we allowed for flooding could be ploughed up and used. The empty extra curves around the riverbed, the water-meadows that flood twice a year, could all be put under his blessed plough to grow more and more of his damned wheat. So Harry listened courteously and politely to all the wise old men, and paid them no heed. My letters of excitable remonstrance he ignored, too. Too clever for his own good was Harry, and the old tenants sent their sons out to build his dam and fit its pretty little sluice gates and dig out its little channels, and they laughed behind their hands at the waste, and the cost and, I dare say, at what Miss Beatrice would have to say when she came home, and the rage she would be in.

What happened next could have been predicted by any fool except the fool who now squired Wideacre. The waters behind Harry's new-built dam backed up in the little valley far faster than he had anticipated. He had measured the flow of the Fenny, but not allowed for the fact that when the snow melts and we have heavy spring rains the whole land becomes wetter and there are streams where he had never guessed streams would flow. The swelling lake drowned a hazel coppice that was older than Wideacre itself, and waterlogged some good dry upland meadow fields. As the waters built up, the nice little sluice gates struggled to open and close to control the flood; the new plaster in the wall melted like springtime ice; the dam crumbled and a great wall of water, high as a house, thundered down the little valley towards Acre.

It knocked out the road bridge in the first splashy roaring collision and Harry could thank his fool's luck that there were no small children sitting on the parapet or old men smoking and staring at the stream when that deadly wall of water ripped the sound old bridge out by its roots.

It spread then, a wide sweep of destruction as careless as a fan brushed across a table of ornaments. Crops, shrubs, bushes and even large shallow-rooted firs were bowled over in a broad swathe for twenty feet on either side of the banks. So Harry's proud new wheat crop on the old water-meadows was ripped out of the earth before it had even rooted, and all his newly claimed fields were littered with mud and rubble and broken trees.

The flood hit the new mill with some of its force spent and, although the yard was flooded, the building had stood firm. Ground-floor windows and doors were staved in and some of the grain spoiled, but the new buildings were sound and strong. The old mill, where Ralph and I had met and loved, and Meg's rickety hovel were swept away altogether. Only two walls of the mill were left standing and that sweet flowering green bank washed clean of our footprints. Even the straw he had picked off my skirts was gone, whirling downstream on the floodtide.

Then the worst of the flood was spent and the river returned to its banks. Harry wrote me that he had been greeted with anxious faces when he rode out the next day, but I knew there would have been smiles behind his back. Every scrounger on Widacre would have profited from the Squire's folly and the claims of flood damage would be sky high. Harry had to find the money and the workers to rebuild the bridge and the road; he had to compensate the tenants whose lands had been damaged and crops spoiled. He had to buy Mrs Green new glass for her windows and chintz for her curtains. When I read his doleful letter describing the damage and the claims he faced I had been hot with rage at his folly and the waste of it all. But now I was just as anxious to be home so I could set all to rights again.

Besides, there were things I could not ask Harry, but could only see for myself. How the young doctor was getting on, and whether Lady Havering had managed to catch him for one of Celia's pretty sisters; if he remembered his passing liking for me. My heart stayed rock-steady at the thought of him – he was not a man who would excite or challenge me – and he could not gain me Wideacre – but his attention had flattered my vanity at a time when I needed a diversion, and he intrigued me. He was so unlike the men I knew – men of the land like squires, bluff farmers and county leaders. But my heart beat no faster at the thought of him. He had no mystery, no magic like Ralph. He did not hold the land and charm me like Harry. He could only interest me. But if he were still single, and still smiling with cool blue eyes at me, then I was happy to be interested.

I gazed out to sea where the waves followed each other like wandering, rolling hills and faced the principal question that awaited me at home: if the villains of the Kent attack had all been rounded up, sentenced and hanged; or whether one – just one, the leader with his two black dogs and his black horse – was still free. The question no longer woke me screaming every night, although the black horse continued to ride through my occasional nightmares. But the thought of my lovely strong Ralph swinging himself about on crutches, or worse still shuffling his body along the ground like a dog in the gutter, would always make me feel sick with fear and disgust. I took care to keep the picture from my mind, and if it came, unbidden, when I closed my eyes for sleep I took a good measure of laudanum and escaped.

If the corn rioters were all taken I could sleep in peace. He might well be dead already. He could have been executed in his disguise and no one ever thought to tell Wideacre, and certainly no one troubled enough to send the news to us in France. The figure who still haunted my darkest nightmares might be a ghost indeed, and I had no fear of dead men.

But if he were dead I felt I would mourn him. My first lover, the boy, then the man, who had spoken so longingly of the land and pleasure and the need to have them both. The clever youth who saw so young that there are those who give and those who take love. The daring, passionate, spontaneous lover who would fling himself on me and take me without doubt and without conscience. His frank sensuality had matched mine in a way that Harry never could. If he had only been of the Quality . . . but that was a daydream that would lead nowhere. He had killed for Wideacre; he had nearly died for it. All I had to hope was that the noose had done what the spring of the mantrap had half done, and that the love of my childhood, girlhood and womanhood was dead.

'Is that – can that be land?' asked Celia suddenly. She pointed ahead and I could see the faintest dark smudge like smoke on the horizon.

'I don't think it can be yet,' I said, straining my eyes. 'The captain said not till tomorrow. But we have had good winds all day.'

'I do believe it is,' said Celia, her pale cheeks flushed with pleasure. 'How wonderful to see England again. I shall fetch Julia to catch her first glimpse of her home.'

And away down the hatch she went and came up with the baby, nurse and all the paraphernalia of infancy so that the baby could be pointed to the prow and face her homeland.

'It's to be hoped she's more excited by the sight of her father,' I said, watching this nonsense.

Celia laughed without a trace of disappointment. 'Oh, no,' she said. 'I expect she's far too young to pay much heed. But I like to talk to her and show her things. She will learn soon enough.'

'It won't be for lack of teaching if she does not,' I said drily.

Celia glanced at me and registered the tone of my voice.

'You don't ... you don't regret it, Beatrice?' She stepped towards me, the baby against her shoulder. Her face showed concern for me and my feelings, but I noticed she had tightened her grip on the baby's shawl.

'No.' I smiled at her suddenly scared face. 'No, no, Celia. The baby is yours with my blessing. I only spoke thus because I am surprised to see how much she means to you.'

'How much?' Celia stared at me, uncomprehending. 'But, Beatrice, she is so utterly *perfect*. I would have to be mad not to love her more than my life itself.'

'That's settled then,' I said, glad to let the matter drop. It seemed odd to me that Celia's instinctive, passionate love for the child, which had started at the news of my pregnancy, had flowered into such devotion. My enthusiasm for the boy I dreamed I carried blinded me to the prettiness of the girl who was born. But then Celia had wanted a child to love, any child. I wanted only an heir.

I got up and strolled across the gently rocking deck to gaze across the sea to England, which was becoming a darker smudge every moment. I leaned against the ship's rail and felt, half consciously, the sun-warmed wood pressing against my breasts. Tonight, or at the latest tomorrow night, I should be in the arms of the Squire of Wideacre once more. I shivered with anticipation. It had been a long, long wait but my homecoming to Harry would make up for it.

The wind veered to an offshore breeze, the sails flapped and the sailors cursed as we neared land. The captain at dinner promised we would dock at Portsmouth in the morning. I dipped my head over my plate to hide the disappointment in my face but Celia smiled and said she was glad.

'For Julia is most likely to be awake then,' she explained. 'And she is always at her best in the mornings.'

I nodded, my eyelashes hiding the contempt in my eyes. Celia might think of nothing but the infant, but I would be surprised if Harry so much as glanced in the expensive cradle when I was standing by it.

I was surprised.

I was bitterly surprised.

We came to Portsmouth harbour shortly after breakfast, and Celia and I were standing at the ship's rails anxiously scanning the crowd.

'There he is!' called Celia. 'I can see him, Beatrice! And there is your mama, too!'

My eyes hit Harry's gaze with a shock like a horse shying. I held to the rail, my nails digging into the hard wood to stop myself from crying, 'Harry! Harry!' and stretching my arms out to him to bridge the narrowing gap between ship and shore. I gasped with the physical pain of demanding, hard sexual desire. I glanced beyond him to Mama leaning forward to look out of the carriage window and raised a hand to her, then found my eyes dragged back to my brother, my lover.

He was the first up the gangplank as soon as the ship was moored and I was first to greet him – no thought of precedence in my head. Celia was bent over the cradle collecting her baby anyway, so there was no reason why I should hang back, and no reason why Harry should not take me into his arms.

'Harry,' I said, and I could not keep the lust from my voice. I held out my hands to him and raised my face for a kiss. My eyes ranged over his face as if I wanted to devour him. He dropped a brief affectionate kiss off-centre on my mouth and looked over my shoulder.

'Beatrice,' he said. And then looked back to my face. 'Thank you, indeed I *do* thank you for bringing them home, for bringing *both* of them home.'

Then he gently, oh so gently, set me aside with an unconscious push and walked past me – the woman he adored – to Celia. To Celia and my child he went, and put his arms around both of them.

'Oh, my dearest,' I heard him say softly, for her ears alone. Then he plunged his face under her bonnet and kissed her, oblivious of the smiling sailors, of the crowd on the harbour wall, oblivious, too, of my eyes boring into his back.

One long kiss and his eyes were bright with love, fixed on her face and his whole face was warm with tenderness. He turned to the baby in her arms.

'And this is our little girl,' he said. His voice was full of surprise and delight. He took her gently from Celia and held the little body so the wobbly head was level with his face.

'Good morning, Miss Julia,' he said in a tender play. 'And welcome home to your own country.' He broke off and said aside to Celia, 'Why, she is the image of Papa! A true Lacey! Don't you think so? A very true-bred heir, my darling!' And he smiled at her and, tucking the baby securely in the crook of his elbow, freed one hand so he could take her little hand and kiss it.

Jealousy, amazement and horror had first of all nailed me silent to the rail, but I found my tongue at last to break up this affecting scene.

'We must get the bags,' I said abruptly.

'Oh, yes,' said Harry, not shifting his gaze from Celia's deliciously crimsoning face.

'Will you fetch the porters?' I said, as politely as I could.

'Oh, yes,' said Harry, not moving an inch.

'Celia will want to greet Mama and show her the baby,' I said skilfully and watched Celia's immediate guilty jump and scurry to the gangplank with the child.

'Not like that,' I said impatiently, and called the nurse to carry the baby, straightened Celia's bonnet and shawl, handed her her reticule and went with them, in a dignified procession, ashore.

Mama was as bad as Harry. She hardly saw Celia or me. Her arms were out for the baby and her eyes were fixed on its perfect little face, framed in the circle of pleats of the bonnet.

'What an exquisite child,' Mama said, her breath a coo of pleasure. 'Hello, Miss Julia. Hello. Welcome to your home, at last.'

Celia and I exchanged knowing glances. Celia might be baby-struck but she had walked all night with the child almost every night since the birth. We maintained a respectful silence while Mama cooed and the baby gurgled in reply, while Mama inspected the tiny perfect fingers and held the satin-slippered feet with love. She raised her head at last and acknowledged us both with a warm smile.

'Oh, my dears, I can hardly tell you what pleasure it gives me to see you both!' As she said the words her eyes cleared of her passion for the baby and I saw some shadow pass over their pale blueness. She looked quickly, sharply, even suspiciously from Celia's open flower-like face to my lovely lying one.

I felt suddenly, superstitiously afraid. Afraid of her knowledge, of her awareness. She knew the smell of birth, and I still bled in secret, a strange, sweet-smelling flow that I feared she could sense. She could not know; yet as she looked so hard at me I felt half naked, as if she was noting the new plumpness of my neck, of my breasts, of my arms. As if she could see beneath my gown the tight swaddling around my breasts. As if she could smell, despite my constant meticulous bathing, the sweet smell of leaking milk. She looked into my eyes . . . and she knew. In a brief exchange of silent looks she knew. She saw, I swear she saw, a woman who had shared a woman's pains and pleasure, who had, like her, given birth to a child; who knew, like her, the pain and the work and the triumph of pushing out, into the uninterested world, a magical new life that you have made. Then she looked hard at Celia and saw a girl, a virginal pretty girl, quite unchanged from the shy bride. Virtually untouched.

She knew, I could sense it. But her mind recoiled. She could not put the knowledge into her conventional frightened mind that her instincts were telling her as clear as a ringing bell. Her eyes saw my plumpness and Celia's strained thinness. Her senses smelled the milk on me; her own motherhood recognized that mark on me: a woman who has given birth, who has taken her part in the creation of life, and her eyes slid from me to Celia.

'How tired you must be, my dear,' she said. 'Such a long journey after such an experience. Sit down and we will soon be home.' Celia had a kiss and a seat beside Mama in the carriage, and then Mama turned to me.

'My dearest,' she said, and the fear and unspeakable suspicion in her eyes had gone. She was too weak, she was too much of a coward to face anything unpleasant; the secret horror of her life would always escape her. 'Welcome home, Beatrice,' she said, and she leaned forward and kissed me, and held my plump fertile body in her arms. 'It is good to see you again, and looking so well.'

Then Harry joined us and he and I loaded the failing wet-nurse into Mama's carriage, and watched the luggage and the servants into the second chaise.

'How well you have managed,' said Harry gratefully. 'If I had known when I left you . . . But I never should have gone at all if I had not known that you would manage, my dearest Beatrice, whatever happened.'

He took my hand and kissed it, but it was the cool kiss of a grateful brother and not the warm caress he had given to Celia. I scanned his face, searching for a clue to his change towards me.

'You know I would always do anything to please you, Harry,' I said ambiguously, the heat still in my body.

'Oh, yes,' he said equably. 'But any man would feel the care of his child, his very own child, to be something special, so precious, Beatrice.'

I smiled then. I could see into his heart. Harry, like Celia, was baby-struck. It would be a tedious period while it lasted but they would grow out of it. I very much doubted if Harry's infatuation would last the length of the journey home, cooped up in a carriage with a squalling, underfed, travelsick baby, an inexperienced mother and a foreign nurse.

But I was wrong.

It lasted the long journey. Their passion for the baby proved so demanding that the journey took long extra hours while the coach dawdled at walking speed behind Harry and Celia who believed the infant's travelsickness would be relieved by a walk in the fresh air. I strolled ahead. Mama stayed, imperturbable, in the coach.

Despite my rising irritation with Harry, I could be angry with no one when I walked in the lanes of Wideacre with the great chestnut trees showering crimson and white petals on my head from their fat candle flowers. The grass grew so green – so brilliant a green it made you thirsty for the rain that had made it that astonishing colour. Every hedge was bright with greenness, every north-facing tree trunk was shadowed with the deep wet greenness of moss or the grey of fat lichen. The land was as wet as a sponge. All along the hedgerows there were the pale faces of the dogroses and the white flowers of the blackberry bushes. In the better cottages, vegetables were thriving and flowers edging the garden paths made even the smallest houses look bright and prosperous. The grass, the pathways, even the walls were speckled with summer flowers growing with irresistible joy in the cracks and crannies.

Yes, Harry and I had a score to settle. No man would walk past me to another woman and not regret it, but on that long, slow journey home I felt, as I felt for the rest of the summer, that I first had to come home to Wideacre; that Harry was the least important issue in this homecoming. That Harry and I could wait until I had met the land again.

Come home I did! I swear not a cottage on our estate but I banged on the door and pushed it open and smiled, and took a cup of ale or milk. There was not one house but I inquired after children, and checked profits with the men. Not one new hayrick did I miss, not one springing field with the soil so rich and wet did I neglect. Not even the seagulls wheeling above the plough-shares saw more than me. My horse was at the door every morning, and while Harry was up early keeping baby hours, I was off to brood like a laying hen over the land.

I loved it still – infinitely more now that I had been elsewhere, now that I had seen the pitiful dry French farms and the ugly rows of vines. I loved every fresh, easy fertile acre of it and I loved the difficult hill fields and the plough-free downs as well. Every day I rode and rode until I had quartered the estate like a hunting barn owl and marched its borders as if it were Rogation Day every day.

Mama protested, of course, at my riding out without a groom. But I had unexpected allies in the happy couple.

'Let her go, Mama,' said Harry easily. 'Beatrice is beating the bounds; she's been long away. Let her go. She'll take no harm.'

'Indeed,' Celia assented in her soft voice. 'Indeed she deserves a holiday after all she has done.'

They smiled on me, the soft foolish smile of doting parents, and I smiled back and was off. Every step of the paths, every tree of the woods I inspected, and I never rested for one day until I knew I had the estate firmly back in my hand.

The estate workers welcomed me back like a lost Stuart prince. They had dealt with Harry well enough for he was the Master in my absence, but they preferred to speak to me, who knew, without being told, who was married to whom, who was saving a dowry and who could never marry until a debt was paid. It was easier to talk to me for so little needed saying, while Harry, in his awkward, helpful way, would embarrass them with questions where silence would have been better, and with offers of help that sounded like charity.

They grinned slyly when they confided that old Jacob Cooper had a brand-new thatch on his cottage, and I knew without being told more that the reeds would have been cut, without payment, from our Fenny. And when I heard that it had been a remarkably bad year for pheasants, hare and even rabbits, then I knew without being told that they had all taken advantage of my absence to be out with their snares and their dogs. I smiled grimly. Harry would never see such things for he never noticed our people as people. He noticed the tugged forelock, but never saw the ironic smile beneath. I saw both, and they knew it. And they knew when I nodded my head that the sparkle in my eyes was a warning against any one of my people overstepping the line. So we all knew where we were. I was home to take the estate, the people, and every greening shoot back in my hand. And it seemed to me, on every hard daily ride, that the estate, the people and even the greening shoots were better for my return.

I rode everywhere – down to the Fenny to see the marshy

water-meadow where the yellow flags were blooming, rooted into the two crumbled walls that were all that remained of the derelict mill. My horse was knee-deep as I urged her up to look. The building where a girl and a lad had lain and talked of love would never shelter lovers again.

It seemed so very long ago now that it felt as if it had happened to someone else, or that I had dreamed it. It could not have been me that Ralph had loved and romped with and rolled with and ordered and plotted with and risked his life for. That Beatrice had been a beautiful child. Now I was a woman afraid neither of the past nor of the future. I gazed unemotionally at the ruined barn, and at the new marshy empty meadow and was glad to feel nothing. Where there had been regret and fear there was now an easy sense of distance. If Ralph had survived, even if he had survived to lead a gang of rioters, he would be far away by now. Those days on the downs and the secret afternoons in the mill would be almost forgotten to him, as they were to me.

I turned my horse homewards and trotted through the sunny woods. The past was behind me, the River Fenny flowed on. I had a future to plan.

I started with my own quarters. The builders had finished in the west wing and it was ready for me. The lovely heavy old furniture, which had been exiled from Harry's bedroom on his return from school to his mock-pagoda, had been bundled into a lumber room at the top of the house, and I had it taken out and polished until it gleamed with the deep shine of Jacobean walnut. Knobby with carving, so heavy it took six sweating men to carry it. 'So ugly!' said Celia in gentle wonderment. It was the furniture of my childhood and I felt a room was insubstantial without it. The great carved bed with the four posts, as thick as poplar trunks, with the carved roof above, I moved to my bedroom in the west wing.

Now I had a room that looked out on the front not the side of the house and I could see from my window the rose garden, the paddock, our wood and the lovely crescent of the downs rising behind it all. The carved chest stood beside it, and a great heavy press for my dresses loomed in the adjoining dressing room.

Once the lumber room upstairs was cleared of the heavy old furniture, I found much there that had belonged to my papa. Servant-like, the maids had bundled away his things into a mess of saddles, riding crops, hacking jackets and thongs of whips. My papa had fancied himself as an amateur saddler and his saddle rack and a wooden horse had also been thrown in the room. Once the furniture was set in the room below, the horse stood, forlorn, in the little room at the top of the stairs. Some whimsicality, some respect for my papa, stopped me throwing it out with the odd saddles and the whip he had been mending. Instead I put them all in the centre of the room and set myself to learning the skills that had come so easily to him. Long afternoons I spent there, my fingers busy with pulling threads through leather, my palms rosy with the sting of the saddler's needle, oddly at peace.

Downstairs I had collected Papa's old rent table: a great round table that looked as old as Arthur's and could be spun so each labelled drawer faced the Squire in the great carver chair. Each drawer bore a letter of the alphabet and all the papers relating to each tenant were kept under the letter of his name. Beside it I placed the great money chest and here, monthly or quarterly, I collected the rents and, weekly or daily, paid out the wages. This was the office, the centre of the great money-spinning business of Wideacre, and I held the keys. I had ordered from Chichester an artist's easel and commissioned a detailed scale map of the estate, so boundaries could at last be precisely recorded instead of being argued out on the spot in the old way. I had also pur-loined my papa's old desk from the library – one with pigeonholes and two secret hiding places – to stand beside the window, so I could look up from the accounts to gaze across the roses to the paddock and the green woods and see the sun roll across the top of the downs, smiling on Wideacre crops and Wideacre profits.

The smaller downstairs room I had been unable to save from Mama's mania for pastel and gold and it was a conventional lady's parlour. She had furnished it for me with a pale carpet, spindly furniture and pretty brocaded curtains. I made sure I had a sweet smile of thanks, and concealed my grimace of distaste at the vapid prettiness. The most important thing about the room, as about the whole wing, was that it was accepted by everyone that I might sit here in the evenings alone, and that I might spend my mornings, or even all day, in the office.

The infant angel contributed to my peace in this. Even Mama agreed I could not possibly work, add up accounts, or write letters of business, with a small baby gurgling or crying in the same room. Since Harry or Celia had her brought into the parlour every afternoon and evening, it was easy for me to be excused attendance on the little treasure for at least a part of that time.

What I could not escape was my own response to the baby. She really was enchanting. She had kept the deep blue eyes she was born with and had soft brown hair, soft as silk to the touch, soft as puppies' coats. In the sunshine one could clearly see the touch of my own rich copper, and when she grew strong enough to rear up in her cradle, I could see the gleam of my own curls on the warm little head.

Celia put her out to sit in the sunshine of the terrace every afternoon in fine weather and on warm days. When I had my office window open I could hear the sound of her coos and gurgles mingling with the buzz of bumblebees and the deeper coos of the wood pigeons from the woods. When I was stuck for a phrase in a business letter, or could not make a column of figures say the same thing more than once, I would look out of the window and see her little legs kicking in the air, or her fists waving as she tried to catch at the sun or the lacy edge of her sunshade.

One day her coos were so resonant and contented I nearly laughed aloud at the noise. She sounded so like me, with my passion for sunshine and warm breezes on my skin. In all this house of people who trod the land as if it were floorboards, it seemed only I and my daughter, Celia's daughter, were the ones who knew where we were. I, and a baby too small to speak, too young to understand. As I watched and listened I saw one of her toys, a well-sucked toy rabbit made of lamb's wool, fly out of the cradle. The contented gurgle was silenced in the sudden disappointment and a note of complaint took its place. Without thinking twice, I opened the tall window of my office and stepped over the window sill on to the terrace.

I picked up the toy and tucked it back in the crib beside her. Ignoring it altogether she beamed up at my face and her legs and arms went into a little frenzy of kicks to welcome me. She gurgled loudly; she reached for me. I chuckled; she was irresistible. No wonder the entire household was demented over her smiles. She was as much of a domestic tyrant as I could ever be. We were much alike, this little baby and I.

I bent to smile at her, before I left her and went back to my study, and flicked her cheek with one careless finger. She caught it with a surprisingly strong grasp and guided it unerringly towards her smiling, toothless mouth. The little gums closed on it and the cheeks hollowed as she sucked vigorously, her eyes hazy blue with delight. I chuckled; the child was an utter sensualist, like myself. And she grabbed her pleasures, like I do, with a firm grip. When I tried to pull away she hung on and was half lifted from the cradle before I relented and scooped her up and placed her against my neck.

253

She smelled so sweet. That delicious baby smell of warm clean skin and soap. That sweet smell lingering around their mouths from drinking only warm milk. That lovely clean smell of newly laundered cotton and newly washed best wool. I tucked her little head securely into my shoulder and swayed a little. Her coos of pleasure started again, resonant by my ear, and when I turned my face to sniff the warm little crease of her plump neck she made me laugh aloud by suddenly fixing her mouth on to my jaw line, like a little vampire, and sucking noisily and with evident satisfaction.

The smile still on my face, my feet still dancing to jiggle her, I turned towards the house. Someone was in the parlour window watching me. It was Celia. She stood utterly still, her face like white marble.

My face was still warm with laughter and affection for the little baby, but as I met her eyes the smile died from me and I felt uneasy and guilty – as guilty as if she had caught me with my hands in her lace drawer, or if she had found me reading her letters. She disappeared and a few seconds later the front door opened and she came out on to the terrace.

Her hands were trembling but her face was set and her walk was swift and direct. She came to me without a word, and lifted the baby from the warmth of my neck with as much emotion as if she were taking a scarf off me.

'I put Julia out for her sleep,' she said unemotionally. She turned her back to me and placed Julia in the cradle. Disappointed, the child started a wail of protest, but Celia tucked her in as firmly as any strict nurse.

'I would rather she were not disturbed when she should be having her rest,' said Celia.

I felt as awkward as a boy in an apple orchard.

'Of course, Celia,' I said deferentially. 'She dropped her toy and I merely came out to give it back to her.'

Celia straightened up and turned to me. 'She would be happy to play that game all afternoon,' she said. 'But you, I am sure, have work to do.'

I was dismissed. Little insignificant Celia, standing tall with the power of her motherhood over the child, had dismissed me like an unreliable maid.

'Of course,' I said, and I smiled like an idiot. 'Of course.' And I turned on my heel and went back down the terrace to where my office window stood open and my desk waited, piled with papers. In the length of that short, awkward walk, I could feel Celia's eyes on my back, Celia watching me with no affection in her gaze.

I should have learned from that, I suppose. But Julia drew me. A little, only a little. I had no great longing for her. When I occasionally heard her cry out in the night I slept better for my deep contentment that it was not me who had to get up to see to her. When she was fretting during the day, or when Celia missed supper and the tea tray because she was up in the nursery, I felt no instinct then to be with the baby. But sometimes – when the weather was hot and I could see her little legs kicking and hear her cooing – I would slink out to the terrace like a clandestine lover and smile at her, and tickle her plump little palms and feet.

I learned discretion. Celia never again caught me hanging over the cradle. But when she went to Chichester with Harry to choose some new hangings for the nursery, and Mama lay down feeling unwell because of the heat, I spent an easy, laughter-filled half-hour playing peep-bo with the baby, dodging round her sunshade and appearing as if by magic on one side of the cradle and then the other, which made her gurgle with laughter so much she nearly choked herself.

Predictably, I tired of the game long before she did. Besides I had to drive down to the village to see the smith. She gripped my face when I kissed her goodbye, but when I actually disappeared she set up such a howl of protest that her nurse came bustling out of the house to see what was wrong.

'She won't settle now,' she said, eyeing me with disfavour. 'She's all awake and playful now.'

'It's my fault,' I confessed. 'What would settle her down?'

'I shall have to rock her,' said the nurse, grudgingly. 'The movement of the cradle might do it.'

'I have to drive to the village,' I offered. 'Would she fall asleep in the carriage?'

The nurse's face brightened at once at the prospect of an airing in my smart curricle and she bustled off to get her bonnet and an extra shawl for Julia.

I had been right. As soon as she was lifted from the cradle, Julia beamed her approval and started her delightful coos of pleasure. And when we trotted down the drive with the bars of sunlight and shade from the roof of trees flickering in her eyes she waved her little hands to greet the wind and the sound of trotting hoofs and the brightness and rush and beauty of it all.

I slowed down on the bridge over the Fenny.

'This is the Fenny,' I told her solemnly. 'When you are a big girl I shall teach you how to tickle for trout here. Your papa can teach you how to use a rod and line like a lady, but I shall teach you how to tickle them and flick them out on the bank like a proper country child.'

She beamed at me as if she understood every word, and I beamed back in mutual approval. Then I clicked to Sorrel and we trotted past the lodge gates where Sarah waved to us and out down the sunny lane to Acre.

'These are the meadowlands, resting this year,' I told Julia, gesturing with my whip. 'I think good fields should be rested every three years and grow just grass. Your papa thinks they should be rested every five. You can be the judge of that for we have rested some for three years and some for five, and when you are a lady, farming the land like me, you can be the judge of which system kept the land in the greatest heart.'

Julia's little sun bonnet nodded gravely as if she could understand every word. But I think she may have caught the inflexion of my voice and heard my tones of love for the land, and of a growing tenderness for her.

Half-a-dozen people were outside the smithy when I drew up, villagers and one farmer tenant waiting for his work-horse to be shod. The women were around the curricle in a second, admiring the pretty baby and the exquisite lace dress. I tossed the reins to the smith, who came out, wiping grimy hands on his leather apron, and passed the baby carefully down to the village women.

They cooed over her, as maternal as broody hens; they touched her lace petticoats and her fleecy shawl and they stood in line so that each might hold her and admire the smoothness of her skin, the blueness of her eyes and the utter whiteness of her clothes.

By the time I had finished with the smith, she had reached the end of the line, a little dishevelled but none the worse for being handed round like some sacred relic.

'Better change her before her mama gets back,' I said ruefully to her nurse, noting the lace trimming on her little gown was grey where it had been fingered by hands ingrained with years of dirt.

'Indeed, yes,' said Nurse stiffly. 'Lady Lacey has never taken her to the village and would never have let those people touch her.'

I glanced sharply at her, but I said nothing for a moment.

'She's taken no harm,' I said eventually. 'Have you, little girl? And these people will be your people, as they are mine. These are the people who make the money that keeps Wideacre prosperous and beautiful. They are dirty so that we can have daily baths and fine clean clothes. You must always be ready with a smile for them, little one. You belong to each other.'

I drove in silence then, enjoying the wind in my face and keeping a careful eye on the road ahead to make sure we struck no stones which might jog her. I was driving so carefully I hardly heard the noise of a carriage and pair and I jumped like a criminal when I suddenly saw, in the road ahead of us, the family chaise. They were just ready to turn into the lodge gate; another second earlier and I might have been home before them. As it was, Celia, gazing out of the offside window, had a perfect view of my curricle trotting briskly down the lane from Acre, with her nurse and her child sitting up bold as brass in the passenger seat.

Her eyes met mine and her face was blank. I knew she was angry and I felt no surprise. I had a sinking feeling in my gut, the like of which I had not felt since I was a child in disgrace with my papa. I had never thought Celia capable of rages. But to take her child out for a drive without permission was, I knew, something she would regard as wrong. And faced with that icy stare I felt extremely guilty.

I did not hurry to follow them up the drive, but there was no enraged mother waiting for me in the stable yard. Nurse and Julia dismounted and went into the house by the west-wing door, to slink up to the nursery for a total change of clothes, I guessed. I handed Sorrel over to the groom and went round to the front door. Celia was waiting for me in the hall and she drew me into the parlour. Harry, discreetly, perhaps obediently, was nowhere to be seen.

I turned to the mirror above the fireplace and took off my hat.

'What a wonderful day,' I said lightly. 'Did you find the things you need in Chichester? Or will you have to send to London?'

Celia said nothing. I had to turn from the mirror to face her. She was standing still in the middle of the room, dominating it with her slight presence and the force of her anger.

'I must ask you never to take Julia out without my express personal permission,' she said evenly, totally ignoring my questions.

I met her eyes but said nothing.

'I must also remind you that Harry and I decided that Julia should not be taken out in a curricle, or any open-topped carriage,' said Celia. 'We, her parents, decided we did not think it safe for her so to travel.'

'Oh, come now, Celia,' I said airily. 'She took no harm. I had the safest horse in the stable between the shafts. I trained Sorrel myself. I just took her down the lane to Acre because she would not settle on the terrace.'

Celia looked at me. She looked at me as if I were an obstacle on her road that somehow had to be crossed over or gone around.

'Her father and I decided we do not wish her to travel in an open carriage and that includes your curricle, whatever horse you are driving,' she said slowly, as if explaining something to a stupid child.

'Further, I do not wish her to be taken out of her cradle, or out of the house, or out of the estate, without my express and personal permission.'

I shrugged. 'Oh, Celia, let's not pull caps over this,' I said easily. 'I am sorry. I should not have done such a thing without first confirming you had no objection. I merely had to drive to Acre and it amused me to take Julia and show her the land, her home, like my papa used to do with me and with Harry.'

Celia's gaze never wavered and her expression did not warm to the casual tone of my apology. 'Her situation is very different from either yours or Harry's,' she said steadily. 'There is no reason why she should have a similar upbringing.'

'She's a Wideacre baby!' I said in surprise. 'Of course she must learn about the land and go out on the land. This is her home, just as it is mine. She belongs here, even as I do.'

Celia's head jerked and her cheeks suddenly flushed scarlet.

'No,' she said. 'She does not belong here as you do. What your plans are, Beatrice, I do not know. I came into this house to live with my husband and with your mama and with you. But my Julia will not live here all her life. She will marry and leave. She will spend her girlhood here, but I dare say she will be away at school for much of the time. Then she will make visits to friends. Widacre will not be the only house in the world for her. There will be very much more in her life than the land and the house. She will not have a childhood like yours, nor interests like yours, nor a life like yours.'

I gaped at Celia, but there was nothing I could say.

'As you wish,' I said in a tone as cold as hers. 'You are her mother, Celia.'

And then I turned on my heel and left her, standing alone in the middle of the parlour. And I went to my office and shut the door and leaned back against the panels. And I stood still in the quiet of my office with my papers around me, for a long time.

Julia was utterly Celia's child. It was all done as Celia wished. Mama would have had the baby's diet supplemented with a spoonful of molasses, or at least honey, at every mealtime. Celia refused and the baby drank only pure breast milk. Harry wanted to give her little sips from his glass of port when she sat on his knee after dinner. But Celia did not allow it. Mama wanted her swaddled, and Celia stood up to her with as much polite certainty as she had ever shown against a wish of my mama's – and she carried the day.

Mama had threatened that Julia's limbs would grow crooked if she were not strapped tightly to boards, but Celia stood against her and even called in Dr MacAndrew for support. He was full of praise for the decision and promised she would be stronger and healthier for her freedom.

Dr MacAndrew's voice in our household carried a great deal of weight. In our absence he had become a friend and confidant to Mama, who told him, I suspected, much about herself and her married life and her ill health. She told him also, I imagined, something about the problems she had encountered in rearing me, for I did not like the gleam I sometimes saw in the doctor's eyes when we met. He looked always as if he liked what he saw, but he looked always as if I might somehow amuse him, in some way I could not fathom. And Mama watched us closely.

The first time we met after our return from France was awkward. I was pouring tea for Mama in the parlour when he came in for a routine call on Julia and made social conversation to me with the skill of a well-mannered man, which ignored my quick flush, that had risen when he first came into the room.

'You look as if France agreed with you, Miss Lacey,' he said. Mama's eyes were sharply upon us and I withdrew my hand from his clasp and sat down again behind the urn.

'Indeed it did,' I said equably. 'But I am glad to be home.'

I poured him tea and handed him the cup and saucer with a hand that was rock-steady. It would take more than a gentle smile from Dr MacAndrew to make me tremble.

'I have made a new acquisition while you were away,' he said, conversationally. 'I have bought a new horse from abroad, a full-bred Arab, as a saddle-horse. I shall be interested to know what you think of him.'

'An Arab!' I said. 'I think we shall not agree on that. I still prefer the English breeds for our climate and our terrain. I have yet to see a pure-bred Arab with the staying power necessary for a long day's hunting.'

He laughed. 'Well, I shall take a wager with you on that,' he said. 'I would back Sea Fern against any hunter in your stables, on the flat or over hurdles.'

'Oh, racing,' I said dismissively. 'I would not argue with you there. I see how well they do in short races, but it is stamina they lack.'

'I have ridden Sea Fern all day on calls and he has been ready for a gallop over the downs in the evening,' Dr MacAndrew said. 'Miss Lacey, you will not fault him.'

I laughed. 'My papa always used to say it was a waste of time to talk sense to a man who was selling land or who had bought a horse. I shall not try to persuade you. Let me see him after one winter and perhaps we will agree then. After you have paid your corn merchant for an animal too high-bred to stomach anything but oats all the year round, you may come to agree with me.'

The young doctor smiled, his blue gaze easy and direct.

'Of course I shall spend a fortune on him,' he said easily. 'One should be proud to be ruined feeding a fine animal. I would rather spend money on oats than in my kitchen or on my cellar.'

'Well, there we do agree,' I smiled. 'Horses are quite the most important thing in a household.' I went on to tell him of the horses I had seen in France – such poor things on the streets and such fine animals in the noblemen's stables. And he told me more about his precious Sea Fern. Then we talked of form and breeding until Harry and Celia came in with Nurse carrying the baby, and all rational conversation was ended for that day, for the baby had learned to hold her toes.

But at parting he took the tips of my fingers in his assured clasp and said, 'So when will you ride your challenge, Miss Lacey? Sea Fern and I are ready. Shall we ride a race? Ground and distance of your choosing.'

'A challenge?' I asked and laughed. Harry heard our voices and looked up from the cradle where he was dangling his watch.

'I think you may lose, Beatrice,' he warned me. 'I have seen Dr MacAndrew's horse and he is not one of the dainty Arabs that you know but something more impressive.'

'I shall take my chance against any Arab in the land on Tobermory,' I said, naming the best hunter in the stables.

'Well, I'll back you,' said Harry with enthusiasm. 'Fifty crowns, sir?'

'Oh-ho! A hundred!' said Dr MacAndrew and then we were all betting. Celia waged her pearl necklace against my pearl earrings; Mama bet me a new bookcase for the office. Harry promised me a new riding habit if I defended the honour of the Wideacre stables and I bet him a new silver-handled hunting whip that I would do so! Then John MacAndrew looked at me and I met the challenge of his sandy-lashed gaze.

'And what shall be our wager?' I asked.

The room went silent; Mama watched us curiously, a half-smile on her face.

'Winner names the forfeit,' he said promptly, as if he had

planned this. 'If I win I shall claim a prize from you, Miss Lacey. And you may claim one from me.'

'An open wager is a dangerous game for the loser,' I said with a gurgle of laughter at the back of my voice.

'Better win then,' he said and left.

The forthcoming race did two things to Harry. It concentrated his attention on me again and he and I spent a happy morning in the office with the new-drawn map of Wideacre before us, planning the course. Then, and this was even better, it inspired him to leave the baby and Celia and ride out with me to check the route where we could see the condition of the ground. It was the first ride we had taken together since my return and I deliberately suggested the bridle-way along the downs that passed the hollow where we had first made love.

It was a sweet day, hot and promising to be hotter, with the smell of new-mown hay blowing off the meadows. On the upper slopes leading to the downs they were harvesting and the heady smell of the crops, herbs and the long-stemmed flowers breathed over us. Every heap of straw gleamed with red poppies, blue larkspur and the white and gold of moon daisies. I hooked up a swatch of a heap with the handle of my crop and sniffed at it with passionate delight. I should so adore to be a horse and eat the stuff. The smell of it is so appetizing, like the very best tea or good quality tobacco. I tucked the poppies under the band of my hat, although I knew they would be faded by the end of the morning. Poppies, like pleasure, do not last. But one should have them, anyway. My riding habit this year was a deep crimson and the scarlet of the flowers, bright as a blacksmith's furnace, clashed wonderfully against the deep darkness of it. If Mama had seen the two reds shrieking at each other she would have smiled and said, 'Beatrice has no eye for colour.' But she would have been wrong. I had such an eye for colour, especially the colour of Wideacre flowers, that no colour can seem wrong to me. Harry smiled at me.

'I can see you are happy to be home, Beatrice,' he said lovingly.

'It is heaven,' I said, and I told no lie.

He nodded and smiled. We rode on upwards, our horses pushing breast-high through the bracken, while flies buzzed around their heads and kept their ears twitching in irritation. Then we broke from the ferns as from a green sea, and scrambled up the crest of the downs like landfall.

The horses lengthened their stride and snorted in anticipation. Harry was riding Saladin, a fresh young hunter, but my horse, Tobermory, was rested and eager and took the lead when I released the tension on the reins. We cantered easily along the track that winds along the crest of the downs and I looked down, as I always look down, to see a miniature Widcacre, like a perfect toy, nestling in the patchwork fields and woods below.

The track wound its way between trees and I lost sight of my home, the home I carried always in my mind. We were in a secluded enough spot. Some earth movement had thrown up a trench on the smooth crest of the downs and hundreds and hundreds of years ago this little wood had taken root and was now grown to tower above us. Sweet green beeches and small oaks made a tiny shelter for us and around their roots pale woodland flowers were like stars in the darkness of the forest floor. It extended for no more than a couple of hundred yards but in that space there were little leafy hollows and the undergrowth was thick. I stole a sidelong glance at Harry and noted with anxiety the firmness of his mouth. He was looking straight forward, unseeing, past his horse's ears. Saladin, on a short rein, shook his head in protest, but Harry's grip only tightened.

'Stop the horses, Harry,' I said in a gentle voice. He reined in but there was no gladness in his face. He was holding Saladin too tightly and the horse pulled back at the bit. Harry's face was grim and there was a hint of desperation in his eyes. I read him like a book. I had known him inside out when I seduced him, and I had known the chance I had taken when I sent him home to England alone. Now I realized coldly that Harry was seeking to make an end with me in order to be clean and guiltless and free to love – not Celia – but the adored baby.

I sat in the saddle, as lovely as ever, as desirable as ever, and I knew with certainty that while I lived in the house that should be mine but that he called his, and rode on the land that should be mine but that he claimed, I had to have Harry. I knew also that I would hate and resent him every day and night for the rest of my life. My passion for him had gone. Why, I do not know. It had

263

faded like a new-picked poppy the second I had his heart to wear in my hatband. Harry was so lightly won, so easily kept. In France, away from the land he owned, but which I needed so badly, he seemed such a very ordinary youth. Good-looking indeed, charming, amusing, not very bright; you could have half-a-dozen Harrys at any English-dominated hotel in any French town. Away from the land and empty of the magic of the harvest, Harry was not special.

But even if my passion had turned to disgust I would still have sought him out. My heart-throbbing, trembling desire for him might have been worn out by the easy conquest and use of his body. But I still needed the Squire. Harry and I had to be lovers to keep me safe on the land.

'Harry,' I said, and I let my voice linger on his name.

'It is over, Beatrice,' he said jerkily. 'I have sinned, God knows, with you and led you into sin. But it is over now and we will never be together in that way again. In time, I know, you will come to love elsewhere.'

A silence fell. My brain was racing like a ferret in a cage to find the spring on the trap of Harry's desire, but there was none at hand. I let the silence ride and watched him. He lifted his head. His face was set and determined. I could see he had set his heart on becoming the loving father, the good husband, the powerful Squire of some maudlin fantasy, and the sly, secret pleasures of our love were not part of this daydream of a virtuous new life.

My eyes on his face were as inscrutable as an emerald snake's, while my mind turned over the problem of this new, moralistic Harry. This time and this place were not the way to come at Harry. He had prepared for an offer of love on this ride; he had armed himself against me. He had his lust on as tight a rein as his horse, which sidled and backed against the merciless bit. The way to Harry was not to let him prepare and consider and reject me in advance. The way to capture Harry was to surprise his lust before his conscience was awake. This little wood, this warm secluded morning would all have to go to waste. Harry would not be taken here.

I smiled with a sweet and open smile, and saw the answering beam of relief on Harry's face.

'Oh, Harry, I am so glad,' I said. 'You know it was never my wish, it was something that happened against my will, against both of our wills, and it always troubled me so. Thank God we think alike on this. I have been in agonies over how I could tell you of my resolve that we should end.'

The godly fool's face lit up. 'Beatrice! I should have known . . . I am so glad it is like this for you. Oh, Beatrice, I am so glad,' he said. Saladin stretched his neck in relief at the suddenly loosened rein. And I smiled tenderly at Harry.

'Thank God we are now both free of sin,' I said piously. 'Now at last we can love each other and be together as we should.'

The horses moved forward and we rode companionably, side by side. We came from the gloom of the wood into God's own sunlight and Harry looked around him at the sweet rolling sunny turf as if he thought the New Jerusalem had dawned on him, with the golden light of a sinless paradise all around us.

'Now let us plan this race,' I said sweetly, and we cantered forward to a shoulder of the downs to overlook the track that rises from the valley floor. From here we could see most of the route I planned for Tobermory and Dr MacAndrew's Arab, and a punishing ride it would be. The race would start and end at the Hall and make the shape of a great figure of eight. The first loop was north from the Hall up the steep sandy tracks of the common land. The ground is soft as sugar there because it is deep sand on clay, and while neither horse would be fast on that going, I thought the shifting ground would tire the Arab. The common is used by the village people for their sheep, for the odd goat or two, for ill-fed cows and, of course, for game: birds, foxes, deer. It is mostly heather with bracken in the sunny, sheltered dips of the ground, and thick solid woods, mainly beech, of course, on the west slopes. The loop across the top of the common took in the open ground where the Arab's quickness of turning would be of little use, and where Tobermory's strong legs might set the fastest pace.

When we dropped down from the common there was a steep track downhill, which I thought could be taken no faster than a slithering canter – and I could trust Tobermory to handle that, for he had hunted over this land for four seasons – then there were two stiffish jumps into the parkland of Wideacre Hall: one over a wall, which was high, and one over a ditch, which was difficult to judge if you did not know it. Then there would be a good thundering gallop along the grass tracks of the woods until we broke free of the trees facing the south loop of the race, which would take us straight up the track to the top of the downs, a good long testing gallop, climbing steeply all the time. I expected both horses to be blown when they reached the top, but whoever had the lead then was likely to keep it. Ahead lay a smooth grassy track of springy downs turf for a couple of miles and then the descent back to the Hall through the beech coppice, which would be a tiring slither for horses and riders, then a thundering finish along the drive to the Hall.

Harry and I thought the entire circuit would take about two hours, and that the worst part for horse and rider would be the steep descent home. We gave John MacAndrew fair warning of this while the grooms were tacking up the horses, but he only laughed and said we were trying to scare him off.

Tobermory came out of the arched sandstone stable doorway like a bolt of copper. He was well rested and anxious to go, and Harry whispered to me to rein in hard or I should find myself halfway to London. Then he tossed me up into the saddle and held the reins while I shook out the crimson skirts of my habit and settled my hat more firmly on my head.

Then I saw Sea Fern.

Dr MacAndrew had told me he was a grey, but his coat was almost silver white with silky, sleek shadows on the powerful legs and shoulders. My eyes gleamed in appreciation and John MacAndrew laughed.

'I think I can tell what I shall lose if you finish first, Miss Lacey,' he said teasingly. 'You would never make a gambler.'

'I should think anyone would be glad to take that horse off you,' I said longingly. My eyes took in the perfect sharp-featured face and the bright intelligent eyes. His neck was a perfect sickle held in by the groom, yet as strong as a bent bow. A lovely, lovely animal. John MacAndrew mounted without using the block in a stylish spring to the saddle. We measured each other and smiled.

Celia, Mama, the baby and Nurse were all on the terrace to see us stand shoulder to shoulder as we waited for Harry's signal.

Tobermory pranced at the bit and Sea Fern sidled with excitement. Harry stood still on the terrace, a handkerchief in his raised hand. Then he dropped his arm and I felt Tobermory jump as I let him go and he felt the spur.

We thundered through the woods at a tightly controlled canter. Sea Fern's white forelegs were first over the park wall and I had expected that. But I had not thought he would hold his pace so well up the punishing slope to the common, nor that he would seem so little tired at the top. At the crest of the hill he snorted at the sand and then took the track at a gallop. It is a long river of sand, widened as a firebreak, and although Tobermory put his head down and thundered at it, Sea Fern held off our challenge, his hoofs throwing silver sand into my face for the two, maybe three miles of it. Both he and Tobermory were blowing, but Tobermory did not pass him until the ground started to slope downwards towards the park.

Some of our people were cutting firewood and at the sudden glimpse of them Sea Fern shied, and then reared. Tobermory, steady as a rock, did not check, and I heard them cheer as I thundered downhill, well in the lead, and Tobermory reared up to leap the wall into the pale of the park. He held the advantage in a long hard gallop through the park and when we started up the hill to the downs. I was sure, with a laugh caught in my throat, that the race was over for Sea Fern. Then we reached the top and the smooth ride was before us. Tobermory was panting but he felt the downs turf under his hoofs and his head went up. We thundered along the track, but I could hear hoofs behind us, and they were gaining on us. Sea Fern was blowing foam and John MacAndrew was leaning forward like a jockey to get every inch of speed from him, urging him harder and harder on our heels. The noise of the chase reached Tobermory and he shook his mane at the challenge and plunged into his fast hunting stride – the top speed of a staying gallop. It was not enough. By the time the track started to slope downwards to the woods, Sea Fern was at Tobermory's shoulder.

As we plunged into the gloom of the woods I tightened my hold on Tobermory, keeping a careful watch under his hoofs for dangerous roots and treacherous patches of mud. I watched on my own account for low branches that might sweep me from the saddle or slap in my face. But John MacAndrew took no care. He took the lead in a mad downward dash and flung his priceless horse at that slippery track as if he no longer cared for it. The beautiful animal slithered and stumbled, held to a relentless pace, and I could not, dared not, match that breakneck speed. Among the jumbling pictures in my mind of splashy puddles and low head-chopping branches, some corner of my mind said swiftly and precisely, 'Why? Why is John MacAndrew riding this playful race so hard?'

By the time we were through the lodge gates with Sarah Hodgett calling, 'Go on, Miss Beatrice!' as I thundered past, the lead was too big to close. Sea Fern's powerful galloping hind-quarters gleamed like white silk in the flickering sun and shadows of the drive as we dashed towards the house, and the doctor on his Arab was reining in at the terrace a clear couple of lengths before me.

I laughed in unfeigned delight. I was dirty; I could feel wet mud caking in spots all over my face. My hat had tumbled off somewhere and a stable lad would have to search for it tomorrow. My hair had come unpinned during the wild ride and was a tangle of chestnut curls over my shoulders. Tobermory was creamy with sweat, his bright coat bathed in it. Sea Fern was shuddering with panting breaths. Dr MacAndrew's fair skin was scarlet with heat and excitement and his eyes – winner's eyes – were sparkling blue.

'What is your forfeit, then?' I gasped, as soon as I could draw breath. 'You rode like a demon for it. What is it that you want so badly?'

He slid from his saddle and reached up to me to lift me down. I slid into his arms and felt my face crimson, fuelled by the breathless excitement of the race and the smell of our hot trembly bodies, and the pleasure of a man's arms around me again.

'I claim your glove,' he said. But he said it with an emphasis that stopped my incredulous laughter and made me look at him intently.

'First the glove,' he said, stripping the scarlet kid gauntlet from my hand, 'and later, Miss Lacey, your hand in marriage.'

I caught my breath on a cry of outrage but he coolly pocketed the forfeit as if men proposed to ladies in this way every day of the year. And before I could say anything, Harry and the whole pack of them were tumbling into earshot and I could say nothing.

There was nothing, in any case, that I wanted to say. While I retired to change my gown, wash my face and pin my hair, I wasted no time in planning a reply. His cool tone made it clear that none was required. I stood in no danger of breaking my heart over a man who owned no land, least of all someone who would neither inherit nor buy Wideacre. If this young, enchanting doctor ever proposed he would find himself gently, kindly refused. But in the meantime ... I twisted the hair nearest my face into ringlets around my fingers and chuckled with unrestrained laughter ... in the meantime, it was all delightful, and I must hurry or I would be late for tea.

It might have meant nothing more to me than a light-hearted jest but the race made the young doctor an accepted member of our family circle. Although Mama never spoke, I knew she regarded him as her future son-in-law and his presence in the house freed her from her persistent, unacknowledged fears. So it was a happy summer for all of us. Harry's worries about the land were lifted once he saw it back under my confident control and knew he could rely on me to protect him from errors of ignorance with either the precious fields or the people. The vines were doing well despite the strange English soil, and it was a triumph of Harry's experimental enthusiasm over my love for the old ways that I was happy to concede. Whether we would have enough sun to turn the little buds of grapes into fat, sweet, green fruit was something not even Harry's confidence could guarantee. But it was a fair chance and one worth taking, which might produce a new crop and even a new product for Wideacre.

Mama was happy in Harry's smiles and in my settled contentment. But her main role was that of doting grandmother. I realized only now how much her tenderness must have been constrained by my hurtful independence, and by the convention of leaving children out of reach in the nursery. Under the loving, indulgent regime of Celia, the little angel was never banished, except for meals and bedtime. She was never left to cry alone in the darkness of the nursery. She was never abandoned to the absent-minded care of servants. Little Julia's life was one long banquet of cuddles and kisses and games and songs from either her adoring papa, her loving mama, or her equally besotted grandmama. And seeing the glow of happiness in my mother's face and the gurgles of delight that came from the cradle, one would need a heart of stone not to see that the love that flowed between them all was a blessing indeed.

I missed her. I was not one of those women whose hip is empty unless they have a child astride it, God knows, but little Julia seemed to me to be a special child. No, more than that. She was the bone of my bone in a way I could not fathom. I could see the glint of my russet in her hair; I could see my easy happy delight in Wideacre in her gurgles when she was left outside in the cradle. She was my child through and through and I missed her when I knew that Celia's eyes were sharp upon me, and that I was not allowed either to raise her from her cradle or play with her, and not – emphatically not – to take her out on the land and give her a little taste, the smallest of tastes, of a proper Wideacre childhood.

As for Celia, she seemed in a haze of happiness. The baby consumed her time and attention and she had developed almost miraculous powers of sensitivity where Julia was concerned. She would excuse herself from the table to go to the nursery when no one but her had heard the faintest cry. The whole upper floor of the house seemed to murmur with lullabies that summer as Celia sang to the baby, and moved around the baby's room in a continual hum of melodic half-laughter. Under Celia's tentative and diffident prompting, one room after another was redecorated and cleaned and the heavy old furniture of my father and grandfather was replaced with the light fragile styles of the fashion. More profit to me, who snapped up the rejected wooden chests and tables for the increasingly cluttered west wing, but no damage to the house, which gleamed with a new lightness.

Celia delighted Mama with her enthusiasm for ladylike pursuits. They worked like scullery maids over a new altar cloth for the church, first designing, then drawing, then stitching. I did a few odd running stitches in the evening in the sections where mistakes would not show, but every day Mama and Celia had the great swathe of material stretched between them and had their heads bent in pious bondage.

When they were not stitching they were reading aloud as if addicted to their own voices, or ordering the carriage to give Baby a little airing, or paying calls, or picking the flowers, or practising songs, or all the old time-wasting, energy-consuming, pretty little activities that compose a lady's life. Why should I complain? They were happy tripping around on the little treadwheel of meaningless duties, and Celia's devotion to her sewing, to her house and to her mama-in-law freed me from many a weary hour in the small parlour.

Celia's girlish diffidence and her ready acceptance of second, nay, fourth place in the household, meant that she never clashed with Mama. She had already learned in France that her wishes and wants would always come second to mine and Harry's, and indeed she never seemed to expect anything else. Now, far from being a confident young wife in her first home, she was more like a courteous guest, or a poor relation allowed to live with the family in return for unremitting civility and little chores. On no area of my power – not the keys and the accounts of the cellar, nor the kitchen, the store rooms and the servants' wages – did she ever encroach. No area of power of Mama's – the selection and training of the indoor staff, the planning of the menus, the decisions about cleaning and care of the house – did she ever threaten. She had been trained hard, Celia. She would never forget the unwelcoming neglect she had met at Havering Hall, and she expected little better of her new home.

With such poor expectations, she was agreeably surprised. Mama was ready to defend her rights against the interloper, but she found that Celia asked for nothing, took nothing, expected nothing. The only time she ever whispered so much as a tentative suggestion was when Harry's convenience and comfort would benefit, and then she had a ready ally in Harry's doting mama, who welcomed any information about her darling boy's preferences.

And Stride, who was an experienced butler and knew Quality when he saw it, would nod his head and advise her. The other servants followed his lead and showed her proper respect. No one would ever fear Celia. But everyone loved her. Her willingness to accept whatever standards or behaviour Harry, Mama or I saw fit made all our lives easier for her sunny presence in the house.

And I, too, was happy. In the morning I generally rode out to see the fields or check the fences, or up to the downs to see the sheep. In the afternoon I did the accounts, wrote letters of business and saw whoever had waited patiently in the lobby room by the side entrance. Before I dressed for dinner I would stroll out with Harry in the rose garden, in the growing shrubbery, or perhaps as far as the Fenny, talking business and gossip. In the evening I would sit opposite Celia on Harry's right hand and dine like a princess on the wonderful food that had come to Wideacre with the new cook.

After dinner, Celia would play and sing to us, or Harry would read, or Harry and I would talk low-voiced in the window seat while Celia and Mama played duets on the piano or tackled another section of stitchery.

All that sweet warm summer we were on a pinnacle of domestic happiness, without conflict, without sin. Anyone watching us, as young Dr MacAndrew did, with a warm steady look in his pale eyes, would have thought we had found some secret of love that we could live so tenderly and easily together. Even my desires were quiescent in that golden time. The warmth of John MacAndrew's smiles to me, the tender tone in his voice when he spoke to me, the respectable excitement of a twilit walk in the garden with him, all seemed enough in that lovely late summer. I was not in love, of course not. But his way of making me laugh, the way his eyes met mine, the way his riding coat sat on his shoulders, all tiny trivial things, added up to some sensation that made me smile when I saw him riding up the drive to dine with us. And his smile on parting, the slight pressure of his fingers and the gentle touch of his lips on my hand, were all part of a stage of courtship too delightful to be hurried.

Of course it would end. If he went on down this road he would make a serious proposal of marriage and have to be seriously refused, and then this innocent, pleasurable time would be over. But while it lasted, while each day brought me a visit from him, or a book he had promised, the loan of his beloved Sea Fern for a treat, or a posy of flowers, I found I woke each morning with a smile and the recollection of some phrase he used, a mental picture of him. And I started my day in a small ripple of pleasure.

I had never before been wooed by a man of my own class and so I was new to the trivial delights of a Quality courtship. The way he touched my fingers when I passed him a teacup, or the way his eyes would meet mine in a room full of people. I liked knowing that the second I came into a room, perhaps at one of the assemblies at Chichester, he would see me and make his way to me. Or if he were in a set preparing to dance I smiled at the secret knowledge that wherever I was in the room, whether before his eyes or behind him, he was acutely aware of my presence. Then, when tea was served, he would be at my chair with a little plateful of my favourite cakes and the eyes of the whole room on us both.

I was so entranced by this courtship of tenths of inches, which progressed invisibly, slowly, that I relaxed my awareness of Celia and Harry. In this new, trivial pleasure I had forgotten my old agonized desire for Harry. In the certainty of my mastery of the land — now accepted by everyone — I no longer needed to dominate the Master of Wideacre himself. Harry could be my partner, my colleague. If I was secure on the land I did not need him as a lover.

Of all people it was Celia, who had done so much to create this oasis of peace, who spoiled it. Of all people who suffered from it, it was she who lost as much as anyone. Of course, being Celia, the mistake came from love and tenderness. But if she had stayed silent that once, stayed silent for that one summer, it could all, even then, have been a different story.

But not Celia. Her mama had tackled her about the separate bedrooms she and Harry occupied. My mama had mentioned the need of a son to follow the triumph of the angel baby. Her own honest conscience reminded her nightly at her prayer time that she had not done her duty by Harry since the baby he loved was not their child. But most importantly for Celia, for Harry and, of course, for me, was that she was learning to love him.

Harry, viewed every day from breakfast to dinner, was neither tyrant nor monster. She heard him being reproved by his mama for being late for lunch; she heard his sister mock his new-fangled ideas on farming; she saw him accept reproof and teasing with unshakeable sunny good nature. The arrangement of their married life he accepted with unswerving cheerfulness. He never unlocked the adjoining door between their two bedrooms, although she knew he had the key. He always entered her room from the corridor and he always knocked first. When he greeted her in the morning he kissed her hand with respect, and when he bade her goodnight he kissed her forehead with tenderness. We had been home three months and he had never said a cross word in her hearing, or showed one spark of malice or one edge of spite. In growing amazement at her luck, Celia discovered she was married to one of the sweetest men ever born. Of course she loved him.

All of this I should have foreseen as clearly as I saw Harry's smile of tenderness when he watched her walking the baby. All of it I should have heard in the way her voice lilted when she spoke of him. But I saw and heard nothing until the late September day when Celia met me in the rose garden. She had a pair of ineffectual but elegant silver scissors in her hand and a basket, and a straw bonnet tied to shade her face. I was walking back from the paddock in my riding habit after checking one of the hunters, who I thought might have sprained a tendon. Celia delayed me on my way to the stable to order a poultice, to offer me a buttonhole of late-flowering white roses and I sniffed their creamy smell, smiling my thanks.

'Don't they smell like butter?' I said dreamily, with the full fat flowers pressed to my face. 'Butter and cream and a hint of something sharp like lime.'

'You make it sound like one of Cook's puddings,' said Celia, smiling.

'Quite right, too,' I said. 'She certainly should make a pudding of roses. How lovely to eat roses. They smell as if they would be melting and sweet.'

Celia, amused at my sensual relish, sniffed a little bud to please me, and snipped another bloom and put in in her basket.

'How is Saladin's leg?' she asked, noticing my dirty hands and the halter.

'I'm on my way to order a poultice,' I said.

Some movement in the first floor of the Hall caught my attention and I stared at the house. Someone was going down the corridor with a great pile of clothing and bedding, followed by someone else with another pile, and someone behind with yet another. As I watched, they passed one window and then another in an extraordinary procession.

I could have asked Celia, but it did not occur to me that she might know what was going on inside the house when I did not. So I said, 'Excuse me,' and went with quick steps to the open front door and up the stairs to the corridor. The place was in utter confusion with bedding everywhere, a wardrobe blocking the door of Celia's bedroom and a great heap of Harry's clothes on Mama's bed.

'What is this?' I asked the chambermaid. She was half buried under a heap of Celia's starched petticoats and dipped a curtsy to me like a linen basket falling.

'Moving Lady Lacey's things, Miss Beatrice,' she said. 'She is moving into your mama's room with Master Harry.'

'What?' I said incredulously. The pile of linen bobbed again as the girl curtsied and repeated what she had said. I had heard her the first time. It was not my ears that had failed to hear, but my mind that could not believe what I was hearing. Celia and Harry moving into Mama's bedroom together could mean only one thing; that Celia had overcome her fear of Harry's sexuality – and that was not possible.

I spun on my heel and clattered down the stairs again and out into the sunlight. Celia was still snipping roses like an ignorant cupid in the Garden of Eden.

'The servants are moving your things into the master bedroom to share with Harry,' I said baldly, and waited for her start of shock. But the face she turned to me under the broad brim of her sunhat was utterly untroubled. She even had the hint of a smile playing around her lips.

'Yes,' she said calmly. 'I asked them to do it this afternoon while you were all out. I thought it would cause you all less inconvenience.'

'You ordered it!' I exclaimed incredulously, and then I bit the inside of my lip and stopped.

'Oh, yes,' said Celia calmly and then her eyes flew to my face. 'I thought it would be all right,' she said anxiously. 'Your mama has no objection and I did not think I should have confirmed it

275

with you. I hope you are not offended, Beatrice? I did not think you would be affected in any way at all.'

Words of complaint died in my mind as I recognized that Celia would think precisely that – that I could hardly be affected if she chose to sleep in the same bed as her husband. But that bed was the great master bed of Wideacre where Squires and their Ladies had lain for years. In that bed Celia became the first lady on the land, and that affected me. In that bed, in Harry's arms, she became a true wife to him and the pleasure of his nights. And that affected me. As his Lady, as his lover, she made me redundant. And the spectre of a suitor riding towards us to take me away was too real for me to risk losing Harry's need for my company.

'Why are you doing this, Celia?' I said urgently. 'You do not have to do this, you know. Just because my mama, or your mama, are anxious for another grandchild, there is no need to do this. You have years ahead of you, you do not have to rush into Harry's bed this summer. You are the mistress of your own house now. You do not have to do any duty with is repugnant to you, to which you object.'

Celia's cheeks flushed as pink as the rose in her hand. And she was definitely smiling, though her eyes were turned down.

'But I do not object, Beatrice,' she whispered very low. 'I am very happy to say I do not object.' She paused and her cheeks flushed more rosy than ever. 'I do not object at all,' she said.

From some recess of lies in my soul I found a smile and pinned it on my wooden face. Celia gave a little gasp of a laugh and turned from me and went out of the garden. At the gate she paused and shot me a quick, loving smile. 'I knew you would be so glad for me,' she said so low I could hardly hear her. 'I think I can make your brother very happy, Beatrice, my dear. And at last now it is truly my happiness to try.'

Then she was gone; loving, light-stepping, exquisite, desirable, and now desiring. And I was lost.

Harry's strong points were not imagination or fidelity. With Celia as pretty and wholesome as a peach beside him in his bed every night he would forget the sensuous delights we had shared. She would become the centre of his world and when Mama suggested a marriage for me, Harry would enthusiastically endorse the idea, thinking every marriage as perfect as his own. I would have lost my hold on Harry when his one desire was his lovely wife. And I had lost the one hold I had on Celia that I thought secure: her terrified frigidity. If she could giggle at the thought of Harry in her bed, she was no longer a child one could scare with a bogeyman. She was a woman and she was learning her own desires. In Harry she would find a loving tutor.

I stood alone in the garden swinging the halter. Somehow I had to salvage some grip on Harry out of this slide into domestic bliss. Celia could give him love; she was overflowing with tenderness and the need to love someone. She was far more loving than I ever could be, would be, would ever want to be. Celia could give him pleasure – a night with her sweet kisses and delicate lovely body would be more than most men get in a lifetime, outside their dreams.

But there had to be something I could do that she could not. There had to be some hold I could keep on Harry even if he was an uxorious husband and a besotted lover. I had held Harry in my thrall for two years and I knew him better than anyone. There had to be some string in my hand that I could pull to set him dancing to my tune. I stood like a statue of Diana the huntress: tall, proud, lovely and hungry, while the September shadows lengthened across the garden and the sun burned low over the roof of Wideacre making the stone slates rosy in the light. Then the swinging halter stilled and my head came up and I smiled into the burning face of the setting sun. I said softly to myself one word: 'Yes.'

The top floor of the west wing, the third, was used as a store room. It is a long, low room that runs the length of the house with windows at either end facing north over the common and south over the garden. When I was a young girl with more energy than outlets, I used to come up here on wet days and shout and sing and dance where no one could hear me. The ceiling is shaped to the roof and the windows set into the roof under gables, so low that I had to stoop to see out of them after my eleventh year. It had been filled with the old furniture banished from the rest of the house, but once that had been polished and set in my rooms this attic store room was empty of all but my papa's old saddlery equipment and his other things.

I had kept it as a retreat, and the new use I planned would not draw any attention to it. I cleared the saddles I had been working on from the saddle rack and it stood like a vaulting horse in the middle of the floor. Papa's coats and his boots, his notebooks on breeding and his diagrams of saddles I packed away in a chest. But I kept his hunting knife and his great long-thonged whip.

Then I called in the Acre carpenter and ordered him to fix two stout hooks to the wall at a man's shoulder height, and another two at floor level.

'I hope I've done right, for if I don't know what they be for, I can't tell if they'll serve,' he grumbled.

'That's perfect,' I said, looking at them. I paid him once for his trouble and once for his silence. A good bargain. For he knew that if he broke it I would know and he would never again work in Sussex. When he had gone I tied leather thongs to the hooks. The room was perfect. It already had a large chaise-longue near the fireplace and no one would notice if I added a candelabra from my other rooms and scattered a few sheepskins on the floor. I was ready.

I was ready, but I could not make a start. It was hardly reticence, but I could not find in myself the necessary confidence or the necessary mania to do it. In this thing I was serving Harry's peculiar tastes and not my own more simple ones. I needed an event to spur me on to action. Even when Celia came downstairs to breakfast too late to pour my coffee, with shadows under her eyes but with a smile like a happy child, I still made no move. A week passed and I was ready, but still unready. Then Harry said to me at supper, 'May I speak with you afterwards, Beatrice? Will you sit with me while I take port?'

'Certainly,' I said with equal formality. I waited while Celia and Mama withdrew from the room and took the seat at the foot of the table. The butler poured me a glass of ratafia and set the decanter of port at Harry's hand, and left us.

The house was quiet. I wondered if Harry remembered another evening, like this one, when we had sat in silence as the house creaked and the flames flickered and died in the stone fireplace, and we had melted into each other on the hard wooden floor. But then I saw the smile on his boyish mouth and the happy clear eyes, and I realized he did not remember at all. It was other kisses and another body that warmed him now. His lovemaking now took place in the Master's bed; our passionate, furtive exchanges belonged to the past.

'I have to speak with you about something which makes me very happy,' said Harry. 'I do not think it will come as a surprise to you. Actually, I do not think it will come as a surprise to anyone.'

I turned the delicate stem of the glass between my forefinger and thumb, my mind blank.

'Dr MacAndrew has approached me, as the head of the house, for my permission to ask for your hand in marriage,' said Harry pompously.

My head snapped up, my green eyes blazed.

'And you said?' I shot the question at him.

He stumbled in his surprise. 'I naturally said "Yes", Beatrice. I thought . . . we all thought . . . I was certain that . . .'

I leaped to my feet and the heavy old chair scraped the polished floor.

'You gave your consent without consulting me?' I said, my voice icy but my eyes green fire.

'Beatrice,' said Harry gently. 'Everyone has seen how you like him. His profession is unusual, of course, but he is of excellent family and his fortune . . . is remarkable. Of course I said he could speak to you. Why ever should I not?'

'Because he has nowhere to live!' I blazed out, my voice almost a sob. 'Where does he propose I should live, may I ask?'

Harry smiled, reassuringly. 'Beatrice, I don't think you realize how very, very wealthy John MacAndrew is. He plans to return home to Edinburgh and I believe he could buy all of Holyrood Palace for you if you had a mind to it. He certainly has the money to do it.'

My mind, ice-sharp with anger, caught at once at the crucial point. 'So I am to be married and packed off to Edinburgh!' I said, outraged. 'What of Wideacre?'

Harry, still confused at my rage, tried to reassure me. 'Wideacre will survive without you, Beatrice. You are all a Squire could be, and more, God knows, but this must not stand in your way. With your life and happiness taking you away to Scotland, Wideacre is the last thing you should have on your mind.'

If I had not been in such a blind rage that made me want to shriek and weep I should have laughed aloud. The idea of my life taking me to some pretentious town house in Edinburgh or my love for some sandy-haired stranger taking me from Wideacre was comically funny – if it had not been stark horror. All horror.

'Who knows of this plan?' I said, fiercely. 'Mama?'

'No one, except myself,' Harry said, hastily. 'I spoke first of all to you, of course, Beatrice. But I believe I may have mentioned it to Celia.' His half-smile revealed that my future exile had been the topic of some marital chit-chat in the master bed.

'But I had no idea, Celia had no idea, that you would be anything but deeply, deeply happy, Beatrice.'

His voice, so controlled, so soothing, so much the chocolate smooth voice of powerful men who marry, and bed, and dispose of women down the long centuries, while women wait and wait for land, snapped the remainder of my control.

'Come with me,' I ordered, and grabbed a candelabra from the dining table. Harry exclaimed, looked around for rescue and seeing none followed me. In the hall we could see the parlour door ajar and hear Mama and Celia's gentle voices as they sewed the altar cloth. I ignored it and turned to the great sweep of shallow stairs, Harry following, bemused but obedient. I led him up the first, then the second flight, then up the narrow stairs where my candles were the only dipping, flickering light.

We reached the locked door to the west-wing store room.

'Now wait,' I said and unlocked the door with the key from my pocket and left him standing outside without even a light. In haste I slid from my evening gown into the green riding habit I had worn as a girl when Harry had first come home from school and caught me, on that hot afternoon, naked on the floor of the old mill barn. The long line of buttons down the close-fitting jacket I left open from throat to navel. I was naked underneath. In my hand I held Papa's old hunting whip – a long black thong of leather coiled wickedly and efficiently, the handle black ebony with silver inlay.

'Come in,' I said in a voice Harry would not dare to disobey.

He pushed open the door and gasped as he saw me, tall and angry in the flickering light of the candles. He gasped again when he took in the deep shadow down the front of my gown, and the saddle rack, and the hooks on the wall, and the sensuously cushioned divan and the scatter of thick sheepskin rugs.

'Come here,' I said. My tone cut him like a knife. In a trance he followed me to the hooks on the wall and when I tapped his legs with the crop he straddled so I could tie both ankles with the leather thongs. Speechless he spread his arms out while I tied him by the wrists – tightly and painfully – to the hooks.

One hard pull and his fine linen shirt was ripped to the waist and he flinched and stood half naked before me. With my bare hand I double-slapped him across the face; left–right–left–right and then, like a stable cat, I scratched his chest from his throat to the belt of his breeches with the sharp fingernails of both claw-like hands. He slumped on his bindings and groaned. It sounded as if he were really hurt. I was filled with deep gladness.

I took Papa's old hunting knife and slit the seams of Harry's fine embroidered evening breeches so they hung in tatters from his waist. The blade had nicked his skin on one thigh and when I saw the welling drop of blood I knelt and sucked it as hungrily as any vampire. If I could have bled every ounce of his male pride and his folly and his power from him, I would have done so. He groaned, then straightened up again, straining against the ties as if he wanted to be free. I stepped backwards and with one expert flick uncoiled the whip so the thong squirmed on the floor towards him like a snake ready to strike. Then I raised it.

'Understand this, Harry,' I said, and my voice was clear with hatred. 'I am never, in all my life, leaving Wideacre. I am never, in all my life, leaving you. We are together for ever. While you are the Squire of Wideacre you have me as surely as you have the land. You forgot that, and that is why I am going to punish you. I shall punish you in such a way that you will never forget and it will be a drug and a longing to you which you will never rid yourself of.'

Harry gasped as if to speak, to beg against the sentence, or to beg for it. I neither knew nor cared. I raised my arm and cracked the whip.

Papa had taught me how to handle a whip in the stable yard when I was ten. With skill and practice you can pick a strawberry without bruising it, or break the hide of a bull. I used Papa's whip to slap Harry hard on the tender skin under the arms and down the flanks of his sweaty, trembling body, and then to tease and caress him around the throat, down his panting chest and barely to graze him between his straddled legs.

'Go to the rack,' I ordered. I untied him and he fell in a heap at my feet as soon as I loosened his wrists. I kicked his ribs without hesitation in one abrupt uncaring move. 'Go to the saddle rack,' I repeated.

He fell on it as if it was his schoolboy bed, and laid his cheek on the smooth polished wood while I tied each wrist and ankle to one of the legs. Then I played the whip over his back and his buttocks and his thighs, so each touch was the lightest sting, but the repetition added to discomfort, then pain, and then to pink, stinging grazes.

I untied him again and he slid from the rack into a crumpled heap on the floor and put out one imploring hand to the hem of my skirt.

I loosened the skirt of the riding habit at the waist and dropped it beside him. His hand closed convulsively on the soft velvet and he buried his face it in with a half-sob. But I left on the short tailored jacket and my soft leather riding boots.

'On your back,' I said mercilessly.

Harry was far gone. He lay like a stranded whale, beached on a shingle spit of unnatural desire. Out of element, out of place, helpless and heaving; I dropped like a scavenging eagle on the burstingly hard shaft of his body and as he entered me he screamed one hoarse shriek of pleasure. His back arched as he pushed up to greet me, and the sore spots on his shoulders and ribs scraped against the bare floorboards and rubbed on the fleece rug. I stayed cool and detached in my mind, but somewhere in the depth of my body some unimportant private crisis of pleasure mounted and was satisfied. The clenching of my muscles as I took my way tipped Harry over the border of his ecstasy of pain and I felt his whole body shudder. His wriggles underneath my hard control became faster and more frenzied, then I saw his eyelashes close on his tear-stained cheeks and his mouth opened to give a great groan of release and pleasure. At that exact second I abruptly straightened up and lifted myself off him. And I slapped his rigid manhood with an open palm as if I was slamming an ill-trained dog to the floor. Harry gave a shriek of incredulous pain at the blow, and I saw that one of my rings had cut the delicate, bursting skin. A fountain of seed and blood, unwanted, rejected, spilled over his scratched, whipped belly, and he gave three great choking sobs of release and loss. I watched him bleed like a hurt virgin, my face as kindly as frozen marble.

I could hardly get up next day, I was so tired. The emotional strain, the great shuddery sexual tension and the effort of dominating and brutalizing Harry had worn me out. I took breakfast very late in my room, sitting up in my wide white bed, and then spent the rest of the morning at my desk at the sunny window of my office. I was supposed to be doing the accounts, but little work was done that day. In truth, I spent the time gazing unseeing out of the window with the picture of Harry's agony and Harry's agonized ecstasy before my eyes.

At midday the parlourmaid brought me some of the strong black coffee we had shipped home from France. On the silver tray was an extra cup, and Harry entered the room behind her. I must confess, he took me by surprise. I had hardly thought he would have the courage to assert himself, and so soon. He walked rather stiffly, but not so badly that anyone would notice who was not watching him like a newly trained sparrowhawk.

The maid poured the coffee and put mine on the desk by my hand, and then left us alone. I said nothing. My tiredness had vanished and I was as wary as a poacher – seeking gain and yet rigid with fear.

Harry put his cup down on the porcelain saucer with a high-toned click.

'Beatrice,' he said, and his voice was a sigh of exhaustion and obsession.

It was as if all the candles in my heart had been lit at once. I had him. I had him safe again. I need never again fear for my place at Wideacre. I had won the Squire to corruption and I had him tight in my net.

'You treat me as if you hate me, but you don't hate me, do you, Beatrice?' His voice had a hint of a beggar's whine. I guessed that this was the voice my clever Ralph would recognize. The voice the schoolboy Harry had learned at school when the hero Staveley had taught his little troop to fetch and carry and fag and fight for him. The voice Staveley had taught him to use when he begged for bullying, or beating, or little treats of reward. If I had known Staveley, or even if I had Ralph to advise me, I should have known better at this moment what I should do – whether to indulge or punish Harry some more. I awaited some clue.

'I was wrong, I have been all wrong,' said Harry like a whipped spaniel puppy. 'But do not beat me again, Beatrice. I shall do better. I shall never offend you again.'

Harry, the Squire of Wideacre, as a whimpering child, made my skin crawl with revulsion. With a sudden stab of memory I remembered the disdain in Ralph's bright black eyes when Harry knelt on the floor of the dusty barn and laid his cheek on Ralph's bare foot. Of course Ralph had looked relieved that we should, so miraculously, escape discovery. But he also looked as I imagined I looked now, as if Harry were some obscene mistake of nature, like a three-headed calf. I saw before me the long years of running the Squire as a puling baby – and I longed for Ralph's uncomplicated, dominating fresh lust.

284

'You disgust me,' I said, speaking the truth, which leaped unstoppable to my lips.

Harry gave a whimper and slid from the pretty salon chair to his knees on the carpet at my feet.

'I know it. I know I do,' he said miserably. 'I cannot help it. I am bewitched, I think. I have been wrong all my life. Only you can save me, Beatrice – though it is you who have done the bewitching. I am caught in your snare and I am helpless before you. For God's sake be merciful with me.'

I smiled, the easy cruel smile of this new role Harry had cast for me in his fevered, oversexed, overeducated imagination.

'You are mine for ever, Harry,' I said. 'Your fumblings with your little bride, your friendships with men, your love for Mama or your work on the land – none of these are the real life. The real life is with me in secret, in a private locked room that only you and I know about. And you will get to that room only when I bid you, for only I have the key. And there I will take you into pain and beyond pain. And we will never, ever part; for I do not wish to go, and you –' I smiled down into his upturned white face – 'you would die without this pleasure.'

He gave a sob and buried his face in my skirt. I touched his head with my hand as gently as our mama would have done and heard his sobs renew at my tenderness. Then I gripped on to the long blond curls and pulled his head up so I could look into his eyes.

'Are you my servant?' I demanded in a whisper like a shard of ice.

'Yes,' he said tonelessly. 'Yes.'

'Are you my slave?'

'Yes.'

'Then go now for I have had enough of you.'

I said it cruelly, and I turned back to my desk. He shuffled to his feet and walked slowly and painfully to the door. His hand was on the doorknob when I said, in the voice I use to call my dogs, 'Harry!'

He turned quickly and awaited my pleasure.

'You will behave at dinner as if nothing at all had ever happened,' I said. 'This is a life and death secret and your silly open face must not betray you, or you will be ruined. Do it, Harry.'

He nodded, like a pauper taking orders at the workhouse, and turned to leave.

'And Harry,' I said with a new, languorous note in my voice, little more than a whisper.

I could see his back tense like a shudder, and he turned again.

'I will unlock the door of my secret room tonight, and you may come to me at midnight,' I said, softly.

He shot me a look of speechless gratitude. Then I let him go.

I was still left with the problem of John MacAndrew and, to tell the truth, the problem of my pleasure in his company, which I was loath to lose unless I had to. One solution was obvious: an easy lie. That Harry had quite misunderstood me, and that I enjoyed his friendship but I feared we would not suit as a married couple. I sat, musing, facing my desk with the papers I should be checking piled under a heavy glass paperweight – a deep red poppy embalmed inside it. I played the scene over in my mind – my dignified regret at rejecting John MacAndrew – and I tried some of the phrases of maidenly modesty in my mind. But my serious face kept breaking into a smile. It was all such fustian! And clever, sharp John MacAndrew would see through it in a trice. I had to find some lie to turn him from his course of marriage to me, and my exile to Scotland. But I would never convince him that I liked him only as a friend when he could see, as everyone could see, that I had a quick smile as soon as I saw him, and that no one could amuse me as he did.

I did not ache for him as I had for Harry. I did not see him with my conscious mind suspended utterly by the power of my body's feelings as I had with Ralph. But I could not help smiling when I thought of him and the idea of his kisses delighted me. Not in my dreams – for I never, ever dreamed of him – but in daytime reveries and in the pictures that came into my mind before I slept.

While I was still turning over in my mind what I could say to him, I heard the noise of a curricle and pair and Dr MacAndrew's expensive carriage bowled up the drive and stopped, informally, impertinently, outside my window. He looked down from the high box-seat and smiled at me. I crossed to the window and flung it wide to him.

'Good morning, Miss Lacey,' he said. 'I have come to kidnap you from your business. It is too lovely a day to waste indoors. Come for a drive with me.'

I hesitated. To refuse would be ungracious and would only delay the proposal if his mind was set on marriage. Besides, now the window was open I could smell the hot end-of-summer scents of full-blown roses and gillyflowers and stocks. In the woods, pigeons were cooing their hearts out and the swallows were swinging and swooping in the air in their last picnic before their travels. We could drive around to watch them breaking the turf in the rested fields to ready them for sowing.

'I'll fetch my hat,' I said with a smile, and I swept from the room.

But I had not considered Mama. She met me at the great staircase, and insisted that I change into a pretty walking-out dress and not clatter about the country in my morning gown. While I fretted at the delay, Mama called her maid as well as mine and laid out a choice of gowns before me on the bed.

'Any one, any one of them,' I said. 'I am only going for a drive to the fields with Dr MacAndrew, Mama. I'm not off to London for the season, you know.'

'There is no reason why you should not look your best,' Mama said with unusual force. And she chose for me a deep green gown, smart jacket and voluminous skirt, which would bring out the green in my eyes and show my clear honey skin to perfection. The little matching bonnet had a veil of green lace, which I complained gave me spots before my eyes but actually delighted me with the way it hinted at the brightness of my eyes and drew attention to my smiling mouth. Mama's own dresser piled up my hair in fat coils and Mama herself pinned on the hat and pulled down the veil. Then she took both my gloved hands in her own and kissed me.

'Go on,' she said. 'You look lovely. I am very, very happy for you.'

Not only Mama seemed to think I was off to hear a proposal. Half the household had found a job to do on the staircase or in the hall that morning, as I made my way down to the front stairs. Every one of them bobbed a curtsy or tipped a bow to me and they smiled as if the whole of Wideacre was in a conspiracy to see me wedded.

The front door was flanked by our entire staff of footmen and parlourmaids as if we were entertaining in state. Both halves of the great double door were flung ceremoniously open by the butler and, gawping out of the parlour window, as Dr MacAndrew handed me up, were Celia, Nurse and, of course, Baby Julia.

'You've had a fine send-off this morning,' he said teasingly, noting the flush of scarlet on my cheeks.

'It's more usual to wait until you are accepted before you make an announcement,' I said acidly, my scene of maidenly refusal forgotten in my irritation.

He choked with laughter at my indiscretion.

'Now, Beatrice, try for a little tone,' he implored, and for all the world I could not check a laugh in response. But this was no way to lead up to a refusal – and besides all the house staff had piled out on to the terrace to see us go, and could see me driving away with my suitor with a smile on my face.

We swept down the drive at a spanking pace. He was driving his matched bays and they were fresh and going well. Although he held them to a trot on the twists and turns, I was looking forward to feeling the speed when we reached the road to Acre. The lodge gates were waiting for us opened wide, and Sarah Hodgett was there with a curtsy and a meaningful smile for me. I glanced accusingly at John MacAndrew's profile as all the Hodgett family crowded out of the house to point and wave at pretty Miss Beatrice and her young man. John MacAndrew turned his head and grinned at me, unrepentant.

'Not me, I swear it, Beatrice. So don't look daggers at me. I said not a word to anyone save your brother. I imagine the whole world has seen how I look at you, and how you smile at me, and has been waiting for us while you and I are taken by surprise.'

I considered this in silence. I disliked the easy tone of confidence but I was interested in whether I was surprised at the proposal. I had been amazed at the day of the race, but I was even more disbelieving of my own behaviour now. Sitting up high on the box of his racing curricle, with a laugh trembling all the time on my lips and no words of refusal anywhere in my mind.

That I should refuse to leave Wideacre was, of course, self-evident. But I could hardly refuse him before he proposed, and every second the assumption that I would accept him, and even the impression that I had accepted him, seemed to be growing. John MacAndrew had been clever enough to let the proposal of marriage become an understood thing between us without chancing a refusal.

As we came out of the drive and into the lane he turned, not as I had expected towards Acre but right towards the crossroads where our lane meets the main road between London and Chichester.

'Where do you imagine we are going?' I inquired drily.

'For a drive, as I told you,' he said lightly. 'I have a fancy to see the sea.'

'The sea!' I gasped. 'Mama will have a fit. I told her I should be back for dinner. I am sorry, Dr MacAndrew, but you will have to go shrimping alone.'

'Oh, no,' he said coolly. 'I told your mama we would be back after tea. So she will not expect us earlier. She agrees with me that too much desk work is bad for young women.'

I gasped again at this further evidence of John MacAndrew's tactical flair. 'Is my health suffering very badly?' I asked sarcastically.

'Indeed, yes,' he said without hesitation. 'You are becoming round-shouldered.'

I choked down a laugh – and then laughed out loud.

'Dr MacAndrew, you are a complete hand, and I will have nothing to do with you,' I declared. 'You may have kidnapped me today, but I shall be more careful of you another time.'

'Oh, Beatrice,' he said, and he turned his face from the road to smile very tenderly towards me, 'Beatrice, you are so very clever, and so very, very silly.'

That left me with nothing to say. But I found I was smiling into his eyes, and my colour was rising.

'Now,' he said, dropping his hands and letting the pair break into a smooth fast canter, 'now we are going to have a lovely day.'

Indeed we did. His housekeeper had packed a picnic that a lord might have envied, and we dined at the top of the downs with all

Sussex at our feet and God's clear sky above us. My extraordinary performance of the night before dropped from my mind as if it had never happened and I revelled in the relaxation of being neither goddess nor witch but simply a pretty girl on a sunny day. After Harry's frenzied worship, it was restful not to have to pretend, not to have to dominate. John MacAndrew's smile was warm, but his eyes were appraising and quick. I should never have him grovelling at my feet in a wet heap of remorse and lust. I smiled at him in easy approval and he smiled back. Then we packed up the picnic gear and drove on.

We reached the sea at teatime. He had chosen the stretch of shoreline nearest to Wideacre – almost due south – where there is a tiny fishing village of half-a-dozen shanties and a most villainous-looking public house. We pulled up outside and John MacAndrew's shout brought the landlord running, very surprised and very certain he had nothing in his house fit for the Quality. So, too, were we. But in the boot of the curricle was a complete tea service with the best tea, sugar and cream.

'I dare say it will be butter by now,' said John MacAndrew, spreading a rug on the shingle of the beach for me to sit. 'But a simple country girl like yourself does not expect everything to be perfect when she condescends to leave her estate and visit the peasantry.'

'Indeed not,' I retorted. 'And you will not know the difference, for I dare say you tasted neither butter nor cream until you crossed the border.'

'Och, no,' he said instantly, adopting the broadest Scots accent. 'All we drink at home is the usquebaugh!'

'Usquebaugh!' I exclaimed. 'What is that?'

His face darkened with some private thought. 'It's a drink,' he said shortly. 'A spirit, like grog or brandy, but a good deal stronger. It's a wonderful drink for losing your senses with, and a good many of my countrymen use it to forget their sorrows. But it's a poor master to have. I've known men, one of them very dear to me, ruined by it.'

'Do you ever drink it?' I asked, intrigued at this serious side to John MacAndrew that I had glimpsed before only in his professional work.

He grimaced. 'I drink it in Scotland,' he said. 'There's many places where you can get nothing else. My father serves it at home instead of port in the evening, and I cannot say I refuse it! But I fear it rather.' He paused and looked at me uncertainly, as if considering whether or not to trust me with a secret. He took a breath and went on. 'When my mother died I had just started at the university,' he said quietly. 'The loss of her hit me hard, very hard indeed. I found that when I drank usquebaugh – whisky – the pain left me. Then I found it good to drink all the time. I think it is possible to be addicted to it – as I warned you some people become addicted to laudanum. I fear addiction for my patients because I've had a taste of it in my own life. I'll take a glass of whisky with my father, but I'll take no more. It is a weakness of mine I do well to guard against.'

I nodded, understanding only dimly what he meant, but knowing well that he had trusted me with some sort of confession. Then the landlord came out from the public house carrying, with awestruck concentration, John MacAndrew's silver tea service, the silver pot filled to the brim with perfectly brewed Indian tea.

'I shall expect to be attacked by highwaymen on the way home, all after your sugar tongs,' I said lightly. 'Do you always travel with such vulgar ostentation?'

'Only when I am proposing,' he said so unexpectedly that I jumped and some of my tea spilled in the saucer and splashed my gown.

'You should be horse-whipped!' I said, dabbing at the stain.

'No, no,' he said, teasing me even further. 'You misunderstand the nature of my proposal. I am even prepared to marry you.'

I choked on a laugh and he rescued my teacup and put it on the tray behind him.

'Now I will stop,' he said, suddenly serious. 'I love you, Beatrice, and I want with all my heart that you should be my wife.'

The laughter died on my lips. I was ready to say 'No' but somehow the word would not come. I simply could not bring myself to spoil this lovely sunny day. The waves splashed and sucked at the shingle; the seagulls called and wheeled in the salty air. The words of refusal seemed a million miles away, even though I knew I could not possibly accept.

'Is it Wideacre?' he asked as the silence lengthened. I looked up quickly in gratitude at his understanding.

'Yes,' I said. 'I could live nowhere else. I simply could not.'

He smiled gently, but his blue eyes showed hurt.

'Not even to make a home with me and be my wife?' he asked. The silence lengthened, and it seemed that I would indeed be forced to frame some sort of absolute refusal.

'I'm sorry,' I said. 'I truly am. Wideacre has been my life, all my life. I cannot begin to tell you what it means to me. I cannot go away from it.'

He reached across the rug and took my hand in both of his. He held it gently, and then turned it palm up and pressed a kiss into the warm, cupped hand, and then he closed my slim fingers over the kiss as if to hold it in.

'Beatrice, know this,' he said, and his voice was very grave. 'I have seen you, and watched you for a year now and I knew you would be likely to refuse me and to choose instead to stay at home. But hear this: Wideacre belongs to Harry and after him to his heirs. It will never, it can never, be yours. It is your brother's home; it is not your home. If you and he should quarrel – I know, I know, how impossible that seems – but if he insisted, he could throw you off tomorrow. You are there only at Harry's invitation. You have no rights at all. If you refuse marriage for Wideacre then you are refusing your future home for a place that is only a temporary place to stay – it can never be either secure or permanent.'

'I know,' I said, low. My eyes were on the sea and my face was stony. 'It is as secure as I can make it,' I said.

'Beatrice, it is a special place, a wonderful place. But you have seen very little of the rest of the country. There are other places equally lovely where you and I could make a home of our own, that would become as dear to you as Wideacre is now,' he said.

I shook my head and glanced at him.

'You do not understand. It could only ever be Wideacre,' I said. 'You do not know what I have done to try to win it, to make a place for myself there. I have longed for it all my life.'

His clever eyes were on my face. 'What you have done?' he said, repeating my indiscreet words. 'What have you done to try to win it that commits you so deeply?'

I hovered between a collapse into a heart-easing conscience-saving confession to this wise, this gentle, lover and a clever, habitual lie. My instincts and my hungry cleverness warned me away, away from confidence, away from trust, away from love, away from real marriage.

'Beatrice . . .' he said. 'You can tell me.'

I paused, the words were on my tongue. I was about to tell him. Then I glanced down towards the sea and saw a man, bronzed as a pirate, looking curiously at us.

'It seems I was right about your silver sugar tongs,' I said lightly. John followed the direction of my gaze and exclaimed and started to his feet. Without hesitation he went towards the fellow, his boots scrunching on the shingle. I saw them exchange a few words, and then John glanced uncertainly back at me, and came back towards me with the man following a few steps behind.

'He recognizes you as Miss Lacey of Wideacre,' John said, rather bewildered. 'And he wants to speak with you about something, but he will not tell me what it is. Shall I send the fellow about his business?'

'No, of course not!' I said smiling. 'He may be about to tell me where to find buried treasure! You count the spoons and repack the tea things and I will see what he wants.'

I rose to my feet and went towards the man who pulled his forelock as I approached. I could tell he was a sailing man; he had none of the heaviness of a farming labourer. His skin was tanned a deep dirty brown, and his eyes narrowed with staring over bright waters. He had a pair of flapping trousers, wide-bottomed, and shoes – not boots like a farm labourer would. He wore a handkerchief tied over his head with a characteristic little plait of hair poking out behind. A complete villain, I judged, and I had a wary smile for him.

'What d'you want of me?' I said, certain it was a loan or some favour.

'Business,' he said, surprisingly. 'Trade.'

His accent was not local and I could not place it. West country, I thought. I started to have a glimmer of an idea what his business might be.

'Trade?' I said sharply. 'We farm, we don't trade.'

'Free trade, I should have said,' he said, watching my face. I could not control the flicker of a smile.

'What d'you want?' I said briskly. 'I've no time to waste talking to rogues. You can speak to me briefly but we don't break the law on Wideacre.'

He grinned at me without a flicker of shame. 'No, miss,' he said. 'Of course not. But you have good cheap tea and sugar and brandy.'

I grinned ruefully at him. 'What d'you want?' I said again.

'We've trouble at the place where we usually store our goods,' he said in an undertone, keeping a wary eye on John MacAndrew, waiting alert by the curricle. 'We've got a new leader and he suggested storing in the old mill on your land. The goods would be there only a few nights each run, and you need know nothing about it, Miss Lacey. There'd be a couple of kegs left behind for you if you would be gracious enough to accept them, or perhaps some fine French silks. You'd be doing the Gentlemen a favour, Miss Lacey, and we never forget our friends.'

I could not look severe at the cheeky rogue and there was nothing unusual in what he was asking. The smugglers – the Gentlemen as they were called – had always come and gone up the hidden deep-banked lanes of Sussex, and the two Preventive Officers, whose job it was to control smuggling along the whole long, inlet-ridden coast, spent their nights snug in bed and their days writing reports. One of them was a professional poet and had been given the job to provide him with time to write. So in Sussex we had the joint benefits of duty-free spirits and fine poetry, an excellent, if comical, result of the muddle over the excise laws, and the gifting of government jobs to deserving young gentlemen.

Papa had permitted smuggled goods in out of the way barns and had turned a blind eye to occasional reports of half-a-dozen horses passing quietly down the lane through Acre late in the night; Acre village itself would keep curtains drawn and mouths shut. The Gentlemen were generous to their friends but they would find and kill a tale-bearer.

So there was very little reason why they should not store goods on our land and the permission was on my lips, but the mention of the old mill and the new leader made me curious.

'Who is this new leader you have?' I said.

The man winked. 'Least said, soonest mended,' he said discreetly. 'But he's a fine planner and good man to follow. When I see his black horse at the head of the ponies I feel at ease.'

My mouth was suddenly dry. I swallowed with difficulty.

'Did he choose the old mill as a store?' I said. My voice was a thread and I could feel sweat making my face clammy.

The man looked curiously into my face, which was suddenly white.

'He did, miss,' he said. 'Are you ill?'

I put my hand to my eyes and found my trembling fingers were wet with sweat.

'It is nothing, nothing,' I said desperately. 'Is he a local man then?'

'I think he was born and bred near Wideacre,' said the man, impatient with my questions and worried at the way my hands were trembling and how my eyes had gone dark. 'What shall I tell him?'

'Tell him that the old mill is washed away and that everything is different,' I burst out, my voice rising with my fear. 'Tell him there is no place for him on Wideacre. Tell him to find another store, another route. Tell him he may not come near me or near my land. Tell him my people will not allow it. Tell him he was always an outcast and I was always loved.'

My knees were buckling but suddenly I found John's hard arm around my waist. He held me up and one hard look from him sent the man scuffling down the shingle to slip between the upturned fishing boats.

John MacAndrew, professional that he was, scooped me up like a baby and tossed me up into the curricle without a word. From under the driver's seat he produced a flask of his Scottish whisky and held the silver bottle to my lips. I turned my head away in disgust at the smell but he forced a couple of mouthfuls on me and I found that it warmed me and stopped my panic-stricken trembling. We sat in silence until I could hear the frightened beats of my heart slowing again. My mind was blank with fear at this sudden apparition – this ghost on a clear day. There were surely a hundred better things I could have done than to break down, and that in front of a man who was led, no doubt, by one of our expelled poachers, or one of Acre's ne'er-do-wells, or by one of the farm labourers pressed into the navy and run off to the smugglers. The black horse alone meant nothing. I was a fool to panic. A fool to be afraid.

But even now, sitting up high in the curricle in the warm afternoon sunshine with hundreds of pounds' worth of MacAndrew silver in the boot, and hundreds of guineas of bloodstock between the shafts, I felt utterly vulnerable and abasingly afraid.

I shuddered in one convulsive shiver, then took a deep breath. I gave the inside of my cheeks a good hard bite and, hidden in my lap, I pinched the palms of my hands with my sharp strong fingernails. Then I turned to John MacAndrew and smiled.

'Thank you,' I said. 'I am silly to have been upset by him. He was a free-trader, a smuggler, and he wanted somewhere to store his kegs. When I said no he was abusive. I don't know why I should let it upset me, but somehow it did.'

John MacAndrew nodded understandingly, but his eyes were sharp.

'Why did you say no?' he asked. 'You're surely not against them?'

'I never was,' I said slowly. But then my fear rose up and choked the truth out of me. 'But I'll have no lawless men on Wideacre,' I cried passionately. 'I'll have no leaders of mobs, no attackers of property, no men who move and work in the night on my land, near my home. He may be a smuggler today, but who knows what he might do tomorrow? I'll have no trained men led by a black horse riding the lanes near my house.' I stopped with a sob, horrified at my outburst. I was too scared and shocked at myself either to retract or to try to reduce the impression I had so clearly given of fright and horror.

John's warm hand covered mine.

'Do you want to tell me why?' he asked, and his voice was sympathetic and tender and low.

I exhaled, and it was almost a moan.

'No,' I said miserably. 'No.'

We sat in silence then, the horses with their heads bowed and the reins slack, the late afternoon sun red among rosy, fleecy clouds, low over the sea.

'I'll drive you home then,' said John and there was warmth and patience in his voice. I knew then that he loved me. That he loved me so much he was prepared to take on trust the things that I did, that should have warned him I was not the straight-forward pretty girl I seemed. He could have guessed I had a secret, a hanging secret. But he chose instead to click to the horses and to drive me home in the sunset, which turned to twilight as we crested the downs at Goodwood and then to star-light along the sweet-smelling nighttime lanes of my land. We followed a new moon home, a slim sickle in the night sky, and when John MacAndrew lifted me down from the curricle I felt the ghost of a kiss on the top of my head.

He never pressed me for an explanation. Not through the final hot days of summer when the hay was stacked and the corn winnowed and the beasts weaned and growing fat, and there was less work on the land and more time for visiting and dancing and picnics.

When we went to Havering with Celia and Harry and Mama, John and I would find ourselves walking alone together in the ramshackle formal gardens, or in the overgrown shrubbery. When we went in to tea there would be a smile between Mama and Lady Havering, instantly wiped off their faces when John or I looked directly at either of them. If in the evening we rolled back the rugs and Mama played country dances and jigs on the Haverings' grand piano, I would always dance the first and the last dance of the evening with my hands in John's. Then, when we waited for our carriages in the night air, which turned cooler at the end of every sweet insignificant evening, he would tuck my wrap around my shoulders, and sometimes gather it around my neck, to brush the side of my cheek, pale and soft as a flower in the moonlight.

Then the carriages would clatter around from the stable yard and he would hand me into the chaise with a gentle pressure on my fingers to say a private goodnight among the general fare-wells. I would lean my head back against the silk cushions and feel the warmth of his smile, the gleam of his eyes, the touch of his hand on my cheek as the horses trotted home, and Mama sat beside me, her face smiling and at peace too.

But I was never so absorbed in this delightful, this easy, courtship that I forgot to hold on to Harry, to hold to the land. At least once a week I would climb the stairs to the room at the top of the house and take Harry into a shivering, private maze of pleasure and fear. The more often I did it, the less it meant to me, until my icy disdain of Harry's plump pantings was real.

I knew now what my earlier passion for Harry had hidden from me. That although I had thought I had bedded him as a free woman I was as bound as if I were a slave. For it was not a free choice. I had wanted him because he was the Squire, not for himself. And now he was losing his fine, clear looks and becoming fatter and softer, I bedded the Squire, not Harry. And it was no free choice because I could not choose to say no. My safety and security on the land meant I had to keep my special, costly hold on its owner. I paid him rent as surely as the tenants who came to my round rent table with their coins tied up in a scrap of cloth. When I lay on my back, or strode round the rooms threatening him with every imaginable, ridiculous pain, I was paying my dues. And the knowledge galled me.

But although Harry had lost his magic, the land had not. Wideacre that autumn glowed like a scarlet leaf of rowan. The summer heat lingered late and even in October John could take me driving with only a shawl around my shoulders. But when the frosts came in November I was glad, for the hard ground held the scent and in the hoar frost I could see the prints of foxes' paws and the hunting season was open. I was back in the saddle for the first time after two long years of mourning and absence, and our hounds were mastered once more by Wideacre's Squire, as they should be. Every day Harry and I checked them and talked of nothing but foxes and hunters and runs. It was Harry's first season and he threatened to botch it badly. But his interest in breeding good animals meant that we had the fastest hounds in the county – you had to follow them at a gallop and jump whatever lay in your path – no time for niceties! So there would always be riders who would want to come out with us and lend a hand with the hounds. Shaw was a good keeper who knew the ways of foxes, and I was always at Harry's side.

12

Between Shaw the keeper, and me, Harry made a reasonable fist of it, and our first day out in October was a long glorious run that started on the common and then chased in a great sweep over the fields back to the common and a kill on the edge of the park where the Wideacre woods are encroaching on the heather and bracken. He was an old dog fox that one. I swear I hunted him one season before with Papa. He got away then from the slower old-fashioned pack but now he was three years older and Papa was dead, and even unskilled Harry, who totally lacks a hunter's instinct, could see that the wily animal was heading for a stream to lose the scent in the water.

'Send them in, Harry!' I yelled above the clamour of the pack and the thunder of hoofs, the wind whipping my words away.

The horn blasted, 'Too-roo! Too-roo!' and the horses leaped forward; the hounds spread out with their final full-cry killing run, and the old fox strained to a final burst of speed. He nearly made it too, but they had him at the side of the stream, and Harry waded thigh-deep among squealing, hungry hounds to cut the brush and pass it, still bloody, up to me. I nodded my thanks, and took the prize in my gloved hand. I have had the first kill of the season every hunt since I was eleven when Papa smeared my face with the disgusting, rank, sticky blood.

Mama had gasped then, when she saw me, as stained as any savage, and she had neared open complaint when Papa sternly told her that I was not to be washed.

'The child smells of fox,' Mama said. Her voice, tremulous with anger, had dropped to a whisper.

'It is the tradition,' Papa said firmly. That was enough for him and it was enough for me too. God knows I was not a squeamish little doll, but when he had rubbed the blood on my face from the base of the hot tail I had swayed in my saddle with sickly faintness. But I did not fall. And I did not wash.

I solved the problem in a way that, looking back, seems typical of my desire to please my papa and yet be true to myself. Papa had told me that the tradition was that the beastly blood stayed on until it wore off. I thought for some hours while the blood congealed into crusty scabs on my young skin, then I made my way down to the old sandstone drinking trough by the stables. I sat beside it, put my face to it, and rubbed the delicate skin of my cheeks and forehead against its rough sides until I was sore and scraped, but clean.

'Did you wash, Beatrice?' Papa asked me sternly when we met at breakfast the following day.

'No, Papa, I wore it away,' I said. 'May I start to wash again now?'

His great lovable, loving shout of laughter rattled the sash windows and the silver coffee pots.

'Wore it away, did you, my little darling!' he roared, and then subsided into chuckles, wiping his eyes on his napkin. 'Yes, yes, you may wash now. You have satisfied tradition; and that's good. And you have got your own way too, and that's comical.'

I seemed years away from this scene and from my papa's love as I sat in the hard winter sunshine and accepted the brush from Harry. The smell of the warm freshly killed fox had brought it all flooding back to me, but it was all long gone. Long lost, and long past.

'A good run, Miss Lacey,' said one of the Havering boys, Celia's step-brother George.

'Yes, indeed,' I said smiling.

'And how you do ride!' he said with worship in his eyes. 'I can't keep up with you! When you took that last hedge I had to shut my eyes. I was certain that low bough would sweep you off!'

I laughed at the recollection.

'I had my eyes shut too!' I confessed. 'I get so excited I forget to take care. I put Tobermory at the hedge without even seeing the tree. When I realized there was no room for us between the hedge and the low branches it was too late to do anything about it except keep my head down and hope we squeezed through. We just did, though I felt the twigs scratch my back.'

'I hear you have been racing too,' said George, nodding to John MacAndrew, who rode up to us. The sun seemed to shine with sudden new warmth, and we smiled into each other's eyes.

'Just a friendly race,' I said. 'But Dr MacAndrew rides for high stakes.'

George's bright eyes flicked from one to another of us.

'I hope you did not lose Tobermory!' he said.

'No,' I said, with a private smile to John MacAndrew. 'But I'll not be betting blind against the doctor again.'

George laughed, and at last took himself off to compliment Harry on the run, and I was left alone with John. But it was the trained doctor, not the lover who spoke.

'You're pale,' he said. 'Do you feel unwell?'

'No, I'm very well,' I said, smiling to reassure him and to support the lie. Even as I spoke I felt a swimmy sensation of faintness and nausea.

'I can see you are not,' he said curtly. He dismounted and held out peremptory arms to me. I shrugged my shoulders and slid down from the saddle and let him lead me to a fallen tree. Once seated I felt better and drew a couple of deep breaths of the sharp autumn air, smelling the bright, cold exciting smell of dry leaves.

'What's wrong?' he asked. He had not released my hand after leading me to the seat, and his sensitive fingers had discreetly taken my pulse.

'Oh, let be,' I said, and pulled my hand away. 'I cannot afford a weekly consultation, doctor. I am queasy and headachey because we have harvested the first of the wine and I was tasting the young vintage last night. It tastes like vinegar; it needs a West Indian island full of sugar to make it sweet enough; it costs a fortune to produce and it leaves me with the vilest headache in the world – on account of the loss we have made on it all, and the damage it does to my liver.'

He laughed out loud at my ill humour, quite unoffended. Then kindly, sensibly, he left me alone. He moved off to chat with some of the others and I was free to lean back against a branch of the tree.

I had lied, of course. We had indeed drunk Harry's bitter unsuccessful wine last night, but that was not the cause of my early-morning queasiness and my faintness, and the tenderness in my breasts. I was with child again, and I felt sick because of that nauseous, tiring condition, and worse at the idea of the condition. It cost me every ounce of courage to smile and joke with Harry and George and John MacAndrew with the sickness from this vile growth inside me.

I was not surprised George could not follow my lead. I had been riding for a fall. A good bruising tumble that would shake this parasite free and leave me blooded and clean and whole again. But Tobermory was too sure-footed and I was too good a rider. I had taken some incredible jumps and was still here in the autumn sunshine, as lovely as ever, as virginal-looking as Diana the huntress – but one month pregnant. My rage at the injustice of my continual fertility while Celia, the deserving wife, could only play host to my cuckoo made the nausea on my tongue taste like fire. In recapturing Harry's slavish adoration, I had created another problem. This beastly, intractable, insoluble growth in my belly had not shaken loose on my hell-for-leather ride so maybe it was as strong a child as Julia had been, who had clung on through many a breathless, dangerous, thundering gallop and been born none the worse for it. I had not had the luck of a tumble. I should have to take some evil old peasant's dirty mixture, and grit my teeth through the ensuing, solitary pain.

She took some finding, for with the disappearance of Ralph's mother Meg from Acre no other old crone had emerged skilled in the necessary borderline arts. Ironically I found her by pretending to Mary, Mrs Hodgett's pretty daughter, that I wanted a love potion. She looked to me like the sort of girl who would hardly need such magic either. But just as I had foreseen, she knew the name of an old dame who lived in a shanty hut on Havering Common.

Forewarned by my knowledge of the ways of the country, I expected a dirty hovel, but the old witch's shanty was worse than the sties where we keep our pigs. Mud-floored, walled with slabs of turf and bits of bracken, and with branches of trees plugged with moss and turf for a roof. As soon as I entered the door, stooping under the low roof, I knew it was a mistake to come, and I did not believe she could do it. But there was nowhere else

302

to go, and no other option to try. So I went through with it. The disgusting old witch produced a stone flask stoppered with a scrap of dirty cloth, and hid the silver shillings I tossed on the floor somewhere among her rags. I carried it home as if it were poison, and in the privacy of my bedroom drank the lot as she had told me.

It was as bad as I had feared. I was ill that night and had a day of retching, and the flux, but no little mess of half-made child came away. I still carried it with me. We seemed utterly inseparable. I was exhausted by the pregnancy and by the forty-eight hours of illness but I still had to ride back to that dirty cottage and see what the old witch could do now.

The true answer was nothing – except another bout of illness. She recommended another try, even put her stale mouth to my ear and assured me that a blunt knife pushed gently inside, as she would promise to do, would cause no pain, or hardly any pain at all, and would free me from the incubus. But I had had enough. I suspected, rightly I think, that for the fees I could pay she would continue trying until the baby was indeed dead – or until I was. I did not trust her dirty room where she mashed the weeds she called herbs. And I emphatically did not trust her with a rusty knife. So I had done with her, and when I felt well enough to think straight again – which took four miserable days – I put my mind to other possible means.

I thought, of course, of Celia. Dear little Celia, so sweet and so loving. I remembered her instant acceptance last time, and her loving response to Julia. It was a possibility that she might be glad of another child. My head lifted, and the glint of a smile crossed my face. It was another chance for me to put my child in the heir's cradle. If I could have avoided the pregnancy, I would have done so. If I could have lost the child I would have done so. But if he was hanging on, determined to grow, then he could inherit the earth indeed – or at any rate the fairest, sweetest corner of it.

I was more cautious this time. My pride and my peace had been dealt a stinging blow by the birth of a useless girl. Never again would I worship my own swelling body, seeing in its new shape the certainty of my future. But I could not suppress a little rising smile, at the thought that having had one girl, surely the chances were greater that this time my brother and I had bred true – had conceived a son.

I could not wait. I had conceived in September, and it was already mid-October – I dared not. Celia had to be told and some plan to explain our departure from Wideacre had to be cobbled together, and it had to be done quickly. I called out to one of the grooms who had followed the hunt with a spare horse. He touched his cap, and lifted me into the saddle. I told him to tell the Master that I was tired and would hack gently home, and I left without saying goodbye.

But I had not reckoned on John. He forced no farewell or explanation from me, but when I glanced back at the ring of huntsmen under the sweeping trees I saw that Sea Fern was standing to one side, away from the bustle of the hounds and the round of silver flasks. He was watching me ride away, and in the tilt of his head I saw not the blind gaze of the lover but the hard, analytical scrutiny of the professional man. I straightened my back in the saddle, conscious of his eyes upon me, and thought yet again that Celia and I would have to hurry. It would be tedious indeed to be off on my travels again, and difficult to arrange. But Wideacre, with the hard sharp eyes of Dr MacAndrew on me, was unsafe for any secret.

I waited to be sure I could have Celia to myself for a good period of time, and after dinner asked her to come to my office on the pretext of some brocades I wanted her to help me choose. The parlourmaid served us Bohea tea at the great rent table and Celia smiled at the contrast of the pretty red porcelain against the heavy masculine furniture of the room.

'Well, it is an office,' I said, half apologetically. 'If I had the labourers into my parlour they would break those delicate chairs and tread mud on the carpet.'

'I don't know how you can do it,' murmured Celia, glancing at the ledgers piled on one side of my desk. 'I should think it is so difficult to work out where all the money is coming from, and where it is being spent! And so boring!'

'I find it hard, certainly,' I said, telling an easy lie. 'But I am happy to do it for it frees Harry from the worry of it. But, Celia, I really asked you to come here because I wanted to talk to you alone.'

Her velvet-brown eyes were instantly concerned.

'Of course, Beatrice,' she said. 'Is there anything wrong?'

'Not with me,' I said firmly. 'It is you I wanted to talk about. My dear, we have been home for four months, and you have shared a room with Harry for nearly two. I just wondered if you had noticed any signs to tell you that you might be expecting a child?'

Celia's little face flushed as scarlet as a poppy and her eyes fell to her clasped hands in her lap.

'No,' she said very low. 'No, no signs, Beatrice. I cannot understand it.'

'Are you quite healthy?' I asked her, with affected concern.

'I thought so,' she said miserably. 'But yet I do not seem able to conceive. Harry says nothing, but I know he must be wondering about an heir. Mama suggested eating a lot of salt and I have done so, but it seems to make no difference. What makes it worst of all, Beatrice, is that you and I know that I did not even conceive Julia. I have been married a full year, and not conceived a child.'

I wrinkled my forehead, my eyes warm with concern.

'My dear,' I said, 'perhaps you should take some medical advice. John MacAndrew or, if you preferred, a London specialist?'

'How can I!' Celia exclaimed. 'Any doctor would be certain to ask about the conception of the first child and I cannot tell him that I have no first child when Julia is in the nursery, and Harry believes her to be his!'

'Oh, Celia!' I said. 'This is what I feared. But what will you do?'

'I can see nothing that I can do,' she said. She reached in the pocket of her little silk pinny and brought out a handkerchief, a tiny scrap of lace. She wiped her wet cheeks and tried to smile at me, but her lower lip trembled like a child's.

'I pray and pray,' she said low. 'But my prayers are not answered. It is a dreadful thought that because of my inadequacy Wideacre will pass to your cousins. If I had known that I would so fail Harry as a wife I should never have married him. I would have spared him that disappointment.' She ended with a little sob and pressed her handkerchief to her mouth.

'But I know so little of these things, Beatrice,' she said. 'And I cannot ask my mama. A year is not so very long, is it? I could just have been unlucky so far?'

'No,' I said, squashing that hope as firmly as I could. 'I believe that most ‚women are most fertile in the first year of their marriage. Since you have not conceived yet, I think it is unlikely that you ever will.'

I gave her a pause for her to wipe her eyes again, her head bowed under the sentence I had delivered. Then I held out a ray of hope.

'What if I were to conceive again, and we were to go away and I were to give you the child?' I said, musing aloud.

Her tear-filled eyes came up to my face and she managed a watery giggle.

'Really, Beatrice!' she said. 'You are too shocking!'

'I know,' I said impatiently. 'But I am thinking of you, you and Harry. If I were to be betrothed, or even married, I would be prepared, indeed I would be happy to solve your most dreadful problem by giving you my child.'

'No,' she said, with a determined shake of her head. 'No, it would never work. It could never work. It could not be arranged.'

'These are just details,' I said, containing my impatience. 'I say it could be arranged. I could arrange it. Would it not be a relief to you to be able to bring another baby home to Wideacre? And if it were a boy you could bring an heir home to Harry!'

She looked at me doubtfully, and I felt a glimmer of confidence and hope.

'Can you be serious, Beatrice?' she asked.

'I am hardly likely to joke, when your life and your marriage are in such desperate crisis,' I said, trying to overwhelm her with despair. 'I see you are miserable; I see Harry anxious. I see that Wideacre will be taken from Harry's line and given to distant cousins. Of course I am serious.'

Celia rose from her chair and came to stand behind me. She put her arms around my neck and leaned over the back of my chair to rest her damp cheek against my hot one.

'That is so very good of you,' she said with emphasis. 'Very generous, and very loving, and very like you and your sweet nature.'

'Yes?' I said. 'So we could do it?'

'No,' she said, sadly and softly. 'We could not.'

I turned in my chair to look up at her. Her face was sad, but she was resigned to her sadness.

'I could not, Beatrice,' she said simply. 'You have forgotten that to carry out such a deception I should have to lie to Harry. I would put another man's child in Harry's home and that would be a betrayal of him as surely as if I had been unchaste. I could not do it, Beatrice.'

'You did it before,' I said crudely. She winced as if I had struck her.

'I know I did, and that was wrong,' she said simply. 'In my fear of marriage and in my concern for you I committed a most dreadful sin against my husband whom I now love more than anything else in the world. I should not have done it, and sometimes I think that my punishment is not only to live with the consciousness of that sin, but also to have to live with my barrenness. I try to atone for it by loving Julia as well as if she were indeed my own precious daughter, and by never lying again to Harry as long as I live. But I know well that I should not have done it. And I should never do such a thing again, whatever the temptation.'

She sighed a deep breath and she wiped her cheeks again with the wet scrap of lace.

'You are so good, so generous, to suggest such a thing, Beatrice,' she said gratefully. 'It is like you to think nothing of yourself and everything of me. But your generosity is misplaced this time. It would not be a great, a generous gift. It would be leading me into dreadful error.'

I tried to nod and smile sympathetically, but my face muscles were stiff. I felt a rising tide of panic and fear of my pregnancy, and with it a rise of nausea. I was terrified of this growing child, which would neither die nor be given away. At the horror I had of the shame if I was forced to confess it. At my fear of what my mama would do, of what Harry would do. I should be sent away from my only home in shame. I should be tucked away in some dowdy market town with a pretend marriage ring on my finger and nothing from Wideacre around me except a monthly pension. I would have to wake in the morning to the noise of carts and carriages, and the birdsong of home would be far away. The sun that ripened the crops on the fields would shine through my dirty windows but its warmth would not feel the same. The rain, sliding down the window panes of my genteel little town house, would be filling the pools and hollows alongside the Fenny, but I would never drink that sweet water again. I could not bear it. This would be the end of me.

I looked at Celia, a slim figure in lilac silk, and I hated her for her obstinate morality, her silent, secret clarity about right and wrong, her wilful resistance to my needs. She was barren and I longed for that empty, clear, uncomplicated state. She was married and had traded independence and freedom for dependence and a quarterly pittance. But she had such security! Nothing would remove Celia; she would die in the Squire's bedroom. While I, who loved the land and needed the land and longed for the land, would die of homesickness in some narow bed in a little room and be buried in soil that did not smell of home.

I had to get Celia out of the room or I would weep before her.

'Good heavens,' I said lightly. 'Look at the time! Julia will be crying for you.'

It was the surest trigger in the world. Celia leapt to her feet and rustled to the door. She went with a light step, the pretty little moralist. Her sorrow was no heavy weight in her belly. Her pathetic conscience had blocked the only escape I could think of, and she had sunk my plan. And I sank too. Sank to my knees on the floor of my office, laid my head on the great carved chair that had always belonged to the Master of Wideacre, hid my face in my hands in that unyielding walnut seat and let my sobs shake me. I was utterly alone. I was desperate.

In the distance I heard a horse's hoofs on the drive and raised my head to listen. Then, to my horror, John MacAndrew's beautiful silver Arab horse was at my window, and John MacAndrew was looking down from his vantage point in the saddle to me kneeling, my dress creased, my eyes red, my head in my hands. His merry smile was wiped off his face and he wheeled Sea Fern around to the stable yard. I heard him shout for a groom and then open the side door of the west wing where the workers came for their pay. Then he was in the room without knocking and I was in his arms.

I should have pushed him away; I should have gone to my bedroom. I should have turned my face from him to look out of the window and said in cold tones that I had a headache, or the vapours, or anything, anything. Instead I clung to his lapels with two desperate hands and wept my heart out on his broad, comforting shoulder.

'Oh, John,' I said miserably. 'I am so glad you are here.'

And he, wise, tender lover, said nothing, not one word other than soothing, meaningless noises like, 'Hush, little darling' and, 'There, there, there.'

No one had smoothed my back while I sobbed since I had shrugged off my mama's caresses at six or seven, and the strange tenderness made me even more weak with self-pity. Finally my sobs subsided and John sat himself in the master chair without a word of by-your-leave, and drew me, unresisting, hopelessly compromised, on to his knee. One firm arm was around my waist, the other hand came under my chin and turned my face to meet his scrutiny.

'You have quarrelled with Harry? With your mama?' he asked.

'I can't explain,' I said, lost for a lie. 'Don't ask me. I just realized, because of something, that it is as you said: that I have no real home of my own. And I cannot bear to leave here.'

'I understand about Wideacre,' he said, his eyes scanning my tear-stained face. 'I understand. Although I cannot imagine feeling the same way about land, I do sympathize.'

I buried my head in the comfortable warm softness of his woollen jacket shoulder. He smelt of cigars and of the fresh autumn air, and also a hint of sharp clean shaving soap. With the tears drying on my cheeks I felt a rising awareness of him as a man, and our sudden, surprising embrace. I laid my face close to his neck and touched his throat, almost shyly, with my lips.

'Marry me, Beatrice,' he said, low-voiced at the first touch of my mouth on his skin. He turned his face down and caught the secret little kiss on his lips. 'I love you, and you know you love me. Say we can be married and I shall find some way to make you secure here, on the land you love.'

309

He kissed me gently on my sad mouth, and then, as the corners of my mouth curved up in a smile of pleasure, he kissed me harder. Then my arms were around his neck and I held his face to mine as he kissed every inch of my face: my sweet-smelling hair, my wet eyelids, my flushed cheeks, my ears, and then he pressed his mouth hard on mine and I tasted him with delight.

Then his mouth was on my face and my hair and the lobes of my ears, and I could not have told what I was doing or what I wanted. I was hardly an inexperienced girl, but somehow that clever man with the lazy veiled eyes had me off his knees and on the floor before the fire before I had decided, before I had even had time to think about what I was doing. And his hands were inside my gown, touching my breasts till I cried out for the feel of his weight coming down hard upon me. And his skilful doctor's hands were ruffling up my skirt and my petticoats before I had time to protest, or words to protest or, God knows, the least idea in my head of protest.

The door was not locked; the curtains were not drawn. Anyone could have driven past the window and glanced in, or any servant could have come to the door with candles. I did not think. I could not think. All there was in my head was a ripple of laughter at the outrageous way John MacAndrew was behaving, and a more serious longing like a cry, a sweet clear cry from my heart to his that said, 'Do not listen to all the refusals I have made to you. Let there be nothing more said between us. But love me, love me, love me.'

And then the one sane corner of my mind that was left noted that I was on the floor underneath him, and that my arms were around his neck, and my eyes were shut, and my lips smiling, and that a voice, my voice, was whispering his name and saying, 'Love me.' And he did.

And after I had cried out in pleasure – too loudly, too clearly, for safety – he said, very quietly but with great easiness and relief, 'Oh, yes, yes, yes.'

And then we lay still for a very long time.

Then the logs on the fire shifted and I jumped out of my trance, and struggled to be up with a guilt-stricken wriggle. And he took his weight from me, and helped me to my feet and pulled my creased skirts down for me with as much courtesy as if we were in a ballroom, and with a little secret smile to acknowledge the incongruity of it too. Then he sat himself back in the master chair and drew me to him again, and I laid my face against his cheek and smiled with secret delight, and nearly laughed aloud for my happiness.

When I opened my eyes we smiled at each other like conspirators.

'Beatrice, you strumpet, you have to be betrothed after that!' he said, and his voice was husky.

'I suppose I am then,' I said.

We stayed in my office as the sun set over the western fields and the evening star came out low on the horizon. The fire burned down to red embers and neither of us troubled to toss another log on. We kissed gently, lightly, and we also kissed hard and with passion. We talked a little, of nothing. Of the run we had out hunting that day, of Harry's incompetence as Master. He did not ask me why I had been crying, and we made no plans. Then I saw the candles lit in Mama's parlour, and the silhouette of the maid drawing the curtains.

'I thought it would hurt,' I said lazily, with one passing thought for my reputation as a virgin.

'After the horses you ride?' he asked with a smile in his voice. 'I am surprised you noticed it at all!'

I chuckled aloud at that, unladylike; but I felt too easy to pretend to be anything other than my sated, smiling self.

'I must go,' I said, scarcely stirring. As idle as a stroked cat on his knee. 'They will wonder where I am.'

'Shall I come, and shall we tell them?' asked John. He helped me stand and smoothed the back panel of my dress where the silk was creased and crushed from our long courting.

'Not today,' I said. 'Let it be just for you and me, today. Come for dinner tomorrow, and we can tell them then.'

He bowed in mock obedience, and let himself out of the west-wing door, with one final gentle kiss. His visit had passed unnoticed by Mama, by Harry and by Celia, but I knew that all the servants in the house and all the stable lads would know that he had been with me, and how long he had stayed. That was why no candles had been brought to my office as the light had faded. They had all conspired to leave John and me to court, like any village girl with her lover, in the gloaming by the fire. So, as is always the case, Wideacre people knew far more than Harry or Mama would ever have guessed.

Next day, when John came to take me for a drive before dinner, Harry, Mama and Celia paid little attention, but every servant in the house was smiling and peeping from the windows or hovering in the hall. Stride announced to me with elaborate ceremony that John was waiting ʌ his curricle in the drive, and when he handed me up I felt as if I were being led to the altar. And I did not mind.

'I trust you are not abducting me today,' I said, and twirled my parasol, sunshine yellow, over my yellow bonnet and yellow woollen dress.

'No, I'll content myself with the sight of the sea from the top of your downs today,' he said easily. 'Do you think we can get the curricle up the bridle-way?'

'It'll be a squeeze,' I said, measuring the shafts and the pair of glossy bays with my eyes. 'But if you can drive a straight line it should be possible.'

He chuckled. 'Oh, I'm a poor whipster, I know. Utterly incompetent. But you can always put a hand on the reins to keep me straight.'

I laughed outright. One of the things I liked about John MacAndrew the most was his immunity to my experimental slights. He had a hard core of resilience that meant he never winced at my attacks. He never even seemed challenged by them. He took them as part of a game we played – and he confessed incompetence or inadequacy without a blush, to bluff and double-bluff me into laughter and confession.

'I beg your pardon,' I said gaily. 'I dare say you could drive your curricle and pair up the staircase without blowing the horses or scraping the varnish.'

'I could indeed,' he said modestly. 'But I would never do it, Beatrice. I would never show you up. I know how ashamed you are of being cow-handed.'

I gave an irrepressible chuckle and gazed into his disconcertingly bright eyes. When he teased me in this way his eyes were as bright as if he were kissing me. Then he pulled the horses to a standstill before the fence and footstile up to the downs, and he climbed down from the driving seat and hitched the reins to the post.

'They'll keep,' he said, dismissing hundreds of guineas of bloodstock as he held an arm to me as I dismounted. He held my hand as I climbed over the stile; walking up to the crest of the downs he still kept it. I should choose no other place for courtship. But I believe I should have been happier on that day if I had not been mere yards from where Ralph and I used to lie, hidden in bracken, or if I had not seen, a dozen yards to the right, the little hollow where I had slapped Harry's face and ridden him to utter pleasure.

'Beatrice,' said John MacAndrew, and I turned my face up to his.

'Beatrice . . .' he said again.

It is as Ralph said. There are those who love and those who are loved. John MacAndrew was a great giver of love and all his wit and all his wisdom could not prevent him loving and loving and loving me, whatever the price. All I had to do was to say yes.

'Yes,' I said.

'I wrote to my father some weeks ago to acquaint him of my feelings, and he has treated me well; I should say generously,' said John. 'He has given me my shares of the MacAndrew Line outright, to do with what I will.' He smiled. 'It is a fortune, Beatrice. Enough to buy Widacre over and over.'

'It's entailed; Harry could not sell,' I said, my interest suddenly sharpened.

'Aye, that's all you think of, isn't it?' said John ruefully. 'I meant only to tell you that it is a fortune enough to buy or rent any nearby property you desire. I have told my father that I shall never return to Scotland. I have told him that I will marry an Englishwoman. A proud, difficult, stubborn Englishwoman. And love her, if she will let me, every day of her life.'

I turned to him, my eyes bright with tenderness, my face smiling with love. After Ralph I had not expected to love again. With Harry, I had thought my passion would last for ever. But now I could scarcely remember the colour of their eyes. I could see nothing but John's blue eyes bright with love and the smile of tenderness on his face.

'And I shall live here?' I asked, confirming my luck.

'And you shall live here,' he promised. 'If the worst comes to the worst I shall buy the Wideacre pigsties for you, so long as we are on the sacred soil. Will that satisfy you?' In impatience and in love he scooped me up into his arms and held me, hard as iron. In a great sweep of my familiar half-forgotten sensuality I felt my knees buckle beneath me when I was held by a passionate man again. When we broke apart we were both breathing in gasps.

'So we are formally affianced?' he demanded tersely. 'You will marry me, and we will live here, and we will announce it at dinner?'

'I will,' I said, as solemnly as any bride. I thought of the baby heavy in my lower belly, and the warmth of desire lighting me up. And a leaping satisfaction in the MacAndrew fortune with which I could do so much for Wideacre.

'I will,' I said.

We clasped hands and turned back to the curricle. The horses had stood quiet, nibbling at the dark leaves of the autumn hawthorn hedge, and a blackbird sang sadly in the wood.

John had to back down the narrow track until we came to a gateway where we could turn, then he held the horses in hard down the length of the bridle-way until we were on the level sweep of the drive and heading for home.

The beech leaves fell around us like bridal rice as we passed slowly up the drive; John was in no hurry to be home. The copper beech trees were purple-black this autumn, while the leaves on other trees that had been deliciously green were yellow and orange, unbelievably bright colours even in the fading light. My favourite trees, or nearly my favourites, the silver birches, were as yellow as buttercups and shimmered like gold against the silver of the white trunks. The hedgerows were ablaze with red hips from the dogroses, and black glossy elderberries nodded where the creamy flower heads had been.

'It is a fine country,' John said, following my loving eyes as I looked all around me at the familiar but always different trees, and hedgerows, and ground. 'I do understand that you love it.'

'You will come to love it too,' I said certainly. 'When you live here, when you spend your life here, you will care for it as I do, or nearly as much as I do.'

'No one could equal your passion, I know,' he said teasingly. 'It is not the same for Harry, is it?'

'No,' I said. 'I think only my papa cared for it as I do, and even he could bear to be away from it for shooting or for a season in town. I would be happy if I never left the estate again as long as I live.'

'Perhaps we may take leave of absence once a year,' said John, laughing at me. 'And when it is a leap year we might go to Chichester!'

'And for our tenth anniversary treat I shall let you go to Petworth!' I said, not to be outdone.

'We are agreed then,' he said, smiling at me. 'And I am well content with the bargain.'

I smiled in return and then we rounded the drive and drew up outside the steps where the candles stood in the parlour windows to light our way home.

The announcement that John made after dinner, when the servants had withdrawn and the fruit and cheese were laid out, was greeted with as little surprise as we could wish. And as much joy. My mama's face was tender with tears and smiles as she held out both hands to John and said, 'My dearest boy, my dearest boy.'

He took both hands and kissed them, and then hugged her to him and kissed her soundly on both cheeks.

'Mama!' he said outrageously, and earned himself a tap from her fan.

'Impertinent boy,' she said lovingly, then she held her arms wide to me and I moved close to her for the first sincere, warm-hearted hug I think we had ever exchanged.

'Are you happy, Beatrice?' she asked under the hubbub Harry was making with the bell, ringing for champagne, and slapping John on the back.

'Yes, Mama,' I said truthfully. 'I really am.'

'And at some sort of peace at last?' Her eyes scanned my face, trying to understand the puzzle that was her daughter.

'Yes, Mama,' I said. 'I feel as if something I have waited for has finally come to me.'

She nodded then, satisfied. She had seen the key to all sorts of puzzles in the dim awareness of her mind. The smell of milk on me when Celia and the baby and I returned from France, my nightmares after my father's death, the disappearance of my childhood playmate, the gamekeeper. She had never dared to grasp the thread and let it lead her through the maze to the monstrous truth. So now she was well pleased to have thread, maze, monster and all safely buried as if they had never been.

'He is a good man,' she said, looking at John who had one arm around Celia's waist, and was laughing with Harry.

'I think so, indeed,' I said, following her gaze. John, ever watchful of me, caught my look upon him and released Celia with exaggerated suddenness.

'I must remember I am an affianced man!' he said, teasing. 'Celia, you must forgive me. I forgot my new state.'

'But when will you be a married man?' she asked gently. 'Beatrice, do you plan a long engagement?'

'Indeed not,' I said without reflection. Then I paused and looked at John. 'We have not discussed it, but I should certainly like to be married before Christmas and before lambing.'

'Oh, well, if the sheep are to be the arbiters of my married life I suppose it should be whenever is convenient to them,' John said, ironically.

'You will call the banns and have a full Wideacre wedding,' begged Mama, visualizing the dress and the attendants and the party and the feasting on the estate.

'No,' I said firmly and with an assured glance at John. 'No, however it is done it should be quiet. I could not stand a full-blown affair. I should like it to be quiet and simple and soon.'

John nodded, a silent gesture of absolute agreement.

'It should be as you wish, of course,' said Celia diplomatically, glancing from Mama to me. 'But perhaps a very small party, Beatrice? With just a few of your family, and John's and your best friends.'

'No,' I said inexorably. 'I know the fashion is changing but I stick to the old ways. I should like to wake up in the morning, put on a pretty gown, drive to church, marry John, come home for breakfast, and be out in the afternoon checking fences. I do not want one of these fashionable fusses made over what should be a private affair.'

'And neither do I,' said John, coming to my support when I needed it.

'They're right,' said Harry with traditional loyalty. 'Mama, Celia, you need say no more. Beatrice is famous for her love of the old ways; it would be an absolute blasphemy for her to have a modern wedding. Let it be as Beatrice says – a quiet, private affair – and we can have our party at Christmas as a joint celebration.'

'Very well then,' said Mama. 'It shall be as you wish. I should have enjoyed a party, but as Harry says we can make it a special Wideacre Christmas instead.'

She earned a smile from me for that compromise. And her son-in-law-to-be kissed her hands with an elegant air.

'Now,' said Celia, turning to the most interesting question. 'We shall have to redecorate the west wing for the two of you. How would you like it done?'

I surrendered then.

'Any way, any way at all,' I said, throwing my hands up. 'Any way you and Mama think is the best. All I specify is that there shall be no pagodas and no dragons.'

'Stuff,' said Celia. 'The Chinese fashion is quite *démodé* now. For you, Beatrice, I shall create a Turkish palace!'

So, between teasing and good decisions, John and I had our way of a private wedding and his removal, with the minimum of fuss, into a broad fine bedroom adjoining mine, a dressing room leading off it, a study downstairs facing over the kitchen garden for his books and his medicines, and an extra loosebox in the stables for his precious Sea Fern.

But we decided to have a wedding trip: just a few days. John had an aunt living at Pagham and she lent us her house. It was an easy afternoon's drive – an elegant small manor house with a welcoming wide-open door.

'There's no land attached to it,' said John, noting my raking glance out of the parlour windows. 'She owns it merely as a house and garden. There is no farm land. So you need not plan your improvements here.'

'No, it is Harry who is the one for the new methods,' I said, returning without apology to the table where John sipped his port and I was toying with candied fruit. 'I was thinking only that if the fields were planted longways instead of in patches as they are, it would make a better run for the plough.'

'Does that make much difference?' asked John, an ignorant town dweller, and a Scot.

'Oh, heavens, yes!' I said. 'Hours in the day. The longest, worst part of ploughing is turning the horses. If I had my way we would farm only in strips. Lovely long reaches so the horses could go on and on without stopping. Straight, straight, straight.'

John laughed outright at my bright face.

'All the way to London, I suppose,' he said.

'Ah, no,' I disclaimed. 'That is Harry again. It is he who wants lots more land. All I want is the Wideacre estate properly rounded off and enclosed, and properly yielding. Extra land is a pleasure to own, but it is new people to know and new fields to learn. Harry would buy it as if it were yards of homespun. But it is different to me.'

'How is it?' he prompted. 'How is the land different from all other goods, Beatrice?'

I twisted the slender stem of my wine glass and looked down at the tawny liquid in the bowl.

'I cannot really explain,' I said slowly. 'It is like some sort of magic. As if everyone secretly belonged somewhere. As if everyone had a horizon, a view, that perhaps they may never see, but if they did, they would recognize it as if they had waited all their lives for it. They would see it, and they would say, "Here I am at last." It's like that for me with Wideacre,' I said, conscious that I felt far more than I could say. 'As soon as I fully saw it – one day, years ago, when my papa took me up on his horse and showed me the land – in that second I recognized my home. For Harry it would be any land, anywhere. But for me it is Wideacre, Wideacre, Wideacre. The only place in the world where I can put my head to the earth and hear a heart beating.'

I fell silent. I had said more than I had meant to. I felt at once foolish, and perilously exposed. My fingers still twirled the glass and I kept my eyes down on them. Then they were stilled, as John put his pale-skinned hand over them.

'I will never take you away, Beatrice,' he said tenderly. 'I do indeed understand how your life is here. It is a tragedy for you, I think, not to have been born the heir to the land. But I do see how you are indispensable on the estate. I hear on all sides how well you manage it, how you change Harry's plans so that they work in practice as well as in theory. How you never give charity, but always give help. How the land and the people who work the land benefit over and over again from your passion. And so I pity you.' My head jerked up in instinctive contradiction, but my protest was stilled by his gentle smile. 'Because you can never possess your beloved Wideacre. I will never come between you and your control of the land, but I am unable, no one is able, to make the land you love absolutely yours.'

I nodded. A few pieces of the puzzle of my new husband had fallen into place. His understanding of what Wideacre meant to me had prompted his agreement to our living in the west wing. His understanding of my obsession had led him to disregard my first refusal. He knew we could be lovers. He knew we could be married. He knew that one of the greatest things in his favour was that he owned no land, no house of his own where I would have had to go. He knew also, for he was so good, this serious, quizzical, desirable husband of mine, that his smile set my pulse thudding, and when he touched me, I melted.

I had never slept all night with a lover in one bed without fear of morning, and that was good for me. But best was his desire, which drew him to me for more times than I could remember in a hazy night of pleasure and wine and talk and laughter.

'Ah, Beatrice,' said John MacAndrew, pulling my head on to his shoulder with tender roughness. 'It's a long while I've been waiting for you.'

And so we slept.

And in the morning, over the fresh-baked rolls and the strong coffee, he said, 'Beatrice, I think I may like being married to you.' I found then that my smile was as warm and spontaneous as his own, and that the warmth on my face was a blush.

So the first days of married life passed as easily, as tenderly, and as full of delight, as the first months, aided by our mutual desire. John had had other lovers (and, God knows, so had I), but together we found something special. A mixture of tenderness and sensuality made our nights sweet. But our days were special because of his quick wits and his utter refusal to cease laughing: at me, with me, because of me. He could set me laughing at the most inappropriate moments: when faced with a rambling complaint from old Tyacke, or when listening to some mad scheme of Harry's. Then I would glance past Tyacke to see John pulling his forelock to me in burlesque imitation of respect, or see him nodding enthusiastically behind Harry's back while Harry outlined an insane plan to build massive glass-houses to grow pineapples for London.

At times like that, and they came every sweet cold wintry day, I would feel that we had been married and happy for years, and that the future stretched before us like easy stepping stones across a slow river.

Christmas came round and the tenants were bidden to the traditional party. The biggest houses in the land let the tenants and labourers watch the Quality feasting and dancing, but the Wideacre tradition is that of a manor farm. We set up great trestle tables and benches in the stable yard, and we build a great bonfire and roast whole oxen. After everyone has eaten well, and drunk deep of Wideacre-brewed ale, we push the tables back, throw off the winter wraps and dance in the pale winter sunshine.

This party, the first since Papa's death, was held under the clear blue sky of a good winter's day, and we danced all afternoon with sunshine warm on our cheeks. As the bride, it fell to me to lead the set and with a half-apologetic smile at John I claimed Harry's hand for the dance. Behind us the set formed, mimicking our handclasp. Behind us, as well, formed the traditions I had meant to set: that the Squire and his beautiful sister always led the Christmas dance in the stable yard. The next couple was Celia, looking breathtakingly pretty in royal blue velvet trimmed with white swan's down, and my darling John, ready with a gentle word for Celia and a private smile for my eyes alone.

They started the music. Nothing special: a fiddle and a bass viol, but it was a fast merry tune and my crimson skirts swirled and swayed as I twirled one way, then another, and then clasped Harry's two firm hands and romped down the avenue of faces. Harry and I stood at the bottom making an archway with our arms and the rest of the set danced through. Then we became part of the smiling, clapping corridor for Celia and John.

'Are you happy, Beatrice? You look it,' called Harry to me, watching my smiling face.

'Yes, Harry, I am,' I said emphatically. 'Wideacre is doing well, and we are both well married. Mama is content. I have nothing left to wish for.'

When Harry's smile widened, his face, increasingly plump from the offerings of Celia's cook, became even more complacent.

'Good,' he said. 'How well everything has turned out for us all.'

I smiled, but did not reply. I knew he was reminding me of my early opposition to the idea of marriage with John. Harry had never understood why my utter refusal had turned into smiling consent. But I knew he was also thinking of my promise and threat that I would be on Wideacre, at his side, for ever. Harry both dreaded and longed for time alone with me in the locked room at the top of the west-wing stairs. However loving he found Celia, however full his life, he would always long for that secret perverse pleasure waiting for him beyond the light of the chandeliers, beyond the usual halls and corridors of the house. Since my marriage I had met Harry in secret there perhaps two or three times. John accepted easily my excuse of late work, and he himself sometimes stayed overnight with patients if he anticipated a painful birth or a difficult death. During those times, while he waited and watched with the birthing and the dying, I strapped my brother to the wall and ill-treated him in every way I could imagine.

'Yes, it is good,' I agreed.

It was our turn to gallop down the set. We had risen to the head again while we were talking, and again we clasped hands and danced down the line. As we reached the end the musicians rippled a chord signifying the end of that dance and Harry spun me round and around so that my crimson brocade skirts flew out in a blaze of colour. I was unlucky the dizziness tipped me from elation to nausea, and I broke from him white-faced.

John was at my side in an instant. Celia, attentive, beside him.

'It is nothing, nothing,' I gasped. 'I should like a glass of water.'

John snapped his fingers peremptorily to a footman and the icy water in a green wine glass washed down the taste of rising bile, and I cooled my forehead on the glass. I managed a cheeky smile at John.

'Another miracle cure for the brilliant young doctor,' I said.

'It's as well I have the cure, since I think I provided the cause,' he said in a low warm voice. 'There's been enough dancing for you for one day. Come and sit with me in the dining room. You can see everything there, but you may dance no more.'

I nodded, and took his arm into the house, leaving Celia and Harry to head the next set. John said not a word until we were seated by the window that overlooked the yard, with a pot of good strong coffee beside us.

'Now, my pretty tease,' he said, handing me a cup just as I liked it, without milk and with lots of brown treacly sugar. 'When are you going to condescend to break the good news to your husband?'

'What *can* you mean?' I asked, widening my eyes at him in mock naivety.

'It won't do, Beatrice,' he said. 'You forget you are talking to a brilliant diagnostician. I have seen you refuse breakfast morning after morning. I have seen your breasts swelling and growing firm. Don't you think that it's about time you yourself told me what your body has already said?'

I shrugged negligently, but beamed at him over my cup.

'You're the expert,' I said. 'You tell me.'

'Very well,' he said. 'I think it well we married speedily! I anticipate a son. I think he will arrive at the end of June.'

I bowed my head to hide the relief in my eyes that he had no doubt that I had conceived on that one occasion before our marriage, and no idea that the child was due in May. Then I looked up to smile at him. He was not Ralph. Nor was he the Squire. But he was very, very dear to me.

'You are happy?' I asked. He moved from his chair to kneel beside mine and slide his arms around my waist. His face nuzzled into my warm perfumed neck and into the fullness of my breasts – pushed up by the unbearably tight lacing of my stays.

'Very happy,' he said. 'Another MacAndrew for the MacAndrew Line.'

'A boy for Wideacre,' I corrected him gently.

'Money and land then,' he said. 'That's a strong combination. And beauty and brains as well. What a paragon he will be!'

'And a month early for the conventions!' I said carelessly.

'I believe in the old ways,' said John easily. 'You only ever buy a cow in calf.'

I had worried about telling him, but no shadow ever came into his mind, not in that first tender moment, nor at any later time. When he discovered how tight I was laced and insisted that I came out of my stays, he merely teased me for my size – he never dreamed that I was five weeks further on in my pregnancy than our lovemaking before the fire would have allowed. All through the icy cold winter when my body was burning at night and so firmly rounded, he merely enjoyed my happiness, and my confident, daring sensuality without question.

No one questioned me. Not even Celia. I announced that the baby would be born in June, and we booked the midwife as if she would be needed then. Even when the long icy winter turned green I remembered to hide my rising fatigue and pretend I was blooming with mid-pregnancy health. And a few weeks after the first secret movement I clapped my hand to my belly to say, in an awed whisper, 'John, he moved.'

I was aided in the deception by John's own ignorance. He might have been qualified at the first university in the country, but there were no women of Quality who would allow a young gentleman near them at such a time. Those who preferred a male *accoucheur* would choose an old, experienced man, not the dashing young Dr MacAndrew. But the majority of ladies and women of the middling sort held to the old ways and used the midwives of the district.

So the only pregnancies John had supervised were those of the poorer tenant farmers and working women, and those only by chance. They would not call him in, fearing the cost of professional fees, but if he was in a Quality house visiting a sick child, the Lady of the house might mention that one of the labourers' wives was having a difficult birth, or that one of the parlourmaids was pregnant. So John saw births only where there were grave dangers, and only those of poor women. And while he looked at me with his tender sandy-lashed gaze I was able to lie, with all my experience, with all my skill, and with a silly hope of keeping our happiness safe: to keep things as tender and as loving as they were.

Love him I did, and if I wanted to keep his love he would have to be out of the way when the child he thought was his was born, supposedly five weeks premature.

'I should so like to see your papa here again,' I said conversationally one evening, while the four of us were seated around the fire in the parlour. Although the blossom glowed in the trees and the hawthorn was white in the hedges, it was still cold after sunset.

'He might come for a visit,' said John dubiously. 'But it's the devil's own job detaching him from his business. I nearly had to go and drag him away by the coat-tails in time for the wedding.'

'He would surely like to see his first grandchild,' said Celia helpfully. She leaned towards the ever-open workbox, which stood between us, and selected a thread. The altar cloth was half completed and I was employed in stitching in some blue sky behind an angel. A task not even I could spoil, especially since I made one stitch and laid down the work every time I wanted to think or speak.

'Aye, he's a family man. He would fancy himself the head of a clan,' John said agreeably. 'But I would have to kidnap him to get him away from the business during the busiest time of year.'

'Well, why don't you?' I said, as if the idea had, that second, struck me. 'Why do you not go and fetch him? You said yourself you were missing the sweet smells of Edinburgh – Auld Reekie! Why not go and fetch him? He can be here for the birth and stand sponsor at the christening.'

'Aye.' John looked uncertain. 'I would like to see him, and some colleagues at the university. But I would rather not leave you thus, Beatrice. And I would rather make a visit later when we could all go.'

I threw up my hands in laughing horror.

'Oh, no!' I said. 'I have travelled with a newborn child already. I shall never forgive Celia for that trip with Julia. Never again will I travel with a puking baby. Your son and I shall stay put until he is weaned. So if you want to visit Edinburgh inside two years, it had better be now!'

Celia laughed outright at the memory.

'Beatrice is quite right, John,' she said. 'You can have no idea how dreadful it is travelling with a baby. Everything seems to go wrong, and there is no soothing them. If you want your papa to see the baby it will have to be him who comes here.'

'You're probably right,' said John uncertainly. 'But I would rather not leave you during your pregnancy, Beatrice. If anything went wrong I would be so far away.'

'Ah, don't worry,' said Harry comfortingly from the deep winged chair by the fireplace. 'I will guarantee to keep her off Sea Fern and Celia can promise to keep her off sweetmeats. She will be safe enough here, and we can always send for you if there is any trouble.'

'I should like to go,' he confessed. 'But only if you are sure, Beatrice?' I poked my needle in an embroidered angel's face to free my hand to hold it out to him.

'I am sure,' I said, as he kissed it tenderly. 'I promise to ride no wild horses, nor get fat, until you return.'

'And you will send for me if you feel in the least unwell, or even just worried?' he asked.

'I promise,' I said easily. He turned my hand palm up, in the pretty gesture he had used in our courtship, and pressed a kiss into it, and closed my fingers over the kiss. I turned my face to him and smiled with all my heart in my eyes.

John stayed only for my nineteenth birthday on the fourth of May when Celia had the dining room cleared of furniture and invited half-a-dozen neighbours in for a supper dance to celebrate. More tired than I cared to show, I danced two gavottes with John and a slow waltz with Harry before sitting down to open my presents.

Harry and Celia gave me a pair of diamond ear-drops, Mama a diamond necklace to match. John's present was a large heavy leather box, as big as a jewel case with brass corners and a lock.

'A mineful of diamonds,' I guessed, and John laughed.

'Better than that,' he said.

He took a little brass key from his waistcoat pocket and handed it to me. It fitted the lock and the lid opened easily. The box was lined with blue velvet, and nestling securely in its bed was a brass sextant.

'Good heavens,' said Mama. 'What on earth is it?'

I beamed at John. 'It is a sextant, Mama,' I said. 'A beautiful piece of work and a wonderful invention. With this I can draw my own maps of the estate. I won't have to rely any more on the Chichester draughtsmen.' I held out my hand to John. 'Thank you, thank you, my love.'

'What a present for a young wife!' said Celia wonderingly. 'Beatrice, you are well suited. John is as odd as you!'

John chuckled disarmingly. 'Oh, she's so spoiled I have to buy her the strangest things,' he said. 'She's dripping with jewels and silks. Look at this pile of gifts!'

The little table in the corner of the dining room was heaped with brightly wrapped presents from the tenants, workers and servants. Posies of flowers from the village children were all around the room.

'You're very well loved,' said John, smiling down at me.

'She is indeed,' said Harry. 'I never get such a wealth of treats on my birthday. When she's twenty-one I shall have to declare a day's holiday.'

'Oh, a week at least!' I said, smiling at the hint of jealousy in Harry's voice. Harry's summer as the pet of the estate had come and gone too quickly for him. They had taken him to their hearts that first good harvest, but when he had come home from France they had found that the Squire without his sister was only half a Master, and a silly, irresponsible half at that.

My return from France had been a return into pride of place and the presents and the deep curtsies, bows, and loving smiles were the tribute I received.

I crossed to the table and started opening the gifts. They were small, home-made tokens. A knitted pin cushion with my name made out of china-headed pins. A riding whip with my name carved on the handle. A pair of knitted mittens to wear under my riding gloves. A scarf woven from lamb's wool. And then a tiny package, no bigger than my fist, wrapped, oddly, in black paper. There was no message, no sign of the sender. I turned it over in my hands with an uneasy sense of disquiet. My baby stirred in my belly as if he felt some danger.

'Open it,' prompted Celia. 'Perhaps it says inside who has sent it to you.'

I tore the black paper at the black seal, and out of the wrapping tumbled a little china brown owl.

'How sweet,' said Celia readily. I knew I was staring at it in utter horror and tried to smile, but I could feel my lips trembling.

'What is the matter, Beatrice?' asked John. His voice seemed to come from a long way off; when I looked at him I could hardly see his face. I blinked and shook my head to clear the fog and the buzzing sound in my ears.

'Nothing,' I said, my voice low. 'Nothing. Excuse me one minute.' Without a word of explanation I turned from the pile of unopened gifts, and left my birthday party. In the hall, I rang the bell for Stride. He came from the kitchen doors smiling.

'Yes, Miss Beatrice?' he said.

I showed him the black wrapping paper balled in my hand, I had the little china owl tight in the other hand. I could feel the coldness of the porcelain and it seemed to make me shiver all over.

'One of my presents was wrapped in this paper,' I said abruptly. 'Do you know when it was delivered? How it came here?'

Stride took the crumpled paper from me and smoothed it out.

'Was it a very little package?' he asked.

I nodded. My throat was too dry to trust my voice.

'We thought it must have been one of the village children,' he said with a smile. 'It was left under your bedroom window, Miss Beatrice, in a little withy basket.'

I gave a deep shuddering sigh.

'I want to see the basket,' I said. Stride nodded, and went back through the green baize door. The coldness of the little owl seemed to chill me through and through. I knew well enough who had sent it. The crippled outlaw who was all that was left of the lad who had given me a baby owl with such love four years ago. Ralph had sent me this ominous birthday gift as a signal. But I did not know what it meant. The dining room door opened, and John came out exclaiming at my white face.

'You are overtired,' he said. 'What has upset you?'

'Nothing,' I said again, framing the word with numb lips.

'Come and sit down,' he said, drawing me into the parlour. 'You can go back to the dancing in a minute. Would you like some smelling-salts?'

'Yes,' I said, to be rid of him for a moment. 'They are in my bedroom.'

He scanned my face, and then left the room. I sat cold and still and waited for Stride to bring me the little withy basket.

He put it in my hands and I nodded him from the room. It was Ralph's work, a tiny replica of the other basket I had pulled up to my window seat in the dawn light on my fifteenth birthday. The reeds were fresh and green, so it had been made in the last few days. Wideacre reeds perhaps, so he could be as close to the house as the Fenny. With his basket in one hand, and his horrid little present in the other, I gave a moan of terror. Then I bit the tip of my tongue and pinched my cheeks with hard fingers to fetch some colour to them, and when John came back into the room with my smelling-salts I had a hard laugh ready, and I waved them away. Smelling-salts, questions, grave looks of concern, I dismissed airily. John watched me, his eyes sharp and anxious, but he pressed no questions on me.

'It is nothing,' I said. 'Nothing. I just danced too much for your little son.' And I would say no more.

I dared not give him reason to stay. With my baby due in three or four weeks, I had to have him away. So I hid my fear under a bright brave front, and I packed his bags for him with a light step and an easy smile. Then I stood on the steps and waved his chaise out of sight, and I did not let myself tremble for fear until I had heard the hoofbeats of the horses cantering away down the drive.

Then, and then only, I leaned back on the sun-warmed doorpost and moaned in fright at the thought of Ralph daring enough to ride or, even more hideous, to crawl right up to the walls of the Hall, and hating enough to remember what he had given me for a present four years before.

But there was no time for me to think, and I blessed the work and the planning that I had to do, and my tiredness during the days and my heavy sleep at nights. In my first pregnancy I had revelled in slothful inactivity in the last few weeks, but in this one I had to pretend to three pairs of watchful eyes that I was two months away from my time. So I walked with a light step and worked a full day, and never put my hands to my aching back and sighed until my bedroom door was safely shut and I could confess myself bone-tired.

I had expected the birth at the end of May, but the last day of the month came and went. I was so glad to wake to the first of June. It sounded, somehow, so much better. I recounted the weeks on my fingers as I sat at my desk with the warm sun on my shoulders and wondered if I should be so lucky as to have a late baby who hung on to make my reputation yet more secure. But even as I reached for the calendar a pain gripped me in the belly, so intense that the room went hazy and I heard my voice moan.

It held me paralysed for long minutes until it passed and then I felt the warm wetness of the waters breaking as the baby started his short perilous journey.

I left my desk and tugged one of the heavy chairs over to the tall bookcase where I keep the record books that date back to the Laceys' first seizure of the land seven hundred years ago. I had rather feared that it would hurt me to climb on to the seat and to stretch up to the top shelf. And I was right. I gasped with the pain of stretching and tugging at the heavy volumes. But the scene had to be set, and it had to be persuasive. So I pulled down three or four massive old books and dropped them picturesquely around the chair on the floor. Then I turned the chair over with a resounding crash and lay down on the floor beside it.

My maid, tidying my bedroom above, heard the noise of the falling chair and tapped on the door and came in. I lay as still as the dead and heard her gasp of fright as she took in the scene: the overturned chair, the scatter of books and the widening stain on my light silk skirt. Then she bounded from the room and shrieked for help. The household exploded into panic and I was carried carefully and tenderly to my bedroom where I regained consciousness with a soft moan.

'Don't be afraid,' said Mama, taking my cold hand. 'There is nothing to fear, darling. You had a fall from a chair in your study and it has made the baby come early. But we have sent for the midwife and Harry will send post to John.' She leaned over the bed and stroked my forehead with a handkerchief that smelled of violets. 'It is too soon, my darling,' she said gently. 'You must prepare yourself for a disappointment this time. But there will be other times.'

I managed a wan smile.

'I am in God's hands, Mama,' I said, blaspheming easily. 'Does it hurt very much?'

'Ah, no,' she said tenderly. 'It will not hurt you, my brave girl. You have always been so full of courage and so dauntless when you faced pain or fear. And besides, it will only be a small baby for it is early.'

I closed my eyes as the familiar grip of the pain closed on me.

'Mama, could I have some lemonade like you used to make when we were ill?' I asked, as soon as it had passed.

'Of course, my darling,' she said, and bent to kiss me. 'I'll go at once and make some. But if you need me you can ring, and Celia will stay with you. Mrs Merry, the midwife, is on the way, and a groom is riding for Mr Smythe, the Petworth *accoucheur*, so you will be well attended, my darling. Rest now, as much as you can. It all takes a long, long time.'

I lay back and smiled. It would not take a long, long time, and Mr Smythe had better stir himself or he would miss his fee. Second babies always come more quickly, I knew, and I could feel the pains growing ever more intense and with less time to rest between them. Celia sat beside my bed and held my hand as she had done once before.

'It is like waiting for Julia,' she said, and I noticed her eyes were filled with tears. She was deeply moved at the prospect of birth, this pretty, barren woman. 'You did so well then, dearest, I know you will manage wonderfully now.'

I gave her an absent-minded smile, but it seemed already as if she were far, far away. I could think of nothing but the struggle going on inside me between the child battling to be free, and my tense body refusing to yield easily. A sudden rush of pain made me groan, and I heard a clatter as a housemaid dropped her end of the family cradle outside the door. Every single servant in the house was dashing around to get a nursery ready for the new unexpected baby: the first of this generation to be born at Wideacre into the Wideacre cradle.

The pains came faster, except they had ceased to be pain and were more like a great strain of heaving a chest of drawers upstairs or pulling on a rope. Mrs Merry was in the room but I scarce heeded her as she bustled around tidying, and tying a twisted sheet from one bedpost to another. My only response was to snap at her when she urged me to pull on it. I wanted none of that lunging, shrieking women's toil when inside me was a secret, private progress, which was my son edging his way through my reluctant tunnels. She took no offence, Mrs Merry. Her wise old wrinkled face smiled at me and her shrewd eyes took in my curved back and the cooing, moaning sounds I was unconsciously making, and the rocking of my body.

'You'll do,' she said, as I would speak to a brood mare. And as calmly as I could wish she unpacked some darning and sat at the foot of the bed until I needed her aid.

It did not take long.

'Mrs Merry!' I said urgently. Celia flew to hold my hand, but my eyes sought the knowing smile of the wise woman.

'Ready now?' she asked, rolling her dirty sleeves up.

'It is . . . it is . . .' I gasped like a floundering salmon as the power of birth once again grabbed my rigid heaving belly like an osprey and shook me in its talons.

'Push!' yelled Mrs Merry. 'I can see the head.'

A spasm overwhelmed me, and then I paused. Another great thrust and I could feel Mrs Merry's skilled, grimy fingers poking around, gripping the baby, and helping it to force its way out. Then another shove of muscle and flesh came, and the thing was done, and the child was free. A thin burbly wail filled the room and from behind the closed door I heard a ripple of exclamations as every servant who could possibly be in the west wing heard the cry.

'A boy,' said Mrs Merry, swinging him by his ankles like a newly plucked chicken and dumping him without ceremony on the quivering mound of my belly. 'A boy for Wideacre; that's good.'

Celia's guileless, suspicionless eyes were on the new baby.

'How lovely,' she said, and her voice was full of love and longing, and unshed tears.

I gathered him up into my arms and smelled the sweet strong unforgettable smell of birth on him. In a rush, suddenly, scalding tears were pouring down my cheeks and I was sobbing and sobbing. Weeping for a grief I could name to no one. For his eyes were so very dark blue and his hair so very black. And in my tired and foolish state I thought he was Ralph's baby. That I had given birth to Ralph's son. Mrs Merry scooped him out of my arms and bundled him, wrapped in flannel, towards Celia.

'Out of the room altogether,' she advised briefly. 'I've a hot posset brewing for her that will have her right as a trivet. It's good for her to have a weep now – it gets it out early rather than later.'

'Beatrice crying!' said Mama with amazement in her voice as she bustled into the room and stopped still at the sight of me face down amid the rumpled sheets.

'It's all been too much for her,' said Celia gently. 'But look at Baby. What a miracle. Let's settle him down and come back to Beatrice when she is rested.'

The door closed behind them and I was alone with my sudden inexplicable sorrow, and with sharp-eyed old Mrs Merry.

'Drink this,' she said, and I choked on a herbal posset that smelled sweetly of mint, lavender and, probably most fortifying of all, gin. I drained the mug and the tears stopped rolling down.

'A seven-month-old child, eh?' she asked, eyeing me, bright with her secret knowledge.

'Yes,' I said steadily. 'Brought on by a fall.'

'Large baby for seven months,' she said. 'Came fast for a first, too.'

'What's your price?' I asked, too weary to fence with her and too wise to try to lie.

'Nay,' she said. Her face creased with her smile. 'You've paid me all you need by calling me in. If the bright young doctor's wife sticks to the old ways then half the ladies of the county will do so too. You've given me my living back, Miss Beatrice. They won't be so quick to call in Mr Smythe when they know I delivered you on my own.'

'You know I keep to the old ways in everything I can. In conception too,' I said with a smile and dawning confidence. 'And what I say on Wideacre is law. There will always be a cottage for you on my land, Mrs Merry, and always a place laid for you in my kitchen. I don't forget my friends . . . but I hate gossip.'

'You'll hear none from me,' she said firmly. 'And there's none that can swear to the age of a child at birth. Not even that clever young husband of yours could do so. And if he's not back inside a week or so, I should think there would be no telling – Edinburgh-trained or no!'

I nodded, and leaned back against the pillows while she changed the wet sheets skilfully, without disturbing me, and then turned and patted the pillows behind me.

'Fetch my son, Mrs Merry,' I said suddenly. 'Bring him in to me. I need him.'

She nodded, and went heavily from the room and came back with a bundle of blankets slung carelessly over her shoulder

'Your mama and Lady Lacey wanted to see you, but I said not yet,' she said. 'Here's your lad. I'll leave you alone together to get acquainted, but you lie quietly in bed. I'll come and fetch him shortly.'

I nodded, but I scarcely heard her. His blue eyes looked into mine unseeing. His face was a crumpled moon with neither shape nor structure. His only clear features were his mass of black, black, hair, and those piercing, near-violet eyes. I threw the covers back and stepped barefoot on to the cold floorboards and walked across to the window with him in my arms. His body was tiny, as light as a doll, fragile as a peony. I flung the window open and sighed as the sweet-scented, flowering, fruiting smells of a Wideacre early June breathed into the room. Before me the rose garden was a mass of dense pink and crimson and white, the heady perfume swelling up the sun-warmed stones of the house to my window. Beyond the garden the paddock gleamed emerald with the lush summer growth, ankle-deep, knee-deep grass. And behind the paddock the grey trunks of the beech trees supported a shifting cloud of melting greenness mixed with the deep, almost violet, splashes of the copper beeches. Above and beyond the tossing heads of the trees were the pale squares of the highest fields on the flanks and shoulders of the downs, and then above them, higher than one can imagine, higher than one remembers, the great head of the downs and the rolling crescent of the green line of horizon that encircles Wideacre.

'See this?' I said to the baby, and faced his little lolling head outwards. 'See this? All this is mine and it will, one day, be yours. Other people may think they own it, but they do not. It is mine, and I endow you with it. And here starts a new battle to make sure that you own it, my son, in full. For you are the heir, you are the son of the Squire, and the son of the Squire's sister, and so you own it doubly. But more than that: you own it because you will know it and love it as I do. And through you, even after my death, the land will be most truly mine.'

I heard Mrs Merry's heavy tread in the corridor outside my room and I slammed the window shut and leaped back to bed like a naughty schoolgirl. I paid the price in faintness when I was back on the pillows, but my son, my lovely son, was taken to Mama and Celia and I was left to blissful sleep and dreams of a future that suddenly seemed so much more of a challenge, and yet so much brighter.

I spent the next week in a world of contented mothering as sensuously delighted as a feeding cat. I lived in a haze of daydreams with only one constant thought in my mind – how to force Harry to make his son the heir to Wideacre without revealing the truth of his parentage. I knew my pernickety brother well enough to know that he would be repelled at the idea of an incestuous child. Even my own pragmatic mind tended to shy away from the thought, and I sensed that any hint of my son's true father would mean only disaster and the end of my plans and hopes. But somehow there had to be some way to give this perfect second child – my son, my boy – equal rights with my first child – Julia. The tangle of injustice and ill luck was the only flaw in my happiness during my moments of solitude. But for the rest I dreamed, and crooned, and sang over my baby, my son, my perfect son.

His fingernails were so delightful. Each tiny slender finger smaller than a twig was crowned with a perfect nail, even a little white tip to it. And each fingertip carried its own perfect little circle. And his tiny feet, so small and so plump and yet with such lovely little bones that one could feel through the firm flesh. And the sweet-smelling crannies of his neck, and his tiny ears curled like shells, and his perfect *ooo* of a mouth. When he was hungry and reached for my hard, oozing nipples his little face contorted and the mouth became a little triangle of longing. Then when he had sucked himself into a collapse of milky unconsciousness his upper lip showed the sweetest blister from sucking so hard.

I revelled in the hot June days so he could lie naked, kicking on my bed, while I patted him with powder, or rubbed him with oils after his bath. And I insisted, as Celia had done before me and at last I understood, that his little legs should not be strapped down with swaddling but allowed to be free. So the whole of

Wideacre now ran to the schedule of two small tyrants instead of one: the perfect Julia, and the equally perfect Richard.

For Richard was to be his name. Why it came to my lips I never knew, except that Ralph's name was in my mind as soon as I saw that jet-black wet head, so perhaps the 'R' was on my tongue before I could catch it. An odd slip for me, and I never make odd slips. But darling Richard made me careless. I dreamed for him, and planned for him, but for the moment I had lost my old angry, lying, cutting edge. I had the folly to fail to prepare for anything. I neither planned nor prepared what I should say if anyone challenged me about his age. For he was a plump, healthy baby, feeding every three or four hours, not a skinny early child at all. Celia said nothing. Whatever would Celia know? But the household knew – in the way that servants always do. And if they knew then Acre knew too – I understood without asking.

But ours is a country area. There are few marriages in the parish church that take place without a good round belly on the bride. For what is the point of a wife who cannot be shown to be fertile? The other way is the Quality way, but you end up with the bad bargain that Harry got – a barren wife and no hope of issue. Everyone in the village, just like everyone at the Hall, and, for all I know, everyone in the county, assumed that John and I had been lovers before our marriage and thought none the worst of me, or of him, for it.

Only Mama dared to face that trivial sin.

'He's such a big baby for his age,' she said, looking at us both as I crooned over him as he lay on my bed, replete after a feed, his little milky face puffed up in delight. His eyes closed in his plump doze.

'Yes,' I said, absently, watching his eyes.

'Did you mistake your dates, my dear?' Mama asked, her voice low. 'He seems so plump and well for a baby born so early.'

'Oh, come, Mama,' I said idly. 'You must see perfectly well. He was conceived when John and I were affianced. I go by the old ways; he was conceived with my betrothed. There's no harm in that.'

Mama's face was a picture of disapproval.

'There's nothing morally wrong with it, Beatrice, I know,' she said. 'And if your husband has no objection it is not my place to make any complaint. But it is typical of your country childhood and your obsession with country values. I should not have dreamed of such a thing. I am glad you are no longer in my charge.'

And with that, she swept out of the room in high dudgeon, leaving me to laugh at her with Richard who neither laughed nor cried, but lay, somnolent in the sunshine, as if his mama could be a self-confessed strumpet every day of her life.

The fiction that he had been conceived by John before our marriage was so persuasive that I did not trouble myself about John's return and what he might think. I knew little of babies, and I thought that three weeks in infancy would make little difference. I could scarcely remember the first days of Julia, but I had a recollection of her filling out once she got to England and looking much the same from birth till then. And the success of the deception with Julia had made me confident. I had done it once. I had spoken vaguely of a baby coming early, of the inaccuracy of a young bride's calculations. It had been done easily and without challenge. I did not think it would be so different with Richard. I could see no reason why my husband, however clever and skilled, should be able to distinguish between a strapping boy child born a little later and one born three weeks early. Some extra days and he might have been sure of nothing.

But he came early.

He came earlier than we expected. He was with us inside the week, travelling post like a demon and bribing the coach boys to ride day and night and not stop for food. He hammered up the drive in a filthy post-chaise and thundered into the house and into the parlour. Mama was at the piano, Celia with Julia on her knee, and I was seated in the window seat with Richard in the wooden cradle rocking beside me. John was white with fatigue, smelling of whisky, his face dirty, and shabby with beard. He looked around incredulously as if he could not believe the existence of this scented parlour, this domestic peace. Then his red-rimmed eyes focused on me.

'Beatrice, my love,' he said, and was down on one knee beside me, one arm around my waist, his chapped dry mouth hard on mine. The door behind him slammed as Mama and Celia whisked out to leave us alone.

'My God,' he said with a deep tired sigh. 'I had imagined you dead, or ill, or bleeding, and here you are, as lovely as an angel and as well.' He raised his eyes and scanned my clear face. 'You are indeed well?' he said.

'Oh, yes,' I said, tenderly and low. 'And so is your son.'

He gave an exclamation and turned to the crib, a smile of wonderment half hovering around his tired mouth. Then the half-smile was wiped from his face and he bent over the cradle with eyes that were suddenly hard.

'Born when?' he asked, and his voice was cold.

'June the first, ten days ago,' I said, trying to keep my voice even; as a man crossing a frozen river tries to spread his weight by sliding.

'Some three weeks premature, I think?' John's voice was as sharp as a shard of cracking ice; I felt myself beginning to tremble with unexpected fear.

'Two or three,' I said. 'I am not utterly sure . . .'

John lifted Richard from the cradle with expert, unloving hands, and unwrapped his shawl. Ignoring my half-hearted protest he undressed him so swiftly and skilfully that the baby did not even cry. He pulled gently at the little legs and on the hands, and he prodded the rounded belly. His taper doctor's fingers encircled the plump wrist and the betraying chubby knees. Then he wrapped the baby in the shawl again and put him gently back in the cradle, holding the head steady until the child was safe. Only then did he straighten and face me. As I saw the look in his eyes the thin ice broke beneath me and I plunged down into an icy blackness of discovery, and ruin.

'That baby was carried full term,' he said, and his voice was a splinter of frozen glass. 'You had him in your belly when you lay with me. You had him in your belly when you married me. You doubtless married me for that very reason. That makes you a whore, Beatrice Lacey.'

He stopped, and I opened my mouth to speak, but no words came. All I could feel was a pain in my chest as if I was drowning in icy water trapped under a low ceiling of ice in a frozen river.

'You are something else, too,' he said, his voice flat. 'You are a fool. For I loved you so much I would have married you and taken on your child if you had asked it of me. But you preferred to lie and cheat and steal my good name.'

I put my hands up as if to ward off a blow. I was ruined. My son, my precious son was ruined too. I could find no words to protect us, nothing to make us safe.

He took half-a-dozen hasty steps to the door and opened and shut it quietly. My nerves cringed, waiting for the slam of the door to the west wing but none came. A hushed click of the library door was all. Then the house was as silent as if we had all been frozen in time, and the ice of my sin had killed even the warm heart of Wideacre.

I sat without moving as a finger of sunlight moved slowly across the room mirroring the sun's slow afternoon pace across the sky. It failed to warm me, and I shivered even while I felt my silk dress grow hot. Every one of my senses was on edge to hear movement in the library, but I heard nothing. The peaceful tick of the parlour clock was as gentle and as regular as a heartbeat, the louder clicking of the grandfather clock in the echoing hall subdivided the slow seconds.

I could wait no longer. I crept from the room and listened outside the library door. There was no sound, but the room was full of a presence. I could sense him, like a deer senses a waiting hound. I stood stock-still, my eyes wide with fear, my breath unconsciously shallow. I could hear nothing. My mouth was dry with terror . . . so I went in. I am, after all, my father's daughter. Afraid as I was, my instinct was to face it and go on into it. I turned the doorknob and it yielded. It opened a crack and I froze in fright, and then, when nothing happened, pressed it open a little further so that I could peep into the room.

He was in the winged armchair with his filthy riding boots on the velvet cushions of the window seat, staring sightlessly over the rose garden. One hand was loosely clasped around a glass and a bottle of the MacAndrew whisky was tucked into the cushions of the chair. The bottle was nearly empty; he had been drinking on his journey and now he was drunk. He turned to stare at me as I walked into the centre of the room, my ivory skirts hushing on the Persian carpet. His face was a stranger's – a mask of pain. There were lines I had never seen before on either side of his mouth and his eyes looked bruised.

'Beatrice,' he said, and his voice was a gasp of longing. 'Beatrice, why did you not tell me?'

I stepped a little closer and my hands moved out to him, palms outspread as if to say I had no answer.

'I would have cared for you,' he said, his eyes luminous with tears, the skin on his cheeks shiny where tears had spilled over and dried. The lines on either side of his mouth as deep as wounds. 'You could have trusted me. I promised you I would care for you. You should have trusted me.'

'I know,' I said, my own voice breaking on a sob. 'But I did not know. I could not bring myself to tell you. I do so love you, John.'

He gave a moan and shifted his head on the back of the arm-chair as if my love for him confirmed and did not ease his pain.

'Who is the father?' he asked dully. 'You were lying with him while we were courting, weren't you?'

'No,' I said. 'No, it wasn't like that.' Under his agonized stare my eyes dropped to the floor. I could see every thread in the carpet under my feet, every strand of the pattern. The white wool gleamed like a fresh-clipped sheep, the blues and greens as bright as kingfisher wings.

'Is it something to do with the china owl?' he asked abruptly, and I jumped at the sharpness of his perception. 'Something to do with the sailor on the beach that day? The smuggler?' he demanded. His eyes bored into me. He had all the pieces of the puzzle in his hand, but he could not see how to put them together. Our happiness and our love were in pieces too, and I could not see how to mend them. Just then, in that cold room by the empty grate, I would have given all I owned to have his love once more.

'Yes,' I said with a shuddering sigh.

'Is it the gang leader?' he asked. His voice was very low, as tender of my feelings as if I were one of his patients.

'John . . .' I said imploringly. His quick mind was taking me helter-skelter down a road of lies and I could not see where I was going. I could not tell the truth. But I had no lie that would satisfy him.

'Did he force you?' John asked, his voice very, very gentle. 'Did he have some power over you, perhaps Wideacre?'

'Yes,' I breathed, and I glanced at his face. He looked as if he were on a rack. 'Oh, John!' I cried. 'Don't look at me like that. I tried to be rid of the baby but it would not die! I rode like a mad woman. I took some horrid stuff. I did not know what to do! I wish, I wish I had told you!' I dropped on my knees beside his chair and covered my face in my hands and wept like a peasant woman by a deathbed. I did not dare so much as touch his hand on the arm of the chair. I could only kneel beside him in an agony of misery and loss.

In the haze of my grief I felt the kindest touch of all the world. His hand on my bowed, curly head. I raised my face from my hands and looked at him.

'Oh, Beatrice, my love,' he said brokenly.

I shifted so I could put my wet cheek against his hand. He turned his hand palm up to cup my face and I laid my face along it, my eyes searching.

'Go now,' he said gently, and there was no anger but a lifetime of sorrow in his voice. 'I am too tired and too drunk to think straight. I think this is the end of the world, Beatrice. But I do not want to speak of it until I have had time to think. Go now.'

'Will you go to your room and sleep?' I asked tentatively, anxious for his comfort and dreading the lines of fatigue and pain on his face.

'No,' he said. 'I will sleep here. But ask them not to disturb me. I want to be alone for a while.'

I nodded as I heard the dismissal of me in his voice and got to my feet with a little sob of pain. He did not touch me again, and I went, slow-paced, towards the door.

'Beatrice,' he said softly, and I turned at once.

'This is the truth?' he asked, scanning my face. 'It was the smuggler, and he forced you?'

'Yes,' I said. There was nothing else I could say. 'As God is my witness, John, I was not willingly unfaithful to you. I would never have betrayed you if it had been my own free choice.'

He nodded then, as if my oath might serve us as a stepping stone across his river of grief, where we could meet on some safe shore. When he spoke no more to me I went quietly out of the room.

I went out. I threw on a shawl and went out bare-headed without bonnet or cap on my chestnut coils of hair. Of course I went outside. Whenever my heart is aching I walk through the rose garden, through the little gate into the paddock, past the horses who come so loyally and lovingly to greet me and nuzzle my pockets for titbits, through the lychgate into the wood and on down to the Fenny. I walked without stopping in my silk shoes, which were stained and muddy by the time I came home, and with my fine afternoon tea gown dragging in the meadow grasses.

I walked with my head high and my hands in fists, with tears drying on my cheeks. I walked as if I were out taking the air, a young wife taking time to be alone to savour her joy at the safe return of her adoring husband. Counting her blessings: a healthy first-born son, a husband who had driven like a maniac to come to her, and a secure and beautiful home. But I was not counting my blessings; I was mourning my loss.

For I loved John. I had loved him as my equal – my equal in rank, something Ralph and I had never had, for I never lost my sense of Ralph's gypsy blood. I loved him as my equal in wits – something I never had with Harry, whose book learning seemed to make him slower rather than quicker. My lean, lovely quick-witted husband had won me body and mind, and that had been a new pleasure to me, which I thought I would never cease to enjoy. And now our peace hung on a thin thread of my own spinning, and a breath of truth could snap it in two. I had won no security on Wideacre, though I had done everything a woman could do to keep myself safe inside its lovely borders. When I paid my rent with Harry, those dark nights had brought me to bed with a child, and that child would be my undoing. My husband could cast me off and I would be sent away in shame, or he could take me away, away from Wideacre.

The pain that had been knocking against my ribs with every step I took rose in my throat then and I groaned and leaned my head against the trunk of a tree. A great spreading horse chestnut tree. I rubbed my forehead on the comforting rough bark and then turned around and leaned my back against it and looked upwards. Against the blue sky of a June afternoon the pink fat candles of the flowers glowed as sweet as icing on one of Harry's puddings.

'Oh, John,' I said sadly.

And there seemed no other words.

Of all the people in the world I would have willingly seen him hurt last of all. He might reject me; we might never again be lovers. I could not believe that it would be me who caused him such unbearable pain. I could not believe that things could not come right between us. My face was still warm from his kiss of greeting; I could still remember the feel of his arms holding me hard against him in his passion and relief at seeing me. It was too soon, far too soon for me to start thinking that this man might turn against me, might cease to love me.

I stood beneath the broad branches and felt the chestnut flower petals drift down on my hair, and brush my cheeks like more tears. I could almost have thrown Wideacre – house and land – into the sea rather than break the heart of that good man who loved me. Almost.

I waited for the comfort that the wood always gave me. I glanced towards the Fenny to see its eternal shimmer between the sweet greenness of the summer trees. I closed my eyes to hear better the loving coo of the wood pigeons, and the distant call of a cuckoo far away, somewhere up on the downs.

But the old easy magic of the land did not work that day, did not ease my sadness. In the library the man I loved and trusted was tumbling into sleep rather than face me and the child I had hoped he would love. And the only way I knew back into his heart and his trust was a massive lie that I would have to find the nerve and the wit to make stick when he was sober and awake again. So I retraced my steps home, dry-eyed and white-faced, and with my heart still crying inside me.

I dawdled through the rose garden and plucked one of the early roses, a white rose, creamy as milk, with dark shiny leaves I kept it with me when I went back indoors and laid it on my dressing table when my maid plaited and powdered my long chestnut hair. When I went down to dinner, as regal as a queen, I held it between my fingers and pricked my hand on its sharp thorns when I felt the tears rising.

Mama and Celia were ready to tease me at John's absence. Celia had ordered his favourite meal of wild duck cooked in limes, and I advised that we eat without him and save his portion for him to dine later.

'He is exhausted,' I said. 'He has had a long, long journey, and no company save a crate of his papa's whisky. He left his valet behind him several stages back, and his luggage will not yet have reached London. He has ridden too fast, too far. I think we had better leave him to rest.'

I kept the white rose beside my plate all through dinner. In contrast with the greenish purity of the deep centre the napery seemed cream, and the candle flames yellow. The talk flowed easily between Harry, Celia and Mama, and I had only to say an occasional word of assent. After dinner we sat before the fire in the parlour while Celia played the piano and sang, and Mama stitched, and Harry and I sat before the fire, and watched the flames together.

When the tea tray came in, I murmured some excuse and left the room. John was still asleep in the library, sprawled in his chair. He had drawn his favourite chair up to the window and had set a table beside it with a glass and the bottle to hand. From where he was sitting he would have seen me walking to the wood and had perhaps understood the droop of my shoulders and my unusual slow pace. If he had felt any ache of love then, he had drowned it well. The bottle was empty, and rolled under his chair dripping a stain of whisky on the priceless Persian carpet. His head was tipped back on the cushions and he was snoring. I spread a travelling rug from the chest in the hall over his outstretched legs. I tucked the folds around him as tenderly as if he were mortally ill, and when I was certain he would not wake I kneeled beside him and placed my cheek to his stubbly unshaven dirty face.

There was nothing more I could do.

My heart ached.

Then I straightened, pinned a calm and confident smile on my face and went back to the candlelit parlour for my tea. Celia was reading a novel aloud to us and that saved me from conversation. Then, when the clocks in the hall and in the parlour chimed eleven o'clock in a clear duet, Mama sighed, and straightened up from the remorseless work of the altar cloth.

'Goodnight, my dears,' she said, and kissed Celia who rose to sketch a curtsy. Then she dropped a kiss on the top of my head, and pecked Harry's cheek as he held the door for her.

'Goodnight, Mama,' he said.

'Are you off to bed too, Celia?' I asked.

Though a wife of two summers, Celia still knew her place.

'Shall I?' she asked the air midway between Harry and me.

'Go and warm my bed,' Harry smiled at her. 'I need to talk some business with Beatrice. But I won't be long.'

She kissed me, and tapped Harry's cheek with her little fan as he held the door for her too. Then he returned to his seat at the fireside beside me.

'Business?' I asked, cocking an eyebrow at him.

'Hardly,' he said with a knowing smile. 'I thought, Beatrice, that you might have recovered from the birth by now. I was thinking about the room at the top of the stairs.'

A great weariness flowed through me.

'Oh, no, Harry,' I said. 'Not tonight. Physically I am well, and we will meet there soon, but not this evening. John is home, and Celia is waiting for you. We will meet there perhaps tomorrow night.'

'Tomorrow John will be rested and you will have no time free from him,' Harry said. He looked like a spoilt child denied a plaything. 'Your only free time for weeks is likely to be tonight.'

I sighed with weariness and distate for Harry's selfish, insistent lust.

'No,' I said again. 'It is not possible. The room is cold and in darkness. I have not ordered a fire. We will meet there in the near future, but tonight is not possible.'

'Here then!' said Harry, his face lighting up. 'Here before the parlour fire. There is no reason why we should not, Beatrice.'

'No, Harry,' I said, with rising irritation. 'John is asleep in the library but he could wake. Celia is waiting for you upstairs. Go to Celia, she wants you.'

'But tonight I want you,' said Harry stubbornly, and I saw the mulish look around his soft mouth. 'If we cannot go to the room we need not do so, but then I want you here.'

The last event I wanted to crown this long lonely day was a romp with Harry on the hearth rug, but the prospect seemed unavoidable.

'Come on, Beatrice,' he said, boisterous as a puppy, and he

kneeled at my feet and hugged around the waist with one arm, and fumbled in my silk skirts and petticoats with the other.

'Very well,' I said crossly. 'But let be, Harry, you will tear my dress.' I loosened my stays with quick fingers, and lifted my skirts and petticoats, and lay before the fire. With Harry in his mood of obstinate insistence I could see that the quickest, easiest way to resolve this conflict was to pay my dues swiftly. Harry was urgent and the whole tedious exercise should not take more than a few minutes. Already, at the mere sight of me, he was breathing heavily and his round face was rosy in the firelight. He had stripped naked from the waist down, and I lay back ungraciously to let him push, unwelcomed, inside me.

'Oh, Beatrice,' he said, and I smiled ruefully at the realization that he actually preferred my unenthusiastic coupling to Celia's loving kisses in the Master's bed. As his body started its well-known rocking pushes I surrendered myself to the easy, familiar pleasure. I raised my hips a fraction and felt him sigh as he eased in yet more deeply. Then I forgot my unwillingness as my body caught the rhythm of his movement, and waves flowed from the very central hot core of my body down to the very tips of my toes. I was caught in the easy seductive pleasure of the moment, deaf and blind to all else.

In the distant back of my mind I heard a sound quite different from Harry's stifled groans, different from my light panting, the sound of a door opening . . . click . . . and then, too late, too late, one hundred years too late, I realized that the noise was the parlour door opening and the click was the latch dropping as my mother's hand fell from the doorknob.

Everything moved so slowly that it seemed pointless to try to respond. My eyes opened as languidly as if they had pennies weighting the lids. With my brother still heaving up and down upon me, I met my mother's gaze.

She was standing frozen in the parlour door, the candles from the hall illuminating as bright as daylight the scene before her. Harry's humping, moonlike, fat, white buttocks, and my pale face, staring speechlessly at her over his velvet-jacketed shoulder. The disaster dawned on us all as slowly as sunrise.

'I left my novel,' she said stupidly, as she stared at the two of us, coupled before the dying embers of the fire. Harry was frozen.

He still lay on me but his head was slewed round to face her, his blue eyes goggling, his red face sweaty.

'I came to fetch my book,' she said. Then the candelabra dropped from her hand and she reeled backwards into the hall as if the sight of us, her two children, meant instant death to her.

Harry gasped, like a punctured bladder of wind, but her collapse had released me from my trance. I moved as fast as I could, but still with nightmare slowness – as if I was drowning in the Fenny and struggling through green weeds under a roof of ice. In one sleek movement I slid up and off Harry and pulled my petticoats and dress down, and retied my laces.

'Get your breeches up,' I hissed at him, jolting him into life, and he scrambled to his feet and fumbled for his clothes. I strode to the door and nearly fell over Mama, who lay in a crumbled heap beside her smoking candles. In the cruel light of the hall she looked not white but green, as if she too were trapped in an under-river world of horror. Some random instinct made me feel for a pulse in her neck, and then for her heart. She looked like death, and I could feel no heart beating.

'My God!' I said incredulously. Then, in rapid decision, I said, 'Harry! Help me carry her to her bed.'

Wig off and wild-eyed, Harry scooped the body of our mother in his arms. I preceded him up the stairs, the single candle flame making hobgoblin shapes of Harry and his burden all the way up. He laid her on the bed and we gazed in joint consternation at her pallor and her deathlike stillness.

'She looks very ill,' said Harry. In my trance of horror even his words seemed to come slowly, from a long way away.

'I think her heart has stopped,' I said coldly. 'I could not feel it beat.'

'We must get John,' said Harry, and moved to the door. I put out a hand instinctively to stop him.

'No, Beatrice,' he said firmly. 'Whatever else takes place we must safeguard Mama's health.'

I let out a long, shuddering, silent laugh.

'Oh, yes,' I said. 'You do your duty, you threepenny-halfpenny Squire.' And I turned my face from his with utter loathing.

Thus they found me, still as a statue, gazing down into Mama's

347

cold face, not touching her. Harry had half carried John up the stairs, John still reeling from fatigue and blind with drink. Harry had said nothing, merely shaken John awake and poured water over him. His real self was still unconscious in a whisky-aided morass of misery. But his professional training burned like a clear torch inside the collapse of his self. God knows it is the truth, and an odd truth; I loved him especially then when his self-discipline surfaced from the sea of fatigue, alcohol and misery, and guided his red-rimmed eyes over Mama's greenish face and placed his shaky hands on her pulse.

'Out, Harry,' he said. His breath was foul with exhaustion and drink, but no one could have gainsaid him. 'Beatrice, my bag is in your office. Fetch it.'

Harry and I fled the room like thieves, Harry to the parlour to set the rug straight, and to tidy up; I to the west wing for John's medical bag. I straightened my dress as I went, but I had not time to clear my mind. It took me valuable seconds to find it, and then I returned, through the door into the hall, up the arching stairs to Mama, where she lay murmuring to the pillows and to the unresponsive roof of her four-poster bed, over and over, 'Harry, Harry, Harry.' I knew with some clear-sighted coldness that she knew what she had seen, and that her voice, her cracked hoarse voice, was calling her son back from the abyss of hell, back from the dark tunnel of sin, back from the embrace of his sister, back from his adult life, to be her boy, her curly-haired sinless child again.

'Harry,' she said in a moan, 'Harry, Harry, Harry.'

In a sudden terror I looked from her to John. His eyes were blank, impassive. He had not yet put his skilled, his knowledge-able mind to what she was saying.

'Harry!' said my mother, in her dreamy monotone.

'Beatrice.'

John's eyes upon me were blank with incomprehension, but I knew it would not last. He would find his way to the centre of the maze. I had chosen this clever, loving man because he was the best I had ever met: the best suited for me, the cleverest mind to meet mine, the wittiest brain to grapple with mine. Now I had launched his wits against me, and I could not tell where he would make landfall.

'I only wanted my novel,' said Mama, as if that explained everything. 'Oh Harry! Beatrice! *No!*'

But John was thinking only partly of what Mama was saying; he was also watching her breath, the movement of her hands across the sheets as they plucked at the counterpane in a ceaseless, worried gesture.

'She has had a shock,' John said to me, as if I were a medical student in the Royal Infirmary interested in diagnosis. 'It nearly proved too much for her, and I do not know what it was. But she is deeply disturbed. If she can be kept from thinking of it, whatever it is, for one, maybe two or three days, it is possible that she will come to face whatever she fears without her heart stopping. It will be a close thing, but I think it can be done.'

He took a phial from his worn bag and a delicate medicine glass with a little spout to help a patient drink. He unstoppered the phial and counted the drops into the glass. His trained, disciplined skill kept his hand steady, though I could see the sweat on his face at the effort.

'One, two, three, four,' he said meticulously, with the alcohol slurring his words. 'She's to have four drops, every four hours. D'you understand me, Beatrice?'

'Yes,' I said.

He scooped Mama's limp body into one arm and expertly fed her the glass, and then laid her back on the pillows, straightening the covers across her and smoothing the pillows beneath her twisting head.

'Harry! Harry! Harry!' she called, but her voice was a little quieter.

'You will have to sit up with her; you, or Harry,' he said carefully. 'In four hours, not before, she may have four more drops. In four hours, not before, four more; until she sleeps naturally without seeming disturbed. Do you understand?'

'Yes,' I said again, my voice empty of feeling.

'Any more, and her heart will simply stop,' he said, warning me. 'She cannot take any more. She needs rest. But too much laudanum and she will slip away. Do you understand?'

'Yes,' I said again in the same monotone.

'Four drops, four-hourly,' he said again. His repeated instructions, the insistent moaning from the bed, the knowledge of my sin and the trap closing in around me made the bedroom like a deep pit. The candles on the bedside table guttered and the shadows of the room wavered towards me. My husband could not meet my eyes. My brother, who had been taken with me in sin, was nowhere to be seen. And in the bed beside me, my own mother droned like a lunatic.

John shut his bag with an effort, and stumbled towards the door.

'No more than four drops, no sooner than four hours. Do you understand, Beatrice?'

'Yes,' I said again.

He staggered from the room to the stairs. The clocks chimed midnight in an ominous chorus as he gripped the polished handrail to keep himself from falling. I held high the candelabra to light him down. His bag banged against each carved stairpost and nearly overset him. He staggered to the library door and nearly fell when it yielded under his hand. I set down the candles and glided downstairs like a ghost.

'Watch Mama,' I said to Harry, who stood, like an overstaying guest, at the parlour door. He nodded, in dumb misery, and I waited until he had climbed the stairs to Mama's room and shut the door, and then, for the second time that day, I gathered every scrap of courage I had, and opened the library door to face my husband.

He was back where he had been all day. But he had a fresh bottle of whisky gripped between his knees, a fresh glass of the amber liquid in his fist, his filthy boots up on the window-seat cushion, his head rolling on the armchair wings.

'What could have caused Mama's attack?' I asked, approaching the chair lit only by icy moonlight pouring in from the eerie silver landscape.

He looked at me, his face as puzzled as a small child who wakens in a darkened room and does not know where he is.

'I do not know,' he said. 'She keeps saying, over and over, "Beatrice" and "Harry" as if you two could help her. But I do not know what she means. Nor why she should keep saying, "I only came to fetch my novel." Do you understand that, Beatrice?'

'No,' I said, hoping that my lie, my certain lie, would carry the weight I needed. 'I do not know, John. Something has obviously upset her, but I do not know what it can be. I do not know what she was reading.'

He turned his face from me then, and I knew that he had forgotten his patient and remembered his wife.

'Go now, Beatrice,' he said piteously. 'You know I long to forgive you and make all well between us, but I am exhausted. I have cared for your mama as well as I am able. Her condition is stable; there is nothing more I can do for her tonight. I promise you she will live. I promise you I will speak to you tomorrow. But right now I feel that I must be alone. I must mourn. I came home a man full of dreams and I cannot tolerate the sudden change. Everything in my life is upside down. Give me a little time. Just give me tonight and I will be myself again.'

I nodded, and bent to kiss his forehead.

'I am sorry,' I said, and I told no lie. 'There is much that I have done wrong – how much you may never know. But I am sorry for the grief I have caused you. I love you, you know that.'

His hand touched mine, but he did not take my fingers in his firm grip. 'I know it, Beatrice. Now grant me a little time alone. I am drunk and tired and I cannot talk.'

I bent and kissed him again, and then I walked as silently as I could from the library. At the door I paused and looked back at him. He was in his own private world of drink and fatigue. As I watched he poured himself another glass of whisky and took a deep draught, holding the spirit in his mouth to savour it. The world seemed very unfair and bitter to me then. If only there could have been a different path to Wideacre.

But I could not sit in a library and say I needed time to think. Upstairs my mother moaned on her bed and my brother listened in mounting fear. Outside the land called and called for a clear master to rule it. I could never rest. There was always work to do for me.

Harry was sitting with Mama, his face as white as hers.

'Beatrice!' he said, as soon as I entered the room. He drew me away from the bed and spoke in a frantic undertone. 'Beatrice, Mama knows! She saw us! She is talking in her sleep, and she knows! Whatever shall we do?'

'Oh, stop it, Harry!' I said abruptly, too exhausted to soothe his conscience while my husband needed to rest from the sight of me, and my mama's heart stopped at my approach as if I were an angel of death.

'Stop it, Harry! It is all bad enough without you playing queen o' the may.'

Harry gaped at me and at the hard tone of my voice, and I pushed him ungently from the room. 'One of us has to sit with Mama and give her laudanum,' I said tersely. 'I'll stay up with her till three or four, then you can do the rest of the night. Go now, and sleep.'

He would have argued, but I gave him another two-fisted shove. 'Oh, go, Harry!' I said. 'I am sick of this night, and I am sick of you. Go and sleep now, so that I can sleep later, and in the morning we will find some way out of this coil. But for pity's sake go now.'

Some tone of desperation in my voice cut through Harry's old-maidish flappings, and he kissed my clenched fists without another word, and disappeared down the corridor to his bedroom. I turned on my heel and went wearily back into Mama's bedroom like a prisoner walking to the scaffold.

She was tossing on her pillows and moaning in horror. Now and again she would say 'Harry!' or 'Beatrice!' or 'No! No!' but the laudanum kept her from saying more. It was no pleasant vigil I spent there beside the shadowy bed. Downstairs my husband dozed and drank rather than look at me. Along the corridor Harry crept into the sheets longing for Celia's sinless honest warmth. In her bed my mama's heart struggled to keep beating despite its deadly knowledge. Only I was awake that night. Like a witch I sat in the moonlight and in the shadows and watched the silvery light make a magic path across the floor from my chair to Mama's bed. I gathered power around me from the sleeping black land outside the windows, and I waited for the moment when it seemed right to move.

The moon's slow pace across the clear sky made a river of light on the floorboards linking Mama and me for the last time. Then I trod lightly down that eerie track and looked at her. She stirred as if she felt my green-eyed gaze on her, but she did not wake. I watched her pale face and heard her rattl-ing, gasping breath, and smiled a gentle smile of certainty. I checked the clock, in another hour she would be ready for her next dose. I would wake Harry.

I slid like a ghost from the room to tap at his door, but it was Celia, not Harry, who opened it.

'Harry is asleep,' she said in a whisper. 'He told me that your mama is ill. Can I come and sit with her?'

I smiled like a woman possessed. It was all coming easily to my hand just as the moonlight had shown me the way to Mama's bed.

'Thank you, Celia. Thank you, my dear,' I said gratefully. 'I am so weary.' I had the phial of laudanum in my hand with the little medicine glass. 'Give her all of this in half an hour's time,' I said. 'John told me exactly what to do before he went back to the library. He said to be sure she takes all of it.'

Celia took the laudanum bottle and nodded her comprehension.

'I will make sure she does,' she said. 'Is John still weary?'

'He is rested now,' I said. 'He was wonderful with Mama, Harry will tell you. And so clear with his instructions!'

Celia nodded. 'You go and sleep now,' she said. 'I will call you if there is any change, but you need your rest, Beatrice. Go and sleep now, and I will give her the laudanum just as John directed.'

I nodded my acquiescence and left Celia at Mama's door. I went soft-footed down the stairs. I paused outside the library door to hear a stertorous breath. I pushed the door open cautiously, and went in.

Daylight was making the windows shady grey and I could just make out the wreck of the man who had once been proud to love me. He was still in his chair, but he had vomited, staining his plum travelling jacket and his riding breeches. At some time he had smashed his glass on the stone fireplace and instead drunk from the bottle, for it was almost drained dry. It had at last put him soundly to sleep. His medical bag was tumbled on the floor beside him, the pills and the little bottles spilling out of its open mouth.

Keeping my eyes fixed on his sprawled, sodden, stained body I held my skirts outwards and stepped backwards, slowly, slowly and silently, until I could close the door and turn the key to lock

353

him in. I wanted no loyal housemaid or young footman cleaning up Miss Beatrice's young husband before she saw him, to spare her pain.

Then, my silken evening gown whispering around me, I glided through the connecting door to the west wing, to my room.

My maid was long since abed, for I encourage no one to wait up for me past midnight. So I shifted for myself and slid out of my gown and sweaty petticoats. Half a lifetime ago, these had been pulled to my waist to enable me to couple with Harry. Now they seemed soiled in the ancient past, and I left them: gown, stays, petticoat, stockings and all, in a heap on the dressing-room floor.

From my cupboard I chose a light morning wrapper, as pink and promising as the rising sun, which I could see warming the rose garden. It was going to be a hot day. It was going to be a long hard day, and I would need my wits about me. The water in the ewer was cold, of course, but I splashed it on my face and all over my shivering body. Of all the people in this sleeping house I would need to be the most awake, the most alive. This day would be a trial in which my claim to Wideacre could turn on the flip of a coin. I would neglect nothing that would make me more alert, or stronger.

I slid on the cold silk wrapper, wrapped a shawl around my shoulders, and settled in my chair to wait. It must have been about an hour since I had left Celia, but I was too wary to creep back to the main part of the house to listen. I was wise enough, and controlled enough, to sit with my feet resting on a little stool, and wait for events to turn the way I had ordered. Then I heard a door bang, and the library door rattle, and Celia's voice sharp with fear calling for my husband.

'John! John! Wake up!'

I heard her bang the door to the west wing and I tore open my bedroom door to greet her on the stairs as if I had leaped from my bed on hearing her call.

'What is it?' I demanded.

'It is Mama,' she said desperately. 'I gave her the laudanum as you said, and she seemed to fall asleep. But now she seems too cold, and I cannot find her pulse.'

I held out my hands to her, and she gripped them hard, her

face absurdly young and anxious, then we turned and fled down the stairs together.

'John?' I asked her.

'I cannot wake him, and he seems to have locked himself in,' she said, despairingly.

'I have a spare key,' I said, and opened the door and flung it wide so Celia could see the chaos.

The morning light picked out the stains on John's clothes and the splashes of vomit on the stone fireplace and on the priceless rugs. In his doze he had knocked over the final bottle and his head lay in a pool of sour-smelling whisky. The chair was kicked over, and there was manure from his boots on the window-seat cushions. My husband, the light of the healing profession, lay like a dog in his vomit, unstirring even when we erupted into the room calling his name.

I strode over to the bell and rang a loud peal, and then picked up a jug of water and threw it into his face. He rolled his head in the wet and groaned. From the servants' quarters I heard a clatter of pans and hurrying footsteps, and from above I heard Harry pattering barefoot down the corridor and down the stairs. He and the scullery maid arrived together.

'Mama is worse, and John is drunk,' I said to Harry, conscious that every word would be relayed to Acre village and far beyond by the girl.

'Go to Mama,' Harry said authoritatively. 'I'll wake John.' He bent over my husband, and hauled him into a chair. 'A bucket of cold water,' he said to the girl, 'fresh from the kitchen pump, and a couple of pints of mustard and warm water too.'

'Then wake the stable lads and Stride,' I said to her as I went towards the stairs. 'Tell one of the lads to ride to Chichester. We need a competent doctor.'

I ignored Celia's gasp and went up to Mama.

She was dead, as I knew she would be.

She had not suffered, and I was glad of that, for Papa's death had been hard and brutish, and Ralph had a long vigil of agony. But this last and, I hoped, final death for Wideacre had been easy drugged sleep. She was lying on her rich, lacy pillows in her fancy new white and gold bed. The drug had seen her on her way smiling at pleasant visions. Under the massive overdose given her by the loving hands of her sweet daughter-in-law she had slid away from the nightmare truth of our lives into a palace of hallucination where nothing could ever disturb her again.

I kneeled at the bedside and put my forehead to her hand, and shed a few easy tears on the embroidered sheet.

'She is gone,' said Celia, and she knew there was no doubt.

'Oh, yes,' I said softly. 'But so peacefully, Celia, I have to be happy she went in such peace.'

'Although I ran for you and for John, I knew it was too late,' said Celia quietly. 'She was just like this then. I think she must have died as soon as I gave her the medicine.'

'John said her heart might not survive it,' I said. I rose to my feet and mechanically straightened the smooth covers, and then went to open the window and draw the curtains. 'But I wish to God he had sat with her.'

'Don't blame him, Beatrice,' said Celia, instantly tender. 'He had a long hard journey. He could not have anticipated that your mama would become ill so suddenly. He had been all this time away, and we have been with her every day and noticed nothing. Don't blame him.'

'No.' I turned from the window back into the shaded room. 'No. No one is to blame. We all knew Mama's heart was delicate. I do not blame John.'

Around us were all the noises of Wideacre awakening, yet curiously hushed, as the servants scurried to prepare the house and pass the news among each other in shocked whispers. Celia and I closed Mama's door, and went down to the parlour.

'Coffee for you,' said Celia tenderly, and rang the bell. As we sat in the parlour I could hear the heavy tread of Harry walking John up and down the library floor, marching him into consciousness. And then a muffled sound of choking as he forced the mustard and water down John's throat, and then a horrid retching noise as John vomited on the emetic and brought up neat whisky. Celia grimaced and we moved to the window seat where we could hear the morning birdsong instead.

It was a perfect, breathless morning with the smell of the roses and the meadows hanging on the warm air like a message of renewal. The fresh leaves of the beeches, still silvered with dew, shimmered in the wood, and in the valleys that intersect the green horizon of the downs the mist was rolling like pale gauze. It was a land worth anything, any price. And I linked my fingers around my cup of coffee with conscious justification, and drank deep of the scalding liquid.

The parlour door opened, and Harry came in. He looked white and stunned, but better than I had hoped. At least he did not look guilty – which was what I had feared. He held out a hand speechlessly to Celia and she ran into his arms.

'John is himself again,' he said to me over Celia's head. 'He could have chosen a better time to drink, but he is sober now.'

Celia disengaged herself, and poured him a cup of coffee. Harry dropped into his chair by the hearth, where the embers of last night's fire still smouldered.

'I have seen her,' he said briefly. 'She looks very peaceful.'

'She was,' Celia assured him. 'She said nothing. She just smiled, and fell asleep.'

'You were with her?' he said surprised. 'I thought it was Beatrice?'

'No,' said Celia, and I lowered my eyelids to hide the gleam of satisfaction at my magical luck. 'Beatrice went to bed after she woke me. I was with your mama when she died.'

I raised my eyes and saw John standing in the doorway listening. He had thrown a dressing-gown over his soiled linen and his face and hair were clean and wet from the soaking Harry had given him. He looked alert and awake. I tensed like a rabbit scenting a stoat.

'She had no more than the proper dose?' he said. His speech was still slurred and his head was weaving like a fighter who has suffered too many blows to the head.

'As you ordered,' I said. 'Celia did as you said.'

'Celia?' he said. His pale eyes squinted against the bright sunlight. He put up one dirty hand to shield his face from the bright light of the Wideacre sun. 'I thought it was you who was there, last night.'

'Get to bed, man,' said Harry coldly. 'You're still half foxed. You left Beatrice and me to nurse her, then Celia took my place. You yourself were little help.'

John stumbled to a chair near the door and stared at the floor.

'Four drops,' he said eventually. 'Four drops, four-hourly; that should not have been too much.'

'I don't know in the least what you're talking about,' I said, and my voice was like a sharp stone skimmed over a frozen river. 'You gave me a phial and told me to give it to her. Celia did so, and then she died. Are you telling us now you made a mistake?'

John squinted at me through his sandy lashes as if he was trying to see something in his memory that had escaped him.

'I don't make mistakes with medicines,' he said flatly, holding on to that one certainty.

'Then no mistake was made,' said Harry impatiently. 'And now get to bed. Mama has just died. You should show some respect.'

'Sorry,' said John inadequately. He stumbled as he rose to his feet. Harry, resigned, went to support him and nodded me to his other arm.

'Don't you two touch me!' he exclaimed, and he spun on his heel for the door. The swift movement was too much for his spinning head and his knees buckled. He would have fallen but Harry grabbed him and I went unwillingly to hold his other arm. We marched him, sagging between us, up the stairs to the west wing and slung him on to his bed.

I turned to go but John grabbed at my wrist with sudden strength.

'Four drops I said, didn't I, Beatrice?' he whispered. His eyes were suddenly bright with comprehension. 'But I know too what she was talking about. What she had seen. What she found when she came for her novel. Beatrice and Harry. I told you four drops, but you told Celia the whole phial, didn't you?'

I could feel the delicate bones in my hand starting to crack, but I made no effort to free myself. I had been readying for this since dawn and he could break my arm, but he could not defeat me. It hurt me still to lie so bold-faced, to the only other man who had loved me honestly, but I gave him look for look and my eyes were like green ice. Energy coursed through me for I was fighting for Wideacre. Against me, he was weak, just a drunk dreaming a nightmare.

'You were drunk,' I said bitingly. 'So drunk you could not choose the medicine. You spilled your medical bag all over the

358

library floor. Celia saw it this morning; the servants have seen it. You did not know what you were doing. You did not know what you were saying. I trusted you because I believed you were a great doctor, a truly great physician. But you were too drunk even to see her. If she had an overdose of laudanum it was you who put the drug in my hands and told me to give it to her. If she died because you gave her too much, then you are a murderer and should be hanged.'

He dropped my wrist as if it had scorched him.

'Four drops, four-hourly,' he panted. 'I would have told you that.'

'You remember nothing,' I said with utter conviction, with utter contempt. 'But what you should remember now, now you are sober, is that if there is any murmur of a question, any whisper of a question, about Mama's death, it needs only one word from me and you will hang.'

His pale eyes were wide with abhorrence and he gazed up at me from the pillow of the big bed as if I smelled of sulphur from the very depths of hell.

'You are wrong,' he whispered. 'I do remember; at least I think I remember it all. It is like a nightmare, so infamous I cannot believe it. But I do remember it, like a dream in delirium.'

'Oh, fustian!' I said, suddenly impatient. And I turned to leave. 'I'll send you up another bottle of whisky,' I said with disdain. 'You seem to need one again.'

And then I wavered.

All the time while I prepared for Mama's funeral, arranged the ceremony, invited the guests, discussed the dinner menu with Celia and organized the servants into black trimmings, I wavered. In the week before Mama's funeral my hand was on the doorknob to John's bedroom, I think, once a day. I had learned to love him so recently; I loved him still, in some small corner of my lying heart, so very much.

But then I would pause and think what he knew about me. I would think with a shudder what would become of me if he spread his foul talk into Celia's ears. If she and he together speculated about the father of Julia. And then my hand would drop from his door and I would turn away, my face hard, my eyes stony. He had seen into the depths of my crime. I saw a reflection of myself in his pale eyes that I could not bear. He knew the humiliating evil price I had paid to make myself secure on Wideacre and before him I was not just exposed and vulnerable. I was shamed.

So in all the bustle and confusion to plan and execute a respectable Wideacre funeral I did not forget to order Stride to take a fresh bottle of whisky up to Dr MacAndrew's bedroom and study every midday and dinnertime. Stride's eyes met mine with unspoken sympathy, and I managed a wobbly smile for him. 'Pluck to the backbone' was the verdict on me in the servants' quarters, and although John had prompt service to his ring for a fresh glass, or more water to take with his drink, he was despised in the servants' hall.

The rumour that his incompetence had caused Mama's death had spread through the Hall and beyond to Acre village, and for miles around. It had reached the ears of the Quality through a thousand tattling maids and valets. When John wished to return to the normal world of visits and parties and dinners he would find doors closed against him. There would be no entry for him into the only world he knew unless I reintroduced him with all my charm and power.

He was not even summoned as a doctor to the yeoman farmers' homes or to the Chichester and Midhurst tradesmen. Even the families of the middling sort had heard the gossip and there would be black looks for him in every village for a hundred miles around: for his drunken incompetence with Lady Lacey, and for grieving Miss Beatrice, the darling of the county.

My grief for a few days was real indeed. But as my fear of him and my sense of shame about his knowledge grew, I found I became colder and colder towards him. By the day of Mama's funeral, only one week after I had threatened him with a hanging if he tried to betray me, I knew I hated him, and I would not rest until he was off Wideacre and silenced for good.

I had hoped he would be drunk on the day of the funeral, but as Harry handed me into the carriage John came out of the front door into the bright June sunlight. He was meticulously dressed in a neatly cut suit of black, his hair perfectly powdered, his black tricorn trimmed with black ribbon. He was pale, pale and cold, despite the hot sun. Or at least he shivered when his eyes met mine. But he had taken no more than he needed to face the day, and to judge from the hardness in his eyes, he was determined to see it through. Beside him, Harry looked plump and bloated and self-indulgent. John came towards the carriage steady-paced like some white-faced avenging angel, and stepped in to seat himself opposite me, without a word to any of us. I felt a touch of fear on my heart. John drunk was a public humiliation for me, his wife. But John sober and vengeful could ruin me. He would have every legal right to order and control me. He could legally watch my every movement. He would know if my bed had been slept in. He had a legal right to come into my room, into my bed, at any time, day or night. Worse, and even more unbearable – I clasped my black-gloved fingers in my lap to keep them from trembling – he could move away from Wideacre and sue me for public divorce if I refused to go with him.

In stealing his name for my fatherless child I had also robbed myself of the freedom any man, married or single, could take for granted. Both my days and nights had to be lived under the supervision of this man, my husband, my enemy. And if he wished he could imprison me, beat me, or take me from my home with the full blessing of the law of the land. I had lost even the limited privilege of my spinsterhood. I was a wife – and if my husband hated me, then I faced the certainty of a miserable future.

He leaned forward and patted Celia's little hands clasped over her prayerbook.

'Do not be too sad,' he said tenderly. His voice was hoarse from the lack of sleep and the continual drinking. 'She died a peaceful, easy death, and while she lived she had great happiness in your company and with little Julia. So do not be too sad. We could all hope for a blameless life of love as she had, and a peaceful, easy death.'

Celia bowed her head and her black-gloved hand returned John's touch.

'Yes, you are right,' she said, her voice low with the effort of controlling her tears. 'But it is a sad loss for me. Although she

361

was only my mama-in-law I felt I loved her as much as if I had been her daughter.'

I felt John's hard, ironic gaze on my face at this artless confession from Celia. Behind my veil my cheeks burned with rage at him, and at this whole sentimental conversation.

'Just as much,' John agreed, his eyes still hard on me. 'I am sure Beatrice thinks so too, don't you, Beatrice?'

I struggled to find a tone of voice that was free from either the rage or the fear I felt at this deliberate baiting of me. He was sliding like a clever skater on the thin ice of the truth. He was daring me; he was frightening me. But I had some power too, and he had best remember it.

'Yes, indeed,' I said levelly. 'Mama always said that she was so lucky in the choices that Harry and I made. Such a lovely daughter-in-law, and so fine a doctor for a son-in-law.'

That hit him, as I had known it would. One word from me and his university would scratch his name from their records. One word from me and it would be the hangman's noose for him and not all his clever spite could save him. He had best remember that, if he drove me to it, I would face down the scandal and the gossip that an accusation of murder would cause, and I would publicly claim that he overdosed Mama while he was drunk. And no one could gainsay me.

He sat back in the carriage beside Harry, careful not to let any part of his coat touch him. And I saw how he bit his lips to keep them from trembling, and clasped his hands to keep them still. He needed a drink to keep his private world of horrors at bay.

All four of us gazed dumbly out of the windows as the tall trees of the drive slid past, and then the fields, and then the little cottages of Acre village. The funeral bell was tolling, one resounding stroke after another, and in the fields I saw the day labourers pulling off their hats and standing still as we drove by. As soon as the carriage was past they set to work again and I was sorry for the old days when every man on the estate would have had a day's paid holiday to pay his respects to the passing of one of the gentry. But the tenants, even the very poorest of cottagers, had given up a morning's work to crowd into the church to be present at Mama's funeral.

She was all there was left of the old Squire, my papa, and with her sudden, unexpected death, the land and the house now belonged to the young generation. There were plenty in the church and in the graveyard to say that Mama's death was the passing of the old days and old ways. But there were even more who said that my papa lived on while I ruled. That on Wideacre at least there was no need to fear change and an uncertain future, for the real power at Wideacre did not rest with the Squire who, gentry-like, was mad for change and profit, but was with the Squire's sister, who knew the land like most ladies know their own parlour, and was more at ease in a meadow than a ballroom.

We followed the coffin into church for the heavy, ominous service, and then we followed it out again. They had opened the Wideacre vault and Mama was placed next to Papa, as if they had been a loving, inseparable couple. Later on, Harry and I would erect some sort of monument to her beside the marble monstrosity already in place on the north wall dedicated to Papa. The Vicar, Pearce, reached the end of the service and closed the book. For a moment I forgot where I was, and I threw up my head like a pointer scenting the wind, and said, with a land-owner's fear in my voice, 'I can smell burning.'

Harry shook hands with the Vicar, and nodded to the sexton to close the vault. Then he turned to me.

'I don't think you can, Beatrice,' he said. 'No one would be burning stubble or heather at this time of year. And it is too early for accidental wood fires.'

'I can,' I insisted. 'I can smell burning.' I strained my eyes in the direction of the west wind. A glow on the horizon, little larger than a pin head, caught my eye.

'There,' I said pointing. 'What's that?'

Harry's eyes followed the direction of my finger and said in doltish surprise, 'Looks like you are right, Beatrice. It is a fire! I wonder what it can be? It looks like quite a wide area – too big for a barn or a house fire.'

Other people had heard me say, 'There' and had seen the ominous redness on the skyline – pale in the sunlight but bright enough to be seen all these miles away. I listened to the murmur and I was quick – perhaps too quick – to identify something more than the usual country curiosity. The cottagers behind me had a tone almost of satisfaction in the low gossiping voices. 'It's the Culler,' they said. 'The Culler promised he would come. He promised it would be this day. He said it would be seen from Acre churchyard. The Culler is here.'

I turned sharply, but the group of closed faces revealed nothing. Then there was a clatter of hoofs and a sweating shirehorse came thundering down Acre street, still harnessed for work, with a little lad bouncing like a cork on its broad bare back.

'Papa! It's the Culler!' he called in ringing tones which brought the murmur to silence.

'They've fired Mr Briggs's new plantation, Papa! Where he enclosed the old common land and drove the cottagers off. Where he planted his five thousand trees. The Culler has fired the new wood, and there will be nothing left but blackened twigs. Mama told me to come and fetch you at once. But the fire will not touch us.'

His papa was Bill Cooper, indebted to us for a mortgage for his farm, but an independent man, not a tenant. He felt my eyes upon him and sketched a bow in farewell and strode towards the churchyard gate. I hurried after him.

'Who is this Culler?' I asked urgently.

'He's the leader of one of the worst gangs of bread rioters and corn rioters and arsonists the county has ever seen,' Bill Cooper said, leading the horse to the lychgate for easy mounting. Forgetful of my new black silks I held the horse's head while he climbed the gate and heaved himself up on to the broad back, behind his son. 'The leader is nicknamed the Culler because he says gentry stock is rotten and should be culled.'

He looked down at me and saw my eyes darken and mistook my fear for anger. 'Begging your pardon, Miss Beatrice – Mrs MacAndrew, I should say. I am only telling you what my labourers told me.'

'Why have I not heard of him?' I asked, my hand still on the reins.

'He is only lately come into Sussex from another county,' said Bill Cooper. 'I only heard of him myself yesterday. I heard Mr Briggs had a note nailed to one of his fine new trees. It warned him that landlords who put trees before men have no right to the land – that the cull of the landlords is starting.'

He tightened the reins and kicked the horse forward. I could feel Harry, Celia and John all staring at my back in astonishment, as I clung to the reins and barred the way. But I had no time for conventions. I was driven by a fear I needed to lay at rest then and there on that sunlit Saturday morning.

'Wait, Cooper,' I said peremptorily. 'What sort of a man is he supposed to be?' I asked. I kept the horse from moving on with a hard hand on the bit, and kept my satin shoes well away from its heavy, shifting feet.

'They say he rides a great black horse,' said Bill Cooper. 'They say he used to be a keeper on an estate, that he learned the ways of the gentry then, and started to hate them. They say his gang would follow him to hell. They say he has two black dogs which go with him everywhere like shadows. They say he is a legless man; he sits oddly on his horse. They say he is Death himself. Miss Beatrice, I must go . . . he is near my land.'

I loosed him. My hand fell powerless from the bridle and the horse brushed past me so close I had the sting of its coarse tail in my face. I knew him, the Culler. I knew him. And the glow of his fire was on Wideacre's horizon. I swayed, my eyes on the unnatural glow, and my lungs, hair and clothes full of the smell of his smoke.

Celia was at my side.

'Beatrice are you unwell?' she asked.

'Get me to the carriage,' I said, miserably. 'I need to be home. I want to be through the lodge gates and behind the front door and in my bedroom. Get me home, Celia. Please.'

So they said I was too distressed at the loss of Mama to shake hands with all the mourners at her funeral, and the kindly respectful faces lined the lane as our carriage drove off. Surely there was no one here who would hide or shelter a gang of desperate men, enemies to the peace of the land? I reassured myself. Not one of my people, not one of them would hide the Culler on Wideacre land. Whatever their private mysterious loyalties and codes of peasant honour, they would surely turn a criminal like the Culler over to a Justice of the Peace if ever he came near my sweet peaceful boundaries. He might burn up to the very parish bounds, hidden and helped by people glad to see their masters humiliated, but on Wideacre I held hearts as well as wealth in my hands. While I was loved the Culler had no chance. Not even if he was Wideacre-born and bred himself. Not even if he had known and loved Wideacre as well as I.

A sob of fear escaped me, and Celia's arm came round my shoulders and held me tight.

'You are tired,' she said tenderly. 'You are tired, and there is no need for you to do any more work for today. You need not take dinner with the guests. You have worked so hard with all the planning and work for this day. There is no need for you to do anything more but rest, my dear.'

Indeed, I was weary. Indeed, I was horribly afraid. My bright, brave relentless courage and anger seemed all burned up like Mr Briggs's woods, leaving nothing but black and smoky ground where no birds sing. With the Culler's work making an ominous grey smudge on the horizon there would be neither rest nor peace for me until he was taken. My head dropped to Celia's shoulder and she patted my back. Under my lashes, behind my veil, I stole a swift glance at my husband, sitting opposite me. He was scanning my pale face as if to read the very depths of my soul. Our eyes met, and I read his sharp, trained, professional curiosity. I shivered uncontrollably in the bright sunlight. The day, which had started so bright and with such a promise of heat, was clouding over and grey thunderclouds blurred with the smoke on the horizon. With the Culler less than a hundred miles from my home and John MacAndrew in my bed, I was endangered indeed.

And the stimulus of my fear, my collapse, was acting on John like a dram of whisky. His own horror was forgotten when he saw the look on my face, when he saw my terror. At once his clever, analytical brain shook free from nightmare, shook free of drink.

He suddenly leaned forward.

'Who is this Culler?' he asked, his speech clear. 'What is he to you?'

I shuddered again, uncontrollably, and turned my face in to Celia's warm shoulder. Her hand tightened comfortingly around me.

'Not now,' she said gently to John. 'Don't ask her now.'

'Now is the only time we might hear the truth!' said John brutally. 'Who is the Culler, Beatrice? Why do you fear him so?'

'Get me home, Celia,' I said, my voice a thread. 'Get me to bed.'

When the carriage drew up to the steps I let Celia lead me to my bedroom and tuck me up in bed as if I were a feverish child. I took two drops of laudanum to keep the clank of the mantrap, the clatter of a falling horse, and the sad soft sigh of my mama's last breath out of my dreams. Then I slept like a baby until suppertime.

The will had been read in the afternoon, and most of the mourners had dispersed, concealing their pleasure or disappointment at the little bequests as well as they could. Mama's small capital was divided equally between Harry and me. She never owned any land, of course. The earth beneath her feet, the rocks beneath the earth, the trees above her head and even the birds that roosted in them never belonged to her. In her girlhood she had lived in her father's house. In her womanhood she had lived in her husband's home, on his land. She never earned a penny, she never owned a farthing that she could in truth call her very own. All the money she left was no more hers than the jewels she had passed on to Celia when Celia married Harry. All she had ever been to Wideacre, to the bank account, to the jewels, to the house, to the land, was a tenant.

And all landlords despise their tenants.

But her rich poverty made the will a simple matter and the reading was over and done by teatime. By the time I emerged for supper at nine o'clock there were only John and Harry and Celia and I to dine with Dr Pearce, the Acre Vicar.

It was the first time that John had been in company since his return home and the night of Mama's death, and for once I blessed Harry's doltish insensitivity to other people's feelings and to the tension in the room. Though slightly subdued by the day, he chatted loudly and easily to Dr Pearce as the three stood before the library fire. No one who looked at Harry, tumbler of sherry in hand, warming his breeches before the fire, would be able to believe that he had ever dragged John out of a stupor of alcohol in this room. Or that he had ever thrown his sister on the hearth and taken her with passionate desperation. But, to judge from John's tense shoulders and scowl, he could imagine both

367

events. Celia remembered his drinking bout too, and I saw her brown eyes anxiously straying to John's face and to the glass in his hand. He turned aside from the window to smile down at her with a suddenly lightened face.

'Do not look so anxious, Celia. I shall not break the furniture.' Celia blushed rosily, but her loving brown eyes met his directly. Anyone looking at her could have seen her honest affection for him, her concern for his health.

'I cannot help being anxious for you,' she said. 'It has been a most difficult time. I am glad you feel able to be with us today. But if you should change your mind and wish to dine alone in your room I should be happy to order a tray for you.'

John nodded his thanks. 'That is thoughtful of you, Celia, but I have been enough alone,' he said. 'My wife will need my company and support, you know, in the days and weeks ahead.' He said 'my wife' as one might say 'my disease' or 'my snake'. His sarcastic voice was hard with detestation when he looked at me. No one, not even little loving Celia, could have mistaken his meaning, and thought his pretended concern sincere. Even Harry paused and glanced curiously at the three of us. John standing, his back to the room; Celia, her sewing falling unnoticed, looking up at him, her colour fading; and I, bent over the round table in the centre of the room, affecting to turn the pages of the newspaper, but as tense as a whip. John turned to the decanter and poured himself another full glass. He tossed it off as if it were medicine.

Then Stride announced supper and broke up the scene, and I enjoyed a small revenge, walking past John, so close that my train swept his legs, to claim Harry's hand to lead me in to supper. Harry sat at the head of the table; I took the foot: Mama's old place. Celia sat where she had been placed since her marriage, on Harry's right, and John sat beside her with Dr Pearce opposite them. John's nearness to me made me icy with affront, but I could tell it sickened him.

He made an effort at distant cold courtesy with Harry, but he could not bear to be physically near him. If Harry's hand brushed his sleeve in passing John shrank as if from an infection. Harry disgusted him, and he loathed me. His hatred expressed itself in direct malice, in biting sarcasm, in concealed insult. All I could do against him was to torment him with my nearness, which reminded him of his past desire for me. He scarcely touched his food and I wondered, with malicious pleasure, how long his use of alcohol would be controlled under the twin pressures of his rage and enforced silence. He had a glass of wine, nearly untouched, at his place and I nodded to the footman to refill it.

Dr Pearce was a newcomer and sensed a little of the tension of this family party. But he was a man of the world and with interest and courtesy he encouraged Harry to talk about his farming experiments. Harry was proud of the changes taking place on our land, and the wealthier tenants were following his lead and making Wideacre known as a pioneer of the new techniques. I had my reservations, and my love of the old ways, and the reputation that Miss Beatrice held by the traditions and spoke for the poor did me no harm with the people on the land.

'When I started farming at Wideacre there were barely two day labourers on the place, and we used ploughs which were unchanged from Roman times,' Harry said, on his hobby-horse again. 'Now we have ploughs that can cut a furrow nearly up to the top of the downs and there are fewer and fewer squatters and cottagers on Acre.'

'Small benefit to us all,' I said drily from the other end of the table. I noted how John tensed at the very sound of my cool, silvery voice and reached unconsciously for his wine glass.

'The cottagers who used to live in the hovels around the village have now become day labourers or even live in the parish workhouse and work in the workhouse gangs. And your new plough has ripped up old, good meadows to make surplus corn-fields, which will create year after year of corn glut. The price of bread tumbles; the corn is hardly worth selling for years in a row, and then in the first bad year there is uproar because the price suddenly soars.'

Harry smiled down the table at me.

'You are an old Tory, Beatrice,' he said. 'You hate all change and yet it is you who keep the books. You know as well as I do what the wheatfields pay.'

'They pay us,' I said. 'They profit the gentry. But they do little good for the people on Wideacre. And they have done no good at all for those we used to call our people – the ones who

369

lived in the hovels we cleared away and kept their pigs on the common patch we have now enclosed.'

'Ah, Beatrice,' said Harry, teasingly. 'You speak with two voices. When the books show a profit you are pleased, and yet in your heart you prefer the old wasteful ways.'

I smiled back, forgetting John, forgetting the tension, my mind on Wideacre. Harry's was a fair comment. Our disagreement was as old as our joint management of the land. If I ever thought Harry's new methods were a real danger to the peace and prosperity of Wideacre then I would stop him in the same second. And there had been plans of his that I had vetoed and we had heard no more of them. What concerned me, as one of the handful of gentry among the millions of poor, was that Harry's schemes and the trend of the whole country were to profit the gentry more and more and to make the poor yet poorer.

'It is true,' I said smiling at Harry with a softness in my voice and a tender light in my eyes for my land. 'I am but a sentimental farmer.'

John's chair scraped harshly on the polished floor as he thrust it back abruptly.

'Excuse me,' he said, pointedly ignoring me, speaking only to Celia. He walked heavily towards the door and shut it with a firm click as if to emphasize his rejection of us, and the candlelit room. Celia looked anxiously at me, but my face never wavered. I turned to Dr Pearce as if there had been no interruption.

'But you come from the higher, colder north where I think there is little wheat grown at all,' I said. 'You must find our obsession with the price of wheat and white flour odd.'

'It is very different,' he admitted. 'In my county, Durham, the poor still eat rye bread; black or brown bread, it is. Nasty stuff compared to your golden loaves, I admit, but they fare well on it and it is cheap too. They eat a lot of potatoes and pastry dishes made with the coarse flour as well, so the price of wheat matters far less. Here I think the poor are wholly dependent on wheat?'

'Oh, yes,' said Celia in her soft voice. 'It is as Beatrice says. It is well enough when the price of corn is low, but when it rises there is real hardship, for there is no alternative food.'

'Then the damned fools riot,' said Harry, with two-bottle

bluster. 'They riot as if we can help the rain spoiling the crop and making it too dear for them to buy.'

'It's not all chance,' I said reasonably. 'We do not profiteer and we do not hoard at Wideacre, but there have been some wicked fortunes made by withholding corn from the market, and by sending it out of the county. When merchants deliberately create a shortage they know full well that there will be hunger and then disturbances.'

'If they would only go back to eating black bread!' sighed Celia.

'These are my customers!' said Harry, laughing. 'I would rather they stuck to white bread and went hungry in the lean years. The day will come when we have more and more land growing wheat and the whole country eats nothing but white flour.'

'If you can grow it, and I say "if", Harry, then good luck to you,' I said. 'But while I keep the books we will plant no more wheatfields. I believe the bottom will fall out of the market. It is all very well one farmer planting wheat, but every single Squire up and down the country is doing so. Come a bad year and there will be many wheat farms ruined. Wideacre will never be a one-crop estate.'

Harry nodded. 'Aye, Beatrice,' he said. 'You are the planner. And we should not be boring Dr Pearce and Celia with this farming talk.'

He sat back in his chair and at a nod from me the servants cleared the plates. Dr Pearce and Harry chose cheeses from the board, and the great silver fruit bowl, piled high with our own produce, was placed in the middle of the table.

'One would be foolish indeed to be bored with such work that produces such wonderful results,' said Dr Pearce politely. 'You eat like pagans in a golden age at Wideacre.'

'I am afraid we are pagan,' I said lightly. I took one of the plump peaches and peeled its downy skin to eat the sweet slimy fruit. 'The earth is so good, and the yields are so high, that at harvest time I find it hard not to believe in magic,'

'Well, I believe in science,' said Harry staunchly. 'And Beatrice's magic goes well with my experiments. But, Dr Pearce, you would burn my sister for a witch if you ever saw her in a hayfield!'

Celia laughed. 'It is true, Beatrice. Only the other day you were supposed to be taking Sea Fern to be shod and I saw him tied to the gate of Oak Tree Meadow and you in the middle of the field, with your hat off and your face tilted up to the sky with handfuls of poppies and larkspur in either hand. I was driving into Chichester with Mama and I had to point something out to her to distract her attention away from you. You looked like Ceres in a mumn..rs' play!'

I laughed ruefully. 'I see I shall become a well-known eccentric and be jeered at by the apprentices in Chichester!' I said.

'Even I had not long arrived in Acre before I heard strange and ominous rumours,' said Dr Pearce, twinkling at me. 'One of your older cottagers, Mrs MacAndrew, told me that he always asks you to take tea and walk in the fields at sowing time. He swore it is a sure way to ward off rust mould on the seeds to have Miss Beatrice take a few steps behind the plough.'

I nodded at Harry. 'Tyacke, and Frosterly and Jameson,' I said certainly. 'A few others like to believe it too. I think a couple of good seasons coincided with the time when I was first out on the land alone after my papa's death, and that convinced them.'

A secret stab of nostalgia touched me at the memory of those good seasons. The first summer of my womanhood when I had met and loved with Ralph under the blue sky of a summer that seemed never-ending, and the second summer when Harry had been the Lord of the Harvest and brought in the corn like a Summer King. Then there was the third hot year and my third good lover, John, who had courted me, and kissed my hand and driven me miles around the estate on one sweet unlikely pretext after another.

'Magic and science,' said Dr Pearce. 'No wonder your crops flourish.'

'I hope it lasts,' I said, without knowing what made me cast such a shadow over the conversation. A flicker of some pre-monition – as insubstantial and yet as ominous as woodsmoke on a distant horizon – touched me. 'There is nothing worse than a bad year after a series of good ones. People become too confident, they expect too much.'

'They do indeed,' said Dr Pearce quickly, confirming Harry's view of him as a hard-headed realist, and my view of him as an unimaginative, pompous man. I knew too well what would follow: a tirade against the poor, their unreliability with rent and tithes, their ceaseless fertility, their unreasonable demands. If Celia and I withdrew now, there was a chance that Harry and Dr Pearce would have finished by the time they came to the parlour for tea. I nodded at Celia, and she left some grapes on her plate and rose with me. Stride went to the door, but Harry put him aside with a gesture and held the door for us both. I let Celia precede me and knew I had read the gesture aright when I saw Harry's warm eyes on me. The talk of the land had reminded him of my power and my beauty. He had buried his horror and fright with his mama, and tonight we would be lovers again.

~~ 14 ~~

It was easier to meet him than I had dared to imagine. John's abrupt departure from the dinner table had signalled, as I had hoped, a return to hard drinking. I had hardly aided his resolution against alcohol, for when he had flung himself into his study in the west wing he had found the dew forming on two icy-fresh bottles of whisky, a pitcher of cool water to mix with a dram, and a plate of biscuits and cheese to bolster the illusion that he was merely taking a small glass with a meal. Casually, as if blind to his own hands, he had broken the seal on one of the bottles and poured a measure, the merest drop, and diluted it well. One taste undid his resolve and he had drunk nearly all of one bottle by the time I came, clear-headed, to peep in on him. He was asleep in his chair by the log fire. The smartness of his early-morning appearance had faded from him the way a poppy crumples after only a few hours. I looked long and hard at him as he lay, mouth half open, snoring softly. His suit was rumpled, his fair hair sticky with sweat from the nightmare that tossed his head and made him occasionally moan in torment. He had biscuit crumbs in his cravat, and the sour smell of whisky on his breath.

No pity touched me. This was a man I had loved, and who had poured on me weeks and months of lawful, generous loving. But he had execrated me, and he threatened my safety at Wideacre. The blackness of my sin had half destroyed him; now I wished it had killed him outright. If he continued drinking at this pace it would indeed have proved a fatal wound, and I would be at peace once again. I held my silk skirts out so the whisper of the fabric did not prompt a sweet dream of remembered happiness, and I stepped slowly and carefully to the door. I locked it from the outside, and he was safe in my power.

I was safe too.

Then I climbed the third flight of stairs to the room at the very top of the west wing, and set a taper to the logs in the grate, and to the candles. I opened the other door that connects with the main part of the house where Harry waited, shirtsleeved and barefoot, in patient silence lit only by the light of his bedtime candle.

We held each other like lovers, not like the fierce sensual enemies we so often were in that room. With my husband drunk and dreaming horrors downstairs, and someone, some enemy, perhaps even an enemy I knew well, sleeping and plotting less than fifty miles from me, I did not feel like a storm of passion with Harry. I needed some loving; I needed some kissing; I needed, with all my frozen, frightened heart, some tenderness. So I let Harry take me in his arms and lay me on the couch as if we were tender lovers, and then he kissed me and loved me with tenderness. In many ways this gentle, marital exchange was the most perverse and infamous act of all that we did.

But I did not care. I cared for nothing, now.

Afterwards, we lay sprawled in an easy tangle on the couch, watching the firelight flickering, and drinking warm claret. My chestnut hair was spread in a tangle across his warm soft-haired chest. My face rested against the plump column of his throat. I was tired; I was at peace. I was bruised but not pained. Any woman in the world would have been deeply satisfied and ready for sleep.

'Harry,' I said.

'Yes?' he said, rousing himself from his half-doze, and gathering me closer into his warm hug.

'There is something I have been waiting to tell you for some time, Harry,' I said hesitantly. 'Something that I am afraid may grieve you, but something you have to know for the good of Wideacre.'

Harry waited, undisturbed. He knew we would not have made love if Wideacre had been endangered by any immediate threat. He knew that my love of the land would always take first place in my mind. He waited to hear what might come next.

'It is about the entail,' I said. 'I am concerned that Wideacre is still entailed on our cousin as the next male heir. If anything, God forbid, should happen to you, Celia, Julia and I would all be homeless.'

A slight frown furrowed his complacent face.

'It's true,' he said. 'I have thought of it once or twice. But there is plenty of time, Beatrice. I do not ride like you do! I may have a boy next time and then he will inherit. I do not think the entail is a pressing problem for us.'

'I was afraid you did not know,' I said. I turned over to lie on my belly and reared myself up on my elbows to look into his face. 'I was afraid Celia had not told you. I do not blame her. It was, perhaps, not made very clear to her in France after the birth of Julia. I fear she is barren, now, Harry. The midwife said it was a miracle she had conceived at all, and that she doubted very much if she would ever have another child. She has some fault in her body that makes her infertile.'

I paused to let the new information sink in.

'After the birth I told her, as gently as I could, but I did not want to upset her, so possibly I did not make the situation sufficiently clear. The truth is, Harry, the honest truth' – I widened my hazel eyes at him in a perfect mimicry of a candid gaze – 'the truth is that I fear Celia will never conceive another child, and that you will never have a son and heir for Wideacre.'

Harry's happy rounded face fell. He believed me.

'This is a blow indeed,' he said, and I could feel him groping for the words to express his thoughts, for some way to make sense of this new view of the world where there would be no son to follow him and, when he died, Wideacre would pass from his direct line to strangers.

'I thought Celia might have fully understood, and might have told you,' I said delicately. 'But it is a bitter thing for both of you to know: that when you die Wideacre will go to our cousin. Little Julia and, indeed, Richard will be homeless.'

'Yes,' he said, as the picture struck him. 'Having been reared on Wideacre, to have to leave it!'

'If only one could change the entail!' I sighed at that remote possibility. 'If only we could find some way to make our two children secure in their home for ever.'

'I have heard of them being reversed,' Harry said doubtfully. 'But it costs an impossible sum of money and involves one in compensating the heirs, as well as the legal fees of changing it.

Few estates could bear that sort of cost, Beatrice, certainly not Wideacre.'

'The cost if we do not change it would be far greater,' I said. I sat up, naked, and crossed over to the fire to throw an extra log on the embers. I turned and smiled at Harry, the firelight throwing flickering lights and shadows on my smooth warm skin. 'I cannot bear the thought of our children miserable and exiled from Wideacre when we are gone, because we failed to provide for them. The two of them – so near each other in age, so like you and me – forced out with no home to go to.'

'Well, they'll hardly be homeless,' said Harry prosaically. 'Julia will inherit my capital and her mother's dowry, and Richard will be one of the MacAndrew Line heirs. Enough cash there to buy the estate many times over, I should think.'

'Which would you rather have, money or Wideacre?' I asked spontaneously, forgetting for a second the way I wanted the conversation to tend.

Harry considered. The fool that he was, he needed time to think. 'Well,' he said in careful, doltish judgement, 'if one had a fortune one could buy places as fine as this. You are Wideacre-mad, Beatrice, but there are some very pretty properties in Kent or even in Suffolk and Hampshire.'

I bit the inside of my cheeks hard. Then I waited until I knew no reckless scornful words would come. Then, and only then, I said in a voice as smooth as silk, 'That's true, I dare say, Harry. But if your little girl is anything like me she will pine and die if she has to live anywhere out of sight of the Wideacre downs. Small comfort a fortune will be to her then, when she has to buy some other hills, and her distant cousins turn her out of the home where she has lived all her life. She'll think you are an uncaring father then, and she will curse your memory, that you failed to provide for her, although you loved her so much.'

'Oh, don't say that!' said Harry, moved as I knew he would be by the prospect of Julia's future reproaches. 'I would we could do something about it, Beatrice, but I can't for the life of me see what.'

'Well, let us decide on it at least,' I said. 'If we decide to aim for the entail, let us set our hearts on it and we will find a way to the money necessary.'

Harry shook his head. 'You don't understand, Beatrice,' he

said. 'We could never raise the sort of capital needed to make such a change. Only the wealthiest families in the kingdom can do such things. It is simply beyond our scope.'

'Our scope, yes,' I said slowly. 'But what about the scope of the MacAndrew fortune?'

Harry's blue eyes widened. 'He never would?' he said, hopefully. 'He would never pour all that money into Wideacre!'

'Not at the moment,' I agreed. 'But he might change his mind. He might consider investing. If we had even half the MacAndrew fortune behind us I think we could consider the change, work out the costs, explore ways and means.'

Harry nodded. 'I'm game,' he said. 'I'd be prepared to sacrifice some of my experimental projects and go for more high-return wheatfields instead of the things I wanted to do. The profit from them could go directly into a fund for buying the entail. We could save for it, Beatrice, and if the worst came to the worst we could always mortgage some land and pay it off later.'

'Yes,' I said. 'I would hate to do that, but it would be worth it in this instance.'

'But you would have to give up your defence of the cottagers and their rights, Beatrice,' said Harry, earnestly. 'There is a hundred acres of common land we could enclose and put under the plough and thousands of pounds to be made if we raised the rents. You have set your heart against those measures, but if we needed to raise money, and a lot of money, then we would have to do things we would not do otherwise.'

I hesitated then, thinking of the lovely rolling common land where the heather grows thigh-high on the sandy light soil, where the little streams run on beds of white sand down the miniature valleys. Of the hollows where the bracken grows in green sweet-smelling peppery fronds where, if you sit still, a dark-eyed snake will come out to bask in the sunshine beside you. Of cold nights when I had walked alone in the empty space under the stars and seen the sharp hoofprints of deer on the loam and seen them moving, soft as shadows, under the great branches of the oak and beech trees. If Harry had his way, all this would be burned and hacked and cleared, and smooth square fields of featureless wheat would grow where the silver birches had shivered and the tall firs had swayed in the wind. It was a big price to pay. Greater than I had thought I would ever have to meet. But it was to get my child into the Master's chair and my blood into the line of Squires.

'And we will have to use the gang labourers on the parish,' said Harry, a certain hard relish in his voice. 'It is sheer waste employing our tenants or people from Acre when we can get all the day labour we need by contracts with the parish. We pay them cash when they work, and nothing when they do not. We would save hundreds of pounds over the year if we left the poor of Acre to find their own work and did not keep them on our books.'

I nodded. I could feel the face of Wideacre changing as I looked into the future. Acre village would be smaller, with fewer cottages. Those that survived would be more prosperous. But the little cottages, where families survived on winter work from us and on casual harvest work, would go. They lived the best lives people could have. In winter they took casual work from us, hedging or ditching or helping with snowed-in sheep or cattle. They lived then on their summertime savings and relied on vegetables from their patch and the milk from the cow they kept on the common. They would keep a pig there, eating acorns from the oak trees, and a couple of hens to run in the lane of Acre.

In spring and summertime they would earn good money sowing seed, moving the beasts, haymaking, harvesting. They would work outrageous hours for two or three days dawn to dusk in the rhythm of the land, and then all of a sudden the work would stop. The fields would be cut, the barns overflowing, the haystacks built, and the whole village would go on a glorious drunken holiday that would last two or three days, until the next job needed doing.

None of them would ever be wealthy. None of them would ever own land. But they lived a life that many a wealthy city-bred man might envy. They worked when they chose and they rested when they chose, and while they would never be rich they seldom feared poverty.

The hens that ran in the lane and the cow on the common were a safe shield against hunger and want. They knew that if they faced a death or an illness in the family there was always a place for the whole family in the Wideacre kitchen, and where a word to Miss Beatrice would see an apprenticeship for the oldest son, and a job for the oldest daughter at the Hall.

But if I went down Harry's mean narrow road then Wideacre would be like any other estate where the poor pulled their forelocks as the carriages went by, and then pulled faces when they were gone; where the faces of the children were white and thin, and those of their mothers were old with worry. Wideacre poor led trouble-free lives because we kept to the old ways. Unchallenged traditions ruled the use of the land and the easy holidays. The common was open to all – even the poaching was a ritual game played with little malice. But Harry's way would mean the common enclosed, the footpaths shut, the cow and pig without grazing. The poor would become poorer. And the very poorest of them would drop through the old traditional supports – and they would starve.

But the end of the road was security for my son. The end of this road was his inheritance. I would have ridden roughshod over every mother in the land – Mary, Joseph, and Baby Jesus too, if necessary – to get my son in the Squire's chair.

'It has to be,' I said. 'I see that.'

'That's generous of you!' said Harry enthusiastically. 'I know how you love the old ways, Beatrice, and they have served us well. It is generous of you to be ready to give them up, and all for little Julia's sake, too.'

'Yes,' I said. I settled back on the couch and wrapped a silk shawl around my naked shoulders. The touch of the cloth was soft on my skin and warm. As I shrugged at the thought of the cottagers who would be homeless and hungry the folds slipped, and Harry leaned forward to kiss one bare shoulder. I smiled at him. He had to go further yet, this night.

'But it still would not be enough,' Harry said. 'To buy out the heir we would have to offer a massive sum of capital. We could start a fund certainly. But we would be unlikely to make enough money quickly enough.'

'I know,' I nodded. 'It has to be the MacAndrew money.'

Harry frowned. He was slow but he was not stupid.

'John would hardly agree,' he objected. 'It is to secure Julia's future certainly, and I hope that while she lived and ruled Wideacre there would always be a home for the three of you, but there is no reason why John should put his private fortune into a scheme that gains him or his child nothing.'

I smiled. One always had to take things so slowly with Harry. But he generally got there in the end.

'Unless we could find some way of making Richard and Julia joint heirs,' I suggested tentatively. 'They could run Wideacre as we do, you and I, together. Everyone can see how well that works, perhaps they too could learn to work together.'

Harry smiled, and traced a line of kisses from the sweet round of my shoulder along the clear line of my neck and up to behind my ear.

'Well, yes, Beatrice,' he said softly. 'But you and I have a rather special way of deciding business matters.'

'They could be partners,' I murmured, lazily, as if I could think of nothing but the rising warmth and pleasure of his kisses. I lay back on the couch, the shawl falling from my nakedness, my eyelids half closed, and my eyes behind them as sharp as green glass.

Harry's movement to kiss a new line, from the fascinating bones at the base of my neck down between my warm tumbled breasts, was arrested at that thought.

'Julia and Richard?' he said in sudden surprise.

'Yes,' I said, pushing his face down to my soft belly, still slack from the birth of my son. 'Why not?'

Harry kissed me, absently, his mind turning over this seed of an idea that could secure Julia the benefit of inheriting one of the sweetest estates in Sussex, which would keep Wideacre in his line.

'You know, Beatrice,' he said. 'That's a rather good idea. If John would accept a half-share of the estate as a return for loaning the capital to buy out Charles Lacey and change the entail we could arrange a contract to make them joint heirs.'

'That is wonderful,' I said, catching his enthusiasm as if I had not been planning this ever since I had recognized myself in little Julia, and felt Richard's rights to the land as sharply as I felt my own.

'How wonderful, Harry, if our two children could rule here after we are gone!'

Harry beamed. 'To give Julia Wideacre would be worth almost

any sacrifice,' he said tenderly. 'And to give your son an equal share in our home makes me almost as happy, Beatrice.'

'You are so right, Harry,' I said, as if I were congratulating him on his idea. 'We should set it in train at once, don't you think?'

Harry rolled towards me in his enthusiasm, and I lay back and readied myself to pay my dues. I could enjoy Harry; when I was full of fear or anxiety, I could even feel a need for him. But once my first easy lust was satisfied I wanted, more than any other pleasure, the delight of being in my own, solitary bed. But Harry was exhilarated at the exercise of his wit upon the problem of the entail, and I wanted him abed and tired and happy tonight, for there would be more to plan in the morning; I wanted him too tired to talk with Celia when he crept in beside her sleeping warmth.

'Come to my office in the morning, and we will write to the London lawyers,' I said, and sighed as if the pleasure of his kisses were too much for me. 'Oh, Harry,' I said, as if over-whelmed. 'After breakfast, tomorrow.'

After Harry left me I had sat for two or three long hours gazing into the red embers, puzzling in my mind, giving myself this time like a gift. I was giving myself a chance to draw back. The next steps before me were like the first steps one takes on the crest of the downs where they slope so steeply that even the grass cannot grow. You take one step, then another, and then the height of the slope catches you and you cannot, cannot stop. And there would be no way of stopping the course I was on. And there would be no laughter at the speed and fright of it.

So I gave myself a few minutes to linger at the top and consider what I was doing. Just a couple of quiet hours beside the fire to test my own determination and to see if I could bear what I was about to do. I had to break the land, break it to pay for that entail. Hammer the earth and the people, and the rhythm of the seasons, until it yielded gold like blood to pay for this daredevil scheme.

You never farm for today. You always think of next season, next year, or the year beyond. You plant wheat for your own profit, but you plant trees for your heir. I was planting trees. I was planning fifty years ahead. I could not pour love and money and care into the land for some damned cousin; it had to be for my bone and my seed.

Whatever the cost.

It was as I had planned. After a night spent lovemaking with me, Harry had tumbled into bed beside his silent, sleeping wife, and barely exchanged more than a dozen words with her until we were all seated around the breakfast table in the warm June sunlight. Celia, dressed in a simple black gown trimmed with black lace, looked as lovely as a young woman who has enjoyed twelve hours' sleep can look on a midsummer morning. Beside her I dare say I looked tired. I know I felt it. I was smiling, for everything that had seemed in conspiracy against me was flowing easily and sweetly my way again. I took a cup of French coffee from Celia with a word of thanks, and a slice of ham from the sideboard. Then the door opened and my husband came in.

He walked with a light and easy step as if he had not been drunk last night, and dead drunk every night for the last twelve. He smiled at Celia's clear prettiness with real affection, and then his face turned to me and the smile became a sneer.

'My lovely wife,' he said, and his words were bitten off as if even speaking to me left a sour taste in his mouth.

'Good morning,' I said evenly, and took my place at the foot of the table.

'Beatrice, I shall come to your office this morning to discuss that matter we mentioned last night,' said Harry pompously, but I wished he had stayed silent.

'Last night?' John asked, his eyes on his plate. 'Something you three talked over together?'

Celia was unruffled behind the silver coffee set. 'No, these two were up all hours talking profit and loss as usual,' she said. 'You know how they are when they are planning for Wideacre, John.'

John shot a hard look at her under his sandy eyebrows.

'I know how these two are together,' he said briefly.

There was an awkward silence.

'Certainly,' I said smoothly to Harry. 'And later I should like to take you to see what the Hale family has done to Reedy Hollow. They have built a little culvert and some drains. It makes that field a good dry field, but I am concerned about the melt-water in spring.'

'You know the water levels better than anyone, Beatrice,' said Harry. 'But do you think they have considered using a water pump?'

Even with John's icy, daunting presence at the table Celia and I could not resist an exchange of smiles.

'Really, Harry,' I said. 'You are too old to play with toys. I think you will have to give up your pumps and your windmills and your ten-crop systems.'

Harry chuckled ruefully. 'It's just that they do such interesting things in the Fens,' he said plaintively. 'I should so like to have a pump at Wideacre.'

'We'll be digging dikes next,' I said, teasing him. 'You stick to Sussex ways in Sussex, Harry, and content yourself with being the most progressive farmer for miles around.'

Harry smiled back at me. 'I will save, Beatrice,' he said earnestly. 'You know I only value these things for the benefits they bring the estate.'

'Save for what?' My husband's tone was like a diamond cutting glass across the warm easy tone of the conversation. 'Do you know what Harry is saving for, Celia?' he repeated.

Celia looked blank, but her instinctive loyalty to Harry kept her mouth shut.

'Harry and I have plans to establish a fund for the future of Julia and for Richard,' I said smoothly. 'To come from some of the profits of Wideacre. We have not any idea of the details yet, and we were proposing to talk about them, and about some rather boring farming plans, this morning. You and Celia are, of course, more than welcome to come to my office after breakfast, but it is hardly the sort of thing that interests either of you. And we are only at the talking stage.'

John's eyes were as sharp as Celia's were bland. 'Planning for the future, Beatrice?' he said, and anyone could have heard the suspicion and hatred in his voice. I shot a hard glance at the footman by the door but his face was correctly wooden. I knew him though; I knew them all. This one was one of the Hodgett lads, a son of the gatekeeper. He had been taken into the house by me after being in trouble with Harry's keeper over a ferret he would set to work in the preserves. I saved him a beating; I saved his father some time and trouble. He adored me. There would be no rumour of this talk outside this room, except as an outburst by young Hal that Miss Beatrice's young husband wasn't worthy to kiss the ground she rode on.

'Of course I plan for the future, John,' I said, and I saw him wince when I used his name. 'I plan for our baby, just like any mother. And I plan for you and me, just like any wife. You can be sure that I will always be thinking of you, and planning for you, just as long as you live.'

Celia looked relieved at the sweetness of my tone, and at the loving nature of the words. But John went pale and looked sickly as he heard the threat behind them. I would hear no more from him today. And I would find a way, I most certainly would find a way, to silence him for ever.

I rose from the table.

'My room, in ten minutes, Harry?' I asked.

Harry rose to his feet and nodded his assent as I made to leave. John was a little slow in rising to show his respect for me, and I waited, motionless, my eyes on him, until he had done so. His pushing back of his chair was like a surly boy and I felt secret pleasure at mastering him, as steadily and as surely as one trains an ill-bred dog. But some dogs are such trouble that one puts a stone around their neck, and drops them in the Fenny.

I went to my office.

Anywhere at Widacre I am at peace, but when I sit in the Squire's chair with the great round rent table before me, and the papers on all the tenants tucked safe in the drawers, the map of the estate on the easel board, and the swallows swooping low outside the window, I am in bliss. This is where the heart of Wideacre beats. In the deep secret hidden places in the woods, in the soft, sandy, sunny common, and on the high thyme-scented downs, but also here where the lives of the people, our people, are recorded in my clear ledgers, and their futures planned on the great charts of the desk. This is where the revenue comes in, in the weekly rents, in records of yields surpassing yields, in the banker's orders from Chichester corn merchants, in the wool sale cheques, in the meat market gold. And this is where the wealth is spent: in the orders for equipment, for new stock, for new seed, and for the ceaseless buying for the house, which Celia seems to think is needed, and which I do not refuse.

We live well on Wideacre, and my ledgers tell me, in reassuring thick black pen strokes on a white page, that we can afford to live well, for this country makes us rich.

And now this wealth, this steady circulation of paper and gold money must be diverted to a new reservoir – a fund to buy my son into the chair where I sit, into the room where I give the orders, into the land and into the power. Richard, my lovely baby, whose bath I would go and watch in a few minutes, would be Master here if any act, any act at all, of mine could put him in this place.

Harry tapped on the door and came in. His kiss on my cheek was the second he had given me that day, but it recognized that our first kiss of greeting at breakfast had been in public, as brother and sister. This one, no warmer or more loving, was a private one between old, familiar lovers.

'Sit down,' I said, and he drew up a chair to the table.

'I shall be writing to the London solicitors this morning to raise the question of the entail with them, and when we know how much they estimate the purchase will cost, we will know better where we stand,' I said in a businesslike tone.

'Good,' said Harry, nodding in assent.

'But I think we should keep this matter between ourselves, until we know we can go ahead,' I said. 'I shall not tell John yet, and I think it would be better if you did not tell Celia.'

'Oh?' said Harry. 'Why not?'

'Oh, Harry,' I said. 'You understand so little about women! If Celia knows you are planning to make Julia your heir, she will know you believe she is barren. I think that would break her heart. Worse, she will know that I told her sad secret to you, so she will feel betrayed by me. Until we know for certain that we can buy the entail, indeed, until the entail is actually purchased and signed over to Richard and Julia, I think Celia should know nothing about it. It would only be a reproach to her for something she cannot possibly help.'

'Very true,' said Harry, with the quick tenderness he always had now for Celia, his pretty wife. 'I should hate her to be distressed. But she will know that I think there will be no more heirs when the contract of partnership between Richard and Julia is signed.'

'But then she will have the comfort of knowing that Julia's future is secure and that at least she has played a part in providing Wideacre with an heir. Julia and Richard will inherit jointly.'

Harry nodded, and got up from the table to gaze out of the window. I heard the scrunch of footsteps on the gravel, and went to stand beside him. My husband was wandering aimlessly towards the rose garden. I could tell from the droop of his shoulders that he had found the drink I had left in the library and he had taken a glass to help him face the day looming ahead. All day without laughter, or joy, or love in a house that stank of sin. He had lost the quickness and lightness of his step. He had lost the pride that made him a swift walker, a fast dancer, a fine lover. I had taken the virtue, the strength and the power from him. If I could see my way to it, I would take more.

'What about John?' Harry asked in an undertone.

I shrugged. 'As you see,' I said. 'I shall tell him of no plans. He is indiscreet, he is incompetent to judge. If he continues to drink in this way then I shall write to his papa and see if you and I can have power of attorney over his MacAndrew shares. He is not to be trusted with a fortune. He could spend it all on drink tomorrow.'

Harry nodded, his eyes still on John's bowed back.

'He is ashamed because he made a mistake with Mama's dose?' he asked.

I nodded. 'I suppose that is it. He does not confide in me. He knows I cannot forgive his behaviour that night. If he had not been drunk our darling mama might have lived.' I rested my head against the window frame. 'I cannot stop weeping when I think of her in illness, and that clown muddling the dose.'

Harry's face was flushed with anger. 'I know,' he said. 'If we had only known! But, Beatrice, we cannot be sure. She always had a weak heart; we all knew that one day we would lose her.'

'What I cannot bear is to have lost her through his folly!' I said.

'I wonder what set off Mama's attack,' Harry said, his cowardly eyes on my face. 'Does John have any idea?'

'No,' I said, lying in my turn. 'Mama collapsed just before she came into the parlour. Perhaps she came down the stairs too fast. John has no idea what caused it.'

Harry nodded. He was greedy for sweet untruths when reality was uncomfortable.

'I know we cannot be sure,' I said. 'But you believe it, and I believe it; the whole house knows how drunk he was. All of the county knows he attended her although he was drunk, and that she was dead the next day. Of course I cannot forgive him. Of course he is ashamed. He has not shown his face off the estate except for her funeral since it happened. And he is not called out even to the poorest houses. Everyone believes he was drunk and made a mistake.'

Harry nodded. 'It must be a bitter thing for him,' he said. John was walking along the paths of the rose garden that led to the little summerhouse. As we watched he dawdled up the steps and sat down inside as if he were worn out.

'It is indeed,' I said. 'His whole life and his pride was in his practice of medicine. I expect he wishes he were dead.'

The relish in my voice penetrated even Harry's dullness.

'You hate him that much?' he asked. 'Because of Mama?'

I nodded.

'I cannot forgive him for failing Mama, for failing me, for failing in his duty. I despise him for his drunkenness that night, and for his drunkenness every night since. I wish I had never married him. But with your support and help, Harry, we will ensure he cannot harm me.'

Harry nodded. 'Aye, it's a bitter shame for you, Beatrice. But you will always be safe here with me. And if his father does indeed invest the MacAndrew shares on you and takes them away from John, then he will be harmless. He will be able to do nothing if he has only what you give him, and has to live where you permit.'

I nodded. 'It will have to do,' I said, half to myself. 'It will do, at any rate, until we know about the entail.'

Two long months passed before we had news. In London the lawyers consulted their dusty files and traced back through hundreds of years the decision to invest only boys of Wideacre stock with the power to inherit. It was the usual way. In the earliest days, when my ancestors first came to Wideacre and saw its dreaming hills and the little cluster of mud and lath buildings, they were fighting men, arrived with the Norman conqueror, hungry for land. Women to them were carriers and breeders and rearers of soldier sons. Nothing else had any value. Of course they settled it that boys and only boys should inherit.

And no one ever challenged it.

Generations of women came and went on this land. Married, bedded, bore children with pain and with courage and were left to run the estate alone. Mothers and daughters-in-law inherited responsibility but no power, as husbands and sons gave the orders, took the profits and took themselves off. Crusading Squires left Wideacre for years in the care of their wives and came back to find the fields peaceful, the crops yielding, the cottages repaired and newly built, and the land fertile. Strangers on their own land, tanned brown from foreign suns, they retired at last to their home and took back the power without a murmur from the women who had poured their own lives and love into keeping Wideacre Hall and Wideacre land strong and thriving.

They are buried in Wideacre church, these absentee Lords. There are great effigies of them in their armour, on their backs, their hands piously clasped over their metal bellies, their feet uncomfortably crossed. Their eyes stare sightlessly at the church roof and I imagine they sometimes lay in bed like that, beside their sleeping wives, gazing at the roof of the great wooden bed that I now sleep in, but seeing in their mind's eye the desert, and the bands of infidels, and Jerusalem on the horizon.

The wives would be as sound and as deeply asleep as I am after a day when I have worked so hard and so long on the accounts that the figures dance before my eyes until I take my candle and go to bed in a haze of tiredness. Or on the days when we have to round up sheep and I spend all day riding around the silly things in circles and bawling like a peasant at the dogs. Or when harvesting goes badly and is interrupted by rain and I have to be out all day to keep the men working and say, 'Hurry! Hurry! Hurry! The storm is coming! The autumn is coming! And the crops are not in!' The crusaders' wives would be as tired as I am after days like that, and they would sleep as I do – the sleep of a woman who runs the house and the land. We have no time to dream, or go riding off to find wars and battles and glory. We are left with the home to run and the land to run, and no glory, no power, and no wealth.

Wideacre Squires were not great Lords like the Havering family, nor great merchants like the de Courceys. They stayed home a little more than the greater men, but still they roamed. With Wideacre at their back and Wideacre wealth at their beck and call they rode out for the King during the war, and lived long years in exile. Wideacre wives ran the estate then too. Writing letters, sending money from coffers that grew steadily more and more empty. Arguing, dealing, persuading the Roundhead army to leave the hay standing, the horses in the field.

In the long years of the Protectorate the Wideacre women were exiles on their own land – staying quiet, staying unobtrusive, hoping that they would be left to live their lives in peace and security. Of course they managed it. What woman does not know how to melt into a threatening landscape so she becomes half invisible and can concentrate on surviving – without power, without wealth, without help?

So when the Stuart Squires came riding home in triumph there was a tired, pale woman on the doorstep ready to welcome the Master home. And he stepped from his horse and into the Master's chair as if he had never been away. And she turned over the books to him, the keys to him, the plans and the orders and the decisions to him, as if all she knew was her needle. As if she had never been anything else but a peg to hang clothes on, an arranger of flowers, and a singer of little songs.

My great-great-great-grandmother was one of those women. I pass her portrait every day of my life, for it hangs on the curve of the west-wing stairs. She has the low-cut gown and the fat white arms of all the women of her day. She has the pretty rosebud mouth that slightly echoes Harry's. But I like to think that she had a strong mouth, a firm chin like mine, which the painter never saw for he was looking for prettiness, not strength. For I know I see something of myself in her eyes. They are not like mine for they are blue, and not feline. But there is something about them. A wariness, a suspicion, that I know mine have when men speak of land and ownership. She learned, as I learned: that women can deserve, or women can earn, but women can never own. And my eyes narrow in recognition when I pass her portrait, and I wonder how well she hid her hatred and her rage when she was moved out of the

Master's chair and into the parlour. And how I can avoid that fate myself.

If I could have seen my way to it I would rather have won Wideacre as my Norman forefathers did: with a straight challenge and a fight to the death to own the land. But we are civilized now, and so women are serfs without hope of recompense. No landed Squire even considers the rights of his wife or his daughters. The only chance I have ever had to own the land that I loved and deserved was by being indispensable to the men who owned it: indispensable to them in the field, like Papa, or – in the case of Harry – in field, office, and bed.

But my son and my daughter would not have to plot and contrive and lie and give their bodies to buy themselves into their rights. They would inherit legally, through men's law, by an act of the men's Parliament, with the blessing of male lawyers and male delegates. And I would smile and smile with my green eyes lidded to hide the gleam of triumph on the day that Richard and Julia were solemnly contracted as equal partners and named as the joint heirs of Wideacre.

The London lawyers' letter outlined how it could be done. The process was as costly as we had feared; it had to be agreed up to the very House of Lords. And then we had to compensate the cousin, Charles Lacey, who would be disinherited. While his hopes could not be high at the moment, for no word of Celia's barrenness had gone beyond the walls of the private rooms of Wideacre, he would guess soon enough when Harry wanted to settle the estate on his daughter and his nephew that Harry knew he would never have a son. Then we might expect a claim of more than a hundred thousand pounds – and we had to meet that claim before the entail could be changed.

'I don't know how we will ever raise that sort of money, Beatrice,' said Harry, the letter in his hand, seated at the rent table. 'We cannot raise it by mortgaging Wideacre for that would be a poor inheritance to pass on to the two of them. And we will never be able to save that sort of money from our revenues.'

'It has to be the MacAndrew fortune,' I said decisively. 'If we could use that to pay Charles Lacey, then I think we could mortgage some land to pay for the legal fees – and pay it off over time. With good management, and high-profit farming, we could probably free the estate from debt in ten or twenty years – certainly before the two children inherit.'

'Yes, but old Mr MacAndrew is hardly likely to buy his grandson into Wideacre at that price,' Harry objected. 'Besides he settled nearly that sum on John only a year ago.'

'It is John's fortune I'm thinking of,' I said musingly. 'If we could get power of attorney over that we could use it however we wished.'

'But on what grounds?' Harry asked, getting up from the table and looking out of the window. The Michaelmas daisies were still blooming beneath my window and their purple smell and the peppery perfume of the chrysanthemums were drifting into the room.

'Because of his drunkenness,' I said crisply. 'It might be possible to have him certified.'

Harry recoiled as if he had been stung by a bee.

'Certified!' he choked. 'Beatrice, it is you who are mad! I know that John is drinking steadily, drinking every day. But he seldom shows it. He is hardly insane!'

'I think his drinking is increasing,' I said, suppressing a fleeting sense of regret. 'I think he will drink more rather than less. And if he drinks much more he will either become incompetent, in which case you can have power of attorney, or he will drink himself to death, in which case I inherit his fortune with you and old Mr MacAndrew as trustees. Either way, his money is ours.'

'Yes, but Beatrice,' – Harry turned back into the rom and his face was serious – 'if this was to come about it would be a tragedy. John is a young man; he has all his life ahead of him. If he were to recover you might still be happy together, and he might well be happy to invest in such a good scheme for his son's future. I know you are angry and distressed with him now, so soon after Mama's death, but I am sure the two of you will be happy again, when John is his old self once more.'

I gave Harry my brightest, most angelic smile.

'It is what I pray for, every night,' I said. 'You heard me then, planning as a business woman. Now you see me as a wife. Of course I hope and believe that this shadow will pass from John.

But if it does not, I will be responsible for my son's future, so naturally I have to plan ahead.'

Harry's smile was relieved.

'Yes,' he said. 'I knew you were thinking aloud and planning for Richard and Julia. And I knew you were not really thinking that John should be certified.'

'Of course not,' I said lightly, then turned the subject away from my dangerous husband's future, and led Harry to think of other things.

But I could not turn Celia so easily. She had been walking Julia in the rose garden when John had seen her from the summerhouse and come out to take a turn. Julia's little bandy legs were eager to take wobbly steps, and she loved holding on to adult hands while she toddled, uncertainly, with many changes of direction and sudden plumpings to the ground on her well-padded bottom.

From my office window I saw them both and could hear Celia's clear voice.

'Do you think she is too young to start walking?' she asked, straightening up from the back-breaking exercise of following the infant prodigy's footsteps.

'No,' said John. He stood beside Celia and detached first one, then another of Julia's little grasping hands from her mama. Celia stood back and put both hands on the small of her back while Julia, welcoming the arrival of a new supporter, set off on one of her little expeditions with John bent over her, keeping her steady.

'If she was in swaddling she would not be walking till she was three or even four,' Celia said, watching their erratic progress.

'Bairns are the same as any young animal,' John said lightly. 'They know their own business best. Tied up in swaddling you can keep them still. But if they can kick and grow strong they are ready to walk at this early age.'

'But she won't hurt her legs, will she? She won't strain them?'

John turned his head and smiled at Celia. 'No,' he said reassuringly. 'She'll go at her own pace and soon be nimble and strong.'

Celia nodded.

'It is so good to see you outside on such a lovely day,' she said. 'And so nice to be able to ask you about Julia. You will start practising medicine again soon, won't you, John? It has been more than three months, you know.'

A shadow passed over his face and he looked back down at Julia again.

'No,' he said softly. 'I dare say I'll never practise again. I have lost my reputation; I have lost the occupation that was very dear to me; Wideacre has cost us all, in different ways.'

I froze, standing by the window. If this conversation grew any more revealing I should tap on the window to interrupt it. John was treading a very narrow line. I would not permit hints and indiscretions to Celia. They both, separately, knew too much. They must never put that picture together.

'But you will stop your drinking now,' said Celia tenderly, persuasively. 'You know how bad it is for you, and how unhappy you are making dear Beatrice. You will try to stop, won't you?'

John straightened up abruptly as Julia sat down, and reached for the golden head of a chrysanthemum.

'I will try,' he said uncertainly. 'These past months seem like a dream, not like reality at all. I keep thinking that one morning I will wake in bed beside Beatrice and she will be expecting our child and that none of this nightmare – my absence, the birth, our mama-in-law's death – will have happened. Then I take a drink because I cannot believe what is happening to me. And when I am drinking I know that it is all unreal, and that my real life is as happy as it was only a few months ago.'

Celia, the odious flirt, put out her hand to him. 'You will try to stop drinking,' she said persuasively. 'Dear, dear, brother John, you will try?'

And my broken drunk of a husband took her hand and kissed it. 'I will try,' he promised. And then he stooped over Julia and set her on her feet, and toddled her round to the stable yard.

And I knew, then, that I had him.

He was in my hand, like a hand-reared foal, because he was half in love with Celia and her child and the whole sentimental nonsense of Celia's life. Repelled by me, appalled by me, he was clinging on to Celia as a devout kisses the hem of a statue of the Virgin. Celia's love of her child, her clear-eyed honesty, her decent warmth, all held John to life when he feared he was going mad, when he longed for death. When he despaired of a world dominated by me, he could always see Celia's clear, lovely gaze and warm himself at the bright clear flame of her purity.

And that gave me a key to manage him. While he stayed on Wideacre through love of Celia, he could not harm me. While he kept his mouth shut to spare her, his discretion benefited me. While he gently, tenderly kissed her hand, he would not harass me. He loved and so he was vulnerable. And I was a little bit safer for that.

I was a little bit more dangerous for that as well. I am not a cold woman and I am not one who easily shares anything she loves, or even has loved once in the past. I never forgot that Celia had once threatened to take Harry from me. That when he could have been my lover he spent time and trouble to bring her willingly to his bed. That in order to keep the two of them permanently estranged I had to don all kinds of disguises and dance to all sorts of tunes to make myself Harry's addiction. If he had not been fatally flawed, early corrupted by the brutality of that school, I should never have been able to keep him from Celia. I knew I was a hundred times more beautiful than she, a hundred times stronger. But I could not always remember that, when I saw the quiet strength she drew on when she believed she was morally right. And I could not be certain that every man would prefer me, when I remembered how Harry had looked at her with such love when we came back from France.

I would never forgive Celia for that summer. Even though it was the summer when I cared nothing for Harry but rode and danced day and night with John, I would not forget that Celia had taken my lover from me without even making an effort at conquest.

And now my husband bent to kiss her hand as if she were a queen in a romance and he some plighted knight. I might give a little puff of irritation at this scene played out before my very window. Or I might measure the weakness in John and think how I could use it. But use it I would. Even if I had felt nothing else for John I should have punished him for turning his eyes to Celia. Whether I wanted him or not was irrelevant. I did not want my husband loving anyone else.

For dinner that afternoon I dressed with extra care. I had remodelled the black velvet gown that I had worn for the winter after Papa's death. The Chichester *modiste* knew her job and the deep plush folds fitted around my breasts and waist like a tight sheath, flaring out in lovely rumpled folds over the panniers at my hips. The underskirt was of black silk and whispered against the thick velvet as I walked. I made sure Lucy powdered my hair well, and set in it some black ribbon. Finally, I took off my pearl necklace and tied a black ribbon around my throat. With the coming of winter, my golden skin colour was fading to cream, and against the black of the gown I looked pale and lovely. But my eyes glowed green, dark-lashed and heavy-lidded, and I nipped my lips to make them red as I opened the parlour door.

Harry and John were standing by the fireplace. John was as far away from Harry as he could be and still feel the fire. Harry was warming his plump buttocks with his jacket caught up, and drinking sherry. John, I saw in my first sharp glance, was sipping at lemonade. I had been right. Celia was trying to save my husband. And he was hoping to get his unsteady feet back on the road to health. Harry gaped openly when he saw me, and John put a hand on the mantelpiece as if one smile from me might destroy him.

'My word, Beatrice, you're looking very lovely tonight,' said Harry, coming forward and setting me a chair before the two of them.

'Thank you, Harry,' I said, as sickly sweet as John's lemonade. 'Good evening, John.' The look I gave him was warm and sensual. I saw his knuckles whiten on the mantelpiece.

The parlour door opened and Celia came in. The blacks of mourning that set off my skin and eyes and hair merely drowned Celia's pale gold prettiness. She never looked her best in dark colours and I foresaw two years when I would shine her down without the least effort. Tonight, while I glowed with health and loveliness and the black velvet was like a jeweller's cloth to show off a warm cameo, Celia seemed aged and worn in her black gown.

Her brown eyes went to John's glass and her cheeks coloured, making her suddenly a pretty girl again.

'Oh! Well done!' she said encouragingly. And when Harry offered her a glass of sherry she chose to take lemonade in some feeble gesture of support. I smiled, my eyes more green and veiled than ever, and accepted the large sherry Harry poured for me, and drank it before John with obvious relish.

Stride called us in to dinner and nodded to me that he wished to speak with me. I let Harry lead me into the dining room and to my chair, then I smiled my excuses and went back out into the hall where Stride hovered.

'Miss Beatrice, I thought I should confirm with you,' he said in an undertone. 'Lady Lacey has ordered that there shall be no wine served this evening, nor any port for the gentlemen after dinner. She has ordered lemonade for the table, and water jugs.'

I gave an irrepressible chuckle.

'Don't be foolish, Stride,' I said. 'Are there wine glasses on the table?'

He nodded. 'The table was laid when she gave me this order and so I did nothing until I had confirmed it with you,' he said.

'Of course,' I said smoothly. 'You did rightly. We will certainly drink wine this evening and Sir Harry will, of course, wish to have his port. You must pour wine for my husband, and if he wishes to continue drinking lemonade he can do so.'

Stride nodded, and I returned to the dining room with a smile on my lips.

'Everything all right?' Harry asked. I nodded, and leaned towards Celia.

'I will explain about the wine later,' I said to her quietly.

She looked surprised at me, and then she glanced instinctively at John. His mouth was white where his lips were pressed together. He had himself in check but one could see the strain. Then Stride came back to the room and the two footmen served the meal while he poured the wine in every glass, as I had ordered.

Celia's gaze came up to me again in an unspoken challenge, but I was looking at Harry and asking him about the newly appointed Master of the Hunt.

'We'll still keep the dogs here, of course,' Harry confirmed. 'And Mr Haller can come over and see them often. I would rather, in any case, see a good deal of him during this year of mourning because although he knows the runs he does not know the Wideacre woods as we do, Beatrice. And I want to make sure the foxes are kept down this year.'

'Good,' I said. Mr Haller was leasing the Dower House, a handsome square-built sandstone house like a half-size Wideacre, which was standing empty, halfway down the drive. He had rented the house for the sport and was delighted to find that the Wideacre Hunt was without a Master while Harry was in mourning.

'How much I shall miss hunting,' I said with longing in my voice. The tone made John's shoulders tense. His wine glass was filled and ruby red before him; he could smell the bouquet.

'Yes,' said Harry. 'And of all people Mama would have wished us to enjoy ourselves.'

I gave a gurgle of laughter. 'Not me, Harry,' I said ruefully. 'She would have broken every convention in the book to please you, but she always wanted to keep me off horses, and indoors.'

Harry smiled and nodded. 'That's true,' he said comfortably. 'And I would not wish to be disrespectful to her memory. But it seems very hard to miss another season.'

He turned his attention to his plate and nodded at Celia.

'This is excellent, my dear,' he said.

She smiled and glowed a little at his praise.

'It is a recipe Papa brought back from one of his London clubs,' she said. 'I thought you would like it.'

John's shoulders had relaxed slightly and he was eating.

'I am so glad to see you eating, John,' I said sweetly to him. 'I was so distressed when you were unable to eat.'

John's fork fell back on his plate, untasted. Harry's eyes on me were tender and sympathetic, but Celia looked slightly puzzled, and was watching my face. I smiled warmly at her and reached for my wine glass. John's eyes were on the claret and I licked my lips in anticipation.

'What shall you do tomorrow, Harry?' I asked lightly, to turn the attention away from me again. 'I had thought of going to Chichester to order a trap or some sort of curricle for me to drive while I may not ride in public.'

'I shall come too then,' said Harry. 'I don't want you thundering home in a high-perch phaeton!'

I laughed, a confident, seductive ripple. John's fork clattered in his plate and he pushed his food away.

'Oh, yes!' I said. 'Something sporty and racy and a pair of matched greys to pull it!'

'I should like to come too, if I may,' said Celia softly. 'Julia needs some new shoes and I don't want to take her to the Acre cobbler; he does not have soft enough kid.'

The servants cleared the plates and Harry stood to carve a brace of pheasants. Celia and I had breast meat and John a couple of legs with rich savoury gravy to pour over the large chunks of meat. He was looking down at his plate, and I guessed he was feeling nauseous, and probably longing for a drink. I waited until he had been served with vegetables, and had a bread roll on his plate beside him, and then I leaned forward.

'Do try and eat,' I said tenderly. 'Don't leave the table and go to your study, John.'

It tipped the scales. He pushed his chair back as if the seat was burning him and took two hasty steps towards the door. He turned and bobbed a bow at Celia.

'I beg your pardon,' he said briefly, and the footman sprang to open the door and closed it with a click behind him. I nodded; John's plate and cutlery vanished smoothly, and Harry and Celia and I were alone.

'It is a shame,' Harry said compassionately. 'You do your best, Beatrice. But, my God, it is a shame.'

I dipped my head as if I were hiding tears.

'I am sure it will get better,' I said in half a whisper. 'I am sure he will learn to conquer it.'

I had thought I might escape a little talk with Celia by sitting with Harry over his port and then going straight to bed. But before breakfast the following day she tapped on my office door and asked if she might come in. In her morning gown of black she looked weary and far older than her twenty-six years. There were shadows under her eyes – she had clearly not slept – and her forehead was creased in a permanent frown of worry. Fresh-faced, smooth-skinned, and as sunny as the crisp blue-skied winter morning, I smiled at her and invited her to take a seat.

'It is about John,' she began. I smiled. Celia diving into a conversation, Celia seeking me out, Celia anxious about my husband, was a novelty indeed.

'Yes?' I said. I had remained seated at my desk and I let my eyes drift to the papers before me.

'Beatrice, he went to his study last night, and he started drinking again, although he promised me he would try to stop,' Celia said in an earnest rush.

'Yes,' I said sorrowfully. The papers were a comparison of yields on Wideacre since I had started keeping records. I thought that they might show the sort of profits we could expect if we followed Harry's idea of farming Wideacre as a business and not as a home.

'Beatrice, I am sorry to intrude,' said Celia. But she did not sound sorry. I was reminded suddenly of her barging into my bedroom in France with words of apology on her lips, but with a hungry baby in her arms and an absolute determination that I should feed the child. There was not one ounce of selfish strength in Celia, but give her someone to mother and she became in an instant a heroine. I should have been wary, but I was only amused.

'You are not intruding, Celia,' I said politely, and let her see that she was. 'Please go on.'

'When John went to his study last night there were two open bottles of whisky on the table. He drank them both,' she said. I showed her a shocked face.

'How did they get there?' asked Celia baldly.

'I don't know,' I said. 'John probably ordered his valet to bring him some. He has been drinking like this for four months, remember, Celia. The servants have just got into the routine of bringing him what he wants.'

'Then we must tell them not to,' Celia said energetically. She leaned forward on the table, her brown eyes bright and her tiredness gone. 'You must tell Stride that on no account is John to be supplied with drink, and we must not have wine on the table, or drink in the house, until he is cured.'

I nodded. 'You may be right, Celia,' I said. 'And John's health must come first. We must find some way to help cure him. Perhaps we should send him away. There are some wonderful doctors who specialize in cases such as this.'

'Are there?' asked Celia. 'I didn't know. But would he agree?'

'We could insist that he goes. We could legally bind him to take treatment,' I said, deliberately vague.

Celia sighed. 'It may come to that, I suppose. But it sounds dreadful. We could start to help him by not having drink here.'

I nodded. 'If you're sure that's the way, Celia,' I said uncertainly. 'I only ordered wine served last night because I thought John should get used to drinking lemonade while other people around him drink wine. When he dines out, there will always be wine at table, and port, you know.'

'Yes,' Celia said. 'I had not thought of that. But I feel sure we should keep drink completely away from him for the first few days. Will you order that, Beatrice?'

I smiled at her. 'Of course I will, Celia. Anything. Anything, to make my husband well again.'

She looked carefully at me, scanning my face. The little, loving Celia, who thought the world as gentle as herself, was learning fast. And the silly child who thought everyone was like herself, spoke like her, thought like her, loved like her, had the pit of otherness opening beneath her feet. She was coming to learn that I was different from her. But she could not begin to understand me.

She returned to her usual good manners. 'I should beg your pardon,' she said. 'I had no right to give an order without your knowledge. It was my concern for John that made me thoughtless. I just wanted to clear the table of wine.'

I blew her a kiss with an airy wave.

'It doesn't matter, Celia!' I said lightly. 'And you were probably right. We will clear the house of drink and that may help John, as you say.'

'I'll go and tell him then,' she said, and slipped from the room with a whisper of black silk.

I returned, with interest, to the yields. I did not need to eavesdrop on the conversation, for I knew, as clearly as if I had been there, how it would be. Celia would beg John to drink no more; John in pain from the whisky he had had last night, in pain at his own loss of manhood, of pride, of control, would miserably agree. Celia, her face glowing with hope and tenderness, would tell him that she had managed to make it easy for him. That the house would be free of drink. That if he came to dinner tonight there would be no sherry scenting the air of the parlour, and no ruby glow of wine cast over his plate at dinner.

That would make him hopeful. He would think that whatever sweet, tempting, teasing smiles I could give him, and however breathtakingly lovely I looked, however desirable I was, at least he would be spared the other sight – of two fresh bottles of whisky dewy-sided in his study, and a key in the lock so he could be alone with them.

So at breakfast we drank tea and lemonade, and Harry huffed into his pint pot, but said nothing. Celia gave up her drive to Chichester with me, preferring to stay home. If I knew my sister-in-law, she planned to tempt John out for an airing, to fortify him with sweet tea, and to keep him by her, with chatter and smiles, and play with Julia until dinnertime. She was fighting for his soul, and she would put all her loving, loyal little heart into it.

So Harry and I drove alone to Chichester and tested our new resolve to save money for Wideacre against the beauties of carriages that the carriage-maker showed us. Harry's resolve, predictably, wavered. But I held firm. What I needed was a smart little gig or trap to get me round the estate, and the well-built low-slung models were both too costly and too unstable for the rutted lanes that I would need to travel on if I wanted to spare myself a walk in the winter snow to check on the lambing.

'I'm exhausted,' I said, affecting a sigh when we had finally reached a decision. 'Let's go and beg some tea from the de Courceys.'

Lady de Courcey was an old friend of Mama's and her two children were only a little older than Harry and me. Of all the Chichester families the de Courceys were the nearest to us in rank, according to Mama's precise calculations. They owned no local land, but they were wealthier. They were an older family, but they had not been in the same house for years as we Laceys. We visited the bishop, whoever the present incumbent might be, of course. We visited two or three other families, but we were friendly only with the de Courceys.

Although we had now lost Mama's chilling sense of social gradations, Harry and I had not yet moved out of her chosen circle to make new friends. Partly it was because we lived at such a distance from Chichester as to make a visit there something of an expedition rather than a regular event. But also it was the nature of our Wideacre life. Like Papa we met only the people who lived close to us, or hunted with us, or kin. The roads were often muddy, and in mid-winter utterly impassable. Our work on the land was time-consuming and physically tiring. And, perhaps more than anything else, Harry and I, and now Celia and John too, were an absorbed self-centred little group. Given the choice, I would have been willing never to leave Wideacre for a single day, and while no one loved the place as I did, they all confessed to being content to stay inside the park walls for weeks and months at a time.

The Haverings were our friends, and the de Courceys. We occasionally had relations of Mama's to stay, or sometimes some of the Lacey family. But, like many families of our rank, we were a little isolated island amid a sea of poor people. No wonder Mama, who saw those beneath her as an anonymous mass, nearly invisible, had been lonely. No wonder I, catching the slightest hint of threat from those surrounding hundreds, thousands, felt sometimes afraid.

It was different for town dwellers. The de Courceys' house stood well back from the road among Scotch firs and was surrounded by a high wall topped with handsome, vicious, metal spikes. When Harry and I drove up there were three carriages already standing on the gravel sweep of the drive and I grimaced at him.

'A tea party,' I said. 'Don't desert me to the old ladies.'

Harry chuckled and handed me up the shallow flight of steps, while our footman hammered on the door. The de Courceys' butler escorted us over the black and white marble floor and threw open the parlour door.

'Mrs MacAndrew, Sir Harry Lacey,' he announced, and Lady de Courcey hurtled towards us from her chair.

'Beatrice! Harry! Darlings!' she said, and kissed us both soundly on both cheeks. I was slightly taller than her, and had to stoop for her kisses. She always made me feel as if she were too young to have been my mama's friend. She seemed to me to be eternally the twenty-year-old beauty who had captured the whole of London for a season and then scooped the best suitor on the market, Lord de Courcey. With no money and no family, she had got to this beautiful house and to her wealth on her looks alone. She struck me, with my keen eye for advantage and ownership, as an adventuress. But there was never a hint of that in her behaviour. She was a pattern card of social graces. It was only my view of her, as having gained wealth and position solely by a pretty face, that made her seem to me a clever cheat.

Now her drawing room was filled with some of the best of Chichester society. Most of the faces we knew, and I was led to make my curtsy to the old tabbies, and to shake the Bishop's hand. Harry, eyeing a plate of cakes, chatted to Lady de Courcey's daughter-in-law behind the tea trolley, and to her son Peter, standing by the fire.

Half a tedious hour we stayed before it was courteous for us to take our leave and then I turned on impulse to Isabel de Courcey and asked her if they would care to dine with us. Peter was keen to come; Lady de Courcey smilingly gave permission; in ten minutes they were ready, and the informal, impromptu invitation excused as part of my impulsive charm.

Celia was watching for us from the parlour window and came out on the doorstep when she saw the second carriage with the de Courcey arms emblazoned on the door following behind.

'How delightful,' she said, with her easy sweet manners. But I saw a shadow on her face, and I knew why.

She had spent all day with John keeping him from alcohol, nerving him for dinner with me, assuring him there would be no wine on the table. Now, dressed for dinner and waiting for him to come downstairs and for us to come home, she discovered with horror that he would be faced with a gay social event, and not the quiet helpful dinner party of a loving family.

I left the de Courceys with Celia and flicked up the west-wing stairs to change. This evening I had a gown of black taffeta, cut low along the square neck, and I wore a pair of jet ear-rings that dangled low and emphasized the length of my neck. I glanced at myself in my glass as I turned to the door and was well pleased with what I saw. The look of me, the perfect shape, would fill any man with desire. I knew, as surely as I knew where I was going, that to see me so lovely and to hate me so much, every night of his life, would destroy John MacAndrew.

404

He had gone through a stage when, fired with drink, he could attack me. He had gone through a stage when he needed a drink to face the sight of me. Now he discovered that the drink that had been his support, that had kept him alive through the nightmare of the recent months, was no help to him at all. He saw now why there had always been a bottle placed by his bedside, always a glass on his morning tray. He saw now that the bottle in the study, in the library, in the gun room, was no accident. That I had ordered it so. And he learned now, slowly, that he had two enemies and they were allied. One enemy was the woman he had loved. And the other was the drink he could not now refuse. He feared he was near defeat. He could feel himself falling. He could not bear his life, filled as it was, with loss. No child, no wife, no work, no pride, no affection from any source except Celia. And she was pouring her love to help him in a reform he feared he could not sustain. He feared also that failure.

I smiled to myself and saw how my mirror showed a woman so radiant that you would think I was still a bride on my wedding day. Then I sped down the stairs, the taffeta billowing behind me. Stride was in the hall, loitering for me.

I smiled at him with my quick awareness.

'I know,' I said, half laughing. 'But we really cannot expect the de Courceys to drink lemonade. Serve sherry in the parlour and wine in the dining room. We will have the best claret with the meal, and I think, champagne with the fruit. The gentlemen will have port as usual.'

'Is Mr MacAndrew's glass to be filled?' Stride asked, his voice neutral.

I showed no flicker of my awareness that Stride, and thus the rest of the household staff, had ceased to call my husband 'Doctor'. He would be 'Mr MacAndrew' to them now for the rest of his life, and they would hear no reprimand from me.

'Of course,' I said, and passed Stride and went into the parlour.

They were all there. John had himself well under control and Celia's eyes were on him full of love. Harry was looking around for the sherry decanter as Stride brought it in, and he poured with a liberal hand for the de Courceys, for me, and for himself.

Celia took a glass of lemonade, and John held the pale yellow drink in his hand, untouched. I could see his head was up, turned towards Harry, and with my keen instinct, I knew he was scenting the air, smelling the perfume of the sherry, warm in the firelight.

Dinner was served and Celia took in the array of glasses on the table with one glance, and a sharp look at me. I shrugged slightly, and nodded my head towards the de Courceys. 'What can I do?' my eyes said, silently to her.

John ate little, but he minded his manners and maintained a stilted conversation with Isabel on his left. I listened to every word as I talked to Peter, who was beside me. John touched neither the white nor the red wine through the meal, and I saw how his eyes followed the glasses when they were taken away. Then the great silver bowl of fruit was placed on the table and there was the promising pop of the champagne cork and the appetizing swish of it bubbling into the glasses.

I was watching John's face; he loved champagne.

'Just one glass,' he said, half to himself, half to Celia. Celia shook her head fiercely at the footman who stood ready to pour into John's glass. There was an awkward moment. He stood with the bottle poised over the tall slim glass. John's eyes fixed on the deep green mouth of the bottle and secret hiss of the good wine fizzing within.

'No,' said Celia in an urgent undertone to the footman. He was Jack Levy – an orphan who would have been in the parish workhouse if I had not given him the job of lighting the fires, ten years ago. Now he was well fed, cocky, and handsome in livery. His eyes went straight to me for his orders, and he obeyed my slight nod. He poured the effervescing golden liquid into John's glass, and moved on. Harry gave a toast. Harry is the sort who always gives toasts. And we drank. John gulped at his glass as if he was parched. Levy glanced at me again and obeyed my nod to refill John's glass. And refill it again. And again.

Isabel was talking about their London season, and about the parties they had attended, and Harry was asking her town gossip. Peter de Courcey was telling me about his plans to buy a shooting lodge in the north, and I recommended he speak to Dr Pearce who knew the area well. No one attended to John, whose eyes were bright and who was drinking steadily. And no one except me noticed Celia, who sat silent, with her head bowed, and tears running down her cheeks.

I waited till her shoulders had straightened, and she had glanced surreptitiously around and wiped her wet face on her table napkin, then rose to withdraw. The men got to their feet, John holding to the back of his chair for support. I suspected the room was spinning around his fuddled head. I led the ladies to the parlour, and we sat by the fire.

The rest of the evening passed but slowly. When the gentlemen joined us they came without John and I cocked an eyebrow at Harry and saw his mouth turn downwards in a grimace.

'The footmen are putting him to bed,' he said in a low voice to me. 'Peter de Courcey saw nothing odd, but really, Beatrice, it is disgraceful.'

I nodded, and moved to the tea table to pour the tea. The de Courceys drank their tea in a rush and left in a hurry to be home while the road was bright in the moonlight. Their carriage was at the door, and they bundled inside with hot bricks at their feet and rugs up to their ears.

'Goodbye,' I called from the doorstep, my breath like smoke on the freezing air. 'Lovely to see you. Thank you for coming.'

Then their carriage rolled away down the drive and I went back into the house. Harry had taken himself off, sleepy with the port and the conversation, but Celia was waiting for me by the parlour fire.

'Did you invite the de Courceys, Beatrice?' she asked. I hesitated. There was a note in Celia's voice I had never heard before. A hardness.

'I don't remember,' I temporized. 'Harry or I.'

'I have asked Harry,' she said. 'He says it was your invitation.'

'Then it must have been,' I said lightly. 'We often have them to dinner, Celia. I did not think you would have any reason to dislike a visit from them.'

'I did not dislike it.' Celia's voice was high with incredulity. 'But whether I should like it or dislike it is not the question, Beatrice. John has been planning all day to drink nothing. Never to drink again. All day I promised him that you had given your word and there would be no drink at Wideacre. All day I assured him that he could sit down to the dinner table and that no one would offer him alcohol to drink. Then he comes to dinner and has to sit with a glass of cool white wine before him, then a glass of red, and finally his favourite champagne. Beatrice, it was too much for him! He is drunk again now, and he will be miserable in the morning! He will feel he has failed, and indeed he has. But he failed because of our selfishness and folly!'

There were tea.. s in her eyes, but there was the bright pink of temper in her cheeks. I scarcely recognized my gentle little sister-in-law in this determined, angry woman.

'Celia,' I said, reproachfully.

Her eyes fell; her colour died down.

'I beg your pardon,' she said, with the discipline of long years of good manners. 'But I am most disturbed about John. I hope that tomorrow night there will be no drink in the house.'

'Of course,' I said. 'But when we have guests we can hardly serve them lemonade. You do see that, don't you, Celia?'

'Yes,' she said unwillingly. 'But we expect no one for the rest of this week, do we?'

'No,' I said with a smile. 'And while there is just you and Harry and me, I think it is right that there should be no drink to tempt John. We will all try to help him.'

She came to me then and kissed my cheek in an empty gesture of courtesy. But her lips were cold. Then she went to bed and left me by the fire looking at the red pyramids and castles, caverns and caves, in the embers, and seeing a long long line of despair and failure for the man I had married for love.

The next night Mr Haller came to dinner so we had to serve wine; John had a glass and then another. Celia and I left him, Harry and George Haller to their port. John's valet put him to bed, dead drunk.

The night after Dr Pearce came up from Acre to take pot luck. 'For a little bird told me you were having hare in red wine sauce, and that is my favourite dish,' he said sweetly to Celia.

'What little bird was that?' she asked, her eyes flickering to me.

'The most beautiful little bird in the parish!' said Dr Pearce, kissing my hand. Celia's face was stony.

The following night we had an invitation to dine with Celia's parents and by common consent it was agreed that John should not come.

Celia spent some time with Stride and I imagined she was making him promise that John should have no wine with his meal and no port thereafter. Stride met me in the hall. He looked patient. His pay was certainly high enough to cover the problem of resolving contradictory orders, and in any case there was only one voice that gave orders at Wideacre, and it spoke now.

'Mr MacAndrew is not to be served wine or port tonight,' I said. 'But you will put two bottles of his whisky with a glass and water in the library for him.'

Stride nodded. His expression did not change by a flicker. I think if I had told him to set up a hangman's noose in Mr MacAndrew's bedroom he would have done so without comment.

'I told Stride, John should have nothing to drink tonight,' Celia said to me as we settled ourselves under the rugs in the carriage for the drive to Havering Hall.

'Of course,' I nodded. 'I only hope he has no whisky.'

Celia looked shocked. 'I had not thought of that,' she said. 'But I feel certain that if he is not actually offered drink he will not order it brought to him.'

'I hope so,' I said piously.

Harry grunted his reservations but said no more.

I made sure the evening was a long one. Lord Havering was at home and was happy to beg his wife for another game of cards when I was his partner, sitting opposite him, my slanty green eyes decorously on my cards but sometimes sliding to his raffish, bloodshot face with a secret smile.

But when we got home every light was blazing and the curtains were not drawn.

'What's this?' I said, my voice sharp with alarm, and I sprang from the carriage before the steps were down.

'Is Richard all right? Julia? Is it the Culler?'

'It's Mr MacAndrew,' said Stride, coming out to the carriage. 'He has set fire to the carpet in the library and smashed some china.'

Harry gave an exclamation and strode past me to the library and flung open the door. It was in chaos. The priceless Persian carpet was blackened and scorched with a great wide hole burned in it. The glass cabinets had been staved in, and some floor-standing flower vases had been flung across the room and smashed. Books had been tipped from the cases and were scattered, leaves curled, in the middle of the room. And in the midst of this wreckage stood my husband, booted and in his shirt-sleeves, with a poker in his hand, looking like the Prince of Denmark in the travelling theatre.

Harry froze on the threshold, too stunned to speak. But Celia dipped like a flying bird under his arm and ran into the room to John.

'What is it, John?' she said, her words tumbling out in her distress. 'Have you gone mad? What is it?'

He pointed the poker. On the little round table, drawn temptingly close to his favourite chair, were the two bottles of whisky and the decanter of icy water. A small plate of biscuits, and a trimmed cigar ready for lighting.

'Who put that there?' demanded Celia, and she spun round on Stride. She seemed suddenly taller, and she held her head high and her eyes burned with anger. 'Who put that there?' she said, and the note of command was clear in her voice.

'I did, your ladyship,' said Stride. He faced Celia without shrinking, but he had never before seen her like this. None of us had.

'Did Dr MacAndrew order it?' she asked. No lie would have been possible to Celia as she stood there, her eyes blazing and her face icy.

'No, your ladyship,' said Stride. He did not volunteer that it was my order. But Celia had, in any case, heard enough.

'You may go,' she said abruptly, and nodded him to close the door. Harry, John, Celia and I were left alone in the wreckage of the room.

The poker had dropped to John's side and he was no longer buoyed up with rage. He was looking hungrily, longingly at the bottles. His shoulders were sagging already with anticipated defeat. Celia strode across the room with fast strides, quite unlike her usual pretty glide, and picked both bottles up by their necks in one hand. With one rapid backward gesture she smashed them against the stone fireplace and threw the broken necks into the grate.

'You ordered those for him, Beatrice,' she said, and her voice was full of anger. Her very dress seemed stiff with her rage. 'You ordered those, just as you have arranged that we should have wine with every meal. You want to force John to drink. You want to keep him drinking.'

Harry's mouth was gawping like a netted salmon. Events were too fast for him, and Celia in a rage was a sight to shock the coolest of men. I was little better. I watched her curiously, as I might have watched a kitten suddenly turn vicious. And I was afraid of this new strength in her.

'I am Lady Lacey,' she said. Her head was up, her breathing fast, her whole face alight with the force of her anger. She had never been angry in her life before, and this explosion of rage was sweeping her along like a spring flood.

'I am Lady Lacey,' she said again. 'This is my house and I order, I *order*, that there shall be no alcohol available in this house for anyone.'

'Celia . . .' said Harry feebly; and she rounded on him, forgetting her habitual obedience as if it had never been. 'Harry, I will not have a man destroyed under my very eyes and do nothing to save him,' she said fiercely. 'I have never commanded in this house. I have never commanded anywhere, nor felt any desire to do so. But I cannot let this go on.'

Harry gazed wildly at me for help but I could do nothing. I stood as still as a fox in the forest when he hears the horns and the yelps of the dogs. But my eyes ranged from John, unmoving, unspeaking, to Celia, bright with anger.

'Where are the keys to the cellar?' she said to Harry.

'Stride has them,' he said feebly. 'And Beatrice.'

Celia walked to the door and tore it open. Predictably Stride and the housekeeper were in the hall and foolish they looked, lingering in earshot.

'Give me the keys to the cellar,' Celia said to Stride. 'All the keys. Miss Beatrice's set as well.'

Stride glanced at me and I nodded. There was no stopping this torrent; it was like being knocked off your feet by a flash flood. You swim with it until it is spent and only then do you worry how to get home.

Stride fetched his keys, and mine from the hook in my office. We stood in silence until the door from the west wing banged and he returned.

Celia took the two bunches in her firm grip.

'I shall keep these until we serve wine again, when John is well,' she said with absolute certainty. 'Harry, do you agree?'

Harry gulped and said, 'Yes, my dear,' like flotsam in the flood.

'Beatrice?' she asked, and her voice was as stony as her face.

'Of course, if you wish it,' I said, my eyebrows raised in an insolent, easy gesture.

She ignored me and turned to Stride.

'We will go and lock the cellars now, if you please. But send Dr MacAndrew's valet to take him to his room. He is not well.'

'Mr MacAndrew's valet has the night off,' Stride started. Celia cut in at once.

'Dr MacAndrew, you mean,' she said, and held his gaze. Stride's eyes fell before her brown bright hardness.

'Dr MacAndrew,' he said.

'Then send a footman,' she said briskly. 'Dr MacAndrew will be tired and needs his sleep. And send someone to clear up in here.' She turned to me and Harry, standing mumchance on the scorched carpet with the smell of expensive smoke around us. I was as nervous as a horse on burned land.

'When I have locked the cellar I shall go to bed,' she said. 'We will discuss this, if you wish it, in the morning.'

And she turned and left us.

And there was nothing I could do to stop her.

In the morning she was the same. In the afternoon she received some callers and while I worked in the office I wondered if the babble of high voices and the tinkle of laughter would tire and undermine her. When I came down to dinner in the evening, my silk skirts rustling, my own head held high, she met me look for look. She was unbending. She was mistress of the house.

I claimed Harry's hand and we went in for dinner with John squiring Celia to her place. He had now been a full day without a drink and his hands were shaking and there was a nervous tremor around his mouth. But with Celia on his arm his head was up and his walk was straight. I glanced covertly at them and they looked like a pair of heroes who had survived the worst of their adventure. They both looked tired: John was in bad shape physically, and Celia had violet shadows under her brown eyes to bear witness that her anger had made her sleepless for another night, but they looked ready to follow any thread into any maze and face any bull-like monster that might be lurking in the darkness there.

There was no wine at dinner. John drank water, Celia sipped at a glass of lemonade, and Harry had a pint mug full of water at his plate. Harry looked sour, as well he might, and I took my lemonade in mutinous silence. None of us made any attempt to maintain the appearance of a normal meal. I would normally set a conversation going and include Harry and Celia, but tonight I was sulky and unprepared for this defeat. The meal was brief and when Celia and I rose to withdraw I was relieved to see that the gentlemen were coming with us. I had not relished the prospect of private time alone with Celia before the parlour fire.

We ordered the tea table early and sat in silence, like suspicious strangers. When I had drunk my tea I put the cup down in the saucer with a decisive click and said to Harry, 'Would you come to my office, Harry, if there is nothing you would rather do? I have had a letter about water rights on the Fenny and I want you to see the problem with a map.'

Celia's eyes were on me, and I saw that she was testing my words for the truth.

'That is, if Celia permits,' I said sharply, and watched her quick rise of colour and her eyes drop in what looked like shame.

'Of course,' she said, softly. 'I shall be going to the library to read in a few moments.'

I did not bother to maintain the pretence once I had shut my office door, but I spun round on it, leaned against the panels and said imperiously to Harry, 'You must stop Celia with this madness. She will drive us all crazy.'

Harry threw himself into the armchair by the fire like a sulky schoolboy.

'There's nothing I can do!' he said with irritation. 'I spoke to her this morning for she would hear nothing about it last night, and she just said again, "I am Lady Lacey and John will not have drink in my house."'

'She's your wife,' I said crudely. 'She has to obey you, and she used to be frightened of you. Threaten her, raise your voice to her. Break some china near her, hit her. Anything, Harry. For we cannot go on like this.'

Harry raised his eyes to me. He looked aghast.

'Beatrice, you forget,' he stumbled. 'We are talking about Celia! I could no more shout at her than I could fly to the moon. She is not the sort of woman one shouts at. I could not possibly try to frighten her. I could not begin to do it. I could never wish to do it.'

I chewed the inside of my lip to control my rising temper.

'Well, as you like, Harry. But we will have a pretty miserable Christmas on Wideacre if Celia keeps the wine locked away. You cannot even have a glass of port after dinner. How will we entertain our guests? What can we offer callers at noon or dinner? This plan of Celia's simply won't work and you must tell her so.'

'I have tried,' Harry said feebly. 'But she just keeps on about John. She is really determined to stop him drinking, you know, Beatrice. She will not hear of any other course.'

His face softened. 'And she is right when she says how happy we were before Mama died. If he did stop drinking, Beatrice, and you and he were happy together again, that is worth any amount of sacrifice, is it not?'

'Yes, of course,' I said sweetly. 'But in the meantime, Harry, it grieves me to see Celia, who used to care for your comfort so well, forbidding you the smallest of innocent pleasures: like a glass of sherry before your dinner, and a glass of port with a friend. You will be the laughing-stock of the county if this gets out. How people will joke about Wideacre gone teetotal, and a Squire so much under the cat's paw that he is not even allowed a glass of his own wine.'

Harry's rosebud mouth turned down still further.

'It's bad, I know,' he said. 'But Celia is determined.'

'But we agree with her!' I said beguilingly. 'We too think John should stop his drinking. It is just that we know that here we cannot ensure that he has no access to drink. The only way to do it is to send him to a doctor who can cure him. I have looked into this and there is a Dr Rose at Bristol who specializes in precisely this problem. Why do we not send John there? He can stay till he is cured, and when he comes home he will be well and we can all be happy again.'

Harry's eyes brightened. 'Yes, and while he is away everything can be as normal again here,' he said, visibly cheered.

'Well, put the scheme to Celia now,' I said. 'Suggest it straight away and then we can have John out of the house within the week.'

Harry bounced from his chair with new energy and left the office. I waited. I reread the letter about the water rights, which is every landowner's nightmare, and checked the claims against a map. It was a farmer further down the valley of the Fenny who was following a new-fangled plan of irrigation to grow some moisture-loving crop on his land. He had dug some fancy channels and was all ready to open the sluice gates from the Fenny when suddenly the water level had dropped. It was our millpond filling up after a period of milling, and if the man had been farming with an eye on the river rather than his nose in a book he would have seen the changing levels of the Fenny before he put his expensive gates in place.

Now his work would have to be redone, and he was blaming

us and insisting on a guaranteed flow as if I could manage the rainfall. I became absorbed in drafting the reply, and barely glanced up when the door clicked.

I had been expecting Harry to return and tell me all was well, but it was Celia. I thought I saw a gleam of tears in her eyes and assumed that Harry had won the argument. But then I saw the purpose in her face, and the look she gave me was not that of a beaten woman.

'Beatrice, Harry came to talk to me, but I think everything he said was what you had told him,' she said firmly. I detected, to my amazement, a slight tone of disdain in her voice.

'I am sure we know each other well enough for you to speak to me directly,' she said. I was right, her tone was scornful. 'Perhaps you will tell me now what is in your mind regarding your husband?'

I pushed the letters to one side, and folded the map carefully while keeping my eyes on this brave child who had left her ladylike pursuits to come so dauntlessly into my office.

'Please sit down, Celia,' I said politely. She pulled one of the hard-backed chairs from around the rent table and sat in it, straight-backed. I moved from my desk to sit beside her; I tried to put a warm compassionate look in my eyes but I found her direct candid gaze too disconcerting.

'We cannot go on as we are,' I said, my voice concerned. 'You saw how uncomfortable it was at dinner today. We cannot possibly have evening after evening like this, Celia.'

She nodded. My reasonable tone was undermining her anger. I was making her see the problem of John as a trouble we all shared. I was detaching her from the idea that he was her responsibility in a world that cared nothing for him, perhaps even with a wife who was happy to do him harm.

'I think we could manage for a short time,' she said consideringly. 'I do not think John's problem is so deep-seated that he needs longer than perhaps a few weeks' freedom from temptation.'

'Celia,' I said earnestly. 'He is my husband. I do think about what is best for him. His health and happiness are my concern.'

Her eyes came up at the tone of tenderness in my voice and she stared curiously at me.

416

'Do you mean that?' she asked baldly. 'Or is it something you are saying?'

'Celia!' I said. But my reproachful remonstrance had not maintained its power.

'I am sorry if I sound impolite,' she said evenly. 'But I simply cannot understand your behaviour. If you do care for John you should be desperate for him to be well. Yet I do not see that.'

'I cannot explain,' I said, my voice low. 'I cannot forgive him for Mama's death. I wish him to be well, but I cannot yet love him as I ought.'

'But you will, Beatrice!' said Celia, her face suddenly lightening with sympathy for me. 'As soon as he is well again, your love will return. I know things will be happy between you once more.'

I smiled, sweet as sugar. 'But Celia, you have your husband to consider too,' I said. 'It is one thing for me to say there shall be no drink served here, but it is hard for you because you will make Harry so uncomfortable.'

Celia's face hardened, and I guessed she had already faced this argument upstairs.

'It is not much to ask of a man,' she said firmly. 'It is not too much to ask of a man, that he should give up drinking for a few short weeks when the happiness, perhaps even the life, of his sister's husband depends on it.'

'No, indeed,' I said nodding. 'Providing he does give up. But what if all you succeed in doing is to drive Harry away from his home?'

Celia's eyes flew anxiously to my face.

'There are many families round here who would be happy to see Harry for dinner every day of the week,' I said. 'They would not trouble him with tragedy-queen scenes when he is tired and wants a quiet drink and a good meal. They would be happy to see him, show him a smiling face, serve him with the best that they have in the house, and make him feel comfortable and beloved. There is young company at some of the houses too,' I went on, twisting the knife. 'After dinner Harry may find himself dancing. And some of the prettiest girls in England are to be found in the farmers' houses around here. And they'd all be more than glad to dance with the Squire.'

When one loves, one gives hostage to the future. Celia, who had once told me that she would have liked Harry to take a mistress, now looked horrified at the thought of him dancing with a pretty girl.

'Harry would never be unfaithful to you,' I said reassuringly. 'I am *sure* he would not. But you could hardly blame a man for dining away from home when his home is made uncomfortable for him.'

Celia turned her head away and rose from the table in a sudden sharp movement that told me that the picture of Harry away from home on pleasure jaunts alone was more than she could face. I sat still and said nothing. I gave her a good few minutes while she stood beside the fireplace resting her head on the high mantelpiece and looking down at the burning logs.

'What do you think we should do, Beatrice?' she asked. I gave a silent sigh. I was in control once more.

'I think we should find a good doctor to take John into his own home to cure him,' I said. 'This drinking is not weakness, Celia. It is more like an illness. John cannot help himself. What I would like would be for him to go away to a really first-class specialist and for us to keep his home safe and happy for him. Then when he returns we can all be as we were.'

'And you will love him again, Beatrice?' Celia's eyes on me were bright with the challenge. 'For I know it is the way things are between you which is the worst of all for him.'

I smiled with relish at the thought of the day-long torture I was to John.

'Yes, indeed,' I said, my voice tender. 'I shall never be out of his sight.'

Celia came back to me, seated at the table, and knelt beside my chair.

'Is that a promise, Beatrice?' Her honest eyes scanned my face.

I held her gaze, my face as clear as my conscience.

'On my honour,' I said solemnly.

Celia, overwrought and anxious, gave a little sob and buried her face in the silk of my skirt. I rested one gentle hand on her bowed head. Poor Celia! She understood so little, and she tried to do so much.

I stroked her hair soothingly. It was soft as warm silk to the touch.

'Silly Celia,' I said lovingly. 'And what a scene you made of it yesterday!'

She turned her face into my lap and then looked up at me smiling.

'I don't know what I was thinking of,' she confessed. 'Something in my head just broke and I was so angry I did not know what I was saying or doing. I have been so worried for John, and so afraid about what was happening. Nobody seemed to be like themselves any more: you, Harry, John of course. It all seemed so different, so strange, when, before, we were all so happy. There seemed to be something poisoning the whole house.'

My smile hid my sudden shock. I had heard this before. Celia was talking just as Mama had done. They both had a sense of the corruption between Harry and me. It was as if our sin were some rotting thing in the house that stank until anyone close to us could smell it, but not know what it was. I gave a little shudder at the thought and bent down to bury my own face in Celia's sweet-smelling hair.

'Let us talk no more tonight,' I said. 'In the morning I shall show you a letter I have had from a Dr Rose at Bristol, and if you agree he sounds like the very person for John then we can send for him to come and see John here.'

Celia got obediently to her feet. She looked tremendously relieved. I had stripped her of her power by using my wits and by exploiting her own trusting nature. She was free again to be the loving wife and the pet of the household. She went lightly to the door and whispered, 'Goodnight, God bless you,' and then left me. I smiled at the embers of the logs and sat before the fire with my feet on the fender. Celia had caused me some alarm, but I had her back in my hand now. I rang the bell for my maid, Lucy.

'Fetch me a glass of port from the hamper that was delivered from Chichester, please,' I said to her. 'And take the bottle into Mr MacAndrew's bedroom.'

Afterwards I warmed my toes, and sipped my glass until I was called to supper. I read in the parlour until the clocks chimed midnight and, at the witching hour, I went to my bed and slept.

*

It was a busy week for me. I replied to Dr Rose and asked him and his partner to come and see John, and, if they thought him likely to respond to treatment, to take him back in their carriage. Left to me, John could have gone into a public hospital for the insane where the lunatics wallowed in their own filth and jabbered like monkeys in corners. But Dr Rose's place was quite different. He had a small manor house outside Bristol and took only half-a-dozen patients. His method was slowly to reduce their alcohol, or drugs, until they were able to face the day with only very small amounts. In some cases they learned to do without their laundanum, opium or alcohol altogether, and could return to their friends and families completely cured.

As soon as that letter had gone off I received one from the London lawyers, who were ready to take steps to buy the entail if I thought the capital to compensate Charles Lacey would be forthcoming. My married name, MacAndrew, inspired a good deal of respect in the City and the letter was positively servile. But they would not be doing their job if they had not cautioned me that the cost of buying the entail was likely to be as much as £200,000. I nibbled the end of my pen and smiled at that. A week ago and I would have been in despair, but now, I thought, with sweet Celia's help, I might be able to find that sum within the month. So I wrote them a guarded reply and told them to open negotiations with Charles and to keep the price as low as possible.

The second letter I had was from a London merchant who had been approached by our solicitors about a possible mortgage to raise the capital we would need to pay the legal fees. The MacAndrew fortune would stretch only so far, and we would have to mortgage some of Wideacre's lovely land to take the whole of the estate for my son. If the figures I had calculated were right, I should be able to pay off the mortgage before Richard was even twenty-one. With extra corn grown on the common, extra rents paid, and bad debts called in, Wideacre could nearly double its profits. But it would be a hard winter for the people if we did all that. The merchant, Mr Llewellyn, offered to drive down to Wideacre to see the land for himself, and I sent him a civil invitation to come within the week.

And then I tired of my office and the four walls around me and slipped upstairs to Richard's nursery where he was in the middle of his breakfast.

There is nothing, nothing in the world messier than a young child learning to feed himself. And, providing you do not have to touch him yourself, no sight more endearing. Richard grabbed unsteadily at his cup of milk and splashed at his face, getting some, accidentally I think, in his mouth. His little fist closed on a slice of bread and butter and he ate from his own hand like a little savage. His buttery, milky, stained face beamed at me through a mask of food and I beamed back.

'Isn't he growing!' I said to Nurse.

'Indeed, yes,' she said, hovering with a wet cloth waiting for Richard to conclude this feast of the senses. 'And so strong and so clever too!'

'Dress him warmly,' I said. 'I shall take him out driving in the new trap I bought. You will come too.'

'There!' she said to Richard approvingly. 'Won't that be a treat!'

She wiped him clean and lifted him from the chair to take him through to his bedroom. I heard his protesting wails as she stripped and cleaned him, and I stood, idle, by the nursery fire smiling at the noise. He has a good pair of lungs, my son Richard, and a will as strong as my own. When they came out together he was dressed as I had ordered, but his hapless nurse looked ruffled and cross.

'Mama!' he said, and scrambled across the room in a little rolling crawl to my feet. My skirts billowed as I plumped down beside him on the floor and lifted him to my face. His gentle little hand patted my cheek and his deep blue eyes were fixed on mine with the unswerving love that only very small well-loved children give. I buried my face in his neck and kissed him hard, and then I play-bit his little bulging tummy, so full of bread and milk, and tickled his warm well-covered ribs until he gurgled and whooped for mercy.

While Nurse found her bonnet and shawl and an extra blanket for him, I romped and played with him like a child myself. I hid behind the armchair and popped out at him to his uproarious delight. I hid his moppet behind me and let him find her. I tumbled him over and rolled him on the floor, then I tossed him up to the ceiling and pretended to drop him in a great giggly swoop down to the floor.

Then I caught him up to me and carried him down the west-wing stairs out through the side entrance to the stable yard. John was just coming in and he froze to see me, my child on my hip, my face flushed with love and laughter. I handed Richard to Nurse, who took him on out to see the horses.

'Thank you for your present of last night,' said John. His face was sickly white. He looked as if he had drunk deep.

'You are welcome,' I said icily. 'You can be sure that I will always keep you supplied with whatever you need.'

His mouth trembled. 'Beatrice, for pity's sake don't . . .' he said. 'It is an awful thing to do to a man. I have seen better men than I end up as puking puppies in the street through drinking continually to excess. Celia thinks she can cure me; she says you all three agreed there should be no drink left in the house. Please don't send me bottles like that.'

I shrugged. 'If you do not want them, don't drink them,' I said. 'I cannot make the whole of Sussex dry for you. There will always be drink around, perhaps one or another servant will always bring you a glass. I cannot help that.'

'You can help it, Beatrice, for you order it,' he said with an invalid's sudden nervous energy. 'Your word is the law at Wideacre. If you had a mind to save me you could ban drink from the whole estate and no one would disobey you.'

I smiled slowly into his red-rimmed eyes.

'That's true,' I said, my face as sweet as a May morning. 'But I will never ban drink from where you are, because I am content to see you destroy yourself. There will be no peace for you while I am here. And every time you open a drawer, or reach underneath your bed, or open a cupboard, there will be a bottle waiting. And nothing you do, or Celia does, can prevent that.'

'I will tell Celia,' he said desperately. 'I will tell her you are determined to destroy me.'

'Tell Celia!' I laughed, a hard scornful laugh. 'Run to Celia and tell her. I shall say I have not even seen you today, that you are dreaming. That I sent no port to you, that the cellar doors are still locked, which they are. Tell anyone whatever you like,' I said triumphantly. 'Nothing will save you from drink while you are on my land.'

I swept past him, my step as light and carefree as a girl's and I caught my son up from his nurse. John heard Richard crow with laughter to be in my arms again, and then heard my sharp order to the grooms to hold the horse steady while I climbed into the trap with the precious burden.

As I took the reins in my gloved hands and clicked to the horse I glanced back at the door. John was standing where I had left him, his face greeny-white, his shoulders slumped in despair. Somewhere, lost in the back of my mind, was a sharp pain to see him so defeated, so driven. But I remembered his attack on me, his affection for Celia, and jealousy, fear, my own driving will, kept me hard. I know no half-measures. I had loved this man most truly; now I hated and feared him. I clicked to the horse and we drove out past him, into the bright sunshine of a Wideacre winter day.

I had him on the run, my husband. He spoke privately with Celia some time while I was out on my drive, and when I came home I noticed her face at the window of the parlour. As I expected, Stride came out to the stable yard with a message from her. He waited while I held Richard up to stroke the horse's nose, and while I fed it a handful of corn from my pocket; then he told me Lady Lacey would like to see me at once, if it was convenient. I nodded, gave Richard a good hard hug, and told him to eat up all his dinner and went with a quick step to the parlour.

Celia was sewing in the window seat and her face was pale and tired again.

'Good afternoon,' I said blithely. 'I have come straight to you smelling of horse and must be quick, for I have to change.'

Celia nodded with a smile that did not reach her eyes.

'Have you seen John today, Beatrice?' she asked.

'No,' I said lightly. 'I passed him on the stairs this morning but we did not speak.'

Her look was suddenly intent. 'You said nothing to each other?' she asked.

'No,' I said casually. 'I had Richard with me, and John looked ill. I did not want him upsetting the child.'

Celia's face was aghast. 'Beatrice, I am so afraid!' she exclaimed. I turned to her in surprise.

'Celia, what is it?' I asked, full of concern. 'What has happened?'

'It is John,' she said, nearly in tears. 'I think he is delirious with drink.'

I feigned shock, and sat beside her on the window seat, taking her embroidery from her still hands.

'Why?' I asked. 'What is happening?'

Celia gave a muffled sob and dipped her face into her hands. 'John came to me just after breakfast,' she said. 'He looked dreadful and he talked wildly. He said you were a witch, Beatrice. That you were a woman possessed by the land. He said that you had killed for the land. That you were trying to kill him. That you had promised that everywhere he went there would be drink until he was dead from it. And when I told him that he was dreaming, he looked at me wildly and said, "You too! She has captured you too!" and he dashed from the room.'

I put my arm around her and Celia leaned her soft pliant body against me and wept into my shoulder.

'There, there,' I said. 'Don't cry so, Celia. It sounds so very bad, but I am sure we can cure John in the end. It sounds indeed as if he is half crazed, but we can help him.'

Celia shuddered with a sob and was still.

'He talks as if it were all your fault,' she whispered. 'He talks as if you were a monster. He calls you a witch, Beatrice.'

'It is often the way,' I said steadily, sadly. 'Men who drink so much often turn against the very people they love most in the world. It is part of the madness, I think.'

Celia nodded, and straightened up, drying her eyes.

'He had a drink last night,' she said sadly. 'I was not able to prevent that. He told me it simply appeared in his room. He said you had cursed him with drink every time he reaches out a hand.'

'Yes,' I said. 'I suppose he would blame me for everything. He loves me still in his heart. That is why he has turned against me now.'

Celia looked at me wonderingly. 'You are so calm,' she said.

'He seems to me to be going mad, and yet you are so calm, Beatrice.'

I raised my head and looked at her tired face with eyes that were filled with tears. 'I have had much sorrow in my life, Celia,' I said sadly. 'I lost my papa when I was only fifteen, and my mama just after my nineteenth birthday. Now I fear my husband is going mad with drink. I weep inside, Celia. But I have learned to be brave while there is work, and plans to be made.'

Celia nodded respectfully.

'You are braver and stronger than I,' she said. 'For I have been in tears all morning ever since I saw John. I simply do not know what we can do.'

I nodded. 'The problem is too great for us to try to handle alone,' I said. 'He must go to some specialist who will be able to care for him properly. Dr Rose should come this week with his partner and they could take John back to Bristol with them.'

Celia's face lightened with hope.

'But would he go?' she asked. 'He was talking so wildly, Beatrice, as if he trusted no one. He might refuse to go with them.'

'If they agree to take him, agree that he needs treatment, we can force him to take treatment with them,' I said. 'They can sign a contract promising to house and treat him until he is well enough to come home.'

'I didn't know,' said Celia. 'I know so little about such things.'

'Nor did I,' I said ruefully. 'But I have had to learn. This Dr Rose writes that if John can be persuaded to meet him and just talk with him he will be able to advise us. Do you think John would take your advice and agree to meet Dr Rose and his partner if you asked it of him? If you gave him your word it was for the best?'

Celia frowned. 'I think so. Yes, I am sure he would,' she said. 'He accused you and Harry of being in some dreadful league for Wideacre, but he does not seem to doubt my affection for him. If this Dr Rose comes soon I am sure John will see him if I promise him that it is in his own interest.'

'Good,' I said. 'Then you must keep my name out of it altogether. Just let him think that they are doctors you have found for him, and then he will trust them and talk to them, and his poor delirious mind will have some peace.'

Celia snatched at my hand and kissed it.

'You are good, Beatrice,' she said chokingly. 'I think I must have been as crazy with worry as John is with drink. Of course I will do whatever you think best. I know all you are thinking of is the good of all of us. I will trust you.'

I smiled sweetly and pulled her face up so I could kiss her cheek.

'Dear little Celia,' I said lovingly. 'How could you ever have doubted me?'

She clung to my hands like a drowning woman.

'You can free us from this madness, I know,' she whispered. 'I have tried and tried but it only seems to become worse. But you can make it all right again, Beatrice.'

'Yes, I can,' I said gently. 'Be guided by me and nothing can be as bad as this again. We can save John.'

She gave another little sob and I slid my arm around her waist. We sat quiet in the window seat warmed by the winter sun on our backs for a long peaceful time.

I left the parlour well satisfied. Celia was snared by her own faith in me, and I had made John's accusations mere evidence of his madness. In the mire of sin that held us all and muddied every clarity, John's solitary clear vision was incomprehensible. They could have as many afternoons as they wished drinking strong sweet tea and trying to keep John from alcohol. Drunk or sober, as soon as my name was mentioned John would sound like a madman. But during those afternoons Celia, loyally and faithfully doing my witch's work, spoke to John of the reputation of Dr Rose, and persuaded him to meet the specialist. She did better than that; she persuaded John that the only way he could be cured of his terror of me and his addiction to drink would be in the haven of Dr Rose's Bristol clinic. And John, drinking and sobering in a haze of nauseous remorse, haunted by bottles tucked into his bed or between his linen, terrified of the gulf that yawned before him, and seeing my witch's smile and my cat's eyes every night and day, promised he would go.

The day of the doctor's visit John had kept sober. I heard him, in the bedroom next to mine, sleeplessly pacing. When he went to throw himself into bed I heard him groan as he found on the pillows a bottle of port. Then I heard the clatter of his boots on the west-wing stairs as he fled the house to the icy garden to escape the lure of the drink. I dozed then, and heard him come in, in the early hours of the morning. He must have been frozen. The December mornings showed a heavy frost and often in the night we had a light dusting of snow. John had walked all night, wrapped in his driving coat, tears freezing on his cheeks, in a panic of fear to be away from the house, to set dark miles between him and me. But he was still on my land.

He came home, teeth chattering with the cold, and I heard him poking the fire in his bedroom for the warmth. He kept his back to his bed, and to the warming drink that was his for the pouring. Dozing in my nest of blankets, I heard him walking, walking in the bedroom, like a ferret dipping and running along the front of its cage. Then I slept, and when my maid came with my early-morning chocolate he was quiet.

'Where's Mr MacAndrew?' I asked.

'In Miss Julia's nursery,' said Lucy with surprise in her voice. 'Mrs Allens says he went up there early this morning to get warm by the fire, and he has stayed there drinking coffee.'

I nodded and smiled. But I minded little either way. John could stay sober today or he could drink. It made no odds. He was in the grip of a nightmare and was starting to doubt the truths he had so painfully learned. Only one person in the house was safe for John: Celia. He trusted Celia. If he could not be with her, he went to be with her child: Julia. Everywhere else there might be a bottle waiting, or some new madness around the corner. But with her child he was safe. With Celia he was safe.

I dressed in my black morning gown and tied a black ribbon around my head to keep the hair back from my face. My skin glowed against the dull sheen of the gown, a cream rose, my eyes dark as pine trees with sadness. I breakfasted alone and then sat in my office. I did not have long to wait until I heard the sound of a post-chaise, and moved to the main part of the house to greet Dr Rose and his partner, Dr Hilary, in the hall. We went into the library.

'How long has your husband been drinking, Mrs Mac-Andrew?' asked Dr Rose. He was a tall man, handsome, brown-haired, brown-eyed, high-coloured. He had been struck by me when he saw me, slim as an ebony wand in the shadowed hall. But now he had pen and paper before him and was doing his job.

'I have seen him drinking since his return from Scotland,' I said. 'That was seven months ago. Since then he has had few days sober – but I believe whisky was always drunk in his father's home, and he drank excessively after the death of his mother.'

Dr Rose nodded and made a note. His partner sat beside him in a hard-backed chair and listened. He was a burly giant of a man, blond, with a stolid face. It would be him, I thought, who could be trusted to restrain insane patients, or to fell them with one well-placed blow behind the ear if they became unmanageable.

'Any reason for him to start drinking?' asked Dr Rose.

I glanced down at my clasped hands. 'I had just given birth to our first child,' I said, my voice low. 'I had known before our marriage that he was madly jealous, but I had not understood how desperate he was. He was in Scotland when our child was born, and when he came home he became obsessed with the thought that the child was not his.'

Dr Rose pursed his lips and looked professionally neutral. But no man could have avoided sympathizing with such a pretty victim.

'That night my mama was taken ill and died,' I said, my voice little more than a whisper. 'My husband was too drunk to care for her properly and blamed himself for that.' My head drooped lower. 'Since then, our lives have been a misery,' I said.

Dr Rose nodded, and stilled the impulse to pat my hand in comfort.

'Does he know we are coming?' he asked.

'Yes,' I said. 'In his lucid moments he is very anxious to be well again. I think he has taken nothing to drink today. So you should see him at his best.'

The doctor nodded.

'I thought you might like to meet him informally,' I said. 'He is in the parlour with my sister-in-law. We could go there for coffee if you wish.'

'An excellent idea,' said Dr Rose, and I led the way to Celia's parlour.

Celia had done a fine job this morning, keeping John out of

the way while the doctors arrived, and then bringing him to the parlour for coffee with her. He was surprised when I entered the room and when he saw the two men with me his hand trembled so that he had to put his cup down on the table. He shot a look at Celia, which she met with a reassuring smile, but it had shaken his confidence in her that I was involved in this visit.

'This is Dr Rose and Dr Hilary,' I said. 'My sister-in-law, Lady Lacey, and my husband, Mr MacAndrew.'

No one commented on the fact that I had dropped John's title from my speech, but Celia's eyes were on my face as she gave her hand to the two men and bade them sit.

I glided to the coffee pot and poured three cups. John watched Dr Rose like a bird watches a snake, and he kept a wide berth from the massive bulk of Dr Hilary, who eased himself into one of Celia's slight chairs like a bailiff on house arrest duty.

'I have heard a little about your problem,' said Dr Rose to John, his voice soft. 'I think we can probably help you with it. I run a small house outside Bristol where you could come and stay if you wished. There are four patients with me now. One is addicted to laudanum and the other three have trouble with drink. They each have a private room and plenty of quiet and privacy while they come to terms with the cause of their problem and learn to resist the craving. I use limited amounts of laudanum in the early days, so the worst period is eased. And I have had some remarkable successes.'

John nodded. He was as taut as a trip-wire. Celia's eyes on his face glowed with support and love. He kept glancing at her as a superstitious man might touch a lucky charm. He seemed reassured by the softness of Dr Rose's voice. But he kept a wary eye on Dr Hilary, who looked at his own boots and sat like a mountain, still on the chair.

'I am willing to come to you,' said John, his voice a thread with strain.

'Good,' said Dr Rose, smiling reassuringly. 'I am glad. I am sure we can help you.'

'I will order your bags to be packed,' I said and slipped from the room. After I had spoken with John's valet I lingered in the hall outside to listen.

'There are just some papers which need to be signed.' I could hear Dr Rose's gentle tones. 'Just formalities. Sign here, please.' I heard the rustle of the documents as he passed them to John and then the scratch of the pen as John signed. I smiled, and went into the room.

It was too soon.

I had mistimed my return. I had been impatient when I should have waited longer. John had signed the first document, agreeing to accept Dr Rose's prescriptions, but he had not reached the power of attorney. My return to the room distracted him, and the pen hovered as he glanced at the close-printed text.

'What's this?' he said, his voice suddenly sharp, his eyes narrowed. Dr Rose glanced across.

'That is a power of attorney document,' he said, his tone still smooth. 'It is usual for people committed to my care to leave their business affairs in the hands of a responsible relation, in case any decision needs to be made while they are with me.'

John glanced wildly around the circle of our reassuring, smiling faces.

'Committed?' he said, his trained mind picking out the one, revealing word. 'Committed? I was coming to you as a voluntary patient.'

'Of course, of course,' said Dr Rose. 'But as a mere formality we always have our patients committed in case their craving for drink becomes too much for them. So we can keep them in, away from suppliers.'

'Locked up?' said John, his voice harsh with shock. 'These papers take my fortune from me and commit me to a lunatic asylum! Don't they? *Don't they?*' He rounded, in a panic, on Celia. 'Did you know of this?' he asked fiercely. 'This was your idea; you persuaded me it would save me. Did you plan this?'

'Well, yes, John,' said Celia, unable to speak coherently while John became more and more frantic. 'But it could be no harm, surely?'

'Who has my estate?' John demanded. He grabbed at the document and the rest of the papers slid in a sheaf to the floor.

'Harry Lacey, and Harry Lacey's lawyers!' he exclaimed. 'And we all know who controls Harry Lacey, don't we?' He shot a venomous but frightened look at me. Then he dropped the paper from his hand altogether as the realization hit him.

'My God, Beatrice. You are stealing my fortune and putting me away!' he said in horror. 'You are having me locked up, and robbing me.'

Dr Rose gave an inconspicuous nod to Dr Hilary but John saw it at once. Dr Hilary rose ponderously to his feet and John screamed like a terrified child.

'No!' he cried. 'No!' and he broke for the door, knocking over the little table and Celia's workbox. Spools of cotton and coffee cups scattered over the carpet and then, moving surprisingly fast for a heavy man, Dr Hilary dived for John's feet and brought him down to the floor in a crashing tackle. Celia screamed, and I clenched my hands in horror as the heavy man pinned John to the floor.

Dr Rose pulled a strait-jacket from his case and handed it to Dr Hilary. John shrieked in panic and terror, 'No! No! Celia! Celia, don't let them!'

Celia snatched at the strait-jacket but I was at her side in an instant. I grabbed her and held her tight. She pushed me away and cried out, 'Beatrice! Beatrice! You must stop them! There is no need for this! Stop them hurting John! Stop them tying him!'

With deft skilful hands Dr Hilary had slid John's flailing arms into the jacket and rolled him over as neatly as a trussed chicken with both hands tied around his belly and strapped behind his back. John's back arched; his eyes bulged in a contortion of terror.

'You are a devil, Beatrice,' he moaned. 'You are the devil itself.'

John's eyes rolled towards Dr Rose. 'Don't do this,' he said. His voice had gone; his throat was so tight with terror he could only croak. 'No! I beg of you. Please don't let this happen to me. It is a plot. I can explain it. My wife wants me put away. She is a whore and a murderess.'

Celia broke from me and swooped down to kneel beside John.

'No,' she said urgently. 'Don't say such things, John. Don't be like this. Be calm, and all will be well.'

John's mouth widened in a soundless scream of horror.

'And now she has you!' he said despairingly. 'You betrayed me to these men, to her henchmen. She set you on to trap me and you did her dirty work for her. *You* . . .!' He broke off and gazed wildly at the four of us, seeking help.

'Beatrice, you are the devil,' he gasped again. 'A devil. God save me from you and from this infernal Wideacre.' He gave a hoarse sob and said no more. I stood in silence. Dr Rose glanced at me curiously. My face was stony, white as milk. Celia had fallen back from John's side as soon as he turned on her, and was weeping with her hands over her eyes to shut out the sight of her brother-in-law bound on the floor of the pretty parlour of her home.

I was as still as a frozen river. I could not believe this scene before my eyes, even though I had known that something like this could happen. I put one hand behind me until I felt the chair and then I sank on to it, my eyes still on John. I saw his eyelids flutter and close and his chest beneath his crossed arms heaved with a sigh.

Dr Rose stepped towards him and raised his head.

'Put him straight in the carriage,' he said to Dr Hilary. 'He's fine.'

The big man lifted John as if he were a child and carried him gently from the room. Dr Rose helped Celia to a chair but she neither looked at him nor stopped her heartbroken, gasping sobs.

'It is very distressing, but not unusual in these cases,' Dr Rose said gently to me. I nodded with a stiff strained movement. I sat bolt upright in the chair as if I were nailed to it. I ached all over from every tense rigid muscle, and my neck and head were hot with pain.

'Dr Hilary and I will certainly sign the committal papers,' said Dr Rose, gathering them from the floor. 'I will need also the signature of a male relative.'

'Certainly,' I said. My lips were numb.

'We prefer our patients to commit themselves to our care, and of course to resign their business affairs until they are well again. But when we are certain that a patient is too ill and too confused to seek treatment we can commit him without his consent,' he said.

'I am quite convinced that he is suffering from delusions brought on by an excessive consumption of alcohol,' said Dr Rose, scribbling rapidly on the documents and signing his name with a flourish. He glanced up at me. 'But do not be too distressed at what he says, Mrs MacAndrew. It is customary for patients like your husband to have exaggerated fears about the very people who are trying to help them. We hear a lot of strange claims from our patients, and when they are cured they forget all about them.'

I nodded again with rigid muscles.

Dr Rose looked towards Celia. 'Should Lady Lacey have some laudanum?' he asked. 'This has been a dreadful shock for you both.'

Celia raised her head from her hands and took a deep breath in a struggle for control.

'No,' she said. 'I wish to see John again before he goes.' She was holding in the sobs with a tremendous effort of will, but she could not keep the tears from rolling down her cheeks. Her brown eyes were continually filled and her cheeks wet with them.

'He will have had some laudanum in the carriage and will be sleeping peacefully,' said Dr Rose. 'There is no need for you to trouble yourself, Lady Lacey.'

Celia rose to her feet with the new dignity she had won in these last few days.

'He thinks I have betrayed him,' she said. 'He trusted me and I let him be held down and tied up like a criminal in my own parlour. He thinks I have betrayed him, and that is not so, for I did not mean to work against him. But I have failed him because I could not stop you.'

Dr Rose stood too, and put out a placatory hand to her.

'Lady Lacey, it was for the best,' he said. 'He will be untied as soon as we get to my house. He will be treated with every possible consideration. And if God wills, and if Mr Mac-Andrew has courage, then he may come home to you all completely cured.'

'*Doctor* MacAndrew,' said Celia steadily, the tears still streaming down her cheeks.

'*Doctor* MacAndrew,' he repeated, nodding his acknowledgement of Celia's correction.

'I shall write a note and I will put it in his pocket,' said Celia. 'Please do not leave until I have seen him.'

Dr Rose bowed his agreement and Celia went from the room,

her head high, her step steady, and the tears still rolling from her eyes.

There was a silence in the parlour. Outside in the frosty garden a robin began to sing its piercing notes, loud on the cold air.

'And the power of attorney papers?' I asked.

'I have signed them as part of the committal procedure,' said Dr Rose. 'He is committed to our asylum until I see fit to release him. And his business affairs will be managed by your brother, Sir Harold.'

'How long do you think he will be with you?' I asked.

'It depends on himself,' said Dr Rose. 'But I would generally expect some improvement in two or three months.'

I nodded. Time enough. Even that slight movement of my head sent needles of pain up my neck and into the throbbing tight skin of my scalp. Everything I had planned was coming to me, but I could feel no joy.

'I shall write to you with a report every week,' said Dr Rose. He handed me a letter describing the hospital and the treatment, and the papers for Harry's signature. I held them in hands that were as steady as his own. But even my fingers ached.

'You may wish to visit him, or to write,' Dr Rose said. 'You, or any one of your family, would be most welcome to stay, if you wished.'

'That will not be possible,' I said. 'And I think it would be better if he had no letters from home, at least for the first month. Recently, the most innocent events have upset him most dreadfully. Perhaps the safest thing you could do would be to send any letters he receives back to me.'

'As you wish,' said Dr Rose neutrally. He picked up his bag and closed it with a snap. I rose from my chair and found that my knees, and even the muscles of my calves, ached as if I had the ague. I walked stiffly towards the door and found Celia waiting in the hall, a sealed envelope in her hand.

'I have written to John to tell him that I do indeed feel that I have failed him, but that I never ever meant to betray him,' she said, her voice even. The tears were rolling down her cheeks but she did not seem to notice. 'I have begged his pardon for failing to protect him from the violence he suffered.'

Dr Rose nodded, his eyes on the letter. As Celia preceded us to the waiting carriage he raised his eyebrows at me and nodded towards the letter in her hand.

'You may take it from his pocket when you have left, and send it to me,' I said, low-voiced. 'It would certainly upset him.' He nodded and followed Celia out to the carriage.

John was stretched along the length of the forward seat, still strapped in the strait-jacket, wrapped in a plaid travelling rug. Above the garish red and blue of the rug his face seemed deathly pale, but his breath was steady and his face, so strained and anguished before, was now as peaceful as a sleeping child's. His fair hair had strayed from its tie in the struggle and curled around his head. There was the trace of tears on his cheeks but his mouth was slightly smiling. Celia climbed into the carriage and tucked the letter into his pocket. Her fumblings with the strait-jacket woke him and he opened eyes that were hazy blue with the drug.

'Celia,' he said, his voice low and slurred.

'Please don't speak, Lady Lacey,' said Dr Rose firmly. 'He should not be distressed again.'

Celia obediently dropped a kiss on John's forehead in silence and stepped out of the carriage. She stayed by the window as Dr Rose got in beside his burly colleague, her eyes fixed on John's face.

His eyes were still open and he gazed at her as if she were a lighthouse at some distant safe port in the middle of a stormy sea. Then his hazy drugged gaze sharpened, and he looked beyond her to where I stood, stiff as a ramrod on the steps.

'Celia!' he said, and his tone was urgent though the words were slurred. 'Beatrice wants Wideacre for Richard,' he said.

'Goodbye,' I said abruptly to Dr Rose. 'Drive on,' I said to the driver.

Celia took three rapid steps to keep up with the window so John could see her white desperate face.

'Save the children,' John said in one choking shout. 'Save the children from Wideacre, Celia.'

Then the horses broke into a trot and the carriage wheels scrunched on the gravel and Celia's little steps fell behind. And he was gone.

*

We dined in silence that evening. Celia had been crying all afternoon and her eyes were red and swollen. Harry at the head of the table shifted in the great carver chair as if he was sitting on pins. Celia had waited in the stable yard for him all morning and had begged him as soon as he appeared to withhold his signature from the documents committing John to Dr Rose's care, and to order them to send John home. Harry retained enough sense to refuse to discuss the matter with Celia alone and told her that I had a right to be the judge of the best treatment for my husband. Celia had nothing to say to that, for all she had were vague impressions, frightened suspicions, that somehow, and she did not know how or why, I was not to be trusted about John.

So she kept her red eyes down, watched her plate and ate hardly a thing. I too had lost my appetite. John's chair stood against the wall, his side of the table seemed curiously bare. I could not clean my ears of the memory of his terrified shrieks when the gaoler doctor had piled on top of him and bound him. The violence that had exploded in that sunny parlour seemed still to be echoing in the house as if a hundred ghosts were alerted by John's screams.

Celia would not even enter the parlour after dinner but said she wanted to sit with Julia in the nursery. I remembered with a superstitious shudder how John too had sought the nursery as if only the children in the house were free from sin and violence and the lingering smell of corruption. But I smiled at her with all the warmth I could bring into my eyes and kissed her forehead to say goodnight. I thought, I imagined, that she shrank from my touch as if it might somehow mark her, leave some smudge of my ruthlessness on her. But I believed that Celia, like Mama, might hold the thread of detection in her hand and still fail to follow it into the maze.

So Harry and I sat alone in the parlour and when the tea tray came in it was my duty to pour and sweeten Harry's tea to his liking. When he had sipped, and munched his way through a whole plate of *petits fours* I stretched my satin shoes out to the brass fender and said, casually, 'Have you signed and posted the documents for Dr Rose, Harry?'

'I've signed them,' he replied. 'They are on your desk. But what Celia tells me about Dr Rose, and about John, makes me wonder if we are doing the right thing.'

436

'It was a most distressing scene,' I agreed readily. 'John was like a madman. If the two doctors had not been so prompt and efficient I do not know what might have happened. Celia thinks she can control John and help him with his drinking but the way he behaved today proves that she has little influence over him,' I said. 'It has been nearly two weeks now since she started trying to make him give up drinking and he has been drunk nearly every night. He even turned on Celia today and accused her of betraying him. We really cannot manage him if he is half mad from drink.'

Harry's round face was downturned with worry.

'Celia did not tell me that,' he complained. 'She only told me that she thought the doctors were too rough with John and that she feared the whole idea of getting him committed. She even seems to be concerned about John's fortune: the MacAndrew shares.'

'She has been influenced by the nonsense John was shouting,' I said smoothly. 'It was a very distressing scene. But dear Celia understands nothing of business and these matters. There is no doubt that Dr Rose's home is the best place for John and of course he has to be committed into their care so that they can make sure he does not run off to buy drink. We should know how impossible it has been to keep it from him! Celia has had the cellars locked for a fortnight and still he has been getting drink from somewhere.'

Harry shot me a sly sideways glance.

'You don't know how he has been getting hold of the drink, Beatrice, I suppose?' he said nervously.

'No,' I said firmly. 'I have no idea.'

'Well, I shall reassure Celia that we are acting in John's best interests,' said Harry, getting to his feet and standing before the fireplace. He hitched up his jacket to warm his plump buttocks before the blaze, for the night was bitterly cold. 'And I shall tell her that his fortune will be absolutely untouched until he comes to take control of it again,' said Harry. 'We have power of attorney over it, but of course we would not use it.'

'Unless we see some business opportunity for him that we would do wrong to miss,' I agreed. 'The whole point of us having control of his fortune is so that his wealth can be properly managed during his illness. Of course we will not use his money to do anything he would not like. But we would be treating him very badly if we did not watch for his interests and act accordingly.'

Harry nodded. 'Yes, of course,' he said. 'But you have no immediate plans, have you, Beatrice?'

I smiled reassuringly. 'Not at all,' I said. 'All this has been so sudden, so unexpected. Of course I have no plans at all.'

'What about the entail?' Harry said nervously.

'Oh, that!' I put a hand to my face and smoothed my forehead in a gesture that contained a trace of theatre.

'Let us leave that idea altogether until we can see our way clearer. John may be home inside the month and we can discuss it with him then. We can continue to increase Wideacre's profits, and to save the surplus. But there is no need for us to rush into trying to change the entail.'

Harry's look of relief spoke volumes. Celia, with no evidence other than her sharp intuition and her sensitivity to untruth, was mistrustful and anxious. And she had imparted a share of her unease. His question about John's supplier of drink, his anxiety about my future plans, all pointed to Celia's half-sense that all of Wideacre was being carried on a tide of my will. That none of us but I knew where we were going. That no one but I was in control. And that no one but I could say who would benefit from this headlong course.

'It has been a bitter blow for you,' Harry said kindly. 'But do not be too distressed, Beatrice. I do believe John may be cured by these people, and then we can be as we were.'

I smiled back at him, a brave little smile. 'Yes,' I said. 'Indeed I hope so. Now go and comfort Celia, Harry. And do assure her that although I am very sad I shall not break down under this.'

Harry gave me a gentle kiss on the top of my head and took himself off. I stayed only to drink one glass of port beside the dying fire, then missed supper in favour of an early bed. I had a day of hard work tomorrow. Mr Llewellyn was coming to look at the estate for a mortgage to pay the lawyers' fees for the change of entail, and I was ready at last to write to the lawyers that they could go ahead: that I had access to the MacAndrew fortune, and that I could use it to buy Wideacre for my son. His to keep, and his to hand on to his son, and his son, and his, in a long, long line for ever. All of them descended from the witch of Wideacre.

I liked Mr Llewellyn on sight. He was a fifty-year-old Welshman who had made a fortune on the little hill ponies of his home mountains. He had bred a string of them and, cunningly, gave them as presents to the cream of the London nobility. Months of relentless training paid off and the ponies carried the heirs of the wealthiest estates in the land with rock-steady safety – and set a new fashion. The craze for the Llewellyn Welsh mountain ponies swept the fashionable world and was not exhausted until every butcher's daughter had one of her own. By the time the fashion had moved on Mr Llewellyn had a fine town house of his own and need never again set foot in Wales, never again go out in the freezing fog of a Welsh winter to break the water on the drinking troughs.

But he had lost none of his sharp peasant cleverness in the huge town mansion. His blue eyes twinkled at the frosty fields of Wideacre and ranged over the view from my office window as if he was pricing every tree in the park.

'A neat estate,' he said approvingly.

'We have made many improvements,' said Harry, sipping coffee with relish. He gestured to the map where the fields we had enclosed were outlined in yellow: the colour of the wheat we would plant this spring. Harry and I had spent long anxious evenings outlining in a dotted orange line all the areas where wheat could grow if the land was cleared. Each time Harry's pudgy finger swept over a wood or a lush meadow I felt dread, and a foreboding of loss.

'We can't possibly enclose Norman Meadow,' I had said. 'It's an old battlefield and the ploughshare will turn up skulls and bones. We'll never get a boy to take a plough in there. The whole of Acre believes it is haunted.'

'I didn't know that,' said Harry, interested. 'What battle would that have been?'

'The one that gained us the land, I think,' I had said ruefully. 'The tradition is that it was there that the Le Says, our ancestors, brought their handful of Norman soldiers and beat the Saxon peasants in a fight that went on for three days until every man in the village was dead. That's the story, anyway.'

'Well, it would make jolly good fertilizer!' said Harry jovially. 'And see, Beatrice! If we turn Oak Tree Meadow over to corn, and Three Gate Meadow over to corn, we cannot be left with a meadow growing hay stuck in the middle. It doesn't make sense.'

None of it made sense to me. To change the shape of a high-profit high-yielding farm where the people who owned the land and the people who lived on it had hammered out some sort of harmony. Where the memory that the landowners came in and laid waste to the village was no more than the name of a field. Wideacre as it stood was a little island of security in a changing countryside. All around us landowners were changing the way they ran their farms. Charging higher rents for shorter leases, withdrawing traditional rights so the poorest of the poor were forced off the land altogether. Using the parish workhouse labour rather than keeping their own people in lifelong security. And building higher and sharper-topped park walls to shut out the sight of the angry faces pinched and thin with hunger and the eyes that burned with rage.

But then I remembered the entail and my son, and my heart hardened. When Richard was Squire of Wideacre with Julia his partner he could make reparation to the people I had been forced to injure in my search for ready money to pay his way to the Master's chair. When Richard ruled the land he could restore the fields for the villagers' vegetables. He could bring back the meadows; he could reopen the footpaths. He could let them snare rabbits, and fish again in the Fenny. When Richard was Squire he could leave the fresh new cornfields to revert to common land. And in a few years (very well, I concede, in many, many years), Wideacre would be again as it was before I conspired with Harry to despoil it. Richard could put right what I was forced to make wrong. Once Richard was in the Master's chair he could make Wideacre good again. And the only way I knew to put him there was to make it bad first.

'It will look so different,' I said.

'Yes,' said Harry. 'It will start to look like a properly planned estate, like one of the plans in my book, rather than a picturesque muddle.'

'Yes,' I said sadly.

The map I had ordered so proudly so that I could resolve the silly squabbles about the use of the land and the precise route of paths or borders was now Harry's delight. He led Mr Llewellyn over to it with an insistent hand on his arm.

'You're planning a lot of changes,' Mr Llewellyn said, scanning the growth of orange-dotted fields, which were spreading like a fungus.

'Yes,' said Harry with pride in his voice.

'You believe in corn then?' said the London merchant, smiling.

'Of course,' said Harry. 'That's where the profits are these days.'

Mr Llewellyn, peasant stock from a hard region, nodded. 'Yes,' he said. 'But you're making a lot of changes very quickly, aren't you?'

Harry nodded, and leaned towards Mr Llewellyn confidentially.

'We have a project in mind that we need capital to finance,' he said.

'And we plan to raise that capital with your mortgage,' I interrupted Harry smoothly. 'We will repay the loan with the profits from the extra wheatfields so the turnover of money from the estate remains at its present high level, despite the loan.'

Mr Llewellyn nodded at me, his shrewd blue eyes crinkling in a smile. He had seen that I had silenced Harry.

'You'll miss your hay crop,' he said. 'How much will it cost you to buy in the extra hay you will need for winter feed?'

I pulled a sheet of paper towards me, for I had done the calculations, not Harry.

'Between eight hundred and a thousand pounds, depending on the going rate,' I said. 'But we will be feeding the sheep on root crops, and on this new silage made from clover. Both the roots and the clover grow in the cornfields when they are being rested for a season.'

'And hay for the horses?' Mr Llewellyn asked Harry. But again I answered.

'The horses will continue to eat their heads off,' I said. 'But we will keep enough hayfields to feed them.'

Mr Llewellyn nodded and scanned the figures I handed to him.

'Let's see the lie of the land,' he said, putting his coffee cup down.

'My brother Harry will show you around,' I said, gesturing to my black silk gown. 'I am still in mourning and I can only drive.'

'Drive me then!' he said genially, and I found myself smiling back at him.

'I should be happy to,' I said politely. 'But I must tell the stables, then go and change. Excuse me for one minute.'

I slipped from the room and called from the west-wing door to a stable lad to harness Sorrel to the new gig. I took only minutes to change into my black velvet riding habit, and then I threw a thick black broadcloth cape on top, for this December weather was bitter.

'You would rather drive than ride?' I asked Mr Llewellyn as he tucked a rug across our knees and we bowled down the drive, Sorrel's hoofs noisy on the frozen gravel and the iron-hard mud.

'I would rather see the land with the farmer,' said Mr Llewellyn with a sly sideways twinkle at me. 'I think it is your footprint on the fields, Mrs MacAndrew.'

I smiled my assent, but stayed silent.

'These are handsome woods,' he said, looking around at the beech trees silvered on the east side with last night's snow.

'They are,' I said. 'But we would never mortgage these. The woods I would like you to consider are higher up, mostly firs and pines, on the north slopes of the downs.'

We took the bridle-track opposite the drive, and Sorrel leaned forward against the collar and blew clouds of steam with the weight of the gig.

The strips of the common plots where the villagers had planted their own crops for the past seven hundred years were white with frost. The little boundary walls and fences were already pulled down, and in the spring we would be ploughing up the vegetable rows that had been tended with so much care for so long.

We gained about twenty acres taking the land back from the villagers. Their land, where they could grow vegetables for the pot, and seed for the fowls: a shield against a poor season, no work, and the spectre of hunger. Their right to their little strip of land was nowhere stated in writing; they had no contract. It was just the tradition that these few acres should always be for the villagers' use. And when I drove into the village and told half-a-dozen of the oldest men that we were ploughing up the land for corn next spring there was nothing they could do to stop me.

I had not discussed the matter; I had not even got down from the gig. I had met them under the chestnut tree on the green and, as I had told them, it started to snow. They had to have their grumble beside their own fireplaces, not at me. And, in any case, the potatoes had already been lifted, the green vegetables cut. They would not feel the loss of the common strips until next winter.

Even then, Acre villagers might count themselves lucky, for almost every cottage had a little garden. The gardens were filled with flowers, often the pride and joy of the house. They would have to go, and the little grass patches where children played would be dug over for vegetables, and planted in straight rows. All this, so that the Wideacre estate might be increased by twenty acres. But all this so that my son Richard would be a week closer to the Master's chair with the extra small profit.

I pulled Sorrel up, and tied her to a fence post and then led the way on a little path along the brow of the downs until we reached the new plantation with the sheep-proof withy fence protecting the young trees.

'How old is it?' asked Mr Llewellyn, the smile gone from his eyes and a hard shrewd look ranging over the tall trees, now standing twenty, thirty feet.

'I planted it with my papa,' I said, smiling at the memory. 'I was five. These woods are fourteen years old. He promised I should have a stool from these trees when I was an old lady.' I shrugged away my sadness.

'Times change,' said Mr Llewellyn, his quick mind following

my grief. 'No one can predict the way things change these days. All we can do is to try to follow our consciences – and to chase profit with a care to others!' He gave me a rueful smile and turned back to the trees.

'Growing well,' he commented approvingly. 'How many trees?'

'About five hundred,' I said. I opened the little gate in the fence for him, and he strode down the straight rows looking carefully at the needles for signs of disease, pulling at the branches to see their healthy spring back into place. Then he walked in a carefully paced square, his lips moving as he counted how many trees to a ten yard square.

'Good,' he said finally. 'I'll certainly lend money on this plantation. I have a contract you may look at in my chaise. Was there some common land as well?'

'Yes,' I said. 'But it's in the opposite direction. We'll drive there.'

We walked back to the gig and with clever courtesy he did not offer to help me as I took Sorrel's reins at the bit and backed him up the narrow path to turn the gig. Only when I had Sorrel facing downhill with the brake on, did he swing into the gig and smile at me.

We drove downhill and then along the lane towards Acre. Before we reached the village we turned left into the park woodland again, along the little track that leads to the new mill. Mrs Green was feeding hens from her front door and I waved at her as we went past and saw her eyes scanning Mr Llewellyn, wondering who he was. She would know soon enough. There are no secrets on Wideacre. I never expect to keep my business quiet.

The track wound through the woods, thickly silent under the grip of the frost, and then broke out into clearer ground as we neared the common. Softly on the air I heard the creaky sound of strong wings and above our heads was a V of geese flying westwards, looking for melted water and feed.

'This is the land,' I said, nodding at the common. 'I showed you the area on the map. It is all as you see here. A little hilly, mainly bracken and heather, a few trees which will have to be felled and two little streams.'

I kept my voice even, but my love for the common, gold and brass under this cold winter light, crept into my tone despite myself. One of the streams was near by and we could hear the trickle of its clear waters as it dripped off icicle waterfalls on its way to the Fenny.

The bracken still glowed bronze under a silvering of white frost. The few trees I would have to fell were my beloved silver birches, their trunks paper-white and their twigs a deep purple-brown in a shape as graceful as a Sèvres vase. The heather still held pale grey flowers under the coating of hoar frost, so every plant masqueraded as lucky white heather. The ground beneath the wheels of the gig was hard as a rock where the wet peat had frozen, but in the little valleys the white sand was as crunchy as sugar and looked as pale and as sweet.

'You can enclose this?' Mr Llewellyn looked at me, his face quizzical.

'There are no legal problems,' I said. 'The land belongs out-right to the Wideacre estate. It has always been used as common land and there is only a tradition of access and use. Our people have always taken the lesser game here; they have always grazed animals here; they have always collected firewood or kindling here. But there is nothing in writing. In the old days it used to be agreed annually by the Squire and the village, but there are no records. There is no written agreement to stop us.'

I smiled but my eyes were cold.

'And even if there were records,' I said ironically. 'They are kept in my office, and there are few of our people who can read. There is certainly no reason why we should not enclose this.'

'You misunderstand me.' Mr Llewellyn spoke softly, but his eyes no longer twinkled. 'I meant to ask whether you felt you could bear to rip up this land with a plough, level the valleys, fill in the stream beds and plant acres of corn here.'

'That is my intention,' I said, my face as grave as his.

'Well, well,' he said, and he said no more.

'You are interested in a mortgage on this land?' I asked neu-trally, and I turned the trap back the way we had come.

'Indeed, yes,' he said coolly. 'It promises to be a most profit-able venture for the estate. Would you wish to have the money paid directly to you, or to your London bankers?'

'To our London lawyers, if you please,' I said. 'You have their address.'

We sat in silence then, and the trap rattled home in the yellow winter sunshine, which brightened but could not warm the icy day.

'A pleasure to do business with you, Mrs MacAndrew,' he said formally, as we drove into the stable yard. 'I'll not come in again. I'll be off now as soon as my horses are put to.'

He went to his chaise and brought the two contracts out to me. I took them, standing beside Sorrel's head, her soft lips gently nipping at my fingers, cold inside the leather gloves. I tapped her russet nose and held my hand out to him in farewell.

'Thank you for calling,' I said politely. 'Good day, and safe journey.'

He got into his chaise and the footman folded up the steps, slammed the door and swung himself up into his seat behind. A cold ride he would have of it, I thought, all the way to London in his livery. I raised a hand in farewell as the carriage moved off.

The day was cold, but I was chilled inside at the change in Mr Llewellyn's manner towards me. A total stranger, he despised me for my attitude to the common land, for reneging on the informal contract between me and the poorest of the poor, for my willingness to destroy the easy fertile beauty of Wideacre. I shivered. Then the carriage was no longer between me and the Hall, and I could see the door to the west wing. Celia was standing there, watching me. She was dressed in the usual black, and she looked thin, and slight, and scared.

'Who was that gentleman?' she asked. 'Why did you not invite him in?'

'Just a merchant,' I said easily, handing the reins of Sorrel to one of the stable lads. I swept Celia in with an arm around her waist. 'It's freezing again,' I said briskly. 'Let's go and warm up beside your parlour fire.'

'What did he want?' she persisted as I stripped off my gloves and cape and rang for hot coffee.

'To buy the timber from the new plantation,' I said with a convincing half-truth. 'I had to drive him up there and it was terribly cold.'

'Selling the timber already?' said Celia surprised. 'But the plantation isn't ready for cutting yet, surely?'

447

'No, not yet, Celia,' I said. 'He's a timber specialist. He offers you a guaranteed price long before the cutting. Actually it is growing well and will be ready for felling soon. You haven't been up there for years, Celia. You don't know what it is like.'

'No,' she admitted, accepting the rebuke. 'I do not get out on the land like you, Beatrice. I do not understand it like you.'

'No reason why you should,' I said briskly, and smiled at Stride as he brought in the coffee. I gestured to him to pour and took my cup to the fireplace to drink it before the blaze. 'Your control over the kitchen is flawless. What's for dinner?'

'Game soup and venison, and some other dishes,' said Celia vaguely. 'Beatrice, when will John come home?'

The suddenness of her question took me by surprise and I jerked my head up to look at her. She was sitting in the window seat with neither darning nor embroidery in her hands, but her eyes were not idle – she was scanning my face – and her brain was not idle. I could feel her trying to think her way out of the incomprehensible situation that seemed to be before her.

'When he is completely well,' I said firmly. 'I could not bear to have to go through that scene again.'

She paled as I had thought she would.

'God forbid,' she said, and her eyes dropped to the floor where John had lain screaming for her to rescue him. 'If I had known they would have treated him like that I should never have supported your idea of sending for them,' she said.

'Certainly not,' I said, matching her fervent tone. 'But once they had him and he was sleeping peacefully it was obvious that the only thing to do was to let them go on with the treatment. After all, it was John's own wish to go.'

Celia nodded. I could see a host of reservations behind her eyes, and I wanted to hear none of them.

'I shall go and change for dinner,' I said, tossing my tricorn hat into the chair. 'It is too cold to go out this afternoon. Let us take the children into the gallery and play shuttlecock with them.'

Celia's face lightened with her quick affection for the children. But her eyes stayed shadowed.

'Yes, lovely!' she said, but there was no joy in her voice.

So at the cheap price of an afternoon of unmitigated tedium

448

playing at shuttlecock with Celia, two doting nurses and with children too small to understand the game, and too little to play it if they did, I won freedom from any questions about Mr Llewellyn, and entails, and my sudden need for capital. And freedom from questions about John, and John's proposed return.

Celia assumed John would come home for Christmas. But Christmas came and went and John was not well enough to return. We could not have a great Wideacre Christmas party for we were still in mourning. But Dr Pearce suggested a smaller party for the village children at the vicarage, which Harry and Celia and I could attend.

I thought we could do better than that; I thought we had better supply it too. Miss Green – the Vicar's housekeeper, the miller's sister – had a spinster's notion of what Acre children should eat, and the sort of amounts that were suitable. So on Christmas Day I drove to church with a bootful of meat and bread and jellies and sweetmeats and lemonade. The party was to be immediately after the church service and Harry and Celia and I walked from the church, saying 'Good morning' and 'Happy Christmas' to the wealthier tenants who had stopped in the churchyard to greet us.

The poorer tenants, and the Acre villagers, and even the cottager children were in the vicarage garden, dourly supervised by Miss Green and by the two curates.

'Happy Christmas, good morning,' I said generally as we entered the garden gate and was surprised at the response. There were no smiles. The men bared their heads or pulled a forelock as Harry and Celia and I walked up the path and the women dipped a curtsy. But the warmth of a Wideacre welcome was missing. I looked around, surprised, but nobody met my eyes, and there were no loving voices calling 'Good day' to me, or muttering with satisfaction how pretty Miss Beatrice was looking today.

I was so accustomed to being the darling of Wideacre that I could not understand the feeling of coldness in that pretty garden. The children were seated on long benches along a trestle table, their parents standing behind them. In a few moments the Wideacre servants would help Miss Green serve them a hearty dinner. It was the Christmas party – one of the jolliest and noisiest events of the year. Yet it was silent, and no face smiled at me. I spotted the midwife Mrs Merry and beckoned her to me with a crook of my finger.

'What is the matter with everyone?' I asked. 'They're all very quiet.'

'It's the death of Giles that has upset everyone,' she said to me, her voice low. 'Had you not heard, Miss Beatrice?'

Giles – my mind went back to the old man who had stooped over his spade to listen to my papa all those years ago when I was a child and thought I owned every inch of Wideacre. Giles, who had seemed so old and frail, had outlived my strong, young papa and had been working right up to the day when I stopped casual labour for the village and called in the parish labour gang instead. Now the old man had died – but that was no good reason to spoil a children's party.

'Why are they so upset?' I asked. 'He was an old man, bound to die some day.'

Mrs Merry's eyes were sharp on my face. 'He did not die from age, Miss Beatrice. He poisoned himself and he will have to be buried outside the churchyard without a service.'

I gasped. 'Poisoned himself!' I exclaimed. My shock made my voice too loud and a couple of our tenants glanced curiously at me as if they guessed that Mrs Merry was telling me the dreadful news.

'There must have been some mistake,' I said certainly. 'Why on earth should anyone think he would do such a thing?'

'Because he said he would,' said Mrs Merry baldly. 'When you stopped the casual work, digging ditches and hedging, he had no money. He lived off his savings for two weeks and borrowed from his neighbours for a week. But then he knew he would have to go on the parish. And he always swore he would kill himself first. This morning they found him dead. He had taken the strychnine he borrowed from the mill, saying he had rats in the cottage. It's a painful death that, Miss Beatrice. His body was bent backwards like a bow and his face black. They were trying to get the body in the coffin as you drove by on your way to church. Didn't you see them, Miss Beatrice?'

'No,' I murmured. I could say no more. Somewhere in the

very depths of me there was a sad little cry at the end of something. Deep in my heart I was mourning for some good thing about Wideacre that seemed to have broken, that seemed to have died. That had been poisoned as surely and painfully as dead Giles. And with as little a dose.

'What's the matter with everyone?' cried Harry, reliably oafish at the worst possible moment. 'I've never seen so many solemn faces. Come along now, it's Christmas morning! Christmas morning!'

The closed resentful looks were turned on him and then the people, my people, looked down at the ground and shuffled their boots in the frozen gravel. Before Harry could make the situation any worse the door of the vicarage opened and the servants came out with the children's dinner.

'Giles is dead,' I said quietly to Harry. 'It seems he killed himself when his savings ran out rather than go on the parish. He was found this morning. You can see that everyone blames us. I think we should wait till they have drunk our healths and then go home.'

Harry's red cheeks went pale. 'My word, that's very bad, Beatrice,' he said. 'Giles had no cause to do a thing like that. He should have known we would never have let him starve.'

'Perhaps he didn't,' I said harshly. 'What he wanted was work, not charity. But anyway he's dead. Let's finish here and get away before some gossip blabs it to Celia. There is no need for her to be upset.'

'Indeed not,' said Harry, glancing quickly around for her. She was holding one of the newborn Acre babies in her arms and smiling at it. The child's mother stood beside, watching the two of them and her eyes on Celia were warm, not cold as the looks I had met.

'We will not stay long,' Harry called in his clear tenor. 'We just came to wish you the compliments of the season, and to hope you enjoy the party we and Dr Pearce have given you.'

Then he turned and touched Celia's arm. Together they walked back to the chaise and I followed a step behind. I could feel the eyes scanning my back and I had the odd fleeting fear that if the Culler or one like him were on my borders now I could not be sure of being safe. But I reassured myself swiftly. It was mid-winter miseries – everyone who works on the land gets tired of the cold weather and the dark days. It was the shock of Giles's death – everyone who is poor is in dread of going on the parish, and even worse, of being forced into the poorhouse. Once spring came life would be easier. And Giles would be forgotten.

In the carriage I leaned forward to look out of the window to reassure myself that nothing had really changed. That the Christmas party was the same as ever. That Giles's death had upset his family and friends but that the rest of the village would soon forget. That once the children had eaten their fill there would be games and dancing and joy at Wideacre as there were at every Christmas time. That nothing on Wideacre could ever change so badly or so fast.

The pretty garden was a shambles. Our move to the carriage had been the signal for a free-for-all. The children were crawling all over the tables grabbing food and stuffing it into their mouths, and their parents were squeezing between them to snatch at food and stuff it into their pockets. It was a small-scale riot; no party. From the doorway Miss Green and the servants watched in horror. At his study window I caught a glimpse of Dr Pearce's white face as his parishioners thumped and pushed and jostled to pull hunks of bread to pieces and to hack and claw at legs of ham. The little sweetmeats I had brought from the Hall fell to the ground unnoticed by anyone except the smallest children who crawled between adult kicking legs to get them. Above their heads on the table their mothers and fathers made desperate lunges for the food as if they were starving.

'Drive on!' I said sharply, with an edge of terror in my voice, and pulled the cord for the coachman. He had been still with amazement at the sight of such a frenzy in the very heart of Wideacre, but jumped at my signal, and the horses leaped in the harness to sweep us away from the scene.

'What is happening?' asked Celia. She could see almost nothing on the far side of the carriage with Harry's bulk between her and my window. I leaned forward to block the view completely.

'Rough party games,' I said quickly, trying to keep the tremor out of my voice. 'And some grabbing by the children.' I glanced at Harry. His cheeks were white, but at my hard look he nodded in support.

'Good heavens, what a noise they make,' he said, trying to sound casual.

Then, mercifully, we were out of earshot and I could sit back in my seat and breathe steadily and quietly to try to control my trembling.

I had not realized, had not thought, that the loss of casual labouring jobs would have hit Acre village so hard so soon. For it was not just our winter chores on Wideacre; we set the pattern for the rest of the neighbours. When Wideacre Hall employed the low-paid gangs of parish workers, recruited by the roundsman from the poorest families who had to live on parish charity, then that practice was sanctioned for the hundred square miles of our influence. Havering Hall had long been paying the lowest possible rates to the parish roundsman's labouring gang and using them for a handful of days a month. Now with Wideacre going over to the parish labourers the last reliable employer in this part of Sussex had been lost.

Giles's shameful death was, of course, the sign of a crazy old man's inability to adapt to a new world. But his belief – that if there was no work to be had on Wideacre, then there was nothing for him but the workhouse – was probably right. The roundsman would take only the fittest of the destitute workers – Giles could never have been employed in the gang. For him it would have been the workhouse – worse than Chichester prison – and the sure road to death. He was a mad old man to take his own life, of course. His death was not a sensible reaction to our attempts to farm Wideacre rationally and profitably. The last thing I needed was a pang of conscience about such an old fool. And I would be mad myself if I even considered that his death should be laid at my door, that I had made his world – Wideacre – unbearable.

So I told myself during the drive home, and when we were inside the Hall with the front door bolted I was ready for Harry's urgent need for reassurance. We stood by the parlour fire while Celia went upstairs to take her hat and coat off, and fetch the children for their Christmas dinner.

'My God, Beatrice, that was terrible,' said Harry. He crossed to the decanter of sherry in two swift strides and poured himself

453

a glass and tossed it off before handing me one. 'They were like animals! Savages!'

I shrugged, deliberately careless. 'Oh come, Harry,' I said. 'You are too nice. There is always a little pushing and shoving at the Christmas party. It is just that we usually do not see it. They generally wait for us to leave first!'

'I have never seen anything like it before!' Harry said firmly. 'And neither, I am sure, have you, Beatrice. They were near rioting. I cannot understand it!'

I wager you cannot, you fool, I thought to myself and sipped at my sherry.

'They are anxious,' I said evenly. 'They are anxious because many of them have lost their winter wages. And Giles's death upset them all too. They think at the moment that they are near starvation, but when spring comes they will realize that there has been little real change.'

'But they behaved as if they had not seen food for a sennight!' Harry objected. 'Beatrice, you saw them! You cannot tell me that those were families who find themselves a little short of cash. They looked as if they were starving.'

'Well, what if they are?' I demanded, suddenly hard; weary of shielding Harry from the consequences of our joint choice. 'You wanted to use the roundsman labour gangs. We both agreed there would be no more casual labour for the villagers of Acre. We both agreed we would keep no hedgers and ditchers and helpers with the sheep on the wage books to be paid in good and bad weather and to be paid if they work or no. We agreed to that. Did you think they worked for the love of it? Of course they are hungry. They are receiving no pay; they are trying to last out on their savings until spring. They think that we will go back to the old ways and that every man in the village will be able to do a day's ploughing, and every lad will be able to earn a penny sowing seed. When spring comes they will find that it is not so. That we shall still use the gang labourers. And if they want work they will have to go to the parish and join the gang and accept the pittance they are offered.

'Are you saying now that you don't want to continue with our plans?' I asked tightly. 'We are saving hundreds of pounds a month, and we are farming as you have always wanted to. Did

454

you think no one paid for your fancy farming ideas, Harry? The poor pay. The poor always pay. But they can do nothing against us. And if you don't like the look of what you are doing then turn your head away and look out of the other window like Celia.'

I spun on my heel and turned my back to him to stare into the fire and regain my temper. I was panting with anger and close to tears. Harry's wilful ignorance about what we were doing to the land enraged me. But also I was boiling with rage at the trap I was in. For the decision to farm for profit and consider only profit had led us to this point and might yet take us farther. The poorer people would have to leave Acre; the estate could not support so many, farming in this new way. And many, many of them would be stubborn and not leave. Then, I supposed, the old people, and perhaps the frailer children, might die. And Giles would be only the first death on the road to make Richard the heir. With the picture of Richard as Master in my mind I would not retract, I would not relent. But I could see, and no one but I would see, the long, slow, painful path the poor of Wideacre would tread barefoot so that my son could be called Squire.

Harry's hand fell on my shoulder and I tensed, but controlled myself not to shake it off. 'This is a bitter time for us both,' said Harry sadly, forgetting the hungry faces and thinking only of himself. 'Of course I agree we should go on. Every landowner has precisely these problems. It is a time of change. Nothing we can do could stop that process of change. The people will just have to adapt, that is all. They will just have to learn to live the way things are. It would be folly for you and me to try to farm in the old ways, Beatrice.'

I nodded. Harry had found a way to still his own conscience, and I had my way to silence mine. I could comfort myself with the thought that all that I now did brought my lovely son closer and closer to owning Wideacre. And Harry could tell himself the convenient lie that he was equally trapped by the changes as the people he had dismissed from their work. Harry had Pontius Pilate's answer that it was really nothing to do with him. He saw himself as part of a process of historical change and he could neither be blamed nor held responsible for what would happen.

'There is just no alternative,' he said quietly. And he even sounded sad that there was nothing he could do.

So when Celia came downstairs with the two nurses and the two children dressed in their best and hungry for roast goose we could all exchange smiles and go into the dining room to eat at a table heaped with main courses and side dishes, as if, five miles away, there were no hungry children picking crumbs from the frozen grass of the vicar's garden.

It was a hard win..er in Acre that year. I went less to the village than I had ever done, for it was no pleasure to me to be greeted with surly faces. Once or twice a woman had burst from a cottage with tears in her eyes and put her hand on the side of my gig and said, 'Miss Beatrice, do take my William to do some hedging for you. You know there's no one like him for hedging in the whole county. I can't keep the children on the wages we get from the parish. They're hungry, Miss Beatrice. *Do* give my man work.'

Then I would have to hold the picture of my own child, my Richard, and his future very clear before my eyes. I would stare hard at the horse's ears and not look the woman in the face and say in an even tone, 'I am sorry, Bessy, but there's nothing I can do. We only use the roundsman on Wideacre now. If your man wants other work he had best go and seek it.'

Then I would click to the horse and drive off before she shamed herself and her man by weeping before me in the village lane. And my face was set and cold, for I knew no other way to do it.

Harry would do nothing at all. When he met someone in the lane and heard the tale of the bad wages the roundsman gave the gang, of the meanness of the parish and of the fear of the workhouse, he would shrug at the man and say, 'What can I do? I am no freer to choose how the world is than you, my good fellow.' And he would put a hand in his pocket for a shilling as if that would help a man with four children and a sickly wife at home, and a long cold winter to get through.

They thought I had turned against them. But that was only partly true. I had to think of other things, of the claim of Richard, and of my desperate need to establish the entail and Richard's and Julia's partnership in the breathing space I had won by John's absence using John's fortune. Even so, I did not enclose the common until spring, so they had a winter's supply of firewood, which they gathered for free, and peat, which they cut for nothing, before I had the fences made that would straddle the footpaths, and ban the whole village from the land they had thought was their own to use.

All winter the fences stood at the back of the stables and I delayed ordering them set in place.

'We really should get on with enclosing the common,' Harry would say to me, leaning over the map. 'Mr Llewellyn's loans are costing us a good deal. We shall be planting wheat this spring, and there will be much work to do to make the ground ready.'

'I know,' I said, glancing up from writing letters at my desk. 'I have it in mind, Harry. I have the fences ready and I have told the roundsman that I shall need at least twenty men for the work. But I wish to wait until the snow is gone. The people are used to getting their firewood for free, and also snaring rabbits there. There may be trouble when the fences first go up. It is bound to be easier for us if we do it when the weather is milder.'

'Very well, Beatrice,' Harry said. 'You know best how it should be done. But really, the people should understand that they have been living in the old ways for too long. I don't know another estate in the county that held to the traditional ways as long as we did. Free firewood, free snaring, free grazing, free gleaning; we have been *robbing* ourselves for all these years, Beatrice. You would think they would be grateful.'

'Odd, isn't it?' I said drily. 'But they are not.'

Indeed they were not. As the winter went on I heard no more appeals from the village women. When I trotted my gig through the village there were no smiling faces or deep curtsys. There was no open rudeness; I would have dismissed anyone from the land if I had seen so much as a flicker of overt insolence. But I was not loved as I had been. And I missed it. The men would doff their caps or pull a forelock and the women make their little bob, but they did not call out 'Good day' to me, and the children were not held up to see pretty Miss Beatrice and her fine horse. It was just another price that had to be paid.

They disliked Harry too, of course. But in the fickle way of ignorant people they did not blame him as they blamed me. They knew he had always been crazy for change, but they had trusted me to hold out against him. Now I was farming for profit they blamed me far worse than they did Harry. They even blamed me for influencing Harry, although if they had consulted their own conveniently short memories they would have known that Harry had always been a fool on the land and I was not responsible for that.

The weather matched the angry desolate mood of Wideacre and the winter dragged on with snowstorms and wet freezing fogs, then high winds and storms of rain all through lambing. We lost more lambs that year than we had done for seasons. Partly it was the weather but also I think it was because the men would not stay out all hours to earn a smile from me and a slap on their shoulders at the end of a long cold evening. While I was there watching over them they did their job helping the sheep in difficulties, checking the nibbled-off cord, ensuring the lambs were accepted by their mothers. But when I was not there I knew that they were away down the hill to Acre with a spit on the ground at the mention of the flock.

So we stood to make less of a profit on the sheep that year than I had calculated. And the prospect of losing that money made me firmer to hold to the plans I had, whatever it cost me in smiles and goodwill.

We had to keep more beasts indoors and there was not enough hay or winter feed. Faced with the choice of killing good stock or buying in feed, I chose to buy. But the hay prices were outrageous and there was no way I could get the money back. We would be lucky to break even on the beasts this year.

I spent one cold dark afternoon after another at my desk. And when Stride brought in the candles in the early twilight my head was aching. We did not seem to be making enough money. And Mr Llewellyn's loans were costing more than I had thought they would. The interest rates were high but the profits were rock-bottom and I was actually paying out more than came in. At this rate I would not be able to buy top quality seedcorn. I would have to borrow to buy seed.

I rested my head in my hands and I knew real fear. Not fear like when you jump too high a gate, hunting, nor even my steady, constant fear of violence, of men coming for me. But business fear. The black figures on white were so uncompromising. And even the feel of the heavy cashbox under the desk did not comfort me. It looked like a lot of money. But I needed more. Wideacre needed more. And I was afraid of the clever London business men. I was afraid to borrow again. But I would have to do so.

Harry was shielded by me from the worry of business. I did not want to frighten him off the plan to change the entail. And I was too proud to admit I was afraid. But Harry could not escape the hatred of the village that grew and grew all the cold winter.

Of the three of us only Celia, the newcomer, seemed to keep their respect. In their prejudiced ignorant way they did not blame her for the empty soup pots and the thin gruel. Like fools they managed not to see Celia's fine woollen cloaks and fashionable bonnets, and saw only that her face underneath the silk trimming was pale and anxious, and that her purse was always open to tide a family over especial difficulties, or to buy a child a blanket for the cold nights. As the weather worsened in January and the ground froze hard, Celia had the carriage out every day to send steaming bowls of stew from the Wideacre kitchens down to families in the village who otherwise would have eaten no meat that week. And I noted, sourly, that they blessed her for it.

She came to know Acre village, my village, and she started to know the people, my people. She started to learn the detail of the kinship and friendship ties. Who was married to whose sister. Which man drank, which father was too rough with his children. Which women were pregnant. And she was the first to know when Daisy Sower's baby died.

'Beatrice, we must do something,' Celia said, walking without so much as a knock into my office. She had come into the house straight from the stables, by the west-wing door, still wearing her driving cape and dress and as she moved to the fire she stripped off her black leather gloves. I was suddenly struck how much she had changed since Mama's death. Her pace was faster, her voice clearer, her whole bearing more purposeful. Now she stood with her back to my fire, warming herself at my hearth and preparing herself to lecture me about my people.

'Do what?' I said sharply.

'Something about the hardship in Acre,' she said passionately. 'It cannot be right, Beatrice. There are families there in want. Now poor Daisy Sower's little baby has died and I am sure that it was because she never had enough milk for it. There was so little food in the house I am certain that she was feeding her husband and the other children first and only then eating. Her baby just got thinner and thinner and now it has died, Beatrice. It is such a wicked waste. It was such a lovely baby!' Celia's voice quavered on a sob, and she turned to the fireplace and brushed her hand across her eyes.

'Surely we can employ more people on the estate?' she said. 'Or at the very least we could give some of the grain to the village. Wideacre seems so wealthy, I do not see how there could be hardship in Acre.'

'Would you like to see the figures?' I said, my voice hard. 'Wideacre seems wealthy to you because up until now you have spent your life indoors where no expense has been spared. The housekeeping is partly your responsibility, Celia, and you know I have never challenged a bill from the kitchen.'

She nodded. The first sign of my anger was enough to unbalance Celia. She remembered too well her horror of Lord Havering when he used to bellow at her in one of his drunken rages. She could not tolerate a raised voice, or even a sharp tone. I used both.

'It is all very well for you queening it in the village with your bowls of soup and blankets, but we have mortgages to meet and debts to be paid. It is no Garden of Eden. This year we have lost dozens of lambs, and the calving is going badly too. If we have a wet spring we will have problems with the corn. It is no good asking me to take on half of the men in Acre village. The estate cannot afford it. In any case I have signed a contract with the parish roundsman and we get our labourers from him. They are generally the very men from Acre anyway, so they are working here, but at proper rates.'

Celia nodded. 'They tell me the parish rates of pay are not sufficient to keep a family,' she said softly.

'That may be so,' I said impatiently. 'It is hardly my fault if the women cannot make the money stretch. It is hardly my job to encourage improvidence. The rates are set by the Justices of the Peace, or the churchwardens. I am not able to pay higher, and I would be foolish indeed to do so.'

Celia looked dashed. But Daisy Sower's baby was still on her conscience and in her barren mind. 'It was just that poor baby . . .' she said.

'How many children has Daisy Sower?' I interrupted harshly. 'Five? Six? Of course there is not enough money to go round. She should stop having children and then she would see she could manage perfectly well. You do the poor a great disservice to encourage them as you do, Celia!'

Celia flushed scarlet and then pale at the tone in my voice. 'I am sorry to have disturbed you,' she said, gathering her scraps of dignity and turning to leave.

I stopped her at the door.

'Celia!' I called, and my tone was kind. She turned at once, and I smiled at her. 'It is I who should apologize to you,' I said tenderly. 'I am a miserable cross sister to you and I beg your pardon.'

She came from the door slowly, and there was distrust in her face.

'You need not say that, Beatrice,' she said. 'I know how much you have to worry you. The sheep and the cows and the worry there always is, I know, in your mind about John. I apologize for troubling you further.'

'Ah, don't!' I said, reaching out a hand to her. 'It is just that I have been worried about money matters, my dear, and it does make me short-tempered.'

Celia's knowledge of money matters extended so far as generally knowing within a pound or so how much she had in her purse, but she nodded as if she understood perfectly.

'Oh, yes,' she said earnestly. 'And your worry about John. Have you had a report from Dr Rose this month?'

'Yes,' I said, making my voice sad. 'He says that John is still far from well but is struggling bravely against the temptation.'

'No word from John himself?' asked Celia tentatively.

'No,' I said, and managed a brave smile. 'I write and write. But Dr Rose said that John is not ready to reply yet, not to any letters. So I am not concerned not to have heard from him personally.'

'Should you like to go for a visit, Beatrice?' Celia asked. 'The roads will surely clear soon and then you could see for yourself how he is.'

I shook my head sadly and leaned my cheek in my hand.

'No,' I said. 'It would do no good. Dr Rose told me quite

specifically that John was not ready to receive visitors and that a surprise visit would almost certainly cause a relapse. We will just have to be patient.'

'Oh yes,' Celia said earnestly. 'Poor John, and poor you too, Beatrice.' She put her arm around my shoulders and gave me a hug. 'Now I will leave you for I know you are busy,' she said softly. 'But don't work too hard, and stop soon and change for dinner.'

I nodded with another of my courageous smiles, and Celia took herself off. I waited until the door closed behind her and I heard her footsteps echo down the corridor to the main part of the Hall, then I opened one of the secret drawers of the desk and took out Dr Rose's reports, and a bundle of letters. They were addressed to my husband. They were from Celia.

Dr Rose had faithfully forwarded every one to me unopened with his monthly reports. These were clear and had done much to increase my tension. If the lawyers did not hurry, if John continued to improve, I should have him back at Wideacre before I had given his fortune away to my cousin in return for the entail. Dr Rose's first report had been gloomy. John had completed the journey in a drugged state but when he woke to find himself in a room with a barred window he had gone crazy with fear. He had sworn that he was imprisoned by a witch, by the Wideacre witch, who had her whole family under some spell and would keep him imprisoned until he was dead.

All this sounded sufficiently lunatic to keep him inside and safely away from Wideacre for years. But Dr Rose's later reports were more doubtful. John was making progress. He still had a craving for drink, but for the rest of his time he was lucid and calm. He was using laudanum in controlled amounts and was taking no alcohol. 'I think we may begin to hope,' Dr Rose wrote in his last report.

I was not beginning to hope. I was beginning to fear. Events were taking place outside the estate where my word was law, beyond my influence. I could not make the lawyers go faster; I could not speed the negotiations with my cousin. I could not set back John's recovery. All I could do was to write letter after letter to the lawyers pressing them to move on with their slow processes, and the occasional sad reply to Dr Rose, assuring him that I would rather my husband stayed with him for a year than prejudice his health by bringing him home too early. I had also a hard task to keep John's father safely away in Edinburgh. As soon as John was committed and power of attorney vested in me I wrote to him to tell him of his son's illness and to assure him that John was receiving the best of care. Using Dr Rose's authority I explained that no one was allowed to visit John, but as soon as he was well enough I would contact old Mr MacAndrew at once so that he could visit his once best talented son. The old man, in a storm of grief and concern, never thought to ask how John's fortune was managed while he was inside the asylum, and I never offered information. If he had asked me I would have said that Harry held the MacAndrew shares in trust for John. But I had been holding to the hope that by the time John was released and ready to reclaim his fortune, it would all be gone. Spent to put the bastard who bore his name into the Squire's chair in the house he hated.

All had to happen at the right time. If only the lawyers would hurry. If only my cousin would sign the contract, surrendering his inheritance. And all I could do was wait. And Celia could only write letters. Eleven letters I had in my drawer in the desk, one for each week that John had been away. Every Monday Celia wrote on one side of one sheet of notepaper, judging perhaps that a long letter might disturb him. Uncertain yet, whether he forgave her for what he had called her betrayal of him. Tender letters they were. They were full of a love so sweet and innocent, the love that two children might share. She started each letter, 'My dearest brother', and she ended each one with the words, 'You are daily in my thoughts and nightly in my prayers', and signed herself, 'Your loving sister, Celia'.

And all the body of the letter was news of the children, a word about the weather, and always the assurance that I was well. 'Beatrice is well and grows lovelier every day,' she wrote in one. 'You will be glad to know that Beatrice is well and, as usual, most beautiful,' she wrote in another. 'Beatrice is well but I know she misses you,' wrote Celia. I smiled a bitter smile when I read them. Then I tied them together and stuffed them at the back of the secret drawer, locked it, hid the key behind a book in the bookcase and went to change for dinner with a light step and my eyes shining.

I held to my private pledge not to enclose the common before the worst of the bad weather was over, and I waited until March before two days of settled clear cloudless days tipped my impatience to have done.

I told the parish roundsman that I would be enclosing two hundred acres of common on the following day and that he should have twenty men waiting for me in the morning. He scratched his head and looked doubtful. He was a plain man, in brown fustian, with the good boots of the labouring man who is making a better living than most, on the backs of the rest. John Brien his name; he had married one of the Tyacke girls and moved into the village. A little freer of village loyalties, with book-learning from his Chichester day school, he had obtained the job of parish roundsman and could now congratulate himself that he was the best-paid and most hated working man in Acre. He had no great love for me. He disliked the tone in my voice when I spoke to him. He thought himself a cut above the rest of the Acre villagers because he could read and write and because he did a job most of them would be shamed to do. Somewhere in my heart I still held to the old ways, and if the villagers despised and disliked a man then so did I. But I had to do business with him, and so I held Sorrel on a short rein when I stopped the gig and explained to him civilly where I wanted the men to meet.

'They'll not like it, Mrs MacAndrew,' he said, his voice expressing contempt for such people who would refuse to work when and where the Quality and their dogs like him bade them.

'I don't expect them to like it,' I said indifferently. 'I merely expect them to do it. Can you get enough men together for tomorrow, or should we wait a day?'

'I have the men to do the work.' His hand gestured towards the shuttered cottages where idle men were sitting, heads in hands beside empty tables. 'Every man in the village wants work. I can pick and choose. But they will not like the job of fencing in the common, fencing themselves out. There may be trouble.'

'These are my people,' I said with the indifference of a local for a stranger's advice. 'There will be no trouble that I cannot manage. You get the men there. There is no need for you to tell

464

them what job they are to do. And I will meet you there. And any trouble I shall deal with.'

He nodded and I held Sorrel in, my hard eyes on him until he turned the nod into the full bow that I expect from my people in my village. Then I gave him a tight smile and said abruptly, 'Good day, Brien, I shall see you at the beech coppice tomorrow, with twenty men.'

But when next day I trotted my gig down the lane and turned the corner to the start of the common land I saw there were not twenty men, there were more like one hundred. Wives too, and children, and the old people too aged for work. And a handful of the poorer Wideacre tenants, and about a dozen of the cottagers. The whole of the poor community of Wideacre was out to greet me. I halted Sorrel and took my time in tying his reins to a bush. I needed time to think; I had not expected this. When my head came up from fumbling with the reins my face was clear and serene, my smile as lovely as the bright morning.

'Good day to you all,' I said. My voice was as bright and as untroubled as the robin in the beech tree over my head who started a clear and lovely warble at the pale blue sky.

The older men were in a little cluster, conferring among themselves. They jostled each other like boys caught in an orchard and then George Tyacke stepped forward, the oldest man in the village, still hanging on to life and his cottage, though he was stooped and bent with rheumatism and his hands shook with palsy.

'Good day, Miss Beatrice,' he said with the gentle courtesy of a patient man who has spent his life at other men's bidding, and yet never lost temper or dignity.

'We have all come out today to speak to you about your plans for the common,' he said. His voice had the soft accent of the Sussex downland. He had been born and bred here, spent all his life within this circle of green hills. His family had never lived anywhere else. It was probably his ancestors whose bones lay in Norman Meadow. It was probably his land before my ancestors stole it.

'Good day, Gaffer Tyacke,' I said, and my voice was gentle. Today might see a hard act, a harsh act, against the poor of Wideacre, but I could never keep a smile from my eyes when I heard the slow drawl of my home. 'I am always pleased to see you,' I said with courtesy. 'But I am surprised to see so many from Acre village, and others, too.' My eyes flicked towards the tenants: my tenants, whose roofs depended on my goodwill, and they shuffled their feet at my scrutiny. 'I am surprised that so many of you should think you have anything to say about what is done by me on my own land.'

Gaffer Tyacke nodded at the reproof, and the tenants looked as if they wished they were elsewhere. They knew that in that one swift glance I had noted every one, and they had an uneasy fear that they would pay for it. As indeed they would.

'We are just worried, Miss Beatrice,' Gaffer said gently. 'We did not want to come up to the Hall and when we first heard of your plans we did not believe that you would do it. So we have left it so long to speak to you.'

I set my hands on my hips and looked around at them. In the winter sunshine my driving dress glowed a deep black. Under my neat black riding hat my hair gleamed as ruddy as an autumn beech tree. They had formed a circle around me but it was the circle of a court, not that of a mob. I was in utter control of this scene and they all knew it. And even old George Tyacke with his dignity and wisdom could not keep the servility from his voice.

'Well,' I said, and my tone was clear and loud so even the most distant of my shrinking tenants could hear me. 'I'm damned if I can see it's anyone's business but my own, but since you've all made a day's holiday to be here, you'd best tell me what it's all about.'

It was as if a flood had broken through a dam.

'It's the rabbits! I can't buy meat, they're the only meat we eat!' said one woman.

'Where am I to get kindling from if I can't come here?' said another.

'I've a cow and two pigs and they've always grazed here,' said one of the villagers.

'I set my beehives out on the common for the heather honey,' said one of the tenants.

'I cut peat for my stove on the common!'

'I gather my brushwood here!'

'My sheep graze here in autumn!'

And above the babble of voices Gaffer Tyacke's old-man trembly tenor carried to my ears.

'Look behind you, Miss Beatrice,' he said. I turned. I had been standing in front of a great oak tree, one of the oldest in the woods. It was a pretty tradition of the village that lovers plighting their troth should seal their engagement by carving their names in its bark. From as high as a tall arm could reach, down to the roots, were love knots and names entwined and hearts carved, sometimes exquisitely carved, in the bark.

'There's my name, and my wife Lizzie,' said George and pointed behind my head. Carefully I stared at the knots and whorls of the tree trunk and made out, as lichened as an old headstone, the heart shape and 'George' and 'Lizzie' carved inside.

'And above them is my pa and ma,' said George. 'And above that is their pa and ma, and the names of my family go back as far as anyone remembers until you cannot read the names but see only a chip in the old bark where a name was.'

'So?' I said coldly.

'Where are my grandchildren going to carve their names when they are courting?' Gaffer said simply. 'If you fell this tree, Miss Beatrice, it will not be like courting at all for the Acre bairns.'

There was a murmur of support from the crowd. The main issues were those of food and fuel, but even the poor have their sentiments.

'No,' I said uncompromisingly. It had been on my lips to offer to leave the tree and to run the fence around it so that the couples of Acre could still walk the dark lane on summer nights and carve their names together, then stop in dark undergrowth to make love on the way home. But it was folly and sentiment. And it was nonsense to put a kink in a straight fence for the happiness of children as yet unborn.

'No,' I said. 'I know you are not in certain ways at Acre and you all know that I have stood your friend in the past. But Wideacre is changing and the way we have to farm is changing. There are still acres of common left that will not be enclosed this season. You may go on grazing your beasts and snaring rabbits, and gathering firewood there. But this area is to be sown for wheat.'

'It will be a bad day when there are wheatfields all around Acre and no one with the price of a loaf inside the village,' called a voice from the back of the crowd, and there was a murmur like a groan of support.

'I know you, Mabel Henty,' I said certainly. 'You owed me three months' rent last quarter day and I let the tally run. Don't you raise your voice against me now!'

There was a ripple of laughter from some of the other villagers and Mabel Henty flushed scarlet and was silenced. No one else took up the cry. I let my gaze roam around the circle of faces until all the eyes had dropped under my hard green glare. They were all looking at their boots. Only Gaffer's head was still up; only Gaffer Tyacke's eyes still met mine.

'I am an old man, Miss Beatrice,' he said. 'And I have seen many changes in my life. I was a young man when your pa was a boy. I saw him wed and I saw him buried. I saw your brother married and I was at the church gate to see you go in a bride. I was at the back of the church when they buried your ma. I have seen as much here as anyone. But I have never seen a Squire at Wideacre who went against Acre village. Nor heard tell of one. If you go on with this when we have asked you, begged you, not to, then you are not the Master as your pa was, nor as his pa was. There's been a Lacey at Wideacre for hundreds of years. But they've never given the poor cause to groan. If you go on with this plan, Miss Beatrice, you will break the heart of Wideacre.'

I nodded quickly to clear my head. A dark mist seemed to swell up from the ground and I could only dimly hear the murmurs of support from the crowd. To fail the land, to fail the people, seemed more than I could bear. In that second as I shook my head like a weary deer surrounded by hounds, I felt afraid. I felt afraid that I had, somehow, lost my way, had mislaid the whole thread and purpose of my life. That the steady constant heart of Wideacre would no longer beat when I listened. I put my hand to my head, the anxious faces around me had blurred into a circle.

John Brien's face stood out. Bright, curious, uncaring.

'You have your orders, Brien,' I said, and my voice seemed to be someone else's, a distant clear tone. 'Put the fences up.'

I took half-a-dozen unsteady steps to the gig and clambered

up into it. I could see little for my eyes were filled with hot tears and my hands were shaking. Someone, Brien, untied the reins and handed them to me. My hands, as automatically skilful as ever, backed Sorrel and turned the gig.

'Don't let him do it!' called a desperate voice from the crowd. 'Miss Beatrice, don't do this to us!'

'Oh, get on with your work!' I said in sudden desperate impatience. 'Enclosures are taking place up and down the country. Why should Wideacre be different? Get on with your work!' And I flicked the reins on Sorrel's back in one irritable gesture and he jumped forward and we swirled away down the lane, away from the circle of shocked faces, away from the old lovely wood, which would be felled, and away from the sweet rolling heather and bracken common, which would be burned and levelled and drained dry.

All the way home I had tears on my cheeks and when I brushed them away with the back of my gauntlet I found my face was wet again. But I could not have said what had made me weep. Indeed, there was nothing. The common would be enclosed as I had ordered, the half-spoken protest of Acre village would be the talk of the ale-houses for half a year and then forgotten. The new fence would soon blend in, greened with moss and greyed with lichen. And the new courting couples of Acre would find another tree for their carvings. And their children would never know that once, through the woods, there had been hundreds of acres of land where little children could hide, and play at war, and picnic and roam all day long. All they would know would be field after flat field of yellow wheat where they would not be allowed to play. And knowing no different, why should they grieve?

It was those of us who had known the common who would grieve. And the next day when I put on my black silk dress I felt I was in mourning indeed. For by now the fences would be up and the men would be cutting down the great lovely trees and hacking out the roots. I would not drive out and see the work done. I did not want to see it until it was so far advanced that no sudden softness of mine could halt the relentless progress of the mindless beast that Harry exultantly called 'The Future'. Neither would I be driving to Acre village for a while. The voices in the crowd had been grieved, not angry, and no crowd led by Gaffer Tyacke would ever be other than courteous. But when they saw the fences going across the ancient footpaths they would be angry. And there was no reason why I should see that anger. I did not choose to.

But after a long breakfast, during which I planned my day, which seemed very empty if I was not to drive out on Wideacre, I went to my office and found John Brien waiting in the lobby by the stable door.

'Why are you not at the common? Has something happened?' I asked him sharply, opening the door and beckoning him in.

'Nothing has happened,' he said, ironically. I sat at my desk and let him stand.

'What do you mean?' I said. He heard the tone in my voice and he heard the warning note.

'I mean nothing has happened because the men won't work,' he said. 'After you left yesterday morning they went into a little huddle with old Tyacke . . .'

'George Tyacke,' I prompted.

'Yes, Gaffer Tyacke,' he repeated. 'And then they said that they wanted to take an early dinner break. So they all trooped home and when I waited for them to come back an hour later no one came.'

'And then?' I said sharply.

'Then I went to look for them,' he said, his voice almost petulant. 'But I could get no answer at any of the cottages. They must all have left the village for the day, or else locked their doors and kept silent. Acre was like a ghost town.'

I nodded. This was a petty rebellion; it could not last. The people of Acre were in a hard vice of needing work, and Wideacre was the only employer. They needed access to the land, and we owned all the land. They needed roofs over their heads, and they were all our tenants. No rebellion could last long under those circumstances. Because we had been good, even generous, landlords they had forgotten the total power the Squire of Wideacre has for the using. I would not want to use the power. But I would certainly do whatever was needed to get those fences up and that common land growing wheat.

'And today?' I asked.

'The same today,' John Brien said. 'No men waiting to work, and no reply at the cottages. They just will not do it, Mrs MacAndrew.'

I flashed him a scornful look.

'Would you ask them to get my gig ready with Sorrel harnessed,' I said in a tone of icy politeness. 'I see I shall have to come out again and get this settled.'

I changed into my driving dress and found John Brien waiting beside the gig in the yard. He was riding his own mare, a horse good enough for a gentleman born.

'Follow me,' I said in a tone I reserve for impertinent servants, and swung out of the yard.

I drove down the lane to Acre. This tale of silent cottages might do for John Brien but I knew that behind every cottage window there would be a pair of eyes watching me go past. I drove to the chestnut tree at the centre of the village green, as clear a signal for a parley as if I was carrying a stick with a handkerchief.

I tied Sorrel to one of the low branches, I climbed back into the gig and waited. I waited. I waited. Slowly, one by one, the doors of the cottages opened and the men came sheepishly out, pulling on their caps and shrugging on their sheepskin waistcoats, their wives and children following at their heels. I waited until I had a goodly crowd around the gig, and then I spoke clearly and my voice was cold.

'We had a few words yesterday and you all explained to me why you wanted things at Wideacre left as they are,' I said. 'I told you then that it cannot be so.' I paused and waited for any comment. None came. 'John Brien here tells me that none of you stayed to work yesterday,' I said. I let my gaze wander around the circle of faces. Not one eye met mine. 'Nor today,' I said.

I signalled to John Brien to untie Sorrel and pass me the reins. 'The choice is yours,' I said flatly. 'If you refuse to work I shall send to Chichester for the labourers from the Chichester poorhouse and they can come and earn your wages and take home your pay while you sit in your houses and go hungry. Or, if there are problems with that, I can bring in Irish labourers and I can cancel your tenancies and give them your houses.'

There was a shudder of horror at that thought. I waited until the spontaneous moan had died, then gazed around the circle of faces again. They were all people I knew so well. I had worked side by side with all of them ever since I had been out on the land. Now I sat high above them and spoke to them as if they were dirt in my road.

'The choice is yours,' I said again. 'You can either take the work that these changes provide. And take the wages that are fairly set by the parish. Or you can starve. But either way those fences are going up. The common will be enclosed.'

I nodded to Brien to stand aside from Sorrel's head and loosened the reins to move off. No one said a word this time, and I had the feeling that they were silent even when I was out of earshot. They were stunned by the ruthlessness of a woman they had loved since she was a tiny girl on a fat pony. They had thought I was their pretty Miss Beatrice who would never fail them. And now I looked at them with a cold set face and offered them the choice between independent starvation and starvation wages.

They went back to work. Of course they did. They were not such fools as to try to stand against one who was landlord, employer and landowner all in one. Brien rode up to the Hall during their dinner break to tell me that the work had started and that the fences were going up quickly.

'You did tell them!' he said admiringly. 'You should have seen their faces. That's broken their spirits all right. I wish we had brought the Irish in. It would wake that village up for once! But they looked pretty sick when you trotted off, Mrs MacAndrew, I can tell you! You slapped them down pretty hard!'

I looked at him coldly. His spite against my people reminded me again of the oddness of the role I had to play. And the disgusting nature of the tools I had to use to do the jobs I had to do. I nodded.

'Well, get back to work,' I said brusquely. 'I want that common ready for spring sowing.'

I did not spare myself the pain of seeing the common this time but drove down to it in the early spring dusk, which came at about four o'clock. In the gloaming I could see little of the common, but the smell of it, the frosty bracken and the hint of icy pine needles, pulled at my heart strings as I sat on the gig at the end of the lane and Sorrel chafed at the bit. Before us loomed the new fences that marked out the limits of this year's wheat-fields. Next year we would enclose and drain more and more until the only fields left to grow hay and the sweet meadow flowers would be the ones that were too high or too steep for any plough. All of the common that rolled in such easy soft valleys would be gone in a few years' time, and this fence, which was causing Acre village so much worry and grief, was only the first of many lessons that would teach them that the land belonged only to us, and that in years to come they would not be allowed so much as to set foot on it without permission. But behind the dark outline of the new fence I could see the soft rolling profiles of the little hills and valleys of the common where it drops down to our woods. And my heart ached for it.

I drove home in a hurry for I wanted to be in time to bathe Richard and to put him into his fleecy little nightshirt. I wanted to tickle his bare sweet-smelling warm tummy, and to tease him by poking my chilled fingers in the soft little pits under his arms. I wanted to brush his hair into black little kiss-curls, and to bury my face in his warm neck and sniff at the sweet pure smell of baby. But most of all I wanted to see him to reassure myself that I did indeed have a son who would be Squire if I could only hold to this one true course, that I was not crazy to tear the heart out of the land I loved.

Next morning John Brien was calling even before breakfast. He was waiting in the lobby before my office and my maid, Lucy, told me he was there as I was dressing. I raised an eyebrow at her as our eyes met in my mirror.

'Don't you like John Brien, Lucy?' I asked quizzically.

'Nothing to like or dislike,' she said abruptly. 'I hardly know him. I only know what his job is, and that he earns twice the wage of anyone in Acre and yet never has a penny to lend his wife's own kin. I only know that he picks out the men who can work and left young Harry Jameson off the gang all through the winter when the lad was desperate for a wage. I don't like him very much. But then, most of them hate him like poison.'

I grinned at Lucy. She was no longer a village woman, for her life was bound up with my life at the Hall and her plate would be always full at the kitchen table. But she had kin in Acre and a good nose for what went on there.

'I've no love for him either,' I said, as she piled my hair on the top of my head, and let a few curls hang down around my face. 'But he should be out working this morning. Have done, Lucy. There's like to be some trouble.'

Obediently, she made two deft touches and stood back.

'Bound to be trouble if you fence off land that's always belonged to the village,' she said dourly.

I gave her a long hard look in the mirror until her eyes dropped.

'The land belongs to Wideacre,' I said firmly.

I gave her one more look, and thought that here was another person I had faced down in so few days. Wideacre might be wealthier at the end of this, and my son might be the Squire, but I would have lost a great deal of love.

I shrugged off the thought and went down to John Brien.

'Yes?' I said coldly. He was twisting his cap in his hands and his eyes were wide with excitement at the bad news he was bringing to me.

'Mrs MacAndrew, 'tis your fences,' he gasped, forgetting his town-bred accent in his haste. 'They've pulled your fences down and hacked some of them. Nearly all the work we did yesterday has been undone. Your fences are down and the footpaths are open again.'

My head jerked up to stare at him as if he was an angel of death.

'Is this the Culler's work?' I said sharply. The fear in my voice made him hesitate and look strangely at me.

'What's the Culler?' he asked.

'An outlaw, a rogue,' I said, stammering in haste. 'He fired Mr Briggs's plantation back in the autumn. Could this be his work? Or is it the village?'

'It's the village,' said John Brien positively. 'There's been no time for anyone else to have heard of the trouble we are having here. Anyway I swear I know who has done it.'

'Who?' I said. My face, which had been white and wet with cold sweat, was regaining its colour and my breath was coming normally again. If it was not the Culler on my land then I could face any danger. For one moment it was as if the ground had opened beneath my feet and the Culler sitting so oddly on his black horse with his two black dogs was coming for me out of the darkness of hell. But then I recognized the sense of what Brien said. It was too soon for anyone outside the village to have got wind of the troubles here. If the Culler was coming, if he was coming for me, and that was a fear I would have to face, then I prayed only to be spared that fear while my mind was so busy, so frantic with so much else.

'Who from the village then?' I said, my voice steady again.

'Gaffer Tyacke's youngest son John. Sam Frosterly, and Ned Hunter,' said Brien certainly. 'They worked slowly and were surly all day. They're known troublemakers. They were last to leave last night and they were in a huddle together all the way home. And they were first there this morning to see my face when I saw the damage. I saw them smile at each other then. I'd lay a week's wages it was them.'

'That's a serious charge, a hanging offence,' I said. 'Have you any evidence?'

'No,' he said. 'But you know they're the wildest lads in the village, Mrs MacAndrew. Of course they had a hand in it.'

'Yes,' I said thoughtfully. I turned to the window and looked out over the garden and the paddock and the high, high hills of the downs. Brien cleared his throat and shuffled his feet impatiently. But I let him wait.

'We do nothing,' I said eventually, when I had taken my time and thought the thing through. 'We do nothing, and you say nothing. I'll not come driving down to Acre every time something happens. Set the fences back in their places and repair the broken ones as best you can. Say nothing to those three: young Tyacke, Sam Frosterly and Ned Hunter. Just leave it. It may be that it was high spirits and bad temper and they'll forget all about it. I'm prepared to overlook it.'

I knew also that if Brien had no evidence we could not move against the three. The village had closed its doors and its face to me. If I arrested three of the happiest, naughtiest, best-looking lads in the whole of Acre I would be more than disliked: I would be hated.

The three had been an irrepressible gang ever since they had been expelled in a giggling heap from the village school. They had stolen apples from our orchards; they had poached game from our preserves. They had taken salmon from the Fenny. But one of them was always the first to claim my hand at a Wideacre dance and, while the other two would hoot and catcall, he would spin me around, his red face smiling. They were bad lads – in the village judgement. But there was not an ounce of vice or spite among the three of them. And any girl in the village would have given her bottom drawer to be courted by any one of them. But they were just twenty and in the uproarious stage of bachelordom when young men prefer each other's company and a pint pot to the prettiest girls in the world. So although they would give and take a hearty kiss under the mistletoe in winter, or behind the hay ricks in summer – they were not the marrying kind.

If I knew them – and I thought I did – then the breaking of our fences would have been done as a dare. If they had no response either from me or from John Brien, the joke would lose its savour. And it would not be repeated, for that would smack of spite. And I believed that they loved me, and would not break my fences, once the thing was beyond a joke.

'Leave it,' I said again. 'And don't let them know that you think it was them.'

John Brien nodded, but the gleam in his eyes told me that he thought I was being weak. I did not care. His opinion mattered nothing to me. If I read this attack as a jest, then I was more likely to be right than he – with his prickly pride about property and his anxiety at being made mock by three wild lads.

But he was right. And I was wrong.

Somewhere I had lost my sense of what was happening in Acre village and on the land. I had been certain that the one attack was one jest, that it would stand alone as Acre's reply to Miss Beatrice's haughtiness. That if I said nothing and did nothing but merely continued to enclose the common, then honour would be satisfied on both sides and the work would go smoothly ahead.

But the second night the fences were thrown down. And the third night they were thrown down and burned.

It was a tidy fire, built with a countryman's care in a clearing, away from the dry tinder in the wood and clear of any over-hanging branches. They had piled up the fences, fired them, and got themselves home to Acre before anyone noticed the flames.

'And then they all tell me that there was nothing they could do!' said John Brien in irritation. 'They say that by the time they got water from the Fenny to put out the flames the fences had been destroyed!'

'They could have made a chain to the common stream,' I objected. 'It's only a few yards away.'

'It's inside the area that's to be enclosed,' John Brien said. 'They said you'd told them to keep off that land, so they did.'

I gave a hard smile. 'It makes sense,' I said.

But I turned to look out of the window and my smile died. 'I won't have this,' I said coldly. 'I gave them a chance, but they seem determined to defy me. If they want to threaten me, with a fire in my woods, then they will have to learn who is Master on this land.

'I shall have to go to Chichester to get new fences. I shall call in at the barracks and get a couple of soldiers to guard the fences until they are up. And if those lads come near them they can have a beating to teach them better manners. I have allowed them their jest. But now there is work to do and the games are over.'

Brien nodded. His eyes bright at the hardness in my voice. 'You could arrest them if we caught them red-handed,' he said. 'They could hang for this.'

'Not Wideacre lads,' I said dismissively. 'They deserve a fright, but nothing more. I'll go to Chichester at once.'

I paused only to find Harry, who was playing with Julia in the nursery, before I ordered the carriage.

'This is very bad, y'know, Beatrice,' said Harry, as he accompanied me to the stable yard.

'I agree,' I said briskly, pulling on my gloves.

'Typical of the poor,' said Harry. 'They simply can't see that this is the way things have to be.'

'They seem to be doing rather well at ensuring that events do not follow this apparently inevitable course,' I said ironically, and stepped into the carriage. 'For a natural process your progress seems to be rather difficult to bring about.'

477

'You are jesting, Beatrice,' Harry said pedantically. 'But everyone knows this is the way things have to be. A couple of crazy villagers cannot stop it.'

'I know,' I said. 'I shall check the law with Lord de Courcey while I am in town. If it goes on we will have to catch them and turn them over to the courts.'

'Absolute severity,' said Harry, inspecting the shine on his top boots. 'No leniency.'

I nodded and waved him farewell from the window. Harry's tone might strike me as pompous and silly but everyone I spoke to in Chichester seemed to share it. Lord de Courcey treated the fence breaking and the mischievous bonfire as if it were an armed insurrection and took me at once to the barracks. I resisted, without too much difficulty, the suggestion that I should have an entire troop of horse quartered on the Home Farm to protect Wideacre Hall from three young lads. But I was glad to accept the offer of half-a-dozen soldiers with a sergeant.

I could have used the Wideacre footmen. But ours is a small community and I knew only too well that while the love and sympathy of the Hall servants might be wholly mine, they would not seize and hold their cousins or even their brothers in a free-for-all over my fences.

I came home in triumph, followed at a lumberingly slow pace by a wagonful of new fences, and at a distance by the sergeant and the troopers. They were to put up at the Bush and it was given out that they were a recruiting party. But they were to be ready for my word to set the trap.

I sent word the very next night. All day John Brien and the grinning villagers had set the new fences and dug them securely into the ground. As darkness fell and the men went home, John Brien, Harry and I met the troopers on the far side of the river. Making no noise, we waded the horses through the water and the soldiers tied their mounts and surrounded the clearing, leaving only the lane to Acre empty. It was dark, the moon was not yet up, and the only light was starlight, and that often hidden with cloud.

I had stayed on horseback and I could see Tobermory's ears flickering nervously at this late vigil. It was cold, a damp bitter cold of a late winter evening. Harry beside me shifted in his saddle and blew into his gloves to warm his fingers.

'How long do we wait?' he asked. He was as excited as a boy and I remembered, with some anxiety, his enthusiastic accounts of the fights at his school led by his hero Staveley. It was all a game to Harry. To John Brien, whose horse was on my other side, it was more serious. Despite his Acre wife he hated the village and thought himself above it. Like any foolish town-bred man he prized his quick wits above the slow wisdom of the country. And like any man climbing up the small and difficult ladder of snobbery he hated the rank of people he was trying to leave.

'We'll give them an hour,' I said softly. I was anxious and tense with the excitement of the ambush, but somewhere in the back of my mind there was a voice saying, 'These are your people, these are your people, and yet you are in hiding with soldiers and with two men whose judgement you despise to ambush them and do them harm.'

I could not believe that I had lost so much of my relationship with Wideacre, with the land, with the people, that I should be out in the dark like some spy to attack them. If it had not benefited Richard! But Richard's rightful place at Wideacre had created a long chain of events that meant that even now my husband was eating his dinner behind bars, and that the face of Wideacre, that beloved smiling land, seemed to be changing as I looked at it. If it had not been for Richard! But . . .

'There they are,' said John Brien softly.

Straining my eyes into the darkness I could see, as he had seen, three figures coming silently down the track that leads to Acre. They were walking at the side in single file and their shadowy shapes sometimes blended with the dark bushes. I saw John Tyacke's blond curls bright in the starlight, and thought I recognized the broad shoulders of Sam Frosterly. I heard John Tyacke say something under his breath and heard Ned Hunter laugh softly. They were quiet because it was night and they were country born and bred. They were not hushed for fear of a trap. They would never have dreamed that there could be a trap laid for Acre lads on Wideacre land.

They moved to the first fence that straddled the land and

readied themselves to push it down. One of them had a spade over his shoulder and he dug out the foundations and then all three rushed at it in a giggling dash and tumbled over when it gave way beneath the charge.

'Now?' said Brien softly to me.

'Now,' I said, my lips so cold I could hardly speak.

'Now!' shouted Harry, and spurred his horse forward as the troopers rose up ʋut of the dark bushes and raced towards the three lads. There were six troopers, a mounted sergeant, Harry, John Brien and I. The lads tumbled to their feet and stared as if they could not believe their eyes, then in a flash they were running like startled deer back towards Acre, heading for home, in the old trust that home was safe for them.

Ned and Sam leaped the broken fence and raced up the track with the troopers behind them and Harry riding them down. But I saw a glint of fair hair and realized that John Tyacke was running in the opposite direction, down towards the Fenny where he could be sure of a hundred hiding places and a dark secret creep home. He did not know I was there, watching him as he ran straight towards me. His ears and his attention were on the noise of Harry throwing himself from his horse on to the two other lads. He was expecting to be chased from behind. He was upon me almost before he knew it and he skidded to a halt in the darkness at Tobermory's side.

'Miss Beatrice!' he said.

'John Tyacke,' I replied. Then he ducked away from me and fled down the little path towards the river.

'Did you see him go, ma'am?' called the sergeant, turning his men from the fight in the lane where Ned and Sam were standing sulkily between John and Harry.

'No,' I said in a quick thoughtless response. He was Tyacke's grandson and I liked Tyacke. He was one of our people and the sergeant was a stranger. He was not to be ridden down like a dog.

'No, we've lost him,' I said.

The troopers took Sam and Ned away to Chichester that very night. I had not thought of that. They were committed to trial at the quarter sessions before Judge Browning. I had not thought of that. By the time Acre woke up the next day there was nothing anyone could do. Two of the best-loved lads of the village had been taken away. And their greatest friend, young John Tyacke, could only sit by his mother's small fire with his head in his hands and mutter that he did not know what he should do.

The whole of Acre knew that if Ned and Sam had been up to some devilry then John would have been with them. But they also knew that the devilry must have gone badly wrong indeed for the three to have been split up. For John was not the sort of lad to leave his friends to face trouble alone. He sat and brooded all day about what he should do, while the fence was repaired and the felling of the trees inside the enclosed land could at last start. Then he went to his grandfather, Gaffer Tyacke, and told him what had happened.

Then Gaffer Tyacke came to me.

I had half expected him, for I had yet to learn that I was no longer the villagers' first call when they faced trouble. Gaffer came in to my office while Harry was there, and if I had been quicker to send Harry out of the room then I might have stopped the downward spiral from error to tragedy. But Stride had served coffee for Harry and me while we worked on some plans, and Harry was intent on some *petits fours* and would have been troublesome to move. So I let him munch at the table while Gaffer Tyacke stood in front of my desk with his cap in his hands.

'I've come to give myself up, Miss Beatrice,' he said.

'What?' I demanded incredulously.

'I've come to give myself up,' he replied steadily. 'I took the two lads into the woods last night and I ordered them to pull down the fences. I ordered them to help me on that one night. The nights before was me alone.'

I stared at him as if one of us was crazy, and then slowly it dawned on me what he was doing.

'Gaffer Tyacke, no one could believe that,' I said gently. 'You are an old man, you could not possibly have done it. I know what you are trying to do, but it cannot be done.'

There was no responsive gleam in his eye. He had known me and loved me since as far back as I could remember. He saw me christened in the parish church, and on my first rides with Papa. But now he looked through me as if I were a smeary window, and said, 'I've come to give myself up, Miss Beatrice, and I ask that you will have me arrested and send me to Chichester.'

'What's this?' said Harry, coming out of his dream of chocolate cakes with a start. 'What's this I hear? Was it you breaking the fences, Tyacke?'

'Yes,' said the old man steadily.

'No!' I said, breathless with irritation and a rising sense of fear. 'How could it be, Harry? Don't be so foolish. You saw the man run last night. It could not have been Gaffer Tyacke.'

'It was me, begging your pardon,' said George Tyacke steadily. 'And I have come to give myself up.'

'Well, you'll have to stand trial and it's a most serious offence,' said Harry warningly.

'I know that, Squire,' said Tyacke evenly. He knew it better than any of us. It was only because he really understood what was happening that he was here. I put out a hand to him.

'Gaffer Tyacke, I know what you're doing,' I said. 'I did not mean it to go this far. But I can probably stop it. There's no need to try and save them this way.'

He turned his face towards me and his dark eyes were as black as a prophet. 'Miss Beatrice, if you did not mean it to go this far you should never have started it. You told us yourself this is the way of the world outside Wideacre. You have brought that world to Wideacre and now it will mean death. You have brought death to Wideacre, Miss Beatrice. And it had better be mine rather than anyone else's.'

I gasped and fell back in my chair, and Harry stepped forward with bullying authority.

'Now see here, that's enough!' he said. 'You've upset Miss Beatrice. Hold your tongue!'

George Tyacke nodded his head, his eyes still upon me burning with reproach while Harry crossed to the bell and ordered the carriage for Chichester.

'Harry,' I said urgently. 'This is nonsense and it must stop now.'

He hesitated at my tone and looked from me to George Tyacke.

'I've come to give myself up to you,' said George. 'But I can go to Lord Havering. I'm prepared to take the punishment.'

'It's too serious to let pass, Beatrice,' said Harry, his tone reasonable but his babyish face alive with excitement at the drama of these petty, deadly events. 'I'll take Tyacke here to Chichester at once and make my deposition. You come along, now,' he said rudely to Tyacke and took him from the room.

I saw the carriage go past the window and I could think of no way to stop it. I could think of no way to stop anything. I sat with my head in my hands by my desk for a long, long hour. Then I went up to my nursery to find my son, the future Squire.

They hanged him.

Poor, old, brave, foolish, Gaffer Tyacke.

The two lads would not agree that it was all his doing but the court was happy to have a man who confessed to breaking fences, trespassing on property and burning wood. So they hanged him. And Gaffer Tyacke went with steady steps to the scaffold and his old shoulders straight with pride.

The two lads, Hunter and Frosterly, they transported. Ned Hunter caught gaol fever and died while he was awaiting transportation. They said that Sam was with him all the time and he died in Sam's arms, his lips black with the fever, longing for a sight of his home and the touch of his mother's hand. Sam Frosterly sailed on the next ship out, and his family had a letter from him, just once. He was in Australia, a hard life and a bitter life for a lad reared in the gentle heart of Sussex. He must have longed and longed for the green hills of home. And they said it was the homesickness, not the heat or the flies or the dreadful bloody brawls, that killed him. He died within the year. If you are Wideacre born and Wideacre bred you cannot be happy elsewhere.

I heard of the deaths – Gaffer's through the trapdoor, and Hunter's on the convict ship – with a thin mouth, a white face, and dry eyes. After Hunter's death, John Tyacke, the young lovely grandson and the pet of the village, disappeared. Some said he had run off to sea, some said he had hanged himself in the Wideacre woods and would be found when the autumn winds came and swept the leaves away from shielding him. He was gone, anyway. And the three of them would roister arm in arm down Acre lane no more. And when they brought the harvest in, John Tyacke would not swirl me round in a leaping jig while the others twisted their caps in their hands and giggled and nudged each other. The three of them were gone.

17

A nd something had gone from me, too.

I could not hear the heartbeat of Wideacre any more. I could not hear the heartbeat; I could not hear the birdsong. As the spring warmed up, slowly, slowly, as if there was a lump of ice at the heart of England that year, I did not warm. The cuckoos were calling in the woods; the larks started to make small experimental upward flights and try their voices, and I did not warm. My heart did not sing. The spring, with all its bobbing wild daffodils in the woods, and its scattering of meadow flowers, with all the leaves and the sweetness, and the rushing of the Fenny, the Wideacre spring came, but I did not melt from my winter coldness.

I could not tell what was happening. I could neither hear nor see. Nothing, nothing in my life seemed real to me any more and I looked out on the greening, damp land as if I were looking through a wall of ice that would separate me for ever from the land I had loved, and the people I had known.

I spent much time gazing out through the window, through the glass pane. Looking incredulously at the greening woods, which were as bright and as fluttering as if everything was still the same, as if my heart still pattered to the tune of the steady thud of my home. I did not dare to go out. I was weary of driving and not yet released from mourning so I could not ride. But I did not even wish to ride. I did not care either to walk in the fields. The warm moist earth that caked on my boots seemed to pull me down like a bog of clay – not like Wideacre's soft loam at all. When I was driving it seemed such an effort to turn the horse's head, to click to him to trot, to hold him steady on the road.

And this spring the countryside was not so lovely; it was too bright. The colours of green this spring hurt my eyes with their vibrant growth. I squinted when I tried to look towards the downs, and the sunshine put hard lines around my mouth and on my forehead where I found I was scowling.

There was no pleasure for me out on the land this spring, I could not tell why. And there was no pleasure for me in the village either. As I had ensured, no one noticed the lack of kindling from the enclosure. I had timed the fencing in of the common carefully. They should not have reproached me for that. No one went cold in the village that spring by my action. So I did not do all things badly.

But they gave me no credit. Just as that year with Ralph the greening of the shoots and the warming of the land had seemed all part of my magic, all part of my good blessings on the land, now everything that went wrong was laid at my door. The Sowers' cow died and that had to be my fault, for she had not been able to graze on the good green shoots of the common. One of the Hills' children fell sick, and that was my fault for my husband doctor was far away and they could afford no other. Mrs Hunter sat by a blackened grate and wept without ceasing for the shame that had taken her son from her. And because he had died calling for her and she could not go to him. That was my fault, they said. That was my fault.

And I knew that it was.

When I had to drive through the village I kept my head high and my eyes blazed with defiance. There was still no one who could meet my gaze then, and they looked away with surly faces. But when I saw Mrs Hunter through her cottage window, sitting motionless beside the black grate, and noted her chimney with no little swirl of smoke, I did not feel defiant. I did not feel ready to brazen out the disaster on my land. I just felt afraid, and comfortless and cold. I pulled up at the cobbler's one chilly afternoon and called out, 'Mrs Merry!' to the group of gossiping women. Their faces turned on me were sulky and closed, and I remembered in disbelief the time when they would have called out 'Good day' and smiled, and crowded around the gig to tell me the village gossip. Now they stood in a circle like a gang of hanging judges and looked at me with cold eyes. They parted to let Mrs Merry come to the carriage and it struck me she came towards me dragging her feet. She did not smile to see me, and her face was guarded.

'What is wrong with Mrs Hunter?' I asked, gathering reins into one hand and fitting my whip into the stock.

'No physical ill,' said Mrs Merry, her eyes on my face.

'What ails her then?' I asked impatiently. 'Her fire is out. I have driven past the cottage three days running and she is always sitting by the empty fireplace beside a cold grate. What ails her? Why don't her friends go in and light the fire for her?'

'She does not wish it lit,' said Mrs Merry. 'She does not want food. She does not want to speak with her friends. She has sat like that since last week when they sent her Sam Frosterly's letter that Ned was dead. I read it to her, for she cannot read. She reached to the bucket and poured it over the fire and sat by the wet ashes till I left her. When I returned in the morning it was the same.'

My face stayed hard, but my eyes were despairing.

'She will recover,' I said. 'It is just a shock for her to lose a son. Her a widow, and him her only child.'

'Aye,' said Mrs Merry.

A cold hard monosyllable from the woman who had delivered my child, who had been with me during that crisis of effort and pain, who had promised me she would not gossip, and who had kept that promise. The woman who had told me I was just like my papa in my care for Wideacre people.

'It is not my fault, Mrs Merry,' I said with sudden passion. 'I did not mean it to happen like this, I did not plan this. I only had to increase the wheatfields; I did not dream the lads would pull the fences down. I meant them to have a fright with the soldiers and cease teasing me. I did not think they would be caught. I did not think Gaffer would go. I did not think he would be hanged, and Ned die, and Sam be sent far away. I did not mean this.'

Mrs Merry's eyes had no pity.

'You're the plough that does not mean to slice the toad then,' she said dourly. 'You're the scythe that does not mean to maim the hare. You go your own sharp way and do not mean to cut those who stand before you. So no one can blame you, can they, Miss Beatrice?'

I put out a hand towards Mrs Merry, the wise woman.

'I did not mean it,' I said. 'Now they blame me for everything. But my son will set it to rights. Tell Mrs Hunter I will see that her lad is brought home to be properly buried in the churchyard.'

Mrs Merry shook her head.

'Nay, Miss Beatrice,' she said with finality. 'I'll carry no message from you to Mrs Hunter. It would be to insult her.'

I gasped at that, and dropped my hands on the reins. Sorrel started forward and I snatched the whip from the stock to flick him into a canter. As I pulled away from the women I heard the clatter of something against the side of the gig.

Someone had thrown a stone.

Someone had thrown a stone at me.

So I cared neither to drive in the woods, nor to walk in the fields, nor to go down the lane to Acre that spring. Harry came and went as he pleased. Celia continued her visits, and it was Celia who made the arrangements to bring Ned Hunter's body home from the hulks at Portsmouth. And it was Celia who paid for his funeral and for the little cross over his grave. Celia and Harry were still met with a bob or a pulled forelock when they went into Acre. But I did not go to the village. Only on a Sunday morning during that warm wet spring did I go past the cottages with the staring windows. Past the smokeless chimney of Mrs Hunter's little home. Past the fresh graves in the churchyard of Gaffer Tyacke, of Ned Hunter. And walked the long slow walk up the aisle of the church past the rows of pews where my people looked at me with eyes as hard as flints.

My work lay indoors that spring. John Brien did the riding and the ordering for me. Daily he came to my office and I told him what work needed doing, and he went off to supervise it. So the land that had never had a bailiff, that had always felt the print of a Master's boot, was watched over and worked by a man who was not a Lacey, who was not even a farmer, but a town-bred manager; who was not even Wideacre born.

With the gang he ordered he had the common cleared and the fields planted with wheat. There was no more trouble from the village. He ploughed up the half-dozen meadows where the children played and the plough cut through the surviving marks of the village's common plot. We planted wheat everywhere a plough could run. And still we were not making enough money.

I was reserving John's fortune to buy off our cousin and I did not want to touch that for the lawyers' fees. But as they dragged on and on, their bills steadily mounted. We had borrowed from Mr Llewellyn to cover the first three months' bills, but then we also had the problem of meeting the repayments on the loans, and no extra money coming in until the wheat crop was sold, the wheat crop that had not yet shown green shoots.

Nothing was coming to my hands fast enough. I had consulted with Harry at the start of the plan, but now I dared not show him the real figures. We were paying out more on the repayment of the loans, and on the lawyers' fees, and John's medical bills, and on the new labour gangs and equipment and seed, than we were earning. We were drawing on our reserves of capital. We were drawing so heavily that I could start calculating how long it would be before the fortune my papa had so slowly and carefully amassed would be exhausted. Then we would have to sell land.

Enough there to keep me indoors, even when the swallows came and swooped low over the Fenny in the morning. Enough there to keep me waiting for the postman every morning in a frenzy of anxiety that today might be the day when Dr Rose would write one of his gentle, but increasingly confident letters saying, 'I am so pleased to tell you that your husband has made a complete recovery. As I write he is packing his bags to come home!'

Every day I expected a letter announcing John's return. Every day I prayed for the letter to tell me that our cousin had accepted the compensation and John's fortune could be paid to him, and the legal work to change the entail could begin in earnest. Every morning I awoke with those two converging processes racing closer and closer together. And every day the postbag was brought to me in my office I opened it with dread, waiting to see if I had won or lost Wideacre for my son.

I had won.

On that sweet April morning with the daffodils nodding golden heads in the garden outside my window and the birds carolling to the spring sunshine, the postbag held a thick cream envelope with our lawyers' crest embossed on the corner, and their pompous seal on the flap. With much self-congratulatory flourish they wrote to say that our cousin Charles Lacey had accepted compensation and was prepared to resign his rights to Wideacre. I had won. Richard had won. The horror and confusion of the past few months could slip behind me and would soon be forgotten. It would be as if this icy spring, this glassed-in shut-out spring had never been. Richard would be reared on the land as the future Squire. I should teach him all he needed to know about the land and the people, and he would bring in the harvest every year of his life. He would marry a pretty Sussex-bred girl of my choice and they would breed new heirs to the land. Bone of my bone, flesh of my flesh. I would have established a line that could stretch down the centuries to the unimaginable future. And I had done it with wit and with cunning and with courage. I had done it, although I had lost the sound of my own heartbeat, of Wideacre's heartbeat, of a voice of love from anyone. But I had done it.

I sat in silence with the letter in my hand and great floods of release and relief sweeping over me as tangible as the spring sunshine that warmed my face and my silk shoulder. I did not move for long, long minutes, savouring the time of victory. Only I knew what it had cost me, what it had cost Wideacre, what it had cost Acre village, to get us to this point where the way was clear for my son. Only I knew that. Even so, there were costs that I did not know, that I did not fully realize. I had won the land for Richard but this spring it had been dead to me. I could not be sure that my feeling for the land could come back to me. The people had turned against me; the grass was too bright a green, even the thrushes' song failed to pierce the wall around me. But it might all be a price that had to be paid to put Richard into my seat. And I was paying and paying and paying, and now the reward was in sight.

I drew the embossed notepaper to me with a sigh and wrote to our bankers ordering them to realize John's entire fortune, to sell all the MacAndrew shares and pay them into our cousin's account. I enclosed the power of attorney document to forestall any query from them at such an extraordinary move. Then I drew another sheet of paper towards me and started a letter to the lawyers to tell them that they could now go ahead with the legal processes to change the entail to favour my son Richard and my daughter Julia as joint heirs.

Then I sat still, with the sunshine warm on my shoulder and gave myself a few silent moments to consider and reconsider what I was doing.

But I was as impatient as I had been when I had been fifteen and said, 'Now.' The price Richard might face, Julia might face, lived in the future. I could deal only with now. I owed it to myself. I owed it to my son that he should sit in the Squire's chair. I was wilfully blind, I had to be wilfully blind, at the price I might be laying on him. The mortgages I had already accepted on the estate he would have to clear. The cost of working all his life with his sister would fall on him and her too. I would have done my duty by him, to her, to myself, and even in some odd way to my papa and the long Lacey line when I put the heir, the best heir possible, in the Squire's chair. Future debts would have to be met in the future.

I blotted the letters, and sealed them, and then I wrote a third. To Mr Llewellyn. I offered him another mortgage on Wideacre: the new meadow lands we had enclosed near Havering. They had come to the estate as part of Celia's dowry and if the worst came to the worst and we had to sell land, I should feel better about losing those newly gained fields. I could not have borne a mortgage on the fields I had ridden with my papa, even for his grandson. But we needed the money. The legal agreement would have to be signed and witnessed in the House of Lords itself and there were many pockets to be lined on the way, as well as legitimate fees to pay. The green shoots of wheat would have to be golden indeed this summer or we would face ruin.

'Beatrice! You look so much better!' said Celia, when I joined her and Harry for breakfast after my morning of shuddering relief.

'I feel better,' I said, smiling. Celia's cook had sugar-roasted a ham with apricots, accompanied by little spicy beef pies. 'What a wonder Mrs Gough is in the kitchen. I really do not begrudge her her wages.'

'No, why should you?' asked Celia, her brown eyes wide. 'All London-trained cooks are expensive. I should think she is rather underpaid here.'

I smiled and shrugged. 'No, don't worry, Celia. I am not about to bring the parish labourers into the kitchen to cook your dinner. I have just been working on the accounts and cannot help pricing everything I see.'

'They cannot be too bad, Beatrice, for your eyes are shining green again and they only do that when you are happy,' said Celia observantly. 'Have you had some good news?'

'Yes,' I said. 'I had a letter that made me very happy.'

Celia's face lit up as if someone had given her a thousand candles.

'John is coming home!' she said, and her voice was full of joy.

'No,' I said, irritated. 'John is not coming home. This good news was business news that you would neither understand nor appreciate. I have not heard from Dr Rose this month, but in his last letter he said that John still had much progress to make before he could come home.'

Celia's eyes dropped to her plate and I guessed that tears were prickling under the downcast lids. When she looked up, her mouth was trembling slightly, both at the disappointment and at the sharp way that I had dashed her hopes.

'I am sorry, my dear,' she said. 'It was thoughtless of me to jump to that conclusion just because you said you had some good news. I think of John and of your unhappiness without him so constantly that as soon as I saw you I thought it could only be his return that could make you so blooming again.'

I nodded ungraciously and turned my attention to my breakfast. Celia, I noticed, ate little and refused some fruit.

'Shall you go to Bristol to see him?' she asked tentatively. 'It seems to have been such a long time. He left in the first week of December, and it is now mid-April.'

'No,' I said, and my voice was firm. 'I feel I should obey Dr Rose's advice on this. He said he would tell me the moment John could receive visitors. It would hardly help John if I were to go pushing in before he was ready to see me.'

Celia nodded submissively.

'As you wish, my dear,' she said tenderly. 'But if you should change your mind, or when Dr Rose says you may go, you know that Richard would be perfectly able to do without you for a few nights. I should make sure that he was happy.'

I nodded. 'I know. Thank you, Celia,' I said.

I need not have been in such a fret of impatience. While the

April days grew warmer and longer and the green shoots that were to pay for my son's inheritance grew stronger and taller, the lawyers in London started the process of hearings and counter-arguments that would take them to the House of Lords. The bankers raised their eyebrows at my letter, but were bound by the power of attorney. One fine morning in mid-April Charles Lacey received into his account £200,000: a fortune for any man. But worth every penny to me and to my son.

On Charles Lacey, who would have come to Wideacre as Master on Harry's death, who could even have expelled me, I showered the wealth of the MacAndrew fortune and kept not a penny back for myself. Not a penny for Wideacre. In one profligate gesture, I threw the MacAndrew fortune into his lap and left Wideacre without protection, without emergency capital.

And I had to write to another London banker to inquire about another mortgage to buy new stock to replace those we had sold in a poor market. It might all be coming to my hand, but it was a near-run thing.

In Dr Rose's Bristol home my husband was growing stronger. His hands stopped shaking and his eyes were losing their feverish brightness. Through the bars across his window he could see the treetops greening and hear the rooks cawing around beakfuls of twigs. He could hear the wood pigeons murmuring over and over. He did not yet know that he was a pauper. He did not yet know that I had ruined him. But as he gained weight and grew stronger, his mind was turning back to me with less dread and less terror.

'He seems to have come to terms with the fact that the unhappiness of recent months was not wilfully caused by you,' Dr Rose wrote to me, with his usual tact. 'He speaks of you now as an ordinary mortal and not as some witch. I know how much this must have distressed you. You will be glad that the delusion passed so quickly.'

I smiled as I read. John's restoration to normality might prove very fragile when he came back and found himself a beggar living on my charity. He should not even have a frank for a letter to his father unless I had seen the contents.

'I think he will soon be ready to come home,' wrote Dr Rose.

'I have discussed this with him and he says he is certain he could live in a normal household again without needing to drink to excess. At present he is abstaining altogether, but he sees drink around him and is able to resist it. In your own household he might learn to take the occasional drink with family and friends. He is confident he could learn to manage this, and I believe he may be right.'

I nodded and turned the page.

John might no longer be half-mad with fear of me but he still would hate and despise me. I knew a certain squirm of fear at the thought of how much he must hate me now, now he had been bound and drugged and imprisoned at my command. And I hated him, and feared him too. If I had my way he should never come home, my quick clever husband with his keen blue eyes. He had all the power that men's laws and men's traditions could give him. I feared that. He knew what I was and he knew a great deal of what I had done, and I feared the bright daylight of his vision. If I had had my way he could have stayed incarcerated for ever. But I had chosen a bad doctor for that. Dr Rose was a good sympathetic practitioner. He had sided with me because my story was persuasive, my face beautiful, and my husband clearly demented. But he could not be asked to hold John for ever. John would have to come home.

And if I knew him, he would be coming home to hate me, and coming home to love Celia and her child. Before he arrived I had to complete the plan that would give Wideacre to Richard. And it had to be done while I had Celia on her own. So she would gain neither support nor, worse, damning information from John. I would find the news of the entail and Julia's and Richard's partnership easier to force upon Celia if she had no help at all, not even the help of such a broken reed as my convalescent husband.

I took up my pen and drew a sheet of paper to me and wrote a swift and easy reply. 'What wonderful news!' I told Dr Rose. 'My heart is overflowing with happiness.' But I had to advise caution. My sister-in-law, who had been so distressed over John's illness, was herself now unwell. I thought it better that John should wait in peace and quiet at Bristol until his affectionate family were restored to their usual harmony.

I signed with my confident scrawl and sealed it, and sniffed the hot wax with relish. Then I leaned back in my chair and gazed out of the window.

The glory of the Wideacre daffodils was lingering on, and the cherry-red shoots in the rose garden were hidden under great clouds of yellow. Paler and daintier, beyond the cultivated daffodils, were the wild ones: self-seeded in the paddock. As I watched, Tobermory bent his handsome head and nibbled at a bunch. He came up, a yellow bloom drooping from his mouth, looking like a clown and I wished I had Richard by me to show him the comical sight of the best hunter in the stables looking so silly. In the banks of the woods beyond the paddock the brown earth was green in lush patches with the new growth of moss and the tiny plants that struggle up to the spring sunshine. Everything was growing and greening and nesting and mating and in all the loud-singing sweet-scented world I seemed the only cold figure in a dark dress, alone indoors.

I jumped up from my desk in sudden impatience and tossed a shawl over my shoulders and went out bare-headed into the garden. I walked through the rose garden, sniffing at the warm gusts of the light scent of the daffodils, which blew, tantalizing, into my face. Through the little gate into the paddock I strolled and Tobermory saw me and came trotting to meet me, his lovely neck arched and his head high.

I reached up to pat him and his gentle huge face came down to nuzzle at my pockets with soft lips, hoping for a titbit.

'Nothing there,' I said to him tenderly. 'I forgot. I'll bring you something later.'

The ice seemed to be melting around my heart as I walked on down to the wood and heard the burble of the Fenny, high and brown, full of spring run-off from the downs. The path has no bridge opposite the Wideacre gate, but there is a fallen tree trunk that serves the purpose for me, though Harry fears he is too heavy and Celia is too afraid. In the middle of it were the Hodgett children sitting dangling their legs over the flood, each equipped with a little stick and a line, hopeful for stickleback. They were the youngest three of the family from the lodge house. Sarah Hodgett had sworn she would have no more after the twins five years ago and had managed to hold to that promise, though often she and her husband looked strained.

'Hello,' I called, my voice as light as the blackbird preening his feathers in the sunshine.

It was as if a dark cloud had come over that sunny wood. The five-year-old twins, mere moppets with a tumble of brown curls and large scared blue eyes, leaped up so suddenly they nearly fell in the water. Their sister, a serious-faced seven-year-old, grabbed a child in each hand and rushed them along the tree trunk to the opposite bank.

'Beg pardon, Miss Beatrice,' she said and started to pull them away, down the path towards their home.

'Don't go!' I called to them. 'You've left your rods!'

The little girl was trailing, looking back at me, and I crossed quickly to the middle of the tree trunk and picked up the sticks and string and smiled encouragingly at her. 'Don't leave your tackle behind!' I said in mock reproof. 'How will you catch the salmon in season?'

The oldest child turned. Her eyes were wide with anxiety.

'We weren't after your salmon, Miss Beatrice,' she said earnestly. 'The little 'uns were just playing fishing, we didn't take anything. We didn't break anything on your land, Miss Beatrice. We used to play here last summer, before we knew we weren't allowed. The little 'uns wanted to come here again. I'm sorry, Miss Beatrice, I'm sorry!'

I could scarcely understand this rush of words, and I jumped down from the tree trunk, the rods in my hand, to gather the children to me and tell them of course they could fish in the Fenny. That they should always have a right to the childhood I had lived. The perfect Wideacre childhood where the woods stretched farther than your little legs could go, and the river flowed faster than you could run alongside.

'Come here,' I said kindly, and started towards them.

The oldest child gave a piercing scream and started to run away from me, dragging the two little ones with her. The baby girl tumbled and fell and her sister snatched her up, an impossibly bulky burden, and staggered along with her, the little boy trotting alongside. I took three swift steps and caught the oldest child by the shoulders and turned her to face me. Her eyes darted wildly and were full of terrified tears.

'What's the matter?' I asked. I was catching her fear and anguish and my voice was high. 'What's the matter with you?'

'Don't send the soldiers after us, Miss Beatrice!' she howled in a collapse into her fear. 'Don't send the soldiers after us and have us hung. We didn't do no harm. We didn't break nothing or fire anything. Please don't have us hung, Miss Beatrice!'

My hands dropped to my sides as if her bony shoulders had burned me. My head rolled back and my eyes shut as I tried to register, to understand this blow to my idea of myself as Miss Beatrice, the darling of Wideacre. While I staggered, with my eyes still shut, the little girl snatched the twins' hands and hurried them away, down the little path to the cottage. And she would not feel safe until they were inside the garden with the gate shut. For out in the woods was Miss Beatrice, whose green eyes could see through walls to what the naughty children were doing. Who could ride down the fastest runners in the village – for who had ever gone quicker than Ned Hunter when he was running a race? Who could hang the most honest man in the village – for who had ever been cheated by Gaffer Tyacke? Out in the woods was Miss Beatrice, dressed in black like the witch she was, guarding the land she now said was hers, and that no one else should have. And little children had better play on the lane, or Miss Beatrice would be after them. And little children had better say their prayers or Miss Beatrice would come for them in the night. And little children had better make themselves scarce for fear that her shadow, her witch's shadow, fall on them. And hadn't they run when they saw me!

I stretched my hands out behind me and felt the rough bark of an oak tree under my icy fingers. I slumped backwards and leaned against it, my eyes looking sightlessly up to the branches and the blue sky beyond, where the courting birds criss-crossed with full beaks. Every time I thought I had reached the worst point of this year, another gulf opened up beneath my feet and I could do nothing but step bravely, bravely into it, and hold on to all my bright courage during the long nightmare tumble. Every little, necessary act I took seemed to be followed with the consequences of a tragedy. The slight decision to turn a little part of the common over to wheat had led me to this oak tree and this black wall of despair. I was hated and reviled on the land I loved by the people I still thought of as mine.

My fingers dug like claws into the bark to keep my legs straight and my mind conscious. But I felt so ill with misery and with this blackness that I could do nothing more than stand. I could not walk home. And for the first time in all my life I wished that I could just go to sleep, here if needs be, on the sweet damp earth of Wideacre. And never wake up to this pain and this loneliness again. I stood, leaning back against the tree, aching with sorrow, and as immobile as if my legs had been caught in a trap and my lifeblood was seeping away as I watched in horror. I did indeed feel that I was bleeding to death. All my wise, loving common sense for Wideacre had drained from me, and all I had left was the empty knowledge that any fool could have. That idiots like John Brien and Harry could have. Men who never heard the deep dark heart of Wideacre beating in the earth. And now I could hear it no longer.

The cold brought me to my senses. At some time I had slid down the trunk and was on my knees in the soft loam. My dress was stained and damp, and the sun had gone down. The chill spring evening awoke me like a jug of cold water over my head and I shook myself like a soaked puppy and clambered to my feet. My legs were useless with cramps and I hobbled across the felled tree like an old lady. I made my slow, chilled, awkward way home and felt like an old lady too. Not the proud matriarch of my fantasy with her children and grandchildren round her, and her line stretching down through the mists of time to rule Wideacre for ever. But a defeated, miserable crone, very near death. And ready for death. And longing for death.

A week later, the post came, and I thought of death no more. It was the deed of entail. The lawyers had finally done it. My eyes scanned it as if I would eat it with my hungry mind. It transferred the entail from Charles Lacey to Julia and Richard. And it provided that the first-born child from Julia's marriage or Richard's line, girl or boy, would inherit for ever. I smiled at that. Another girl might yet come to own Wideacre outright. If my first grandchild was a copper-headed girl with green slanty eyes, she would own the land and have to pay no price for it. She would inherit by acknowledged right, and ride over the land with no thought of a threat to her ownership. If she had my wits she would marry some poor Squire to give her children for Wideacre, and then pack him off to Ireland or America with half an unkept promise to follow. And if she was like me – but did not break her heart and her wisdom as I feared I had done – she would laugh out loud in her freedom and her spirits and her love of the land. And the people of Wideacre would laugh too – for joy at having a good Mistress, fair pay, and food on the table.

Pinned to the change of entail deeds was the contract that would bring all this about. One half-written piece of vellum trimmed with the usual rash of red seals and glossy ribbons. But simple enough paragraphs considering what they would bring. And considering what they had cost.

It said only that herein and hereinafter was a contract between Richard MacAndrew and Julia Lacey, now aged one year and two years. That the estate, hereinafter known as 'the estate', should belong to the two of them jointly, and be inherited, jointly, by the first-born child of the marriage of either party.

I held it in my steady hands and sniffed at the smell of the wax and felt the texture of the thick vellum between my fingers. The red ribbons along the bottom were silk and they felt soft and warm to the touch. I scarcely read the two paragraphs; I savoured instead the very existence of the piece of paper that had cost me so much.

I dipped my head and laid my face against the document. The vellum was warm, smooth but textured. The seals were scratchy like scabs along the bottom. The ribbons smelled faintly of perfume as if they had been bought by the yard in some haberdasher's whose perfumes and powder were kept beside his silks. A tear rolled down my face and I lifted my head to wipe it so that it should not blot this most precious piece of paper. Only one tear, no more. And whether I was weeping for relief that this struggle was now over and I could rest a little or because I had succeeded, I could not have said. The haze of pain that had cut me off from Wideacre had also cut me off from myself, and I no longer knew whether I was winning or losing. I could only go on and on and on. The sharp plough in the furrow, the sharp scythe in the field. And whether it was a toad killed, or a hare maimed, or my own life-blood on the bright blade, I could no longer tell.

Then I rang the bell and ordered the carriage for Chichester that afternoon, and bade Stride tell Harry that I needed him to escort me into town to transact some business.

And even at this late, last, final fence, Harry would have jibbed.

'Why don't we wait for John's return?' he said pleasantly ..s we howled down the hard high road to Chichester, through the pretty downland villages, and dragged more slowly around the steep slopes of the shoulder of the downs.

'Well, we don't know how long he will be, nor in what state,' I said, my tone equally light. 'I should rather get this signed and sealed while it is still fresh in our minds. Then we can tell Celia and John together as a surprise.'

'Yes,' said Harry hesitantly. 'But it's damned bad from John's point of view, y'know, Beatrice. I know he's keen on Wideacre but we have spent his entire fortune to make Richard the heir. I do wish we could have consulted him.'

'Oh! So do I!' I said emphatically. 'But what could we do? If we had left it very much longer there would have been rumours about Celia's barrenness, and that would have distressed her beyond belief. Those rumours would have made Charles Lacey increase his price because they would have made him hopeful of inheriting the estate. We simply had to go on with it when we did. John will understand. It's the decision he would have taken.'

'Well, if you're certain,' Harry said comfortably. The carriage rocked slightly as he settled back in his corner. Harry was gaining weight alarmingly fast. He would have nothing in the Wideacre stables that could carry him if he continued to eat at his present rate and spend lazy afternoons with the children on his knee or taking them for little walks around the garden. And if his heart was weak like Mama's, it must be strained.

'But there's no reason why we should not wait for his return to sign the contract,' Harry said, still uneasy. 'It looks so odd, Beatrice. It says "signature of Julia Lacey's parent or guardian", and there I put my name. And then it says "signature of Richard MacAndrew's parent or guardian", and there's my name as well!

499

Anyone who did not know us would think we were up to some sort of cheat.'

'Yes, but everyone knows us,' I said easily. 'It is so obviously the most sensible and best arrangement for everyone, there could be no slurs cast on it. The only person who loses at all is Charles Lacey and even he has been well compensated.'

Harry chuckled at the thought. 'Poor old Charles, eh?' he said. 'He must have started to get hopeful, d'you think, Beatrice?'

'Yes,' I smiled. 'You outwitted him finely then, Harry!'

'*We* did,' said Harry generously.

'Well, it was your excellent idea that started the plan,' I said. 'And now it is coming to fruition. How well you have ordered the future, Harry! What a certainty of happiness lies before the two children.'

Harry nodded and gazed out of the window. We were coming off the high ground now, dropping down a thickly wooded road which leads to Chichester from the north. The de Courcey mansion stood behind high walls on our left, other great houses further down the road. Then there was the sprawl of little cottages of the poor. Then the wheels were rattling on the paved roads and we were among the town houses of the prosperous Chichester townsfolk with the spire of the Cathedral towering over it all.

Harry's pride in his own quick wits walked his legs up the steps to the attorney and moved his hand across the precious piece of paper until he had signed it, as it had to be signed, in two places.

'It looks a little odd,' said our solicitor, presuming on our long relationship to challenge our actions. 'Is it imperative that it be done without the signature of Dr MacAndrew?'

'My husband is ill,' I said, my voice low. The solicitor nodded. A grey man in a shady office, even he had heard the gossip, and had pitied me, the prettiest girl in the county, married to a drunkard. 'We felt we should press on without him,' I said. 'We cannot tell when he will be well enough to come home again.' I stopped because my voice had become hoarse with suppressed tears.

The solicitor pressed my hand. 'I do beg your pardon, Mrs

MacAndrew,' he said kindly. 'I wish I had not voiced my concern. Think no more of it, I beg of you.'

I nodded and gave him a sweet forgiving smile on parting when he took my hand in a warm handclasp and bent and kissed it. I drooped ever so slightly down the stairs and then laid my head against the cushions of the carriage as if I were weary. Harry saw my face and took my hand comfortingly in his.

'Don't be too sad, Beatrice,' he said. 'John will soon be better, I am sure. Perhaps you two can be happy again. Celia is certain there is a future for the two of you together. And whatever happens to your husband, you and your son at least are safe on Wideacre.'

I nodded and returned the squeeze of his hand.

'Yes,' I said. 'We have done a good day's work today, Harry!'

'Indeed, yes,' he said. 'When shall we tell Celia?'

I thought fast. I did not want to tell Celia, but equally I knew I never would be ready to tell her. When we announced the joyful news of the change of entail and the inheritance of Julia and Richard as contracted partners I anticipated opposition from her. She knew of them only as half-brother and sister, both of them my children. She could not know, would never guess, that they were both sired by her husband. But she did not like their intimacy. And she did not like my touch upon Julia.

'Let me speak to Celia first, Harry,' I said, considering. 'She is bound to be distressed to learn that you know she is barren. I think it would be better if I told her that although you know, you are not troubled, because you have so cleverly found a way to make Julia your heir.'

Harry nodded. 'Whatever you think best, Beatrice,' he said. 'You sort it out as you please. All I can think of is my dinner. How cold these April evenings are. D'you think there will be soup?'

'Almost certainly,' I said equably. 'I shall speak to Celia in the parlour after dinner, Harry, so you may sit long over your port. Don't come in until I send for you.'

'Very well,' he said, obediently. 'I shall have some cheese with my port. I shall be in no hurry to leave, I can assure you.'

Harry's cheese proved to be so potent that Celia actually suggested that we withdraw as soon as it arrived at the table.

'I agree,' I said, laughing. I got to my feet and pocketed an apple from the fruit bowl. 'I would rather have my fruit in the parlour than share a table with that cheese, Harry!'

Harry chuckled, quite unrepentant.

'You are far too nice,' he said. 'Go and have your talk. Celia, I think Beatrice has some good news for you which I know will make you happy.'

Celia's eyes flashed to my face and her ready smile illuminated her.

'Oh, Beatrice, is it John?' she said as soon as the parlour door had closed behind us.

'No,' I said. 'Not yet. But the last letter I had was most encouraging. Dr Rose was talking in terms of months rather than an indefinite stay.'

Celia nodded, but the light had died from her eyes. She looked bitterly disappointed. I could not help wondering, with the spice of my habitual malice, if Harry's increased interest in food, and his growing bulk, was turning him from the golden prince of their early married life into a dreary, unexciting gourmand. And whether John's thin tension, his desperate grief, his nervous, passionate struggle against his drinking and against my control of him had inspired a love in Celia that was more than sisterly.

But I was not ready to tease that truth out of Celia. I had to take a most difficult fence, and all the thought and care I had put into the approach might not carry me safe over.

'It is good news though,' I said. I crossed to the fire and sat in the winged armchair beside it. I pulled up a footstool and lifted my feet up so they felt the warmth of the fire. Celia sank into a chair opposite, her eyes on my face. In the flickering firelight and lit by a branch of candles behind her she looked like some young serious schoolgirl. Far too young to be enmeshed in this complex conspiracy of lies and beguiling half-truths. Far too serious to be able to break away and be free when I had her in my grasp.

'Harry knows that you are barren, and he has despaired of having a male heir,' I said baldly.

Celia gave a little gasp and her hand flew to her cheek as if the pain in her heart was toothache.

'Oh,' she said. Then she was silent.

'But he has hit on the most wonderful plan to sign the estate over for Julia,' I said. 'It was all his idea, but I have helped with it, of course. We kept it from you in the early stages because we needed to discover first if it could be done. But it can be done. It is possible for Harry to buy the entail from our cousin Charles Lacey and to entail it instead upon Julia. She and Richard are jointly to inherit Wideacre, and to run it together.'

Celia's face was a picture of amazement, then dawning horror.

'Run it together?' she said. 'How would they be joint heirs?'

I kept my voice steady and cheerful, but I was conscious of choosing my words with care. I felt awkward. I felt nervous. It was like taking a horse you do not know to a fence you do not know in a county you do not know.

'As joint partners,' I said lightly. 'Like Harry and I do now.'

'Like Harry and you,' said Celia. 'Like Harry and you,' she repeated. She had turned back to me but her eyes were on the fire. Something in their hazy brownness made me wonder what she was seeing in a pile of glowing logs.

'No,' she said abruptly.

I jumped in unfeigned surprise.

'What?' I asked.

'No,' she said. 'I do not give my consent, I do not wish it. I do not think it is a good idea.'

'Celia, what are you saying?' I said. I disliked the speed of her words. The breathlessness, the stillness of the little figure in the pale parlour.

'I do not wish that this contract be signed,' she said clearly. 'I am Julia's mother and I have a right to a voice in the decision on her future. I do not wish this to go ahead.'

'Celia, why not?' I asked. 'Whatever are you thinking of, to stand against Harry's intentions in this way?'

That did not stop her, though it should have given her pause. But her eyes were fixed on the fireplace as if reflected on the coals she could see Harry and me frantically coupling on that very hearth, as my mama had done.

'It is hard to explain,' she said. 'But I do not wish Julia to be involved in the running of Wideacre in the way that you have been.' I could hear the restraint in her voice, which came from

503

her anxiety not to hurt me. But I would have been deaf not to hear the certainty too.

'Wideacre means so much to you, Beatrice, that you cannot understand that there is any other life open to a girl. But I should like Julia to love this place as her girlhood home, and to leave it with a light heart when she marries the man of her choice.'

'But this way she is an heiress, Celia!' I exclaimed. 'She can marry the man of her choice and he can live here as John and I and you and Harry do. She will be joint owner of Wideacre. You could not bless a child with a better gift!'

'You could! You could!' said Celia, speaking fiercely though her voice was low. 'The greatest blessing I shall give Julia will be to keep her free from the idea that Wideacre is the only place in the world to live. That it is the only thing in the world that could make her happy. I want her to be happy anywhere. I want her to be happy because she leads a good life and has a clean conscience and because she can freely give and freely receive love. I don't want her to think that her life's happiness is bound up with a handful of acres and a starving, miserable village!'

'Celia!' I gasped, and I stared at her in horror. 'You don't know what you are saying!'

'I do,' she said emphatically, looking at me directly now. 'I have thought long and hard on this, Beatrice. I have thought about it ever since we came home to England. I should not want Julia to share her home with another couple, however dear they may be to her. When she marries I should want her to live with her husband and live with him alone. I should not want her to come into another woman's house as I did, and to see her husband absorbed and working with someone else as I did. If she loved him with her whole heart I should want her to have all his time and all his love.'

'But we have been so happy,' I said weakly. 'We all were so happy.'

'There was something wrong!' burst out Celia. She took three swift strides to my chair and pulled me to my feet to scan my face as if she would read my soul. 'There was something wrong,' she said certainly. 'You know what it was and I do not. John knew what it was, but he could not tell me and I think it was that which sent him half mad and made him drink. I can feel it everywhere I go in the house. I can breathe it in the air. And I do not want my child touched with one feather of it.'

'This, this is nonsense,' I stammered. I was overwhelmed by the memory of my mama's sense of sin, of something dirty and black in the house that she could smell but not see. I had trusted my mama to be too much of a coward, too much of a fool, to track down the foul thing and look it in the face. When she saw it, the two-backed beast before the fire, she had died with horror.

But Celia might almost dare to track it into its very lair and face it. Armed with her love for her child and her courage, Celia might go where my mama's nervous thoughts had failed her.

'Stop it, Celia!' I said abruptly. 'You are distressed. We will talk no more of this tonight. If you really dislike the whole idea we will change it. But let us have tea now, and then go early to bed.'

'No, I won't stop here, and I won't have the tea tray, and we won't go to bed until I understand more. How was Charles Lacey compensated? What are the terms of the contract?'

'Oh, my!' I said lightly. 'Business, then? Well, very well, if you wish it.' I snowed her under then, with rack-rents and revisions of tenancies, and long leases made short, and cottagers' rights, and enclosure acts and the price of corn. How to sell when it is standing in the field, how to gamble on the growth and on the rise of the market when other farmers have poor crops. I even threw in the battle I had won over the water rights until her unlearned head spun.

'So we have changed our farming system slightly to make greater profits, and we used the MacAndrew money too,' I finished.

She nodded only to clear her head; there was no assent there. She could not have understood a word of the garble.

'John's money?' she asked.

'Yes,' I said. 'That is Richard's contribution, as it were, towards being made heir of Wideacre, jointly with Julia.'

'You have used John's money without his consent?' she asked. Her voice was even but her face was appalled.

'As a loan merely,' I said with assurance. 'The whole idea of the power of attorney is to safeguard the patient's interests. Obviously it is in John's interests – and mine as his wife and the mother of his son – that he should get maximum interest. The loan he has made to Wideacre is paying far more than the MacAndrew Line dividends. And it secures Richard's future, too.'

'You have used John's money without his consent and committed his son to Wideacre without him knowing?' she asked incredulously.

'Of course,' I said, challenging her, face to face. 'Any proper parent would be delighted, as Harry and I are, that the entail can so be changed.'

She smoothed a hand over her forehead as if to wipe away the confusion. It was ineffectual.

'That is a matter for John and you,' she said, her mind in a whirl. 'I cannot think it right. I cannot believe that Harry could have so used John's entire fortune, and that while he was ill, but if the contract is not signed, perhaps it can all wait until John returns from hospital?'

'Perhaps, perhaps,' I said soothingly. 'I am not exactly sure. Harry has been making the arrangements, not I. I undertook only to reassure you, that although Harry was grieved to understand that you are barren there should be no unhappiness between the two of you, because he has found this way around that sorrow. That your lovely little girl can inherit her father's land.'

'You plan that she and Richard will be joint owners?' Celia repeated slowly. 'That she and Richard should grow up together on the land, learning about the land together?'

I nodded.

'And you and Harry would take them both out on the estate, looking at the land and learning to farm. And all the time they would be growing closer and closer. And only you and I would know that they are not just partners, and not just cousins, but half-brother and half-sister?'

'Yes,' I said. 'But Celia . . .'

'But we would not be able to tell them that!' she said. 'They would be best friends and playmates and business partners. They would think they were first cousins, but they would be close kin. They would learn to love each other, and their interests would lie together. How could they then turn aside from each other and learn to love the people they will be betrothed to marry? How can my Julia have the life I had hoped for her and planned for her as a girl of Quality if she is an heiress from the age of two in a partnership with a boy who is neither husband nor distant relation?'

She spun on her heel so she did not face me and buried her face in her hands.

'It is a nightmare,' she said. 'I cannot tell what it is but some danger is threatening Julia from this. I do not know what!'

'You are being foolish, Celia,' I said coldly. I took her shoulders in a firm grip and felt a shudder run through her like a terror-struck foal. 'Wideacre is a family business,' I said levelly. 'Julia would always have had obligations to meet on the estate. She will simply work with Richard as Harry and I work.'

That reassurance tripped her control.

'*No!*' she said, and it was nearly a scream. 'No! I forbid it! You gave her to me and said that she should be *my* child. I claim my right as her mother to decide her future. She shall not be with Richard as you and Harry are, for I am afraid of something about you and Harry, even if I have no words for it but only a dread that chills and frightens me when I wake in the night. I do not know what I am afraid of, and I make no complaint against either of you. But I am afraid, Beatrice! I am afraid for Julia! I do not want her to be part of another brother-and-sister partnership. *No.* I do *not* give my consent. I shall tell Harry.'

I leaped for the door and spread my arms so that she could not get past me.

'Celia, wait,' I said. 'Don't dash out to Harry like that while you are distressed. He will think it most odd. He will think we have quarrelled. Calm yourself and consider what you mean to say. If you do not want Julia to be joint heir with Richard she can always sell him her share when they are older, or he can sell his. There is no need for you to become so upset over this, Celia.'

She had heard none of it. She was looking at me as if she had seen me for the first time. She was looking at me curiously, with disbelief, as if there were some mark scrawled on my face, or as if I had spiders crawling in my hair, or some other horror.

'Stand aside, Beatrice,' she said. Her voice was low and hard. 'I want to speak with Harry.'

'Not while you are so overwrought,' I pleaded, and I did not move.

'Stand aside,' she said again. And I remembered her before the library fireplace with two smashed bottles of whisky dripping from her hand.

'You will distress Harry,' I said. 'He planned this to make you happy.'

'Stand aside,' she repeated, and her eyes flickered towards the bell pull. For one brief moment I wondered if she could face the scene of the butler coming and her ordering him to push me out of the way by forcing open the door. But I saw the look on her face and knew I was arguing with a woman on the edge of hysteria.

'Beatrice, I have asked you three times,' she said and her voice was tight with control that might break at any moment. I feared Celia in a panic more than I feared her when she could judge to speak or be silent. If she screamed out that Richard and Julia were brother and sister then I would be irreparably lost. But if she kept herself under control, and if I went with her, I might manage this scene still.

I opened the parlour door for her with a little ironic bob curtsy and followed, hard on her heels, as she swept across the hall to the dining room. A footman was coming through the door from the kitchen bringing more biscuits for Harry, and I scowled at him so he turned on his heel and went back behind the baize door again. Celia saw nothing, heard nothing. She flung open the dining-room door and made Harry jump with the bang. He had a plate before him heaped with cheese and biscuits, and the flagon of port by his hand. He had butter on his chin. I could trust him as far as I could flick water.

'I do not consent to this arrangement,' said Celia in her high, hard voice. 'The documents are not to be signed. I do not wish it for Julia.'

Harry's blue eyes were wide with surprise.

'But it's done!' he said simply. 'We signed them this afternoon. The entail's changed, and Richard and Julia are joint heirs.'

Celia opened her mouth and screamed, a thin wail like a small animal trapped. She stood motionless, her eyes on Harry's face, his cheeks still full of biscuits. I was frozen too. I could not even think what I could say to stop Celia's mouth. But her horror and her fear of the unknown thing that hid in the corners of Wideacre and that one could almost feel breathing among us kept her wordless.

Her mouth still open, she gave a little whimper like a child with a finger trapped in a door. Her eyes rolled from Harry, motionless at the head of the table, to me, silent behind her. She found one word in her panic-stricken mind. She said, 'John.' Then she picked up her silk skirts in her hands and whirled from the room.

Harry bolted his mouthful and looked wildly at me.

'What's the matter?' he demanded. 'What's wrong with her?'

I shrugged. My shoulders were stiff and I could feel the gesture was wooden. My face must have been as white as a sheet. I could feel the control and the power slipping through my fingers like the sands of the common.

'Listen!' I said. I heard the door to the west wing bang and straight away thought of my desk and the incriminating bundle of Celia's letters to John, which had never reached him. Without a word to Harry I dashed after Celia and to my office. The room was in darkness; she was not there.

I called sharply, 'Celia!' but I had no answer. I could not think where she might be. I checked my west-wing parlour but although the candles and the fire had been lit there was no Celia weeping on the pretty sofa. I ran up the stairs to my bedroom, to John's room; I even glanced into the nursery to see my son sleeping like a tousled angel. But no Celia. Then I heard the sound of wheels on the paving stones of the stable yard and ran to the window. The coach was out and Celia was stepping inside.

'Celia!' I called. 'Wait!' With fumbling desperate fingers I struggled with the catch and the window swung open.

'Stop!' I shouted. The stable lads looked up at my voice even as they were shutting the door to Celia's carriage.

'Stop!' I said. 'Wait!'

Celia's head appeared at the window and I could see she was repeating the order to drive on to the coachman. I knew the coachman. I had given him a chance when Papa had been looking for a new man only six years ago. I had told Papa then that Ben was one of those people that can charm horses into the shafts. I could not remember his surname. He had been 'Coachman Ben' to us for what seemed a lifetime. But he was Wideacre born and bred. I had given him his job. I paid his wages. I knew he would stop, and Celia would have to climb down out of the carriage; then, between us, Harry and I, we could pet her and bully her, and confuse her and mislead her until this show of courage and activity was knocked out of her. And I could carry on, ploughing my straight furrow, scything in my straight line. Whatever stood in my path.

'Coachman Ben!' I called in my clear tone. 'Wait! I am coming down!'

I slammed the window shut and swirled round for the stairs. It took me less than a minute to be downstairs and through the west-wing door to the stable yard. But I heard the clatter of wheels as the coach rolled away, and I saw the lights go round the corner to the front of the house, to the drive, to Acre lane, and from there, if I guessed aright, to Bristol, to John.

'Stop!' I shrieked like a fishwife into the wind of the April night at the vanishing flickering lights. I gazed wildly round for a stable lad to send after them, to order Coachman Ben to stop. To tell him Miss Beatrice demanded his return this instant. But then my angry orders died on my lips and the rage in me died. I stood very still in the cool April night and shuddered from the cold that was in my chilled heart.

I knew why the coachman had not stopped.

I had remembered the coachman's surname.

It was Tyacke.

He was Gaffer Tyacke's nephew.

I turned on my heel and walked slowly, slowly back inside. Harry was still seated at the table, though he had been sufficiently disturbed to stop eating.

'Where is Celia?' he asked.

'Gone,' I said heavily, and threw myself into the chair at the foot of the table. Harry and I faced each other down the long length of the dining table, as we had the first night after our first lovemaking on the downs. That seemed very far away now, and very long ago. He pushed the decanter of port towards me and I fetched a clean glass and slopped a generous measure in. I threw it off with one gulp. It warmed my throat and belly but it did not touch the cold weight of fear beneath my ribs. Who could have imagined that one afternoon of sweet passion on the downs could have led us down this road? Each little step had seemed so easy, so safe. Each little step had led to another. And now the youth who had filled me with irresistible desire was a plump, ageing Squire. Too stupid to lie to his wife. Too foolish to manage his own affairs. And the dazzling, dazzled, girl that I had been was gone. I had lost her somewhere. She had died a little in the fall that killed her papa. Then a little bit more in the trap that bit off Ralph's legs. A little of her had been blown out like a candle when her mother had sighed her life away. And drop by drop, like an icicle growing, the girl that I had been had slipped away, and this ice that was my heart had been left.

'I don't begin to understand what is going on,' said Harry petulantly. 'Why was Celia so upset? Where has she gone? She can't have gone calling at this hour, surely? Why did she not tell me she was planning to go out?'

'There is no need to be quite so dense,' I said sharply. 'You can see perfectly well that Celia and I have had a quarrel. No one is asking for your support, so there is no need to pretend that you do not understand what it is all about. Celia would rather that Julia lost Wideacre than ran it with Richard in the sort of partnership that you and I have. I took offence at her tone and we had words. Now she has flounced off. I expect she is going to see John. I imagine she is going to tell him that we have spent his fortune and to ask him to help her to reverse all our trouble and to revoke the contract between Julia and Richard.'

Harry gaped. 'That's bad,' he said. I pushed the decanter back to him and he poured himself a glass and returned it to me. The room stank of conspiracy. Harry did not know much, but he knew when his comfort and his wealth were in danger. And he knew that in any battle over Wideacre business he would be on my side.

'They can't do that without our consent, can they?' he asked.

'No,' I said. 'And they cannot persuade Charles Lacey to give back the MacAndrew money. So they can do nothing.'

'You said John would be pleased,' Harry said petulantly. 'You said Celia would be pleased too.'

'How could I have guessed they would not be?' I said. 'I dare say John would have been happy enough about it. But not if Celia bursts in on him with tales of his being robbed behind his back in order to benefit your daughter.'

'She would surely never say such a thing!' protested Harry. 'She knows I would never do such a thing. Celia is too loyal to turn against me so.'

'Yes, but I think she caught something of John's madness from him,' I said. 'By the time they took him away she was almost ready to believe that I was having him locked up out of spite, or perhaps even to gain his fortune. Madness, of course.'

'Of course,' said Harry uneasily.

'I don't think either of us realized how close those two had become,' I said. 'Celia spent a great deal of time with John after Mama's death. They were always talking in the parlour or wandering together in the rose garden.'

'She loves him dearly,' Harry said stoutly.

'I hope she does not love him too dearly,' I said. 'It would be a terrible thing if her loving nature had led her astray. If she was even now thinking not what would make you and your child happy but worrying about John and the MacAndrew fortune.'

Harry was aghast. 'That's just not possible,' he said.

'No, I'm sure it is not,' I agreed swiftly. 'It is just that this dash of Celia's off to Bristol looks so much as if she was joining forces with John against us. Against you and me and Wideacre.'

Harry reached for the decanter again, and buttered himself a biscuit with fingers that trembled.

'This is all madness!' he burst out. 'Nothing has been right since Mama died! John went crazy and now, as you say, Celia is behaving most oddly too. If I have any nonsense from Celia about business arrangements you and I have seen fit to make, I shall be very clear with her indeed. She knows nothing about the land. Indeed, I have been happy to let her know nothing about the land. But she cannot now try to interfere in perfectly proper business affairs.'

'That is right, Harry,' I said. My tone was calm but I was panting with relief. 'You have been too sweet, too gentle with Celia, if she thinks she can dash off into the night without even taking her maid, to speak to your brother-in-law, my husband, about our personal and confidential affairs.'

'Indeed, yes!' said Harry. 'I am most displeased with Celia. And when she comes home I will tell her so.'

'Good,' I said. 'I think it needs to be said.' I paused. Harry was seething in his chair, stimulated with temper. I knew what would come next and I resigned myself to a tedious hour or two in the room at the top of the stairs. I knew the signs in Harry. We were together in the secret room seldom these days, for I had my security on the land through the money and through the lawyers, and Harry was too lazy and too idle to think of it often, but it still held its old lure for him. He poured himself another glass and reached a hand out for my glass. I half stood to slide it to him and as he leaned forward to pour his eyes were on my breasts.

'Mmm, Beatrice?' he said, slumping back in his chair. I smiled a heavy-lidded lazy smile at him.

'Yes, Harry?' I said.

'With both Celia and John away . . .' He let the request trail off. His breathing was shallow and a little faster. I shot him one unwinking look from under my dark eyelashes. A look that was both a challenge and an invitation.

'I will go and light the fire,' I said. 'Ten minutes, Harry.'

He gave a sigh of anticipation and buttered another biscuit. I slid from the room like a snake and closed the door softly. 'Carry on eating like that, Harry,' I thought wryly, 'and you will be dead within three years. Then my son Richard and my daughter Julia will be joint heirs, and I will be their guardian and the only Master of Wideacre until I hand over to my darling son. And neither Celia nor John will be able to stop me.'

I did not send an express letter post-haste after Celia. I did not send a footman riding after her to catch her. If quiet, conventional, mousy Celia could whirl out of the house with only a shawl over her head like some demented peasant woman, then she could travel non-stop, and no letter could reach Dr Rose before she did. With Coachman Ben Tyacke driving, no footman with my order would make him stop and turn against the order of Lady Laccy. And, given that Ben was a Tyacke and had loved his uncle dearly, the fact that I wished Celia to return would be enough to make him whip up the horses.

All I could count on was John's instability, on Celia's confusion and despair, and on Dr Rose's prejudice against the two of them, which I had instilled without even planning to do, but which now came, like the witch they called me, unbidden to my hand. I could do nothing, I decided, as I sat back in my morning bath before my bedroom fire. Lucy had rung for more cans of hot water and took them from the footman at the door and poured the scalding jugful down my back. My toes were resting on the rounded lip of the bath, my body curled in the boiling sweet-scented water.

'Miss Beatrice, you will scald,' said Lucy predictably as I waved for another hot jug.

'Yes,' I said happily and felt the near-unbearable heat wash around me. My ten toes were rosy pink with heat; my buttocks and body would be scarlet. After a night of beating and threatening and cursing Harry into a frenzy of whimpering pleasure I felt a certain need to boil myself clean. I might have all the crimes of Wideacre on my copper-curly head – and a few I had not done as well – but at least I lacked Harry's confused messiness. When I needed that sweeping flood of sexual pleasure all I wanted was an honest man to tumble me in bed or grass. Harry seemed to need an unending repertoire of threats and promises and a cupboardful of tricks. And his plump heaving body filled me neither with lust nor hatred, but with a certain cool disdain that excited him all the more. I waved for more hot water. I felt a need to scrub and scald Harry's wet kisses off my skin.

I had done nothing, and I could do nothing, I thought, as Lucy poured the water, and at my gesture massaged the back of my neck with sweet perfumed soap right up to the damp hairline in hard slow circles.

'Mmmm,' I said in pleasure, and closed my eyes.

At the very, very worst Celia and John would come home a pair of avenging angels to destroy Wideacre and the garden of deception I had grown here. John had guessed that Harry was Richard's father, and Celia's secret – that Julia too was my child – would be another piece in the jigsaw. The two secrets together would ruin me.

But I looked at that prospect with my fighter's gaze. I thought I might survive it. John was fresh from the cool sanity of a well-run asylum, unready for the craziness of his real life. I had established him as insane, I might be able to tar Celia with the same brush. Theirs was an insane tale. No one would believe it. It would be far more convincing to claim that their guilt and desire had driven John to drink and overset Celia's senses. That together they had dreamed of a nightmare world of terror: of monsters in mazes, of toads crushed beneath a plough, of wounded hares. It was nonsense. No one would believe them if I could hold my head as proud as a queen and face down every truth as the vilest calumny.

But I did not think they would put the two halves of the picture together.

'Don't stop,' I said to Lucy, who obediently moved the piping cloth over one shoulder and then the other.

John was fighting with one hand tied behind him because of his tenderness to Celia. I knew that. I had watched him in his first days of horror-stricken knowledge when he wavered between drunken despair, hatred for me, and horror at the web that enmeshed us all. If he had been going to expose me to Celia, to wreck her marriage, to break her heart with the disgusting truth of her beloved husband, he would have done it then. But he did not. Not even when he was writhing in a strait-jacket on the floor of her parlour had the secret escaped him. He was not shielding me. He was protecting Celia from the horror that undermined her life so that the very ground beneath her feet was an eggshell cover over a maze of sin. Celia herself might expose me to John in her first gabble of panic, but I could trust my cool steady husband to see the full picture and yet keep his own counsel.

And I did not fear Celia. If she returned alone or decided to act alone I did not think she would expose me. She had given her word of honour and I imagined that would count for much with her. She had loved me once and that might make her pause. She loved respectability as much as my foolish mama, and to expose me would be my ruin and the shame of the Laceys. But more than all of that, more than everything, was her total love for Julia, which, I imagined, would transcend every other thing. If she exposed me as Julia's mother, even in my shame I could claim Julia and take her away. Whatever pain and confusion boiled in Celia's mind I knew, as I knew my own clear-headed calculations, that she would never risk losing Julia. One hint of that danger and Celia would withdraw.

I bent my knees so that the hot water washed over my soaped shoulders and rinsed me clean. I had them both. They both loved and so they were both vulnerable. Compared to that bondage of devotion I was free and unbound. My love for Richard neither contained nor controlled me. I still went my own way. I might plot for him, but I would not sacrifice myself for him. But Celia and John were not their own masters. And as such I did not fear them.

'Towel, please,' I said to Lucy, and she fetched the coarse, linen wraps from where they were warming before the fire. I rubbed myself as hard as I could, until my pink skin stung, and then I brushed my hair free in a silky copper mane, soft as satin on my back. My body showed no signs of two pregnancies. My belly was flat and hard, my breasts round and still firm, my legs as long and as slim as ever with no disfiguring veins.

I smoothed my palm down from my neck, over the jutting swell of my breasts, down over my belly with the soft curls of hair between my legs. I was lovely still. And soon I should need a lover. A real lover, not a chore like Harry, but a man who would laugh with me and romp with me and hurt me and pleasure me. I turned with a sigh and snapped my fingers for Lucy to fetch my petticoats. The hard fighting loving I remembered were those passionate struggles I had with Ralph. God alone knew where I would find another like him. I supposed I should have to resign myself to missing him and longing for him.

And waiting. Waiting for this hard time to be done. Waiting for the profits to show on the land so that Wideacre could be eased, if only slightly, from this drag of debt that I had put on the land. Waiting for the great golden glut of corn to release the land and the people from this struggle for money. So that I could restore a little, instead of snatching away. So that people would forget this one bad year of my mastership of Wideacre and remember instead the good years that had followed each other, one after another, since I had run the land.

Today I should spend another morning in my office trying to make sense of the figures. Mr Llewellyn now had three mortgages on our land: the common land, the plantation, and Celia's dowry lands. But to service the loan to him, when the beasts did so badly, I had borrowed from our bankers. Their rates were lower and I had been pleased with my cleverness at winning Wideacre a little breathing space. But they had the right to alter their rates as they pleased, and now I was paying more to borrow their money than the rate I was paying Llewellyn. I was in the ludicrous position of borrowing money to service a loan. And if I was late with either debt there were penalty clauses to meet.

Last month I had been forced to sell some fat lambs in an early market and had earned less than they deserved, because I was desperate for cash. This month, with Llewellyn's repayments and the bankers' loan both falling due, I would have to face the prospect of selling land – I could not keep on selling off stock out of season. There had to be some way to break free of this downward spiral of debt; yet I could see none. And I had no one to advise me. Only one man I knew understood the ways of the London money-men. Only one man I knew could tell me if it was indeed as I feared, that they were playing with me like a clever fisherman plays with a salmon; that, although I spoke privately to only two or three, they all heard my words; that the message was out: Wideacre was headed for ruin and some skilful fisherman could net it with a flick of his wrist. Only one man could advise me on this. And he was advising Celia on how the two of them could wreck my plans, as they drove home together.

I counted the days that Celia had been away as I went downstairs to breakfast. A day to get to Bristol, since she had started in the early evening. A day or two days to see John and to persuade Dr Rose to release him. Two days to drive home. Heads together in the carriage. Minds together, pitted against me. Planning my downfall, driving closer.

I thought four or five days, and I was right. On the afternoon of the fourth day since Celia had dashed from the house, the carriage came bowling up the drive: muddy, and with one lamp broken. And the two of them inside.

'They are here,' I said tersely to Harry. 'You know what you have to do. We have talked it over, and I am sure you are right.

517

She had tried to meddle with our business. She dashed out of the house to go to another man, and that man my husband. She ran away like a mad thing. She has exposed the Laceys to comment in the county.'

Harry nodded. He was breathing fast and there was a certain brightness in his eyes. 'She should be punished,' he said, and I remembered his early training in bullying at his vicious school.

'Yes,' I said. 'She has been treated like porcelain by us all. Take her at once and take your pleasure on her. You are her husband. You have the right. Go and break her.'

He nodded again. 'But no man could hurt Celia,' he said, wanting to be convinced and loving to hear the words.

'Any real man could,' I said tempting. 'You of all people could, Harry. Remember the little boys at your school? Besides, Celia may be precious to you but you cannot allow her to behave like this. She fled from you to John. If you want to keep her you had best show her who is Master. You are the Squire. You are her husband. You can do anything you like to her. But do not listen to a word she says. Just reclaim her.'

Harry's eyes were wide and blue and his breath came fast. He walked past a tray of cakes without even seeing them. He blundered to the front door alight with cruelty and lust. We heard the noise of the carriage draw up and Harry was at the door before Stride could be there. Celia tumbled out, not waiting for the steps. She was wearing the dress she had left in, and it was creased and shabby from travelling. She looked nothing like the Lady Lacey who had dominated Harry and me. She looked exhausted and a little afraid.

'Harry?' she said hesitantly and went up the steps towards him where he stood, unmoving, by the front door.

He was magnificent. He said not a word. He looked like some fat hero in the travelling theatre. His face was stony. She came beside him, and put her little hand on his arm.

'Harry?' she said again. He scooped her up into a hard grip and I saw her face blench white as he hurt her. Then, still without a word, he swept her into the house and up the main stairs to the first floor. I heard his heavy tread along the corridor to their bedroom, the door open and close, and the double click as he locked it. Then I turned back to the carriage. Whatever was happening behind that door I cared not. Celia would be humiliated and would be forced down to face the mire of Harry's twisted desires. If she refused him he could strike her or rape her. If she consented she would carry the filth of his perverse pleasure on her soul and never again would she meet John with unshadowed eyes or stand before me in my own office and lay down the law to me. She would be humbled to dust.

I smiled.

John caught that smile as he stepped down from the carriage. The sunshine was bright but he shivered as if a cold wind had blown down the nape of his neck. He was looking well. The strained, desperate look had gone from his face and he had put on weight and was lithe and fit again. The hollows under his eyes had gone, and the muscle that used to twitch in his cheek was still. His ordeal had graven two hard lines either side of his unsmiling mouth and two deep frown lines above his eyebrows, but his face was serene, strong. He was dressed immaculately with his usual neatness, in black with the whitest of linen, and a thick black travelling coat. I met his blue eyes and we measured each other in a long hard stare. He might have the look of the man I had loved, but we were sworn enemies. I said no word of greeting but turned on my heel and walked back to the parlour.

I poured myself a cup of tea and my hands were steady. Unbidden, the parlourmaid came in with another cup and a plate, and behind her, as if he had taken tea with me every day for the past five months, came John my husband. He shut the parlour door with a click and I wondered why that little noise should give me such a shudder of dread. I was alone with my husband.

'Tea?' I asked courteously. 'Some cakes? Or some fruit bread?'

'Let us have some straight talking, if you please,' he said, and his voice was even and clear. He was cured of his terror of me, and of his need to drink when my shadow fell on him. I had lost my old power over John and I rose to stand by the mantelpiece so that I could casually rest my arm along it, to hide the fact that my knees were shaking with anxiety.

John moved into the centre of the parlour and dominated the pretty room. His driving coat with the great capes seemed too bulky for the small space. His high black polished boots seemed to straddle the carpet. His hat on a chair filled the lady's room with male power and male threat. I held on tight to the stone of the mantelpiece and kept my face impassive.

'I have nothing to say to you,' I said. My voice did not quaver. He would not know I was afraid. I guarded myself too well.

'No, but I have some things to say to you,' he said. I glanced towards the door. He would be able to catch me before I reached it. I thought about pulling the bell on the pretext of more hot water, but then I thought better of it. This was as good a time as any to face John. And he would have to be faced some time this day. Now I had him without Celia, without Harry, and tired from the journey. Also, with a warm flicker of relief, I felt my anger growing, and I knew that if he threatened me I would challenge him and beat him down. I was no longer the woman who could not move for grief and horror because children fled at her approach. I was a woman fighting for myself and my child, and my child's inheritance and my own home. I had not desolated Wideacre, enclosed the fields and murdered the sweetest lads in the village, to collapse in a repentant heap because my husband looked hard at me with his pale blue eyes.

'I know what you have done,' he said. 'Celia told me all she knew, and with the knowledge that I have, I could understand what you have done.'

'What do you fancy I have done?' I said, my tone icy.

'You have had two incestuous bastards sired by your brother,' said John, his voice as cold as mine. 'One you passed off on Celia who presented it to Harry as her own. One you tried to fob off on me. Then you had me committed to a lunatic asylum – oh, yes, that is what it was, thank you, my dear – so you could rob me of my fortune to buy your son into the inheritance and to lock your two children in partnership on the land.'

My knuckles gleamed white as I gripped the mantelpiece. But I said not a word.

'What I shall do is to untangle this thread of sin and deceit and set us all free of you,' John said. 'Some of your legal contracts and agreements will be breakable, and I shall break them,' he said. 'The children should be cleaned of the taint of you, and of this damnable land. Celia shall be freed of this morass of sin and complicity you have tricked her into. And she may save Harry from you.'

'You are ready to hang then?' I asked drily. 'I promised you I would swear you had killed Mama. The noose would be round your neck the second you speak one word against me. You are tired of life then, John? You are ready for death?'

His eyes met mine without a shadow of dread and with a dawning coldness down my spine, along my shoulders, I realized I had lost that hold on him too.

'I'll take my chance,' he said, and his eyes met mine with a strength that was greater than my own. 'I'm prepared to stand trial to expose you, Beatrice. No court in the land could try me for manslaughter, or even murder, without hearing why your mama's heart stood still on that night. Then you would be exposed to the world as an incestuous whore, as the mother of two bastards, and a thief. Are you ready for that, my pretty wife?'

'You won't get your money back,' I said spitefully. 'You've lost that for ever. It's in Charles Lacey's hands and if I know him it's already half spent.'

'No,' he acknowledged. And he was not looking at me, but out of the window, towards the green line of the horizon. 'No, but I can save the children from you . . . and Celia.'

'A strange way to free them,' I said harshly. 'To free them with your death. I might be shamed, but Celia would have nowhere to live but here. Harry might be disgraced but he would still be Squire. We would all live on here without you. Are you ready for a death that changes nothing?'

'It is not I who am ready for death, Beatrice,' he said. He had turned back and was looking at me, hot with hatred, but with a sharp interest. His eyes were those of Dr MacAndrew again, the quickest-witted physician ever to come out of Edinburgh. 'I see it on you,' he said acutely. 'You have lost yourself somewhere down this weary evil road that you have travelled. The life has gone out of you, Beatrice.'

He reached my side in two quick strides and took my chin in his hand. I suffered him to turn my face to the light and my green eyes were scornful, but I was biting the inside of my cheeks to hide my fear.

'Yes, you are as lovely as ever,' he said dismissively. 'But you have lost a sparkle from your eyes, and there are lines around your mouth that were never there before. What is it, my dear? Have your dirty steps in filth bogged you down so deep you cannot get free? Has the land turned against you? Can you no longer magic the yields you need? Or is it that the people spit on the ground when you pass and curse your very name for the damage and the death that you have brought to Wideacre?'

I broke free of his grip and turned to the door. My hand was on the latch when he called my name.

'Beatrice!'

I turned, as if I had hoped he might say something gentle to me. Or at least something that would give me a clue to hold him in my grip again.

'Death is coming for you, and you are ready for it,' he said quietly. 'As I drove home with Celia I thought I should come home and kill you, to free us all from the horror that is you. But I will not need to make my hands stink with your blood. For Death is coming for you, and you know you are fit to die. Don't you, my pretty Beatrice?'

I turned without a word and left the room. I walked with my head high, my steps long, my skirt shushing round me with every dancing stride. I walked like a lord on his land all the way down the corridor to my office, and then I shut the door behind me and leaned against the panels. At once my knees buckled and I slid down the door into a heap on the floor. I rested my face against the panels. The wood was cold and ungentle to the aching cheekbones where the skin felt too tight.

Death was coming for me, John had said so; he had seen it in my face. And I knew how Death was coming. He was coming on a great black horse with two black dogs, one running before, one following behind. He was coming on horseback, for he had no legs to creep along behind me. He would ride up to me, Death, and I would see his face before I died. Death was coming for me. The rich people, the gentry who feared for their lives and their property called him Death; the poor people who followed him called him the Culler. But I would look in his face and call him 'Ralph'.

*

I sat with my back to the door, unmoving, until twilight darkened the room and I saw the first little star, low on the horizon with the thin moon beside it. Then I clasped both hands around the doorknob and hauled myself to my feet. I was bone-weary, but I did not dare miss dinner. I had to be there.

John had changed. He was free of me. He was free of his love and his dream of love for me that had driven him to drink so he could forget the bitter reality. He was free of his horror of me. He could touch my face with hands that did not tremble. He could turn my head to the light so that he could see with his cruel surgeon's eyes the new tiny maze of lines in my skin. He had lost his love for me, his fear of me. To him now, I was, as Dr Rose had assured me, an ordinary mortal.

And John was confident with ordinary mortals. I was no longer the woman he loved above life itself. I was no longer the woman he feared because she seemed the embodiment of evil and death. Now I was an ordinary mortal with a body that would die, with a mind that could make mistakes.

From now until the day of my death John would be watching for that: for my lovely young body to walk towards death, and for my clever, obsessed mind to make mistakes. And I could do little to mislead him. He had loved me, and he had watched every shadow across my face in the days of our happiness. He knew me, as no other man, save one, had known me. And he had knowledge too. He had learned how to see the truth about people; he had dedicated his life and his wisdom to understanding what makes people as they are, the infections in their bodies, the illnesses in their hearts, the madness in their minds. To John now I was neither love-goddess nor devil; I was instead the most fascinating specimen he had ever studied at close quarters.

And also an enemy to be defeated.

It was not a role that I could face very easily.

I rang for Lucy and she exclaimed when she saw me.

'I'll ask for your dinner to be sent to your room. I'll tell them you are unwell,' she said, as she helped me up the stairs to brush my hair.

'No,' I said. I was so tired it was an effort even to talk. I could scarcely impose my will on my own maid. However could I manage Harry and Celia and John? 'No,' I said again. 'I will go to dinner. But hurry, Lucy, or I will be late.'

They had not waited for me in the parlour but had gone in to the dining room. The footman opened the door for me as I rustled down the hall, my steps smooth again, my face pale and drawn, but a serene smile on my mouth. I stopped stock-still in the doorway and stared.

Celia was seated in my chair.

She sat where she should be, where she had a right to be.

In the chair of the Squire's Lady at the foot of the great dining table where she could see the servants standing in readiness against the walls of the room, keep an eye on the blaze in the hearth, see that the plates of all her guests were filled, and their glasses charged, and meet the eyes of her husband with a warm, loving smile.

Harry glanced up as I entered and his face was half apologetic. 'I hope you don't mind, Beatrice?' he said to me in a low voice, as he rose to meet me at the door and conducted me to a seat opposite John, the seat that used to be Celia's. 'I understood from John that you would not be coming to dinner tonight and so Celia naturally took the foot of the table.'

I smiled neutrally and paused by the chair, looking at Celia, waiting for her to leap to her feet and to move to her place to make the chair of the Squire's Lady free for me. She did not move. She simply smiled at me with her pansy-brown eyes wide and said, 'I am sure you would rather sit opposite John, would you not, Beatrice? It is just like your courting days when your mama was alive.'

'I would rather have Beatrice opposite me,' John said to clinch the decision. 'I like to have her where I can see her!'

They laughed at that, the fools. As if John had never drunk himself into a stupor at this very table. As if my place could be challenged with impunity. As if I should take a seat down the board and give way to Harry's child-bride. I smiled, a sour smile, and sat where they all wished me to be. And I noted with an inward promise of vengeance the quick exchange of looks between the youngest footman and a new lad. They would be looking for work after next pay day.

That night belonged to Celia.

And I saw she had earned it. A bluish bruise shadowed her cheekbone but her eyes were serene. I guessed that Harry had struck her, in anger or passion, but once, and then dissolved into apology and reconciliation. She had no glimpse of his real needs and thought that blow the single lowest moment of her married life. She did not know there was a pattern of punishment forming around her. She thought that blow the first and last she would ever have from Harry. And she thought she could bear it. With the life of Wideacre hanging on a thread she thought she had to endure it.

So she took her place at the foot of the table.

Her beloved brother-in-law drank lemonade on her left, and her husband beamed down the table at her. She bloomed in the candlelight like a carnation in sunshine. Her worries and her sense of horror had been stilled firstly by John's calm acceptance of her garbled, hysterical story, and then by promises Harry had made her while they lay in bed. John had told her that he had not known of the plan to change the entail but he was not surprised. And that the contract could certainly be changed. That, as Richard's father, he could and would resign Richard's rights to inherit jointly with Julia. That Julia could inherit with his blessing, and that they would find some way of compensating Richard or himself for the use of the MacAndrew fortune.

John's calm acceptance of the news, his easy packing and friendly departure from Dr Rose, pulled Celia back from the entrance to the maze. She began to think she had been mistaken. She forgot the evidence of her senses: the smell of sin around the house, the prickle on her skin when Harry would look at me during dinner and ask if I could spare him some time later that evening for business. The sight of a strawberry-red bruise on Harry's back. And her bewilderment when she woke late one night and put her hand out to where her husband should be and found the bed cold. All that she could forget when John smiled at her with steady honest eyes and said, 'Trust me, Celia, I can make it right.'

She had come home on a cloud of relief in her shabby dress, and with a growing anxiety that Harry would be angry with her; that he would not overlook her scream in the silence of the dining room; that he would press her for an explanation of her horror. For Celia and John, and Harry and I, all had our little deceptions and secrets. And we were all jealously guarding them.

But Harry had been easy. They had both conspired to silence. His blow had shocked her but had been followed by a string of kisses. With her love and loyalty half transferred to John she paid her dues to her husband, just as I paid rent to my landlord. Harry thrust himself into her like a fat foot into a silk slipper, forgave her indiscretion and asked nothing more.

They cleared the soup plates and served the fish. John was eating with relish. 'This is wonderful,' he said, nodding to Celia. 'Salmon! How I have missed Wideacre food.'

'Poor fare at the doctor's, was there?' asked Harry, his attention caught. 'I feared there might be. You'll be glad to be home.'

John smiled a warm smile at Celia, whose signature and passionate insistence had brought him home, but his voice when he answered Harry was cold.

'I am indeed,' he said.

'What was it like there?' Harry asked, tactless as ever.

'It was well run,' said John. 'It was well organized. It was a good place for treatment. It was lonely.'

Celia's hand twitched. She had been about to stretch it out to him in an instinctive gesture of sympathy.

'I hoped my letters would help,' she said.

'What letters?' said John. 'I received no letters.'

My fork in my hand, I hesitated, but then moved steadily on, ate the piece of salmon and reached for my wine glass.

'Did you receive my letters?' I asked.

John's eyes met mine with a hard, ironic, insulting smile.

'No, my dear,' he said politely. 'Did you write to me often?'

'Every other day,' I said blandly.

'And I wrote every week,' Celia put in. 'What can have happened to them?'

John's eyes were on my face, his eyes like pale stones.

'I can't imagine. Can you, Beatrice?'

'No,' I said shortly. 'Perhaps Dr Rose thought you were not well enough to receive letters from home. He forbade visitors, you know.'

'I guessed there must be some reason I heard from no one,'

said John. It was like swordplay, talking to him. It was like an unending duel. But I was weary.

I gave up. I was almost ready to give up on the rest of my plans too. I was certainly ready to let one evening go without my controlling every move.

'Excuse me,' I said to Celia. 'I am tired. I will go to my room.'

I rose to my feet and the footman sprang to pull back my chair for me. Harry rose and gave me his arm to the west-wing door.

'It wasn't Celia in your chair, was it?' he asked with his usual doltishness. But I was too tired even to fire an opening shot in a battle over a chair, when my husband had looked at me with trained eyes and saw Death in my face.

'No, it wasn't the chair,' I said wearily. 'She can sit in the damned thing all night if she chooses.' I turned from him and slipped through the door of the west wing. Lucy undressed me and I dismissed her. Then I took the key from my dressing table and locked the door. I jammed the chair under the handle for good measure. Then I fell into bed and slept as if I wanted never to wake up.

18

But I had to wake up. There was always work to do, and no one but me who could do it. I had to wake, and dress, and go down to breakfast and sit opposite John, with Celia at the foot of the table, and Harry smiling, at the head, and exchange inanities. Then I had to go to my office and pull out the drawer of bills and spread them out before me and puzzle and worry at them until my head ached.

They were a morass of demands to me. I could not see how we had got there; I could not see how to get free. The first simple debts with Mr Llewellyn I had understood well enough. But then the bad weather had come and the sheep had done so badly. Then the cows had some infection and many calves were still-born. So I had borrowed from the bankers on some of the new wheatfields. But then that had not raised enough, so I had mortgaged some of the marginal lands – the fields on the borders with Havering. But the repayments on those loans were heavy too. I was borrowing and borrowing against the wheat harvest. Praying that the wheat harvest would be such a golden glut that I need never borrow again. That the barns would overflow with wheat in such a surplus that I could sell and sell and sell, and all my debts would vanish – as if they had never been. I spread the bills before me like some complicated patchwork before an inadequate needlewoman, and I sighed with anxiety.

I carried this burden alone. I dared not tell Harry how the scheme for the entail had committed us to one debt after another. I mentioned casually that we had obtained credit on the basis of one field or one small farm, but I dared not tell Harry that I was borrowing to repay loans. And then I was borrowing to service loans. And now I was borrowing just to pay wages, to buy seedcorn, to stem the tide of bankruptcy that was lapping at my feet. I dared not tell Harry, and I felt so much alone. The scheme

Ralph had planned for Harry: the erosion of his profits and the seeping away of his wealth, I had played on myself. In my one great gamble for total ownership of the land – to have it myself and to see my child in the Squire's chair – I had gambled everything on the Wideacre harvest.

And if that failed: I failed.

And if I failed Harry and Celia and John and the children would go down in one resounding crash of debt. We would disappear like all bankrupts did. If we could salvage anything we might buy a little farmhouse in Devon or Cornwall, or perhaps in John's beastly Scotland. Anywhere where land was cheap and food prices low. And I would never wake to see the hills of Wideacre again.

No one would call me 'Miss Beatrice' with love in their voice. No one would call Harry 'Squire', as if it were his name. We would be newcomers. And no one would know our family went back to Norman times, and that we had farmed and guarded the same land for hundreds of years. We would be nobodies.

I shuddered, and pulled the bills towards me again. The ones from Chichester tradesmen I let run. Only the purveyors of the household did I pay regularly. I did not want Celia to learn from the cook or from a housemaid that the merchants were refusing to deliver until their bills were met. So that made a pile of bills that had to be paid at once. Beside them were a smaller pile of creditors' notes that had to be met this month. Mr Llewellyn, the bank, a London money-lender, and our solicitor, who had advanced a few hundred pounds when I badly needed cash to buy some seedcorn. They had to be paid at once too. With them also was a note from the corn merchant, to whom we owed a few hundred guineas for oats, which we did not grow, for the horses, and a note from the hay merchant. Now we grew fewer meadows I was having to buy in hay, and it was costlier than I had believed possible. It would make sense to reduce the Wideacre stables, which were filled with underworked horses. But I knew that the first Wideacre horse on the market would be seen as a sign that I was selling up, and then the creditors would rush to be first with their notes. They would foreclose on me, in a panic not to be left with a dishonoured note-of-hand, and in their rush for little sums of money, Wideacre would bleed to death from a hundred minor stabs.

Each small, irresistible demand added to a total I could not meet. I had no money. I felt the creditors gather around me like a pack of nipping wolves and I knew that I must free myself of them, and free Wideacre of them, but I could not see how.

I shuffled the final pile of papers into a heap of debtors who could wait, who would wait. The wine merchants, who knew we had their bill's worth of wine in the cellars, and who would be circumspect in their demands. The farrier, who had worked on the estate since coming out of his apprenticeship. The carters, who had been paid on the nail for years and years. The cobbler, the gate-mender, the harness-maker – the little men who could beg that their bills be paid but who could do nothing against me. It was a large heap of bills, but they were all for small sums. My failure to pay might ruin the little tradesmen, but they could not ruin me. They could wait. They would have to wait.

It made three tidy piles. It got me no further forward. I folded them up and stuffed them back into the drawer. I did not have to see them to remember that I was drowning in debt. I remembered it every waking moment, and my nights were full of dreams of strange men with town accents saying to me, 'Sign here. Sign here,' in a long dream of horror and fear of the loss of Wideacre. I slammed the desk drawer shut with sudden impatience. There was no one to help me, and I was alone with this burden. All I could hope for was the old magic winds of Wideacre blowing my way again and a warm wind blowing out of a hot harvest sun to make the land golden, and set me free.

I rang the bell and ordered that Richard be dressed for a drive and brought to me in the stable yard. I could not stay indoors. The land no longer loved me, I could not take Richard at a whirling trot down the drive and show him the trees with the confidence of my papa on the land he owned outright, but I could still go out. It was still my land. I might still escape the intractable, unanswerable sheets of bills by driving out under a clear blue sky with my son.

He came to me beaming, as he always did. Of all the children I have ever seen Richard was the most sweet-tempered. One of the naughtiest too, I admit. At the age when Julia used to hold her toes in her warm cradle and coo to the delight of her grandmama and Celia, Richard was heaving himself up with chubby arms, and trying to climb out. Julia would play with a moppet in her cot for hours, but Richard would hurl it out on to the floor and then bawl for it to be returned to him. If you were fool enough to go to him he would play the same trick again. And again. Only a paid servant would return the number of times Richard thought necessary, before his dark eyelashes would close on that smooth and perfect cheek. He was the bonniest baby. The naughtiest, the sweetest, child. And he adored me.

So I caught him from his nurse's arms and hugged him hard and smiled when I heard his crow of delight at my sudden appearance. I passed him up to her when she was settled in the gig and made sure she held him tight. Then I put his rattle in his grabbing little hands and swung up beside them.

Sorrel trotted down the drive and Richard waved the rattle at the flying trees and at the flickering shadows and sunlight. On either side of the silver toy were little silver bells and they tinkled like sleighbells and made Sorrel throw up his head and step out faster. I drove at a spanking pace down the drive and then up to the London road. We were in time to see the mailcoach go by in a whirl of dust and Richard waved to the passengers on the roof and a man waved back. Then I turned the gig and we headed for home. A small enough outing, but when you love a child your world shrinks to a proper size of little delights and little islands of peace. Richard brought me that. If I loved him for nothing else, I would have loved him for that.

We were nearing the turn of the drive when he choked. A funny sound, unlike his usual open-mouthed barks of coughs. He gave an open-mouthed retching, a sort of gasping for air, a sound unlike anything I had ever heard before. I hauled on the reins and Sorrel skidded to a halt. My eyes met those of his nurse in mutual bewilderment and then she snatched the rattle from his hands. One of the tiny tinkly silver bells on the end was missing. He had swallowed it and he was gasping, reaching for his life's breath around it.

The gig lurched as I grabbed him and laid him over my knees, face down. Without knowing why, I slapped him hard on the back and then grabbed his little feet and held him upside-down with some vague memory of his birth and the little choking noises he had made then.

He squawked some more, but no little silver bell fell on to the floor of the gig. I half flung him back at his nurse and cracked the whip at Sorrel, and shouted, 'Where's Dr MacAndrew?'

'In the village, with Lady Lacey,' she gasped, and clutched Richard to her shoulder.

The noises he was making were more painful now, more shocking to hear. He was retching and choking and his little gasps were less and less effective. He was getting no air. He was dying, in my gig, on Wideacre land, on a sunny morning.

I lashed Sorrel and he put his head down and went from his well-bred canter into a wild gallop. The gig bounced and bobbed like a boat on flood water but I held to the speed, not checking. The wind streamed into my face, I could scarcely see. But one glance at my son told me that none of this rush of air was finding its way into his little body. His gasps were quieter and he was hardly coughing at all. His lips were blue.

'Where in the village?' I yelled above the noise of Sorrel's thundering hoofs and the creaks of the speeding gig.

'At the vicarage, I think,' shrieked Mrs Austin, her face as white as her collar, clinging to Richard in fear for him, and in terror at the headlong pace.

We whirled into the village and I saw nothing, but heard the slap of a hen, neck broken under the gig's wheels. I pulled Sorrel up so hard he half reared as he skidded to a halt, and I flung the reins at Mrs Austin and snatched Richard from her. It was too late. Too late. He was fighting for his breath no more.

I ran up the garden path to the front door, his body limp in my arms, his eyelids as blue as his lips, his little chest so still. The door was opened as I ran, and Dr Pearce's startled face was there.

'Where's John?' I said.

'In my study,' said the Vicar. 'What is wrong . . .?'

I slammed open the door and scarcely saw Celia, Mrs Merry and old Margery Thompson bent over the table. I saw only John.

'John,' I said, and held out the limp body of my son to him.

He had never touched him, though Richard was now nearly a year old. But now he snatched him from me, taking in the blue eyelids, the blue lips, in one fast raking glance.

He laid the child on the table. Richard was limp; his head banged on the wood as if he were already a corpse. John was patting his waistcoat pocket for a little silver penknife he carried.

'What?' he asked, monosyllabically.

'The silver bell, off his rattle,' I said.

'Buttonhook,' he said to Celia. She was beside him, her eyes on my son's face. He took Richard's chin in one hand and forced it brutally upwards until the delicate skin of his neck was tight. And then he cut his throat.

My knees buckled beneath me and I slumped in a chair. For one crazed moment I thought my husband had killed my son, but then I saw him jam the stem of one of Dr Pearce's pipes in the little hole and I heard a rasping breath. He had slit a hole in Richard's windpipe and Richard was breathing again.

I dipped my head in my hands, unable to look, then peeped through my fingers to see John staring down Richard's mouth, with his right hand outstretched towards Celia, as imperious as any Edinburgh surgeon.

She had rummaged in her reticule and come out with a slender pearl-handled buttonhook and a little crochet hook. She put the buttonhook flat in his palm and stood beside him. Without a second's hesitation she took Richard's pale face in her own two hands and straightened him so that the pipe stem was not obstructed. His lips were turning pink again. John bent low, and probed down the tiny throat with the buttonhook. Behind me in the doorway Dr Pearce's boots suddenly creaked as he shifted his weight in the silent horror of the room.

'Too big,' said John, straightening up. 'What else?'

Without a word Celia took one hand from steadying Richard's head and offered John the crochet hook. He smiled, without looking away from my son.

'Yes,' he said. 'Perfect.'

Everyone in the room held their breath. Mrs Merry, who had sneered at the clever young Edinburgh-trained man, Margery Thompson, the village gossip, Dr Pearce and me. John poked down Richard's tiny throat with the slender silver hook and only he and Celia seemed unaware of the agony of tension in the sunlit study.

There was a thin, incongruous tinkle. The little bell knocked against Richard's milk teeth as John drew it out. And then, there it was, suspended on the silver hook.

'Done it,' John said, and he pulled his silk handkerchief from his pocket, pulled out the pipe stem from my baby's throat, tied the handkerchief in a bandage around his neck and turned him on his front on the hard table. Richard retched and coughed, a wheezy hacking cough, and began, hoarsely, to cry.

Celia said, 'May I?' to John and, at his nod, scooped my son into her arms and laid his head on her shoulder. She patted him on his back and whispered loving words while he wept for the confusion and the pain in his throat. Beside his curly head her face was alight with pride and love, and she met John's look with her heart written in her eyes.

'You were good,' he said, sharing the credit. 'The buttonhook was too big. We would have lost him if you had not thought of the other.'

'You were good,' she said. Her eyes met his in frank love. 'Your hand was steady as a rock. You saved his life.'

'D'you have some laudanum?' John asked Dr Pearce, not taking his eyes from Celia's bright face.

'No, only a little brandy,' said the Vicar, watching the two of them as intently as the rest of us.

John grimaced. 'Very well then,' he said. 'He needs something. He's had a nasty shock.'

He took Richard from Celia's arms as gently as a father and held the glass for Richard to sip. When the child squirmed he held his face still and tipped down the little measure with one practised gesture. Richard was soothed at once, and when Celia took him back into her arms, his head nodded on her shoulder and he dozed.

Celia and John looked at each other for a brief, magical moment, then John turned to me, and the spell was broken.

'You have had a shock too, Beatrice,' he said coolly. 'Would you like a glass of ratafia? Or port?'

'No,' I said dully. 'I need nothing.'

'Did you think you had lost him?' asked Mrs Merry. 'He looked so blue!'

'Yes,' I said desolately. 'I thought I had lost him, the next Squire. Then all this, all this, would have been for nothing!'

There was a silence. They all turned shocked faces to me. Every one. Every one of them looked at me as if I was an exhibit in some show of freaks.

'You thought of him as the Squire?' asked John, incredulous. 'Your baby was dying in your arms, and you thought that your work would go for nothing?'

'Yes,' I said. I stared at the empty fireplace. Not caring what they thought of me. Not caring for anything, anymore.

'If he had died, what would have become of Wideacre? The entail specifies them both. I have put everything on the two of them. And then I thought he was dead.'

I dropped my face into my hands and I shuddered with deep soundless sobs. No one put a hand out to comfort me. No one said one kind word.

'You are shocked,' said Celia at last, but her voice was cold. 'I came in the carriage. You can go home in it. John can drive me in your gig. Go home now, Beatrice, and you can put Richard to bed when you get home. Then you can rest yourself. You cannot know what you are saying. This has been a shock for you.'

I let her walk me to the carriage and help Mrs Austin with Richard. Then I saw her step back from the window and Coachman Ben drove me home with my son's warm sleepy body in my arms.

As the trees of the drive flickered past the window, green in the April sunshine, I remembered the look that had passed between Celia and John when he had praised her quickness in thinking of the crochet hook, and she had praised his skill. And I thought also that when she said, 'Your hand was steady as a rock,' she had spoken not for his ears alone. She had praised him, and restored him as a first-class doctor. She had told that quiet room, and thus the village, and the wider world outside the village borders, that Dr MacAndrew was indeed the best doctor that the county had ever seen. She had restored John to society. The trick that I knew he could never have done alone, that I had sworn I would never do for him, Celia had done with one easy sentence.

Wideacre might think that his fatigue and drunkenness had killed my mama, but that tale would be swiftly replaced with the story of how, when my child was in danger, I had driven like a devil to reach him. How I had run up the drive with my son in my arms. How I had asked for 'Doctor' MacAndrew, not 'Mister'. And how John's quick, nerveless skill had saved the life of my son.

The carriage stopped at the front steps of the Hall and Stride opened the door and checked as he saw me inside and not Celia.

'Lady Lacey is coming later in my gig,' I said. But it was an effort to speak at all. 'There has been an accident. Please send coffee to my room. I do not wish to be disturbed.'

Stride nodded, as impassive as ever, and handed me down into the hall. I went wearily through the door to the west wing, not even waiting to see Richard's nurse inside. She would know to put him into his cradle at once. She would know to watch over him while he slept. He did not need my care. And now there was a barrier between him and me. I had known and I had said aloud, that my son, my lovely son, was most important to me as the heir to Wideacre.

I might love the shadow of his eyelashes on his cheeks, or his curly hair, or the sweet, sweet smell of him. But when I thought he was dying it was Wideacre I had thought of first.

Wideacre. There were times when I thought the land had driven me quite mad. I shut my bedroom door and leaned my back against it, and sighed. I was too tired to stop and think. Too tired to consider what I was doing. Too tired even to wonder what had become of me if I cared for Wideacre first and foremost, even before the life of my darling son.

John had left a bottle of laudanum by my bed. I looked at it dull-eyed. I felt neither threat nor fear. I measured out two drops into a glass of water and I drank them slowly, savouring them like a sweet liqueur. Then I lay back on my bed and slept. I did not fear dreams. The reality of my life seemed worse than anything I might meet in sleep. I would rather dream than wake.

In the morning I wished I had not woken. There was a grey mist over everything. I could not see the hills from my window; I could not see the woods; I could not even see the start of the rose garden. The whole world seemed muffled and hushed. Lucy bringing my cup of chocolate found the door locked and called out, 'Miss Beatrice? Are you all right?' and I had to get out of bed on to a cold wooden floor and shiver across to open the door for her.

Her eyes were bright with curiosity but there was no sympathy in them as she watched me jump back into bed and huddle the covers up to my chin.

'Send for the kitchenmaid to light my fire,' I said snappishly. 'I forgot when I locked the door that she would not be able to get in this morning. It's freezing in here.'

'She's not here,' said Lucy without apology. 'She's away down to Acre. There's no one to light your fire. There's only the upper servants left in the house. Everyone else has gone to Acre.'

The mist seemed to have penetrated my very room, it was so damp and cold. I reached out for the hot chocolate and drank it greedily, but it made me no warmer.

'Gone?' I asked. 'Gone to Acre? What on earth for?'

'It's the funeral,' said Lucy. She went to the tall wardrobe and took out my black silk dress for morning wear, and a sheaf of clean fresh-pressed linen.

'Whose funeral?' I asked. 'You are talking in riddles, Lucy. Put those things down and tell me at once what is going on. Why have the servants taken a morning off without leave? Why did no one ask me?'

'They'd hardly be likely to ask you,' she said. She put my gown on the foot of the bed and spread the linen on the clothes-horse before the cold grate.

'What on earth do you mean?' I said. 'Why not?'

'Because it's Beatrice Fosdyke's funeral,' said Lucy. Her hands were free and she put them on her hips. Arms akimbo she looked challengingly at me. Not at all respectful. I sat in my bed more like a cold child than the Mistress of a great estate.

'Bea Fosdyke isn't dead,' I contradicted her. 'She ran off to Portsmouth.'

'Nay,' Lucy said with a gleam of superior knowledge in her eyes. 'She ran off to Portsmouth all right. But she ran off to shame. She thought she'd get a job as a milliner or a shop girl. But she had no references and no training and she could not get work. She lived off the money she had been saving for her dowry for the first week. But her lodgings were expensive and she had no friends to give her a meal. Soon all that was gone. Then she gathered pure for a week or two.'

'What's "pure"?' I asked. I was listening to this tale as a fairy story. But some coldness, the mist, just the mist, seemed to be drifting down my spine. I drew the blankets a little more closely, but I felt a finger of dread, like a draught down my neck.

'Don't you know that?' Lucy's look at me was almost a sneer. 'Pure is the filth of dogs and the human filth that they throw out in the streets and into the gutters. The pure collectors pick it up and sell it.'

I put my cup down. I could feel the rise of nausea at the thought. I made a pout of disgust at Lucy. 'Really, Lucy! What a thing to talk about at this time in the morning,' I said. 'What on earth is it bought for?'

'For cleaning booksellers' leather,' Lucy said sweetly. She stroked the calf-bound volume I had by my bedside. 'Didn't you know, Miss Beatrice, that they make the leather smooth and soft so you love to touch it, by rubbing it and scrubbing it with human and dog filth?'

I looked at the book with distaste and back at Lucy.

'So Beatrice Fosdyke became a pure collector,' I said. 'She was a fool not to come home. There's little enough work here but the parish money would be better than that. She was a fool not to come home.'

'She didn't keep that work,' said Lucy. 'While she was walking the streets with her little bag, a gentleman saw her and offered her a shilling to go with him.'

I nodded, my eyes a little wider. But I said nothing. I was still cold. The room was somehow damp too. The fog outside made ghostly shapes. It loomed up against the window.

'She went with him,' said Lucy simply. 'And the next gentleman, and the next. Then her father went down to Portsmouth seeking her. He found her waiting down by the stagecoach inn, waiting for men to sell herself to. He smashed her face, in the open street, and he got back on to the coach and came straight home.'

I nodded again. The mist was like a grey animal rubbing against the window. Its cold breath was icy in the room. I could not get warm. I did not want to hear about this other Beatrice.

538

'She went back to her lodging house and borrowed a penny off the woman to buy a pennyworth of rope, to tie up her box, she said. She said her pa had come to rescue her. That she was going home. That she would never leave her home again.'

Bright in my mind against the grey window was the picture of Giles, his corpse bent like a bow, because he would not go on the parish.

'She hanged herself?' I asked, to get the story over and to break the spell of Lucy's malicious sing-song voice.

'She hanged herself,' Lucy repeated. 'They cut her down and they've brought her body home. But she cannot lie in the churchyard. She will have to be buried outside. Next to Giles.'

'She was a fool,' I repeated stoutly. 'She could have come home. No one gathers filth on Wideacre. No one sells themselves for a shilling to strangers. She should have come home.'

'Ah, but she would not,' Lucy said. I felt again that prickle of dread at the rising inflexion of Lucy's voice. 'She would not come home to Wideacre because she would not tread the same earth which you tread, Miss Beatrice. She said she would not breathe the same air as you. She said she would rather die than live on your land.'

I gaped at Lucy. Bea Fosdyke, this girl, of my own age, bearing my name, christened in compliment to my parents, had loathed me so?

'Why on earth?' I asked incredulously.

'She was Ned Hunter's girl!' said Lucy in triumph. 'No one knew, but they were betrothed. They had exchanged rings, and carved their names in the oak tree you felled on the common. When he died of the gaol fever she said she would not sleep another night on Wideacre land. But now she will sleep here for ever.'

I lay back on the pillow, trembling with the cold of that freezing room. The chocolate had not warmed me, and no one would light my fire. Even my very servants were against me and had gone to honour the shameful grave of a prostitute who had hated me.

'You may go, Lucy,' I said, and there was hatred in my voice.

She bobbed a curtsy and went to the door. But she turned with her hand on the knob. 'The patch of ground outside the church wall has two heaps of stone there now,' she said. 'Old Giles . . . and Beatrice Fosdyke. We have a graveyard for suicides now. They are calling the suicides' graveyard "Miss Beatrice's Corner".'

The mist was coming down the chimney like a swirling cloud of poison. It was stinging in my eyes. It was behind my throat making me want to retch. It was clammy on my forehead and my face. I slumped back on the white lace pillows and pulled the fleecy blankets right up over my head. In the friendly dark under the covers I gave a great wail of pain and horror. And buried my face in the sheet, and waited for a sleep as deep and as dark as death.

The fog lasted until May Day, a whole long grey week. I told Harry and Celia that it gave me a headache, and that was why I was so pale. But John looked at me with his hard clever eyes and nodded, as if he had heard something he had known all along. On May Day morning it lifted, but there was no joy in the air. Acre village usually had a maypole, and a queen o' the may, a party, and a football fight. The Acre team would take a ball, an inflated bladder, up to the parish bounds, and they and the Havering men would struggle and kick it back and forth over the parish boundaries until one team triumphed and carried it home as a prize. But this year Acre was all wrong.

The cold grey mist hung over everything and people coughed in the coldness and hugged damp clothes to them. Last year's queen o' the may had been Beatrice Fosdyke, and there was some nonsense about it being unlucky to be the prettiest girl in the village and to follow in her shoes. The Acre team could not muster enough sound men. Those who were on the parish dared not be away from their cottages in case John Brien was making up a labour gang and they missed the chance to earn a few pence. And many of the others had coughs and colds because of a long wet spring and poor food. Acre had nearly always won the ball because the team was led by the three tearaways: Ned Hunter, Sam Frosterly, and John Tyacke. Now Ned was dead, Sam on his way to Australia, to his death, and John had gone missing with broken honour, broken loyalty, and a broken heart. So Acre felt indisposed either to dance or wrestle, to court or to make merry.

I dreaded the coming of my birthday in this dismal weather. I always thought of my birthday as the start of spring and yet it was like November when I awoke. I walked slowly downstairs knowing that I would find presents from Harry and Celia beside my plate. But the doorstep would not be heaped with little gifts from the village children. And baskets of spring flowers and posies would not arrive all through the day. And everyone would see what everyone knew: that I had lost the heart of Wideacre. That I was an outcast on my own land.

But, incredibly, it all looked the same. Three brightly wrapped presents sat beside my breakfast plate, from Harry, Celia and John. And on the table at the side, as ever, was a heap of small presents. My eyes took them in with a leap of gladness and a sigh, almost a gasp, escaped me. I felt a sudden prickling under my eyelids and could have wept aloud. Spring was coming then. The new season would make amends. And Acre had forgiven me. Somehow they had understood what I had never dared tell them outright. That the plough breaks the earth, cuts the toad, in order to plant the seed. That the scythe slices the hare while it is cutting hay. That the losses and deaths and grief and pain that had soured Acre all this freezing miserable winter and spring were like the pains of birth, and that the future, my son's future, and Acre's future were safe. But they had understood. They might have turned against me in bitterness and hatred for a while. But somehow they had understood.

I smiled and my heart was light for the first time since John had looked at me as he would look at a dying patient. I opened the presents by my plate first. I had a pretty brooch from Harry: a gold horse with a diamond inset as a star on its head. An ell of silk from Celia in a delicate lovely pewter grey. 'For when we are in half-mourning, dearest,' she said, kissing me. And a tiny package from John. I opened it with caution and then stuffed it back in the wrapping before Harry and Celia could see it. It was a phial of laudanum. On it he had written: 'Four drops, four-hourly'. I dropped my head over my plate to hide my white face and shocked eyes.

He knew that I sought to escape the world in sleep. And he knew also that my sleeping and sleeping through these foggy weeks was a longing for Death. And he knew that I believed him when he had told me that Death was coming for me, and that I was ready. He was now giving to my hand the way to hurry towards it. And the corner outside the graveyard for suicides would be 'Miss Beatrice's Corner' indeed.

When I gathered my courage and looked up, his eyes on me were bright, scornful. I had shown him the way. When he was struggling against drink he had found everywhere, at every hand, a dewy bottle with an unbroken seal. Now I knew that by my bedside every night would be a liberal supply of laudanum. And that the young doctor, who had loved me and warned me against the drug, would now supply me with as much as I wanted, until I slept and never woke again.

I shuddered. But my eyes slid to the little table heaped with presents.

'And all these from Acre!' said Celia marvelling. 'I am so glad, so very glad.'

I nodded. 'I am glad too,' I said, my voice low. 'It has been a hard winter for all of us. I am glad it is over.'

I walked to the table and unwrapped the first little parcel. Each one was no bigger than a cork from a wine bottle, all surprisingly uniform. All wrapped in gay paper.

'What can it be?' Celia exclaimed. She soon had her answer. From the pretty wrapping rolled a flint stone. It was white, and the grey shards on it showed where the white had chipped away. It was a flint from the common where the villagers could no longer go.

I dropped it in my lap and reached for another parcel. It was another flint. Harry exclaimed and strode over to the table. He opened half-a-dozen, ripping at the papers and scattering the wrapping on the floor. They were all flint stones. My lap was soon full of them. I counted them mechanically. There was one for every cottage, or house, or shanty, on our land. The whole village and every poor tenant had sent me a flint for my birthday. They did not dare stone me. Only one pebble had ever been shied at my gig. But they sent me, wrapped in pretty paper, a lapful of flints. I stood abruptly and showered them to the breakfast parlour floor. They clattered on the wood like monstrous hailstones in a storm of ice. Celia's face was aghast. John was looking at me with overt curiosity. Harry was champing on his words, speechless with rage.

'By God!' he spluttered. 'I'll have the troops into the village for this. It's an insult, a deliberate calculated insult. By God, I'll not let it pass!'

Celia's brown eyes suddenly filled with tears.

'Oh, don't let's talk like that!' she cried out in sudden passion. 'It is we who have brought this on Beatrice. It is our fault. I have seen the village getting hungrier and more despairing and angrier. And all I have done is to try and ensure the very poorest families survived the winter. I never challenged what you and Beatrice were doing, Harry. But now I see the result of it. We have been all wrong, Harry. All wrong.'

I looked at her, my face blank. Everywhere I went I seemed to hear echoes of the message that Wideacre had gone wrong, had gone badly wrong. Whereas I believed, I had to believe, that it was all coming right. With fifty flints on the floor around my feet I stared at Celia, reproaching herself for the sorrow and hardness that had come to the land, and at Harry, speechless with anger. And at John, staring at me.

'There's one you missed,' he said quietly. 'Not a stone, a little basket.'

'Oh, yes,' said Celia hopefully. 'A pretty little basket like the children make with reeds from the river.'

I looked at it dully. It was Ralph's basket, of course. I had been waiting for it all day. Now it sat on the table and I noted with dark eyes that he had lost none of the skill with his fingers, even if he would never walk or run or jump again. It was exquisitely made. He had taken time and trouble to make his threat to me delightfully pretty, inviting.

'You open it, Celia,' I said. 'I don't want to.'

'Are you sure?' she asked. 'It cannot be anything bad. Look at the work that has gone into this lid, and the exquisite little catch.' She slid back the little splinter of wood that served as a bolt and lifted the latch. She raised the lid with gentle fingers and parted the straw packed inside.

'How odd,' she said in surprise.

I had expected a china owl, like the last present. Or some horrid trick like a model of a mantrap or a china black horse. But it was worse than that.

I had braced myself for months, knowing that my birthday

was coming, sensing Ralph somewhere near my land. I had expected some warning from him. Some coded threat. I had imagined all the forms that it could take. But it was worse.

'A tinderbox?' asked John. 'A little tinderbox? Why would anyone send you a tinderbox, Beatrice?'

I drew a deep shuddering breath and my eyes turned to Harry, the plump pompous fool who was my only help and support in this hating world that I had made all around me.

'It is the Culler,' I said in despair. 'He sends me that, to tell me he means to fire the house. He will come soon.' And I reached out to Harry as if I were being swept down the Fenny on a flood tide and the waters were closing over my head. But Harry was not there. The mist was in my head and before my eyes again, and this time the greyness was not damp and cold, but hot.

And it smelled like smoke.

I took to my bed like some London miss in a decline. I could think of nothing else to do. I feared and hated the village and did not want to go there. I could not hear the heartbeat of the land so the woods and the downs were no comfort to me. I knew that somewhere, in some secret hollow, Ralph was hiding, watching the house with his hot black eyes. Waiting for me. My office and my maps, my rent table and my accounts were just so much paper that would blaze up if someone set a tinderbox to them. There was nothing for me to challenge so I stayed in bed. I lay on my back and looked at the great carved canopy over my head, at the profusion of fruit and flowers and animals and I longed for a land like that. Where good things grew and one could eat and enjoy without starving another. And I knew, in my secret, despairing heart, that Wideacre had been a land like that before I had gone mad, and lost myself, and lost the heartbeat, and lost the love, and lost the land. All I had left to cling to was the future, was Richard and Julia and the world they might make if I could keep Wideacre long enough to hand over to them. But I was lost.

They treated me like an invalid. The cook dreamed up delicate little dishes to tempt me. But I had no appetite. How could I have? I had eaten hearty on days when I had roamed the land like a gypsy and come home dog-tired and starving. They brought Richard in to see me, but he would not sit still beside me, and the noise he made hurt my head. Celia sat by my bed by the hour, sewing in the window seat with the warm May sunshine lighting her brown hair, or reading a book in companionable silence. Harry came in, clumsily tiptoeing, twice a day. Sometimes with a sprig of hawthorn for me or bluebells. And John came in, night and morning, with a cool hard look at me on his entrance. A phial of laudanum if I asked for it, and an expression in his pale eyes that was sometimes akin to pity.

He was working against me. I knew it without having to steal his letters or check the postbag. He had been in touch with his father, and with his father's sharp Scottish lawyers, to see if they stood a chance of reclaiming what was left of his fortune. To see if they could disinherit my son. But I knew I had tied that rock-solid. I trusted my lawyers to have forged a contract that could be broken only by the signatories. And while I held Harry in the palm of my hand, Wideacre was safe for my son. And John could do nothing against me. But he stopped hating me throughout May while I lay in my bed dozing the warm days away. He was too good a doctor. All he could do, all his disposition and training and habits forced him to do, was to watch me and note the paleness in my cheeks and the shadows under my eyes, and the way I stared sightlessly at the wooden ceiling of my bed.

Under my pillows in the great bed were two things hidden. One, hard and square, was the tinderbox. I had taken the flint from it, and the tinder, for I had a fear now of fire, and every night I would insist that Harry went around the fireplaces of the Hall to check that they were all safely doused. Inside it I kept a twist of curl-paper with a handful of Wideacre earth in it. It was the earth I had clenched in my hand all the trembling walk home; I had kept it in the bottom of my jewel box all these long years. Now I put it with the tinderbox the Culler had sent me. Ralph's earth in the Culler's box. If I had been the witch they called me, I would have made magic with them. And the magic I would choose would have made me a girl again and this pain and hunger and death would not have been.

I lay like a tranced princess in a daydream of death. But Celia, pitying, forgiving Celia, laid little plans for me and tempted me from my bed.

'Harry said the wheat was looking very well,' she said one morning towards the end of May as she sat in the window seat of my bedroom and gazed over the rose garden and paddock to the woods and the high, high downs behind.

'Yes?' I said languidly. I did not even turn my head. Above me was the carved roof of the bed showing corn standing tall, fat sheep, cows in calf and a tumble of fruit and sheaves of wheat from a great twirly shell. A carving to bless the master of the land with a constant reminder that the land was fertile and easy.

'It is high and silvery-green,' Celia said. Somewhere, among the mist in my mind, the shape and colour of the rippling fields came back to me.

'Yes,' I said with more interest.

'He says that the Oak Tree Meadow and Norman Meadow are growing a crop the like of which has never been seen in the country. Great fat heads of wheat and straight tall stalks,' said Celia, her eyes on my suddenly brightening face.

'And the common field?' I asked, raising myself a little in bed and turning to look at Celia.

'That is doing very well,' said Celia. 'It is so sunny there, that Harry says it will ripen early.'

'And the new fields we enclosed up to the slopes of the downs?' I asked.

'I don't know,' said Celia slyly. 'Harry did not say. I do not think he has been up that far.'

'Not been up that far!' I exclaimed. 'He should be up there every day. Give those damned idle shepherds one chance and they'll let the sheep in to graze it down to the root to try and show us that the downs should be left for sheep! Let alone the rabbits and the deer. Harry should be checking the fences around the corn fields every day!'

'That is bad,' said Celia ingenuously. 'If only you could go and see for yourself, Beatrice.'

'I'll go,' I said without thinking, and tossed back the covers and slid from my bed. The three long weeks in bed had made me weak, and my head swam when I leaped up. But Celia was at my side, and when Lucy came into the room they had my pale grey riding habit laid out for me.

'Shouldn't I still be in black?' I asked, pausing at the sight of the pretty dress in the lighter material.

'It has been nearly a year,' Celia said, temporizing. 'One would not wish to be lacking in attention but it is far too hot for your black velvet riding habit, Beatrice. And you always looked so lovely in this one. Wear it today, you are not going off the estate, and you will feel so much better in it.'

I needed no persuasion but slid the silk skirts over my head and buttoned the smart jacket. Lucy brought the little velvet cap that matched the outfit and I piled my chestnut curls into it carelessly, and pinned it securely. Celia gave a half-sigh as I stood before the mirror.

'Beatrice, you are so beautiful,' she said earnestly. I turned and looked at myself in the mirror.

My eyes looked back at me, the mouth curved in my quizzical smile. As I grew older and harder I had lost the magical prettiness that had been mine when Ralph loved me, and my beauty was like a luminous sunbeam in a dark barn. But the new lines around my mouth and the little trace of lines above my nose on my forehead from scowling had not robbed me of the beauty that comes to women with clear, lovely bones under smooth, glowing skin. I would be a beauty from now until the day of my death. Nothing would ever rob me of this. But in many ways it was changing. In some ways it was soured. The new lines did not matter, but the expression did.

Ignoring Lucy and Celia, I stepped closer to the mirror so my reflected face and my real one were just inches apart. The bones, the hair, the skin were as perfect as ever. But the expression had changed. When Ralph had loved me, my face was as open as a poppy on a summer morning. When I had desired Harry my secrets did not shadow my eyes. Even when John followed me, and courted me, and held my wrap for me after dancing, the smile on my mouth showed warm in my eyes and turned his heart over when he saw me. But now my eyes were cold. Even when my mouth was smiling, or when I was laughing, the eyes were as cold and sharp as splinters. And my face was closed in on the secrets I had to carry. My mouth had new lines because the lips pressed together, even in repose. My forehead had new lines because I frowned so often. With surprise I realized that when I was old, my face would fall into the expression of a discontented woman. That I should not look as if I had enjoyed the best childhood anyone could have, and a womanhood of power and passion. I might think I had made a life to give me every sort of pleasure. But my face when I was forty would tell me that my life had been hard and my pleasures all paid for.

'What is the matter?' asked Celia gently. She had slipped from her window seat and come to stand beside me, her arm around my waist, her eyes on my face.

'Look at us,' I said, and she turned to look in the mirror as well. It reminded me of the day we were fitting for her wedding and my bridesmaid's dress, so long ago at Havering. Then I had been a pattern for any man's desire, and Celia had been a pale flower. Now as we stood side by side I saw she had worn the years better than I. Her happiness had put a bloom in her cheeks, a constant upturning of her mouth. She had lost the scared look she had worn at Havering Hall, and was ready to laugh and sing like a carefree bird. The battle she had fought and won, over John's drinking, against her husband and Lord, Harry, and against her best friend, me, had put an aura of dignity around her. She still had her childlike prettiness, but she had cloaked that vulnerable girlishness with the dignity of knowing her mind when others did not. And being able to judge, and judge rightly, when those around her were ready to do wrong. She would be an old lady beloved for her charm, but also for her uncompromising moral wisdom.

It was not in Celia's nature to be unforgiving, but she would never forget the selfishness I showed and Harry showed when John trembled at the sight of a bottle, and we drank before him and praised the wine. She no longer depended on me, and she would never trust me again. There was a little distance between us that not even Celia's loving spirit would attempt to bridge. And as she watched my eyes in the glass I could no longer predict with certainty what she was thinking.

'I think you could ride to see the wheat crop,' she said temptingly. 'I do think you could, if you wanted to, Beatrice.'

'Yes,' I said, smiling. 'It has been nearly a year. I should love to ride up to the downs again. Tell the stables to get Tobermory ready for me.'

Celia nodded and took her dismissal from the room, pausing only to gather her sewing. Lucy handed me my grey kid gloves and my whip.

'Better already,' she said, and her voice was cool. 'I have never known a lady who could recover like you, Miss Beatrice. Sometimes I think that nothing will stop you.'

My weeks in bed had rested me well. I took Lucy by the arm, just above the elbow in a hard, pinching grip, and I pulled her a little towards me.

'I don't like the tone of your voice, Lucy,' I said confidentially. 'I don't like it at all. If you want to look for a new place without a reference, with a week's wages in your purse, and far away from here, then you have only to say.'

She looked back at me with villager's eyes. Hating and yet craven.

'I beg your pardon, Miss Beatrice,' she said and her eyes fell below my blazing green ones. 'I meant no harm.'

I let her go with a little push and swung out of the door and pattered down the stairs to the stable door. John was just outside, watching the tumbler pigeons on the stable roof.

'Beatrice!' he said, and his cold eyes scanned my face. 'You are better,' he said definitely, 'at last.'

'I am!' I said, and there was a gleam of triumph in my face that he could no longer look on me as a patient that he was nursing to a slow and painful end. 'I am rested and well again, and I am going out riding,' I said.

One of the lads led Tobermory from the stable door. In the hot sunshine his coat gleamed exactly the colour of my own chestnut hair. He whickered when he saw me and I stroked his nose. I gestured to John and there was nothing for him to do but to cup his hands for me to put my booted foot in then, and to toss me up into the saddle. I had a thrill of pure joy when I felt his white hands, doctor's hands, under my boot, and I beamed down on him from Tobermory's high back, as if I loved him.

'Do you see Death in my face today, John?' I said teasingly. 'You were in rather a hurry to think that I would die to please you, weren't you?'

John's face was serious and his eyes were as cold as flints.

'You're healthy as ever,' he said. 'But I still see Death coming for you. You know it, and so do I. You feel well now because the sun is shining and you are out on horseback again. But things are not the same for you, Beatrice. And you are not such a fool you do not know when everything around you has been destroyed, and that the only thing left to die is you.'

I bent down and patted Tobermory so that John should not see that my face had blenched when he spoke to me in that prophet's voice.

'And what shall you do?' I said, my voice hard and under control. 'When you have talked me into an early grave or into madness with boredom at this theme of yours? What do you do then?'

'I will care for the children,' he answered easily. 'You hardly see Richard these days, Beatrice. You have either been plotting the downfall of Julia and Richard and Wideacre, or you have been ill in bed.'

'And you care for Celia,' I said, finding the point at which I could wound him in return. 'That is why you did not tell her the whole package of crazy ideas you have about me and my life. When she came to you all in grief and all in terror you did not tell her she should be grieved, she should be terrified. Even though you yourself were grieved and terrified, did you? You soothed her and petted her and told her it could all be made right. And then you brought her home to be reconciled with her husband as if nothing were wrong.'

'As if there were no monster in the maze,' John said softly. 'Yes. There are some sights and some thoughts that a woman – a good woman, Beatrice – should never have to think, should never need to know. I am glad to protect Celia from the poison that is in her house. It is possible to do because I know that this time of endurance will not go on for ever. The maze will collapse. The monster will die. And in the rubble I want Celia and the children safe.'

'Fustian!' I said impatiently. 'It sounds like a scene from one of Celia's romances. What do you think causes this collapse? How are Celia and the children safe? What nonsense you talk, John. I shall have to get you committed again!'

His eyes went hard at the jest, but his face stayed serene.

'The collapse will come about through you,' he said certainly.

'You have overreached yourself, Beatrice. It was a good plan and a clever one. But the price was too high. I do not think you can service the loans and then Mr Llewellyn will foreclose. And he will not only foreclose on the loans you made with Harry's consent, he will foreclose on the others: that only you and he, and now I, know about. And he will refuse to accept the land. He will insist on money. And you will have to sell. And you will have to sell cheap, because you will be in a hurry. And all your promissory notes will fall due at once. And you will not be able to pay without selling land and more land. Then Wideacre will be stripped of its land and its wealth. And you will be lucky if you hold on to the house, but all the rest of this' – he gestured to the garden, the green paddock, the shimmering pigeon-cooing wood, and the high pale hills, streaked with the white path – 'all this will belong to someone else.'

'Stop it, John,' I said, my voice hard. 'Stop it. Stop the way you curse me. Any pain, any threats from you and it will be I who smash the maze. I shall tell Celia that you are in love with her and that is why you drank. And that is why you came home with her. And I shall tell Harry that you and she are lovers. And Wideacre will be destroyed for you and her. She will indeed be in the rubble. And you will have brought the wreckage on her when she is divorced and parted from her child, and thrown off the estate, and shamed. If you threaten and curse me, if you meddle in my financial affairs, if you contact Mr Llewellyn and threaten my ownership of the land, I will ruin Celia. And that would break your heart. So do not threaten me, and do not curse me as you do.'

John's eyes were bleak and distant. 'It is not I who lay the curse, Beatrice,' he said. 'You are your own curse. For every road you tread has a snake coiled in the path. If Death comes for you, if ruin comes for you, it will be because death and ruin are all that you know, all that you plan for, everything around you. Even when you think you are planning for the future, for Richard, for life, all you can produce is death in the village and desolation on the land.'

I jabbed suddenly at Tobermory's mouth in a spurt of rage and I whipped him. He reared up in the old trick I had taught him and his front hoof caught John a glancing blow on the shoulder. It sent him spinning against the door but did him no great harm, and then I set my heels in Tobermory's side and we thundered down the drive as fast as if I was riding a race again, but this time against John's words and his keen sharp insight. Not against John, the man who once rode to win because he loved me so.

Tobermory was in high fettle and as glad to be out of his stable as I was glad to be on his back and not in the gig. The sunshine was as golden as champagne on my face and I flushed warm as he cantered past the new corn meadow up to the slopes of the downs. The birds were singing with summer madness and somewhere up in the hills a pair of cuckoos were calling in their two-toned notes like a pipe played by a child. The larks were singing their way up into the summer sky and the earth was breathing, a warm lush smell of grass growing and flowers blooming and hay readying. Wideacre was eternal. Wideacre was the same.

But I was not. I rode like a city girl. I looked around me and saw all I needed to see, all I had come to see, all there was to see. But it did not speak to me. It did not chime in my heart like a clear-toned bell. It did not call to me like one loving cuckoo to another. It did not sing to me in a lark's voice. It was eternal, eternally lovely, eternally desirable. But it no longer needed me. I rode on the land as a stranger. I rode on Tobermory like someone who has just learned to ride. I did not breathe with him. When I whispered his name his ears did not flick back to listen to me. The saddle felt stiff and awkward under me and the reins too big for my thin hands. Tobermory and I did not move as one, an unthinking half-human half-horse animal. And his hoofs did not cut into the land like the Fenny cuts out its riverbed. We were not part of the land. We were merely on it.

So I looked at the corn with conscious care, with extra care, because I knew I could no longer know by instinct whether the crop was healthy. I rode along the line of the fences and when I saw a gap where a sheep could push in and ruin the crop, I hitched Tobermory to a tree and slid from the saddle. I heaved a branch over the gap and stared at it with my experienced dry eyes. It would keep a sheep out. The job had been done. But the branch had seemed very heavy, and I felt weary through and through.

I trotted along the top of the downs and dropped down by the Acre track into the village. In my numb cold mood I had forgotten that I had not been in the village for nearly a month. Not since the base threat of my birthday presents. They would know that the breakfast parlour floor had been scattered with flints, for the servants coming home to Acre on their day's holidays would have spread that rich piece of gossip. And they would know that Miss Beatrice had gone to bed stumbling like an old woman and had not got up for weeks. I had not planned to come home this way; Tobermory's head had turned to Acre out of habit and I had been in a daze and not stopped him. Now I rode down to the village on a slack rein and let who dared threaten me. I could face down Lucy when she challenged me and I was fresh from my bed, but to be on Wideacre land and not to feel at home drained my strength from me like life-blood into the earth. My shoulders drooped, but my back was straight as ever, as my papa had taught me to ride. My head was up, but my fingers holding the reins were numb. Tobermory felt the change in me and he picked his way carefully, his ears flickering uneasily.

The track drops down into Acre past the churchyard, around the corner they call 'Miss Beatrice's Corner' with the graves of the two, the only two, suicides in the long history of Wideacre. Someone had put fresh flowers on both of the little mounds. But there was neither headstone nor cross. Not even a wooden one. Dr Pearce would not have permitted it. Once they grew careless and forgot the flowers, the graves would hardly show. And then they might forget. And then they might cease calling those two little heaps by my name.

We turned left, past the church, and rode down the lane. I half expected, half feared some sign of the villagers and I faced that thought not with courage but with dull numbness. What more could they do? They had ceased to love me; they had learned to hate me. They dared do nothing against me other than hidden threats and childish cruelty. I might ride down Acre street every day of my life. If they did one thing to displease me I had the power to raze the whole village. I could burn the roofs over their heads. And they knew it.

As Tobermory walked down the street a woman in one of the gardens looked up from the pitifully short row of vegetables she was weeding. She took in the handsome hunter and my smart grey habit in one swift glance, and then she gathered up her child and swept indoors. Her cottage door banged, like a shout. And I could hear the sound of the bolt being shot. As if to distract me from her rudeness – although I knew her name, Betty Miles – a barrage of bangs followed me down the village street. They had seen me from the little windows of their unlit cottages. They had heard Tobermory's hoofs as they sat beside their empty fireplaces with little in the stew pot and no wage coming in, and then they had gone to their front doors and banged them sharply two, three times. Acre was shut against me, as the land was closed to me.

I rode Tobermory home, and stopped only briefly to look at the great wheatfield where the common land had once been. As if by some spell you could see the old landmarks under the blanket of the pale green wheat crop. The two valleys showed as indistinct lines. Even the great hollow, where the oak tree's roots had spread, showed as a dip. And the two footpaths that led from where I sat on my horse showed as two little trenches leading from the oak tree's gap up to the hills where the heather was budding and the ferns showed green. In my clear tired mind I knew that the infilling had been done badly because I had not been on the land to check it; that another year's ploughing would wipe out all traces that the land had been open and loved and free to all the village.

But sitting on my high hunter with my pretty cap perched on my head, it seemed to me that I might plough and plant this field every season for a thousand years and you would still be able to see where the village children had driven the geese, and where the oak tree had stood for courting couples to carve, announcing their betrothal.

I turned Tobermory with heavy hands and headed for home at a jolting trot. It was a warm scented humming summer afternoon. The silk of my dress was rippling in the breeze of the trot that lengthened into a canter as I dropped my hands and Tobermory lengthened his stride. I moved in the saddle like a lump of wood, and under my ribs felt like a frozen stone.

*

Only Harry welcomed me back with blind good humour. They were taking tea in the parlour when I came in, unpinning my cap for it seemed suddenly too tight.

'Good to see you out on the land again!' he exclaimed, his voice muffled around some fruit bread.

Celia's eyes were on my face, worried at my pallor. I saw her glance at John and he scanned me with his measuring, professional, unloving stare.

'Have a cup of tea,' Celia said, gesturing to John to pull the bell pull. 'You look tired. I'll order another cup.'

'I am perfectly well,' I said with some impatience. 'But you were quite right, Celia, it does look like being an excellent crop. With a good summer we should clear many of the outstanding debts of the estate.'

I shot a look from under my eyelashes at John as I said this. He looked scornful, and I was certain, as I had guessed, that the MacAndrew fortune had bought even lawyers' and merchants' secrets, and that John alone of the three of them knew that one season would not clear our debts. Four or five good ones would be needed. And whoever had good weather when your survival depended on it? I was running on the spot with Wideacre, like one of those dreadful dreams when you cannot flee from a threat coming for you.

'Excellent!' said Harry heartily. 'I am especially glad that you are up and about, Beatrice, because I wanted you to take the London corn merchant to the fields next week.'

I frowned at Harry, but the damage was done.

'A London corn merchant?' asked John quickly. 'What can he want here? I thought you never sold direct to the merchants?'

'We don't,' I said promptly. 'We never have done. But this man, a Mr Gilby, wrote to say that he was in the area and would like to look at our fields to give him some idea of the standard of Sussex wheat.'

Harry opened his mouth at the lie, but at a look from me closed it again. But that single betraying gesture was enough for John, who looked hard at Celia in an unspoken message that as good as called me a liar to my face.

'Perhaps it would be better if you did not see him, Harry,' Celia said, her soft voice tentative. 'If he were to offer a very good price you could not help but be tempted, and you know you have always said that local corn should be locally sold and locally ground.'

'I know,' said Harry impatiently. 'But one has to move with the times, my dear. Wideacre is farming in the way that all sensible land is now run. And the old idea of little markets and a pennyworth of corn for the poor is really not good business sense.'

'And hardly a conversation for the parlour,' I suggested smoothly. 'Celia, could I have another cup? This warm weather makes me so thirsty. And do you have some sugar biscuits there?'

Celia bustled behind the urn, but I could tell by her face she had not finished. John stood still by the fireplace, his eyes on Harry, and then looking in turn at me. He looked at us both with a detached curiosity as if we were some specimens in his university medical training that were interesting, but rather unpleasant, examples of some lower animal life.

'So you will not sell to him,' he said flatly. He knew very well we had to. I had to sell to the top bidder to start to clear the backlog of debts.

'No,' I said firmly. 'Or at the very most we will sell only a small part of the crop. The wheat off the new fields, which would not have been in the market last year anyway. There can be no objection to that. It would be madness to flood the Midhurst market with corn and bring the price down, after all.'

'Indeed?' said John, with affected interest. 'I should have thought that after the winter the poor have endured you would be glad that they should have cheap bread this summer and autumn.'

'Oh, yes!' said Celia with emphasis. 'Do say that it will be a good harvest and the benefits will be passed on to the poor, Harry! Beatrice! It has been a terrible winter for them, as John says. But one good summer and I am sure all of Acre would be happy and well fed again.'

I sipped my fresh cup of tea and said nothing. She was Harry's wife and he had sworn he would have no ill-informed sentimental meddling with our land. He shuffled his feet and looked back at me to give him a lead. Like a cat's green unwinking stare, my eyes were on his face, challenging him to make a stand against Celia's mistimed Christian spirit.

'I won't discuss it,' Harry said at length. 'Celia, you and John are very right to care for the poor; I care for them myself. No one wants anyone to go hungry. But if they are so improvident as to marry and have huge families without knowing how they are to support themselves they can hardly expect cheap wheat. Of course there will be no starvation in Acre. But I cannot support a whole village as well as run the estate as it should be run.'

'Should be run?' John queried.

'Oh! Let's change the subject!' I said with abrupt playfulness. 'Harry the Squire has spoken! And indeed there is little hardship in Acre now the good weather is coming. Let us talk instead about some visitors or amusements now summer is here. I long to take Richard down to see the sea; shall we make a party of it?'

Celia looked still uncertain but she could not face an open clash with Harry, and the topic was safely closed. I saw John's hard eyes on me and knew I had not turned him from his dogged pursuit of the truth of my plans, of the trail of my deceptions. But without Celia's gentle support he did nothing. He merely sat in silence and watched my face. Only when his eyes were on Celia did they soften.

After that, I took good care that Celia and John should be off the estate on the day I expected Mr Gilby. I reminded Celia of the urgent need for new shoes for both children and the toughness of the village cobbler's leather — good enough for Harry and me when we were small, but quite inadequate for the little princess. Celia decided to take both children to Chichester for a day's shopping and we all agreed to go. At the last moment I feigned a headache and cried off, and had the satisfaction of seeing the three of them, and the two children, bowling off down the drive a clear hour before I expected Mr Gilby.

He was punctual, which I like. But that was the only thing I liked about him. He was a slight man, a townsman with natty, almost dandified, well-cut clothes, snowy linen, and boot-tops so bright you could see his weasely little face upside-down, looking up at you when he bowed low. He bowed often. He knew, and I knew, that Wideacre wheat had never before been sold while it grew in the fields. That Wideacre wheat had always been offered first to the people whose labour had made it tall and proud and golden. He knew that every prickly, self-important Squire of Wideacre had suspected and disliked London merchants, the clever money-men who might bluff or cheat an honest man out of his profits. And he knew also, as I feared half the City knew, that the estate was overcommitted, that our notes and mortgages were in the hands of Mr Llewellyn, the bankers, and two other London merchants. That we had to deal with the people we had despised because we were locked into a trap of debts and loan repayments. He knew all this as well as I. But no shadow of it appeared on his smooth pale face as he handed me into the gig and I drove him down the drive.

He glanced around the woods mentally pricing them, and he looked left through the hedge and the line of trees to the old meadows, which were now featureless, flowerless, with green tall corn.

'All this?' he asked.

'Yes,' I replied shortly and, taking one hand from the reins, swept a gloved finger over the wide acreage shown on the map on the seat between us.

He nodded and asked me to stop the gig. I waited on the driver's seat while he strolled among the fields like a lord on his own land, and plucked a handful of green ears of wheat, and peeled back the silvery-green sheath, and popped the raw unripe kernels into his mouth and chewed them like a thoughtful locust that I had been fool enough to invite on to my land. The only way to keep the distaste off my face and out of my voice was to be as cold and as bloodless as he. And that was easy. The pain of driving a merchant around the land, where my papa had sworn no business man would ever tread, was turning me to ice; even though the afternoon sun was blazing down on my head and I was hot and stuffy in my long-skirted driving gown and jacket.

'Good,' he said, as he swung back into the gig. 'Excellent crop. Promising. But it's an uncertain business, buying the crop before it's cut. You have to make allowances for the risks, Mrs MacAndrew.'

'Indeed I do,' I said civilly. 'Would you like to see the down-land fields now?'

He nodded his assent, and I drove him down the drive and up the bridle-way to the slopes of the downs. The plantation on our left was thriving, but I could scarcely glance at it without a sinking feeling of guilt in the pit of my stomach. Wideacre water and earth were feeding these sweet dark springy trees. But the trees no longer belonged to Wideacre. They were Mr Llewellyn's, and the wide, lovely crescent of the plantation my papa had ordered with such pride was not a source of wealth for the future, with limitless wood for building and burning. It was gone. Sold as it stood. Before it even reached its mature height. Now I was selling the corn while it was still green. Nothing seemed to belong on Wideacre any more. Not the trees. Not the corn. Not even me.

Mr Gilby climbed down again and walked among the wheat. On these north-facing slopes the crop was later, and the little kernels he put in his mouth were as small as rice grains, still pale green with an unripe pod.

'Good,' he said again. 'But a risky business. A very risky business.'

The quality of Wideacre wheat against the chances of its being spoiled were his themes all the long afternoon while I sweated inside my stays and shivered from the dread I felt.

He strolled in my fields, and looked at my sky as if he might buy it as well, in a job lot. No doubt the blue sky and the hot white clouds were 'good, but risky' too.

He wanted to see the common land fields and we had to drive through Acre. I would have preferred to take the track through the woods but the bridge by the mill was up, and there was no easy way around for the gig. No doors were slammed at the sound of my horse's hoofs this time, but Acre village was as silent as if it had been itself enclosed and the people gone on the tramp.

'Quiet place,' said Mr Gilby as the unearthly hush penetrated even his money-box brain.

'Aye,' I said drily. 'But not empty, you can be sure.'

'Having trouble with the poor?' He cocked a knowledgeable black eyebrow at me. 'They won't adapt, will they? They just won't learn to change.'

'No,' I said shortly.

'Bad business,' he murmured. 'Don't have any rick-burning round here, do you? No crops spoiled in the fields? No attacks on barns?'

'We never have,' I said firmly. 'They complain but they would dare nothing more.'

'Good,' he said. 'But risky,' he said after a pause.

'Risky?' I said, clicking Sorrel into a trot once we were clear of that ominous deserted village street.

'Risky,' he said. 'I can't tell you how much trouble I have getting my grain wagons through the countryside on the way to London. I have had mothers lying down in the road before them with their babies in their arms. I have had fathers surrounding the wagons and cursing the carriers – as though anyone was to blame! I've even been caught by the mob myself once or twice. One time I actually had to sell half a wagon to them at the market price before they would let me through!'

'We don't have any of that here,' I said firmly, a superstitious shiver down my spine.

'Aye,' he said. 'Sussex is quiet at the moment. They'll come to heel.'

We pulled up in the stable yard and I took him in by the west-wing door into my office.

'Handsome room,' he said, looking round as if he were pricing the furniture.

'Thank you,' I said shortly, and rang for tea.

While Stride brought the tray and set up the urn Mr Gilby wandered along my bookshelves, inspecting the red leather bindings with approval. He put a flat hand on the rent table and turned it experimentally to feel the smooth movement as it spun. He fingered the backs of the chairs and shuffled his boots in the plain deep-pile carpet. Even while he sat and drank his tea his eyes flickered around, looking out of the window where the birds sang and the bees hummed in the rose garden, at the door with its polished walnut wood, at my desk and the great cash box beside it. At the comfort and elegance of a room furnished with goods hundreds of years old.

'Here's my offer,' he said, scrawling on a piece of paper. 'I won't haggle with you, Mrs MacAndrew, you're far too good a farmer. You know the value of your crop. It's good, but it's risky. I like the crop but I don't like the look of the road that leads from Acre to the London road. There are too many places there for trouble from men who think they know more about farming than their masters. I like your crop, but I don't like the look of your village. So I think it's good, but risky, Mrs MacAndrew. And my price represents that.'

I nodded, and looked at his paper. It was less than I had hoped, rather a lot less. But it was treble what we would get in the Midhurst market, and double what we would get at Chichester. More to the point he would pay me now, not in six weeks' time when the grain was ripe; then a bumper crop could bring a bonus. The money chest beside my desk was nearly empty, and the loans would fall due again in July. I could not refuse him, even if I had wanted to. But his talk of shady lanes, and a silent village, had me shivering again.

We had never sold the crop away from our people before; but if he thought our people might turn against me, might threaten me to my face, then I would not hesitate to save the land for me and my son, the only way I knew. I did not wish them to starve; I did not mean them to suffer. But they had to play their part in winning Wideacre for Richard. And when Richard was Squire everyone would agree that it would have been worth the price, even this cruel price of fear for me and hunger for them.

But, in truth, when he spoke to me of shady lanes and angry men I felt such blind fear, and unreasoning fear, that I would have starved the whole of Acre. Somewhere, near or far, from Wideacre land, was the Culler. He had threatened me last year. This year he had sent me that terrible little tinderbox. He was telling me as clearly as he could that there was fire coming for me. That the cull of the gentry would start with me. And so I cared nothing for anyone who might help the Culler, or succour him, or point him to the Hall and say, 'Take her, she is our beloved Miss Beatrice no longer.' And while he was near my land, or while his mind was on me, even if he were far away, I would rather have money in the chest than corn in the fields or grain in the barns. He could not burn gold. He could not attack me safe in this room.

'I agree,' I said neutrally.

'Good,' said Mr Gilby. 'You'll have a draft on my bank within two days. You'll reap it yourself?'

'Yes,' I said. 'But you had better send your own wagons down. We don't have the carts or the beasts to take it all to London.'

'Good,' he said again, and gave me his soft hand to shake on the deal. 'A handsome place you have here, Mrs MacAndrew,' he said, gathering his hat and gloves.

I smiled and nodded.

'I am looking for a place like this myself,' he said. I raised my eyebrows and said nothing. It was the way of the counties around London, but I had not thought Sussex would suffer so soon from these city-bred merchants setting themselves up as Squires. They brought their city airs and graces into the country. They understood neither the land nor the people. They muddled along with farming and they wrecked the land by forgetting to rest it. They spoiled whole villages by taking servants up to London and then sending them home again. They lived on the land but they had no heart for it. They bought and sold it as if it were a length of cloth. They belonged nowhere, and bought anywhere.

'If you were considering parting with Wideacre . . .' Mr Gilby started engagingly.

My head jerked up. 'Wideacre!' I said outraged. 'Wideacre will never be for sale!'

He nodded, an apologetic smile on his face.

'I am so sorry,' he said. 'I must have misunderstood. I thought you were selling the crops and the woods preparatory to selling the estate. If you had been I would have paid a very fair price, very good indeed. You'd not get a better one, I assure you. I had the impression that the estate was rather overcommitted and I thought . . .'

'The estate is managing wonderfully,' I said with a tremor of rage in my voice. 'And I would be bankrupt before I parted with it. This is the inheritance of the Laceys, Mr Gilby. I have a son and a niece who are to come after me. I would not sell their home. I would not sell my own home.'

'No, of course, of course,' he said pacifically. 'But if you should change your mind. If Mr Llewellyn were to foreclose, for example . . .'

'He will not,' I said with an assurance I did not feel. What talk was there about Wideacre in the money-men's clubs? Would they form a ring against us and foreclose on the estate to win for themselves one of the biggest prizes in Sussex? Had my borrowings not been discreetly spread around London at all, but had played straight into the hands of a ring of cronies who even now calculated the months before I should be ruined? And what did Mr Gilby, a corn merchant, know of Mr Llewellyn, a dealer in land and wood from the other side of the City?

'Even if he did, I have sufficient funds. I am a MacAndrew,' I said.

'Of course,' said Mr Gilby, his black eyes betraying his secret knowledge that the MacAndrew money was closed to me. He might even know that the MacAndrew fortune was working against me.

'I'll bid you good day then,' he said, and he took himself off without another word.

He left me still. He left me silent. He left me cold with dread. It was bad enough to know that the Culler and all the lawless men of his rank might be planning against me, waiting to come to me. But if my own people – those who slept between linen sheets and ate off silver plate – were plotting against me, then I was lost indeed. If the hard-faced money-men knew of me, knew of the mounting pile of debts and the empty cash box, then Wideacre and I were both in jeopardy. I had not thought that they might all know each other. I had forgotten that men like to make little clubs, like to be in packs, like to bully as a gang. Alone and isolated from the outside world I had not realized that there might be eyes watching me, ears listening for the first note of hesitation, and smiles exchanged as they heard of one heavy debt after another, and no sign of my getting clear.

I could fight them with the easy productive wealth of Wideacre at my back, and a village full of people who loved me and would work for free rather than I should lose a battle against strangers. Or I could fight an angry village, a bitter workforce. But I could not fight the lower orders and the people of my own rank at once, and hope to win. And while I was undermining and attacking the poor, the wealthy were undermining and attacking me. With a sullen, silent village on one hand and a secretive ring of creditors on the other I was surrounded by peril. And in the middle of it all – like a bone between two dogs – was Wideacre. And I could no longer feel for Wideacre.

I gave a little moan of sorrow and exhaustion and laid my face on my hands on my hard desk and stayed still until the summer evening grew grey outside my tall windows and bats criss-crossed the evening sky. Somewhere, from the wood, a nightingale started singing. I longed only for rest.

I had not reckoned with Celia. I began to think I had never properly reckoned with Celia. She came into my office as soon as the carriage returned. She came in, taking off her bonnet, and never even glanced at the mirror over the mantelpiece to see if her fair hair was smooth.

'We passed a post-chaise on the drive with a gentleman in it,' she said. 'Who was he, Beatrice?'

I glanced at the papers on my desk and looked at her with raised eyebrows as if to imply that I found her curiosity impertinent. She met my eyes look for look. And her pretty mouth was not smiling.

'Who was he?' she asked again.

'It was someone come to see a horse,' I said blandly. 'Tobermory's foal out of Bella. It seems that the fame of the Wideacre hunters is spreading.'

'No, it wasn't,' Celia contradicted me, her voice even. 'It was a Mr Gilby, the London corn merchant. I stopped the carriage and spoke to him.'

I flushed with irritation but I kept my voice steady. 'Oh, him!' I said. 'I thought you meant another gentleman. I have had two visitors this afternoon. Mr Gilby was the last.'

'He told me he had bought the wheat as it stands in the fields,' said Celia, ignoring my lie. 'He told me you are indeed going to forestall the market.'

I rose from my desk and smiled at her. I knew there was no warmth in my eyes, and her face was like stone.

'Really, Celia, this is hardly the business you were brought up to,' I said. 'The business of managing Wideacre is a complex task and one in which you have previously shown little interest. It is too late now to start meddling with the way I run the estate.'

'You are right to reproach me for knowing little,' she said. Her breath was fast and as she spoke one of her easy blushes coloured her face and neck. 'I think it is a great fault that ladies are taught to know nothing of the lives of the poor. I have lived all my life in the country and you are right when you say I am ignorant.'

I tried to interrupt her, but she talked over me.

'I have lived in a fool's paradise,' she said. 'I have spent money without ever thinking from whence it came or who had earned it.'

She paused. I moved to the bell push as if to order tea.

'I was brought up to think like a child,' she said, speaking half to herself. 'I was brought up like a baby who eats food but does not realize someone has had to cook it, and mash it, and serve it in a bowl. I have spent and spent Wideacre money without ever realizing that the money came from the labour of the poor.'

'Not entirely,' I contradicted her. 'You should speak with Harry on the theories of political economy, but we are farmers, remember, not merchants or manufacturers. Our wealth comes from the land, from the natural fertility, from nature.'

Celia waved away the argument with an impatient gesture and put her palm flat down on my rent table.

'You know that is not true, Beatrice,' she said. 'You take the money here every month. People pay us because we own the land. Left to itself the land would grow weeds and meadow flowers. We invest in it as surely as a merchant, and we pay people to work it for us as surely as a mine owner pays miners.'

I stood silent. Celia had changed so much from the shy girl who had watched the reapers and blushed when Harry looked at her. I said nothing, but I felt a growing unease.

'The mine owner pays them a fraction of what they earn,' she said slowly as if she was working out her ideas aloud. 'Then he sells what they have dug, at a profit. He keeps all of that profit. That is why he is rich and they are poor.'

'No,' I said. 'You do not understand business. He has to buy equipment and he has to pay back loans. Also, he has to have a return on his investment. If it did not profit him to mine, then he would invest his money elsewhere, and his workforce would have no wage at all.'

Celia's honest gaze was on my face and, surprisingly, she smiled as if I was jesting with her.

'Oh, Beatrice, that is such nonsense!' she said with a ripple of laughter. 'That is what Harry says! That is what Harry's books say! I would have thought you of all people would have known what nonsense that is! All the people who write about the need for a man to have profit are rich people. All they wish to prove is that their profits are justified. That is why there are hundreds of men writing thousands of books trying to explain why some people go hungry and others get richer and richer. They have to write all those books because they will not accept the answer which is there before their eyes: that there is no justification.'

I moved restlessly, but she was looking out of the window past me.

'Why should the man who invests his money have his profit guaranteed, while the man who invests his labour, even his life, has no guaranteed wage?' she said. 'And why should the man who has money to invest earn so very much more with his capital than a man could earn working at the very top of his strength, all day? If they were both to be rewarded equally then after the debts had been paid and the new equipment bought, miners would live in houses and eat the food of the mine owners. And they clearly do not. They live like animals in dirt and squalor and they starve while the mine owners live like princes in houses far away from the ugly mines.'

I nodded emphatically. 'The conditions are dreadful I am told. And the moral danger!'

Celia's brown eyes gleamed at my shift of ground.

'It is as bad here,' she said baldly. 'The labourers work all day and earn less than a shilling. I do not work at all and yet I have an allowance of two hundred pounds a quarter. I have taken no risks with capital. I replace no machinery. I am paid simply because I am a member of the Quality and we are all wealthy. There is no justice in that, Beatrice. There is no logic. It is not even a very pleasant way to live.'

I plumped down in my chair, the Squire's chair, and I drew my papers towards me. I had forgotten that I had ever thought the world should change. I had forgotten that a landless man had ever persuaded me that the people who know and love the land are those who should make the decisions about it.

'It is a wicked world, Celia,' I said, smiling. 'We are agreed on that. But it would do little good if you were paid a labourer's wage. It would make no difference if we were a Leveller's commonwealth. The Commonwealth of Wideacre would still have to pay its way in the outside world.' I tapped the drawer, which held the sheaf of bills due for settling this month. The wood no longer sounded hollow: it was packed tight. 'It is the outside world that is massing against Wideacre,' I said. 'It is the outside world that sets the pace of change.'

'Sell land,' said Celia abruptly.

I gazed at her, open-mouthed.

'What?' I said.

'Yes,' she replied. 'Harry tells me that you two have borrowed so heavily to buy the entail and pay the lawyers' fees that you have no choice but to profiteer and farm in this new way. Clear the debts by selling land, and then you need farm no longer in a way that starves Acre, and has wrecked the life of Wideacre.'

'You do not understand, Celia!' I burst out. 'We will never, never sell Wideacre land while I manage the estate! No landowner ever parts with land unless he has to. And I, of all people, would never sell a Wideacre field.'

Celia rose from the table and went to stand behind the bureau, looking down on me. She leaned her arms along the top.

'Wideacre has two great strengths,' she said fiercely. 'The land, which is fertile, and the people, who will work their hearts out for the Laceys. One of these assets will have to be wrung dry to pay for this mad scheme to which you are committed. Let it be the land. Sell some land – however much is needed, and then you will be free once again to treat the people in the old ways. Not with justice, but at least with tenderness.'

'Celia,' I said again, 'you simply do not understand. This year we are desperate to make a profit. But even if we were not, we would be starting to farm in the new ways. The less we pay the labourers the more profit we make. Every landowner wants to make as much profit as possible. Every landowner, every merchant, every business man, tries to pay as little as possible to his workers.'

She nodded then slowly, as she finally understood. But the colour had gone from her face. She turned and went with a slow step towards the door.

'What of your allowance?' I said, taunting her. 'And your dowry lands? Shall I pay your allowance to the parish poor rates, and do you wish your couple of fields to be declared a commonwealth?'

She turned back to me, and I saw with surprise that there were tears in her eyes. 'I spend all my allowance on food and clothes for the village,' she said sadly. 'John matches it with what his father sends him, and Dr Pearce pays in the same amount. We have been buying food to give the women, and clothes for the children, and fuel for the old people. I have spent every penny you pay me, and John and Dr Pearce have matched it.' Her shoulders drooped. 'We might as well not bother,' she said dully. 'It is like the dam of Harry's that broke when the spring floods came. It is all very well giving a little charity when the men are in work and the village is prosperous, but when the landlords are against the tenants, as you are, Beatrice, and when the employers have decided to pay the least they can, charity has no chance. All we are doing is prolonging the pain of people who are dying of want. At best we are rearing children for the next Master of Wideacre to work and to pay as little as he can. Their mothers tell me they cannot see why their children are born. And neither can I. It is an ugly world you and your political economists defend, Beatrice. We all know it should be different and yet you will not do it. You and all the rich people. It is an ugly world you are building.'

She waited to see if I had an answer to that sad-voiced condemnation and then she went out to her room. I pursed my lips as if I had a sour taste in my mouth. And then I opened that bursting drawer and took out the bills to look at them again.

The news of the forestalled corn went fast around Wideacre and Celia's was merely the first of three visits I had to endure. She was in some ways the hardest to answer because she feared me now not at all, and her honest brown eyes had a certain knack of looking at me as if she could not believe what she saw.

My second visitor was easier to manage. It was Dr Pearce, the Acre Vicar, who entered with apologies for disturbing me, but would I make allowances for a worried man?

He knew who paid his tithes and he was anxious not to offend me. But he was driven, like Celia, by the poverty that met his eyes every day in Acre. He could not, like Harry and me, simply

568

avoid the village. He lived there, and his high-walled garden was no refuge when children cried for hunger in the lane that ran before his house.

'I hope you do not think I am exceeding my position,' he said nervously. 'I hold no brief for improvidence. No one who knows me or my connections could ever doubt for a moment my proper feeling on the treatment and discipline of the poor. But I must speak to you about this wheat crop, Mrs MacAndrew.'

I smiled then, conscious of my power.

'Speak then, Vicar,' I said. 'And I will do what I can.'

'They are saying in the village that the crop is sold already,' he said, his eyes on my nod of assent. 'They are saying in the village that the whole of the crop, every wagonload, will be sent away to London.' I nodded again. 'They are saying in the village that they do not know where they will buy their corn to grind for flour to make bread.'

'At Midhurst market, I assume,' I answered coolly.

'Mrs MacAndrew, there will be a riot!' exclaimed the Vicar. 'Of the three major suppliers of corn, two of you – Wideacre and the Havering estate – are sending grain out of the county. Only the little Tithering estate is selling locally. There will be hundreds of families needing corn and only one farm selling at Midhurst. The corn will simply run out.'

I shrugged, and made a little grimace. 'Then they will have to go to Petworth, or Chichester,' I said.

'Can you not stop this?' Dr Pearce's tone was suddenly ragged with fear, his urbane smiling face suddenly naked with concern. 'The whole village has changed almost overnight, it seems. The fences went up and the heart went out of it. Can you not take the fences down and restore the land? When I first arrived here, I heard from everyone that no one knew the land like you. No one loved the land like you. That you were the heart of Wideacre. Now all I hear is that you have forgotten your skills, forgotten that these people are your people. Can't all this be restored?'

I looked coldly at him through the wall of glass that now separated me from everyone.

'No,' I said. 'It is too late. They will have to pay dear for corn this year or do without. You may tell them that next year it will be better, but this year Wideacre has to sell to the London market. If Wideacre does not prosper, no one prospers. They know that. I am ensuring their ultimate prosperity. The way of the world is that the poor survive only if the rich prosper. If the poor want to eat, the rich have to be enriched. That is the way the world is. And Wideacre is not nearly wealthy enough to be safe.'

Dr Pearce nodded. The opulent dinners at Oxford, his landed friends and family, the shooting parties, the dances, the balls, had been his world. He was one of those who do indeed believe the world is a better place for the rich becoming wealthier. And he had read a hundred clever books written solely to prove that point. He himself longed to increase his tithes on the back of our bumper crop. He belonged, like me, to the rich. And his eyes glistened, despite his concern, at my picture of an inevitable process whereby we gained and gained and gained, and no one could blame us or gainsay us.

'It is the children,' he said weakly.

'I know,' I said. I reached into a drawer in my desk and found a guinea. 'Here,' I said. 'Buy the children some toys, or sweetmeats, or food.'

'The coffins are so very tiny,' he said, more to himself than to me. 'The father generally carries it in his arms. It is so light, you see. They do not need pallbearers. For the children who are dying are so small, and when they die of hunger they are as light as babies by the time they die – little arms and legs like dry sticks. When they lower it into the grave it is such a little hole.'

I tapped the bundle of papers on my desk with a sharp click to recall him to his surroundings. He was gazing out of the window, but not seeing the budding tea-roses and the fat boughs of white sweet lilac.

'Was there anything else?' I asked abruptly. He jumped, and reached for his hat.

'No,' he said. 'I apologize for troubling you.' Then he kissed my hand without a shadow of reproach, and he was gone.

So that was the champion of the Acre poor! I watched his glossy bay cob amble down the drive, its plump haunches rolling. Small wonder they dreamed of revenge, of a man to ride like a devil before them to lead them against the people with plump faces who lived on dainties and drank only the very best of wines. While the comfort-loving, biddable, Vicar of Acre stood between them and me, they had scant protection indeed. They must think, indeed by now they should know, that the whole of the world was against them. That for me, and for people like me – the ones who ate four times a day – the poor were there to work. And if there were no work? Then there was no need for them to live.

There was a knock at the door, and Richard's nurse came into the room. 'Do you wish to see Master Richard before dinner?' she asked.

'No,' I said wearily. 'Take him out for a walk in the garden. I can see him through the windows.'

She nodded, and a few minutes later I saw her stooping over my son, helping him to toddle from one bright rose bush to another, and patiently, repeatedly, putting a petal in his hand and then, reprovingly, taking it out of his mouth.

The thick glass of my office window muffled the sound. I could scarcely hear my son's clear lisping voice. I could not make out at all the words he was struggling to say to express his joy at the gravel beneath his feet and the petal in his hand, and the sunshine on his face. Through the thick glass of the window all the colour seemed drained from the landscape. And the little flaws in the glass made him and his nurse seem a long way away. The window pane was like the lens of a telescope held the wrong way. As I watched him he seemed to recede even further. Further and further away from me. A little boy in the sunshine, too far for me to recognize as my own. And I could not hear his voice.

19

The news Dr Pearce took back to the village only confirmed their fears and when we drove to church, in summer silks and satins, the faces were no more surly than usual. Celia and I led the way, our trains hissing up the aisle to the family pew, followed by Harry and John, and then the two nurses with the children. Julia toddling slowly, and with many an unpredictable swerve, and Richard carried in Mrs Austin's arms.

As I passed up the aisle, my grey silk rustling around me, my new bonnet of twilled satin tied with a silky fat bow framing my face, I could feel a stir of unease like a wind in the top of the pine trees on a still summer's day. I slid my eyes to one side and then another and what I saw made me draw in my breath in horror.

On the pew sides, all the way down the church, I could see the callused hands of our workers. As they heard my heels tap on the stones of the aisle, they all clenched into a protective fist, with the index finger crossing the thumb. The sure defence against a witch. The one-handed secret sign of the cross. I walked, smoothly, stately, between the avenue of pagan fists. I looked neither to left nor right again. But their hatred and their fear of me followed me like a court train on a ball dress.

Once I was inside the pew, and the door safely closed behind us, all anyone could see of me was the grey silk bow on the top of my bonnet. I dropped my head on my hands then as if in prayer. But I had no prayers. I was just resting my burning forehead against my icy fingers and trying to blot out the sight of all those honest dirty hands making the sign of the cross against me. Trying vainly to ward off the evil they thought I carried with me.

Dr Pearce preached a good sermon. I listened, stony-faced. His theme was that wonderfully ambiguous instruction of rendering unto Caesar, and he made a persuasive case for resting content under the civil authorities – whatever they chose to do to their people. I doubt if any of his parishioners heard a word. There was a continual clatter of the dry coughs that indicate consumption, and a muffled choking from a child with pleurisy. A hungry baby cried unceasingly at the back of the church, a thin despondent wail. Even in the richly panelled, well-cushioned Wideacre pew there was no peace. Even when the Vicar told us, his uncertain eyes on Harry and me, that the word of the Lord said we might always do as we pleased.

After the final psalm I walked down the aisle again. Conscious, at every step, of the dull, resentful eyes on my face, and the rare warm glances directed at Celia, half a step before me. We no longer lingered in the churchyard to say good day to the tenants. That tradition had somehow vanished. But while we walked to the carriage I saw, from the corner of my eyes, the rotund figure of the miller, Bill Green, burst from the church porch and march determinedly towards the carriage.

'Miss Beatrice!' he called. 'Good day, Squire, Lady Lacey, Dr MacAndrew,' he said in an afterthought, recollecting his manners. Then his anxious eyes were on my face again as I settled myself in the carriage.

'Miss Beatrice, I need to speak to you. May I come to the Hall today?'

'On a Sunday?' I asked, my eyebrows raised in genteel disapproval.

'I have called on many a working day and you have been too busy to see anyone from Acre,' said Miller Green, breathlessly. 'But I must have speech with you, Miss Beatrice.'

The other parishioners were coming from the church door, staring curiously at the miller, whose usually happy face was now strained. One hand on my carriage door, begging for one moment of my time.

'Very well,' I said with my new dislike of the Acre poor when they were all together in a group staring at me. 'Very well. Come to the Hall at three this afternoon.'

'Thank you,' he said. He stepped back with a little bow and I saw that his plump cheeks were sagged and that his bright skin colour had gone. He looked sallow and ill.

I did not need a visit from him to tell me what was wrong. I had seen this meeting coming from afar off, as soon as Harry and I agreed to send Wideacre corn out of the county.

'This will ruin me, Miss Beatrice,' Miller Green said desperately. 'If Acre people have no corn they will not bring it to me for the grinding. If your tenant farmers sell all their corn in the grain they will not use my mill to make flour. If you send the whole crop out of the county, where am I to buy my grain to grind for flour to supply the bakers who buy from me?'

I nodded. I was sitting at my desk, the window to the rose garden open behind me. The two children were playing in the paddock and John and Celia were strolling behind them, watching Richard's nurse steering him along the footpath towards the wood. Celia's cream parasol was an echo of the daisies, cream roses, and rare white poppies. I had seated Miller Green at the rent table and ordered him·a glass of small beer, but it stood beside him, untouched. He twisted and turned on the chair like a dog with fleas. He was a proud man, a rising man. But now he was a man in a panic. He could see his plans and his newly won prosperity sliding away from him as water slides over his millwheel.

'Miss Beatrice, if you do not want the millwheel, which your grandfather built, to lie idle, if you want the poor to eat, if you want our lives here to go on at all, you must, you must, reserve some of the crop for sale locally,' he said desperately. 'Miss Beatrice, there's me and my wife and our three lads, all three working on the parish gang now for poor parish rates. Little money coming in from them, and much shame for them. If we lose the mill, it will be the workhouse for us, for we will be penniless and homeless in one night.'

I nodded again, my eyes towards the garden. John and Celia had reached the gate to the wood. With tender patience they turned back towards the house so that the children should have the smooth grass of the paddock under their tottery feet. I saw Celia nod, her little bonnet tip in emphasis, and saw John throw his head back to laugh at her. I could not hear them. The window was open but there was still a wall of glass all around me. The glass made it possible for me to watch my son learning to walk holding another woman's hands, with utter indifference; to tell this good man, this old friend, that he would indeed have to go to the workhouse and die in poverty and sorrow; to tell him that my will was as strong and unstoppable as the grinding stones of the mill. And that he and all the grasping, desperate, poor of Acre should be crushed and powdered so that a little boy, just learning this day to walk, should ride tall over the land.

'Miss Beatrice, do you remember the harvest three summers ago?' Bill Green said suddenly. 'Do you remember how you rested in our yard while we got the harvest supper ready? How you sat in the sun for an hour, listening to the wheel turning and the Missus's doves cooing?

'D'you remember how the wagons came singing up the lane and how you let the harvest into the barn with the Squire so young and handsome riding high on the sheaves?'

I smiled in nostalgia. Unwillingly, I nodded.

'Yes,' I said tenderly. 'Of course I remember. What a summer that was for us! What a harvest it was that year!'

'You loved the land then, and all of Acre would have laid down their lives for one smile from you,' Bill Green said. 'That year, and the year before, you were a goddess in Acre, Miss Beatrice. Since then it has been like you were under a spell and everything has gone wrong. Wrong. All wrong.'

I nodded. I had the papers under my hand that showed it was all going wrong. Ruin was on the way. As surely and as steadily as the coming of the Culler. I could smell the hint of smoke in the summer air. The creditors were presenting their bills before the quarter day. They knew; I knew. Wideacre was over-stretched. They could smell ruin like horses can smell a storm in the air. As I can smell smoke.

'Set it right!' Bill Green's Sussex drawl was a longing whisper. 'Set your hand to it, and make it right, Miss Beatrice! Come back to us, come back to the land, and set it right!'

I gazed at him blankly, dreaming of a return to the land, of a return to the old ways. But my face was as hard as one of his stones, and as cold as his millpond.

'It is too late,' I said, and my voice was dry. 'The corn is already sold. I have already been paid. The agreement is made, and I can do nothing. This is the way farming is done these days, Miller Green. You may indeed face ruin. But if I do not farm as the other landowners farm, then I would be ruined too. I do not choose how the world should be run. I have only to find my way in it.'

He shook his head like a stunned prize fighter.

'Miss Beatrice!' he said. 'This isn't like you. It's not your voice that could say these things. You were always for the old ways. The good ways when men and Master worked alongside and men were paid fair and had a little land, and a day off, and kept their pride.'

I nodded. 'Yes, I was,' I said. 'But the world is changing, and I have to change too.'

'That's the Quality!' he exclaimed with sudden bitterness. 'Never say, "Aye, I did it. I want more money and I shall get it whatever the cost to the poor." It's always "the way of the world". But the way of the world is the way you, and the Quality like you, decide it should be, Miss Beatrice! All of you – land-owners, squires, and lords – make the world the way you want it and then say, "I can't help it, it's the way of the world." As if it were not you who decides how the world should be.'

I nodded, for he was right.

'Well then, Bill Green, have it your way,' I said coldly. 'I chose that Wideacre should be wealthy. That my son and Miss Julia shall inherit. And if it costs you your mill, if it costs every life in Acre, then so be it.'

'So be it,' he muttered, as if he could not understand. He fumbled for his hat, his Sunday hat, and put it on his head. His glass of beer was growing flat and stale.

'Good day, Miss Beatrice,' he said like a man in a dream, a dream of misery.

'Good day, Miller Green,' I said, honouring him with the title he would not keep long.

He walked from my office like a man half dead. Soundless, speechless, incredulous.

His dappled grey mare was hitched outside, and he heaved himself into the saddle, still in his dream. I saw him ride past the window and saw John call out to him as he and Celia came through the gate into the rose garden. Miller Green tipped his hat instinctively at the sound of a Quality accent, but I doubt he heard or saw anything. His horse ambled down the drive on a loose rein, the stocky rider slumped in the saddle. He had tragic news to take home. There would be tears in the pretty sunny parlour of the mill this afternoon, and dinner would be spoiled.

John and Celia dawdled at toddler pace through the rose garden and then walked to the terrace up to my office window, Celia pausing to see that Nurse had Julia's hand over the sharp stones of gravel.

'What did Miller Green want?' asked John through the open window, as if it were his business.

'Arrangements for the harvest dinner,' I said blandly.

'He came all this way, on a Sunday, to plan a dinner his wife has organized for years?' asked John in his most sceptical voice.

'Yes,' I said, and added cruelly, 'I said Celia would make all the arrangements.'

Celia jumped as if she had been pricked with a pig-sticker and I could not conceal the gleam of my amusement. 'Set it in hand will you Celia? You know so much about the village these days. It should be about three weeks on Saturday. That should be nearly the right time. A day or so here or there makes little odds as long as there is enough fresh food for eighty or a hundred people, and it keeps fresh.' She looked utterly aghast, and I could not repress a short spiteful laugh.

'Excuse me, I have work to do,' I said to the two of them. And I leaned forward and banged the casement shut in their faces. John's eyes met mine through the glass. But even he seemed so very far away.

I had been right when I predicted a good crop. But wrong when I thought it would be reaped in three weeks. Even with a hot, hot sun that made midday work a torment, and an extra reaping band from the Chichester parish, it was the second week in August before we were done.

My heart should have been singing. It was a wonderful harvest. We started on the newly enclosed common fields and the reapers marched in a great wide sweep, up and down, up and down, the three gentle slopes of the levelled field. Wave on wave of greeny-golden, sound, dry corn rippled down before them. In the mornings of the first days, now and then, a voice would start a song, forgetting, in the pleasure of the smell of the ripe corn, in the crackle of the dry stalks, in the rhythm of the line, that this wealth and beauty were not, this year, a promise of a safe hunger-free winter.

'I love to hear them sing,' said Harry, reining in beside me after he had been for a ride on the downs. I had been all day in the field. I trusted this crop, which could save Wideacre, to no other.

I smiled. 'So do I,' I said. 'They keep time better and the work goes faster.'

'I might take a sickle out myself,' said Harry. 'It's years since I went reaping.'

'Not today,' I cautioned him. 'Not on this field.'

'As you wish,' he said, dense as ever. 'Shall we wait for you at dinnertime?'

'No,' I said. 'Tell them to leave something for me in my office. I may well stay over their dinner break to see they are back to work promptly after they have eaten.'

Harry nodded and wheeled away. As his horse passed the reapers who had reached the end of the field he pulled up to watch them straightening their backs, with a grimace from those who were crooked with rheumatism. They cleaned their sickles with weary sad faces, and fell into line again like pressed infantrymen. Harry cried a cheery 'Good day! Good harvesting!' to them. I doubt very much that he noticed no one replied.

They worked until noon and still the field was barely half cut. They were not going slow – I would have been on to that in a flash and they knew it. And they were too unused to the idea that this harvest would profit them not at all to cheat on the work. They still loved the great pale forest of wheat as I did, and they swung along in a steady easy river of movement expressing their joy in the great fertility of the land in every purposeful, painful swing. But still the field waved high. It was so huge! Only now, when I saw the gang reaping and reaping for half a day, did I realize what a massive acreage I had laid to wheat, and what a triumph this wheat harvest was.

The women and the children and the old folk followed the reapers, clasping great heaps of wheat to their bodies, banging the stalks against their knees and twisting a plait of wheat around to make a tight heavy-headed stook. The women had fewer illusions than the men about this explosion of fertility from the new field, and I watched them like a covetous hawk as they snapped off the odd head of wheat and stuffed it into their apron pockets. Poor beggars! Turning their backs to me that I should not see them pocket the traditional favours of the harvest. Gazing around with innocent-seeming, sly eyes and dropping a few stalks of wheat to the ground so that one of them, not even the culprit, might have some good gleaning later.

It was the tradition, always had been the tradition, that the gleaning at Wideacre was generous. The land grew so rich, the crops so tall, that no Squire had ever done more than smilingly grumble at the rituals of the informal robbery.

But now it was different.

It had to be different.

I waited until the little children had come down the lane with the pitchers of ale and the hunks of bread and cheese for their parents' dinners. This year I saw the bread was greyer than it should be, made with as little flour as possible eked out with powdered pease or grated turnip. There was no cheese for anyone. And the pitchers held only water. These men and women were working under a burning July sun with only a hunk of grey bread to eat, and water to drink. No wonder they looked pale beneath the grime and the sweat. No wonder the dinner break was no longer a time for laughter and jokes and sharing of gossip and baccy. They were smoking hawthorn leaves in their pipes. And when they laid back to doze, the younger men put their hands behind their heads and stared silently at the sky as if they longed to see a future there that might free them from this unending round of poor drudgery.

After they had had thirty minutes, to the second, I called in my clear confident voice 'All right! Back to work!'

The men and the women got to their feet as willingly as pigs coming out of mud to the killer. They glared at me, surly and cross, but no one did more than mutter. The sun was at its highest now. Mounted on my horse, unmoving, I could feel the heat of it baking on the coiled hair at the nape of my neck and the sweat making my silk gown damp. The men who had been hobbling, bent-backed, back and forth through the corn, swinging their sickles, looked like fever patients, so white and drenched in sweat. And the women look drained, mortally ill.

'Gather round,' I said peremptorily, and waited until they stood around me docile as cattle in a head-bowed half-circle. I noted, with a shiver of displeasure, that no one stepped on my shadow. When Tobermory shifted his weight so the shadow moved, the crowd swayed like a wheatfield with him, so my shadow touched no one.

'Turn out your pockets,' I said baldly. And my gaze drifted over every head bent with weariness and humiliation at this fresh shame.

'Turn them out, I say.'

There was a dull silence. Then one of the young men, one of the Rogers lads, stepped forward.

'Those are reaper's rights,' he said. His young voice clear as a mellow-toned bell.

'Let's see yours,' I said instantly on the attack. 'Turn them out.'

He clasped his hands over the pocket flaps of his leather breeches.

'Those are reaper's rights,' he said. 'You should not muzzle the ox that treads the corn. We're not oxen in Acre, yet. We're reapers, skilled reapers. And a handful of corn, morn and night, is the reaper's due.'

'Not any more,' I said coldly. 'Not on Wideacre. Turn out your pockets or turn out of your cottage, young Rogers. The choice is yours.'

He glared at me, baffled.

'You're good for us no longer, Miss Beatrice,' he said in despair. 'You held to the old ways once, and now you're worse than a workhouse ganger.'

He pulled up the pocket flaps of the breeches and took a dozen heads of wheat out of one pocket, and a dozen from the other.

'Throw them down,' I ordered. He did so without another word. But he kept his eyes to the ground. I had a fleeting insight that he would not look at me so that I should not see that he, a youth earning a man's wage, was weeping.

'And now the rest of you,' I said without emotion.

One by one they stepped forward like mummers in a play and threw down the heads of wheat until it made a tiny, insignificant pile in the deep rich field before me. A meagre theft. Enough to make little more than a couple of loaves. They would have used it for thickening soup, to stretch the bacon and water a little further. To make some gruel for the children, or some pap for the unweaned baby who cried and cried at a dry breast. Altogether it was little gain for the village, and a loss to the estate of a few pence.

'This is thievery,' I said.

'Reaper's rights!' someone called from the back of the crowd.

'I heard you, Harry Suggett,' I said, raising neither my eyes nor my voice so there was a ripple of fear at my instant identification of the anonymous challenge.

'This is thievery,' I said again quietly. 'You know what Dr Pearce says about thievery: that you will go to hell. You know what the law says about thievery: that you will go to gaol. Now hear what I say about thievery. Anyone I catch with one grain, just one grain, of wheat in their pocket will be handed over to a Justice of the Peace at once, and his or her family, every one of them, will be homeless that same night.'

There was a breath from the crowd, almost a groan, a great 'ooohhh', instantly stifled.

'And there will be no gleaning for Acre until the Chichester workhouse gang have been through the fields gleaning for me first,' I said firmly. 'Only when the field is cleared as I wish may you come to see if there is anything left.'

Again there was the sigh of consternation. But they could say nothing. At the back of the crowd was a woman, a young girl, Sally Rose, a mother but no husband to provide for her and the babe. Her coarse apron was up over her head and she was weeping very quietly.

'Now get to work,' I said gently. 'If there is no thieving, and no cheating, you will not find me unfair.'

At the softer note in my voice their eyes flashed to my face. But they were full of suspicion and unease, and all around the circle hands were clenched in the old sign against black magic.

I stayed out in the field all day, and we still had not cut it all. It was an unbelievable harvest, a miracle of a harvest. The untouched common land grew corn as if it had been longing all those innocent heather-filled years to burst into ripple upon ripple of pale yellow. No one filched wheat as far as I could see, and my eyes were sharp enough to see all around the field, although my mind was sluggish and cold and slow.

When the sun started sinking, late in the afternoon, and the sky was like warm mother-of-pearl with fleecy clouds of pink and the pearly greyness of twilight, I said, 'All right. You can stop now.'

I waited while they cleaned their sickles and stacked them tidily on the wagon. Then they put on their jackets and the women threw shawls over their shoulders for the weary walk home. I watched them file out of the field, all silent, as if they were too tired and too sad for speech. A newly wed couple walked as a pair, with arms around each other, but she rested her head on his shoulder in a gesture that seemed more like sympathy than passion. The older couples walked side by side with a yawning gulf between them that comes from poverty miserably shared that has no ending. A lifetime filled with regrets. I checked that they had fastened the fence carefully behind them, and watched them down the track towards Acre. I kept my horse still until they were out of sight around the corner and I was alone in the glooming wood. Then I set Tobermory to ford the Fenny and cantered along the track towards the drive and my home.

My mind was calm. A good day's work and a yield better than I had a right to expect. If my luck held and I could be the goddess of good weather just once more, just one more year, the gamble would have paid off.

If I could pay off the most pressing creditors entirely and make prompt repayments on other debts, I could restore faith in Wideacre among the money-men. Once they believed that I could service my debts they would plot against me no more. The spreading of a little gold and the harvest of my fertile fields would serve as good security. These men were foxes – they fed off dying animals; they killed only weak prey. They surrounded Wideacre when they thought it would fail. At the first sight of success I would be offered generous credit again.

The balance between utter ruin and total triumph now rested on whether I could get the wheat in with a surly, rebellious, undernourished workforce, before the good weather broke and spoiled the standing crop. If I did, I should draw a bounty payment from Mr Gilby and Wideacre would be secure for at least a year. The wind seemed set fair, the sky a faithful promise of clear weather on the morrow. The chances were good.

My heart was not light, for my heart was a shard of heavy glass these days, and I despaired of ever again feeling it lift with joy at simply being alive. But my mind at least was calm. And my courage was as dauntless as ever.

So I clicked to Tobermory and he lengthened his fast stride while the shadows and the ghosts slid past us and we saw the lights of the house through the dark pillars of tree trunks of the wood.

'Gracious, how late you are,' said Celia, as I clattered into the stable yard. 'Had you forgotten we were going to supper with Mama?'

'Forgive me, Celia,' I said, sliding from the saddle and tossing the reins to a stable lad. 'I had forgotten altogether.'

'I can make your excuses if you wish. But won't you be dull all alone at home?' she asked. The carriage stood waiting for them; Celia scanned my face in the twilight, exquisite in her evening gown, Harry and John immaculate behind her.

'Not at all,' I said, smiling at the three of them without affection. 'How very grand you are! It would take me hours to achieve such a pinnacle of elegance. Leave me in my dirt, and tell me all about it tomorrow.'

'We could send the carriage back for you,' Celia suggested, as she mounted the steps and spread her grey silk dress carefully over the seat.

'No, no,' I said. 'I do indeed assure you. I am tired and longing for my bed. And I must be up early to be in the field with the reapers tomorrow.'

Celia nodded, and Harry bent and kissed my cheek as he passed me.

'Thank you, my dear,' he said. 'Squire of Wideacre!'

I smiled at the jest, but my eyes were wary when John took my hand. 'I'll bid you good day and goodnight too then,' he said civilly. His sharp eyes scanned my face. 'You look tired, Beatrice.'

'I am bone-weary!' I laughed. 'But a hot bath will set me to rights. And a huge supper. I would eat Lady Havering out of house and home if I came.'

John's smile reached his eyes no more than my mirthless performance warmed me.

'Yes,' he said. 'It is indeed a hungry harvest this year.'

He dropped my hand and got into the carriage with Harry and Celia, and the odd little threesome rolled off. I saw nothing more of them that night. After I had scalded the aches out of me with one of my boiling baths, I ate a supper big enough for two, and rolled into my bed like a hedgehog ready for winter. Before I slept the thought of the hidden tears in young Rogers's eyes gave me a strange sharp pain, somewhere beneath my ribs. But then it passed. Nothing touched me much these hot, sad days.

I saw little of Harry, Celia or John the next day, or the next. The August social round was starting, and that meant picnics and fêtes and fairs in Chichester, and midsummer revels and late balls. For me it meant the wheat harvest, and that alone. Indeed the only time I noticed the gay life Celia was leading was when she wanted the coach horses when I had ordered them to be harnessed to an extra wagon. I refused to allow her the horses and Celia, the sweetest summer merrymaker that ever was, renounced the picnic without a frown, and made a summer ball for the children instead. She laughed and danced in the little summerhouse in the rose garden while John strummed a guitar, as if she cared not whether she was at a ball or alone with the children. I could hear her laughter, and her light step on the wooden floorboards while I made up the accounts and readied the wages at my desk. Through the glass I could see my son, and Julia, and Celia, hand-clasped, ringing-a-roses all afternoon.

I felt no regret at being behind the window while they were out in the sunshine and little Richard's knees grew browner and his face bloomed with speckles of freckles like a lapwing's egg. I did not mind seeing them through glass. My work this summer would mean I need never worry again when I opened the drawer that held the bills. Under one heavy glass paperweight were the terrifying quarterly demands from the money-lenders, the mortgage-holders, and the creditors. But under another was a sheet of paper with a list of yields from the wheatfields. And every sun-filled long day, while the workers sweated and swung the sickles, and I sat motionless on Tobermory in the shadow of a hedge if I could find one, Wideacre was growing and ripening its way into breaking even. If the weather held, if the uncut fields yielded equally well, we might even make a tiny profit.

This summer I might be living the life of a despised bailiff, but next summer I should be as blithe and as beloved as Celia. For one season, for one season only, I had to be either indoors counting the gains, or out on the fields watching for treachery. Next summer I would be the prettiest girl in the county again. Next year I should teach Richard to dance with me, not with Celia. Next year I should not feel this sluggish coldness. I should feel joy again, I would be as happy, as easy, as uncomplicated as Celia.

There was a tap on the door and it was Harry, dressed to cut the corn. Instead of his dark silken breeches and waistcoat he had trews of homespun. But he had kept his fine linen shirt, and his polished leather riding boots. He looked like a painter's idea of a farm labourer. He was a cruel travesty of the young golden god who had brought in the harvest only three years ago. His face then had been round and golden, now it was plump and flushed with the heat. His features then were as clear as a Greek statue and now even his profile was blurred, with fleshy cheeks and a double chin. And Harry's lithe young god-like body was now that of an ordinary man, a little older-looking than his years: over-indulged, overweight, under-exercised.

He had lost his early promise of intelligence, too. The Harry who had gone to school had been a scholar with a keen love of books and learning for its own sake. He came home with the sharp wits knocked out of him by the school's corruption and by the discovery of his own perverse taste for pleasure. All he read these days were books on farm machinery, the odd fashionable novel, and occasionally stories about punishment and pain, which he kept in a secret box in the room at the top of the stairs.

He was like our mama. He would always avoid an unpleasant scene or an unpalatable truth; he complained they gave him a pain in his chest. He was a great one for the convenient lie, or for accepting another's untruths rather than braving reality.

But he was also like me. We were both obsessed children. But when I learned that the most important thing in my life was the land, this Wideacre, Harry learned that the most important thing in his life was his pleasure, his indulgences. So he grew fat on rich food and sweet pastries, and red-faced on too much port. And he grew lazy and slobbish about his body for he sought to be fit for punishment – not fit for clear, free, equal love.

Now he dressed like a pauper prince in the travelling theatre and planned to work alongside ill-paid hungry men. I thought of our lads in the fields with enough material for perhaps one decent shirt among them, and sighed at Harry's bright foolish face.

'I thought I'd ride down on the wagon and do some reaping,' he said boyishly. 'They're working on Oak Tree Meadow, aren't they?'

'No,' I said. 'That was two days ago. They're in Three Gate Meadow now. I'll be down later. You can keep an eye open for gleaning if you're there. I told you that I've warned them I'll not stand for it.'

'Very well,' said Harry. 'I shall probably stay till dinner. You might send one of the stable lads down with something for me to eat if I'm not back by three.'

It was in my mind to caution Harry again, but I let it pass. If he chose to play gentleman farmer then it could do little more harm. The bitterness between us and the village could hardly grow more sour. Besides, I reckoned I had taken all the blame for the changes on the land. If Harry stole their hearts and became once more the demigod of the harvest, he might make them less surly. A rather plump deity, this year, and less bronzed and muscled. But if they liked having him in the line, it might make them go a little faster.

Harry took himself off singing what he fondly thought was a country song with many a 'Hey-nonny-no', a sound I have never heard any countryman make, even in his cups. Then the wagon went creaking down the drive with Harry sitting up beside the wagoner and waving goodbye to Celia and the children.

He was back within the hour, his face grim as he drove the wagon past my window. I pushed the letter I was writing aside, and waited. The west-wing stable door banged and I felt the gust of hot wind as Harry came into my room without a knock.

'They insulted me!' he said. His lower lip was trembling with rage and distress. 'They would not speak to me. They would not sing the reaping songs we used to sing. They did not give me a

586

place on the line of reapers. They squeezed me up against the hedge. The girls didn't smile at me. And when I said, "Come on, lads, let's sing," one said, "We're not paid enough to breathe, Squire, let alone sing. You get that flint-eyed sister of yours to pay us the proper rate, the fair rate, and we'll sing like bloody blackbirds to please you. But while we hunger, you can sing to yourself!" '

'Who?' I said swiftly. 'I'll have him off the estate at once.'

'I don't know!' said Harry petulantly. 'I don't know all their names like you do, Beatrice. I can't even tell them apart. They all look the same to me. They don't seem to have proper features. It was one of the older men, but I don't know who. The others would know.'

'And it's likely they'd tell me!' I scoffed. 'Well, what did you do?'

'I came home!' said Harry indignantly. 'What else could I do? If I can't harvest my own fields I might as well come home for dinner. You'd think they'd be glad to have a Squire to work alongside them. If it's the old ways they want, what could be more traditional than that?'

'Odd indeed,' I said drily. 'How far had they got?'

'Oh, I hardly noticed, I was so upset,' said Harry uselessly. 'Really, Beatrice, it is too bad. I can tell you, I shan't go into the fields again this season. You'll have to do the supervision, and if it's too much for you it must be John Brien. It really is quite wrong I should be exposed to such insult.'

'Very well,' I said wearily. 'Now go and have some coffee and biscuits, Harry. You'll feel better after that.'

'But why should they speak to me so?' he demanded, his face working with distress. 'Don't they realize that this is the way the world has to be now?'

'They certainly don't seem to.'

'I get a pain in my chest when I am upset,' Harry said, the sickly-child whine in his voice again. 'I should not be exposed to a scene like that. It is time they realized we are doing our best. When I think of all the work we provide for them. And the charity too! There's Celia spending pounds every week on soups and bread for the poor. And this harvest dinner too! A pretty penny that will cost. And no thanks for it, you know, Beatrice!'

'Harvest dinner?' I said sharply. 'There is to be no harvest dinner this year.'

Harry looked blankly at me. 'Celia is organizing one,' he said. 'You asked her to make the arrangements, she said. It's to be at the mill, once the last field is cut, and they bring the last wagon in, as usual.'

'No!' I said aghast. 'Harry, it cannot be! Bill Green himself faces ruin and he will hardly welcome merrymakers at the mill. It will be the Christmas party over again. We cannot tell what will happen! Besides, it is hardly bringing the harvest home when we are merely storing it, and threshing it at the mill and Mr Gilby's wagons will come and take every grain of it out of the county!'

'Well, it's all arranged, Beatrice,' said Harry awkwardly. 'And I told all the people about it today, before they would not let me reap. I suppose it would only make everything worse if we said now that it would not take place.'

I scowled dreadfully. 'I never meant Celia to take me seriously,' I said. 'It will have to be cancelled.'

'As you wish,' said Harry uncertainly. 'But everything is prepared, and everyone seems to be planning to come. It might be easier to go through with it than to cancel outright.'

I nibbled the tip of my finger, lost in thought.

'Oh, very well,' I said. 'If it is all planned, and Miller Green has not refused, I suppose it should go ahead. But it is odd, midway between the old ways and the new like this.'

'Perhaps when they have brought the corn in they will all cheer up and have a good party,' Harry said witlessly. 'Perhaps it will be like that first wonderful summer.'

'I doubt it,' I said. 'One never gets the same summer twice. And Wideacre is all different these days. And you are different. And I would not know myself.' I paused, my voice had sounded so sad. 'Anyway,' I said briskly, 'if it is all planned it will have to go ahead. And we can leave early if there is any unpleasantness.'

Harry went off to change and take coffee, a little soothed, and was able to pour out the tale of his wrongs to Celia's sympathetic ear. But when she, prompted by a hard look from John, suggested that the men would not have been so rude if they had not been in despair, Harry was quickly up on his high ropes.

'Now, Celia,' he said, wagging a plump finger at her. 'You must let Beatrice and me run the land as we see fit. If they have to tighten their belts in Acre for a few days that will do no great harm. It will give them an appetite for your harvest supper! Beatrice and I know best on this.'

Celia opened her mouth to reply, but then thought better of it. She shot a swift glance at John from under her eyelids. They needed nothing more. They understood each other so well. John now took up the debate, knowing, without being told, that Celia could not challenge Harry further than she had done.

'Celia is right, you know, Harry,' said John. He was hiding his distaste of Harry in his anxiety to get Harry to see reason about the land.

'Celia and I have spent much time in Acre recently,' said John. He spoke with his old incisive authority. 'We have set in hand a system so the food we give is distributed first to the families with ill children, then to the old people, and then to the other families in need. But it is evident to me that we can do nothing effective while there is no long-term solution to the problem of poverty on Wideacre.'

'No one denies that!' said Harry. 'It is a hard time for all of us who are dependent on the land.' He took another cake and bit into it with resolution.

'It's not just "hard" in Acre,' John said patiently. 'There will soon be many deaths through starvation if nothing is done. The supply of food we have provided can keep some families going, but there are more of them in need than we can satisfy.'

'That is because they insist on having large families,' I said coldly. 'They bear children with no idea how to support them. All you two have been doing is encouraging them to live in a fool's paradise. While you give them free food they will never understand the way of the real world.'

John shot me a hard look 'This real world of yours, Beatrice,' he said in a tone of detached interest, 'this is the world where you can employ every man in Acre for hundreds of years, and then suddenly refuse to keep any, save two skilled workers, on the wage books?'

I said nothing.

'This real world is one where there is no way of preventing the conception of children and yet the bastards of Quality wear silk and can look forward to inheritances? Yet the legitimate children of the poor go hungry?'

I knew he was thinking of two bastards, two incestuous bastards, in this house. I said nothing again, but I shot a murderous glance at Harry who was licking his fingers and looking at John.

'No wonder they do not understand the real world,' said John, 'for this real world of yours baffles me. I have never been anywhere like Wideacre and I have travelled all around England and Scotland. In less than a year this estate has gone from being one of the most profitable, happiest places in the county. Now it is in the hands of the creditors, and the poor are starving. Which picture is real? The reality you inherited, or this horror you have made?'

'Now, now,' said Harry, blustering after catching my look. 'It is no use blaming Beatrice simply because we now farm in the way of everyone else. Of course we farm for maximum profit. Beatrice has simply employed the obvious methods.'

'It seems to me that there is a choice,' said John. He was still infuriatingly cool, as if he were conducting a debate at his university chambers. I walked to the fireplace, leaned one arm along the cool mantelpiece and watched him.

'There is the choice between saying the important thing in life is to make as much money as possible and saying the important thing is trying to live without abusing other people. Perhaps even to try to make their lives a little better. You and Beatrice – forgive me, Harry – seem to be committed to profit at any price. I find I don't admire that.'

John's look at Harry and me was like a lance on a gangrenous wound. He made me feel filthy. I gave an affected sigh.

'Really, John, for a nabob's son your moral obligations to profit sit rather oddly! You can enjoy the luxury of a conscience because someone else did the dirty work of earning the wealth for you. You were born and bred to a massive fortune. It is easy enough for you to despise wealth.'

'I *had* so much,' he corrected me, a gleam in his eyes. 'You had better pray I do despise wealth, Beatrice. For I have my wealth no longer.'

Celia leaped to her feet, then checked herself. She had been about to run from the room but she hesitated and turned to Harry.

'We all seem to be talking about different things and even quarrelling,' she said sadly. 'But while we talk things get worse and worse in Acre. Harry, I do implore you to stop this headlong dash for profit and at least give the poor the chance to buy Wideacre wheat at a proper price.

'We all know that forestalling the market is wrong. Your papa never did it. You promised that you would never do it. Please, please, sell the wheat to the village.'

'Now, Celia!' said Harry, falling back on the reliable weapon of a loud-voiced bluster. 'Are you accusing me of breaking my word? Are you challenging my honour?'

'Oh, no!' she said. 'But . . .'

'That's enough!' said Harry, with a bully's abruptness. 'Beatrice is running the land as we see fit. And I shall go harvesting another year, when Acre has come out of this fit of the sullens. This conversation is closed.'

Celia dropped her eyes to the coffee jug and I saw a single tear fall like a raindrop on to the silver tray. But she said nothing. And John, after one compassionate glance at her downcast face, said nothing more. I waited until I was sure they were completely silenced and then I went back to my office. I had work to do.

At last the prospects seemed to be brightening. The fields were being cut faster than ever before and I was out every day in a fever of impatience to get the job done.

Not only could I see the chance of a great bounty on the way for Wideacre, and a chance to be free, utterly free, of the creditors but I also felt a storm in the air. It prickled on the horizon. I felt it on my skin. The skies were clear, I could not wish for clearer. But I could feel the clouds massing against me, somewhere over the horizon.

The days were hot, too hot. They had lost their honest summertime heat and were sultry, threatening. Tobermory's neck was streaked with sweat even while he stood in the shade and the flies buzzed ominously low about his head. The men in the field suffered as it became hotter and damper. One day a reaper fainted – Joe Smith, old Giles's son. He fell on his sickle like a fool and the line broke as they ran around him. I rode over. It was a nasty wound, open nearly to the bone.

'I'll send for the Chichester surgeon,' I said generously. 'Margery Thompson can bind it up for now, and I will send for the doctor to stitch it for you.'

Joe looked up at me, white with shock, his dark eyes hazy.

'I'd rather have Dr MacAndrew if I may, Miss Beatrice,' he said humbly.

'Get in the wagon then,' I said with sudden temper. 'It's going up to the Hall. I think your beloved Dr MacAndrew is in. If he's out doing good deeds in Acre you can sit in the stable yard and wait for him. I hope you don't bleed to death while you are waiting.'

And I wheeled Tobermory and trotted back to my patch of shade by the hedge, and watched them help Joe into the wagon. He was in luck, John was in the garden and saw him as soon as the wagon drew up in the stable yard. He treated him for free and with such skill that Joe was out gleaning two days later. Another proof of John's skill. Another reason for them to love him. Another enemy of mine.

I was surrounded by them. I worked all day in a field full of men who hated me and women who feared me. I slept at night with only a door between me and a man who wished for my death. And I woke every dawn to know that somewhere, out on the downs, was another enemy who was planning my death, who was readying himself to come for me.

The weather seemed to hate me. The heat held but there was no wind. The wheat barely rustled before it was cut down. In the hot humid days there was utter silence. The men did not talk in the fields; the women did not sing. Even the little children, twisting the stalks for tying the stooks, played and spoke in whispers. And if I rode Tobermory over towards them, they backed away with silent mouths agape, black stubs of teeth showing, and melted, like diseased fox cubs, into the hedgerow.

Not even the birds sang in the heat. You would think they shared Wideacre's baking despair and were silent for sorrow. Only in the cool ominous dawns and in the uneasy twilight would they start up and their voices sounded eerie, like the whine of a whipped dog.

The light seemed wrong to me, as well. I was coming half to believe that it was my eyes and senses that were deceiving me, tricking me into fearing a storm when I so desperately needed a settled calm. But if I had mistrusted the prickle down my sweaty spine, and the wet smell of the heavy air, I could not be wrong over the brightness of the day. It stung my eyes. It was not the brightest honest yellow heat of a Wideacre midsummer, but something with a sickly dark core. A bluish light, a purple light hung over us. A sun like a red wound in a yellowing sky. When I opened my eyes in the morning I shuddered instinctively as if I had a fever. I dressed in my hot full-skirted habit with no joy. The sky was like an oven above me, and the ground as hard as iron beneath my feet, all the moisture baked from it. The Fenny was shrunk so small I could not hear its ripple from my bedroom window, and when it flowed through Acre it stank with the slops thrown into it, and the cattle fouling it. I too felt desiccated: as dry as an old leaf, or an empty seashell when the smooth little wet animal that lived inside it is dead.

So I hurried the reapers. I was there first in the field every morning, and last to leave every night. I rode them as I would a sluggish horse and they would have kicked out if they had dared. But they could not. Whenever they halted the line to wipe their heads or to rub the stinging sweat from their eyes they would hear me call, 'Reapers, keep moving!' And they would groan and grasp the handle of the sickle – slick with sweat and turning painfully even in their callused hands. They did not murmur against me. They had not even breath enough to curse me. They worked as if they just longed for the whole miserable job to be done, the harvest in, and winter to bring cold starvation and quick death to end it all.

And I sat high on the sweating horse, my face white and strained beneath the cap that cast no shade on my eyes, and knew that longing for myself. I was bone-weary. Tired with days and days of watching and worrying and driving them, and driving myself. And tired with a deep inner sickness that said to me as slowly and as firmly as a funeral bell, 'All for nothing. All for nothing,' as if the words made any sense at all.

But we were nearly done. The stocks were piled in the centre of the field awaiting the wagons, and the men had collapsed, gasping in the airless shade of the hedge. The women and the old people stacking the stooks were nearly finished, and the men watched their bent-backed wives and parents with lack-lustre beaten eyes, without the strength to help them.

Margery Thompson, who had been at the vicarage when John saved Richard's life, had ceased her work already. I watched her under my eyelashes, my attention suddenly sharpened with unease. She had seated herself on the bank by the hedge and was twisting stalks of corn on her lap. It is the tradition on Wideacre that the last stook, the last one of the whole harvest, is a corn-baby, a corn-dolly. Woven by the cleverest old woman, the doll represents the leader of the harvest. Season after season I had loaned my ribbons to make the circle of magic between the harvest and me complete. I had seen a little corn-dolly Beatrice triumphant at the top of the pile of stooks. In the year Harry brought in the harvest the corn-dolly was bawdy, with a scrap of linen for its shirt and a head of wheat between the stalk legs, grotesquely erect, and everyone had roared. Harry had taken that one home, grinning, and hid it from Mama. The corn-dollies they had made for me were pinned on the wall of my office. Proof, if ever I was near forgetting, that the world of papers and debts and business was the pretend life, and the real world was the corn and the goddesses of the fertile earth.

The corn-dolly tradition had slipped from my worried, money-mad mind, but as I watched the old woman's nimble fingers moving so cleverly and so quickly among the stalks I knew a twinge of dread warning me of some fresh disaster, that some magic against me was brewing.

The clouds had come out from hiding at last and were piling up on the horizon like great walls, blocking out the eerie sunlight and making a premature dusk. It had held off long enough to save me. As long as the wagons came safely through, and took Wideacre's corn to the richest market in the world, the rain could pour down and wash Acre and all Wideacre into the Fenny for all I cared. I had done what I set out to do, and I cared little if the storm drowned me.

Tobermory shivered in the breeze, not because it was cold, for it carried no freshness, but it blew like the breath of a threat. It was as hot as if it blew from India with the black magic of distant dangerous places. Margery Thompson had the corn-dolly on her lap and was muttering to it as if she were nursing a baby, and chuckling to herself. The others had finished piling the stooks and were looking at her curiously. The stooks were heaped in an unstable pyramid in the middle of the field, wanting only the corn-dolly to top it off and to mark the end of the harvest.

'There. 'Tis done,' she said, and tossed it high in the air. She threw it accurately and it balanced on the top of the pile. The reapers moved forward, drawn by the old tradition as if they hardly knew what they were doing, their sickles sharp in their hands.

The game was that they stood some distance from the heap and shied their sickles at it. The sickle that stuck in the dolly belonged to Bill Forrester and he walked wearily towards the stooks to claim his prize and bring it to me. But when it was in his hand he flushed scarlet to the roots of his hair and chucked it, like a football, to the man next to him. They tossed the dolly down the line and then one skilful hand, I don't know whose, sent it whirling into the air towards me. Tobermory threw up his head in fright and I tightened one hand on the rein and caught the dolly – faster than thought, which would have warned me to let it fall.

It was not one corn-dolly but two. It was two figures coupled. It was the two-backed beast Mama had seen before the fire. A piece of grey ribbon filched from me was round the neck of one of the dollies, and a scrap of linen to indicate Harry was twisted around the other. The head of wheat that had been such a good bawdy joke four seasons ago was now obscene. The phallic sheath of corn was stuck between the other dolly's straw legs. She was meant to be me; he was meant to be Harry. The secret was out.

Not out as gossip, I thought, shaken to stillness by this horror made from good Wideacre wheat, that seemed to stink in my hand. But out of something sensed. Something as threatening and permeating as woodsmoke. Something as indescribable yet as certain as the feel of thunder on the way. Margery Thompson, the clever old woman, had listened with her inner ear, and made a joke that hit the mark. The truth had come to her despite herself. She had not spoken it of her own free will. She had just smelled the stink of lust and incest that lingered around my skirts, that Celia feared and Mama had sensed. And she had fashioned a horror from good Wideacre wheat to show that everything was wrong.

I tore at the delicate bodies and dropped them to the ground beneath Tobermory's hoofs.

'You disgust me,' I said to the thickening air over their heads. 'You are scum. You deserve to be treated like pigs for you think like swine. The treatment you have had from me has been the best I could do. But now I shall feel nothing, nothing for you. If we are at war then well and good. I shall enclose all the common. Indeed I shall enclose and flatten Acre village itself. I shall clear my land of you altogether. And the good clean land will grow pure without your stinking cottages, and your fearful children, and your dirty minds.'

The men had hunkered down again, and only the women sighed like fir trees when the first breath of a storm moves the feathery tops. But they did not weep or call out. The baking air was draining us all, sucking the strength from us in unpredictable eddies of little hot whirlwinds.

'Now go,' I said. My voice was full of hate but cracked with weariness and the dryness of my tense throat. 'Go. And when I come to the harvest dinner this afternoon remember that the man there who does not doff his cap to me and the woman who fails to curtsy is penniless, homeless, and jobless, from that moment.'

They sighed again like a forest when a woodland fire is taking hold, licking like a lover up the young saplings while the tops of the trees flutter as if to call for help.

I wheeled Tobermory round and left them in the stubble. The wagons were lumbering over the fields towards the pile of stooks and I could see John Brien in the leading cart.

'I'm away to change,' I said. 'I will come down to the mill later.'

'There may be trouble at the harvest dinner,' he said warningly, his strange town face forever fearful on the land, sharp in this early gloaming. His face was greenish yellow from the uneasy storm light. I heard a crackle, sharp as fire, in dry bracken behind me, and his face was suddenly blazing like a white angel as the sheet lightning dropped like a shard of glass on the upper horizon of the downs.

'There is always trouble,' I said wearily. 'We can always arrest some young lads. We can always hang another old man. They can start trouble but we always finish it. I have men from Chichester to guard the corn tonight and till it is threshed. And Mr Gilby will send guards with his wagons. I do not fear Acre's spite. And tomorrow I shall speak with you about expelling them all from Acre and firing the village. I want it no more. I need it no more.'

His weasel eyes glinted at the prospect of violence to the people he despised.

'I shall see you at the mill,' I said. 'Make haste to get this load into the barn. I think the rain will hold off, but when it comes it will be a great storm.'

He nodded and cracked his whip at the horses but he need not have hurried. I was right about the rain. It held off for all of my wearisome ride home when I could scarcely breathe the hot air. I felt as if someone was holding a damp muffler over my mouth and if I could have breathed I would have screamed for help.

Even inside the Hall the light made everything strange. Celia's parlour was an undersea green, and her face was white coral, a drowned virgin. Her eyes were like brown hollows in her head and when she poured my tea her hands were shaking.

'What's the matter, Celia?' I asked.

'I scarcely know,' said Celia. She tried to laugh but the lilt in her voice had a hard edge. John was alert, his eyes on her strained face.

'Are you unwell?' he asked precisely.

'No,' said Celia. 'I suppose it is just this horrid weather. This endless threat of storm that never comes weighs and weighs on me. I feel hot and then shivery. I have been down in Acre today and it feels all wrong there too. Some of the women seemed to be avoiding me. I feel certain that there will be trouble over the grain wagons, Beatrice. The air is full of threat. I feel almost fearful. I feel that something most dreadful is going to happen.'

'It's going to rain, that's what's going to happen,' I said drily, to shake Celia out of her fancies. 'It's going to pour. We had better take the carriage to the harvest dinner and not the landau.'

She nodded. 'Yes,' she said. 'I ordered the coach. One does not have to be as weather-wise as you, Beatrice, to feel this storm coming. I feel like a cat with my fur rubbed all the wrong way. I have felt thus for days. But I fear more than a storm. I fear the mood of Acre.'

'Well, I shall soothe my nerves with a bath and a fresh dress,' I said with pretended indifference. But I knew I had John's eyes on my face, and I knew my eyes were dark with fear at Celia's forebodings. 'And then, I suppose, we will have to go. When did you plan we should be there, Celia? The carts will be unloaded within an hour.'

'As soon as you wish,' she said absently. As she spoke there was a rumble of thunder along the heads of the downs. Another flash, so bright it stabbed our eyes, lit the room with a blaze of blue and then vanished, leaving us blinking in total blackness. Celia laughed at her jump, but her voice had a high note of hysteria.

'I will be quick then,' I said. But I could not move fast. The air was too thick for me. It quivered around me with meanings and resonances with a stink of horror I could not face. I swam through it to the door and tried to smile casually at them. My teeth were bared in an awkward grimace and my eyes were dead and cold. John moved to open the door for me, and his fingers brushed my hand.

'You are icy cold, Beatrice,' he said, his professional interest kindled, but malice in his voice. 'Have you a fever? Or are you, too, afraid of this storm? Do you also feel the tension, the hatred all around us?'

'No,' I said wearily. 'I have been bringing in the corn for what seems like all my life. I have been out in the fields every day. While you two sit in the parlour and plot against me, and drink the tea my labour has paid for, I am out there in the baking sunlight trying to save Wideacre. But I would not expect anyone to understand that.'

'I say, steady on,' said Harry, roused at last from the plate of cakes on the little table before him. 'You know why I cannot help, Beatrice. They pay no mind to me, and I cannot bear insult.'

My lips curved in a disdainful smile. 'No reason why you should, Harry,' I said. 'I go out and bear it for you. For all of you.' In my mind I saw again the obscene dollies and the wheathead cock and the crafty skill of the making, as they seemed to roll over and over with their perverse passion, falling from the stook in the middle of their thrust.

'I am tired,' I said with finality. 'Please excuse me, all of you. I should go and wash my ill-temper away.'

But I should have known better than to hope for decent service while there was a party starting at the mill. Every one of the kitchen staff had taken leave without one word of permission from me. The cook had taken a day off and gone to Chichester with Stride in the gig. Only Lucy was left to serve me and she complained bitterly about every hot water can she had to lug up the two flights of stairs and along three corridors.

'That's enough, Lucy,' I said finally when I felt rested and brave again. 'Now tell me again, who is in the house?'

'Only the valets, Lady Lacey's maid and me,' said Lucy. 'All the others have gone down to the mill. There's a cold collation laid for your dinner.'

I nodded. In the old days the staff shared in every party and feast that the village could dream up. Sometimes they begged permission to borrow the paddock for Wideacre's own sports events. But now the easy uncounting, uncalculating days were past.

'I'll dock them a day's pay,' I said while Lucy draped a towel around my shoulders, unpinned my hair and brushed it in long sweeps. She nodded. Her eyes meeting mine in the mirror were cold.

'I knew you would,' she said. 'They knew you would. So they asked Lady Lacey, and she said they might go.'

I met her gaze with a long hard look that I held until her eyes dropped to her hands.

'Warn them not to push me too far, Lucy,' I said, my voice even. 'I am tired of impertinence in the fields and house. If they push me too far they may be sorry they ever started. There are many servants looking for places, and I no longer have much attachment to people born and bred on Wideacre.'

She kept her eyes on the tumbled silk of my copper hair and brushed it in steady even sweeps. Then she deftly bunched it into one hand and twisted it into a smooth knot on the top of my head.

'Beautiful,' she said grudgingly. I looked at myself in the glass. I was lovely. The days in the field had bronzed me into my usual summer honey and now that the strained weary look had gone from my face I once more looked like a pretty twenty-year-old. The colour was back in my cheeks and there was a dusting of tiny freckles over my nose and upper cheekbones. Against the honey tea of my skin my hazel eyes gleamed greener than ever. My hair, burnished with the sun, was bronze as well as copper, and some of the curls around my face had even been sun-bleached to red-gold.

'Yes,' I said coldly, acknowledging like her the physical perfection of the oval face in the glass.

'I'll wear the green silk,' I said, rising from the glass and dropping the damp towel on the floor for her to stoop and pick up. 'I'm sick of greys and dark colours. And no gentry will be there.'

Lucy opened the wardrobe and shook out the deep green sack dress. A matching green stomacher tied tight at the front and a wide swaying panel shimmered loose at the back.

'Good,' I said, as she slid it over my head and tied the stomacher tight. 'But I cannot breathe in here. Open the window, Lucy.'

She threw open the casement window but the heat and the damp air flowed in like a river of steam from a kettle to scorch the inside of my mouth and nose. Involuntarily I gave a little moan.

'Oh, if only this weather would break,' I said longingly. 'I cannot breathe this air. I cannot move in this heat. Everything is so unbearably heavy all around me!'

Lucy looked at me without sympathy.

'It's affecting the children, too,' she said. 'Master Richard's nurse asked if you would step into the nursery when you were changed. He is fretting and she thinks he may be cutting a tooth.'

I shrugged my shoulders. The fresh silk was already feeling too warm and sticky.

'Ask Mr MacAndrew to go,' I said. 'I have to get ready to go to the mill. Mr MacAndrew will know what to do, and Richard minds him.'

Lucy's eyes met mine and I read her instant condemnation of a woman who would not go to her own child when he was in pain and calling for her.

'Oh, stop, Lucy!' I said wearily. 'Just tell him to go to the nursery at once, and then you come back and powder my hair.'

She went, obediently enough, and I moved to the window to try to breathe. The rose garden was drained of colour. I could not even remember how pretty it used to be before this nightmare light closed in. The green grass of the paddock was grey and ghostly looking. The scarlet roses in the garden looked green and sickly. The belly of the storm was leaning on the rooftop of the house and I looked up to a ceiling of purple clouds as billowing and claustrophobic as a tent. It stretched from the top of the downs to the top of the common without a break, without a chink to admit either light or air. The only light was the great dropping wall of sheet lightning that cracked as if the back of Wideacre had broken in two on the rack of my plans. The white light burned my eyes. I was still dazzled while Lucy powdered my hair and handed me my wrap.

'I'll take nothing. It's too hot,' I said. The merest touch of the pure wool on my fingers had me sweating and itchy.

'You don't look well,' said Lucy coolly. She cared nothing for me now. I could be dying and she would not care.

'I am perfectly well,' I said coldly. 'You may go, Lucy. I shall not want you any more tonight. Are you and the valets and Lady Lacey's maid going down to the mill?'

'If we may,' she said with a hint of insolence in her voice.

'You may,' I said, too weary to challenge her again. I had worn out any affection for me. I had worn out all the love that everyone had felt for me. I was still only a young woman but I had already lived too long. I had enjoyed my best years, the years when I was surrounded with love and everyone adored pretty Miss Beatrice. Now I was old and tired and longing for sleep. I swept past her, my silk train hushing behind me and rippling like a flood of green poison all the way down the stairs. I had lost my quick easy stride; I felt less like a pretty girl than a snail with its sticky trail over everything it touches.

They were waiting for me in the hall and the carriage was at the door. Harry, portly and pompous in his grey silk with a black

601

embroidered waistcoat and silver grey stockings. Celia, drained of colour in a navy silk dress, which made her strained face haggard in the yellowish storm light. John, handsome and meticulous as ever, and glowing with the knowledge that none of this could go on for much longer; that, like the storm, something was certain to break. Their faces turned to me as I came through the west-wing door and, in a sudden spurt of rebellion, I said to myself in horror, 'My God! What have I done? I have planned my life and waded through blood; I have wilfully killed and accidentally killed and gone on and on with my heart growing harder and colder, so that this useless trio should live here in wealth and ease with clean consciences. So that I can see them every dreary day for the rest of my life. So that my long struggle should have as its goal seeing Harry, Celia and John every day until I die.'

I mastered my face with an effort and put my fingers to my forehead to smooth out the skin and the sudden expression of despair from my face.

'I am sorry to have kept you waiting,' I said. 'Shall we go?'

Only Coachman Ben was there to drive us. The footmen were down at the mill released by dear Celia for a night out with the villagers. So John pulled in the steps and shut the door. The rocking of the carriage in the eerie light reminded me of my sickness at sea, and I pressed my lips together. Celia and John spoke in an undertone about the failure of their charity to make any real difference to Acre, and I heard again the rising note of panic in Celia's voice when she said privately to John, 'Whatever we do is simply not enough. However much we spend we seem only to delay a crisis. We solve nothing, and winter is coming.'

Her anxious voice set my teeth on edge and her words made me tense with foreboding. I bit my lips to keep my anger quiet.

The carriage rolled in the mill yard and a hundred pinched faces, greenish in the storm light, turned towards us. Celia alighted first, and there was a gentle murmur of called greetings for her. I came down the steps into a stony silence as cold as the millpond, but every woman dropped into a curtsy and every man doffed his cap or pulled his forelock. John was greeted with a few 'Good days', but Harry's bluff shout, 'Good day! Good harvesting!' fell into an icy well of resentful silence.

'Better get it over and done with,' he said in a loud undertone to Celia, easing a finger under his tight stock.

'Very well,' she said. 'Will you say grace?'

Harry looked abashed but strode over to the trestle table and waited until everyone was settled on a bench. Then he gabbled a string of Latin, which he may have understood once, and waved to Mrs Green at the kitchen door.

She marched out, her face set, carrying shoulder-high the great tray of sliced ham and chicken and beef, and crashed it on the table. Behind her came the Wideacre kitchenmaids all carrying great platters of cheeses and, behind them, the footmen with great loaves of our golden bread. There was no ripple of pleasure at the sight, no cheers as the enormous amounts were laid on the table. The heart was out of Wideacre. They were hungry; they were starving. And they had forgotten the taste of meat. There was no fighting. They were too exhausted to fight. Their good behaviour was partly a courtesy to Celia and John, but also because they had gone beyond fighting. They were resigned now to dying of hunger together, and there was no one sufficiently angry or sufficiently hopeful to grab his neighbour's portion. The natural leaders of the village – old Tyacke and the three lads – were gone. All there was left were the miserable poor, enduring their hunger in silence. Expecting death this winter, and fearing it no more. They were so hungry – it gave me a shiver to see – they could not eat.

At the Christmas party they had scrambled for food, clawing like savages, as wild as hungry animals. But now at the harvest dinner the sharp new hunger had gone from them. They could eat little or nothing. They had forgotten how to relish food; the tasty cheese and the sweet-cured ham had lost their savour. And their poor shrunk bellies could manage proper amounts of food no more. They were used to famine. And they could eat only little.

Instead they shamelessly folded great doorstep slices of bread and meat and cheese and stuffed wedges of food in every pocket and handy corner of their clothes. They took food like squirrels preparing for a hard winter – in enormous amounts. But even then they did not grab. They helped each other now, and the frailest older people were given their share by young men whose

603

own cheeks were pinched and white. Saddest of all was the way that these old people in their turn pressed extra pieces of meat on the mothers with small children. One girl, with a look of blank despair on her face, was pregnant, and with tender courtesy her neighbours on either side of the bench ensured she had wrapped up meat and cheese in her kerchief to take with her. They no longer grabbed food from each other's mouths. They had learned the discipline of hunger, and they had been shocked by wintertime deaths. Now they shared, even when their own bellies rumbled and pained them.

The ominous dark sky billowed overhead but here on the lower ground we could not even feel the slight breeze that had blown at the Hall. We could see its passing in the way the treetops swayed and the pine trees moaned as it grew stronger. Then there was a crash like a thousand trees falling and the scene was suddenly frozen in a snowy glare and the thunder roared at us. Celia beside me suddenly swayed, and grabbed my arm.

'I can't stand this,' she gasped. John instantly had an arm around her waist supporting her.

'Get her away!' he said abruptly to Harry, and supported Celia the few steps to the carriage. Coachman Ben, a hearty eater at the Hall kitchen, had not joined his hungry family at the table but came out of the purple shadows when he saw we were ready to leave.

'We will be off then!' said Harry, his voice like a foghorn above the rising wind. 'We will say goodnight, and thank you for your labours.'

I stepped into the carriage and sat beside Celia. Her hands were as cold as ice and she kept twisting them in her lap as if she were trying to pull invisible rings off her fingers. She shuddered every now and then, and gasped. I thought then that we might have got away with it, but I had forgotten Harry's infallible instinct for doing the wrong thing.

He climbed into the carriage and then turned to call from the open door.

'So Wideacre is not so bad, hey?' he shouted. 'There's not many estates left where they still bring the harvest in with a free dinner, you know!'

The rising wind moaned and the muffled voices moaned with

it. The hollow hungry despairing eyes lifted from the table and fixed themselves on Harry at the steps of the carriage, and me at the window as if they could burn us up with the hatred of their gaze.

'What about the corn?' yelled one voice, and the rabble's chorus of hate swelled beneath it.

'Wideacre grown should be Wideacre sold, Wideacre milled, Wideacre fed!' they rumbled. At the kitchen door of the mill I saw Miller Green appear and his eyes met mine in a message of cold hatred.

Harry hesitated, as if to shout down the rising hum of voices, but I tweaked his jacket and said quickly, 'Harry come!' and he pulled in the steps and slammed the door. The carriage tipped as he slumped back in his seat opposite me. Celia was gasping like a beached salmon and her face was ashen in the darkness of the coach.

'I cannot stand it,' she said again.

'What's the matter?' I asked, my voice arid.

'I cannot stand living like this any longer,' she said. Her eyes were burning. She grabbed my hand and held it so hard she hurt me.

'I will not live like this,' she said. 'These people are dying of hunger. The children are starving and their arms and legs are like sticks. I cannot eat in the Hall while there is starvation in the village.'

The coach was wheeling around; we would soon be away. There was another flash of lightning and every detail of the death's-head feast was as bright as white noon. They were still seated at the trestle and every great platter of food had been cleared; there was not even a crumb left behind. In one corner of the yard a hungry child was retching desperately, choked on his first decent meal in half a year. His mother was holding the little heaving body, tears pouring down her face. The young girls in stained and ragged linen were not flirting with the lads. They had laid their dirty weary heads on the table, or were staring dully into space as if they had no interest in courtship and love, with their hunger and the fear of hunger a hollow under their ribs.

It had taken less than a year to turn the thriving, jolly, noisy, courting, wedding, bedding village of Acre into a graveyard for the walking dead with hollow eyes and sad faces. They looked ready for the workhouse. They looked like labourers fit for the new workhouses where they like quick fingers, no strength, but a dogged determination to get through the day, to collect the penny to buy a crust of loaf and some gin to get through another despairing night.

These were the walking dead from Harry's great vision of the future. I had known it would be like this. I had killed them.

The carriage rolled forward, and another flash of lightning cracked over our heads and made the horses shy. The villagers saw my white face staring from the window, and Harry's fat head near mine. They saw the horror but no pity in my eyes. From the back of the yard I saw an arm swing and I jerked back from the window in an instinctive reaction. The stone smashed into the glass and splinters and shards shattered into the coach like ice. Celia's fine silk and mine were sprinkled with splinters of glass and John and Harry's boots crunched on the shards on the floor of the coach.

A scratch on the back of my hand welled red, and I dabbed at it with a ribbon, feeling a sliver of glass dig deep into the cut, but feeling no pain.

Neither pain nor resentment, while the coachman whipped up the frightened animals and Harry exploded with rage. Celia hid her face in her hands and wept like a comfortless child. The carriage swayed, the horses near bolting in their fright at the thunder and the wind lashing the trees. Over the noise of the rumble of wheels was the louder rumble of thunder as it rolled around the top of the downs, but still it did not rain. Through the jagged hole of the window hot air blew in my face making me gasp with the stifling heat of it.

'If only it would rain,' I said absently.

'Rain!' Celia cried out, and her gentle voice was harsh. 'I wish it would rain a flood and sweep the whole of this cruel country away and Wideacre with it!'

'I say!' said Harry feebly. 'You're upset, Celia, and no wonder! Villains they are! I'll have the whole village cleared! I'll not have them on my land!'

Celia turned on him, her eyes blazing. 'It is we who are the villains, not they!' she said, half stammering in her rage. 'How could you, how *could* you, have let such a life come about? On your own land, Harry! We treat the poor worse than a northern coal baron! We feed the horses in our stables with more care than those little children are fed! We should be the ones who are chased by soldiers in the wood and hanged. It should be us who go hungry, for it is the four of us who let this plague of unhappiness loose on Wideacre. John and I are to blame as well as you, for we stood by and tried to help in foolish little ways. But it is you and Beatrice who are most at fault, Harry, for you should never have farmed in this way that kills people. You are ploughing lives into Wideacre, not seaweed. You are sowing our downfall, not seeds. And I will not have it!'

The carriage stopped outside the Hall and Celia pushed past me, swung open the door and jumped down in a shower of glass. I would have grasped Harry's hand for a few urgent words but John swept him in after Celia and there was no time to prompt him.

'We farm Wideacre in the only way there is to produce a good yield,' said Harry defensively, standing before the empty grate of the parlour. The thunder rumbled outside in a nightmare contradiction, half drowning his words.

'Then we must content ourselves with less yield,' said Celia sharply. She was riding the storm of her anger. Her moral force was based on her certainty of being right. Celia never spoke as a stratagem; she only ever spoke out when her stern, unswerving conscience told her she must.

'Yields are hardly a matter for you, my dear,' said Harry, with a warning note in his voice.

'They are when the carriage is stoned with me inside!' Celia retorted, her colour blazing in her cheeks. 'They certainly are when I cannot pray in my parish church because behind me there are hungry people, dying people, facing starvation.'

'Now!' said Harry, raising his voice. 'Now, I won't have this, Celia.'

I nodded at John. 'Come,' I said, and turned towards the door.

'Oh, no,' said John not moving. 'This is not a private affair between Harry and Celia that they should settle in privacy. This is an issue that concerns us all. Like Celia I cannot live here while this starvation goes on. Another winter is coming, and the last one took famine within a hair's breadth of that village. I won't leave this room until we have decided to restore the common plots for vegetables and you have agreed to open up the common land again.'

'What do you know about farming?' I demanded rudely. 'Either of you! All you have seen, John, have been the Edinburgh drying greens; and all you know, Celia, is the inside of your parlour. If we do not farm in this way we will lose Wideacre!' I stopped on a shaky half-laugh as a great crack of lightning lit up the room and showed me Harry's aghast face.

'I am not exaggerating,' I said. 'We are desperately over-stretched and we have to keep on this course or we will lose all. No Wideacre for us, no Wideacre for Julia. The poor carry the brunt of it, of course they do. The poor always do. But once the profits of this season come in we will be able to ease the burden a little. And then yearly it will get better.'

'No,' said Celia. She was standing by the window, the sky livid behind her, the black clouds underlined with the garish orange light of the setting sun.

'This is not a time for gradual improvements,' she said. 'We must change completely. It is not right that we should eat well at table while people starve on our land so that we can grow rich. It is not Christian, it is not right, that there should be such a great gulf between rich and poor. I will not accept that this is the way it has to be. You are a tyrant on Wideacre, Beatrice; you can decide absolutely how things are to be. But you may not decide that the poor starve – I will not allow it!'

'I manage Wideacre in the only way there is to increase yields . . .' I started but Celia's voice broke in over mine, clear and sharp with her anger.

'You do not manage Wideacre, Beatrice,' she said, and her voice was full of scorn and disdain. 'You ruin it. You ruin everything you love. You are a wrecker. I have loved you and trusted you and I was mistaken in you. You adored Wideacre but you have destroyed every good thing about it. You loved the meadows and they are gone. You loved the woods and they are sold or uprooted. You loved the downs and your ploughs are going higher and higher. You are a wrecker and you destroy the very things you work for.' Her eyes flickered from me to John and I knew she was also thinking of how I had tried to wreck him too, the man I loved.

I took a deep breath that sounded like a harsh groan as she held up this hard mirror to my life. And I knew she was right.

'I will not live with you while you persist in this destruction,' she said as cool as a judge with a hanging sentence in mind. 'I will not permit you to destroy the morality of our life by forcing us to be party to this horror. I will not attack the people who look to us to shield them. I will not starve people who have no defence.'

She stopped and in the silence Harry's eyes went from her flushed face to my white one. But he said nothing. I bit the inside of my cheeks to steady my breathing and then I drew breath to defeat her. I had words, I had power. I could beat her down.

But John's sharp eyes had been on me all the time, and he spoke first.

'You are wrong, Celia,' he said, and I quickly glanced at him, an unexpected ally. 'You are wrong,' he said. His eyes were bright, and very sharp on my face. 'They do have a defender,' he said slowly, watching me. His emphasis surprised Celia and she was looking at me too. Even Harry was alerted.

'They do have a defender,' said John again. 'The Culler is on Wideacre.'

'No!' I said, and I crossed the room with two quick strides and took John's lapels in a hard grip, scanning his face, wide-eyed.

'It is not true,' I said. 'You are trying to torture me, as I tormented you. It is a lie.'

John's look at me was empty of any compassion. 'No, Beatrice,' he said. 'The Culler is on Wideacre. I heard them say so tonight. Who is he? And why is he such a terror to you?'

I half closed my eyes and near swooned. John put two ungentle hands under my elbows to support me and scanned my white face with his hard, questioning gaze. I opened my eyes to look past him, to the familiar safe landscape of my home.

And then I saw them.

Two black dogs in the rose garden. They were still, as still as

609

well-trained keeper's dogs when he has ordered them to stay and has an eye on them from some dark shadow. The spaniel was sitting, ears cocked, eyes bright on the house, black as mourning velvet. The black lurcher was lying, head up like some heraldic monster, watching the house, watching me.

'He is here,' I said, and took one staggering step to the chair by the fire before my legs gave way and I sank into it. A hard hand on my shoulder twisted me around and I raised my dazed eyes to see Celia bending over me. But her touch was hard, and her eyes were cold.

'Who is he?' she said. I could hear a little insistent echo of the question over and over again, which said 'Who is he?' 'Who is he?' 'Who is he?' in my frightened whirling head.

'Is he coming for Julia?' she asked. Her hard little hand on my shoulder tightened and she half shook me in her own fear. 'Is he coming for Julia?'

I gazed blankly at her. I could scarcely remember who Julia was. In the grip of my own terror all I could see were the two dogs with their eyes fixed on the parlour window, waiting for their master to send them in like a hunting pack.

'Is he Julia's father? Is he coming for her?' Celia's voice, sharp, with an edge of hysteria, still could not get through to me.

'Yes,' I said, neither knowing nor caring what I was saying. 'Yes, yes.'

Celia gasped as if I had slapped her, and stretched a hand to John.

'What?' said Harry, utterly bemused. His secure world was shattering too fast. His life was being undermined from too many sources at once. 'What are you all talking about? I am Julia's father.'

'No,' said Celia dully, one hand held by John, tears pouring down her cheeks. 'This is just more of your sister's wreckage, Harry. Beatrice cheated you, and she cheated me. I am not Julia's mother. She is Beatrice's child. And now her father is coming for her.'

Harry's frightened eyes turned on me.

'Beatrice?' he said, as if he meant to call for his mother. 'Beatrice, tell me, this is none of it true?'

'It is true,' I said. I was in my own private hell and I cared not

610

who else plunged into their own nightmares. 'Julia is my child and the Culler is her father.'

'And who is the Culler?' asked John, following the thread through the tortuous maze of lies. 'Who is this Culler?'

I met Harry's eyes.

'The gamekeeper's lad,' I said. Celia and John looked to Harry for it meant nothing to them. There was a second while Harry's face was blank and then his pitiful confusion was replaced with a look of pure terror.

'He is coming for us?' he said. 'He is coming for you? He is coming to get Julia?' The tone of terror in his voice tipped Celia over the border from fear to panic.

'I am going,' she said. 'I am leaving here and taking the children at once.'

I slumped back in the chair. It was all wrecked, as Celia had said it was. The maze was falling in, and the Culler's dogs waited in my garden.

'I'll harness the horses,' said John and he left the room without another glance at me. Questions were still burning in his mind, but one look at Celia's aghast face had sent him running to save her from the horror that I knew, and that Harry confirmed.

John had been waiting for this moment, when the maze would be wrecked and he would pull Celia and the children she loved out into safety. He thought I lied about Julia's father. He thought I lied when I confirmed Celia's long secret fear that one day the mysterious father would come to snatch Julia from her. But he knew the sound of terror in my voice, and he knew the world of Wideacre was crumbling around us. And all he cared for was that the innocent should be out of the wreckage when the world caved in.

Harry had turned his head into the stone mantelpiece and was weeping in silence. He was like a child left alone among a ruin.

Celia left the room without another word. I heard her run up the stairs to Julia's nursery, and then come down slowly, carefully, carrying the sleeping child. Then I heard the door of the west wing bang as she went for Richard. I went into the hall like a sleepwalker.

Harry shambled after me, still weeping.

John came in from the stables; he took Richard from Celia and she turned to pick up Julia from the sofa. My son had not even stirred. He slept wrapped in a blanket, his dark lashes on his pink cheeks, one thumb firmly embedded in his sweet pursed mouth. Now and then he sucked noisily and settled into sleep again. I put my nose to his sweet-smelling forehead and felt the soft tickle of the baby hair. But I felt nothing, nothing, nothing, in my icy private well of fear.

John's eyes on my face were curious.

'No,' he said, as if agreeing with something I had said. 'There is nothing left for you, is there, Beatrice? It is all gone.'

I straightened and looked coldly at him. Nothing could touch me now. I was lost.

Celia walked past me without a word, without even a backward glance, and Harry followed her like a good foal his dam. He was blind and deaf and dumb with shock, all he could do was follow in Celia's small determined footsteps until his own haze of horror lifted. Then my husband walked past me without a word. The door to the west wing clicked; I heard them go down the corridor to the stable door. Then the stable door banged in the keening wind. I was alone.

The hall was almost as black as nighttime in the gloom from the storm, but I feared no shadows. The terror I had hidden in my mind for year after year after year was here. It no longer threatened me as some horror for the future. It was here and I could face it. Half blind, half dazed with shock, I at least was free of a fear of ghosts, of shadows that moved, of dreams that could terrorize me. My worst fears, my utter terror, were all coming for me. I need fear the unknown no more.

And the house, my lovely Wideacre, was at last mine. Mine alone. Never before had I been utterly alone in the house like an insect in the heart of a deep sweet-smelling rose. Never before had there been silence from the kitchen quarters, silence from the bedrooms, silence from the parlour. Not a sound. Nothing. No one was here but me. I was the only person in the Hall, the only person on the land. And my ownership was undisputed.

I walked around the Hall like a woman in a trance. I touched the carved newel post of the staircase, fingered the intricate carvings, which showed corn, a bag of fleeces, a cow in calf, all the great easy fertile wealth of Wideacre. I crossed to smooth the polished top of a straddle-legged table with the flat of my hand. The wood was warm and gentle, good to stroke. A silver bowl of flowers stood on the table, the drooped heads of the roses gazing at their own pale reflection in the polished top. I touched them gently with one fingertip and the soft petals showered off the flower heads leaving the cluster of dusty stamens. I thought of what Celia had said: 'You are a wrecker, Beatrice.' And I smiled without humour, and turned away.

The parlour doorknob was a little miracle of round warmth under my cupped palm. The panels smooth and cool to my forehead. I ran my fingers along the stone mantelpiece and felt the sweet rough texture of Wideacre sandstone. I touched the delicate pretty china Celia had brought back from France, and the rose-pink pebble I had once found in the Fenny that I had insisted should be displayed on the mantelpiece. Some conscientious parlourmaid had put the little china owl on the mantelpiece with the other porcelain. I touched it now without fear. He was coming for me. He would be here soon. I need fear no more secret messages.

I rubbed the back of my hand along the smooth brocade of the winged chair, the one I like to sit in to watch the fire. And I tinkled the keys of the piano – a ghostly sound in the silent house. Then I left the parlour and went through the hall, trailing my fingers in the bowl of pot-pourri and catching up a handful of dried flower petals as I passed. I went to my office. To my own special safe room. The fire was laid but not lit and the room was dark. I walked in, as if it were an ordinary day, with a steady heart and a light step. I was just moving a little more slowly than normal. I was thinking a little more slowly. And I could see nothing clearly. There was a mist around the periphery of my vision that meant I could see nothing except what was immediately before me. I was in a long, long tunnel. And I did not know where it was taking me.

Before I lit the candles I went to the window. The storm had rolled along the head of the downs and was no longer close to the house. A fitful light showed through the breaks in the storm-clouds; the rose garden was empty. The Culler's dogs had gone. He had been here to see the house, perhaps to see who was there and who had fled. He would know I was here alone. He would know I was awaiting him. He would know that I was aware of his nearness, as he was of mine. I sighed, as if that knowledge made me content, then I turned from the window and lit the candles and set a spill to the fire, for the room felt damp. I pulled down a cushion from one of the chairs and sat myself before it and watched the logs burning. I was in no hurry. My life no longer required planning. Tonight would go according to his plan, and I need, at long last, do nothing.

20

The dream started at once, I think.

I know, I know it was but a dream. But some real days have seemed less real than those moments. Every day of this weary harvest has seemed less real than this dream. As I gazed blank-eyed into the fire I heard a noise unlike the thunder rolling. I heard a window creak. The light from the stormy cloud-chased sky was blocked and the room went utterly black for someone had blocked out the light as he climbed through the window. I turned my head languidly, but I did not call for help. I opened my mouth but I could not scream. I could only freeze, half sitting, half sprawled, and wait for what was coming to me.

He came silent to me and he pushed the chair from behind my shoulders so I lay flat on the floor. I trembled as if his very touch was an icy wind, but I did not move. Only my eyes blinked and gazed in a gleam of moonlight.

He kissed my collarbone in the hollow at the base of my neck. He opened my gown and kissed one breast, the nipple as hard as a blackberry, and then he kissed the other. I found my voice but I only made a soft moan of longing. I found I could move, but my hand did not reach for a weapon but went straight to him, and felt his familiar, his beloved hardness. Hard as bone.

He brushed my hand away like a troublesome fly, and slid his face down my body, over the curve of my smooth, well-fed belly, and then he took me in his mouth.

He was not gentle. He did not kiss. He did not lick. He sank his teeth into me as if he was starving for meat and he bit deep until his teeth ground on the core of my body and closed on my most private, most secret, flesh.

I screamed then, but there was no sound. And it was not a scream of pain, but of pain and pleasure, shock and delight, and a certain terrified acceptance of my fate. He sucked at me, his cheeks hollowed. He rubbed his face against me, his stubble scratching the inside of my gripping thighs. I tried, with all my will, to lie passive against this outrageous dream-like assault but when his teeth closed on me again and again in little biting thrusts, I moaned as if I were going mad and put both hands down to his head to force his face into me. His tongue slid inside me in a teasing thrust, and I cried out in lust. Then my hands closed on his head and clenched in his hair and I held his cheating, wicked curly head still and rubbed myself against him as hard as if he were the carved newel post on the stairs. He shook his head when he needed to breathe, and I pulled his hair to clamp him closer back to me. Then in one agonizing second after another he closed his jaw and his lower teeth scraped the soaked aching length of me and I shuddered on a deep hoarse cry of pain and said, 'Ralph.'

Then I opened my eyes and I was alone.

Alone.

Always alone.

It was nearly dawn. The candles had burned out. The storm-torn sky was getting lighter but the storm was still unsated. It had ringed the downs and was coming back towards me. I felt the tension in the air like a bruise on scalded skin. I did not know if I had been dreaming.

The casement window was open. It had been on the latch last night. I knew it. I knew that. But it had been a stormy night; it could have rattled free. Or Ralph could have slid a thin blade beneath the catch and flicked it open. He could have swung a leg over the window sill and stepped down into the room. He could have stepped . . .?

I cried out. The Ralph of last night had been whole – surely? I could remember his hard thighs when I rubbed my hands against him. But below his knees? I could not remember. I had not thought. Once his hard, sharp, fox's teeth had closed on me I had thought of nothing except his name tolling in my head like a firebell, and his thick black curls clenched in my grabbing, desperate hands.

'Ralph.'

I went to the window, to the open casement creaking on a hinge, and looked towards the high hills of the downs. Some conviction, some need, as blinding as the distant lightning, was shattering the southern horizon, was growing on me.

'Ralph.'

It had all gone wrong since I lost him.

I ached. Not just the pain I had awoken with, of bruises in my softest, wettest, most vulnerable flesh. But the pain beneath my ribs, which I had lived with so long that I had thought it my nature to long and long and long until I was sick and exhausted with my unfulfilled passion. Until I grew dull and tired. Until every season was the same, until every plan was hollow, until every road led nowhere, and all there was was the absence of Ralph, and my lack of him, and my unswerving, unceasing, passion for him.

And now, they said, he was coming.

It had been the same for him. I knew. Not as a pretty woman knows, with the tactics of courtship, the easily broken promises, and easily told lies. It had been the same for him because we were two halves of a trap. We could only snap together. And even that death-toothed real trap could break only his legs, could break nothing between us. He was mine even though I had tried to kill him. He was mine even though I had sliced him in two as neatly as one slices a peach. He was mine even if he came to murder me.

And I would be his.

The window suddenly banged beside me and my eyes lost their impassioned haziness, and focused on the drive. I could see, I thought I could see, a glimmer of torches moving in a line under the shadows of the trees. They were coming up the drive. I was quite calm. Ralph, or a dream of Ralph, had lain with me and I was finished with longing and clinging to life and hoping to escape him. I was the child Beatrice again, who feared nothing.

I turned to the mirror over the fireplace, lit only by the flashes of lightning, and unpinned my hair, shook out the powder, and let it sweep in a great glorious wave of copper and brass down over my shoulders nearly to my waist, as I had worn it when I was a child playing with another child in the woods of Wideacre. I smiled into my own reflection. If I had been superstitious, or if there had been any sense left in me, I should have made the sign of witchcraft against myself when I saw that smile in the mirror. My eyes had a blank greenness, rinsed of humanity. My smile was that of a madwoman. My face's pale clear loveliness was so utterly corrupted from within that it was the face of a fallen angel, of one who has supped with a devil and used no spoon. I looked like a she-devil, as lovely as an angel from heaven but with eyes as green as a cat's, as green as jade, as green as a snake's. I felt an insane ripple of joy in my heart. The distant rumble of thunder sounded more like the salute for a queen than a warning.

The thunder was coming nearer.

I could smell rain on the wind, which was now cold. A good night wind, cool with a smell of rain falling on distant meadows. A cleansing rain to wash this pain and confusion away. Great heavy drops of rain to wash the wreckage clean.

The rain was coming.

And so was Ralph.

I walked to the window seat, my gown shimmering in the repeated flashes of lightning. It was a night for demons. I could see some of the torches before they were hidden by the sharp bend of the drive, just before the house. They would be here soon. The lightning flashed again and I settled in the window seat where the casement opens like a tall door on to the terrace. I would see them rounding the bend from here.

The torchlight bobbed as they came up the drive. Then the lightning flash split Wideacre's sky in two with a great *crack-crack!* First, I saw his dogs, black as devils: one black lurcher, one black water-spaniel. One before, and one behind him, scouting as they had learned to do when he walked in the woods after poachers. The lurcher was in front, its black coat shiny with the rain, which was lashing down like black silver bolts from a low black sky.

Then I saw him.

They had not lied when they had told me about him. The horse was high, a thoroughbred and strong. Black without a single fleck of white on it. Utterly black. Black mane, black head, black eye, black nostrils. And toweringly high. Bigger even than Tobermory. And atop it 'the Culler', sitting 'so oddly'. His legs stopped short at the knees, but he rode like one accustomed to holding his seat. He rode like a lord, one hand on the reins, the other clenched on his hip, holding something. Something I could not see. My Ralph with his black curls all wet with rain.

A shaft of lightning made the scene noontime bright and showed my white face at the window. The dogs scouted up the terrace as if they were sniffing out a witch, and the lurcher came without a check to my window, and paused, and scratched, and whined. Then it reared up on its hind legs, and scrabbled at the window, and barked, bayed, at me.

And Ralph turned his head.

He saw me.

His great horse reared and leaped up to the terrace as if it were no more than a grassy bank. When the lightning crashed again and the thunder bellowed, Ralph was between me and the light and his body shielded my eyes.

I climbed up on the window seat like a girl slipping out to greet her lover. I swung open the window and stepped out. The rain was sheeting down in great thick rods, a wall of water. I gasped as it poured on my head. I was soaked in seconds, my silk gown a second skin.

Beyond Ralph the mob had stopped, watchful, fearful. The torches hissed, sizzling in the rain, paled by the great blinding flashes. I was deaf with the barrel-rolling thunderclaps, and blinded by the light, but my eyes were on Ralph's face and his smile, as I walked towards him, my head high, right up to the great horse's head. The lightning split the sky and shone bright on the knife in his hand. His gamekeeper's knife, for slitting the throats of cornered deer.

I smiled and in the sharp blue light he saw my eyes gleam as he leaned down to me, as if he would catch me up to him, and hold me, and hold me, and hold me, for ever.

'Oh, Ralph,' I said with a lifetime of longing in my voice, and I held up my arms to him.

And then his knife hand came down like a thunder blow. And the lightning itself was black.

~ EPILOGUE ~

Wideacre Hall faces due south and the sun shines all day on the yellow stone, illuminating mercilessly the great black scorch marks on the two walls left standing, and the blackened, charred roof timbers.

When it rains the smoke stains run in great black smears down the honey-coloured walls, and the scattered rubbish from the house – Beatrice's papers, even her map of Wideacre – blows around the garden, sodden, breaking into mushy scraps.

As winter comes and the nights are longer and darker the villagers from Acre will not go near the Hall. Mr Gilby, the London merchant, wants to buy the estate from the widowed Lady Lacey but he is hesitating about the price, afraid of the reputation of the local poor, afraid of the mob. If he buys, he will have to wait until summer to rebuild; and bring in labourers from outside the county. No Sussex labourer would touch the house. Neither will the villagers go into the Wideacre woods, although the old footpaths are reopened. Miss Beatrice's body was found in the leaves in a little secret hollow near the garden gate, a childhood hiding place. And now they say the whole wood is haunted by her, crying and crying for her brother who died the same night, when his heart – weak like his mother's – could not stand the bolt to Havering Hall. Crying and crying for the land goes Miss Beatrice, a swatch of corn in one hand and a handful of earth in the other.

If Mr Gilby does buy he will care neither for ghosts nor for profit. He is too practical a business man to mind the rumour of a ghost on his land. More important for the village, he cares little for profit. His money is made on guaranteed returns in the City. He does not put his faith in the weather, or the health of beasts, or the unreliable treacherous gods of Wideacre. He wants only to live in peace and enjoy his notion of country life. So his leases would be long, and the rents easy. But while he dithers, the footpaths are reopened and the new cornlands have self-seeded and gone back to meadow. If he does not come to Wideacre before spring he will find that the village has replanted the common strips again, and Acre is as it was; as if there had been no hard years, as if Beatrice had never been.

It will take more than a spring for the children and Celia and John to recover. Celia went in the night from the Squire's Lady to an impoverished widow, living in the little Dower House. She is in mourning for another year, but her face beneath the black veil is serene. The children are a quaint pair, solemn in their black clothes. They hold hands on their long walks and their little heads are close together when they pray: Julia's brown hair glinting with a tinge of copper, Richard's curls glossy as a black horse. John MacAndrew also lives in the Dower House, to care for his son and help the widow adjust to her new life. All he has is an allowance from his father. There is some rumour that Miss Beatrice squandered his money on an entail and an unbreakable contract for his son. But in this part of Sussex there is nothing they would not say against Miss Beatrice.

She has passed into legend. The Wideacre witch, who turned the land to gold for three sweet seasons, and then scraped it dry in two cold years. How, when she walked in a field as a young girl, you could see the seeds growing in her footprint. How the fish swam to the bank when she walked along the Fenny. How the game was fat and easy to shoot when she had been in the woods. How she was a very goddess of Wideacre, as sweet and as bitter and as unpredictable as all goddesses.

So when she turned against the land men died. When she stopped loving, the sweetness of Wideacre went sour and people went hungry. No vegetables grew. The footpaths closed. And an old oak tree crashed down, rootless, when she lost her temper under it one uneasy summer's day.

No man could have stopped her. Acre would have died of hunger in her second cold winter. Only another of the old gods, a legless man, half-horse, half-man, could have ridden like a centaur to the window of her house and plucked her out like a lover his lass. He rode away with her across his saddle and they found her body, but never heard of him again. He was gone.

Back to some secret place where the old gods live. Back to some heartbeating core of the earth where he and Miss Beatrice are golden once more, and smile on the land.

Wideacre Hall faces due south. It is a ruin now, and no one goes there. No one except little Richard MacAndrew and Julia Lacey who like to play in the broken summerhouse. Sometimes Julia looks up at the ruin with her wide child's eyes. And she smiles as if it were very lovely to her.